# Robert the Bruce

# Jack Whyte

# Robert the Bruce

WITHDRAWN

A TOM DOHERTY ASSOCIATES BOOK
NEW YORK

ROBERT THE BRUCE

Copyright © 2012 by Jack Whyte

Originally published under the title *The Renegade* in Canada by Viking Canada, an imprint of the Penguin Group

A Forge Book
Published by Tom Doherty Associates, LLC
175 Fifth Avenue
New York, NY 10010

www.tor-forge.com

Forge® is a registered trademark of Tom Doherty Associates, LLC.

ISBN 978-0-7653-3157-1 (hardcover)
ISBN 978-1-4299-2267-8 (e-book)

Forge books may be purchased for educational, business, or promotional use. For information on bulk purchases, please contact Macmillan Corporate and Premium Sales Department at 1-800-221-7945 extension 5442 or write specialmarkets@macmillan.com.

First U.S. Edition: August 2013

Printed in the United States of America

0  9  8  7  6  5  4  3  2  1

*This book, like every other I have written,*
*is dedicated to my wife, Beverley,*
*for who and what she is.*

# AUTHOR'S NOTE

On a beautiful autumn morning in the early stages of writing this book, I found myself sitting in the sunshine gazing at a portrait of the middle-aged Robert the Bruce, King of Scots, and remembering two grand old men I had known as a child. They were brothers, Edward and Michael O'Connell, and their youngest sister was my maternal grandmother. They were both fierce-looking, hawk-like men in their fifties, tall and gaunt and broad and stern, with big ears, prominent, beaky noses and a proud, independent air about them. The portrait of Bruce reminded me forcibly of both of them, not merely the physical elements of their heads and faces but their unyielding expressions of determination and uncompromising strength of what used to be known as character.

Those two upright old men shaped me when I was a boy too young to be aware of it, and one of them, the one I came to know best, became the model on whom I built one of my earliest protagonists, Caius Cornelius Britannicus of "A Dream of Eagles."

On that particular day in 2010, though, it was the elder brother, Edward, whom I could see in the face of Bruce, and as I sat there wondering why, and why the thought should have occurred to me, I experienced one of those quasi-mystical flashes of understanding and enlightenment that is known as an epiphany.

I had been wrestling for weeks with an anomaly that, though seemingly trivial at first notice, had nevertheless perplexed me to the point at which it had become intolerable and was seriously affecting my approach to my story. It had occurred when I realized, almost incidentally, that in reading everything I could find on the Bruce I had become aware that academic historians (not speculative fiction writers like myself) were virtually unanimous in admitting, to varying degrees, that they were at a loss to explain why Robert the Bruce, at several crucial and seminal times in his life, behaved as he had, apparently in defiance of all logic. In each of those instances (and all the historians agree on what they were), his decisions and subsequent actions appeared to lack an identifiable purpose or an attributable motivation.

And then I saw those grand old men and saw that Bruce, too, had his exemplar.

Bruce was the seventh of his name, the seventh consecutive Lord Robert Bruce. The fifth of those was Robert Bruce of Annandale in southern Scotland, known as Bruce the Competitor, because in the aftermath of the death of King Alexander III and then of his heir, the seven-year-old princess known as the Maid of Norway, Bruce of Annandale had one of the two strongest claims to the throne of Scotland and came within a coin's toss of being crowned King of Scots. But the astonishing thing was that, in an age when most men were dead by the age of forty, the old Competitor was seventy at the time of the competition. He was one of the greatest and most admired nobles of his time, not only in Scotland but throughout Christendom—for Europe, as we know it today, lay years in the future. He bore the royal blood of several countries, including England and France, and lived a life of unimpeachable honour and integrity. He must have been formidable, but he has been entirely eclipsed by the fame and the glory of his grandson, Robert the Bruce, King of Scots, and history has largely forgotten Bruce the Competitor. His grandson Robert, though, could never have forgotten him, reared as he was at the fierce old warrior's knee and eager to learn everything the old man had to teach him. Therein lay my epiphany that morning. Considering those two, pupil and teacher, and knowing the tenacity, nobility, integrity and strength of purpose of the elder, how could anyone doubt or question the decisions the grandson made at any stage of his brilliant career, when they were underpinned and rein-forced by the lessons learned at the old man's knee?

And so I started again, at a new beginning, and went looking for the story of the boy who would be king.

Jack Whyte
Kelowna, British Columbia
July 2012

# PROLOGUE

Thursday, May 16, 1297

Robert Bruce awoke in a foul humour on the day that was to change his life. He had no inkling that it was to be a day of days, but he was acutely aware from the moment he opened his eyes that he would be glad when it was over, for he had no illusions about the unpleasantness of what lay ahead for him that day, and the hissing drumbeat of heavy rain on the roof of his tent in the pre-dawn darkness seemed to set the tone for what was to come.

"Fires are a' oot an' everythin's arse deep in mud, so there nae hot toddy for ye this mornin'." Thomas Beg's rumbling voice came from the darkness beyond the foot of the narrow cot and was followed by a muffled clank of metal from the firebox. "Shite! It's nearly out. Haud still now and let me get a light."

Bruce lay unmoving in the darkness and thought about rolling out of bed, then relaxed and forced himself to ignore the noise of the rain, listening instead to the underlying sounds of his manservant tinkering with the firebox, and picturing the huge man blowing on the embers as he fed them gently with wisps of dried peat moss, coaxing them into flame.

"There! That's got the bugger."

A tiny halo of light sprang up in the pitch-blackness and grew steadily stronger. The metal door of the firebox clanked softly as Thomas Beg set the device carefully on the ground by his knees, grunting in concentration as he worked. Bruce waited, visualizing the care with which the big man would be extending a candle towards the tiny flame inside the box, then seeing the result immediately as the wick caught fire and sprang into life.

"God-cursed, pishin' rain." The big man rose quietly to his feet, one hand holding the candle while the other cupped the flame protectively, then moved cautiously to where a second candle stood on the small table beside Bruce's bed. Moments later the light from both wicks flooded the small tent, and Bruce pushed himself up on one elbow.

"Early," he mumbled, scrubbing at his eyes with his free hand.

"Early's what ye wanted, was it no'?" Thomas Beg was looming above him, looking down with a frown.

"Aye, it was, and I thank you. How long have you been up?"

"Long enough to see it's been a whore o' a night and it's gaun to be a whore o' a day, forbye. There's no' a fire left burnin' in the whole camp. If I hadna thought to bank the fire in the box afore I went to bed, we'd be stumblin' aboot like blind men. And rain? I've never heard the like o' it. Woke me up, it was comin' doon that hard. An' ye know I dinna wake up easy or often. But ye'd best be up yersel', gin ye want to be ready afore that whore o' an Englishman comes out o' his tent. Mind yer feet, noo."

"Hmm. I'm up." Bruce threw back his blanket and swung his legs over the edge of the cot, then flinched and hissed, lifting his feet hurriedly at the shock of the chill groundwater that instantly soaked into his thick stockings.

"I warned ye." Thomas Beg shook his head and handed him his heavy boots, then stood watching as his earl struggled into them, forcing his wet stockings into place and then lacing the boots up tightly before he lurched to his feet, shivering as he tugged at the long, quilted undercoat and drawers he had worn to bed.

"I need the latrine," Bruce murmured.

"Wait till ye go ootside, then, and wear your cloak," his companion said as the earl went to the tent flaps and held them open for a moment before shrugging into a foul-weather wool cloak that hung from a peg there.

Thomas Beg watched as Bruce stepped outside, and listened to the soggy sounds of the earl's boots in the grass until they faded into the rain-soaked night. He quickly set about folding and rolling Bruce's bedding. It was a task he could do in his sleep and he did it mindlessly, rolling and tucking and strapping until he had made a tightly compact bundle, then folding the trestle legs of the light, sturdy campaign cot and setting it on its side for collection by the camp crew. He poured water from the jug into the washbowl and laid a rough towel ready on the bedside table. Then stepped to the T-shaped wooden frame that held Bruce's armour and took down a belted pair of mailed leggings.

He was holding the leggings spread and ready when the earl stepped back inside, his head bent as he fumbled with the lacings at his crotch before he raised his arms to allow Thomas to feed the belt of the leggings around his waist. The earl buckled and cinched it tight and turned his back to allow his man to fasten the straps that held the leggings tightly in place from mid-thigh to ankles, then wriggled until he felt the heavy garment settle comfortably. When he was satisfied with the feel of it, he bent over the bowl on the table and rinsed his face and eyes, scooping water over his short-cropped hair and rubbing it into his scalp and the back of his neck before reaching for the towel. He wiped his eyes first and then held both ends as he scrubbed the nape of his neck from side to side vigorously with the rough cloth before dragging it down over his wet crown and drying his face and hands.

"There," he said. "Better. Never fails. No matter how cold and miserable you are, a cold douse and a rough towel on the back of your neck will warm you up."

"Aye, so I've heard ye say … Every mornin'."

Bruce managed his first smile of the day as he turned to face his man, who was now holding out the chain-mail hauberk he would wear over the thick under-tunic he had slept in.

"Let's get ye into this and then we'll eat," the big man growled.

"Eat? Eat what, in this weather? Wet grass?"

"Sheep like it. Come awa now."

They worked together in silence, both of them frowning in concentration as Bruce shrugged awkwardly into the bulky, confining garment, thrusting his head through the neck opening, then struggling to insert his arms before pulling and hauling until the iron-heavy body and mailed skirts fell into place. A man could dress himself in a mailed hauberk unaided, but it was a sullen, thankless task, and most preferred to work at it in pairs, sharing the difficulty. Thomas Beg, over years of working with Bruce, had developed a knack of settling the job quickly, and Bruce was grateful for his skill. Thomas himself preferred to have his huge arms free of encumbrance when he swung the heavy axe that was his primary weapon, and wore only a short-sleeved mail shirt beneath his leather jerkin. His only concession to armouring himself below the waist was a thick set of bull-hide thigh coverings, strapped to cover front and rear and reinforced with riveted, overlapping strips of steel. The boots he wore were similar to Bruce's own, made by the same boot maker but reinforced, like his thigh greaves, with more of the steel strips that were strong enough to repel a swung blade.

Bruce waited patiently while Thomas deftly snugged the straps that held the hauberk fastened at his back—the most difficult of all to fasten alone. The long, chain-link coat, reeking with the familiar mixed odours of human and equine sweat, raw metal, and the thin coating of oil that kept the links from rusting, was split to the waist at front and rear, permitting its wearer to sit astride a horse, and Thomas Beg stepped back, examining the hang of it critically. He nodded, satisfied, and turned away to bend over the metal firebox that still sat in a corner of the tent, where he picked up a cloth-wrapped bundle that had lain there on top of it, unseen by Bruce. He unfolded the cloth to reveal a steaming treasure that made Bruce grin with pleasure: a juice-rich slice of meat compressed between two inch-thick slabs of bread and cut into twin portions.

"Glory be to God," Bruce said reverently, feeling the saliva squirt beneath his tongue. "Where did you get that?"

Thomas Beg sniffed. "Where d'ye think? I saw ye arguin' wi' that damned Englishman last night, afore ye walked awa wi'oot eatin' a thing, an' I knew ye'd be sorry. So I wrapped up some o' what was left an' took it wi' me. But I never saw ye after that. Ye must hae came straight to bed."

"Aye, I did. Damn the man, he drove the thought of eating out of my mind. Sweet Jesus, the fellow is insufferable. I had to walk away or I'd have felled him. Upstart bastard. Aye, well, anyway, I'm obliged to you, Tam … Again."

Neither man spoke after that until they had finished their food, and then, still in silence, they completed the task of armouring the earl, seating the tight-fitting, leather-lined coif of mail comfortably on his head with its skirts covering his neck and shoulders, and lacing it beneath the chin before adding the heavy casing of steel that protected Bruce's back and chest.

Thomas Beg was hauling at the last of the buckled straps at Bruce's waist when the roaring drum rattle overhead abruptly died away, leaving only the sluicing sound of running water being shed from the sloping roof.

"Well," Thomas growled, "thank the Christ for that. We'll still be arse deep in mud out there but at least we winna get soaked on top. Unless it starts up again." He stepped away and opened the tent flaps, and stood peering out for a while and listening to the splashing sounds of unseen people moving around in the darkness. A loud clatter of falling pikes and a bark of profanity announced that someone had blundered into a pile of stacked weapons in the dark, and he turned back to Bruce. "Darker than it should be," he said, "but there's no use in carryin' a torch, even if we had one. The clouds must be awfu' thick. Are ye set?"

"As close as I'll ever be," Bruce answered, tugging at his sheathed sword until it hung comfortably. "Let's see if we can find that clerkly, whining bastard Benstead, then, and make a start to this *auspicious* day."

Thomas Beg looked askance at him, ignoring the heavy irony in Bruce's emphasis. "Benstead?" he asked instead. "I thought ye put him in his place yesterday, for good. Why would ye seek him now?"

Bruce grunted, the sound heavy with distaste. "Because of what his true place is. He's Edward's official representative. I can't change that, nor can I ignore it, much as I'd like to. So we'll go and find him before we set anything in motion, see if he has anything to say. I doubt I'm going to like whatever comes out of his mouth, for the man's a venomous reptile. But this is a matter of duty, and I owe it not to him but to his master. Come on, now, lead the way."

# Book One

# Encounters

# 1284

# CHAPTER ONE

# THE COUNTESS

"Ow! Ye wee brute!" Marjorie Bruce, Countess of Carrick, arched her back and pulled away from the infant suckling at her breast, but her youngest was teething and was not at all inclined to relinquish his hold on the nipple. The baby's nursemaid sprang forward, her face twisting in sympathy as she took the baby out of its mother's hands.

"Take him away, the wee cannibal," the countess said, adjusting her bodice to cover her breast. "He's finished, anyway, so he'll sleep all afternoon, and I have to start getting ready. Mother of God, what a morning. Make sure you break his wind, or he'll howl like a wolf. And send Allie in when ye leave. I'll need her to help me, for Earl Robert should have been here by now and I hae no wish to greet him looking as though I've spent the night in the byre wi' the kine. The King himself will be here come tomorrow and our Nicol should be bringing young Robert and Angus Mohr this afternoon, and God knows there's much to be done ere any of them arrives, so hurry you up, and be sure the rest o' the bairns are fed and clean."

The nursemaid bobbed her head and hurried away, clutching the baby tenderly in her arms, and her mistress stood up with both hands on her hips and flexed her spine, back and forth. She was pregnant again, and though it had not yet begun to show, she was starting to feel it, aware of the familiar changes in her body. This child would be her eighth, God willing, and there were times when she was tempted to wonder, slightly ruefully, if there had ever been a time in her adult life when she had not been heavy with child. She would never complain about that, though, for Marjorie of Carrick believed, with all her being, that she had been put on God's earth to mother a large and happy brood in a time when many women despaired of ever birthing and rearing a single child successfully. In that, she believed herself blessed. She had spent too long a time, earlier in her life, fearing that she might never mother a child. Now, thinking about that, she lowered herself into a firmly upholstered chair by the big stone fireplace and looked around the comfortably furnished family room on the second floor of the castle keep, making a mental list of all that needed to be done to make the place clean, presentable, and welcoming for her husband's return. A discarded garment caught her eye, and she bent and scooped it up, a tiny knitted woollen cap, still retaining a trace of warmth from the baby's head. She sat staring down at it, kneading it with her fingers and smiling to herself, wondering about the ways of God and the futility of trying to discover what He had in store.

As the sole heir to Carrick, her widowed father's only child, Marjorie had been married, at the age of eleven, to a man fifteen years her senior, and had then been abandoned before she reached the age of puberty, when her headstrong husband rode off with Prince Edward of England to join the Christian armies bound for the Holy Land in the ill-fated Ninth Crusade. He had died at a place called Acre, killed in some pointless skirmish against the Mameluke Sultan Baibars—a name still incomprehensible to Marjorie— leaving her both virgin and widow at the age of fourteen.

Devastated by the news of her husband's death, she had come close to despair over her situation, isolated and alone as she was, miles from anywhere in her father's remote seaside fastness of Turnberry with little prospect of ever meeting anyone else who might take her to wife. Her father the earl was a fine man, but he seldom ventured far from home, and Turnberry, with its ancient and massive sod-built walls and austere, almost inaccessible location, received few visitors of any kind, and almost none were marriageable, eligible males.

Marjorie's very real fear of a manless, childless future began to seem justified over the three years that followed, for her mother's only remaining sister, a thin-lipped and humourless man-hater called Matilda, had been a nun since girlhood, and she took it upon herself to ensure that the young widow would find solace in becoming a bride of Christ.

Thanks be to God, Earl Niall disagreed with his good-sister. He had no sons, but he took great pride in his boisterous, hard-working, and irrepressible daughter, who was, he liked to claim, his natural heir and the equal of any man around her, blessed with strength of mind and body and the determination that was needed to look after her lands and her people and to make her way in the world. And all of that, he would add fondly, in spite of the undeserved misfortune thrust upon her by the tragic loss of her husband while she was yet scarcely old enough to understand what had befallen her.

Earl Niall died soon after Marjorie's sixteenth birthday, of a lingering putrefaction from the tusk of a wild boar that had savaged him in a hunting accident, but thanks to his friendship with King Alexander, he had made sure, long before his death, that the succession passed to his beloved daughter in her own right as Countess of Carrick, with the blessing and support of the King himself. Marjorie was as nobly born as the man she soon married, the sixth Robert Bruce, and perhaps even more so, for her nobility stemmed from the royal blood of the ancient Gaelic kings, while his was entrenched in the Norman French heritage that gave him his mother tongue.

The door opened at Marjorie's back and Allie, her housekeeper, bustled in, muttering to herself as she always did and carrying the big wooden-handled woven bag that went everywhere with her. She and her husband, Murdo MacMurdo of Stranraer, who acted as factor, were the joint force that kept the entire world of Turnberry Castle functioning smoothly. The pair had done the same for the countess's father, supervising the myriad details of the earl's household affairs and the castle estate.

"Earl Robert's late," Allie announced, before her mistress could turn around. "But the way things are goin' this day, that's a blessin'. Kirsty was right—that young sheep boy Hector broke his leg fallin' off that cart when the axle went frae underneath it, but the break wis clean and Brother Callum put splints on it, so the boy will no' be runnin' much for the nex—" Her eyes widened at the sight of her mistress's face. "What's the matter wi' you? Is somethin' wrong, lassie?"

Marjorie blinked in surprise, for she had not been aware of anything being wrong. "There's nothing the matter," she responded with what she imagined to be an impatient frown. "I was just thinking about all that's to be done before the earl comes home and I drifted into a bit o' a daydream. I didna hear ye come in and ye startled me, that's all."

Allie sniffed loudly and her expression softened. "Aye, well you're right enough about a' that's to be done. The last thing we needed here this mornin' was a bad accident. But the boy's well enough, as I said, and we hae an extra lamb that we hadna counted on to feed the visitors tomorrow. The daft beast fell out o' the cart when it tipped, an' then juked back under the wheel just far enough to get itsel' killed when the whole thing smashed down. Broke its neck and Cook has it now, cleaning it for the spit. Forbye that, Murdo's had three men workin' all mornin', choppin' logs and cartin' dried peat, so there's nae shortage o' fuel, an' the larder's well stocked wi' meat, baith beef and deer, forbye fowl and game, grouse an' ducks an' geese and hare. There's a crew o' men out fishin' in the bay and anither nettin' trout in the river. The bakery ovens are a' well fired and we'll hae enough bread to feed the multitude. Murdo's ale kegs are full an' ready to be tapped, but we hinna seen hide nor hair o' that useless gowk o' a wine merchant frae Ayr. He was supposed to be here last week and he'll probably come by next month, but in the meantime, gin the King o' Scots wants wine when he's here, he'll either hae to bring his own or whistle for it and mak do wi' Brewster's ale like the rest o' us. Jessie said ye wanted me, to help ye. Wi' what?"

"Wi' the whole campaign, Allie, for a campaign it is. We're to entertain MacDonald o' Islay and the King himsel' at the same time, and Earl Robert's no' here yet, so come wi' me an' help me get changed, and then we'll set about seein' how things are workin'. It sounds like Murdo's well aware o' what needs to be done on his side, so that will make it easier for us to see to what's to do on ours. Here, help me fold these covers."

Between them they gathered up the brightly coloured woollen blankets that were scattered over the chairs and couches—the nights were cold inside the stone-walled castle tower, even in the height of summer—and set about folding them and setting them on top of the long table against one wall.

"How many o' them will there be, d'ye ken?" the housekeeper asked.

Marjorie shrugged as she set the last of the folded blankets down. "As many as come," she said. "Nicol will bring Angus Mohr, and Angus will no doubt have a flock o' his peacock chieftains in tow, anxious to set eyes on the King o' Scots, though they'd never let on. An' the King, of course, will bring who he brings, though I'm no' expectin' that many. A few o' the elder earls, I'm thinkin', probably MacDuff and Lennox an' Mar. They seem to be his closest cronies, and there might be a bishop or two, since he'll need witnesses for whatever he means to propose to Angus Mohr. And of course they'll a' hae others in their trains. We might hae as many as thirty."

"Mother o' God! I thought a score at the outside, but *thirty*?"

"Aye, and mayhap more. I've no way o' tellin' until they arrive. There could be another half score, for all I know."

"But where will we put them a'?"

"Come, and I'll tell you."

The countess led the way through a heavy doorway that was padded with felt to keep out drafts, into her private dressing chamber, which had no ceiling and so was open to the daylight that streamed in through the high, narrow windows overhead on the east and west walls of the castle tower.

"Now, let's see," she said and quickly began sorting through the hanging garments in the heavily carved wooden wardrobe that dominated the room. There was hardly a profusion of clothes there, and most of them were gowns of vibrant colours, but a highly unusual collection of accessories was tucked into boxed shelving beside the wardrobe: silken scarves and woollen wraps and leather belts and jewelled accoutrements of all colours, shapes, and sizes, for Marjorie of Carrick intuitively understood the feminine art of making less appear like more through the simple means of ornamenting her basic clothing.

"What were we talking about? Oh aye, where to put the camp followers, as Earl Robert calls them. We'll put them where they've always been put." Her eyes narrowed as she scanned the hanging gowns and assessed the options available to her. "This isna the first time Carrick has played host to the King o' Scots, and we've never had any trouble in the past, so there's nae use in frettin' about it." She picked out a few choices and passed them to Allie before starting to remove the gown she was wearing.

"The King's chamber is ready for him, I've seen to that already, and Angus Mohr will have the other big guest room. Apart from that, I couldna care less." She picked out a long, narrow ribbon of pale yellow with a pendant attached and held it against one of the two gowns she had chosen. Satisfied that her eye had been true, she handed it, too, to Allie and turned back to her undressing. "The earls and bishops will sleep in the great hall, where there's room to spare for them a', and the rest, the followers and the hangers-on, can sleep outside on the grass. They're used to that, and it's high summer.

"I remember the time my cousin Janet was married here—I was just a bairn. We had so many people here we couldna keep them a' inside the gates and they ended up building what seemed to be a whole new town o' tents along the riverbank. An' they were a' here for a week and more. So folk can go, and will go, where they need to go. It's no' my job to be hostess to all o' them, especially when I invited none o' them. This is a house. It's a big house, I'll grant ye, but it's no' a hostelry." She undid the last of the buttons holding up her gown and let the garment fall around her ankles. She stepped out of it, wearing only a simple, knee-length shift, and turned to face the wall beside the wardrobe, where she had had Murdo hang a long, framed, and polished mirror made from a single flawlessly smooth sheet of brass that Earl Robert had bought for her years earlier, in

York, on one of his visits to England. It was her pride and joy and the single concession in all of her household to her womanly vanity.

She stood silently for a few moments, looking at her reflection, still amazed, after all those years, at the fidelity of the mirror, and gazing critically at the changes that those years—and seven healthy, breast-fed children—had wrought on her body. She was still well shaped, she knew, and still attractive to the man she loved. Her waist, despite a decade of bearing children, was still remarkable, and she worked every day to keep her belly taut between pregnancies, short though those intervals had been. There were stretch marks, inevitably, on her abdomen beneath the shift, but they were few, considering the realities of life, and the paunch her pregnancies had caused was smaller than it might have been, barely noticeable beneath her clothing. Her thighs, legs, and buttocks were strong and well formed and, like her arms, devoid of fat or sagging flesh, because she walked for miles almost every day, visiting her tenants, and worked as hard as any of her people in the upkeep of the castle estates. Since girlhood, she had never shied away from physical labour, be it bringing in the harvest from the fields outside the castle walls or turning her hand to cleaning out the stables and the byres.

She raised one hand and poked her fingers into her hair, testing it for cleanliness and deciding she would have to find time to wash it before the men arrived. Marjorie of Carrick was proud of her hair and of the fact that it had been the subject of more than a few songs and tributes from visiting bards over the years. Her eyes were startling, too, a gift from her mother's side, wide and arresting beneath arching brows, and more green than blue, with lustrous whites that often appeared to be a pale, pale shade of blue against the natural darkness of her skin. Sighing, she gathered up one of the gowns she had selected, shrugging into it quickly and shimmying as she pulled it into place.

"Anyway," she said, "I intend to look my best if we're to entertain both King and lord. In that, at least, I hae some control."

Allie busied herself picking up and folding the discarded gown before turning back to her mistress, ready to help her dress again, but Marjorie's dismissal of her concerns had not put her mind at rest. "My God, though, the expense o' it," she breathed, almost silently, as she pulled the back of Marjorie's gown into place. "What was Earl Robert thinkin', to invite the King to come here to do somethin' that ought to be done by rights in Dunfermline?"

"The expense o' it?" Marjorie twisted to face her, smiling and frowning at the same time as she tugged at the waist of her gown. "Here, see if ye can pull out those creases, smooth them down. I'm getting big again and I'll soon no' be able to squeeze into this thing at all, for a while, at least."

Allie eyed her mistress's waistline and pursed her lips. "Ye dae no' bad. Good enough to keep yer man nudgin' at ye."

"Aye. That's why I'm expectin' again. But the expense o' it, ye were sayin', havin' the King come here instead o' bidin' where he belongs?" She smiled. "It's no' that great an expense, Allie, when ye consider what Earl Robert will gain by it. The cost wouldna beggar the House o' Carrick, and ye can be sure it winna make a dint in the coffers o' the House o' Bruce. Besides, the cost is no' important. It's the King's dignity that's at hazard here. Angus Mohr would never set foot in Dunfermline town, it being Alexander's seat. It's a matter o' pride, as such foolish things always are wi' men. Angus calls himsel' the Lord o' Islay, but in his own mind I hae no doubt that when he says 'Lord' he thinks 'King.' And so for him to go to Dunfermline, he would be lowering himself to meet the King o' Scots, at least in his own eyes. Alexander understands that full well, I'm sure, but for whatever reason, he has made up his mind that he must meet face to face wi' Angus Mohr, and must therefore meet him elsewhere than in Dunfermline. Earl Robert knows that, too, and he knows that Turnberry is the perfect place to ease the minds o' both men. Neither one o' them can doubt his welcome here, and each o' them trusts Robert or myself—I should say *and* myself— Earl Robert because he has proved himself time and again to the King, and me because I've known both men, lord and King, since I was a bairn." She stopped to cock her head, listening, and held up her hand. "Who's there?"

The door opened a crack and one of the women from the nearby castle town of Turnberry stuck her head timidly into the room, managing, for all her timidity, to scan her eyes from side to side, seeing and noting everything there was to be seen in the countess's brightly lit dressing chamber. Every woman in the castle town, and most of their men as well, had been conscripted into service for the coming royal visit, and the main building, which was normally tended by a small crew of caretakers, was overrun by more temporary servitors than Marjorie could ever remember seeing at one time.

"Well?" she asked the woman. "It's Bella, isn't it? What do you need me for?"

The woman bobbed her head. "Forgi'e me, mileddy, but one o' Earl Robert's men just arrived in the kitchens wi' word for ye."

"D'ye ken the man?"

"Aye, lady, it's the big laddie who aey rides wi' the earl, him wi' the missin' ear."

Marjorie had an instant vision of the youth they called Wee Thomas because of his great size. He was not the cleverest of her husband's followers, but he numbered high among the most loyal— and fearless. A giant at fourteen, to be sure, but still a mere child in years, he had earned the earl's undying esteem and gratitude by the selfless ferocity with which he had attacked three men who had sprung from hiding and attacked Earl Robert, having evidently been dispatched to kill him, though by whom no one knew to this day. Armed with only a rusty old dirk, the boy had cut down one of them and wounded another before any of them knew he was among them, and his attack had given Earl Robert the brief time he needed to gather his wits, unsheathe his own weapon, and deal with the remaining attacker. By that time, though, the boy would have been dead had the hard-swung sword stroke that glanced off his skull and severed most of his left ear hit its target, the crown of his head.

She became aware that the woman was still poised in the doorway. "My thanks, Bella. Is he still at the kitchens?" The woman nodded. "Good. Tell him to stay where he is and eat something. I'll be there directly, as soon as I'm done here."

Not long after, Thomas Beg lurched to his feet, flushing, as he always did, when his employer, whom he believed to be the most beautiful woman he had ever seen, entered the kitchen and came gliding towards him at the plain wooden table where he sat. He had been ravenous, devouring a meal of savoury game stew piled atop a thick slab of fresh-baked bread and loving every bite of it, but the moment he saw the countess he lost all awareness of what he had been doing a moment earlier.

"Thomas," she said, smiling in recognition and ignoring his reddening face as she approached him. "I'm told ye have word for me from Earl Robert."

The boy dipped his head, speechless.

"Speak up, then. What d'ye have to tell me? Or is it somethin' ye canna say here?"

The giant boy flushed even deeper and stammered out, "The Earl winna be comin' this day. But he'll be here soon, wi' the King. He wanted ye to ken, so he sent me on ahead, wi' a letter for ye."

"A *letter*? Ye have a letter for me?"

Thomas reached deep into his shirt and pulled out a leather wallet. Marjorie took it from him and flipped it open, seeing the parchment folded inside, but then she closed it again, resisting the urge to snatch the letter out and read it right there in front of everyone. Instead, she merely inclined her head to the boy. "My thanks for this," she said. "Am I to answer it, do ye know?" Thomas shook his head and half shrugged, and she bit down on the urge to snap at him, knowing that being impatient with him would only make matters worse. "What are you to do now, Thomas?" she asked then, keeping her voice gentle. "Are ye to stay here, or does Earl Robert expect ye back? Where was he when you left him?"

Thomas Beg shook his head, his eyes wide with something approaching panic, a condition that Marjorie had remarked upon whenever she had spoken to him directly, but he managed to answer her question. "He's in Dunfermline, mileddy, wi' the King, but he sent me on in front o' him, to bring you that."

Marjorie sucked in her breath. "Aye, I see. Well, let me read it. Sit ye down and eat."

She walked away and seated herself on a sturdy chair at a smaller table that held a thick, burning candle, and opened the letter, schooling her face to betray nothing as she read, aware that she was being watched. The letter was written in Latin, and not in her husband's bold, spiky hand, so she knew it had been written by a monk or a priest at the abbey in Dunfermline. Its brevity, though, marked it clearly as having been dictated by Robert himself, and she read it slowly and carefully, one hand over her mouth to mask it from curious eyes as she formed the Latin words.

*My love, this in haste, knowing you need to be aware of how matters have changed—not in substance but in scope. England is here in Dunfermline—Edward himself, accompanied by Queen Eleanor and their train. His friend Richard of Ulster accompanies him with his wife Margaret, who is big with child and close to her term. The occasion is a Royal progress to mark the end of Edward's Welsh war with a visit to his cousin Scotland, before he undertakes a new campaign in Gascony.*

*Upon hearing that we are bound for Turnberry to meet with Angus Mohr MacDonald, he decided to accompany our King, to Witness the business being done and to do Honour to our house, citing that he has not set eyes upon you in person since our attendance at his Coronation in London six years ago. So he will accompany Alexander, bringing de Burgh of Ulster with him. Queen Eleanor and her ladies will stay here in Dunfermline with Queen Margaret, the Countess of Ulster being in no condition to travel at this time, within a month of birthing as she is. Even with both Kings present, the royal party will be small enough, but significant none the less, with de Burgh and a few others attending the monarchs, plus a royal English escort of ten men-at-arms. Closer to three score I fear than to the score and a half we had thought.*

*Knowing you will be aware that I have no choice in this matter, I can but send you advance warning in the knowledge that you will take the steps required to prepare yourself for our advent, my Love, accomplished worker of miracles that you are. I will delay our*

*arrival for as long as may be by arranging a hunting party to divert*
*our guests on the way, and to provide much-needed venison for our*
*larders. B.*

Worker of miracles, indeed. Marjorie scanned the letter again, noting the different flourish of the final "B" that proclaimed Bruce himself had signed the missive, and grudgingly admiring, not for the first time, the way in which her scholarly husband could capture words to explain himself clearly and briefly. Her thoughts quickly returned, though, to the hard kernel of the message. Sixty people, descending on her within the day. She folded the letter back into its original creases, giving herself time to think and to clear her face of all expression before looking at anyone else. Young Thomas had sat down again, but he was still staring at her, cow-eyed, and the other four people in the kitchen were pretending not to be watching her.

"So, Thomas, when did you leave Dunfermline?"

"Yesterday morn—" The lad cleared his throat noisily before continuing. "Lord Robert telt me to ride like the wind and no' to stop atween there an' here."

"And how far behind you will the others be?"

"They wis to leave this mornin', and to stop this night in Stirlin'. Then Lord Robert said they wad stop again, the next night, at Kilmarnock, and come on down here the day after that."

"You're sure o' that? They'll no' be here tomorrow?"

"No, no' tomorrow. Earl Robert said it wad tak them three days … I think the Kings want to hunt deer on the way."

"Thanks be to God for that, then. We'll need every minute o' time between now and then." She moved quickly to the door, then turned at the threshold. "My thanks, Thomas," she said. "Earl Robert will be pleased wi' how ye've done. Run now and find Murdo for me and send him to me directly. *Directly*, mind—I need him this minute. I'll be upstairs, tell him. Away wi' ye now." She went out, her head filled with arrangements that would have to be seen to at once, and made her way straight to the family quarters.

The first problem was one of protocol, and Marjorie of Carrick was realistic enough, and feminine enough, to see the inherent irony, but she was far from amused by it. Edward of England's unexpected advent meant that she would have four proud and powerful men beneath her roof for several nights, but only two suitable bedchambers in which to accommodate them. Two of the four, Alexander and Edward, would naturally claim precedence based upon their regal titles, but what, she wondered, was she to do with the other two? De Burgh, the Earl of Ulster, was the most powerful man in Ireland, and they would all be worse than foolish if they expected Angus Mohr MacDonald of Islay to be abashed by that distinction. Within his own domain of the western mainland and the hundreds of islands that made up the Isles, Angus Mohr was every inch the monarch, as powerful in his own territories as the other three were in theirs, and no one there doubted—or flouted—his authority. Moreover, Angus was the one whom King Alexander had specifically invited to attend this gathering, so he was, in fact, the guest of honour and entitled to the finest accommodations available. Marjorie had no idea how she would work out that problem, but she refused to be overwhelmed by it.

Murdo arrived within moments, and she immediately waved him to a seat at the large table where she and Earl Robert both worked in the administration of their daily affairs. With no more reaction than a mildly raised eyebrow, the factor lowered himself into the chair and waited. He had known his mistress since she was a child learning to walk and speak, and had witnessed every form of tantrum, mood change, and caprice and every fit of pique she had added to her woman's arsenal along the way, so that now, as Countess of Carrick, she had long since lost any capability of surprising him.

Marjorie launched directly into bringing him up to date on all that had changed since they had last spoken, early that morning. Murdo listened solemnly, making no attempt to interrupt her until she eventually fell silent. Then, when he was sure she had no more to say, he nodded judiciously and cleared his throat.

"Aye," he growled. "The Blessed Mother o' God had the same problem—three kings chappin' at her door and a' she had was a bed o' straw in a stable. But that bed was for her and the Bairn, and naebody kens to this day where the wise men slept while they wis there."

Marjorie opened her mouth to snap at him, thinking he was being flippant, but she stopped short as he held up an open hand. "I'm no' bein' foolish, lassie. I'm just tellin' ye what came into my head as ye were talkin'." He lapsed into silence, staring down at the tabletop, and now it was Marjorie who sat waiting for him. Murdo was the only man she knew who would dream of calling her "lassie," as though she were still a child. But in his eyes, Marjorie knew, she *was* but a child, countess or no, and she knew he meant no disrespect. The old man never spoke to her that way in front of anyone else.

"It's remindin' me o' the time Earl Niall had the fower bishops here," he continued. "The same kind o' thing, that was. Fower bishops to your fower kings. Fower lords o' the Church then, fower lords o' Creation now. D'ye recall what he did?"

"Murdo, I don't know what ye're talkin' about."

His eyebrows rose. "I'm talkin' about the time the earl—" He stopped, and his eyes narrowed. "Aye," he murmured. "Aye, mayhap ye werena born yet, now I think o' it. It was a while ago an' I was young then, mysel' … What happened was that fower bishops cam to Turnberry. Fower important bishops, a' at the same time. There was Richard Inverkeithing o' Dunkeld, Clement o' Dunblane, Bondington o' Glasgow, an' auld Gamelin o' St. Andrews … God, they've a' been dead these twenty year an' more. But that's neither here nor there. What I'm sayin' is, the fower o' them turned up here, uninvited, all o' them on their separate ways to a gatherin' in the north o' England and each one o' them expecting to be treated according to his rank. Truth was, though, that they were a' equal, even though each o' them thought he was more important than the other three. Fower bishops … "

"And? In God's name, Murdo, what does this hae to do wi' anything?"

"Rein in your horse, lassie, an' listen. Each o' these men sent a priest wi' a message, to tell Earl Niall he would be comin' within the week, and as it turned out, the fower messengers a' turned up here on the same day, hours apart. So the earl knew he couldna board the fower o' them—he had no more room than ye hae now, an' yet he would hae to treat them a' the same. For a day or two after that, frettin' about what to do, he wasna fit to live wi', until your mother, God rest her soul, came up wi' the solution."

"My *mother*?"

The old man nodded. "She told him the story o' the three wise men. They were kings in their own lands, to be sure, but they were men first and foremost, and they were wise—wise enough to ken that lookin' after them wasna somethin' that the Mother o' God should have to fret about. Forbye, they had come a long way, to see the Christ Child, so they had brought their own tents. An' if the wise men set an example, your mother said, and found their own lodgin's, how could these bishops complain about havin' to do the same thing? An' she was right, of course, but what she said reminded Earl Niall o' somethin', and he saw what to do.

"His father had been a great sailor when he was young, wi' two fine galleys o' his own. But when his father died and Nicol became Earl o' Carrick himsel', he quit the sea. He traded the biggest galley for a prime herd o' sheep and then years later, when he was an old man, he lost the other one, destroyed at anchor right here, in a great winter storm. What Earl Niall recalled was that his father, who was a frugal man, had set his sailmaker to turning the big galley sails— there were six o' them, huge—into fower great tents—pavilions, they called them—to sell to knights bound for a crusade. That crusade never happened, and the tents wis still in Turnberry, safe stored in the big stone bothy down by the pier."

"You mean the oar bothy?"

"Aye. And so Earl Niall had them set up, on the lea outside the walls. One for each bishop. And nary a one complained."

"Hmm. But how does that help me?"

Murdo grinned. "Same as it helped your da. They're still there. I looked at them the month afore last, to see if they were worth keeping or if I should burn them. They were in fine shape, better than I had expected, poles and ropes and a'. And they're *big*. I doubt even Edward o' England will hae any bigger."

Marjorie stared at him. "And we could use them for this?"

"Aye, ye can, lassie—one for each o' them. We'll set them up on the lea, same as before, as the corners o' a square, a hundred paces apart. That way, they'll all be equal and they'll a' hae plenty o' room to stretch their legs."

"My God, Murdo McMurdo, ye've saved my life. How long would it take to set them up?"

The old man shrugged. "If I set the men to work on it this afternoon, the tents should be up by this time tomorrow."

"Pavilions, Murdo. We'll ca' them pavilions. I like that word. It's French and it sounds grander than tents."

"Aye, if ye like. The bishops can hae the two extra rooms and the earls and high-ups can a' stay close to their various kings. And we'll set up space for the sodgers and men-at-arms down by the river. Can I go now an' get started?"

"You can, and God bless you. You're an angel sent from Heaven."

"No, lassie, I'm a factor who's good at his job, that's a'." He stood up. "Right, then, I'll be away."

His mistress was suddenly radiant. "Young Rob will be thrilled. He'll no' soon forget the day he turned ten, surrounded by kings and barons and earls. Run, then, and do what ye must, for God knows I've a wheen o' things to do myself."

# CHAPTER TWO

# THE BOY

Less than fifteen miles southeast of Turnberry, just as the Countess of Carrick dismissed her factor, a horse and its rider stopped on a steep path up the side of a hill. The rider's eyes followed the deep marks where another horse's hooves had dug into the hillside as it fought its way up the high, sloping bank. He hesitated only slightly, then yanked hard at the reins, pulling his mount towards the close to sheer incline. The animal's ears flicked at the insistence of the reins, then it turned obediently and launched itself at the steep slope, hooves digging firmly into the crumbling earth of the shale bank as it fought its way towards the crest. Its rider bent forward and murmured encouragement, his feet firmly braced in the stirrups, enjoying the thrust of the beast's powerful haunches as it bounded upward, four and then five mighty surges before it gained the top of the incline and stamped its feet triumphantly on the heather-clad summit.

"Good beast!" the boy on its back cried in Gaelic, clapping his hand on its neck appreciatively. The animal arched its neck and snorted, stamping its feet again as its rider turned to grin at the man who had been waiting for him on the hilltop.

The man dipped his head slightly in acknowledgment. "It took you long enough. I thought for a minute there I was going to have to come looking for you." The liquid, rippling Gaelic rolled off his tongue, its lilt perfectly capturing the raillery implied in the comment.

"I'm here, am I not?"

"Aye, you are. And you did well, that last wee bit. You could have taken the easy way."

"Why would I do that? You didn't," the boy answered. "I saw where you came up."

"Aye … " His companion's voice faded away, and he sat straight-backed, his narrowed eyes moving constantly as he scanned the bleak landscape of the moor that stretched around them on all sides. "But then I'm a man grown. You're just a wee boy."

"I am not." There was just the slightest tinge of protest in the boy's voice. "I'll be ten tomorrow. That's more than halfway to being a man grown."

The beginnings of a smile flickered at the edges of the other's mouth. "Right enough, I suppose. But you still have a way to go along that path. Still, you show promise. Faint, mind you, faint, but there none the less."

"Where are we going, anyway, Uncle Nicol?"

The man turned in his saddle, his smile widening until it made his eyes crinkle. "Well now, I was hoping you could tell *me* that, seeing that you're nearly a man and all. Where do you think we're going?"

The boy sat straighter, his face turning thoughtful. He twisted to one side and then the other, looking back the way he had come and then gazing at the hills of the western horizon. "To the coast, I know," he said, almost to himself. Then, in a louder, more confident tone, "We left Dalmellington at daybreak and we've been riding ever since. That's more than four hours, so we've come nigh on twenty miles, heading west the whole way. Maybole's to the north, so we must have passed that already and … " He hesitated. "And we're heading southwest now, so we can't be going to Turnberry. We're going to Girvan."

"There," his uncle grunted. "I knew you would tell me. And you're nearly right. We're going *close* to Girvan, to the north of it, to a place I know."

"What for?" No answer was forthcoming, so the boy persisted. "Uncle Nicol? Why are we going to this place that you know?"

"To meet a man, a friend of mine, though in truth he was a friend of my brother, your grandfather, God rest his soul." Nicol's grin had vanished, his face now wearing his normal expression of calm thoughtfulness, and even the tone of his voice changed, as the tenor of his Gaelic words became more reverent. "His name is MacDonald, Angus Mohr MacDonald, and he calls himself the Lord of Islay."

"Is he old, then?"

"Old enough, I suppose, but don't ever let him think you think that. He's far from being a doddering old fool. His lineage stretches back forever and he wields great power in the west, especially since Haakon, the King o' Norway, quit the Western Isles after the sea fight at Largs thirty years ago and withdrew to Orkney. There have been great changes in the Isles ever since then, with the Scots from the mainland takin' over more and more from the few Norsemen still there. Old Somerled, who ruled Skye a hundred and more years ago, was Norse, and one of his line married John, chief of Clan Donald, who called himself the first Lord of Islay and was Angus Mohr's father. And now Angus rules there." Nicol smiled, his voice changing again. "And as far as I know, he has never met a Bruce in all his life. Nor any other Englishman, for that matter. It will be interesting to see how he reacts to you."

The boy's eyes went wide with outrage. "I am no Englishman! I'm a Scot, born and bred right here in Carrick."

"Aye, but Angus is a *Gael*, and his folk have been here since before the Romans came. And mayhap you are a Scot, as you claim, but there's more accident than intent in that. Your mother has the blood, God knows, but your father and all his folk are English by descent, though they will argue that their ancestors were Norman and French, with not a Saxon Englishman among them. To Gaels like myself and Angus Mohr, though, they are all alike. Ill-bred foreigners to a man, stumbling and mumbling in their awkward, ill-sounding tongues. And those of them who do have the grace to speak the Gaelic have been fortunate to be born here and thereby be gifted with the Tongue." He scanned the horizon again. "Anyway, as I said, it will be interesting to see how Angus reacts to meeting you.

I will introduce you as my kin, of course—my great-nephew, son of my brother Niall's daughter—but he will see you immediately for what you are. I might name you, for the folly of it, plain Rob MacDuncan, but Angus Mohr will not heed that for a moment when it's clear to his eyes that you are an incomer, young Robert Bruce of the House of de Brus."

He cocked his head, waiting for a response, but when it came, it was not what he had expected.

"I know who Angus Mohr is, and you make him sound like an ogre," the boy said. "But he can't be that bad, because my mam likes him."

"He is an ogre, boy, and don't you ever think otherwise. No man comes to be as powerful as Angus Mohr is by being kind and gentle. Besides, your mother can find a good word for anyone. That is why she's my favourite kinswoman."

"Not everyone, not by a mile. My father has friends she won't let in the house, so she's not that tolerant."

"Friends? Or do you mean people who work for him? I've seen some of them myself and I wouldn't let them into my house, either."

"Aye, but she has always liked Angus Mohr, ever since she was a babby. So he can't be as black as you would stain him."

Nicol turned his head away to hide a smile and spoke towards the distant western hills. "Perhaps she may be right. We'll see. But one way or the other, once we have the great man safely in hand, along with whoever might find honour in being with him, we will make our way up to Turnberry, where you will be a Bruce again—for a while at least, until they pass you back to me. It's just a few miles north of where we are headed, and your mother will be waiting for you. Tomorrow is your tenth birthday after all, as you said, and ten years is a whole decade—worthy of celebration—so we're taking you home to be with your family. You will remember the day you turned ten, though. You will recall it forever after as the day you met the King."

"The King? King *Alexander*?"

"Aye. Is there another that you know of? Alexander the Third, of the House of Canmore, King of Scots. You will not have met him before, I suspect, eh?"

"No." The boy was wide-eyed with wonder. "And he's coming to Turnberry?"

"Aye, he is. And he'll be there for your birthday." His grin grew wider and then he shrugged. "Mind you, he's coming to meet with Angus Mohr as well. The two of them have matters to discuss. But he will know your face, from tomorrow on."

Rob was stunned, for he had never met anyone his own age who had met the King. Alexander had been King of Scots for more than twenty years, he knew, but few of his common subjects were ever fortunate enough to meet him, especially here in the wild southwest. And now King Alexander himself would be in *Turnberry*, there for his birthday …

Rob had known he would be returning home for his birthday, because he did so every year. This year, though, he had not been altogether sure he wanted to go back, and he had been feeling guilty about that, uncomfortable with what he suspected were stirrings of disloyalty. Now, though, he felt a great wave of relief sweep over him, banishing his earlier feelings and filling him instead with eager anticipation. Notwithstanding the King's visit and the excitement it would engender, he found himself thrilling to the thought of seeing his mother again, and even his father, Earl Robert, though the man seldom recognized Rob's existence other than to growl a warning at him from time to time when his patience grew thin. And it would be good to see his brothers and sisters again, though most of them were too young to be of any real interest. His elder sister, Christina, he knew, would be happy to see him, and so would his closest younger sibling, Isabel. Even Nigel, the sturdy, smiling, sunny-natured child whose name was really Niall, after their maternal grandsire, would make him welcome. Isabel was eight now, and Nigel must be six and a half, but below them in line, spaced roughly a year apart, came three more boys, Edward, Thomas, and the recently born Alexander. All three of those, in young Robert's eyes, were little more than sources of never-ending noise, ranging from screams of rage to whines and bleats of complaint, separated by unintelligible outbursts of squabbling.

No wonder, he thought for the first time, that his father was so impatient and short-tempered all the time. Robert Bruce of Carrick was a conscientious, studious man who took his duties as the earl seriously and was consequently seldom at home. Whenever he did come home, though, the constant noise of brawling, squabbling children must have driven him mad. Realizing that he shared that much in common at least with his father, Rob decided, then and there, that meet the King or no, he would far rather spend more time with his uncle Nicol, in his home at Dalmellington, than among his own clamouring brood in Turnberry Castle, and he was surprised, for a moment, by how happy the decision made him feel. He turned his eyes slightly to glance at his uncle and was relieved to find that Nicol was deep in his own thoughts, his narrowed eyes gazing off towards the west as though they could pierce the hills and show him the distant sea.

Rob Bruce could not remember when he had decided that his uncle Nicol was his favourite person in the world, but for as far back as he could recall, no one else had come close to claiming his esteem in the way Nicol MacDuncan had. He had done it effortlessly, too, simply by being the only adult male in the boy's life who treated him as a person, rather than as a simpering, unformed, half-witted child. Nicol had never spoken down to his nephew and never belittled him. He had always treated him as a real person—not as an equal, certainly, for Rob knew he was no such thing, too young even to lay claim to such consideration. Yet none the less Nicol had always treated him as a thinking being, someone whom he expected to have an opinion on any subject, no matter how ill informed that opinion might be. And not only did he assume that Rob *had* opinions, he insisted upon hearing them and discussing them. He never scoffed at what he heard, never sneered, never belittled anything his young charge said. Instead, he would fill in the gaps in the boy's knowledge, enlarge upon the pros and contras of each element of

Rob's opinion and frequently end up leaving several more options in his nephew's mind for further consideration. Looking at him now, Rob felt a flush of warmth and affection for the man.

Nicol was really his mother's uncle, her father's youngest brother by almost twenty years, which meant, in truth, that he could never have really known his eldest brother, Niall, the former Earl of Carrick, at all, and he had never known the father, Nicol MacDuncan, whose name he bore. That Nicol had been the son of Duncan, the first Earl of Carrick, and had not lived long enough to see the boy child of his old age birthed. In fact, Nicol was no more than a year or two older than his favourite niece, Marjorie, Earl Niall's formidable daughter, and he had taken an active, avuncular interest in the welfare of her eldest son since the first day he saw the boy, when young Robert was only four weeks old and Nicol decided the child looked like the son he had always wanted. Nicol had married young, to a woman who died childless a few years later, and then he had wed a widow with three daughters, but he and she had never had any children of their own, and since the widow had clearly demonstrated her own fertility beforehand, it soon became clear that Nicol, and not his wife, must be at fault. No one thought any the less of him for that; it was simply accepted and ignored.

Nicol's initial interest in his niece's firstborn son had never abated, and for the past three years it had resulted in the boy's being given over into his young great-uncle's care for several months, from early spring until midsummer, before being returned to the family fold in time for his birthday on the eleventh of July. Those months, from the beginning of March all the way through until mid-July, had become Robert's favourite and most jealously guarded time of the year, when he would learn more about everything around him than the rest of his brothers and sisters combined would absorb in an entire twelvemonth. He grunted quietly, deep down in his chest, then kneed his horse forward gently until he sat beside Nicol, staring out with him over the wild landscape below.

To say that the lands of the earldom of Carrick were hilly would be a deceptive description; *rocky* and *bleak* and *inhospitable* were far more accurate words. The name Carrick sprang from *carraig*, the Gaelic word for a rock or a rocky place. The Carrick lands were almost completely lacking in arable areas that might offer sustenance for farmers, but they offered fine grazing for the hardy local sheep, and because of that the people of the Carrick region were mainly wool producers—just like everyone else the length and breadth of Scotland. Young Rob, the seventh consecutive Robert Bruce of his line, had been born here, in his mother's ancestral home of Turnberry Castle, overlooking the Firth of Clyde and the Isle of Arran and the distant Mull of Kintyre. To the north lay the town of Ayr, and to the east, the earldom's main town of Maybole. Rob loved Carrick, and he was always excited to be reminded from time to time that it would one day be his. These were his own lands, his inheritance, and the knowledge of that never failed to thrill him. For the time being, though, the lands were his mother's. Rob's father, though he held the title Earl of Carrick, held it solely by virtue of his marriage to the countess.

"Are you ready, then?"

Rob glanced at his uncle and nodded, then kicked his mount forward to follow Nicol down from the summit and into the trackless reaches of the moors. There were no roads across the moorlands. In truth there were few real roads in all of Scotland. The boy thought about that as he allowed his horse to make its own way at the heels of Nicol's mount, for the matter of roads—or rather the lack of them—had been brought to his attention only a few weeks earlier—by his uncle, of course. Roads were something he had never had cause to think about. His people went everywhere on foot, and could travel five miles in a single hour over trackless land. When greater distances had to be travelled, those who had horses used them, but even so they were all inured to dismounting and leading their animals slowly through the treacherous, boggy, and wildly uneven terrain of the moors, where a single misplaced hoof could result in a broken leg and a lost mount.

That conversation, which had lasted throughout an entire afternoon, had resulted, as such talks with his uncle Nicol nearly always did, in a far broader understanding of things in the boy's mind, prodding him to think about matters he had never considered before. The Romans in ancient times had built wide, straight roads throughout England, as they had throughout the entire world, for the sole purpose of moving their armies quickly and efficiently, and those roads had made it possible for men to build towns everywhere along their lengths. Scotland had few such roads, because the Romans had never made a determined attempt to conquer the remote and inhospitable territory they called Caledonia. As a result, Nicol had pointed out, Scotland had far fewer towns than England and only a few port cities. The revelation had fascinated the boy.

In and around the villages and hamlets of the Carrick region there were beaten paths, created by the coming and going of the local folk. But there were no large settlements worthy of being called towns in Carrick, other than, perhaps, Maybole, the administrative centre, and there were no roads. England lay mere miles to the south of where Rob and his uncle rode now, but on the entire western seaboard there was only one real route between the two countries, and that was little more than a winding track, unusable at the border crossing much of the time because it was under water. Travellers coming north from England did so along the single narrow road that ran north from Carlisle to the border, but then they had to wait for low tide before crossing the wide, sandy estuary of the Solway Firth that separated the two countries.

It was a tedious and inconvenient route for travelling merchants, but at least they could use it. Armies, on the other hand, could not, so the Solway crossing was never considered seriously as an invasion route. The firth was as safe as a wall in shutting out large armies, because the shifting tides and treacherous sands made crossings impossible for large numbers of soldiers and supplies, and the lie of the land on the north side of the firth made it possible for small numbers of defenders to destroy any advance guard that might have crossed from the south before the next low tide allowed the invaders to be reinforced. Rob knew that was true because his uncle Nicol had taken him all the way down there the day after their talk, and they had spent the night on a low hill overlooking the wide, wet sands of the firth so that Rob could see for himself how straitened and dangerous the crossing was, even at low tide. He had asked his uncle when an army had last tried to cross there from England.

"Eighty-five years, I've heard. That seems a long time even to me. But it's not that long at all. There has been peace between Scotland and England for all that time, and life has been good in these parts. But in truth that could all change tomorrow, for any one of a hundred reasons. All it would take is for some idiot on either side—and not even a king, just some powerful baron or earl—to offend, or threaten, or cross some other fool on the opposite side, and we could have English armies trotting towards us across those sands within a month. So look well at what I'm showing you and remember it. This route will lead any enemy who crosses here directly into Carrick, into your lands and towards your folk. Take heed, then, and don't ever lose sight of the dangers of having an open door at your back."

Rob, for all his youth, felt certain he would never have to worry about such a thing.

Lost in his thoughts and the places they led him, the boy fell into a daydream, content to allow his horse to follow Nicol's, his body adjusting mechanically to the lurching of the beast's back as it picked its way across the tortuous landscape and began the long climb up the last sloping hillside between them and the sea. He came back to attention, though, as they crested the hilltop and he heard his uncle speak.

"They're here already. But we haven't kept them waiting."

A hundred feet below them, on a shallow, sandy beach, a long, sleek, wide-bellied galley was drawn up onto the strand, its sail already furled and secured to the enormous spar that braced it, and a number of men were busy around it in the shallows, some of them up to their waist in water as they laboured at transferring horses from the vessel to the shore. Two beasts had already been unloaded and were being tended on the pebbled shore above the wrack by a boy whom Rob gauged to be about his own age. A third horse was about to be swung over as he looked, hoisted in a wide cloth cradle slung beneath its belly, and a fourth stamped nervously on the small cargo deck that seemed barely large enough to have held four animals. Nicol kicked his horse forward, leading the way down the grassy hillside as Rob shortened his reins and followed.

The boy on the beach with the horses was the first to notice them, and he shouted something to the others, so that within moments everyone was looking up the hill to where Nicol and his young companion were wending their way down. Rob saw row upon row of upturned faces staring at them from the rowing benches on both sides of the galley's central aisle, but though he was close enough to see the colour of their hair and beards he was still too far away to see any faces clearly. Above the oarsmen, on a platform in the prow, a dozen more men were working around the hoist being used to transfer the animals from the ship to the shore, and six more, besides the boy and his horses, were on the beach, four of them unloading the beasts from the galley, standing up to mid-thigh in the water but soaked to the waist as they waited for the suspended horse to be lowered to them. Their interest in the two newcomers had been brief, little more than a quick glance in response to the boy's shout, and quickly abandoned in the need to maintain a secure footing among the waves that broke over the submerged stones of the shelving shoreline.

The remaining two men on the shore stood on the pebbled beach above the waterline and were clearly, even at the distance from which Rob first saw them, of a different rank to the others. As he and his uncle drew closer to the water's edge, and details began to grow clearer, Rob saw what it was that set these two apart from their companions. Their clothing seemed little different from that worn by the rest of their party, but it was brighter, the colours bolder, more vivid, and the decorations adorning their garments—feathered crests and jewelled brooches—were larger, richer, and more elaborate, so that the pair stood out from their fellows like two of Earl Robert's beloved cock pheasants among a brood of dowdy hens.

"Which one's Angus Mohr?" Rob whispered to his uncle.

"Which do you think? The older one. The other's his good-son, a MacRory lordling, married to his daughter Morag. I only met him once and I can't recall his name but it will come to me … " Nicol spoke from the side of his mouth without turning his head away from the bustle below. He was smiling, though, and Rob knew the smile was for the people watching them.

"Why would they land here, when Turnberry's only four miles up the coast?"

"I can make a guess. Angus Mohr trusts no one—and believe me, he has learnt that to his cost. He has known your mother all her life and would probably trust her, but he does not know your father, other than as an English-born incomer, and therefore I would guess he is loath to sail blithely into Turnberry harbour without a guarantee of being able to sail back out again. Now say no more about it."

The hillside beneath them began to level out, and as they neared the shore Rob kept his eyes on the fierce-looking older man of the pair awaiting them. The man called Angus Mohr was imposing, so much so, in fact, that the man beside him, his son-in-law, faded into insignificance, appearing slight and nondescript. The Lord of Islay was every inch what his title proclaimed him, tall and broad in the shoulders, but where both height and width should have demanded depth and weight, the man was slim and agile-looking. He was stern-looking, too, Rob thought, the space between his brows showing a single crease that, while not quite a frown, looked as though it might easily become one. His hair was thick and black, with a single blaze of white above his left eye, and it hung in ringlets to his shoulders. There was no trace of a curl in his short, neatly trimmed beard, though, and his sun-darkened skin emphasized deep-set eyes that were startlingly, brilliantly, blue. His thin-ridged nose was more like a beak than any Rob had ever seen. A brimless black cap with a silver ring brooch that secured a hackle badge of distinctive black-cock tail feathers hung from his left hand.

Rob felt the change in his horse's gait as it stepped onto the yielding surface of the pebbled beach, and he tightened his reins, remaining slightly behind Nicol until his uncle reined in and slid from his mount's back, stepping forward with hands outstretched to welcome his guests, the elder of whom was now smiling broadly. By the time the boy dismounted and followed him, their greetings had been made and Nicol was waiting for him, half turned to him with a beckoning arm. The tall man stood glowering down at him.

"Angus, may I present my great-nephew Robert de Brus. He is firstborn son to my niece Marjorie, whom you know well, and he has been spending time with me these past few months. Robert, this is Angus Mohr MacDonald, Lord of Islay, and beside him is Lachlan MacRuaridh of Garmoran, goodman to Lord Angus's daughter Morag."

Both men nodded soberly at the boy, and Lord Angus's eyebrow twitched. "You would be what," he drawled, "the *seventh* Robert de Brus?"

Rob nodded, too young to be surprised by such knowledge in a foreign potentate. "Aye, sir," he said. "My father is the sixth of our name."

"As *his* father is the fifth. Aye, I know the man. Your grandsire, I mean. But you are born here in Scotland, are you not?"

"Aye, sir. In Turnberry."

"Aye, indeed. And not in England. Your father was born in England, if I remember rightly. In Writtle, is that not so?"

Rob had no idea if that were so or no, but he knew that his grandfather held lands at Writtle in Essex, and so he merely nodded, noncommittally. The Highland chief, watching the boy keenly, almost smiled, then shifted his gaze to Nicol, who had been watching the interplay.

"So, Nicol MacDuncan, are we to stay here all day or are you to take us to Turnberry to meet this King of Scots?"

"We are for Turnberry. We can leave as soon as you are ready."

The third horse scrambled ashore at that moment and was led to join the others while the last one aboard was moved into place to be fitted with the sling, and the three men began discussing other things that were of no interest to Rob. Knowing they had lost awareness of him, he looked about him curiously, and his eyes were drawn back to the boy holding the horses nearby. He was unsurprised to find the other gazing back at him levelly, his face expressionless. Rob glanced at his uncle, then, leading his mount, walked over to where the stranger stood clutching the reins of the newly landed horses.

"Hello," he said when he was close enough to be heard.

The other boy simply stared at Rob, his eyes empty of all emotion, then turned and led the horses away. He did not go far, though, barely more than a score of paces, before he stopped again and stood staring down at the pebbles at his feet. Rob watched him, unsure whether to ignore his bad manners and follow him or to take offence, turn his own back and walk away, too, leaving the lout to curdle in his own ungraciousness. He decided to follow and see what happened, telling himself he had nothing better to do. He drew level with the other boy again and found himself greeted with that same empty look, but this time the other's eyes slid away over Rob's shoulder towards the men talking behind them, and he spoke without moving his lips or looking again at Rob.

"I'm no' supposed to talk to ye," he said in Scots. "I havena been permitted."

Rob felt his eyebrows rise. "Permitted?" he said. "Ye mean ye're no' allowed to *talk*?"

The other boy continued to avoid his eyes, watching the distant trio of men. "No, I'm supposed to be workin'. And until they tell me to stop I canna do anything but work."

"Are ye some kind o' slave, then? A bonded servant?"

A smile, remote and bitter, flickered over the other boy's face. "No, but I might be better off as either one. I'm but my father's son. And my task is to see to his wishes at all times, until he gies me leave to stop."

"And who is your father, some kind of king? A tyrant?"

The half smile flickered again. "Sometimes he is. But at other times he's well enough. That's him, talking to the man you came wi'."

"Angus Mohr? That's your father?"

"Aye. Angus the Old since I was born. I'm called Angus Og—Angus the Young. Who are you?"

"Rob Bruce."

The other boy turned to look at Rob, his eyes suddenly full of curiosity, and he spoke unthinkingly in Gaelic. "Bruce? You mean like the Englishman who married into Carrick?"

"The Earl of Carrick, you mean," Rob responded in the same tongue. "Aye. He's my father. The countess is my mother, and that's where we're going. To Turnberry Castle. That's where I live."

Angus Og was wide-eyed. "You speak the Gaelic?"

Rob grinned. "I should. I was born here. Will you be coming to Turnberry with us?"

Angus Og's glance flitted from Rob to his father, whose back was to them. "I ... I don't think so. I'll have to stay here with the boat."

"Why?"

"Why? Because I have no choice. I'm in training."

"For what?"

The look that drew was almost pitying. "For life ... "

"We're all at that. Would you like to come? To Turnberry? D'you want to?"

"Aye, of course I'd like to come, but I know better than to ask."

"Then don't. I'll ask for you, and I'll ask my uncle Nicol, not your father. You're about the same age as me and there's nobody else around who's my age, and besides, tomorrow's my birthday. Nicol will say yes, I know, and your father will be hard put to say no after that."

"No," the other said quickly. "Don't ask my da. He'd never let me. Tell your uncle to ask Ewan, the captain, over there by the water's edge—the big fellow in the red jerkin. I'm ship's boy in his crew, but he'll let me go with you."

"Good, then I'll go and ask." He hesitated. "Ship's boy, you say. Can you ride?"

"Aye, but only a pony, smaller than these." He indicated the horses he was holding. "Nothing near as big as that thing of yours."

Rob grinned and patted his own horse's neck. It was a strong and well-built gelded bay, a biscuit-coloured crossbreed almost as large again as the stocky garron that had foaled it. "This fellow's not so big," he said. "You should see the horses the English knights use. Now *those* are big. Destriers, they call them. Giant warhorses, twice as big as this and more than three times the weight."

"Get away!" the young Islesman said.

"No, I swear by the Holy Virgin, it's the truth."

His listener was unconvinced. "No horse could be that big. Have you *seen* one? It could be an English lie, to keep us all in awe."

"They're real—I've seen some. Two years ago, when we visited Lord Bruce in Lochmaben. Four English knights rode in while we were there, and they were mounted on destriers."

Now Angus Og frowned in puzzlement. "Lord Bruce? You call your da Lord Bruce?"

"No, I told you, my father is the Earl of Carrick. Lord Bruce is *his* father, my grandsire." Only then did it occur to him that he never thought of his grandfather by any other name than Lord Bruce, but he saw nothing strange in that. "He lives in Lochmaben," he went on. "D'you know it? It's a fortress near the border with England."

Angus squinted into the sun, tilting his head. "What age will you be tomorrow?"

"Ten."

"I'm eleven, nearly twelve. Your uncle would let me come, think you?"

Rob smiled. "Aye, he would, and will. But will your Captain Ewan? Wait here."

Less than half an hour later the two boys, double-mounted on Rob's big bay, sat off to one side as the rest of their party left the beach and struck out along the coast for Turnberry Castle. They would be there by mid-afternoon, and the talking among adults would begin almost as soon as they arrived, depending on who was there to meet them. Rob knew his mother's time would be completely consumed by her duties as hostess and castellan, so she would have no time for him, but she would be happy to see him home and he knew she would make his new friend feel welcome. What excited him most, though, was that the affairs of the adults would leave him with plenty of time to show Angus everything he wanted him to see in and around the castle.

They waited for the mounted members of the party to pass by, Angus Mohr and his good-son MacRuaridh of Garmoran riding with Nicol, and two other men whom Angus Og named to Rob as MacDonald chieftains following close behind, and then Rob kicked his stocky bay forward to ride behind them and ahead of the score of heavily armed clansmen who formed Angus Mohr's guard. Turnberry lay less than five miles to the north, and the summer afternoon was perfect.

# CHAPTER THREE

# THE KINGS

From where she stood on the roof of the castle keep, Marjorie of Carrick could clearly see the royal party approaching from the northeast, the late-afternoon sunlight glinting off metal and reflecting back at her in shimmering waves of colour and movement. They were still too far away for her to make out individuals, but she had no doubt that her husband was among them, riding at the head with the two kings.

"They'll be here within the hour," she said quietly.

Beside her, Murdo cleared his throat. "There's more o' them than we thought."

"Aye, it looks that way, though ye've better eyes than me if ye can count them frae here. Still, we'll be able to take all of them. Ye've done well, Murdo."

"I hope so. It's lucky we were to have thae big tents—we'd hae been hard put to find room for them a'. An' thanks be to God the big fellow down there's the only one likely to need furnishings for his place. I think we can be sure the other three have their own comforts wi' them." He nodded to where a number of men were carrying basic furnishings from the castle into the pavilion that would house Angus Mohr of Islay for the next few days, and his mistress turned with him to look down at the four massive tents that now dominated the broad, grassy plain in front of the castle gates.

Angus Mohr's personal standard had been anchored firmly in front of his temporary abode where no one could fail to see it: a white banner showing a black galley under sail, suspended from a cross-brace and mounted upon a high pole. The Islesman had chosen the pavilion himself on his arrival, indicating bluntly, after a quick glance around him, that this one would be his, and it seemed to the countess that there was more than a little subtlety involved in the choice. With no advantage to be gained from choosing first among four seemingly equal pavilions, Angus faced no possibility of being asked to move later, in order to give precedence to someone else. But two of the pavilions were, of necessity, closer to the castle and its gates. In choosing the pavilion farthest from the entrance, Angus Mohr had made sure that the two kings would take the rear two, leaving Richard de Burgh in the one to Angus's left as they walked from the castle to the pavilions. And rank, as Angus Mohr well knew, declined from right to left in matters of protocol.

Marjorie smiled as she saw Angus Mohr himself walking with her uncle Nicol, both of them strolling head down, their hands clasped behind them, and she wondered what they were discussing; wondered, too, if she were giving the Lord of Islay too much credit for his suspected subtlety.

There was no sign of the two boys, she noted, for young Robert had taken his new friend to explore the seaside caves in the high cliffs a mile to the north. Her eyes moved onward, scanning the space beyond the men and taking in the arrangements that had been made there, where a formally outlined military encampment, complete with horse lines, cooking pits, and piles of fuel, now stretched along the gently sloping meadow that led down to the river about a quarter of a mile away from where she stood, just before the riverbed began its final curl westward towards the sea.

Murdo and his crew of workmen had achieved a miracle within the day and a half that had elapsed since he'd told her of finding her father's forgotten trove in the oar bothy. The enormous tents had been carried outside and spread out over the stout, wide frames on the beaches where the fishermen dried and repaired their nets, then left to air in the July sun while the men set about making sense of the mountainous coils of rope—more than fifty of them in varying lengths and thicknesses—and the bound stacks of sturdy poles that had been stored with them, some of them more like tree trunks than poles, six paces long and a foot thick at the base. It was a daunting task, and the men might never have succeeded in making sense of the profusion at all had Murdo not had the presence of mind to invite the oldest man in the Turnberry community to come and offer his guidance. Thorgard One-Arm, as he was called, had come to Arran from Norway seven decades earlier as a babe in arms, and in his youth had worked in Turnberry as a sailmaker for Earl Niall. He had also been the man responsible for turning the massive, carefully stored sails into tents almost forty years earlier. Too old now to share in the work himself, Thorgard was puffed up with renewed pride to find his skills and knowledge in demand again. Under his supervision the masses of poles and supports were quickly sorted into the correct order, and soon the first postholes were being dug.

Watching the pavilions being hauled laboriously into place by teams of sweating, cursing men, old Thorgard had sniffed disapprovingly at their stained condition and suggested that they should be treated with a coat of weatherproofing. And though far from happy with the delay, Murdo, a pragmatist above all else, had set his people to yet another task to which they were unaccustomed: preparing a mixture of diluted glue and whitewash as dictated by the old sailmaker, and brushing it over the coarse woollen fabric of the tents. It had been almost dark by the time the last of the peaked and now sodden pavilion roofs was hauled into place atop its poles, but when the morning sun rose the following day, its beams reflected warmly from the four magnificent pavilions in the meadow beyond the castle gates.

"Right," Marjorie murmured, more to herself than to her factor, "there doesna seem much else we could do. The pavilions are ready and everything that's to go in them will come wi' our visitors. The kitchens are stocked, the cooks are set to go, and the hall's set, wi' the tables in place and the floor freshly rushed. From now on, whatever happens will be out o' our hands. Our lives are going to be dictated for the next while by kings and bishops."

She met Murdo's eye when he turned to look at her curiously. Murdo, she knew, had no interest in the protocols governing visiting dignitaries. To him, kings were merely men of a different rank, and left to his own devices, he would, in his dour Scots manner, treat them as almost equals. That thought brought a tic of a smile to her lips as she envisioned Edward Plantagenet's reaction to being spoken to bluntly by her factor. Alexander, a Scot himself, might deal easily enough with it, accustomed as he was to the Scots lack of deference, but Edward's majesty would be severely challenged were he addressed truculently by a menial.

"Ye'd better go down and assemble the folk, Murdo. Make sure they're clean and presentable to welcome our guests, then line them up in front o' the gates. I'll go and tidy mysel' up while ye're at that, and then I'll come down and wait wi' ye."

"Aye … " Murdo's hesitation was almost unnoticeable. "Angus Mohr has two pipers wi' him. D'ye think it might be fitting to hae them playin' as the King arrives?"

Marjorie of Carrick grinned mischievously. "A Gaelic welcome for the King of Scots? And why no'? It was Alexander's idea to invite Angus Mohr to the mainland, and I know he likes the sound o' the pipes, for I've heard them played in his own great hall in Dunfermline. So be it the pipers are willing, then let them blow away. But be sure ye ask them properly. We canna let them think we expect it o' them. It must be their choice."

As soon as Murdo had hurried away she turned back towards the approaching cavalcade and narrowed her eyes. The party was close enough by then that she could see the flashing colours carried by the standard-bearers, and the distant sound of a trumpet indicated that the approaching party considered themselves close enough to Turnberry to be heard. She became aware of the size of the group and noted its composition, with kings and armoured courtiers in the forefront, bishops and priests in upholstered carriages behind them, and the mounted men-at-arms of the King's Guard preceding the motley array of baggage carts and wagons and extra horses that brought up the rear.

She drew in a sharp breath. Time was flying past her. She turned away and hurried down the narrow spiral staircase to her own quarters in the corner tower. Quickly as she moved, though, she was unable to stop her mind from pursuing a perplexing train of thought.

Edward Plantagenet had introduced an entirely new element into the situation she had been thinking about for weeks. The two original principals, King Alexander and Angus Mohr, might have been governable enough, sufficiently intent upon their own interests to overcome any strangeness between them. But the unforeseen addition of the English King had added a very different element. Edward spoke no Gaelic. Angus Mohr spoke neither English nor French. Every word that passed between them, then, would have to be translated by an interpreter. Her own husband spoke but little Gaelic, having come to learn the language as an adult and finding that it was not an easy tongue to master. Thus Robert might speak to either King easily, and with difficulty to Angus Mohr. Angus Mohr, in his turn, would speak easily with Alexander, and Alexander effortlessly to his brother-in-law Edward. But the gulf between the Gaelic Lord of Islay and the King of England might be unbridgeable, since neither one knew the other at all, engendering a fundamental lack of trust aggravated by Angus Mohr's well-known disdain for all things English. She wondered if the Ulster earl spoke Gaelic—it seemed likely that he might, and if he did, she thought, he might serve as a translator between the two.

Her thoughts were cut short when she reached her chambers and found her three women waiting for her, anxious to begin transforming her into a regal hostess. She looked wryly at them. "We have little time to transform me," she said, "so I expect miracles from you. Let's be about it."

Less than an hour later, looking radiantly confident and not at all matronly, Marjorie of Carrick took advantage of a momentary lull in the buzz of conversation to cast her eyes over the brilliant assembly in the main hall of Castle Turnberry. Everyone present was engaged with someone else, and the hum of conversation was sustained and pleasant. Even the taciturn Angus Mohr was deep in conversation with Robert Wishart, who had been Bishop of Glasgow for the past twelve years. Marjorie allowed herself a tiny sigh of relief, at ease, though still apprehensive, for the first time since the English King's party had arrived at her gates.

They had approached the castle in formal order, a walking thunder of heavy hooves amplified by jingling, clinking metal and creaking saddlery and augmented by the rumble and squeaks of heavy baggage wagons, and no one had said a word until the spar- kling, brightly coloured but dusty and weather-worn front ranks had reached where she stood waiting for them. As he drew near, her husband patently ignored the new pavilions on his threshold, failing to acknowledge them with as much as a glance, as though such princely accommodations were commonplace at Turnberry. His countess had watched as the earl dismounted along with the two Kings and stepped forward, smiling, his hand outstretched to bring her forward and reacquaint her with the monarchs, both of whom she knew from former occasions, and with Richard de Burgh the Earl of Ulster, whom she had never met. She had known King Alexander all her life, but she had also accompanied him to London, years before, with Earl Robert and a hundred other Scots lords, to attend the English King's coronation in Westminster.

As the royal guests and the senior members of their entourage greeted their hostess, all smiles and cordiality, the churchmen behind them climbed down from their carriages and came forward in their turn to do the same. Someone at the rear then shouted orders to the baggage train and escorts to break formation and disperse, and Murdo and his team of ushers moved among them to guide the various contingents towards the areas set up for them.

Angus Mohr MacDonald had stood slightly behind and to the left of Marjorie throughout these proceedings, side by side with her uncle Nicol, and though the Islesman had nodded graciously and acknowledged the newcomers wordlessly one by one as they were presented to him, his obvious lack of warmth and his inscrutable expression had been enough to unsettle her. And so as soon as she had finished her formal welcoming greetings and before any awkwardness had a chance to develop, the countess had invited all the principals into the great hall, where food and drink awaited them.

Now the food had been satisfyingly depleted and most of the men had consumed at least one drink from the supplies of home-brewed ale, honeyed mead from England, and wines imported from France, and Marjorie found it easy to smile at Earl Robert as he detached himself from the group surrounding the two Kings and made his way towards her.

"Ye've done well, lass," he said, slipping an arm about her shoulders. "Later on ye can tell me where you found those damned tents."

"You left me little choice but to improvise, Husband. Do you approve?" Her speech had changed from the broad, localized Scots she used in speaking to the local folk of Carrick to the more formal, smooth-flowing, English-enriched variant that she used with her husband. Earl Robert, aristocratic and English-born, and raised in Scotland's far southeast, spoke Gaelic reluctantly and with great difficulty, and Marjorie had always deferred to his preference for the anglicized Lowland tongue.

"Approve? I was thunderstruck, but I could hardly show my surprise in front of everyone. They are wondrous, my love. And *four* of them!"

"I thought them big enough to serve as venues for your talks. Supposing, that is, that they all came here to talk … "

"Oh, they'll talk, my love, you may depend on that. Kings and bishops do little else."

"Is it cold in here? Should I light the fires?"

"God no, lass. It's high summer out there. Tonight will be time enough, when the sun goes down."

She nodded towards a small group of men in the corner beyond the Kings. "I've never seen so many bishops in one place at the same time. I know Bishop Wishart, but who are the others? Oh, I know, I met them when they arrived—but I met too many people at once, so their names are all gone and I can't recall which is which."

The earl grinned. "The skinny one in the red cap is Fraser of St. Andrews. He's younger than he looks and I don't know him well but the King thinks highly of him. The tall man talking to him is not a bishop at all, but he is one of the most powerful churchmen in the realm. That is Master Nicholas Balmyle and he's the Official—that's his title—of the Archdeaconry of Lothian, the Sub-Diocese of St. Andrews. That makes him nominally subordinate to Bishop Fraser, but from what I've heard, I would not wager on his subservience—to Fraser or to any other prelate. He's not what I expected. Far more friendly and approachable than I would have thought."

"Hmm. He doesn't look awe-inspiring. What's so special about him?"

"His mind, my love. They say he's more mind than man. I wouldn't know, but the man is impressive enough for me. The other two with them are abbots—Arbroath on the right and Dunfermline in the brown and blue robes."

"Jesu!" Marjorie hissed, astonishing her husband by tugging sharply at his sleeve. "Come with me, quick!"

She had watched Bishop Wishart nod, smile, and back away respectfully from Angus Mohr before turning to join Fraser of St. Andrews and the other clerics in the corner, but then she had seen Edward of England watching Wishart, too, and as the bishop crossed the room, the English King left the group around him and King Alexander to cross to where Angus Mohr was talking quietly with Marjorie's uncle Nicol. Marjorie reached them, her bemused husband in tow, just as the two men came face to face and Edward, smiling slightly, said, "Angus Mohr MacDonald, let us talk, you and I."

Angus Mohr had drawn himself up to his full height as he saw the Englishman approach, and he answered in Gaelic. "I am Angus Mohr, and you are Edward, King of England … I can see why they call you the Longshanks."

Edward blinked, clearly not having expected the rolling Gaelic response, but before he could open his mouth Marjorie laid a hand gently on his forearm. "My lord Edward," she said pleasantly, "I doubt you speak the Gaelic tongue—would be surprised indeed if you did—and I know for a fact that my lord of Islay here has not a word of English or French, so may I offer my services as interpreter between you?"

The slight smile on Edward's face widened. "You may do that, Countess, and I will be even more in your debt than I am already," he said. He glanced at her husband and winked conspiratorially as he continued. "Few things are more frustrating than for two men to be unable to converse easily together. What did my lord of Islay say?"

Still smiling but filled with stirrings of apprehension, Marjorie glanced from one man to the other. "Angus Mohr acknowledged your recognition of him."

"Aye, and what else did he say? I'll warrant there was more." The King's smile was one of genuine amusement.

Marjorie felt a tinge of colour rising to her cheeks. "He said he can see why they call you Longshanks."

Edward laughed and turned his smile on Angus Mohr. "Tell him I can make no secret of it and that he himself is no dwarf. There are few men at whom I can look levelly, eye to eye. And express my pleasure at meeting him, if you will, for I have heard much about him these past few days."

Marjorie translated, then listened to the flood of Gaelic that poured out of Angus Mohr in response before she turned back to Edward. "That was well said, and the two of you well met, he says. He, too, has heard much of you and your exploits, in the Holy Land in your youth and in Wales these past few years. The name of Edward Plantagenet is well respected everywhere, he says. Perhaps not always loved, if one thinks of Wales, but respected even there."

"Hah!" Marjorie stiffened as the English King punched a clenched fist gently into Angus Mohr's shoulder, but his eyes were alight with good humour. "Good man!" he said. "I admire a man who speaks his mind—always have." He turned again to Marjorie. "Tell him, if you will, that I suspect we could be friends, we two, upon sufficient acquaintance and were we able to converse, and though his time will be much taken up by my royal brother Alexander tomorrow, I hope I might have the pleasure of talking to him at more length in the days ahead." Without waiting for Marjorie to translate his words, he inclined his head graciously to the Islesman and returned to join King Alexander.

Angus Mohr's face had remained expressionless as Edward administered the gentle punch, but Marjorie was acutely aware of Edward's unwitting breach of protocol. No one, ever, was permitted to lay hands upon the Lord of Islay. The Islesman, however, had plainly chosen to accept the gaffe, clearly aware that the Plantagenet had committed his sin unknowingly. Now he looked at her, one eyebrow slightly elevated, awaiting her translation. When he had heard it he gazed speculatively at Edward, who now stood with his back to them, conversing with his brother-in-law.

"I think I might enjoy talking to the man," he admitted, "though until this moment I would never have believed it. So be it if we can find a man we can both trust to translate for us. My thanks to you, Countess, for interceding here, and for your timing. Earl Robert, I am told you are learning our tongue."

"Poorly, I fear, Lord Angus," the earl said haltingly in Gaelic. "I came too late to the study of it. But I work at it, since it is my lady wife's tongue, and my children speak it fluently, being born into it here in the west, but I fear I will never be aught else than a plodding stammerer."

Angus Mohr smiled lopsidedly. "You do passing well, for an Englishman. Better than your English King."

Once again Marjorie felt herself go tense in the face of Angus Mohr's disconcerting bluntness, and awaited her husband's response.

"My King is Alexander Canmore, my lord, the man you have come here to meet. Edward of England may claim to be my feudal liege, in that my family holds great estates in England by his pleasure, but not to be my royal one. I am a Scot by birth, as is my father, and Alexander is the King of Scots."

The earl spoke evenly, evincing no displeasure, but Robert Bruce was not noted for either his patience or his tolerance, and his wife knew how angrily he would normally have reacted to such provocation, mild though it was. But Angus Mohr was not yet finished speaking his mind, and she saw his eyebrow quirk up before he mused, "By your own admission, though, you hold two loyalties, and one of them is to your family and its estates in England. We can but hope that nothing untoward should ever force you to choose between the two. Someone once said—and I can't remember who it was—that no man can serve two masters." He held up a hand before Bruce could respond. "I am not criticizing you, Lord Bruce. We all have tasks to perform and expectations we must meet in the eyes of others."

The earl's response was as temperate as before. "And what might change, to affect those loyalties, my lord? The two Kings could not be closer in friendship, allied as they are by love and marriage and mutual esteem. Nothing is like to change that."

"Agreed," said Angus Mohr, nodding slowly and scratching his chin with one fingertip. "Nothing is likely to change that. And yet things change and are altered constantly. That is the way of life, the bishops like to tell us. Let us both hope, then, that you are never forced to consider otherwise."

"Lord Robert! A word with you, if you please." The voice was Alexander's, calling from across the room.

"You'll pardon me, my lord, but I am summoned." The earl dipped his head to Marjorie. "My dear, permit me."

On the point of turning back to Angus Mohr, she saw Murdo standing by the doorway, trying to catch her eye. She hesitated, but Angus Mohr had followed her glance and seen Murdo, too.

"That's your factor, is it not?"

"It is. Murdo. I expect he'll be wanting to talk to me about supper."

"Then go you and talk to him, Countess, and have no concerns about me. I will not cause you grief, here in your own house. Nicol here will share another cup of mead with me and we'll be fine, the two of us. Away you go."

She threaded her way among the groups of guests to where Murdo stood waiting. She was scanning the factor's eyes and stance as she drew near him, looking for signs that he was troubled, and she felt her heart lighten when he caught sight of her and smiled.

"Is all well, Murdo?"

"Aye, Countess, it is. The boys came home more than an hour ago and I sent them to eat in the kitchens, for I jaloused ye wouldna want them in here wi' a' the grand folk. They were tired out and wearin' half the dust an' dirt o' Carrick on them. Allie will see them to their beds. But she sent me to ask what time ye'll be wantin' to sit down to sup, for she wouldna want the food to be less than perfectly hot. D'ye know?"

"No, I don't. What hour is it now? I confess I've lost track o' the time."

"Late afternoon … about fower, I'd guess. I hinna checked. But on any ordinary day we'd serve supper about two hours frae now."

"Aye, that sounds right." Marjorie checked over her shoulder, and her guests seemed content to be as they were for a while. "We'll gie it another hour or so here, to let the serving folk get the rest o' the tents ready for the lords, and then we'll send them to their tents for an hour longer while the hall is made ready for supper. Two hours will be about right, then, so ye can tell Allie to be ready when she would on any other day. Away ye go now, and thank ye for seein' to the boys."

Every table was filled at dinner in the hall that night, and the food was tasty and plentiful, and welcomed by everyone. The only unexpected event of the evening came at the end of the meal, when the platters had been pushed away and the assembly had settled down to drink at length and to enjoy the remaining entertainment. A sudden stir at the entrance marked the arrival of the sergeant of the guard, followed by a pair of guards shepherding a dishevelled, travel-stained, and tired-looking courier between them. They marched directly to the head table, where the sergeant announced to King Alexander that the man between them had ridden up to the gates a short time earlier carrying dispatches that he had refused to surrender for proper delivery. He had dispatches for King Edward, he said, and his duty would not be complete until he had placed them directly into the hands of the King himself.

King Alexander nodded to the English King, and Edward returned the gesture and extended his hand to the courier, beckoning him to come forward and deliver his packet. The man shrugged free of the guards' hands and stepped towards the table, opening the thick bag slung across his shoulders and pulling out a bulky, wax-coated packet, which he placed on Edward's outstretched hand. It was sealed with a wax stamp and marked in its lower left corner with a large red dot. Edward hefted it gently.

"I thank you," he said. "How long have you been on the road?"

The courier straightened his shoulders and thumped his right fist against his breast in a salute. "Eight days, Majesty."

The King raised an eyebrow, aware of the attentive silence in the hall. Even the ancient bard from Arran had fallen silent in the middle of his singing, his fingers stilled upon the strings of his harp. "Eight days?" he asked. "And why so long?"

"I missed your royal presence by ten hours in Dunfermline, where I went first, thinking you to be in residence. It was late, growing dark, and I was persuaded by your commander there to spend the night and set out again come morning. Since then, I have ridden two more days to find you here."

"Good man, then, and again, my thanks." He raised the packet he still held. "Does his lordship of Bath and Wells require a response to this?"

"I know not, Majesty."

"Hmm. Well, you had best bide a while, until I discover that for myself." He looked then at the sergeant of the guard. "See that this man is treated well, Sergeant. He has earned his bread and board." The sergeant, stiff as a spear shaft, saluted, and Edward spoke again to the courier. "The sergeant will find you food and a place to sleep. Present yourself to his lordship the Earl of Norfolk on the morrow and inform him that I have awarded you two silver shillings for your services. He will pay you, and then I would have you await my further orders."

He nodded in dismissal, and the man rejoined the guards, who saluted the royal party and then wheeled and marched away, the courier between them, and every eye in the hall followed them as they went. King Alexander clapped his hands in the silence and told everyone to continue as before.

As the bard began to sing and play again and the buzz of voices resumed, Edward sat musing, hefting the packet in one hand again as he stared at it. It was apparently dense with contents, wrapped in a thickly woven envelope of coarse wool that had been dipped several times into melted wax for waterproofing and security and then sealed with the insignia of the sender. Edward had barely glanced at the seal, for the wide, red dot beneath the final coat of wax told him from whom it came. He was more interested in guessing how much of the weight in his hand was coarse woollen wrappings and wax, and how much was written content.

"Affairs of state?" The question came quietly from Alexander, expressing what Edward knew everyone was wondering.

"Aye, brother." His response was equally quiet. "I fear so. And weighty, it seems." He tossed the packet to the Scots King. "From Burnell. The red dot is a sign that the matters contained are urgent. We have a pact between us, Robert and I, that he will never waste my time with anything less." Alexander tossed the packet back, and Edward turned it so that the people sitting closest on his left, his host and hostess, could see the dot. He had no need to say more, for everyone listening was already nodding sagely. Robert Burnell, the Bishop of Bath and Wells, was Edward's Lord Chancellor of England and one of his closest friends and advisers.

Alexander shrugged. "So be it then, brother. Best make your farewells."

Edward grunted, trying to imbue the sound with regret, for he had long since grown bored with the unintelligible Gaelic moanings of the old bard, and turned to his host and hostess. Before he could speak, though, Marjorie of Carrick smiled. "Clearly you must go, Your Grace. Such a shame, since I know full well how you must have been enjoying old Seumas's saga."

The King found it easy to grin back at her, a tacit acknowledgment of her barb's accuracy. "I fear I must, Countess, much as it grieves me to deprive myself of your company this evening. Accept my gratitude for this wondrous meal and for your hospitality at large, if you would, for I have enjoyed it thoroughly and look forward to rejoining you tomorrow. In the meantime," he leaned forward slightly to address the Earl of Carrick beside her, "my lord of Carrick, my thanks are no less due to you. And now, with your permission, I will leave you."

He rose to his feet, tucking the waxed packet of dispatches beneath his arm, and waved in a broad, unmistakable gesture to the English lords who had been watching him and had risen as one to follow him. His meaning was unequivocal. They hesitated, then all but one resumed their seats, leaving only Roger de Bigod, the Earl of Norfolk, standing. As captain of the King's Guard, it was Bigod's duty to accompany Edward everywhere, and now he moved resolutely to join the King before Edward reached the hall door.

Edward frowned, but accepted that the man was merely doing his duty. "If you must come with me, then you must. I am but going to my tent, to read this. You may see me safely there and then return here. De Blais will attend me thereafter."

"As you wish, sire." Gervais de Blais was Edward's personal attendant on this journey, a senior squire in the final preparations for knighthood, and Bigod knew Edward trusted him completely.

The King inclined his head. "I do wish it, my lord of Norfolk." He paused on the threshold and turned back to scan the hall once more, then waved to Alexander, who was watching him from the head table, and strode out, clutching his packet.

Several hours later, once the high-born guests had returned to their pavilions and the household was asleep, the Countess of Carrick and her consort earl sat comfortably side by side in their candlelit bedchamber, holding hands loosely in front of the stone hearth as they enjoyed the warmth of a leaping fire and discussed the events of their day. It was a habit they had developed years earlier, communing with each other at the end of each day without having to fret about being disturbed, and they had both come to relish the quiet luxury of it, since it was frequently the only peaceful time they had together from one day to the next.

Content with the easy silence between them, Marjorie turned her head slightly to look at the man who had shared her life and her bed for the past ten years. He was unaware of her look, staring into the flames with a thoughtful scowl on his face, and as she gazed at his fire-lit profile she felt herself smiling at the changes in his appearance since they had first met. They were not greatly pronounced, but they were there to be seen in his greying, unkempt hair and close-trimmed beard, and in the fine lines deepening into wrinkles of crow's feet at the corners of his eyes. He was forty-one now, she thought, a mere three years younger than Alexander and four years younger than Edward of England, and though the years had been good to him, the changes she remarked would surely grow more visible in the years ahead. But the face she knew so well was a strong one, firm of chin beneath the short beard and dominated by a strong, narrow, straight-edged nose and a high, clean forehead above deep-set, piercing eyes.

He turned suddenly, alerted perhaps by her stillness. "What are you thinking, Wife?"

She shrugged slightly. "Oh, I was just looking at you … wondering if I will look as well as you do when I reach your age."

Earl Robert grinned. "God, lass, that's fourteen years away. We could all be dead by then. You are but seven and twenty. Enjoy that while you can, for it won't last long. I would wager you can't imagine being thirty, let alone forty, can you?"

She laughed and lapsed into Scots. "That's true, and I hae to remind myself sometimes that I'm wed to an auld man, for thank God there's that lusty part of you that hasna aged the slightest bit. Makes me wonder how many mair bairns ye'll hae got on me by the time I'm forty."

"A few more, I hope. But in ten years' time you'll be too old to have any more."

She was on the point of telling him that she was quickened again, but she stopped, recognizing that there would be time enough ahead, once their royal guests had departed and he had time to enjoy such news. Instead, she tilted her head back and looked down her nose at him. "*I'll* be too auld? By then you'll be a dodderin' five and fifty, Robert Bruce. Ye'll be lucky if ye're able to throw a leg across a horse, let alone a willin' woman." His mouth opened to protest, but she leaned across and stroked his cheek. "But that's fourteen years i' the future, dear yin, and by then I'll no' begrudge ye your rest. In the meantime, though, ye're still hale and hearty."

"Aye," he growled, half laughing, then gazed at her, his look sharpening, "and ready for you, too, this minute."

She pushed him away fondly, switching back to English. "Curb yourself, my love. We have the whole night ahead of us. And before we bed we have things to talk about. Were you pleased with how matters went today?"

"I was."

"What about tonight's supper?" They had had upward of thirty guests in the hall, including the Kings and their retainers, the Islesmen, and the various bishops, abbots, and priests, and the entertainment throughout had been non-stop, provided by a trio of harpists who accompanied the Kings and interspersed with bagpipe music, plus an old saga provided by the bard from Arran, brought in especially for the purpose.

"It could not have been better, lass. Even your Islesman behaved himself perfectly."

"*My* Islesman? Why would you call him mine?"

"Because he is here, and so are you, my love—not the wife and mother but the countess, presiding as hostess, in all her tawny-haired glory, over the affairs of mere men. I doubt there's a man alive who could resist being your slave, seeing you thus."

Marjorie sat silent for a moment, digesting that, and then dipped her head. "That, my lord, was the perfect thing to say to ensure a pleasant … *welcoming*, before you go to sleep this night."

"Excellent. Then let's be about it, woman." He reached out for her, but she caught his hand before he could grasp her breast. "In a minute, I promise. Just be patient with me. Did you speak to Murdo?"

"No, not yet. I will tomorrow."

"Will you have time?"

"Why would I not?"

"I was thinking about the King. Will he not require your presence at his meeting with Angus Mohr?"

"I doubt it. The proceedings will all be in the Gaelic and you know how useless I am with that. No, he'll have Gaelic-speaking witnesses enough for what he is about, without my being there. I'll probably attend him for a while in the morning, to make sure they have everything they need, but I doubt I'll be expected to stay, any more than Edward will."

"What will they need that they might not have already? What's to happen there, anyhow, between Alexander and Angus Mohr?"

"Talk … Little more than talk."

"Talk aimed at what? Are you allowed to tell me, or is it a dark secret?"

"It's no secret. At least it won't be after tomorrow. In the meantime, though, few people know what Alexander intends."

Marjorie straightened in her chair. "And what *does* he intend?"

"To honour Angus Mohr."

"To honour him … The King of Scots seeks to honour Angus Mohr MacDonald? Honour him in what way and to what end?" She held up a hand. "Bear with me. I'm trying to answer my own question, but all that's coming to me is another: why now? It seems to me our King might find better things to do for the good of the realm than go out of his way to meet and honour a man he barely knows— and one, forbye, who shows little affection for him."

"By the living God, Wife, you have a man's head on your shoulders, for all your womanly shape and softness. You see right to the heart of things where most men would stop short. I think you are wrong in this particular case, though. I believe Alexander could find *nothing* better to do at this time than what he intends." He hesitated, weighing his next words. "Why, you ask, and to what end? The answer is plain and simple. He does it for the good of the realm. Think about it, Marjorie. Angus Mohr MacDonald is a canny and powerful man, with soaring ambitions that could make him dangerous. He is absolute Lord of Islay, but his influence reaches far into the other Western Isles—into Jura and Mull to the north, and beyond that as far as Rhum and Eigg, and even east to mainland Argyll and Kintyre and the Isle of Bute. Indeed, almost to Arran itself, just across the firth in front of us. He is close to becoming a threat, growing more powerful with every year that passes, as his Islesmen spread his influence and the island folk accept him. And that is what Alexander seeks to check, here in Turnberry."

For long moments the crackling of the fireplace was the only sound in the dark room as Marjorie thought about what her man had said. Finally she spoke. "So, how does he intend to check him?"

"By making an ally of him, rendering him beholden to the King's grace."

"And how will he do that? Angus is no fool. He'll see to the heart of it."

"I agree the man is no fool, nor will Alexander treat him as one. But as I said, Angus has ambitions. Tomorrow, the King of Scots will ennoble Angus Mohr."

"*What?*" Marjorie snorted. "How will he do that? By *knighting* him?" The scorn with which she emphasized the word embodied the contempt with which the Gaels regarded the Norman French notion of knighthood.

"No, that would be folly. He intends to bestow upon Angus Mohr the title of Lord of the Isles, in perpetuity."

The countess's mouth fell open, and her eyes grew wide as she began to perceive the implications of what her husband had said. "Sweet Jesu," she breathed eventually. "Sweet, sweet Jesu … That is either the most brilliant idea I have ever heard or the greatest, most tragic foolishness ever dreamed up by man. Alexander is playing with fire, juggling live coals … "

"Aye, but juggling brilliantly, based upon what needs to be done. Angus Mohr's ambitions must be set at naught, and peacefully, before he gains sufficient influence to require stronger measures to restrain him. And what better way to do it than by pandering to his lusts? The man already sees himself as an island potentate.

"Alexander's solution is pure diplomacy, inspired strategy, and magnificent politics all in one. The lordship of the Isles will set the seal on Angus Mohr's pretensions. It will grant him the equivalent of an earldom in rank and possessions, but without the formal status of earl, and as Lord of the Isles he will be established as the dominant puissance, the presiding force, in the Western Isles. We do not believe he will be able to resist the lure, even though he sees the hook built into it: in accepting the lordship, he will be acknowledging Alexander's right as King of Scots to grant it to him, and that will make him the King's man in the eyes of all, Church and state, both in this realm and in England, with Edward himself as witness to it. And it will cost Angus nothing, save the time and effort of travelling to Dunfermline for formal investiture at some future date. But it will make him, beyond dispute, the King's representative in the Isles of the west. And that in turn will set him and his Islesmen up as defenders of the King's realm against any insurrection among the Macdowells of Galloway or any other. A powerful ally to have, think you not?"

"I am impressed," Marjorie said eventually. "As a stratagem it appears to be both sound and sensible. I can find no fault in it. And it should work, providing Angus Mohr accepts. And I believe he will, for the reasons you say. But ... " She frowned. "There's already strife enough between MacDonald and the Macdougalls. How will Alexander of Lorn react to this?"

"That's the beauty of the whole thing." She heard the enthusiasm he had been at pains to conceal before. "He has no choice, cannot object. Alexander is already sheriff of Argyll and Lorn, in the King's name, and therefore this development strengthens his position, too. When Angus Mohr accepts the lordship of the Isles, he will accept, publicly, the task that goes with it. He will be pledged to support the

King's interests in the west. And that in itself practically ordains alliance between him and Alexander. It will bring peace to the west for the first time in a hundred years."

In the fire's flickering light he saw his wife's private doubt expressed in the faint pout of her mouth.

"Oh, it won't happen overnight," he continued smoothly. "No one expects that. Those two warhorses have been prancing around each other too long for either one of them to take to the notion of alliance easily. But it will happen, my love, over time. By this time next year it should be well in hand, and we believe—"

"*We* believe? Had you a hand in this?"

"A small one. There were others involved. But yes, I was part of it."

Now Marjorie turned sideways to look over at him. "Well, Husband," she said, "you were right. It is a brilliant solution to a problem few beyond these parts knew to exist. We can but hope Angus accepts the title, though he would have to be blind not to see how a refusal will hobble him. Aye, he would have to be blind … and foolish. A blind fool." She sighed loudly and rose to her feet, stretching a hand out to the earl. "So be it, then. Take me to bed now, goodman, and show me how young you are."

Later, when they lay contentedly intertwined before separating to sleep, the countess murmured, "I hope this all goes as well as you predict, my love. It will set the seal upon this week and this place of ours and change the lives of many folk, not only ours. I wonder what was in King Edward's packet … " She waited for his reply, but Robert Bruce of Carrick had gone ahead of her and his only answer was a gentle snore. She smiled and gently eased her long legs free of her husband's, then turned on her side and snuggled her buttocks against him, enjoying his habitual response as he grunted and fitted himself to the curve of her back. "It must have been of import," she murmured to herself, "for I thought he might come back, but he never did …"

# CHAPTER FOUR

# MEETINGS

Late in the afternoon of the next day, Alexander Canmore, King of Scots, emerged with a smile on his lips from the great pavilion where he had spent long hours in council with his followers and guests. In the full light of mid-afternoon, he looked about him, breathing in the scents of the summer day, the sweet, salty tang of the seaweed on the nearby shore mingled with the familiar odours of fresh hay and warm dung from the horse lines on his right. He heard the swelling sound of voices at his back as the other men began to spill out from the pavilion, their day's business concluded, and he draped an arm amicably over the shoulders of the Gaelic chief, Angus Mohr, who came up beside him. Both men stood talking quietly, their heads close together as the others filed by them without seeking to interrupt, and it was clear from their easy intimacy that they were both satisfied with the outcome of their deliberations.

The Scots King laughed aloud and slapped Angus Mohr gently on the shoulder, and as he did he saw Edward of England standing close by, watching him, and in unfeigned pleasure he opened his arms to his royal kinsman, calling out his name. Edward moved forward to embrace his brother-in-law as the Gaelic chief stepped back, giving him room. As they exchanged pleasantries, Angus Mohr cleared his throat and spoke in Gaelic to Alexander, bowing his head slightly but none the less deferentially to the Scots monarch, who listened graciously and answered him in the same language. The MacDonald chief then glanced at Edward, nodded pleasantly, and left the two Kings together.

They watched him leave, and when he was safely beyond earshot Edward asked quietly in English, "Well, cuz, did you get what you required of him?"

"Aye, brother, I did. A good day's work, indeed, from both our viewpoints. Angus Mohr is now my official ally in the far west, Lord of the Isles by royal decree and ten times richer than he was when he set foot here in Turnberry to meet us. From this day forth he will prosper greatly, enriching me and this realm with his friendship—which might conceivably prove fickle, though I doubt that—and with his championship, which will endure if for no other reason than that his future welfare will depend on it. We have had concerns, these past few years, about the activities of certain people in the far west whose ambitions I have found difficult to curb from Dunfermline. We have few good roads here in Scotland, as you know, and none at all in the west and armies progress too slowly when they have to march overland, picking their way over trackless wastes, around lakes and mountains. Now I will have MacDonald there, ready to protect my interests in concert with his own. Those others I spoke of are his enemies—traditionally so—but now that he is my man, beholden to me for all that he owns from this day forth, he will protect my welfare and that of my realm in furthering his own. And so I am well pleased."

He took a step backward, eyeing his royal guest. "What about you? Is all well?"

"Aye, it is," Edward answered. "But why should you suspect otherwise?"

"Why? Because I saw you take your chancellor's dispatch from the hands of his messenger and I know you spent hours walking and thinking about it, fretting over it. Your man Norfolk told me that you left before dawn this morning and when you returned earlier this afternoon you were caked with dust and sweat. A long walk alone in the hot summer sun bespoke grave concern, but I was happy to see you looked well content when you came back."

"I was and I am. I found a solution and I am happy with it."

"And am I permitted to ask what it concerned and what you determined?"

The English King grinned. "You are. Burnell directed my attention to a matter beyond my realm and yours, in Sicily. There's a threat of war looming there, he says—a war that might threaten us in England if left unchecked. That disturbs him, and he is a man not easily disturbed. In consequence it concerned me even more. I have troubles enough of my own without being forced into more at the whim of others overseas whose affairs hold no interest for me."

"And so a resolution came to you?"

"Aye, with God's help. I will write to the Pope immediately and offer my services as a mediator, to negotiate a peace that will be acceptable to everyone. It should work. I'm uninvolved in the dispute, and those who *are* involved all know I have no interest in what's being fought over. Add to that the consideration that the Pope will be eager, I believe, to throw the full authority of the Church behind me, since he has more to lose in this affair than any of the principals." He chuckled. "My regal brothers in Christendom are all wise and noble men, and who but a fool would seek to wage a ruinous war when an honourable settlement can be arranged without disgrace?"

Alexander grinned. "Who, indeed? And we all know there are no fools among the Kings in Christendom. I'll wish you well then, brother."

It was later that same afternoon when Rob Bruce and his new friend returned to Turnberry after a long day of explorations and adventure. They had taken a boat that morning and rowed northward along the coast to one of Rob's favourite spots, where a high cliff plunged down to a narrow strip of beach that was reachable only when the tide was ebbing. The entire face of the cliff was riddled with caves, the interior so honeycombed that once inside at beach level, an enterprising boy could make his way up to the very top by climbing from cave to cave without ever going outside. It was dangerous, because the tide below went out and came back quickly, leaving only a narrow space of time for entering and getting out again, and as the returning waves swept back, the lower levels were flooded with lethally swirling water.

They had had almost two full hours in the caves that day because this was the season of what the fishermen called neap tides—the lowest that could occur—and they had beached their boat high and dry a hundred paces from where the cliff began, then made their way along its base to the entrance to the first cave. Rob could not remember ever having spent such a long time in there, and they had explored the caves extensively, though they found nothing of value. Merely being there, in peril from the incoming tide, had been adventure enough to satisfy them both, and they had judged their escape finely, scuttling like crabs along the base of the cliff until they reached the safety of the shelving bank beyond, with spuming breakers threatening to sweep the legs from under them over the last few scrambling yards.

"We've got caves on Islay," Angus Og said in a hushed voice when they were safely at the top of the sandy slope beside the upsweeping cliff. "But we've nothing like that. Our caves are just caves, and the biggest you ever get is three linked together. But this place … I've never seen anything like it."

"There *is* nothing like it," Rob answered, his voice equally quiet. "Nicol says it's the kind of stone that makes so many caves possible. It's soft and hard together, if you can imagine that, and the waves have just scoured out the soft bits and left the hard bits standing. Nicol says someday the whole thing's just going to collapse, rotted from the inside out. I think I believe him, too. I just hope I'm not in there when it happens!"

Angus Og was wide-eyed imagining it, and soon he began to giggle, flapping his arms as if to knock away the tumbling roofs and walls. His antics quickly had Rob laughing, too, and in moments both boys were rolling around and sobbing hysterically, hugging their sore ribs.

They fished from the boat for the remainder of the day, and before they knew it their midday meal was a long-forgotten thing and they were hungry again and still five miles at least from home.

Murdo the factor saw them as they reached the main gates and called them over to him. He asked them where they had been and then sent them back to haul the boat up beyond the tide line and to empty it and secure it properly. When he was satisfied that they had left everything in order, he dispatched them indoors by a side entrance to report to his wife. Rob went obediently, Angus Og tailing along behind him in silence, and Allie examined them both for cuts and dirt stains, then sent them off to the kitchens to be fed, warning them to behave themselves and to stay well away from the busy cooks and from the main body of the house, where the earl and countess were entertaining their royal guests.

Rob had noticed that his friend had very little to say around grown men and women, even when they were as warm and friendly as Murdo and Allie and the other members of the countess's household, and though he had been tempted to say something about it, he had wisely decided to keep silent. He sensed somehow that Angus Og's upbringing among his forbidding father's Islesmen had taught the boy to be wary of all adults. Rob had only ever felt that way himself on his infrequent visits to his paternal grandfather, Lord Robert Bruce of Annandale, but while he was there he felt that way *all* the time. The old man frightened Rob, even though he knew there was no reason for his fear, so he was prepared to accord the same tacit understanding to his quiet friend Angus.

Freed again from the constraints of having to behave acceptably, the boys charged around the corner of the main house and raced directly for the kitchens, Rob in front and Angus Og hard on his heels. They were approaching the outer doors to the main house when they looked up and almost skidded to a halt, their eyes growing wide as they saw that they had almost hurtled full tilt into Someone Important.

There were in fact two men before them. One of them, an armoured knight with a frowning face, had thrown out an arm as if to fend them off, and he snarled at them now, ordering them to get back. The other man, though, who looked older and was a full head taller than his companion, laid a restraining hand on his arm.

"Let it be, my lord of Norfolk," he said. "Wait for me inside."

The other looked at him askance, then shrugged and stepped through the open doorway, leaving the two boys gaping openly at the magnificence of the rich, white, heavily embroidered tunic that the man now facing them was wearing. Rob was squinting at the coat of arms on the broad chest, deciphering the elements of the red, gold, and blue escutcheon and racking his brains for what he had been told by his tutor about the premier coats of arms.

"That's the royal coat of arms," Rob said in English to the tall man. "Are you the King of England?

"I am," Edward Plantagenet said evenly. "And who are you?"

Rob felt himself flush, but he returned the monarch's gaze steadily and spoke with confidence. "I am Robert Bruce, my lord," he said. "Seventh of that name. This is my mother's castle and they call me Rob." He turned slightly, indicating his companion with a wave. "And this is my friend Angus, from Islay. His father is Angus Mohr."

"Ah, the new-named Lord of the Isles." Edward nodded at the frowning boy. "I have met your father. Do you understand the honour accorded him today by King Alexander?"

The young Gael gazed back at him, but there was not the slightest hint of awe in his look, and Edward pursed his lips in the beginnings of disapproval, but before he could say anything Rob spoke again.

"Angus does not speak English, sir King." He flicked a glance at his friend and added, "That's why he looks so … unfriendly. He doesn't know who you are and didn't understand a word you said to him."

"But he does know about the honour extended to his father today, does he not?"

"Aye, sir, he does. Murdo the factor told us about it just now."

"And is he proud of it?"

The response came after a very slight hesitation. "I cannot answer that, my lord King. He and his father are ... not close."

"I see."

Rob's gaze did not flicker as he watched the English King meet Angus Og's eye squarely, then nod graciously to the lad and turn directly back to Rob. "He does look ... unfriendly. But now I understand why. How old are you, Robert Bruce?"

Rob blinked. "I'm ten. I was ten yesterday. Halfway to being a man, my uncle Nicol says."

"More than halfway," the English King replied. "Much more, I think, from the look of you." He glanced again at Angus Og, who was still gazing stolidly at him. "A pity that your friend does not speak English. He should learn it someday."

Rob shrugged. "He might, someday," he said, unconscious of any impertinence, and then he frowned. "Sir, I don't know what to call you."

"Most people address me as sire."

Rob nodded slowly. "Aye, but they're English and I am Scots. I would call King Alexander Your Grace if I met him, but not sire. We don't call anyone sire in Scotland."

The English King cocked his head. "Does that mean you never have met the King?"

Rob shook his head. "No, not yet. I was supposed to, on my birthday, when he arrived. But he was too busy."

"Call me my lord, then, and I will see to it that you do meet him. Have you ever been to England?"

"No, my lord."

"Your father has great lands there. Does he never visit them?"

"No, my lord. Not much, anyway. They are my gransser's lands—Lord Robert's."

"Ah, Lord Robert's. Of course. Well, one of these days your father the earl will come again to England—he attended my coronation, you know, with your lady mother—and I will tell him that when he does, he must bring you to visit me in Westminster. Would you like to see London?"

Rob nodded solemnly. "Aye, my lord, I would."

"Then so you shall. But now I must go and join your parents. Where are you two going?"

"To the kitchens, my lord." Rob hesitated then, frowning again. "Can I ask you something else?"

For a moment he thought the English King was going to smile, but he maintained a straight face and merely nodded. "You may."

"Why are you called King Edward the First? There were three other kings of England before you."

The King's eyebrow shot up. "There were. That is true. I am wondering how you knew that."

"My tutor, Father Ninian, told me."

"I see. And did he tell you their names, these three former kings?"

"Aye, sir, he did. Edwards three—the Elder, the Martyr, and the Confessor."

"All of them named, but none of them numbered. Did you ask why?"

"I did, my lord, but Father Ninian didn't know."

"It is very simple, young Bruce. The custom of numbering kings is a French one—a Norman one, in fact. I am the first king called Edward to rule in England since the days of my great ancestor the Conqueror William. Therefore I am Edward the First. The others you named were Anglo-Saxon Kings, the elden Kings of England, and hence they had no numbers to their names. Do you understand now?"

Rob nodded, and the King of England waved a hand. "Excellent," he said. "Go then, and sup well. We will speak again. Farewell." He nodded kindly, including both boys in the gesture, and made his way inside the heavy doors, leaving them staring after him.

"That was Edward Longshanks, the King of England," Rob said quietly in Gaelic, his voice tinged with awe. "Did you see the height of him?"

"Aye," Angus Og said equally quietly. "What was he saying to you?"

"He invited me to come and visit him in England, at his palace of Westminster in London."

Angus Og blinked in surprise. "Will you go?"

"Of course I'll go—if my da will take me. D'ye think me daft enough to say no? My da says London is bigger than Dunfermline and Perth together."

"He might keep you there," Angus said, his expression dubious. "My da says there are too many Scots folk who go down there and never come back."

"That's not true," Rob said. "Who would want to stay down there anyway, among Englishmen? I'd surely come back if I went. But I want to see Westminster. Mam says there's a church there that's bigger than any other church in England or Scotland. Westminster Abbey, they call it."

"I'm starved."

"Me too. Race you to the kitchens."

Supper was long past, and by the rules of the Bruce household, Rob should have been safely abed hours earlier, but on those magnificent late July days in the year 1284, thanks to the gathering of so many distinguished guests and their retinues, there was nothing of the normal in effect within Turnberry Castle, and Rob and Angus Og had taken advantage of the general confusion to slip out of doors again almost as soon as they were sent to bed. No one saw them leave and none paid them any attention as they walked through the encampments for the lesser visitors. They wandered among the long rows of tents, listening to all there was to hear, and Rob was amazed by the range and variety of dialects and languages being spoken. Some of the conversations were incomprehensible to him, but all of them, save for the Gaelic of the Islesmen, were gibberish to Angus Og. Awash in the sea of foreign-sounding tongues, the two drifted without purpose, driven by their curiosity and gazing avidly at the heavy, gleaming armour and polished weapons of the soldiers and men-at-arms around their fires, none of whom were even aware of the gawking boys.

In one spot between two separate encampments for horse and foot soldiers, men were gaming, pitting their skills against one another in contests ranging from wrestling to throwing horseshoes at iron spikes set in the ground, and the open spaces between the major contests were busy with smaller games involving dice, tossed coins, and bone tokens. The air was filled with raucous voices shouting and laughing, exchanging gibes and friendly insults and imprecations, and all too often, as bets changed hands, with jeers and bitter cursing that awed Rob with their range and fluency.

It finally grew too dark for the horseshoe games to continue, and as the boys left the ordered lines of tents with their roaring fires, it was approaching the tenth hour of the night. In the west, silhouetted against the lingering light in the summer sky, the distant mountains of Arran were sculpted in black. Encouraged by the invisibility the coming darkness would afford, the boys were making their way towards the seashore, attracted by the distant, melancholy sound of bagpipes. They were off the common path, skirting a cluster of stunted, wind-bent hawthorn trees on a grassy knoll, when Rob, leading the way, found himself suddenly close to a fair-sized knot of men—all Gaels, wearing shawls and plumed bonnets—who appeared to be quarrelling among themselves, their raised voices muffled by the distant breaking of the waves on the beach at their backs. He reached out a hand to stay Angus Og, but before he could alert the other boy he felt a heavy hand clamp onto his shoulder.

Rob twisted in the grip to look back. "Uncle Nicol!" he gasped in Gaelic, his knees threatening to give way. "I thought you were my da."

"Aye, I can see that. You're as whey-faced as a caught thief. What are you up to?" Nicol MacDuncan had turned his nephew to face him and now stood with his arms folded over his chest. "You two should be abed long since. If anyone notices you're missing, the earl will plant his boot firmly in your arse, my lad, as ought I."

Rob opened his mouth to reply, but before he could say anything he heard an angry curse and the sound of a heavy blow behind him, followed immediately by the rasping slither of a blade being drawn.

He spun around, and what he saw was branded into his mind: two snarling men faced each other, one of them brandishing a long, bared dirk while the other tugged to clear a sword from the scabbard behind his shoulder.

The dirk-wielder leapt forward, the thrust of his entire body behind the stabbing lunge, then seemed to stop in mid-leap as his blade hit the solid bulk of the swordsman's breast. The stricken man gasped at the suddenness of it and his upper body hunched violently, his shoulders seeming to curve down and around the weapon that had pierced him. He stayed there, motionless, for several heartbeats, poised as if held up on the dirk's hard blade. Then, his teeth bared savagely, eyes glaring in rage that swiftly changed to disbelief, he turned slowly, stiffly, sideways to face Rob, as though to show him the thing that was lodged in his chest. He teetered grotesquely and his face changed, going slack and empty as the high, extended fingers of his yet upraised hand released his unused sword. Unable to look away, Rob watched the weapon fall, its heavy hilt and guard sending it tumbling, spinning within its own length to strike the ground point first between the two men and lodge there, swaying.

The murderer seemed appalled by what he had done, for he made no effort to pull his dirk free, merely releasing his grip on it as his victim turned away from him with the lethal blade protruding from his chest. The wounded man's arm came down slowly, feebly, fumbling at the dirk's hilt as though to grasp it and pull it free, but he had no strength in him by then. He made a gurgling sound in his throat and toppled forward, rigid as a tree, to hit the ground face down, driving the long blade home hard enough to punch clean through him.

Rob heard the meaty rip as the knife tore through the body, its exposed point strangely bloodless and bright between the dead man's shoulders in the fading light; heard, too, the utter silence that followed, brief and quickly banished as a voice rang out in grief and fury and a third man sprang at the killer, whirling a short, broad-bladed axe above his head. The killer, empty-handed, did what Rob would never have expected. Instead of trying to leap away, he sprang at his attacker, almost on his toes, to place himself inside the axe's sweeping arc. And as he went, quicker than thought, he snatched up the dead man's swaying sword and thrust it straight-armed at his assailant, driving its point beneath the fellow's chin. The blow was deadly, amplified by the momentum of both their bodies. The axe-wielder's head snapped back as the blade pierced his neck, but his own hard swing and his determination were unstoppable. He was dead before his strike landed, but the lethal edge of his hard-swung axe took his opponent high on the shoulder, cleaving through cloth and flesh and bone and smashing him to the ground.

Another silence followed. Rob heard it clearly, as if in a waking dream. Sharp-edged yet less profound than the one before, it was disturbed by the shuffling of rapidly moving feet. All the men were moving quickly now, splitting into two groups and baring weapons, readying themselves to die if need be, crouching and sidling, searching for weaknesses among the others facing them. He heard his uncle shout in protest and felt himself pushed strongly back as Nicol stepped past him.

But the voice that stopped all movement was not Nicol MacDuncan's. It was a roar of outrage, voiced by Angus Mohr MacDonald himself as the newly named Lord of the Isles strode into the gap between the opposing groups. He was closely followed by another Gaelic chief—defined as such by his dress and bearing—whom Rob had never seen.

Weaponless, MacDonald held his arms high, the look of fury on his face defying any to ignore him or challenge him, and the unexpected sight of him, appearing at that spot and in that moment, froze every man there. He was dressed splendidly, as he had been earlier that day when meeting with the King of Scots, in a bright, belted tunic of buff-coloured leather over a high-necked bright green shirt, with leather boots and leggings dyed to match. He looked every bit the Lord of the Isles, and no man there would meet his eye as he stood, arms raised, glaring around at the carnage.

"What started this?" His voice emerged now as a deep, angry growl, and no one answered it. He looked directly at one of the men in the forefront. "You, Donuil Dhu. What happened here?"

The man addressed, Black Donald in the English tongue, shifted from foot to foot, gripping his bared dirk, his eyes cast down before his leader. He muttered something to the ground.

Angus Mohr's next words cracked like a thunderclap. "Look at me, man, and use the voice God gave you!"

Donuil Dhu drew himself erect and looked at his chief. "They had words," he said. "Fergus and the Macdougall ... Ill words."

"Ill words ... *Ill words*, you say?" The MacDonald scanned the crowd, and even from where he stood watching, Rob saw the fury in him, marked the bitter scorn that changed his voice. "Four dead men, over *ill words*?"

What he said brought frowns of perplexity to every face in the crowd, for all of them could see that the dead men numbered only three.

The thoughts of young Rob Bruce, though, had abruptly snatched his attention elsewhere. *They had words ... Fergus and the Macdougall.* Suddenly Rob understood the bloodied corpses on the ground to be a mere consequence of who and what these people were. The MacDonalds of Islay and the Macdougalls of Argyll and Lorn were ancient enemies, goaded by mutual hatred bred and fed through generations of fear and well-deserved distrust. He had always known that; he had heard it spoken of throughout his life. The Macdougall lands lay to the north, largely on the western main-land bordering the MacDonald holdings in the Isles, and their people were a folk who, for a hundred years and more, had defended their long sea lochs against incursion and usurpation by MacDonald Islesmen. He knew that this spilling of blood was far from being the first such, but he nevertheless saw it as oddly inappropriate—the notion of irony lay years in the future for the boy—that this eruption should occur here in the neutrality of his mother's Turnberry, and on such an occasion.

He sensed movement by his side and saw that Angus Og had moved closer, standing right beside him.

"Are you going to be sick?" Angus asked in a whisper, sounding both concerned for Rob and awestruck by what they had seen.

"No," Rob answered, somewhat surprised that this was true. "Are you?" he whispered.

"No."

"Who's the chief with your da?"

"I'm not sure, but I think he's the Macdougall."

*Of course he is*, Rob thought. Alexander Macdougall was the King's sheriff of Argyll and Lorn. And a strong Macdougall contingent had arrived with King Alexander's party, that he knew. Since then, Macdougall's followers and those of Angus Mohr had avoided each other. But it was clear to Rob now that the two rival chiefs must have been conversing close by when this fight broke out, and in apparent amity, since neither one was armed. And that explained how the rival parties had ended up together—each group was nearby as escort to its chief.

Angus Mohr's voice suddenly rose again. "Hear me, all of you!" They were all watching him, not a man stirring, and he waved towards the bodies at his feet. "This is the worst kind of madness."

Someone at the rear of the crowd dared to speak, muttering what sounded to Rob like an imprecation.

Angus Mohr stiffened, and his eyes sought among the crowd for the speaker. "Say that again." His tone was reasonable enough, but Rob sensed pent-up anger lying beneath it. "Come, then. Speak up."

Someone stirred towards the rear, glancing sideways at the man nearest him, and Angus pointed at the man thus singled out. "You. Iain. Was that you who spoke? What did you say?"

The man Iain, hulking and low browed, scowled. "Ye said four dead men. But that's no' right. There's but the two. Tam's no' dead." His speech was guttural, his words slurred and malformed, but everyone understood them.

All eyes went to the man felled by the axe. Sure enough, he was stirring, blood welling copiously but sluggishly from his shoulder wound, indicating that no artery had been severed. Someone hurried forward and knelt beside the man.

"Stand away!" Angus Mohr's voice was icy.

The kneeling man looked up at him in astonishment, opening his mouth as though to protest, but his indignation withered before the chief's flint-hard gaze, and he pushed himself erect and backed away as the Lord of Islay extended his hand. "Your dirk," Angus Mohr commanded. "Give it."

The other hesitated, then drew his weapon and held it out tentatively, hilt first. Angus Mohr took it wordlessly and reversed his grip on it, holding the point downward as he turned to face the man clearly dying on the ground nearby. Amid an appalled stillness he stepped forward, dropped to one knee, and used the index finger of his free hand to guide the dirk's point to a precise point on the body beneath him. He gripped the hilt in both hands, braced himself above them, and thrust down quickly, the entire weight of his upper body behind the blade. The man on the ground convulsed, his legs kicking spasmodically, then went still.

Someone among the watchers moaned, a strangled, tortured sound, and Angus Mohr stood up and turned to them, his face white and expressionless.

"Murderers die," he said, holding up his bloodstained hand. "It is the law, and I, his chief, have seen to it." He waited, but no one moved or spoke. "He who takes any man's life without just cause forfeits his own, and this man here killed twice, over *ill words*. You enjoy hearing ill words? Well here are more: two men were slain here needlessly and both were Macdougall. In redress, one MacDonald now faces his God, answering for the crime of that. But one is not enough. As I am your chief and that same God is my judge, one more of you will hang this night, for you were all involved in this abomination. I care not who it is, but one must die to make redress. Draw straws among yourselves, do what you will, but make your choice now."

Rob sucked in his breath and held it, knowing instinctively that this moment was a defining one in the life of Angus Mohr. The new

Lord of the Isles, at the very outset of his tenure, faced the threat of rebellion here among his own people unless he could convince them of the rightness of what he was proposing—and the outcome could alter everything in Scotland's west. Rob felt, could almost hear, the drumbeat of a pulse in his neck, and the silence seemed to him to stretch unbearably as every man of the MacDonald group fought indecision, debated loyalty within himself, and searched for a response to something unforeseen, unimaginable. And throughout it Angus Mohr stood facing them alone, tall and straight-shouldered in the gloom of onrushing night.

"Angus of Islay!" The voice, loud and authoritative, was Alexander Macdougall's, and all men's eyes turned to him. "May I speak?"

"Say what you will." Angus Mohr's voice was harsh.

"I have no sympathy with what has happened here, but it was not one-sided," Alexander began, turning to address the others. "Two of your number died, but only three men drew steel at the start, and the man who died last was fastest. Ranuff and Sian Morningstar were brothers, always hotheaded, as you all know, and that has cost them dear. And now the death of one more man has been ordained, a bystander like all of you, in expiation." He stopped, and turned to look at Angus Mohr before addressing his own men again. "As witness to what has now been done and said, and speaking both as your chief and as high sheriff of Argyll and Lorn, it is my belief that the *intent* of that order is sufficient. All three dead men are gone and cannot be brought back. What's done is done, and nothing worth-while can be gained in throwing another life away solely to make amends." He turned back to Angus Mohr and raised his voice yet higher. "And so, Angus of Islay, I would put to you two requests: take back your order on the hanging … And tell these men what we two have been doing while they waited on us."

The MacDonald chief gazed at him in silence, his expression grave. Then he nodded. "So be it. No hanging will take place. And I thank you, Alexander of Argyll, for your forbearance." He raised his voice. "Donuil Dhu, had you a fire back there?"

"Aye, lord, we did."

"And have you readied torches against the dark?"

"We have."

"Stir up the flames, then, and bring us some light, for soon we won't be able to see a thing out here."

As the guardsman hurried away to fetch the torches, Angus Mohr turned back towards the Macdougall chief, but stopped, catching sight of Nicol MacDuncan, who was still standing close by him, not having moved since the moment Angus Mohr arrived to stop the fighting. "Nicol," he said. "How long have you been here? Come and join us. We may have need of an impartial witness."

Rob felt a swelling of relief, for he had been worried that at this point—a natural end to one thing and the start of another—Nicol might remember that he and Angus Og were there and hustle them away to bed. Now, watching his uncle clasp his hands at his back and lean forward to listen to the two chiefs speaking quietly between themselves, he tugged at Angus Og's sleeve, and they moved back quietly to disappear around the small grove of stunted hawthorn trees at the base of the hill, where Rob found a place for them to sit beneath the low-sweeping branches. No grown man would follow them in there, he knew. They would be safe enough, and still close enough to hear what Angus Mohr would say.

"Your da's a brave man," Rob said.

The other boy looked at him. "I know," he said.

"D'you think he knew you were watching?"

Even in the dark beneath the trees there was sufficient light for Rob to see the small grin that twisted his friend's mouth. "He scarce knows I'm alive. My da has too many grand affairs to tend to, to take notice of an ungrown, unimportant son. Don't fret about *my* da seeing *me*. Look to your own father."

While the boys were whispering, Donuil Dhu had returned with others, bearing lit torches that were quickly distributed. Now Angus Mohr MacDonald stepped among them again, taking his place this time within the half circle of flickering brands, his back to the boys.

The others' talk died away. Nicol MacDuncan, Rob noted, was no longer with them.

"Alexander Macdougall has asked me to tell you what he and I have spoken about today," Angus Mohr began. "And I will. But first I must speak to you about yourselves." He waited, hearing the curiosity in their silence. "You were hand-picked for this," he continued. "Every man of you. By the two of us, Alexander of Argyll and Angus of Islay. That means we trusted you, above your fellows, to look to our safety while we talked." He was speaking more quietly this time, so Rob had some difficulty hearing him, but he could clearly see what none of the others could see: the tendon-taut clenching and unclenching of the big man's fists behind his back, concealed from everyone as he fought to control … What? Rob wondered. Anger?

"You were all with us this day when we met with the Scots King. You witnessed what we undertook, even if you did not understand all the words of it. I took up a new responsibility this day, to work with Alexander Macdougall who is sheriff of Argyll and Lorn, and I undertook it willingly, with an eye to your well-being and your families'. Between the two of us we swore to see to the peaceful governance of our lands in the west and northwest, Islay and Bute, Kintyre and Mull, Skye and Barra, Argyll and Lorn." Rob could sense him looking each man in the eye, one after another. "On this day I, Angus MacDonald of Islay, was named Lord of the Isles by the King of Scots." He took a step forward, closer to his clansmen. "I accepted the rank for the same reasons the Macdougall accepted his—honouring and being honoured by the King of Scots, who rules his people from Dunfermline. And I took up the responsibilities that accompany that title."

Still the fingers flexed and clenched at his back. Macdougall of Argyll stood motionless beside him.

"Do any of you know what those responsibilities are? Or do you think, perhaps, that titles like Lord of the Isles and Sheriff of Argyll and Lorn come without any duties? Do you think me free of all obligation, now that I have a fine new title, or Alexander of Argyll?

If you do, you are bigger fools than this day's slaughter would make you appear.

"Your task here was to guard our privacy while we talked—not to fight among yourselves like diseased wildcats in some Highland cave." Those hands at his back still flexing, kneading. "We had much to talk about, the Macdougall and I—still have—and little of it, you must know, for your ears and tongues to ken of. But we were speaking of an end to the warfare that has plagued our people for countless years. An end to hatred and needless, wasteful killing like this killing here. You wonder that I was angry when I saw it? Thank God instead that I was here to stop it before all of you lay bleeding." He looked around at all of them, the Macdougalls as well as his own, and bellowed, "This folly, this madness, ends now! This minute! There will be no more of it, on pain of death. From this time forth, any fighting between the sons of Donald and of Dougall—*any* fighting—will bring death to the men involved. Do you *hear* that? Is it *clear* to you?"

He began pacing back and forth, holding himself straight as a blade and looking at their faces, watching for Rob knew not what, but then he stood still and added, in an almost whimsical tone, "It will not be easy."

The listening men, hard, doughty fighters all of them, broke into sardonic laughter. It was not much of a jest, but it acknowledged the realities of who they were.

The MacDonald let them laugh, and when the silence had returned he repeated, "No, it will not be easy. But it must be done. We made agreement today to stop it, and to work *together* to stop it. And our solemn word was witnessed by this gathering of Kings, princes, and earls, from Scotland, Ireland, and England. We gave our bond, the Macdougall and myself. And within the same God-chosen day, your folly and these murders gave the lie to both of us, making us appear fools and liars. If word of these events reaches the ears of any who is not here present, I swear every last one of you will answer to us in person with your lives. When I am done, you will take these three men and bury them, away from any watching eyes, and if any man asks after them tomorrow, you will say you know not where they went."

A voice came from among the MacDonald men.

"Ye should've told us, Angus Mohr."

It was the same uncouth voice Rob had heard earlier.

"They are not always right to call you daft, are they, Iain?" Again a ripple of laughter arose. "And what should I have said? That you were to have no more fights among yourselves with the Macdougalls? You would have laughed at me!"

They did, louder this time, and he waited for them to fall quiet. When he spoke again, Rob was aware of a difference in his voice, an altered, deeper resonance.

"Listen now. Much needs to be done after today's great matters, and none of it to be easily achieved. We have old hatreds to bury, new alliances to forge, old customs to be abandoned and new ones to establish. We all—even you sorry rogues—stand now on the sill of a new age for our people. Our *united* people. This very day I pledged, on your behalf, to keep the peace here in the west, in conjunction with Macdougall here, for Alexander Canmore, King of Scots." He whipped up a hand, intent upon silencing a protest that he believed must come, but no one even moved.

"Now, some may say—*will* say—that the Scots King has no presence here in the west, and thus no right to claim allegiance of any of us. Those people are wrong *now* and will be more so in time to come. Like it or not, Alexander Canmore *is* the King of Scots—it is his rightful title—and he claims this west of ours as part of his realm, with the full support of Holy Church. And *that* is a matter of great import. You might resent that, might deny it and rebel against it. But you will forfeit your own soul's salvation if you do, in denying God's own right to dictate the affairs of men."

Rob listened, rapt, knowing beyond a doubt that he was hearing more of great matter in this darkened place than he had ever heard before. He was aware that the man he was listening to was a warrior chief whose reputation lent itself to pillage, piracy, and arrogance rather than to diplomacy and subtle politics, but his words were holding everyone spellbound—and with that thought the boy realized that he had missed something the man was saying.

" ... damn yourselves, that is your own affair," he heard. "But damned you will be. Make no mistake on that. And there is no *need*. The Scots King offers us no ill. He seeks our goodwill—our friendship and support here in the west. His own, true realm lies in the east, and there, from Dunfermline town, he has his work cut out for him in governing to the north and south, the towns and burghs and the fertile lands that feed and support the people there—far, far more people than our isles and mountains could support."

A new thought tugged at young Rob Bruce as he heard those words, but even as it came to him it vanished. Annoyed, he tried harder to grasp it, but by then it was too late.

"East, south, and north," the Islay chief was saying, gesturing dramatically in each direction with both hands as he named it. "The Scots King's realm lies there—with us, our high mountains, lochs, and glens, at his back in the west. He sees no risk from us, and he is right. All of us Gaels combined would not suffice to raise an army big enough to conquer his. But he needs us to guard his back. To keep these mountains safe from threats to him. And to gain that help from us, he offers us the right to govern ourselves as we see fit, without threat of interference from him. So be it we conduct ourselves as worthy allies, the man will leave us alone and in peace. The King's peace, he calls it. And I, for one, have no quibble with that, so long as the King who claims that peace leaves *us* in peace."

Slowly, someone in the assembly began to applaud and moments later he was joined by a second man and then another, until all of them were clapping their hands together in approval. Angus Mohr MacDonald bowed his head, then raised his arm high and brandished his fist. And then he turned to Alexander of Argyll and placed an arm about his shoulders.

Rob Bruce lay awake in the darkest hours of the night. He could not remember ever being awake at that time. The previous day, though, had been unlike any other, and it had been close to the middle of the

night before he and Angus Og had arrived back in the castle to find
the housekeeper waiting for them in Rob's small room. She was in
her nightclothes, pacing the floor angrily when they walked in. But
Rob, who had known Allie since he was a baby in her arms, knew
how to read her moods and sensed that she had not been too worried.
She was wise enough to know that the presence of so many grand
and unusual guests and armed encampments would have been irre-
sistible to curious boys forced to retire early when so much was
going on around them.

Despite his exhaustion, though, sleep had eluded Rob, and he'd
lain on his back for hours, staring wide-eyed up into the darkness
long after his candle had guttered out. He saw again and again the
sudden, brutal violence and the blood spilt from appalling wounds.
He heard the explosive, hate-filled sounds and watched again and
again as the raised sword fell from the dying man's fingers. And he
saw Angus Mohr again and again: those long, tense fingers flexing
behind his back as he poured scorn on his guards; heard again the
milder voice he had used when he spoke to his men in the light of
the new-lit torches. And suddenly a door swung open in his mind,
showing him what it was that had been tugging at him as he had
watched and listened beneath the hawthorn tree: it was a word, once
obscure but now more clearly understood, that had been thrust upon
him several months earlier by his tutor.

It had been the first warm day of spring. Rob, who would be
leaving home within days to spend the springtime with his uncle,
was chafing at having to sit inside and study when he might have
been outside in the sunshine. In desperation he had asked the old
priest—it would be decades yet before he realized how young Father
Ninian actually was, though the man had tutored Rob's own father—
why they could not conduct their lessons outside, on the grass.
Ninian had straightened up and peered at him before muttering,
more to himself than to Rob, "I have enough trouble keeping your
mind upon your work in here. Why would I add to it by taking you
outside into the distractions of the world? And why would you even
ask me to? Do you believe me so easily manipulable?"

Seeing the blankness on the boy's face he added, in his customary didactic way, "Manipulable. From the Latin *manus*, a hand. Surely you know it?"

Rob had shaken his head. "No, Father."

"That is ridiculous, Robert, and unacceptable. This is a word you should surely know, coming from a family adept in its applications." He paused, blinked, and continued. "Manipulation means moving something, or controlling it, by hand. That stylus you are clutching—when you write with it you are manipulating it. And since you *can* manipulate it, it is therefore manipulable—able to be manipulated. Do you understand?"

Robert nodded, his yearning to be outside ousted by a strange word. Ninian had taught him to love words, so that he was constantly learning new ones and searching for others newer yet. But then he frowned. "If you please, Father? You said my family is ... " he hesitated over the word, knowing it but unaccustomed to pronouncing it, "adept at it. Why should that be?"

His tutor sucked in a great sigh and released it with a grunt. "Because your grandfather is Bruce of Annandale."

"Are you saying, sir, that other people's families can't manipulate things?"

The priest's face broke into a fleeting smile. "No, Robert," he said more quietly. "That is not what I meant at all. Everyone who has hands can manipulate. But the word is a rich one, complex with layers of meaning. Every family has its manipulators, of differing abilities, but your family has Lord Robert, who has more aptitude in such things than any other I could name." He stopped again, seeing the utter bafflement on his student's face, and then he sighed a second time and closed the massive Bible from which he had been reading to the boy.

"Very well then," he said, the half smile flickering again. "I will accept that you are not attempting to manipulate me at this moment, so let us leave the Blessed Paul—a great manipulator in his own right—and proceed elsewhere." He raised a hand towards Rob, spread his fingers wide and then clenched them, repeating the gesture several times with variations, moving the hand around. "Manipulation. In its most basic sense it means moving and controlling things with your hands, often moulding them as a potter moulds his clay. Have you watched our potter, Fergus, at his wheel?" Rob nodded. "Then you understand what I am saying, no?" Again Rob nodded. "Excellent. So, the most basic level understood, we move forward. Come here now and sit at the table with me."

Rob hurried to obey, oblivious now to the seductive sunshine outside. This was always his favourite part of his lessons, when Ninian warmed to an incidental topic and his enthusiasm spilled over to engulf his student.

"At its most *exalted* level, manipulation entails a far more mysterious talent than simply using one's hands. It involves the ability to use your *will* to shape, control, and mould *people*—to influence their behaviour and even their beliefs, bending them to your requirements and to your way of thinking. And *that*, Robert, means you are controlling their *minds*—their moods, their beliefs, their emotions. It is an ability few men possess. On a small scale we all attempt it every day, we try to manipulate the others in our lives, to make them do what we want them to do—let us leave this classroom and sit outside in the sunlight, for example—to make the lives of everyone about us useful to our own designs. I believe the need to do so is born in us."

He spread the fingers of his right hand. "You failed, of course, in your manipulation. After all, I have authority over you and no need to be responsive to your wishes. Few people ever attain the needed skills to influence others in any significant way, and most of those who do succeed have spent their entire lives learning how to do so. The very best of those, the adepts as I have come to think of them, are all leaders, men of power and influence." He tilted his head and looked at Rob with eyes that twinkled with a kind of mischief. "But what I ask myself frequently is this: are they powerful and influential leaders because they are adept at manipulating people, or have they learned to manipulate people as a result of being leaders? That is a question you should ask yourself in the times ahead, Robert.

Whatever the answer might be, you should know that your grandsire is such a man. Lord Robert Bruce of Annandale ranks first among his peers in this respect. I have often watched him play with people's minds the way a cat plays with a mouse, manipulating them by using the strength of his own personality and the passion of his beliefs to persuade them to do what he wishes them to do. Your father is quite similar, although to a lesser degree, as he lacks the primal fire, the *urgency* that motivates your grandsire."

Rob could find no words to express his astonishment, but Father Ninian was already busy with his tools, wrapping his pens with care and closing the tightly hinged lid on his inkhorn.

"And now you may go outside," he said without looking at Rob. "We will return to Paul's letters to the people of Corinth tomorrow. But in future, bear in mind what I have told you and try to look beyond the faces that your eye encounters, to discern what really lies behind those bland expressions. The day will come, not too long from now or I miss my guess, when you will need to know such things, if only to safeguard yourself against manipulation by others. Now go, and leave me to my work."

Rob had had no time to dwell on that lesson in the days that followed at his uncle Nicol's home in Dalmellington. Nicol MacDuncan was completely without guile, as open and honest as a man could be, and his household was run for him by his two step-daughters, neither of whom appeared to have the slightest wish to wed a man of her own. They both loved Rob and demonstrated it by bullying him as delightfully and mercilessly as they did their amiable stepfather. Any efforts those two made to manipulate Nicol or his nephew were loud, assertive, and entirely lacking in subtlety, so the boy had no opportunity to practice the kind of assessments urged upon him by his tutor, and he soon forgot about them alto-gether.

Only now, in the dark hours of this sleepless night, did revelation wash over him like sunlight from a gap in heavy clouds. He had watched Angus Mohr MacDonald manipulate his small crowd of listeners effortlessly. Now he saw the Islesman chief again, using his hands expressively—those same hands he had worked so hard to keep concealed earlier—as he talked to his men in a voice that suddenly rang and echoed with changing, soaring notes and falling cadences. He had *manipulated* them, easily and deliberately, and now Rob was bemused by his failure to see it sooner. He understood now that Angus Mohr had kept his hands out of sight at first not simply to hide his anger but to maintain control, not of himself but of his listeners. Showing too much anger would have weakened the lesson he wished to deliver—it would have made him too much like the men he was admonishing, railing at them for their lack of discipline when he himself could not control his own emotions.

He knew, too, that Angus Mohr had used the band of guards to practise on, saying to them what he would also have to say, soon and with more conviction, to his chieftains and his supporters and subordinates. He recalled the exact words the man had used: *Now, some may say*—will *say*—*that the Scots King has no presence here in the west, and thus no right to claim allegiance of any of us … Those people are wrong* now *and will be more so in time to come.* That argument was one that Angus Mohr would need to win if he was to maintain control of his own.

Rob Bruce stared into the darkness and smiled at his own cleverness, and resolved that someday he, too, would manipulate men with ease.

# Book Two

# The Noble Robert

## 1290

# CHAPTER FIVE

# A LAYING ON OF HANDS

"**J**esus! Move!"

The warning came too late, for the hurtling speed of the bulky figure descending the narrow, winding stone staircase made nonsense of any effort the man coming up might have made to avoid him. With no time to do anything else, the runner threw himself to the inside of the staircase, where the vanishing wedges of the tightly winding steps made footing impossible, and as his shoulder hit the wall he rebounded across and down the narrow space of the well, striking the other man as he went and throwing out his hands to cushion the impact with the outer wall. The man ascending, a castle servant, was thrown back against the same wall, the breath driven from his lungs, but before he could topple he was hit again as the other man rebounded once more from the wall. The servant's legs gave way beneath him and he fell, clutching at the stone steps above him as he gasped for air. The wooden bucket he had been carrying flipped end over end, hurling water against the curving wall before plummeting down the spiralling stairs, splintering into pieces and narrowly missing the other man, who was already several steps below. He had managed to right himself, bracing himself awkwardly against the wall and listening to the distant clatter of the heavy bucket. There was no sound from above, and as soon as he had regained his balance he launched himself back up the sodden stairs, scrambling on all fours until he saw the feet of the other man. He hesitated, afraid he had killed him, then quickly moved up higher, placing his feet carefully to get around the fallen man as he peered down at him.

The whimper he heard next would return to him later as being perhaps the most beautiful sound he had ever heard, and he almost moaned aloud himself as he knelt closer to the sprawled figure.

"Are you hurt? Can you move?"

The servant raised himself up slightly and looked at his questioner wide-eyed. "What happened? Who are you?"

"Robert Bruce. My father's the Earl of Carrick. I knocked you down. I was late, running, didn't expect to meet anyone on the stairs. I'm even later now, so I have to go. Will you be all right?"

The man pushed himself around on one elbow and sat up slowly, shaking his head, and Bruce dug into the scrip at his waist and pulled out a coin. It was a silver mark, more money than the other man would see in a year. He pressed it into the fellow's palm and closed the unresisting fingers over it. "Look, sit here and get your breath back. Someone else can bring the water up again, but I have to go. I'm in trouble enough as it is. If anyone is angry at you, tell him to come and find me, Rob Bruce of Turnberry, guest of the King. I'll make it right for you. Farewell."

He set off again quickly, this time keeping well to the right, where the steps were widest, and he felt the rough material of his shoulder covering scraping against the wall as he went. He was wearing thickly padded practice armour of sized sackcloth, reinforced with leather at shoulders, elbows, and knees and strengthened underneath with layered thicknesses of compressed straw and heavy fustian. Sufficiently strong to protect against hard-swung quarterstaves and blunted swords, the covering was none the less light enough to offer little restriction to his movement—far different from the chain mail and plate steel that would replace it when the time came to fight in earnest. Yet even as he went, his mind reeling with all that had occurred to him in the short but memorable period before his encounter on the stairs, he was aware of a loose flapping at his right shoulder and at his lower legs where he had not had time to buckle the straps of various parts of his coverings.

As he leapt down the last few steps into the narrow, open doorway, blinking against the sudden brightness from outside and hopping on one foot, he fumbled for the loose straps below his right knee. Gripping one end of a strap in each hand, he shuffled past the door and looked for a place to rest his foot while he threaded the buckle and secured the legging. Beyond the doorstep to the Squires' Tower the rocky outer yard fell away steeply, and he lowered himself to sit on an outcrop while he quickly fastened the buckles at knee and ankle on one leg and then the other, cursing Humphrey de Bohun under his breath and yet smiling as he did so. Had de Bohun not tripped him, toppling him into a muddy, water-filled ditch, Rob would not have been forced back to his tower room to change his sodden clothes, and he would not have had the adventure that had delayed him so wondrously and then required his mad dash down the stairs.

He was fumbling awkwardly at the loose straps of his upper right armguard, making heavy weather of the left-handed task, when he was distracted by the brassy noise of several concerted trumpets in the distance. He quickly made his way crabwise under the curved sweep of the wall of the tower in which he was housed, heading towards the grassed courtyard that fronted the main buildings of the palace. Trumpet calls were far from unusual here, for this was the King of England's home, but such announcements were usually single blasts, heralding the arrival of some visitor or supplicant to the King's favour. A multiple, disciplined fanfare such as this, on the other hand, indicated the advent of someone of importance, and Rob was curious to see who it might be, forgetting, for the moment, that his own long-overdue arrival at his destination was likely to over-shadow the incoming visitor's, at least in the disapproving eyes of his tutor, Sir Marmaduke Tweng.

Rob Bruce liked Sir Marmaduke Tweng, finding him to be the embodiment of knighthood and chivalry: well bred, well dressed, and always well disposed towards those with whom he had dealings, even servants and menials. The knight was renowned for being civil tongued and even tempered, yet few men—and absolutely none of his youthful charges—would ever dare to arouse his wrath. Unmastered in the lists or in single combat, Tweng was lethally proficient with every weapon he picked up, and when called upon to fight he was implacable and, many said, invincible. Reputed to be one of the most gifted soldiers and commanders in Edward's entire realm, he had proved himself in battle and on campaign many times, both in the Welsh Wars and on the King's external campaigns in France as Duke of Aquitaine and Gascony.

Now, recalling that he had justifiably earned Sir Marmaduke's displeasure, Rob abandoned his wish to identify the newcomers and instead headed down towards the drilling grounds where his companions were training. He found them gazing, though, at the spectacle unfolding on the expanse of open ground fronting the main entrance. The incoming cavalcade was at least three score strong, all of them brightly caparisoned with heraldic colours, with weapons and burnished armour glittering in the late-morning sunlight. They had captured the attention of everyone in the palace yards, so that Bruce was able to take his place with his three companions without being noticed. Or so he thought until Sir Marmaduke turned and eyed him coolly.

"Ah, Master Bruce," the knight drawled, his voice showing no trace of anger or displeasure. "We are honoured that you should deign to join us, albeit belatedly." One of his eyebrows twitched slightly and he scanned Rob quickly, from head to foot. "I trust you are sufficiently dry and warm by now?"

Rob felt himself flush as he nodded. "Yes, thank you, sir, I am."

"Excellent. Then you should be ready for a lesson." The knight held a long, bare sword loosely, its point resting on the ground by his foot. Rob recognized the training sword, its edges blunted to prevent it cutting through the padded armour worn by the pupils.

Rob nodded again. "I am, sir."

"No, sir, I fear you are not, and I will not ask how you came by the blood on your face."

Bruce blinked in surprise. He raised a spread hand to his face and felt a slick wetness on his forehead. "A scratch," he said, hearing the surprise in his own voice. "I ... stumbled on the stairs and must have grazed it." Then he saw the direction of his tutor's look and remembered that the buckles under his right arm were still unfastened. "I ask pardon, sir. I came in haste and I fear I could not run and fasten these left-handed while I did."

"Hmm. Master Percy, assist Master Bruce."

Henry de Percy, who had evidently been pitted against the tutor before Bruce arrived, since he was the only one of the pupils holding a bared blade, sheathed his weapon and moved to face Rob, where he set about fastening the delinquent straps, pulling them tight and settling them comfortably. He was the oldest of their group, a year Rob's senior and the grandson of Sir John de Warrenne, the Earl of Surrey. With his back to Tweng, he looked curiously at Rob while he worked, plainly wondering what had happened. The unformed question had to wait, though, for a man-at-arms came running from the main gate, calling Sir Marmaduke's name as he approached. The two men stood close together while the newcomer addressed the knight in a muffled whisper, and as soon as the messenger departed, Tweng turned back to his charges.

"Gentlemen, I must leave you to yourselves for a while. I am summoned to the King. While I am gone, you may practice the quarterstaff—but no blades, you hear? I will send Sergeant Bernard to attend you and ensure your diligence. Carry on."

Henry Percy crossed to the pile of quarterstaffs on the ground nearby and lobbed one of the cumbersome weapons to each of them in turn. Rob hoisted his, twirling it in one hand and gauging its weight and balance almost without thought as he squinted towards where the newly arrived group was now disbanding. The leaders had already dismounted and gone through the gates, and the mounted troopers of the escort, under the command of their sergeants, were deploying in order, wheeling their mounts away towards the distant stables on the far side of the outer walls.

"Who was that?" Bruce asked, jerking his head towards the main gates.

Percy looked at him with wide eyes. "You didn't recognize the colours? Bek, of Durham."

"Bishop Bek?"

"*Prince*-Bishop Bek," John de Bigod interjected, his voice wry. "Mere bishops do not ride with a private army."

"I thought he was in Scotland," Rob said. "My grandfather met with him in Glasgow, two months ago, just before I came down here with my father. Bek had just been named the King's deputy in Scotland, in dealings with the Guardians over the royal wedding."

"Well, much may happen in two months and he's here now. Plainly has pressing business with the King. Mayhap the Scots Queen has changed her mind."

They all laughed at Percy's comment, for Princess Margaret of Norway was seven years of age and not yet crowned. Known as the Maid of Norway, the child was the sole granddaughter and acknowledged heir of King Alexander III, who had left the realm without an heir when he was killed in an accident two years before. The daughter of the Norwegian King and Alexander's deceased daughter Margaret, she lived in Norway and had not yet set foot in her future realm, though she would do so soon. Directly following her lawful coronation at Scone, in Fife, she was to be wed to the five-year-old Edward of Caernarfon, Prince of Wales and heir to the English throne. That union would be a historic one, for the legal progeny of the match would inherit the joint Crowns of Scotland and England for the first time in history. The details of the coronation and the subsequent marriage between the crowns had been under negotiation for more than a year now, and Bishop Bek had been delegated to negotiate with the Guardians of Scotland on behalf of King Edward.

"Who was the Scot who rode with him?" This was de Bohun, the future Earl of Hereford, his voice truculent as always.

Percy glanced over at him. "What Scot?"

"The young one, at Bek's back."

"I saw no Scot. That was Rob Clifford, and he's as English as you are. Lord of Skipton in Yorkshire since his grandfather died. Bek is his mentor nowadays, takes him everywhere."

De Bohun scowled. "I'm not talking about Clifford. I mean the other fellow, at his back—the one wearing the outlandish green and red."

Percy frowned. "I didn't notice anyone like that. But I was watching Bek." He turned to John de Bigod. "Did you see a Scot?"

Bigod shrugged. "I wasn't paying attention to anyone in particular."

"What about you, Bruce?"

"Don't ask me. I missed them coming in. By the time I got here, they were all huddled at the gate, already dismounting." He looked at de Bohun. "You mean *crossed* red and green, like green patterned on a red cloth?"

"Aye, or red on green cloth—big, ugly squares."

"Must be a Gael, then, a Highlander from Scotia, north of the River Forth."

Percy reached out to tap his quarterstaff against Rob's. "Enough of Scots. We have work set for us. If the Claw comes by and finds us chattering like women we'll all rue it. De Bohun, you and Bigod. Bruce, you're with me."

As they faced off and began to circle each other cautiously, weapons at the ready, Bruce, half smiling, said, "Enough of Scots, you said? We Scots are not to be dismissed so easily, my lord Percy."

"D'you say so?" Percy leapt forward, his staff whirling up and then down in a wicked chop, but Bruce parried it easily and pivoted smoothly, passing Percy rearward as the other lunged, exposing his back fatally. Percy was agile and unbelievably fast, though; he checked himself instantly and leapt to his left before Rob's stabbing thrust could hit him, so that instead of striking the centre of his back the blow merely glanced off his padded shoulder.

He spun back to face Rob, dropping again into a fighting crouch, his teeth bared in a grin of sheer enjoyment. "Don't look around," he said. "The Claw's coming."

"Behind me?"

"Aye, where else?"

Bruce grinned back. "God bless you, then, for your cautious fears for your craven English arse." He swung up his guard and went to the attack and for a few moments there was nothing but the whirling blur of Percy's staff and the clattering impact of hard ashwood as they parried and slashed. And then Rob saw an opening and struck, only to find himself upended and crashing to the ground as Percy's staff struck him behind the knees and swept his legs from under him. The Englishman had set a trap and Rob had lunged at it, coming to grief through his own eagerness.

"I think you have just been easily dismissed, my Scots friend." Percy held out his hand, smiling, and helped his fallen opponent to his feet just in time for Sergeant Bernard to reach them.

"A pretty trick, that," the sergeant growled to Percy. "But if you ever try it against a man with a real sword you won't live long enough to wonder why it didn't work." He paid no heed at all to Bruce, who was brushing himself down ruefully, but turned to speak to the other two, who had grounded their weapons to watch. "All of you, listen. Sir Marmaduke's with the King and I am to attend him, so hear me: the rest of the day is yours, to spend as you will. But I want you here tomorrow at first flush of dawn, you hear? A moment later than that and I'll have you running in full mail all day long, so be sure it's yet dark when you get here."

He stalked away without another word.

Bruce found himself smiling again, and not just because he had been set free. He was struck as always by the man's sheer, unrelenting truculence. He knew him only as Bernard, sergeant-at-arms and nicknamed the Claw—though never within his hearing—because of his deformed left hand. He had heard the tale: years earlier the man had interposed his arm between King Edward and a hard-swung falchion in a skirmish in Wales, saving the King's life at the cost of his own limb. But where many another man would have died of his wounds or retired from fighting, the sergeant had fought grimly to retain his arm and regain his health, and against all odds, he had succeeded. His hand was permanently twisted into a gnarled claw, but he could still use it for any task that did not require him to flex his fingers, and his bravery had earned him a permanent posting as a sergeant-at-arms in Westminster from a grateful monarch.

Wondering if he himself would ever have the courage to make such a sacrifice, Rob became aware that one of his companions was standing close beside him and he turned to see the nephew of the Earl of Norfolk watching him curiously. "What took you so long to come back?" Bigod asked.

Rob grinned, the Claw forgotten. "I'd tell you, but I doubt you would believe me."

"Try me."

"Aye, where were you all that time?" This was de Bohun. "You were gone long enough to have tupped a woman, let alone changed your clothes."

Bruce's grin widened. "I did both, thanks to you," he said. "I owe you a debt, de Bohun. Perhaps I'll tell you why someday." He turned as though to walk away, but all three of his companions surrounded him, determined to have an explanation. He let them clamour a bit and then threw up his hands in mock resignation.

"So be it, so be it! I'll tell you. But I'm not going to shout over all of you." They fell silent immediately, and he looked around, seeing several people who were close enough to overhear what he might say. He beckoned the others to follow him. Sensing a story worth hearing, they followed quietly as he led them to a small copse of trees on the near bank of the brook that meandered through the castle precincts. He seated himself against the straight bole of a young oak and nodded to them to join him on the lush grass.

"You tripped me well, de Bohun, right into the ditch," he began. "My fault, of course, for trusting you to walk behind me. I should have seen it coming." He eyed the youth from Hereford who, although a year younger, was of a size with Bruce and the others. Humphrey de Bohun glared back haughtily, unsure if he was being insulted.

Bruce laughed, then turned to the others. "Well, as you know, I was soaked to the skin—and chilled to the bone. That ditchwater is icy, as well as filthy, fouled with dung and horse piss. So I don't mind telling you—not even you, Humphrey—that I was feeling mightily sorry for myself.

"As I neared the tower, carrying my armour in both arms, I saw the launderer's people boiling bedsheets down by the bank of the stream, and I stopped and asked leave to cleanse myself in one of their vats. They thought I was mad, of course, but they mixed a bath for me, with boiling water from their kettles cooled with stream water. That got rid of the stink on me, but my clothes were ruined. The fellow in charge told me to leave them there and they would wash them, and then he threw me a torn old sheet to wear the rest of the way. The sheet was damp on my skin, and I was freezing, on top of which I had my arms filled with my whoreson armour while I was climbing up the stairs in the dark."

The others listened intently, nodding as he spoke, for all of them lived in the same tower, in tiny, partitioned rooms on the upper floors set aside for squires, and they were intimately familiar with the long, grinding climb up the dingy, twisting staircase.

"By the time I reached the top I was furious—with you, in part, Humphrey, but mostly with myself for being so stupid as to let you walk behind me." He looked at Percy, with whom he shared his quarters, then went on. "I dropped the armour on the floor inside the door and tried to dry myself with the sheet, but the damned thing was too clammy, so I snatched up the blanket from my cot and dried myself with that, thinking I might never be warm again. Then, with the blanket over my head, I let myself fall straight back onto my cot, shivering like a done man ... "

"And?" de Bohun prompted.

"And I was attacked by three females! They must have been hiding behind the curtain dividing Percy's cot from mine. I heard them giggling just before they leapt on me, but my head was covered by the blanket and I had no chance to see them. Before I could sit up, one of them landed by my head and held me down, pressing the blanket over my eyes. Then they twisted it, tightening it behind my head, blindfolding me."

For long moments no one made a sound, until Percy asked quietly, "*Three* of them?"

"That's what I said."

"Who were they?"

"I told you, I didn't see them, so I don't know."

"Were they servants?"

"Hardly. Servants would never dare such a thing. At least not without encouragement."

"And you had not encouraged them," Bigod said.

"John, I didn't know they were there until they leapt on me."

"That is no answer."

"You asked no question. But no, I have never encouraged any servant girls to be familiar with me."

Bigod said, "But if they weren't servant girls ... then they must have been ... "

Bruce nodded. "Aye, they must have been. Three of the Muses."

A profound silence ensued, with no one among the stunned listeners inclined to break it. Nine young noblewomen were staying with their parents as guests at the Palace of Westminster, all of them living in the royal apartments and far removed from the remote defensive tower where the squires were lodged. The girls ranged in age from thirteen to seventeen, and the four young men referred to them as the Nine Muses because they were as distant and ethereal as their classical counterparts, kept strictly apart from the avid young men by ever-vigilant and suspicious parents. The name was doubly apt, though, for each of the young women had provided inspiration, at one time or another over the course of the previous month, for at least one of the small group of nobly born squires who worshipped them from afar. The two groups never spoke or even mixed socially, but their eyes conversed eloquently whenever chance brought them within sight of one another, and the amount of silent flirting that occurred on such occasions provided the four lads with much to talk about in the hours between supper and sleep each night.

Now Bruce's tale left his three companions wordless as they grappled with the implication: the notion that these divine young creatures—or three of them, at least—might be less than supernaturally chaste. It was an astounding thought, for it contravened everything their knightly code had taught them to believe about noblewomen.

"Not this time, Bruce," Henry Percy said with a slight smile. "This is one of your tales I'm not going to be gulled by."

"What," Bruce said. "You don't believe me?"

Percy laughed. "Believe you? Would I risk offending a fellow squire's honour by calling him a liar? Not at all. But let me say instead I've learned that your imagination sometimes leaps beyond the edges of our little world and our daily drudgeries. How many times have you enthralled us of an evening with your flights of fancy and your talk of women and the delights they have to offer, taking us with you to places in our minds where we would never venture by ourselves? This time, though, it's taking place in daylight, and I fear the magic suffers without darkness to enhance it." He glanced to where de Bohun sat glowering at them. "What say you, Humphrey?"

"I agree. He's a liar." His voice was flat, the insult coldly provocative.

Bruce sprang to his feet, about to leap at de Bohun, but then he stopped and narrowed his eyes, and he raised a hand to his face, splaying his fingers over his mouth and nose. Finally he leaned forward, extending the hand to de Bohun, fingers widespread. "Smell that, then tell me again that I lie."

De Bohun scowled at the proffered hand, but reached out and took it, drawing it slowly to his nostrils. He sniffed deeply, then frowned and tensed visibly, and sniffed again, avidly this time, his eyes growing round with the shock of recognition.

Percy scrunched forward quickly on his buttocks and seized the outstretched wrist, bringing it to his own nostrils. "Sweet Jesus," he breathed. "It's true." He turned slightly, offering Bruce's hand to Bigod, but the young Norfolk shook his head, his features stiff.

"I believe it," he said. "But I mislike it greatly. This whole thing smacks of sin and unknightly conduct."

"How so?" Bruce asked sharply.

"How can you even ask that question? It is the deepest and most shameful sin to dishonour any woman by decrying her in such a way."

"Decrying who, John? I named no one, so who have I maligned? No names were involved, nor will any be. I merely spoke of an encounter with three unknown women. I *saw* nothing. I *knew* none of them. I only know what happened."

"And what *did* happen?" Percy's voice was low. "Tell us … exactly."

Bruce shook his head. "I can't, because I don't really *know* what occurred, apart from the obvious. I told you, I was on my back, on the bed, believing myself alone, and I was naked and unthinking. I heard, or felt, a sudden rush of movement, and before I could move I was jumped upon and held down. I had no hope of seeing who they were. They pinioned me, giggling and whispering. One of them lay across my neck, holding my head down. I could smell the scent she used—verbena or some such thing. Two others pulled my arms wide and knelt on them—"

"You made no attempt to fight them off?"

Bruce looked straight-faced at the questioner. "I know you called me a liar, de Bohun, but d'you think me truly stupid, too? They were girls. Women. Three of them. Soft and warm and wriggling. Laughing and whispering. Climbing all over me. Would *you* have fought them off? You probably would have, now that I think of it. But I?" He paused, as though considering the question, and laughed. "I made the best of it and did nothing. I lay there on my back and enjoyed everything they did to me. I grew excited, as any of you would, rearing up at them in plain sight, and they grew quiet. The measure of their stroking changed, moving down from my chest and belly as though drawn by the sight of what was there in front of them. And then one of them, the boldest, took me in hand … " He cleared his throat noisily, willing a sudden tremor to leave his voice, then resumed in a calmer tone, his eyes moving from face to face among his spellbound audience. "I think it was the one on my right side, though I cannot be sure. Her hand felt very small, her fingers almost cold. And then there were other fingers there, beside hers. I've never been so exalted, and it did not take long. I exploded. The hands withdrew and they watched in silence, not even breathing, as the hardness drained from me. And then I heard a whisper—something I did not catch—and they were gone. I heard their voices dwindling down the staircase."

Henry Percy shook his head in wonder. "Did you not follow them?"

"Follow them? I couldn't *move*. I doubt I would have had the strength to stand, had I tried at that moment. No, I did not follow them. I lay there for a time, my head still muffled in the blanket, reliving all of it and wondering what it meant. And then I remembered that I was supposed to be drilling. I pulled on fresh clothes and a clean tunic, and started putting on my armour. By then, though, I was too anxious to be able to buckle it all up properly and I decided to fasten the straps as I went. I ran into a servant on the stairs and almost killed myself and him … And the rest you know."

"You saw no sign of any women when you left the tower?"

"God, no! They had been gone for ages by then. I looked, but there were only men in sight."

"By the Christ, Rob, it might have been a waking dream," Bigod said quietly, all thoughts of unknightly conduct long since vanished and now replaced with an expression of awe. "It could have been, if you but think on it. You were chilled and in pain, and tired. You fell back on your bed. You could have passed out and been visited by a succubus while you slept. A spirit of lust, immortal and intangible."

Bruce extended the spread fingers of his right hand again. "Intangible?" he said. "I think not, John. Immortal spirits leave no human scents behind when they depart."

Percy pointed at the hand. "How came you by that … scent? You made no mention of it."

Bruce heaved himself to his feet, swaying awkwardly for a moment in the heavily padded armour until he found his balance. "I had no need to mention it, and no one asked." He waited as they all regained their feet, but before they could move anywhere de Bohun barked, "I'm asking now, then."

Bruce shrugged. "They knelt on my arms," he said. "I told you that. Well, when the stroking began in earnest and I started to respond, I could tell they were paying less attention to me and more to what was happening to me. The one on my right parted her knees, freeing my arm. And my hand was beneath her skirts. She made herself available to me right willingly … and that was what made me lose control and spill myself."

"Jesu! And you will never know who she was."

Bruce smiled. "Oh, I will know, Humphrey, if I ever find my hand in there again … "

The royal summons arrived later that afternoon, delivered by a household steward who was plainly displeased at having had to spend his valuable time searching for a petty squire; a squire, more-over, who had been in none of the places where a squire ought to have been in the middle of the afternoon. He had finally found the four young men sprawling wet and half-naked on the grassy bank by a deep swimming hole in the stream that meandered towards the castle walls to feed the moat fronting the main entrance.

"Bruce!" he bellowed as he swept towards them, radiating displeasure. "Is one of you called Bruce?"

Henry Percy raised himself on an elbow and scowled up at the fellow, shielding his eyes with his free hand. "What does that matter to you, peacock? We have leave to be here, on our own time and about our own business."

"Are you Bruce?" The question dripped with disdain.

Rob rolled over onto his belly and raised himself to his elbows, looking up at the bad-tempered messenger. "I'm Bruce. You have a message for me?"

"You are to present yourself in the Throne Room before supper. The King commands you." The man sneered down at the haphaz-ardly piled clothes and practice armour nearby. "I would suggest you make yourself *present*able before you *present* yourself," he said, smirking at his own wit, and then turned away.

Before he could take more than a step, Percy surged fluidly to his feet and tripped him from behind, sending him sprawling. The fellow sprang back to his feet quickly enough, his long white robe stained with grass and dirt, and spun around to face them, almost spitting with outrage, but his demeanour changed swiftly when he found a long-bladed sword at his throat, the point pressing beneath his chin. His mouth snapped shut and the colour drained from his face as he rose on his toes, wide-eyed. It was plain to Rob the man had no idea the sword was a practice weapon, blunt and useless, but Percy maintained an upward pressure on the dulled point to keep the fellow on his toes and witless with fear.

"You are what, fellow, a steward? Not a serf, I can see, but a servant none the less, with too high an opinion of yourself. Sufficient to persuade you to insult your betters. Stand still now—no, don't move—and learn the extent of your prancing folly! I am Henry Percy, grandson of the Earl of Surrey. The smiling fellow over there on your left is John Bigod, heir to the earldom of Norfolk. Beside him is Humphrey de Bohun, who will one day be Earl of Hereford, and the fellow you have just insulted unforgivably with your spite and your surly speech is Robert Bruce, heir to the earldom of Carrick in Scotland and a close favourite of the King's Majesty. Four future earls, halfwit. Four … *earls*." His voice was almost a whisper. "Four solid causes for you to wonder how long you will survive as a *scullion*, let alone a steward, when we come into our own. Four powerful enemies for one mere fool to acquire in a brief moment of ill-tempered pettiness, think you not? Now get yourself out of our sight. Quick now, without another word, lest you have further cause to rue your stupidity. Run!" He swept up the practice sword as though to strike and the steward fled.

Rob was shaking his head. "I know he was an offensive idiot, Percy, but don't you think you were a bit hard on him? Four earls, in God's holy name. We are four squires, my friend, not yet even knighted, and I doubt that I, for one, shall ever hold an earldom.

John never will, I know. He's Norfolk's nephew, not his son, and we Bruces are a long-lived clan. My grandsire's still a formidable man and he must be seventy." He broke off and frowned. "I wonder what the King wants of me."

"Probably to do with that Scots lad Humphrey said he saw come in with Bek," John Bigod said. "If he's really there, and if he's young, the King will want you to look after him, protect him from dangerous future English earls like us."

Rob shook his head. "No, I don't think so. Besides, he came in with another lad—the fellow Percy named. What was it, Henry?"

"Clifford. Robert Clifford." Percy shrugged. "I know Clifford is definitely there, but I wouldn't wager on any Scot being in his company. I saw no one." He looked Rob up and down. "That flunky was right, though. You'd better make ready to meet the King. You can't go into the Throne Room dressed like that."

"They probably won't let me in now anyway. That steward, oaf or not, was a King's messenger. He's probably complaining now to the seneschal and they'll arrest me as soon as I show my face."

If he expected any sympathy from the others he was disappointed, but Bigod looked at him levelly. "I agree with Percy," he said. "You had better change into something suitable for a royal execution."

"Shit," Rob muttered, but he knew they were right and he went off to change into his best tunic.

Soon after, he was standing in front of the heavily guarded doors fronting the main building of the Palace of Westminster, the Great Hall. He was reluctant to move forward, wondering if the surly steward might, indeed, have lodged a complaint against them. He noticed one of the guards looking at him suspiciously, probably because he was the only person standing still among the tide of bodies shuffling towards the entrance, and so he drew himself up, squaring his shoulders and tugging beneath his light blue silk cloak at the folds of the dark blue French-style quilted tunic he was wearing for the first time. He took a deep breath and stepped forward, directly towards the guard who had been watching him.

Without altering his expression beyond a querying twitch of one eyebrow, the guard lowered his spear shaft sideways, just enough to bar the way as Rob reached him.

"Bruce," Rob said. "Robert. Of Turnberry in Carrick. Son of Robert Bruce, Earl of Carrick. Summoned by His Majesty."

The guard blinked once, impassively, and raised his spear to the vertical again, allowing Rob to pass through the open doors at his back.

Inside the main doors the vast anteroom was crowded with people, a brightly coloured confusion of noise and movement. Rob stopped just across the threshold, taking it all in with stirrings of awe. This was the first time he had ever approached the Throne Room alone and unescorted, merely one of the throng of hopefuls seeking admission to the world of power behind the tall, wide carved doors in the far wall. He recognized Sir Robert FitzHugh, the King's seneschal, standing head-down at his post by the high lectern in front of the doors, candlelight reflecting off his thick, silver hair as he consulted his list of attendees. Behind Sir Robert, a sextet of Household Guards flanked the entrance itself, three on either side. Two of them had their hands on the doors' handles, ready to pull them open. The other four, under the watchful eye of a plumed and polished sergeant-at-arms, stood vigilantly, their eyes scanning the crowd.

Rob made his way to the front, where he stopped, watching Sir Robert as the seneschal dealt with the importuning of a heavy-set, florid-faced merchant, whose equally portly wife stood at his side, frowning. Sir Robert murmured something soothing and glanced away, his eye meeting Rob's by accident as he did so, and the change in him was immediate. His face lit up and he smiled and drew himself erect.

"Sir Robert," he said loudly, causing every head within hearing to turn towards the young man. "His Majesty has asked for you. Be so good as to come this way."

Rob heard the muttering behind him as he followed the seneschal obediently. *Sir Robert?*

The guards pulled the doors of the Great Hall open to reveal a gathering larger and more brilliant by far than the throng in the ante-room, and in the first moments of what was a revelation unlike anything he had ever seen before, Rob thought he heard stringed music underlying the babble of voices, and his breath caught at the rich mixture of odours and perfumes that filled the air: the unmistak-able sweet aroma of hundreds of burning beeswax candles and the hot-waxen smoke from lamps and guttering wicks; sharper woodsmoke from what must be enormous fireplaces; and every-where eddying smells of delicious foods and spices and the scents of laughing, excited women, all mixed with the musk of sweat and unwashed bodies. He heard the music again, faint and far away though in the room somewhere, but he did not even try to look for the source of it, for the floor was packed with people, many eating, most drinking. He heard snatches of French and even Catalan among the swirling voices on all sides.

The seneschal paused only briefly at the top of the two shallow steps inside the doors to stretch up on his toes and look over the crowd before he reached back and took Rob by the wrist, pulling him along as he swept down the steps into the vast hall, said to be the largest anywhere. Forty feet above their heads, supported by massive, arching rafters atop walls that were six feet thick, the ceiling was masked in darkness that the lights below could never hope to penetrate.

Rob followed on Sir Robert's heels, weaving in concert with the older man and trying not to step on the skirts of the seneschal's robe as FitzHugh twisted and wove expertly through the crush of bodies, skirting one group, sidestepping another, and, despite an occasional smile or tip of his head to one person or another, speaking to no one.

They were making their way towards the enormous arched window that filled the entire south wall ahead, its soaring panels gleaming with multicoloured glass, and Rob knew that the royal thrones sat on a dais beneath it, for he had been here several times before. But on those occasions the Hall had been partitioned with folding screens and there had been fewer than a score of people in attendance on the King and Queen, so that the atmosphere had been cordial and relaxed, in fitting with Her Majesty's gracious presence. When he drew close to the dais, though, he saw that, despite the swarming courtiers in the massive room, both thrones sat empty.

Sir Robert turned sharply sideways, still clinging to Robert's wrist. There was a single door in the corner, and he led Rob directly to it, releasing his wrist only when he reached out to open the door and step quickly inside. Rob followed him. This room was much smaller, and had two entrances, the second at the rear, facing the one they had used. The only furniture was a single square table in the middle, with an upholstered wooden armchair on one side. The table's broad surface, large enough to accommodate four seated men on each side, was covered with books, bound scrolls, piles of writing paper, pots of pens and quills, and a full dozen stoppered inkhorns. A heavy chandelier hung over the table, suspended by chains, and the light from its several dozen candles warmed the entire room.

"Now, let's have a look at you, young Bruce." The seneschal studied Rob with narrowed eyes, then nodded. "Good. Most excellent. Her Majesty's tailor has surpassed himself. The Queen will be most pleased."

Rob felt himself flushing under Sir Robert's appraising smile, aware that the seneschal knew the story behind his finery. About a month earlier, at Westminster, he had been engaged in a friendly scuffle with Humphrey de Bohun when he was peremptorily summoned to the palace by his father. Running to avoid keeping his father waiting, Rob had encountered King Edward and Queen Eleanor. He had skidded to a halt and had greeted the royal couple respectfully, not even mildly embarrassed. There was no formality or protocol in such informal encounters when they occurred. He was their guest, or his father was, and he was well liked by both of them and returned their affection. The embarrassment had occurred when he bowed and turned to leave them. The Queen immediately called him back and asked him what had happened to his tunic. He was unaware that the back of his tunic, between his shoulders, had been ripped out and hung behind him in a ragged flap. Queen Eleanor, gracious at all times, had insisted that he remain with her while a servant went running to find the seneschal, who was in turn instructed to take Master Bruce to the royal tailor and see to it that he received some new clothes, suitable to his station as her honoured guest. Thus, informally and almost accidentally, was Robert Bruce introduced to the pleasures of wearing stylish and beautiful clothes designed for him by gifted craftsmen. It was a self-indulgence he would take delight in forever after.

"The gathering tonight is for Her Majesty's pleasure, and the King indulges her," FitzHugh was saying now in his dry way. "This day marks the forty-sixth anniversary of the day she first heard His Majesty named as her husband-to-be. They were wed in November that same year, in Castile, in the Abbey of Santa Maria la Real, and a blessed match it has proved to be. Her Majesty has celebrated this anniversary every year since then, for, unofficial as it is, she holds the memory dear. Forty-five times, and each year the celebration grows larger. But the King is meeting privily with others at this moment, for the affairs of the realm take no heed of celebrations, and we are to join them—*you* are to join them—as soon as may be." FitzHugh hesitated. "Something is troubling you, I can see."

Rob waved vaguely towards the door through which they had entered. "All those people out there … Did the King and Queen just leave them there?"

"Leave them there? No, that would be ungracious. Their Majesties have not yet made their entrance. Nor will they until the King's business is concluded and Queen Eleanor announces herself ready. Now, shall we go? Are you ready?"

Rob drew a deep breath. "I am, sir. But for what? What does the King need with me, on a night like this?"

The seneschal merely smiled and led the way to the far door.

Another large room, its walls draped with brightly coloured tapestries that glowed in the light of hundreds of massed candles, some in heavy chandeliers above the heads of the crowd and others ranked in sloping banks along the walls and against the central pillars like votive racks in churches. Leaping flames from a pair of roaring fires in the great hearths at each end added to the flickering light and shadow, for though the summer day outside yet had hours to run, in this windowless room it was night. There was no music here, though, other than the deep, murmurous sound of rumbling male voices.

Rob looked about at the score or more of richly clad men, many of them clerics, standing in separate groups, some talking quietly among themselves, others plainly waiting, though for what he could not have said. Sir Robert FitzHugh was already striding towards the largest group, near one of the fires, and as he hurried to keep up Rob saw the tall figure of Edward Plantagenet among the cluster of men there, dominant even had his height not been enhanced by the crown he wore. The monarch was in full regalia, and Rob noted that the coronet of heavy gold, with its studding of precious stones, appeared to sit very comfortably and naturally on its wearer's head.

Edward was talking to the elderly John de Warrenne, seventh Earl of Surrey and grandfather to Rob's friend Henry Percy. To the King's right, Humphrey de Bohun, the Earl of Hereford, was listening intently, his heavily jowled, saturnine face scowling in the habitual frown he had passed on to his son. Roger de Bigod of Norfolk was there, too, on the King's left and flanked in turn by Antony Bek, the Prince-Bishop of Durham, and two other clerics, both wearing the pectoral cross and crimson *scapulae* that marked them as bishops, too. There was one more man among the coterie, almost concealed from Rob's view by the trio of bishops, and although he caught only a glimpse of him Rob recognized him at once from a previous encounter. William de Valence, Earl of Pembroke, was one of the most powerful men in Edward's realm, notwithstanding his French birth. He owned vast territories in both France and England and was a close associate of the King. As Rob approached behind FitzHugh, he looked more closely at the Anglo-French earl, noting the air of barely suppressed ennui with which he listened to the voices surrounding him.

The seneschal's hand waved backward in a signal to Rob to stop where he was, and Sir Robert went on alone, clearing his throat deferentially as he approached the royal presence. A flash of garish colour to his left drew Rob's eye away from the encounter, and he saw a youth of about his own age move into view from behind two others. Bare headed, with long, dark hair that hung smoothly to his shoulders, he was unmistakably a Highland Gael, and a wealthy, privileged one. Where Rob would have expected him to wear the normal brogans of his people, this young man wore burnished, calf-high boots that were laced up their open front over tight trousers of saffron-coloured deerskin. He wore an open-collared shirt made of the same soft skin, its deep-cut front laced loosely over his bare chest and secured at the waist with a heavy belt of gold-studded leather. A fringed shawl of light wool in alternating squares of red and dark green hung down his back to his heels, anchored by a brace of magnificently jewelled brooches at his shoulders that were connected by a thick pendant chain of gold links.

Whoever he was, he seemed very sure of himself and completely unaware of Rob, his attention focused on the tall man who stood beside him, talking intently. Rob recognized that man as Sir Gervais de Blais, Edward's personal attendant, a former Gascon cleric whom the King had knighted a few years earlier. Rob had first met de Blais six years before, when the Gascon, then a squire, had accompanied Edward on the King's visit to Turnberry, but he knew him well enough by now to be on easy, first-name terms with him. The Gascon knight met his eye, though whether accidentally or not Rob could not have said, and inclined his head amiably but unobtrusively in recognition before turning his gaze to the last member of their trio, another young man of about Rob's age who was richly dressed in the normal fashion of the English nobility. Rob assumed him to be the new English arrival, Bishop Bek's protégé, Robert Clifford.

"Robert! Come forward, lad." The sound of the King's voice snapped him back to attention and he went forward, receiving a quick wink from Sir Robert FitzHugh as the seneschal passed him, returning to his post in the anteroom. As a man, the entire group surrounding the monarch turned to Rob, and he felt himself flushing, knowing he could not return all their looks eye to eye without neglecting the King. He had an impression of hostility in some of their gazes, open dislike on de Valence's face, and curiosity in the eyes of the two unknown bishops. Bishop Bek merely stared at him impassively. Edward, however, was paying attention to none of them.

"By God, boy, you look impressive, for a heathen Scot." The King was smiling as he spoke, removing any sting from his words. "That tunic's French, is it not? De Valence, what say you?" He did not wait to hear what the French earl might have to say, but carried right on. "Our Queen will be most pleased with what you have inspired her tailors to achieve. My lords, have any of you not yet met young Robert Bruce, firstborn son of our good friend Robert, Earl of Carrick?"

"I have not yet met young Master Bruce, Your Majesty," said one of the bishops, and his companion added quickly, "No more have I, my lord King."

The King's eyebrows rose, whether in real or feigned surprise Rob could not say. "D'ye say so? The son of one of Scotland's foremost earls and unknown to the realm's two most prominent churchmen? Well, we can remedy that. Robert Bruce, I present to you their eminences Bishop William Fraser of St. Andrews and Bishop Robert Wishart of Glasgow." Rob immediately wondered if a mere bishop could be an eminence, but he had no time to dwell on it. "When the time comes for you to inherit your estates, these two, or their successors, will be bound to make great demands of you. It is their nature and their duty. Master Wishart here is a long-standing friend of your grandsire."

Rob, feeling the tips of his ears burning now, bowed to each of the prelates in turn and managed to murmur that he was honoured to meet them. And in a way he was, for he had heard much of both of them throughout his life. Robert Wishart of Glasgow was the heavier and stockier of the pair, his voice gruff and deep in keeping with his bulk. His bishopric of Glasgow lay within the territories of James

Stewart, the High Steward of Scotland, commonly known as James the Stewart, and he had been a Bruce adherent all his life. William Fraser of St. Andrew was taller and much older, almost frail-looking, with white, wispy hair and a stoop that made him seem shorter than he was. His voice reflected his age, thin and high pitched with the slightest hint of a tremor, and his loyalties, never doubted, lay with the House of Comyn and their political affiliate, John Balliol of Galloway. On the death of King Alexander, with the Scots throne fallen vacant, Rob's grandsire, Lord Robert, had been considered a legitimate successor, and Balliol perceived to be his strongest rival.

"Master Bruce," Wishart began, "I am delighted to meet you, having heard much about you from your noble grandsire, Lord Robert. I would have you call on me while I am here in London, should you have the time."

"He will make the time," King Edward said, the edge to his voice reminding all of them that this was his royal gathering and he had no wish to hear others speaking out on matters that did not directly concern him. "But not here and not now, Master Wishart. Robert, I have a task for you—the guidance and care of another of your own race, brought here by Bishop Bek." He raised a hand and crooked a finger, and Rob sensed movement from behind. Unable to restrain himself, he glanced back and saw Sir Gervais de Blais approaching them, accompanied by the two youths Rob had seen him speaking to earlier.

"Gervais, make haste then. Will you keep us waiting?" The comment was voiced mildly enough, but none there failed to note the implicit rebuke.

De Blais increased his pace a little and bowed when he reached the King. "Majesty," he murmured, bowing slightly from the waist. The two young men flanking him stopped when he did, and one of them, the Englishman, bowed low to the monarch. The other stood silent and arrow straight, gazing calmly at the English King as though he were his equal. Rob felt a stirring of gooseflesh as he awaited Edward's reaction, sensing the same anticipation among the others. Edward, however, merely arched an eyebrow at the young

Gael before beckoning him closer, then waving the same hand towards Rob.

"You two will not know each other, I am sure. But that will change within the coming days and you will learn to be friends beneath my roof." Rob immediately heard the ambiguity in the words. One interpretation was straightforward: *I am glad to have the opportunity to bring you together in friendship.* But the other was ominously different: *You may be as you wish elsewhere, but beneath my roof you will be friends.* One look at the newcomer, though, and Rob had decided that the second meaning was by far the likelier of the two. The Gael kept his face utterly blank, and yet his entire demeanour radiated arrogance and disdain, the wide mouth quirking rigidly at one side in what barely escaped being a sneer.

*No friend of mine, this one,* Rob thought. *Not now, not ever. I might spend a lifetime kicking his arse and never get that look off his face.*

"Take note, my lords," Edward said to the group around him. "These two young men are sometime heirs to the proudest, noblest, and most puissant houses in Scotland—houses notably at odds with each other down the years, though both are now sworn to uphold the realm and honour of their future Queen, whose welfare brings our brethren of Mother Church to meet with us this day. I have no doubt these two will stand shoulder to shoulder in the days to come, gladly sharing the honours of fealty to monarch and realm. Robert Bruce of Carrick, bid ye well-met to John Comyn of Badenoch and see to it that he enjoys his visit here beneath our roof."

It was a royal command—the monarch's slightly altered tone emphasized that. Rob tried to keep his face unreadable as he turned to greet the Comyn. He knew he ought to muster a smile of welcome, no matter how false, but the words in his mind were rebellious, and the muscles of his face refused to yield to his insincere efforts.

*I'll greet him as you command, my lord*, he thought. *But I will be damned if I'll bow or scrape to the self-loving whoreson.* "John of Badenoch, I bid you welcome to the Palace of Westminster, in the name of the King," he said, his lips feeling wooden.

The other nodded, his eyes fixed on a point beyond Rob. "Comyn will do," he answered, his voice clipped and curt as though he were speaking to a menial. "Badenoch is my father."

*Aye, and welcome he is to that distinction.* Rob nodded. "So be it. Comyn you will be."

"And Robert Clifford will go with you for the time being, until Bishop Bek has need of him." The King spoke as if completely unaware of any strain between his two young guests.

Rob glanced at Clifford, who nodded coolly but amiably enough. "As you wish, Majesty," he said levelly, looking directly at Edward. "Have we your royal permission to retire?"

"Aye, and our express wish that you should. We have men's business to conduct here. Away with you now. De Blais, see them out."

All three boys bowed deeply and took the requisite three steps backward from the royal presence before straightening up and turning to follow de Blais, who headed for the nearest door. They followed him along a short passageway that led to the Throne Room, and the noise of the assembled courtiers there grew louder with every step. But de Blais turned left at the door and led them through a maze of intersecting passageways, some narrow, some wide, threading his way deftly with the ease of long experience until he reached a narrow, reinforced door that opened onto an enclosed courtyard. Not a word had been spoken among them since they left the audience chamber, but when they were all outside, blinking in the light of the late-afternoon sun, de Blais closed the door behind him and leaned back against it, gazing at his temporary charges with narrowed eyes.

"Well," he said, more to himself than to any of them, "that was interesting. We have a word in France that I never hear over here. *Nuance.* You know it?"

None of them answered directly, but Rob shook his head, intrigued as always with an unfamiliar word.

"It means many things, *nuance*, but all of a kind. Nuance is subtlety—shades of meaning, complexities of mood and … " He wagged one hand, searching for an English word. "How do you say … Texture? Substance? And all of it conveyed in speech, in tone of voice. Sometimes in silence." He eyed each of them again and then shrugged. "Clearly none of you cares, but take my assurance, there were many nuances in that brief encounter you two had with His Majesty. Many subtleties, much left unsaid but deeply meant none the less. I hope you will be friends, as the King wishes. It would vex him did you not."

John Comyn threw Rob a withering sidelong glance and said, "*I* choose my friends." He sounded different this time, and Rob was surprised at the new richness and strength of his voice, a deep and pleasant baritone unlike the terse, high-pitched voice he had used in the audience chamber. He had been anticipating some kind of whine.

"I'll wager you do, and easily, too, for there must be precious few eager to be chosen."

The blood drained from the other's face and he dropped his hand to where his dagger's hilt should be. But weapons were forbidden in the audience chamber, and he clutched for his blade in vain. *By the Christ*, Rob thought. *He's as sudden-tempered as I am.*

Before either of them could move again, de Blais was towering between them. In the space of a heartbeat he had shed the easy air of tolerance Rob admired and was transformed into an angry knight in his prime, one large, steely hand gripping each of the young Scots by the shoulders.

"*Nom de Dieu!*" he snarled, jerking both of them towards him as though they were weightless. "Have you gone mad, fool?" He was glaring at Comyn, who returned the look with loathing.

"Take your hands off me."

"Not hands. One hand, but it has you." Rob saw the muscles in the knight's thick forearm tense as he increased the pressure of his fingers.

Comyn grunted in fury and whipped a fist up and over, pivoting to put his full weight behind the blow to the knight's face. Rob was barely aware of the speed with which the Gascon's other hand released his shoulder and shot out to intercept the strike. Comyn's driving fist stopped short, clamped in the vise that had closed around his wrist, and there it remained immobile while he strained to wrest it free. De Blais's grip was relentless, forcing the younger man's clenched fist back and away, turning him until the two of them were chest to chest, Comyn with his face against the French knight's sternum as he wriggled and fought like a clean-hooked fish. De Blais was immovable, his face expressionless as he held the other effortlessly and waited for his struggles to die down. When they did, he released the young Scot.

"I called you fool," he said, so quietly that Rob had to listen closely to hear every word. "But I do not think you really are foolish. Proud and pigheaded, yes, that you are. Intolerant, certainly. Ill tempered and lacking in manners, manifestly. And arrogant beyond belief for one your age … But not a fool. And because I do not know you, I have to ask myself why you have played the fool's part when you must know it can bring you nothing but grief."

"From whom? You? From this new *friend* I have had thrust upon me? I think not." Comyn shrugged, exaggerating the gesture, then tugged fastidiously at his clothing, adjusting the gold chain of his woollen cloak so that the garment hung properly again, then smoothing the leather shirt over his arms and chest. As he did so he looked again at Rob and sneered. "I certainly have no fear of suffering *grief* from a Bruce."

Rob bit his tongue, willing himself not to respond and not to look at Comyn. He looked instead at Robert Clifford, who was staring at Comyn wide-eyed. Once again Gervais de Blais intervened.

"No one has suggested that you should," he said quietly. "Come, let me show you something."

The Gascon knight gently touched the shirt that the Gael had just finished smoothing. He used the backs of his fingers, his movements unhurried as he stroked the softness of the brushed leather just below the twin badges securing Comyn's cloak. Then, before any of the boys could even guess at his intention, he seized two bunched handfuls of the garment and lifted Comyn off his feet, holding him effortlessly at eye level.

It was the most striking display of sheer strength that Rob had ever seen, and he *felt* the startled widening of his eyes. It had taken Comyn equally by surprise, for he hung unmoving from the Gascon's outstretched arms for several moments, a look of shock on his face. But then he regained his wits and began to struggle, chopping at de Blais's ears with both hands as though to deafen him. He might as well have tried to slap the wind, though, for the big man pulled him close and the flailing hands met harmlessly behind his head as he shook his captive like a child's plaything, barking a single explosive word: "No!" Again the mighty arms bunched and heaved, and Comyn was hoisted even higher as de Blais stepped back with one foot and pivoted, swinging the younger man effortlessly around in a half circle to slam his shoulders flat against the wall by the door. He held him there with ease, leaning into him straight-armed, pinning him against the stones, and Comyn made no further attempt to struggle.

De Blais was not even breathing heavily.

"The day may come, when you are in your prime, that you might seek to chastise me for this little nonsense, and by then I might well be too old to prevent you. But that lies far in the future, Master Comyn, and for now I am twice, perhaps thrice your size and strength, and you are no match for me, so please do not try to make me angrier than I am. You lack manners and good breeding and would have benefited years ago from the good arse-kickings that you so evidently never received." Comyn opened his mouth. "Be quiet! And listen to someone else for once in your silly, over-privileged life."

Comyn glared, and de Blais continued. "You are here as the guest of our King—*my* King—and he has voiced no more than one requirement of you: that you accept his hospitality and learn something of his court and its ways from another like yourself, a fellow Scot, like you, under the King's sufferance ... A simple thing, others might say, and easily accepted. And yet you choose to see it as an insult to your dignity, offensive to your honour. *What* honour? You are but a boy, an unformed, uncouth, foreign newcomer in a civilized land, an outlander. Think you, perhaps, that we should all change our behaviour in deference to your ideas? Answer me."

"I will not be subjected to supervision by a *Bruce*."

"A Bruce! I see." The giant Gascon lowered Comyn to the ground, then smoothed the leather of his shirt again with two slicks of his hands. "Now I can call you fool indeed—and if you dare to move I will drop you where you stand. You have no wish to be supervised by a Bruce? And what of Bruce? How does he feel, think you? Look at him! He is sick of the sight of you and has not known you more than a quarter hour ... yet suffice, I think, to last him a lifetime. But hear this, laddy-buck. Bruce was given a duty. He was ordered to befriend you. He is not your overseer and he is not a spy set to report on you."

Rob had to stop himself from smiling when he heard the Gascon say *laddy-buck*. It was one of King Edward's own favourite expressions, and Rob doubted that de Blais was even aware of having used it.

The French knight was still speaking. "I— Look at me. Look in my eyes ... *I*, Gervais de Blais, am your *overseer*, my arrogant young friend, charged with that duty by King Edward himself. Why else do you think I have been with you since you first arrived? For love of you? No, you show me little to love. The King set me to watch you from the outset, to see how you would conduct yourself within his royal home. You are a stranger, unknown to him, and he wished to see you through the eyes of someone he trusts. Therefore I am required to report to him with my findings. Do you expect me to lie for you? To deceive the man who raised me to knighthood by telling him what a fine fellow you are?"

He drew himself up to his full height, unsmiling, and for the first time Comyn's face flushed. The young Gael's bristling stiffness left him, and his shoulders slumped.

"I beg your pardon," he said quietly.

"Granted. But what of Master Bruce? He is the one you have offended more than me."

Comyn turned his eyes to meet Rob's and dipped his head briefly. His mouth opened but nothing came out. Rob did not mind. His own anger was gone, and it was plain to see that Comyn's had, too. He nodded in return. "So be it," he murmured.

"Good. Then shall we begin again?" De Blais's voice was gentle now, yet it was to Robert Clifford that he looked for concurrence. The young Englishman nodded and smiled faintly. "Excellent," the Gascon said. "So, let me think."

He turned his back on all of them and looked about the court-yard, his right hand cradling his left wrist behind him. "Here is what happens next. Master Bruce will take you two to your quarters in the Squires' Tower. There are others there already, most of them of an age with you, so you will not lack for company. Take note of who they are, Master Comyn, for they represent the cream of this realm, the next generation of the ducal and baronial families of England. All of you will reach manhood within a year or two of one another, which is why you are all here. Edward Plantagenet is a prudent King who has no time for, or patience with, surprises within his realm. To that end he studies all of you, being a believer in the philosophical tenet that the ways of manhood are set deep in childhood. Get to know the others, then, while you are here. But be back here, in amity, to meet with me in one hour from now, and we will start again from there. Am I understood? So be it. I will see you all in one hour."

Rob led the other two towards the squires' quarters in silence that none of them sought to break. He was remembering the tone of the King's voice when he had made his double-meaning comment about their friendship beneath his roof. There had been a new, hard quality in Edward's voice that Rob had never heard the King direct towards him. He had heard Edward's wrath expressed before, many times, for the monarch had a notoriously short temper, but the King had never used such a tone with him in all the time Rob had known him, and it bothered him deeply, the more so since Edward, on this occasion, had not been even slightly angry. And now he remembered the word de Blais had used, *nuance*. The Edward who had spoken to him that afternoon was a different man than the King Rob had grown to love and admire these past few years. And though he could hear the difference in his mind now, he found himself unable to understand what it was that troubled him about it. It had been but one sentence, but Rob had not doubted for one moment that it held a veiled threat. It made him realize that there were hidden, dangerous depths to the English King that he had never suspected, and it made him wonder about how dark and unpredictable those depths might be.

# CHAPTER SIX

# THE LAIRDS OF LOCHMABEN

At the age of sixteen Rob Bruce was long familiar with the awe-striking sensation that gripped him every time he caught sight of his grandfather's fortress of Lochmaben after a long absence—a sense of wonder mixed with the fear-tinged, reverential awe he felt for his formidable grandfather, the master of the place.

Robert Bruce of Annandale, at something more than seventy years of age, was one of the last great feudal lords of Scotland and England, with the royal blood of both countries in his veins. Rob knew him as a daunting, brooding, black-garbed presence with a sharp-boned face that might have been chiselled from stone. Grey-bearded and grim, the Bruce patriarch had always been an intimidating apparition to his grandson, a stern presence with bristling, bushy eyebrows above glaring eyes deep-set on either side of a hard-cdged beak of a nose. But the most sinister aspect of the forbidding old man, in the boy's eyes, was the pair of large, gristly ears that thrust, parchment thin, from his wild grey hair like translucent bat wings. In Rob's earliest memories, the Lord of Annandale had always been aloof, achingly unknowable to the child who had watched him since infancy with fearful eyes, waiting for the frown of disapproval that would announce the old man's awareness of his presence. The frightening old patriarch and the ominous, ancient fortress were as one in Rob's mind, and together they affected him as nothing else could.

Now, riding ahead of everyone else at mid-morning on the seventh day of October in the year of our Lord 1290, Rob watched the earth-and-log fortifications loom into view again as his horse breasted the last low hill, and he felt the familiar, eerie shiver of recognition at the sheer scale of the place.

Lochmaben was nothing like a castle in the English sense. Nor was it comparable to any castle Rob had ever seen. He had heard his father talk of how new castles were springing up everywhere in Scotland and England nowadays, insisting that they were all military installations. They were the emerging fashion, the Earl said: display pieces used for intimidation and serving as assembly points and launching areas for sorties rather than for defensive purposes. Most of them were built of palisaded logs and carefully sited ditches, but an increasing number, among them the crowned heights of Stirling and Edinburgh, were being gradually fortified with stone walls. Edward of England was a great believer in stone castles and was building a number of them in his newly conquered lands in Wales, and his enthusiasm for the strength they offered had convinced his good-brother Alexander of Scotland to follow his example in his own realm, so that someday soon, according to Earl Robert, the entire country would be dominated by massive, modern stone fortifications.

Lochmaben, on the other hand, was a true fortress, ages old, like those in Edinburgh, Stirling, and the other great defensive bastions of Scotland. Like them, it was a natural structure, hewn from the timeless crags of the upflung land and fortified by countless generations of local folk who had dug its maze of defensive ditches deeper and thrown up ever-higher palisaded breastworks around the motte, the rocky summit of the hill at its centre. That summit was now crowned by an immensely strong tower, its walls built of great oak logs and surrounded by groups of thatched huts and sturdy buildings of framed mud and wattle. The site was virtually impregnable, and anyone intending to attack it would have to think long and hard on the costs entailed, for the place was too massive to be besieged without a great deal of planning and limitless resources.

Rob halted his horse on the summit and sat there for a while, watching the activity of the folk around the fortress. In the cleared acres below the first line of defences, teams of people with scythes were working together in lines in the bright sunshine, reaping the harvest of ripened grain, while others gathered up the scythed stalks and bound them into stooked sheaves that stretched in neat rows to dry. He saw no signs of any soldiery in the rustic scene, or any weapons, and was not surprised. Scotland had been at peace for almost thirty years under King Alexander's rule, and since his death the council of Guardians, a group appointed by the community of the realm and comprising six of the country's most powerful men, two of them earls, two more barons, and the last two bishops, had quietly maintained the peace of the realm until such time as another monarch could be crowned.

He glanced towards his father, who was now riding past him, knee to knee with Nicol MacDuncan and talking to him in a voice too quiet for Rob to hear. The others in their party, including the twenty mounted troopers at the earl's back, rode in silence, the muffled thudding of their horses' hooves stirring up clouds of dust from the sun-dried ground. They were alert, all of them, their eyes on the mass of earthworks and wooden buildings that was Lochmaben.

*Bruce men, all of them.* Rob wondered what kind of escort Comyn of Badenoch might be travelling with today, for the Highland Gaels had few horses and went almost everywhere on foot.

In the weeks that followed their meeting in Westminster, the two young men had learned to live in apparent friendship, despite their intense awareness that they would never like each other. That was understood by both of them from the outset. They had nothing in common, other than their mutual dislike and hostility. But they had been under royal command to behave as friends while they were in Westminster, and neither of them doubted the folly of doing otherwise. Knowing they were under scrutiny at all times, they went to great lengths to be courteous and even amiable to each other. Edward made no secret of his propensity for fostering and rewarding favourites while dispossessing and punishing others whose behaviour he deemed unacceptable. And, despot that he was, the range of things he considered unacceptable was expansive and capricious.

Rob and Comyn had been together for four weeks, until Bishop Bek's affairs took him north to Scotland again, with Comyn in tow, within days of the enactment of the Treaty of Birgham, on August 28th at Northampton. Almost two years in the making, the treaty assured both the continuity of the Scots Crown in the person of the seven-year-old Queen Margaret, and the future joining of the Crowns of England and Scotland under the heirs of the royal marriage that would follow, between the young Queen and five-year-old Edward of Caernarfon, the heir to the English throne. The celebrations after the signing were brief but heartfelt, with everyone concerned believing it a job well done.

Rob's father's official affairs in England had concluded with the signing of the Birgham Treaty, but he had family business to attend to after that, and so he and Rob had travelled south and east again, beyond London into Sussex and then Essex, to inspect his own father's properties there. Rob had enjoyed the journey, seeing his father's birthplace and his own future inheritance of Writtle, in Essex, for the first time and meeting an entire clan of English-born relatives whose existence he had barely suspected. There had been no urgency to their journey, and they had been made welcome at Writtle, spending two pleasant weeks in the southern English countryside in magnificent September weather, Rob hunting and fishing with his newfound cousins while his father conducted his audit of the family's English affairs. When they eventually left to return home, they made their way back unhurriedly up the eastern length of England to the border at Berwick, where they crossed into their own country and headed west to visit the earl's father.

Rob kneed his horse into motion and guided it to join his father and Nicol, who turned in their saddles as he approached. The earl nodded, cordial but reserved as always.

"Well," he said, "here we are again. How long has it been since you last saw your grandfather?"

"Almost two years, sir."

"He'll be glad to see you. You've grown much since then."

Rob noticed how his father had used "you" instead of "us." No one had ever said anything on the topic, but Rob had been aware for years that there was something missing in the relationship between the two senior Roberts. His grandfather had never been the kind of man to show emotional attachment, even to his elderly wife, but even so there was something more than a simple lack of warmth between Earl Robert and his stern-faced sire. Rob had heard tenuous, infuriatingly tantalizing hints at earlier strife between father and son when the elder Bruce had married for the second time, at the age of fifty. That wife was still alive and thriving, two decades later, but Rob did not know her well at all, though he spoke with her every time he came to Lochmaben. She was a withdrawn woman who said little to anyone and notably less to Rob's father.

Rob knew from his own investigations that his father, for some unknown reason, objected to the union. That objection had earned the earl his father's displeasure and, Rob had come to believe, his dislike, perhaps even his mistrust. Yet his father, Earl Robert, was a good man, Rob thought; a gentle if somewhat reserved parent, a fond and faithful husband, and an able administrator of his own affairs. He had been a friend and confidant of the late King Alexander, and was well regarded by his own tenants and liegemen in Carrick. It was true that he lacked the volatility, the fire and unbridled passion, of his noble father, but there seemed nothing unnatural to Rob in that, and he could see no reason why the earl's own father should consider him untrustworthy because of it.

"Is Grandfather expecting us?"

"He should be," his father replied. "I sent word on ahead from Berwick."

"Good, because I'm hungry. Let's hope he has told his cook to throw an extra hare into the pot."

The earl barked out one of his rare but welcome laughs. "Oh, he'll have more than that. Even his enemies concede that Annandale's larder is generous. Look, there's someone coming out to meet us. A party of five, with standards. That is encouraging, for it means we are awaited, and I could eat a haunch of venison myself. What say you, Nicol?"

"Swine," MacDuncan answered in the sibilant English he used only when speaking to Earl Robert. "A juicy haunch of pig, with crackling rubbed in flour and salt, and roasted apples." He was looking away as he spoke, his eyes narrowing as he watched the approaching riders. "These folk look agitated, Robert. Does your father always send an escort to meet you?"

Rob turned with his father to look more closely at the approaching men and felt a swift rash of gooseflesh on his nape as he saw that Nicol was right. The riders had an undeniably martial look about them, and the banners they bore were the chivalric pennons of the House of Bruce, pennons normally unseen in times of peace. The man at their head was Sir James Jardine, one of the old lord's staunchest followers, and he wasted no time in pleasantries beyond a stern nod of recognition.

"You are expected, Earl Robert, but your faither has grave need of you. You are to come with me at once."

"What's wrong, Sir James?"

"It's no' my place to say, Earl Robert. The Bruce will tell ye that himsel'. Best no' keep him waitin'. Come awa." He rowelled his horse brutally and wrenched it around to face the fortress in the distance, and the beast took off with a whinny of outrage, leaving the rest of them with no choice but to follow at the gallop.

The level of activity in and around the fortress increased alarmingly as they approached, with parties of mounted riders suddenly erupting from the main gates like angry bees and swarming down the sloping roadway to the plain, where they dispersed rapidly, one grim-faced group of ten passing the Bruces with hardly a glance as they rode on up the hill and along the road towards Berwick.

They followed Sir James through open gates into the main court-yard to find it seething like a nest of ants, people scurrying in all directions and an air of tension and excitement everywhere. Earl Robert paid no attention to any of it, but swung down from his horse, dropped the reins to the ground, and strode towards the tower doors that hung open on their huge hinges. Rob followed close on his heels, aware that Nicol MacDuncan had not dismounted and was staying behind with the others of their party.

The vast hall beyond the doors was only slightly less crowded than the yard outside, but in the sparse light that penetrated the gloom from the open doors and the few tiny windows above them, Rob saw that the half score of heavy black oak tables that normally filled the room had been dragged aside to clear the central space, evidently to accommodate the mass of men he suspected had been in here only a short time earlier. One man, his grandfather's factor, Alan Bellow, stood alone by the far wall, glowering down at a scroll he held open in his hands. He raised his head to them and nodded curtly. Earl Robert nodded back, but he did not stop moving forward.

"Where is my father?"

"I'm in here!" Lord Robert's voice came from the room he referred to as his den, as though it were the lair of some wild beast. Rob had always thought the name appropriate. It was a dark, deep, and surprisingly spacious cubicle under the broad stairs that soared up to the floors above. Permanently lit with racks of thick, stubby candles mounted in sloping iron holders, its rear wall, a sweep of solid stone, was hung with the cured pelts of animals, mainly bears, wolves, and wildcats. One great hanging rack of tanned and worked deer hides served to divide the den into two parts, the nethermost of which held a chimneyed brazier. This room, Rob knew, was where his grandfather spent most of his time, tending to the affairs of his lands and their swarming folk at all hours of the day and night.

The old man had not raised his head as he shouted, but stood looking down at his worktable, his body bent forward as he tapped the point of his dagger on a parchment that lay there, its corners weighted by four fist-sized smoothly polished stones. Rob recognized the pose and the dagger, for the latter was never far from Lord Robert's hand and he invariably used it as a pointer whenever he was deep in thought.

The earl stopped in the doorway, as though reluctant to disturb his father. The old man glanced up at him and beckoned him inside, and he stepped through the open doorway. Rob hesitated, unsure whether he should follow or wait, and his grandfather's eyebrows rose as he caught sight of him.

"Robert? Is that you? You've grown."

"Good day to you, my lord."

His father half turned and waved him away.

"No," Lord Robert growled. "Let him stay. He's a Bruce, and if he's not grown now he will be after this. Close that door and listen, both of you. Sit down, Robert."

Rob moved quickly to close the heavy door at his back as his father seated himself.

"What's amiss, Father?" the earl said. "Where is everyone going? We must have passed thirty riders on the way up."

"More than that. They went out by both gates, front and back, to raise my host, and I'll need you up and away to Turnberry, too, as soon as may be, to turn out your own men."

"To turn out—? In God's name, Father, what has happened?"

"God's work, though some might gauge it otherwise. The Queen is dead … The lass from Norway. I had the word but hours ago, direct from Dunfermline, two horses killed in the bringing of it."

"But … But—" The news was so staggering that neither of the younger Bruces could accommodate it. "But the treaty … Birgham … It's but newly signed … "

"Aye, and all of it a waste of time. Man's plan, God's decree. Now we have to move, and quickly."

"Are you sure, Father?"

"Sure of what? The tidings? Or the need for haste?" There was an impatient edge to the old man's voice.

"The Queen's death."

"As sure as I can be. The word arrived in Dunfermline mere days ago, and by sheer chance the Stewart was there. As soon as he heard of it, he sent the tidings on to me, bidding me look to myself."

The Earl of Carrick braced himself. "And what *was* the word?"

"Unclear, but a sudden sickness at sea, in foul weather between here and Norway. They put in at Orkney and the child died there. Nothing anyone could do to save her. They sent word to Dunfermline, to the council, and then turned back to take the body home to the wee lass's father for burial."

"And now you are doing what, precisely?"

The elder Bruce's face was stony, his fierce eyes focused upon his son's. "Looking to my interests—and yours, and his," he said, lifting his chin towards Rob. "And thanking God I was here when the word arrived."

"What difference would it have made had you not been?"

Annandale glared at his son in astonishment. "You ask me that? What *difference*? In Christ's name, boy, are you besotted? You see what's at stake, surely?"

"No, Father, not as clearly as you evidently do. What *is* at stake?"

"The *realm*, in holy Jesu's name! The Queen is *dead*. Are you addled, boy? See you not what this means?" His eyes flicked to Rob. "Do *you* see it?"

Rob nodded. "Aye, sir. There's no other heir in direct line. The closest is yourself and … Lord Balliol."

"Exactly! The House of Bruce stands next in line for the throne, and Balliol comes second. But Balliol has the Comyns at his back to enforce his claim, thousands of them, and all drooling at the mouth at the thought of having the kingdom fast in their claws. We have but ourselves and a few loyal supporters—James the Stewart and the Earls of Fife, Lennox, and Mar, but that will be to our advantage, gin we move hard and fast. The Balliols will no' have heard the news yet, and once they do, they'll dither and debate. John Balliol was ever loath to make decisions. If his mother Devorguilla was still alive, things would be different, but as it stands the Lord of Galloway will seek guidance from others, and that will give us a few days."

"A few days to do what, sir?"

The question earned Rob's father a look of fleeting scorn. "To be decisive, sir! To *move*. To stake our lawful claim to what is ours by right of blood and birth." Again the pale blue eyes beneath the bushy eyebrows returned to his grandson. "There is a council called at Scone—has been for months—to convene eight days from now, a gathering of the Guardians of the realm, meant to arrange the coronation and the wedding after it. We need to be there early, and in strength, for our own protection. The place will be awash with Comyns, from Buchan and Badenoch and the whole northeast. They'll move to consolidate themselves as they foregather, and so we have to beat them to the mark. If we fail, if we are lax or tardy, they'll steal the throne from under our noses and leave us begging for scraps despite the strength and rightness of our claim."

Rob understood exactly what his grandfather meant and he felt his insides clench with excitement, so he could not quite believe his ears when his father continued to demur.

"Do you not think it might be better to wait, Father? If you move too quickly, too strongly in the wake of this tragic news, you could convey the wrong impression."

The old man straightened up and slid his dagger back into its sheath without looking, the movement perfected over decades of repetition. "Wait?" he asked, his voice ominously quiet. "You would have me *wait*? Balliol and the Comyns would laud you for those words. Wait for what, to lose everything? Look at me, man. I am seventy years old and I have the strongest claim to the kingship in this entire realm. If I wait, I lose my chance—and you lose your crown. Aye, *your* crown, I said, for it is yours by right. If I fail in this, you fail, and young Rob fails with both of us.

The earl studied the floor, and then looked up at his father. "What, then, would you have me do?"

"I told you. Ride for Turnberry and raise your men, then bring them to join me at Scone. I will take the Stirling road and will watch out for you. How many men can you raise?"

The earl shrugged. "Sixty, I would say, perhaps seventy within a day. The more days I had, the more men I could raise. When will you leave?"

"The day after tomorrow. I'll be on the road by dawn."

"Fine, then. If you can provide me with fresh horses, I can be in Turnberry by tomorrow forenoon and I'll have the word spreading as far and as fast as may be. It'll take the next day, at least, to assemble and supply everyone … How many men will you have?"

"Of my own, five hundred, give or take a score. The lairds of Annandale will come to me—Bruces and Johnstones; Jardines, Kirkpatricks, and Herrieses; Dinwiddies, Armstrongs, and Crosbies. At fifty men apiece, a piddling number, there's four hundred already, forbye a round hundred of my own Lochmaben folk. But the Stewart will send his people out to join us, even if he canna come himself, and so will MacDuff of Fife and Domhnall of Mar, so we should number a good thousand, and mayhap half as many again, by the time we get to Scone. Suffice to do what needs to be done and to guarantee we'll no' be murdered in our cots."

Rob had listened to the familiar Annandale names roll off his grandfather's tongue, recognizing each one as it came, from family lore. These were the descendants of the men who had followed the very first Lord Bruce into Scotland, and they had settled here, never to leave the service of the Bruce family. Fiercely loyal with a feudal devotion seldom to be found beyond their dale of Annan these days, they were proud people and ferocious warriors in defending their own.

"So be it," his father said. "I'd best be away, then, if we're to catch up to you before you reach Stirling."

Annandale crossed to open the door and lead them out, beckoning his waiting factor. "Fresh horses for Earl Robert," he instructed, but then stayed the fellow with an upraised hand. "How many men will you take with you?" he asked his son.

"There are two and thirty of us."

"Hmm. I doubt we have that many horses left. Do we, Alan?"

The factor grimaced. "We hae ten, I ken that. But I wouldna be willin' to swear beyond that."

"Well, that takes care of your escort. Take your nine best men and leave the others here."

"I'll take eight. Rob will need a horse, too."

"No, Rob will stay here and travel wi' me. It's time he and I came to know each other. Away wi' you now, quick as you can, and we'll be watching for you by Stirling."

The sun broke briefly from between massed banks of heavy, rain-filled clouds as Rob stood on the knoll that protected the fortress's main gates and watched his father's small force dwindle into the west. He thought about the name he had so recently overheard applied to his grandfather. The Noble Robert. He had always been aware of his grandfather's nobility. Now he realized it had been the nobility of birth and lineage that he had acknowledged, whereas the title he had heard used a mere hour before had been of another nature altogether. The knights of Annandale were dour, blunt men with scant regard for the pretensions of the world beyond their valleys, and courtesy of any kind meant little to them. Tempered by the harsh realities of life in their rough countryside, they had no time for the proprieties of courtly behaviour in faraway places, and titles meant nothing to them. They gauged a man by what he did and what he was, and they were scornful, to a man, of titles and honours that were conferred by kings and not earned by merit. And yet the manner in which he had heard them refer to his grandfather as the Noble Robert had been completely lacking in either irony or conde-scension. The title had been used respectfully. It had emerged with the ease of long and proper usage and with all the dignity of great regard. And it occurred to Rob that there must be a great deal more to his forbidding grandfather than he had ever suspected.

As his father's party dwindled into the distance, they were replaced by newcomers arriving from widely differing directions, some alone, some in groups. He turned and looked back at the great bulk towering behind him, idly wondering whether he would see his grandfather again before they set out in two days' time. Even as he turned again to look back down the hill, the first of the approaching riders had reached the road leading up to the summit, and he knew that Lord Robert would be far too involved with his own plans to have time to spare for an inconvenient grandson. Unsure whether he ought to be relieved by that, he moved away in search of Nicol MacDuncan, hoping that his uncle would help him while away what promised to be a long and barren afternoon. He had seen no one even close to his own age since his arrival in Lochmaben, but even had the place been swarming with young people, he would have been too preoccupied with his own concerns to approach them. Nicol, he knew, would find plenty of things to occupy both of them for as long as was necessary.

And so he did, beginning with an hour-long, bone-jarring bout of practice with the quarterstaves that had become the insignia of trainee swordsmen from the far north of Scotland to the southern-most shores of England. Rob had been training with the quarterstaff from the age of eight, beginning with a small one suited to his size, and though it had been a puny thing compared with the heavy, five-foot-long ash dowel he now used, it had taxed his muscles fully and started his unflagging growth towards the status of knight and warrior. Now, at the age of sixteen, he weighed three times more than he had eight years earlier, and all of it, every pound of weight and rope of muscle, was in peak condition, so that he fought his uncle as a man, giving no quarter and expecting none. Nicol was now on the downward side of his middle years, but few watching him fight could have noted any loss of speed or stamina in his performance. Eventually, though, he dropped the point of his staff to the ground, waving a hand in surrender.

"Enough," he gasped. "I'm spent. I couldn't lift this thing again if my life depended on it."

Rob, feeling no whit less tired, grinned through bared teeth. He dropped his staff and bent forward to rest his hands on his knees. "Thanks be to God," he wheezed. "I thought you were going to keep at me till I dropped, which would have been at any moment now." He lowered his head and concentrated upon his breathing until it grew less laboured, then looked up at Nicol. "What now?"

Nicol straightened up and placed his hands on his hips, then arched his back and rotated his torso as far as he could from side to side, grunting with the effort before he stopped. "Well," he said quietly, straining to breathe normally, "two possibilities I see. One remote, the other necessary. You could go and find your grandfather, spend some time with him … "

Rob grimaced and waved a hand in the direction of the main castle yard, now crammed with men and horses. "I think the Noble Robert has his hands full at the moment. What's your second possibility?"

"A long, hard run followed by a bath in a friendly stream before the heat goes out of the sun. What say you? We haven't had a long run together in months and it'll do both of us good. Might kill me, mind you, but I'll be too exhausted to fret over it."

"I would enjoy that, if I had the strength to stand upright. Can we cool off for a while before we start?"

Nicol shrugged. "Aye, but the chances are fair that we'd stiffen up … Or I would. Better to start out walking right away, until we find our wind again. Then we can start running."

Within the quarter-hour they were at the base of the fortress hill, where they swung right to follow the southerly track they had crossed earlier. There were still several hours of daylight remaining, and the reapers were still working diligently in the fields, the air heavy with the rich smells of dusty, newly cut oats and barley. Rob was fully refreshed by then, feeling as though he could run forever, but he said nothing that his uncle might take as a challenge, content to leave it to Nicol to change from walk to run. Another party of four riders came sweeping along the road from the south at full gallop, and the pair moved aside to let them pass.

"Right," said Nicol, when the riders had gone. "Are you ready for the road?"

They struck off the sun-baked track and ran overland for what Rob guessed to be a circular ten miles at an easy, loping pace that varied from time to time as one goaded the other to race on a particularly challenging slope. When they broke from a dense copse of trees and found the tower of Lochmaben in view again, and less than a mile away, Nicol called a halt and led the way back through the trees to a looping stream they had passed before entering the woods, noting its steep banks and a pool deep enough to swim in. Rob threw off his belt with its sheathed dagger and took a shallow, running dive into the water fully dressed, and for the next quarter of an hour they bathed and played the fool together like a couple of schoolboys.

It was growing dark quickly by the time they entered Lochmaben again, and the temperature had dropped sharply as soon as the sun set, a humourless reminder through their still-damp clothes of the winter's chill that lay in the months ahead. Tired to the bone after their long day—seven hours in the saddle and then heavy physical exercise all afternoon—Rob agreed without demur when Nicol suggested they beg something to eat from the kitchens and then get themselves to sleep as quickly as possible. And so they shared a fresh-baked loaf of crusty bread and a large clay bowl of hot venison stew that they washed down with fresh spring water from the fortress's deep well.

They ate in silence, Nicol staring aimlessly into the distance, engrossed with his own thoughts, while Rob found himself almost fearing the prospect of spending a number of days in the company of his grandfather. It would be the first time he had ever been phys-ically close to the old man for anything longer than a few hours, and he wondered how long it would be before he tried the gruff patri-arch's patience sufficiently to attract the rough edge of his tongue.

# CHAPTER SEVEN

# THE PATRIARCH

Rob awoke suddenly, gasping for air and flailing wildly at the threatening face that hovered over him, but even as he swung his arm he knew that the despairing strength of his blow was false and that his arm had only flapped weakly. He had been dreaming, a vivid, terrifying dream, and its aftermath was sharp, filling his throat and chest with flaring panic before he remembered where he was: in his grandfather's stronghold of Lochmaben, in the family quarters of the great tower.

He breathed in deeply, squeezing his eyes tight shut for a count of three, then pushed himself up onto one elbow, only to see an apparition standing by the foot of his bed, a gaunt figure, muffled and spectral, glowing in flickering, fitful light. His breath caught sharply in his throat as the dreadful dream came surging back to life.

"I startled you. Forgive me. There is no worse way to come out of a sound sleep."

Rob blinked. "My lord, is that you?"

"Aye. The others have all left and we have time to talk, if you so wish."

Rob shook his head, trying to dislodge the last of his sleepy witlessness. "What hour is it?" he asked. "Should you not be asleep?"

He could have sworn he saw the old man's mouth twitch in the beginnings of a smile, but he knew it could only have been a trick of the shifting light.

"No," the old man rumbled in his deep voice. "I don't sleep much nowadays. And depending on my mood and the number of things I have to do, I find that to be either a blessing or a curse of age. So, will you come and help me pass an hour?"

"Aye, of course, my lord."

"Good. Get dressed, then, and come downstairs. I'll be in the den. There's a fire in the hearth. Old bones like mine need warmth, but I think it is cold enough tonight to be welcome to you, too. Here, I'll light your candle. Come down when you are ready."

As soon as the old man had gone, Rob swung his legs out of bed and sat hugging himself and shivering. It was not the chill that had him shivering. His mind was still in the half grip of his dream, and he knew beyond question that the frightening figure that had threatened him was his grandfather. He sat there, frowning into the candle flame. He had often been afraid of the Lord of Lochmaben, but there had been nothing frightening or threatening in his grandfather's presence here.

Realizing that he was wasting time and keeping his host waiting, he rose and dressed quickly, muffling himself from neck to knees in a warm, shapeless coat of soft, thick wool before taking his candle and making his way down the wide, wooden stairs to the main hall. It was dark and quiet now, the huge stone hearths at either end holding nothing but glowing embers, but bright light was spilling out from the massed banks of candles in Lord Robert's den under the stairs, and Rob went forward quickly, announcing himself in a voice that sounded strangely calm and resonant to his own ears.

Lord Robert was seated in his padded wooden armchair, close to a blazing fire in a brazier set into a small hearth by the one stone wall.

"Cold enough for winter," he growled as his grandson entered, then pointed to the empty chair beside him. "Come, sit here beside me." The pointing finger changed direction, indicating a table that held a small jug. "But before you do, bring me that jug and the two cups there."

Rob did as he was bidden, and the aroma from the jug caught sharply at his nostrils.

"Good," his grandfather said, pouring from the jug into each of the cups. "Now bring that kettle, but mind you don't burn yourself. Use the cloth."

Rob wrapped the iron handle of the kettle in a much-singed pad of cloth that hung by the fireside and, directed by Lord Robert, poured hot water carefully into each cup.

"Aye, that'll do it." The old man picked up his cup in both hands and held it to his nostrils, sniffing appreciatively. "Aye," he murmured again, "there's nothing like toddy to keep the chills away on a cold night. Drink up."

Rob sipped with great caution, knowing the water was very hot, but even so the sharpness of the drink snatched at his breath and closed his throat, and he had to set the cup down quickly lest he spill it in the coughing fit that racked him. His grandfather watched him in astonishment.

"What—what *is* that?" he gasped eventually.

The old man's eyebrows were still arched in surprise, but now his expression was altered by an unexpected smile. "It is *uisqhebaugh*. Have you never had it?"

"No, sir, I have not."

The old man's smile grew wider. "Well, don't sound so scunnert, boy. You will soon grow used to it. But it is a taste to be learned, and that is truth. It is the distilled spirits of barley, and it is powerful stuff. When served hot like this, though, mixed with honey and boiled water, it is medicinal. Try it again, but wi' care. You'll find it grows on you."

Rob sipped again, and found that the liquid, while still tasting alien and bitter, was not as unpleasant as he had thought. He lowered his cup slowly. "It's … good, I think … Sweet. Warming."

"Aye, it's all of those. Try some more."

He did, and this time found it almost pleasant. "May I ask a question, sir?"

"That's what you're here for, boy. Ask away."

Rob frowned down at his cup. "This drink. If it's medicinal when it's served hot like this, what is it when it's served cold?"

That brought a bark of a laugh that Rob could scarce believe he had heard. "It's dangerous," the old man said. "And many's the thousand men who have learned that to their cost, to say nothing of the tens of thousands who went to their deaths having learned it too late. It is called the water of life, but it can drown a man more quickly than any other water. It breeds drunkenness far quicker than ale or mead. But you won't be drinking it cold in this household. Stand up. Take off that covering and let me look at you."

Rob rose and shrugged out of the heavy woollen robe, then stood as the old man scanned him up and down.

"Put it back on," the old man said when he had finished. "You're big. Near as big as your father, even now. How old are you, seventeen?"

"Sixteen, your lordship."

"I'm not your lordship, I'm your grandsire. Call me Grandfather."

"Grandfather."

Another abrupt laugh. "You sound as though you're tasting it on your tongue for the first time, like another new drink. You've never liked me, have you?"

Cautiously, his slow movements belying his racing thoughts, Rob sat up straighter and pulled his shoulders back. He looked directly into the fierce old eyes.

"You have never given me reason to, sir."

"Explain. What do you mean?"

There was no passion in the question, no anger. And that gave Rob the courage to continue. He set his cup down with great care on a small table by his chair.

"In all my life you have never spoken to me directly, other than to order me out from under your feet when I was a child ... Except for once, in the stables when I was seven. I was passing through on my way to the tower, and you came in the far door, in haste. I stepped aside to give you room and came close to some fresh hay, and you shouted at me to stand away from it and not make a mess of it. And then you saw it was already scattered and you cursed at me for having done it ... I felt unjustly condemned, since I had touched nothing, and I cried as you rode away, still muttering to yourself. That is my single clearest memory of you."

Lord Robert stared at him, his face expressionless. "I did that? I don't remember it. But you most obviously do, and I don't doubt you … I cursed you? What did I say?"

Rob shrugged. "I don't remember that, sir. I knew only that you were angry at me without cause, and I was hurt … by your readiness to think ill of me."

"Hmm … " The patriarch looked down at his cup for long moments, then raised it and sipped deeply before looking back at his grandson's pale face. "That memory has festered in you these what, nine years?" he growled. "I jalouse it's too deeply rooted now to be pulled out easily. But hear what I am going to tell you now, for I speak not only as your grandsire but as the Lord of Annandale and chief of the House of Bruce. I *am* Bruce, and I never lie. Many resent me for that. It makes them uncomfortable. But it is a part of me that none can question or deny. My word is my worth and I do not deal in falsehoods. Do you hear me, boy?"

Rob nodded.

"Then hear me further. I was not angry at you that day, all those years ago, no matter what you thought. Had I been, I would not have forgotten it." He held up a hand, as though to cut short a protest. "I am not saying I was not angry. In all probability I was, for I anger easily, even now, and I was worse when I was younger, unwilling to accept the behaviour of fools or the uselessness of idiots. Someone else must have angered me that day and you but caught the brunt of it, I fear. But you were certainly not the cause of my foul temper, though you fell victim to it. So I would make amends, if that is possible. Is there something that would serve, this late, to counterbalance the hurt you took that day?"

Rob sat numb, overwhelmed by the differences so quickly shown between the man who had spoken those words and the man he had believed him to be. He shook his head. "No, sir," he said quietly. "You have already healed it. I see now that the fault was more mine than yours. It was the child who saw what was not there, too young to see or understand the reality of things."

"Partly so," the old man said. "But that does not excuse the heedless hurt of it. You would not have been the first innocent I treated so … nor the last. Your father believes I think too much, brooding and ever mulling, scheming and anticipating things that never come to pass, forbye trying to live other people's lives for them. And he may be right. But in my own mind, within the conscience that the churchmen tell us we all have, I sometimes rue my *lack* of thought, the thoughtlessness that leads to needless hurt such as we are talking about." He broke off suddenly, peering keenly at the boy. "What is it? You look troubled."

"No," Rob said, but even to himself he sounded less than certain, and the elder Bruce leaned closer.

"Don't start hesitating now, boy. Remember who you are and speak out, whatever is on your mind."

The words, and the stern gaze that accompanied them, made Rob want to squirm, but instead he merely shrugged. "There's nothing wrong, Grandfather. It was but a thought—a question—that came into my mind while you were speaking … But it's a question, I think, that I have no right to ask."

The old man's eyes narrowed and he leaned slightly closer, leaning his weight on the arm of his chair. "Every man with a brain has a right, and at times even a duty, to ask questions of anyone, Grandson. Questions demand answers, and understanding those answers leads to greater awareness of this world we live in. Even a refusal to answer will tell much to the man who is wise enough to watch and listen closely, for from the very silence he can jalouse why no answer is being given. Besides, while we're talking of rights, I might dispute your right to take your old grandsire to task for past failures, but you did it and I respected you for it. That took courage— the more so since you expected me to rend you from top to bottom, if I suspect correctly. So ask away. What was your question?"

What *was* the question, exactly? Rob knew he could not simply blurt it out in the crude words that had sprung to his mind, not without angering the old man. The matter was impertinent already, without adding insult to the form of it. He bought some time by sipping again at his neglected drink, enjoying the taste of it more now that it had cooled, but he could feel his grandfather's eyes watching him. He coughed gently, feeling the fiery liquor catching at his throat, then shuddered and set the cup down again.

"It was what you said about thoughtlessness, sir," he began. "You said you sometimes rue it, your lack of thought about people's feelings … And you were speaking of my father at the time." He drew a deep breath. "Is that why … Is that why you and he are not close?"

The old man frowned. Then he sank back into his chair. His eyes narrowed to slits, and Rob sat waiting for the quiet wrath that he was sure must come. But his grandfather merely pursed his lips and scratched at his beard as he had done before, and when he did speak his voice held no trace of anger.

"I was about to ask you why you would think such a thing," he said, "that we are not close, your father and I. But to you it's clearly obvious that we are not, and I won't insult you by pretending you are wrong. Your father is my firstborn son and I love him dearly, as a father does. But I also perceive his weaknesses, as fathers do in their sons, and that is what has led to our … estrangement. It is a frequent thing between fathers and their sons, a clash of wills and ongoing petty quarrels that can grow into deep resentment and in turn breed dislike. And yes, to answer your question, there are times when I rue the gulf that stretches between us now, for my own thoughtlessness, my lack of concern for his true feelings over too long a time was largely what drove us apart."

"But he is a good man, Grandfather."

"I know he is, Grandson. As the Earl of Carrick he has prospered and conducted himself in a way that is beyond reproach. His marriage to your mother was the best thing that ever happened to him. It made a man of him when I had despaired of ever seeing him become a man. But by then, of course, the damage had been long done." He sipped from his cup, and then continued. "He is a different kind of man than I was—not worse, nor better, I see now, simply different." He gave a matter-of-fact shrug. "And truth be told, though it pains me to say so, I did not want a different kind of man, even when he was yet a boy. I wanted a reflection of myself. Do you know the words 'alter ego'?"

"Latin," Rob said. "Father Ninian explained it. It means another self."

"Good lad. That is precisely what it means, and it was precisely what I wanted in my son. Another self. And when I saw it was not to be, I was … displeased would be one word for it. Your father was my firstborn son by my first wife, Isabella. She was a de Clair, the daughter of Gilbert de Clair, who was both Earl of Hertford and of Gloucester, and her mother—your great-grandmother—was Lady Isabel Marshall, a daughter of the great William Marshall, Earl of Pembroke, Marshal of England, and, some say, England's greatest hero. He was tutor and master-at-arms to King Richard the Lionheart."

He grunted then, his expression wryly amused, and pushed himself out of his chair. Rob twisted around and watched him as he reached up and took down a large, sheathed sword that hung from a stout peg on the partition behind the door, drawing the long, silver blade from the scabbard as he returned to his chair. "He was also your great-great-grandsire—one of eight from whom you can claim descent—and this was his, the marshal's own sword, given to me by your great-grandmother herself on the day I wed her daughter. She told me she believed her father's sword would lose no honour in my hand." He swung the heavy weapon gently, then sat down again, resting its point on the floor between them, close to the fire. "You would think, with such an illustrious heritage behind her, that Isabella would have bred fiery sons. But that was not to be, for she bred much of herself into her children and too much, I thought, into her firstborn son. I was a brash, ambitious young hothead, and Isabella was a delicate and gentle creature—too much of both, you might have thought, to live long in this brutal world, but she lived for thirty-eight years and was my wife for twenty-four of those, from the age of fourteen, bearing me two daughters and four sons."

He sighed deeply. "To my own shame, though, I believed the sons she gave me fell far short of what I needed. I suppose had I been a different man that might not have mattered greatly. But I was who I was, Robert Bruce, the fifth Lord of Annandale, and I had vast territories to govern and the need for a strong, hard son to stand with me and follow me. I had high hopes for the *sixth* Bruce of Annandale—a son to be forged and shaped and tempered by me, as I had been by my own father. He reared me to govern strongly and dutifully, to live solely as he expected me to live. And when I found out that I could not forge my son in the same way, I became bitter. And harsh. And cruel … "

The old man fell silent, his face, which had been so animated earlier, now empty; his eyes dull and unfocused. But then he shivered and clutched at the woollen shawl that draped his shoulders, pulling it closer about him, and only then did Rob notice that the brazier fire had dulled. He rose quietly and stooped to replenish the fire, thinking that his grandfather had no need of being watched in his grief. He chose short, thick logs of apple wood from the rack by the hearthside and thrust them deep into the glowing coals, one by one. When he was satisfied and went back to his seat, he found Lord Robert watching him, all evidence of his temporary lapse gone from his eyes.

"Well," his lordship said in a more normal tone. "There's time enough to fix all that, eh, boy? Especially with your help, for I assume you will help me, eh? To make amends?"

"I will, Grandfather."

"Good, then we'll do it together. Now, where were we, before that?"

*I was crying in the wilderness, like John the Baptist.* Rob felt his throat swell painfully from the realization of how wrong he had been in his lifelong dislike and fear of this man.

Lord Robert sat up straighter, stretching his hands towards the newly rising flames, and Rob took note of those hands. Old they might be, but they were huge and still powerful, as evidenced by the casual way the old man had swung the enormous sword that now rested against his chair.

"You heard the talk between your father and me this morning. How much do you know of what's going on today?"

"The Queen's death?" Rob shook his head. "Only what you told us, sir, and I was shocked to hear of it. I have talked about the Birgham Treaty with my father, though, on several occasions, and I understand what it entailed. It seems a shame that all that effort should have been for naught."

"You approved of the treaty?"

"I did, sir." He hesitated. "Did you not?"

"I did, but that is neither here nor there. What did you like about it? Was there anything in particular that appealed to you, or perhaps troubled you?"

"Troubled me?" Rob frowned. "No, sir, nothing that I can think of. I liked the provisions for the marriage between our new Queen and young Prince Edward of Caernarfon—two realms, each free and independent of the other, yet ruled in unison and amity by man and wife. And I liked, too, that the council of Guardians did not quibble over approving the girl's claim."

"Nor should they have," his grandfather said. "She was the true heir. King Alexander was her grandsire. How could they quibble?"

Rob shrugged. "Because she was female, a woman and a child at the same time, too young to rule."

Lord Robert's eyebrows rose. "You're right, but she would have had a regent to guide her, as I guided her grandfather Alexander, standing as his regent while he was but a boy. Did you know about that?"

"I did, sir. It was before you went on crusade with young Prince Edward, before he became King.

"Aye, so it was. You've met King Edward, have you not? What is your opinion of him? And do *not* tell me you have no right to an opinion."

"I admire him, sir. I believe him to be a great man and perhaps an even greater King."

"Why?"

"Because of who he is and what he has done since becoming King. He is a warrior and a conqueror."

"He conquered Wales," his grandfather conceded. "But he still has his hands full, trying to control his own barons after decades of his rule. And he gave a good account of himself on crusade, until brought down by an assassin's poisoned blade. But he has troubles with the King of France and with rebels in his own Duchy of Gascony, and the combined costs of those campaigns in France threaten to beggar him and his kingdom. His barons know that better than he does, which does nothing to help his case with them. What else do you admire in him?"

Rob shrugged, as if dealing with self-evident truths. "His laws and reforms. He has reorganized his whole kingdom. You must admit, Grandfather, that his ongoing efforts there have been magnificent."

"Ongoing, yes, I'll grant that. But magnificent? I wish I still possessed your youthful optimism. To an old cynic like me it appears as though Edward's entire legal efforts since the beginning of his reign have been to win back the freedoms lost to him when his grandsire John Lackland ceded power to the barons in Magna Carta. And it's a losing fight, no matter how heroic his struggle. The barons will not support his wars across the sea and they will never relinquish the powers they gained in the Great Charter."

He held up a placating hand, seeing the confusion in his grandson's face. "Differing points of view, Robert. No more than that. Life is all about discerning such things and adjusting to them, whatever it may take. I am but offering my opinions versus yours, in the spirit of debate and temperance. Personally, I like the Plantagenet as a man. As a king, though, I find he has many characteristics that I wish were different. Did you know that he annexed the Isle of Man three months ago?"

The words meant nothing to Rob. "The Isle of Man?" he said.

"Aye. It's ours, part of this realm, has been so since sixty-six, when Alexander made treaty with Haakon of Norway after we drove his minions out of the Isles, after the sea fight at Largs ... "

"But—" Rob sought for something profound to say, to express his grasp of those events, but gave up. "I don't understand what you are saying, Grandfather."

"You will if you think about it. The Isle of Man is an important place, with a significance beyond its size to anyone who thinks in terms of kingdoms. And you, Robert Bruce, must now start to think that way, as I do. Man was Norwegian for centuries, but then it fell to us. Consider that now from England's point of view: a large island, strategically placed thirty miles from England's coast, fifty miles from Wales, and set square across the sailing routes from England to Ireland. It could offer a very real threat to England's trade and commerce, should any conflict ever develop between our two realms. Edward did not like that development. But there was little he could do about it without offending Alexander, his friend and kinsman."

"While Alexander was alive, you mean."

"Aye, that is exactly what I mean." The old man paused, as though to allow that thought to settle. "But Alexander died without an heir, his realm to be governed by a female child dependent upon others who might be less well disposed to England than King Alexander was. Do you understand me now?"

"I think so. The Isle of Man became a threat, if only in theory. But what happened in truth? You said King Edward occupied Man three months ago. How could he do that without starting a war? It would be theft, would it not? Invasion?"

"Trickery is how. Subtle, as such trickery usually is. It seems the people of the isle—Manxmen, they call themselves, though they're Norwegian almost to a man—petitioned Edward for his protection. They were unhappy with the lack of guidance and government from Scotland, they said, and afraid that Norway might return to claim the isle again, now that Alexander is dead and his granddaughter named to Scotland's throne. And so, considering themselves to be no more

Scots than Edward is himself, they besought his intervention for their common good. In writing. A formal request to the monarch whom they believed to be the natural and most appropriate man to lead them."

Rob's eyes had grown wider as he listened. "And no one here complained or sought to intervene?"

His grandfather shrugged. "The thing was done before anyone in Scotland heard a word of it. And I include myself, along with the council of Guardians. What could we do, faced with an accomplished deed, particularly with the Birgham Treaty in the balance? That pact had already been more than a year in the making, and we were faced with the undoing of it all. We could hardly declare war in outrage when all the Manxmen had decided to rebel against us if we did. And to have done so would have thrown all of Scotland into chaos."

"And so it was … accepted, just like that?"

"Aye, it was. An acceptance under duress, and after the fact."

Rob suddenly felt much older than he had been a short time earlier. "So the council debated and accepted this turn of events *after* the fact, as you say. Then why would you feel the need to speak of it now to me?"

"Because you are a Bruce and heir to my lordship of Annandale someday. You are my grandson, blood of my blood. And you are yet very young … Apt, I jalouse, but unskilled, as yet, in seeing faults in others. I brought this up now because I need to free your eyes of the veil that clouds them."

"What veil, sir? My eyes are fine."

A wolfish smile split the older man's face. "Fine, I agree, but very young. Think about it. An island province, peopled by folk whose fatherland was Norway. Their fathers were Norwegian, as were all their ancestors. Then ask yourself how such a simple folk, untaught and unlettered, could conceive of, let alone draw up, a formal petition to a foreign king, begging his intercession on their behalf. Intercession into what, in the first place? There was no conflict anywhere. The Manxmen might have been unhappy, I'll not argue against that. They've had scant recognition from any of us here for the past score years. But they have not been badly treated. They have not even been taxed. They've been … neglected, nothing more."

"But it makes no sense. Unless … Are you suggesting, sir, that they might have been tutored in forming such a petition? By someone from outside? From England?"

Lord Robert spread his palms. "Can you suggest a better explanation? King Edward loves the forms of law."

"But … that is treachery. Infamy. Theft. I cannot believe—"

"Believe it, Grandson. And it was not infamy, nor was it treachery. It was inspired kingcraft, and Edward is a king above and before all else. You might make a solid case for theft, but were I in his position, I might have done the same thing, had I had the wit to think of it. He secured the safety of his realm against a potential threat, increased his holdings at the same time, and did it all without a drop of blood being shed. When I heard of it I was as outraged as you are, but once I had thought about it for a while, I admired his foresight. And his daring."

"And what did the other Guardians think?"

"In private? I know not, for I am not one of the council—have not been for years. Publicly, though, they did the only thing they could and accepted it with such good grace as they could muster, much as they are doing now with this Bek development, though again the death of the Queen must alter that."

Rob frowned. "Bek development? Do you mean Bek of Durham?"

Lord Robert looked at his grandson in surprise, for his reference to Bek had been little more than a thought mused aloud and he had not expected a reaction to it. "Aye, Bek of Durham. Does the name mean something to you?"

"I've met him, Grandfather. In London. He came to meet with the King while I was there, and he stayed for weeks, then returned to Scotland after the signing of the treaty."

"Aye, that's what happened … How did he impress you? Did you speak with him?"

"No, sir, scarce at all. King Edward made me known to him when he arrived and I gathered that he had been assigned to Scotland on the King's behalf, to prepare for the royal wedding. But I had no conversation with him other than to exchange greetings on that one occasion. He struck me as being more prince than bishop, though. A silent, disapproving, judgmental man, I thought, likely to be quick tempered and intolerant."

"Aye," Lord Robert growled, "that is Bek, all of those things and more. He is Edward's man, head to foot, and dangerous ... Were you aware that he had been promoted while he was there in London?" Rob shook his head. "Aye, well he was. He had been here for months, off and on, seeing to the arrangements for Birgham, but as soon as the treaty was signed he was dispatched back here, bearing a letter to the Guardians from Edward. It asked the council—supposedly—to ratify Bek's appointment as Edward's lieutenant in Scotland on behalf of his son Edward and Queen Margaret. In consideration of the need to preserve the peace and tranquility of the Scots realm is how I'm told he phrased it."

"Could he *do* that?"

"He did it. And the Guardians bowed to it. It was a strange letter, from what I have heard, all flowery profusion and protestations of love, as is Edward's way, and all thinly veiling an open warning not to challenge him in his wishes. None of the Guardians knew quite how to respond, for there was nothing blatantly unreasonable about the request, other than the letter itself and the fact of its delivery by Bek. You yourself would have seen no ill in his request. But believe me, it was a demand, an ultimatum lacking only an open threat. And that is what I need you to understand in all of this, Grandson—that your eyes are not yet old enough to see what is really there in front of them."

He raised a finger, pointing for emphasis. "There is no fault in that and I am not blaming you for anything. You've done nothing wrong. You are merely young, seeing things with a boy's eyes, and time will change all that. In the meantime, though, you have much to learn about men and kings, and because you are not merely a boy but a future Robert Bruce in this time and in this place, you will have to learn it all more quickly than others your age. You are my grandson, and you and I have not been close ere now, but from this day on I will do what I can to teach you in this craft, for craft it is, and learnable like any other. I had to learn it myself at your age, and I've profited by it. It has served me well, as it will you.

"Edward of England is all you see in him, make no mistake on that. But he is much, much more than you perceive and, in some ways, admittedly minor ones, he is far less. He is a king and he does what a king must do, manipulating everyone about him to his own ends … everyone. Because the plain truth is, a king can have no friends, as other men know friends."

Rob's frown became a scowl, and when he spoke next his words were directed as though to an equal. "That can't be so. King Alexander had close friends. I saw them with him when he came to Turnberry. And one of them was King Edward himself. And I know he, too, has friends."

"Name them."

Rob hesitated, thinking quickly, drawing from his memories of Westminster. "The Earls of Suffolk, Norfolk, Hertford, and Hereford. I've seen them with him. Relatives, family, and close companions."

"And who were Alexander's friends?"

No hesitation this time. "My father, the Earls of Mar and Buchan, James the Stewart, and the bishops, Fraser of St. Andrews and Wishart of Glasgow."

Lord Robert smiled and stooped forward to pick up a fresh, thin log of apple wood from the fuel rack, then used it as a poker to stir up the glowing coals before he thrust it deep into the fire.

"You have named vassals, every one," he said, "save for the bishops. The others are all liegemen, barons and earls, each with his own needs dependent on being pleasing to the King. That is not friendship, Robert, and the few friendships that can persist against such needs are precious indeed and scarce as dust motes in a cloud-burst. As for the bishops, their prime allegiance is to God and His Holy Church. Their King may be God's anointed, but they themselves are God's wardens, and their sworn devotion is to His eternal Church's welfare, not to the brief, uncertain rule of any mortal man." He paused, and when he resumed, his voice softened into the common, slightly slurred Scots tongue of his people. "Ye'll have heard the auld saying that nae man can serve twa maisters, have ye no'?"

Rob nodded, and his grandfather's speech changed again, his tone now wry.

"Aye, well when one of those two masters is God Himself, which one will the bishops choose, think you?" The old man's face was grave. "Yet Edward of England has one true friend, I believe—two, if you count his wife, Eleanor, who has been his bedmate, soulmate, and keeper of his conscience these forty years. But there is one man who is closer to Edward than a brother and has nothing to gain from his friendship or from duplicity. Can you guess who that man is?"

"No, sir. Who is it?"

"A bishop, against all odds. The man is Robert Burnell, Chancellor of England and Bishop of Bath and Wells. He's a quiet man. You might live in Westminster for a year and never see him, but he is the King's friend in every sense of the word. He is incorruptible, steadfast, and loyal beyond suspicion, and he and Edward have been fast friends for decades. Alexander Canmore had no such friend in all Scotland."

The boy blinked. "Not even you, Grandfather?"

The old man laughed. "Least of all me, boy. I was his regent when he was a boy half your age, and I served him well, but before he confounded everyone by being born, when everyone thought his mother barren, his father named me heir to the Scots throne. Then the boy was born and I was dismissed as heir potential. I became, instead, a threat in the eyes of many. The Bruce holdings were among the largest in Scotland, as well as numbering among the largest in England, too, and I was directly descended from Isobel, the second daughter of the Earl of Huntingdon. I was descended, too, on my father's side, from King David—a second cousin, by relationship—and that won me the title Tanist, or heir-presumptive to the throne by ancient Gaelic law should anything happen to the King himself. So the King and I, you may see, could never be true friends, if for no other reason than that others mistrusted my motives."

"You mean the Comyns."

"Aye, I do. There has never been love between our houses."

"I met one of them in London, too. He came down with Bek."

The old man's eyebrows shot up. "Did you, by God? Which one?"

"The youngest, I think. John, of Badenoch."

"The Red cub," his grandfather murmured. "In London?" His voice changed again. "What did you think of *him*?"

"What you said a moment ago, sir—there has never been love between our houses. I think that is not likely to change in my time."

"Hah! You disliked him?"

"From the moment I set eyes on him, sir." Rob hesitated. "No, that's not quite true. By the time I looked at him he was already looking at me, and the sneer on his face was what decided me."

"A sneer … "

"Aye, sir. As though he had detected a bad smell, and I was it … something stuck to the sole of his boot."

"God's blood, boy, you have captured the essence of the Comyn character: a twisted face and an insulting leer. It is the mark of their bloodline. I can see it as though I had been there. And how did you respond to him?"

"With dislike to match his. I ignored him, sir. But King Edward was displeased—more with me than with Comyn, I think. He ordered us to be friends while we were under his roof and made a point of announcing his wish for all to hear."

"And can you tell me why?"

Rob thought for a moment about the ominous command the King had uttered on that occasion, when his words said one thing but his demeanour dictated another. *Beneath my roof you* will *be friends.* He sucked in a deep breath. "No, Grandfather," he said. "But I can tell you what I heard."

His grandfather raised a questioning eyebrow, and Rob detailed the situation, and the words said, as precisely as he could recall them. When he had finished, Lord Robert sniffed and scratched at his beard, then drew his long-bladed dagger unconsciously and began to twirl it around in his fingers.

"I think you grasp the point he was making, even if you fail to see it clearly. Were your feelings hurt, that he should blame you more than Comyn?"

Rob dipped his chin. "Aye, a little."

"Then you missed it. There was a valuable lesson there, Robert. He was not berating you, other than for effect. He was demonstrating to his vassals how easily he could control the heirs to the two most powerful houses in Scotland, even there in England. He was manipulating you in order to manipulate them even more. In that moment, Grandson, you saw, but failed to recognize, the true face of England's King. An ill man to cross. Why are you frowning?"

Rob's voice was barely above a whisper. "Because I see the truth of what you said earlier … I have much to learn about reading men."

Lord Robert held his dagger out like an extended finger, then flipped it expertly and slid it back into its sheath beneath the folds of his shawl. "And so you have, but you may smile saying it, for at least you *know* it now, and that's a worthwhile start. From this time forward you will view men differently. You'll pay closer attention when they speak and you'll seek and gauge the meanings beyond the surface of their words. You'll draw information from the way they hold themselves, the way they shift their eyes, and you'll quickly learn to see beyond the moment to the real intent."

"You truly think so, Grandfather?"

His grandfather leaned forward with surprising speed and punched him lightly on the shoulder. "I know so, boy. You're bright and you learn quickly, and that's a blessing in itself. Trust your old grandfather, for I told you I do not deal in lies. I would not say these things if I didna believe them. You'll do fine. You're a Bruce, and one day soon you will enjoy all the power that goes with that name—lands, wealth, honour, and reputation. What the ancients called *dignitas*. In the meantime, though, I'm glad I sought you out tonight."

As Lord Robert spoke the words, the fire in the brazier collapsed upon itself with a soft, crunching roar, sending a whirl of bright sparks spiralling up into the chimney draft. Both Bruces, eldest and youngest, gazed into the embers silently, each with his own thoughts, and then the old man sighed and looked away.

"Two full fires since we sat down. God knows what time it is, and the toddy's long since cold. When will you be knighted, do you know?"

Rob shook his head, feeling perfectly at ease now. "No, sir, but probably two years from now. I'll be eighteen then."

"And have you been assigned as squire to a good knight?"

"Not yet, Grandfather. I have been squire to several, but to none of them for long. My father wished it thus. He would rather I learned widely, from many masters, until the last two years of my training, so I expect to be committed to a final teacher any day now."

"Is there anyone you would choose yourself?"

"In Scotland? No, sir. I will go wherever I am assigned."

"What did that mean, *in Scotland*? Do you know someone in England?"

"I do, sir." Briefly Rob told his grandfather about the English knight, Sir Marmaduke Tweng, who had impressed him so greatly and so quickly, and the old man listened gravely, nodding from time to time.

"I have heard much good of this man," he said when Rob fell silent. "He is regarded as something of a paragon."

"To be his squire would be a privilege. I wonder who will confer my knighthood when the time comes—now that we are again without a king, I mean."

His grandfather smiled. "We will not be kingless for long. I intend to press my claim. Had you forgotten?"

Rob's eyes grew wide. "Aye, sir, I had. Forgive me."

"For what? No one remembers everything at this time of night. But it's true, I could be King of Scots when your time comes, and if

I am, then I will knight you myself. Now, get you off to bed, for I think I might sleep myself for an hour or two."

Rob glanced at the narrow cot that lay against the rear wall. "Here, sir?"

"Aye, here. I often sleep down here. 'Twould scarce be politic to wake my lady wife at this hour, eh? And if you wish you may spend time with me tomorrow. I'll have much to do but you can come with me and watch and listen. Forbye, I want my men to have a look at you. Away you go now, and sleep well."

Rob woke up the next morning with his grandfather's invitation fresh in his mind and he leapt out of bed. He knew that the old man's invitation, absentminded though it had sounded at the time, was a test of some kind—of his willingness or commitment—and he was determined not to fail it by appearing to be indifferent or lazy. No time had been specified, but his grandfather's day began early, and Rob intended to be there before the old man could notice his absence. He ate a quick breakfast and made directly for the great tower of Lochmaben.

He listened avidly as his grandfather and his vassal knights made their plans for taking the road north towards Stirling and Scone the following day, and he was fascinated with the meticulous attention to detail that Lord Robert brought to everything. He marvelled, too, at the magnate's tireless repetition of what he deemed to be most important: the painstaking recitation to each successive newcomer of the importance of the logistical details needed for equipping, feeding, and maintaining a party large enough to be an army, for many days and nights over long distances. He listened admiringly as his grandfather catechized his leaders individually on the arrangements each had made, seldom raising his voice but harping insistently on the need to be aware of the most minute but necessary and well nigh unforeseeable details.

"Details, details, details," he told his men, time after time. "You have to feed your people every day. And feed them well, every man of them, and even the folk that feed *them*, and any women that might be with the cooks. You know from your own experience that you can leave nothing to chance. You have to equip yourself as completely as you can against sudden needs you might never foresee—extra weapons, saddles, supplies, and the equipment to repair broken equipment. You wouldna think of going on a campaign without an armourer in your company, would you? Well, we are going on a campaign, to claim a kingdom! But where's the good of having an armourer if he leaves half his tools behind him because he can't carry them? Your armourer will need a cart, equipped wi' everything he might need at any time. *Might* need, mind you, and hear me well on that, for God alone can foresee what might happen out there on the road."

Most important to Rob, though, was that his grandfather introduced him to each man of the group of knights known as the lairds of Annandale in the course of that long day, and though several of the grim-faced veterans eyed him askance, all of them acknowledged him and, grudgingly or otherwise, accepted his presence among them. For his part, Rob worked hard to memorize their names and traits from the moment of first meeting them, analyzing them by appearance and demeanour and fixing their names, faces, and voices firmly in his memory.

When the business of the seemingly interminable day was over and all the lairds had departed to their homes to organize the next day's expedition, Rob met again with his great-uncle Nicol MacDuncan to share his table at supper, the pair of them drawing odd looks from their seated neighbours as they spoke quietly together in rippling, lilting Gaelic. Nicol had all their own arrangements well in hand, he told Rob, and the remaining score of Carrick retainers were prepared to leave in the morning with the Lochmaben contingent—but he was itching with curiosity about what had happened that day between Rob and his grandfather. Nicol listened without interrupting as Rob told him everything in detail, watching his nephew enjoying his own recollections of what he had evidently decided had been the single most exciting and exhilarating day of his life.

"So," he said when Rob had finished, "it's clear your grandsire is a different man to you today than he was yesterday, and you—you're bubbling over with excitement like a pot on the boil. What changed your mind about him?"

"I don't know," Rob said quietly. "A new feeling of rightness, of belonging?" He shrugged. "That sounds silly, but I think it's true … I felt, today, like a real Bruce, one of the family, as though I belonged where I was, sitting by Lord Robert's side while he planned for our future. I didn't do anything other than sit there, but I felt welcome and I learned more about … about being a Bruce, I suppose, than I had ever thought to learn. And it felt natural. As though I was taking my rightful place."

His uncle said nothing, and after a moment Rob added, "My father has always treated me with kindness and my grandfather never has, in the past. And yet since last night all of that has changed, for now I see that my father has never *involved* me in anything—nothing of importance anyway—seeing me, I suppose, as yet a child. Lord Robert, on the other hand, has brought me into his life after a lifetime of silence and taught me more than I have ever known of who I am and where I belong. And all within a single day." He smiled, shaking his head again. "I find it hard now to believe I could ever have been afraid of him, Nicol, and I want to spend all my time with him from this point on. Impossible, I know, but that's what is now in my mind and in my heart. But am I being disloyal to my father, or to you?"

"No, to both. But your life and the disposal of it is still your father's to command, for years to come. And knowing how his life and his father's seldom cross paths, I can see he might not wish to see you spend too much of your time with the sire he himself knows none too well. He might resent that, might simply be reluctant to see you enjoy a knowledge and a privilege that he himself was never asked to share." Nicol shrugged. "I can't say anything on that matter, for God alone knows how this will all work out. But I'm glad, none the less, to see you over your fear of the old man. Enjoy it while you can, and to the full."

Rob grinned. "I intend to. Tomorrow will bring great adventures, I pray."

"Don't pray too hard, Nephew." Nicol's tone was matter-of-fact. "Adventures sometimes bring surprises, and too many of those can be of the unpleasant kind. I would suggest you remain content as you are, and simply accept what comes along. We'll be marching north in force, sometimes through lands whose folk care nothing for Bruce interests. Did you have any indication that your grandfather foresees armed hostilities?"

"He hopes not, but he's prepared to fight, if fight he must. It will depend, I suppose, on what he finds at Scone."

"Aye, that's what I'm afraid of." Nicol looked around and was unsurprised to discover that they were almost alone, most of the others having gone inside, leaving the clearing up to the kitchen helpers. He cleared his throat and pushed away the wooden platter that held the scraps of his meal. "Come on, let's leave these people to their work. It's dark outside already and I'm cold. Bed beckons, lad, and the dawn will come too soon. We'll need all the sleep we can get this night."

# CHAPTER EIGHT

# A RIDE TO PERTH

No one paid Rob the slightest attention as he emerged from the kitchens in the pre-dawn gloom of the following morning, hitching his travelling pack up higher on his shoulder and reaching down to adjust the sole weapon he carried, a dagger sheathed at his waist. The Lochmaben men were assembled in the main yard outside the tower as planned, and the noise was deafening: the snorting and whinnying of horses; the stamping and clatter of shod hooves on stony ground; the creaking and clinking of saddlery and harness competing with the sounds of steel armour and rattling weaponry, all mixed with the clamour of voices as men shouted loudly, trying to make themselves heard above the cacophony. The entire walled gate yard was brightly lit by the flames leaping from two massive iron cressets that dominated the yard, each containing its own bonfire.

Ahead of him, beyond the fires, the horsemen, some fifty of them, were drawn up in two distinct groups, facing the outer gates, their shadows dancing wildly in the firelight. Beside them stood the foot soldiers, far more of them than Rob had expected. Given what his grandfather had told Earl Robert, he had anticipated that there would be perhaps fifty to three score of infantry, rounding out the hundred-strong force from the fortress itself, but at first glance he saw that this muster was far bigger. The men were ranged in separated groups of twenty or so. Rob's first swift scan of them registered at least seven groups, amounting to no fewer than a hundred and fifty bodies, all of them heavily armed. And finally Rob saw his own small contingent of Turnberry retainers, with Nicol MacDuncan mounted at their head.

A gust of wind whirled over the walls, filling the yard with bluster and making the fires bellow even more loudly, and his eyes followed the explosions of sparks that flew upward against the grey, paling sky where the flush of the approaching day was a faint stain of pink on the horizon. And then the scene in front of him was transformed as every man there raised his arms and shouted in salute, calling the name of Bruce over and over.

Rob turned to look behind him, and his jaw dropped. The main doors of the tower had swung open at his back and two lines of identically uniformed guards were now marching shoulder to shoulder down the wide steps to the courtyard, carrying burning flambeaux mounted on long poles. The front pair stopped at the bottom step, and the entire column behind them split to line both sides of the steps, the swirling smoke from their torches creating the effect of a downward-sweeping ground fog. They were followed by two standard-bearers, each carrying a banner depicting the arms of the House of Bruce. The first, a blue lion rampant on a white field, was the ancient emblem of the Bruce family, brought north to Scotland a hundred years before in the service of David, Earl of Huntingdon, who became King David I. The other, magnificent in its richness, was the personal standard of Robert Bruce of Annandale: a blood-red saltire on a field of gold, with the blue Bruce lion embedded in the right corner of the red bar across the top. This pair stopped at the head of the stairs and then moved to each side, leaving sufficient space for the man at their back to pass between them and stand looking out over the cheering crowd that filled the great yard.

Rob had expected to see his grandfather as he had always seen him—gaunt, stooped, and grim-visaged, unkempt and soberly dressed in his muffling, workaday clothes of black and grey. What he saw instead left him awed. Lord Robert was fully armoured in magnificent black steel helm and corselet worn over a knee-length mail hauberk of the same colour. Heavy black boots covered his legs to the knee, and a black mantled cloak was turned back over his shoulders to expose the blood-red silk lining. In his steel-gauntleted right hand he held the sword he had shown Rob the night before, the sword of the Marshal of England. He raised it high, then brandished it in a salute to his men, and the volume of their cheering rose to new heights. The old man looked, Rob thought, like a warrior in his prime, no vestige of his seventy years visible in the spectacle he presented. The armoured figure brandishing his blade between the standards was not the aging Robert Bruce V, his grandsire. He was *the* Bruce, patriarch of his house and of all his folk and vassals. He had summoned them here to do his bidding and give him their support, and it was only proper that he should present himself thus to them, in recognition of the trust they placed in him and he in them.

Watching the man, and hearing the storm of enthusiasm at his back, Rob felt himself in the grip of a strange and novel sensation as his skin flushed and the short hairs all over his body stirred. A great lump swelled in his throat, and only as he fought it down did he recognize that what he was feeling was pride—pride in his stern old grandfather and in his own name, and in what that name signified within the realm of Scotland.

The cheering continued as Lord Robert sheathed his sword and moved swiftly down the steps to the mounting block, where a sturdy black horse awaited him, caparisoned in black and gold and held in check by two grooms. As he came he caught sight of his grandson and stopped, beckoning Rob to come forward.

"Get rid of that pack and mount up," he said. "Then come and ride by me."

There was no prouder young man in all Scotland than Rob Bruce when he passed through Lochmaben's gates a short time later, riding on the right of his noble kinsman in the new dawn's light.

The sun rose in a clear, blue October sky, glinting off the gear and weapons of the party that surrounded Rob and Lord Robert's command group as they left Lochmaben. They turned north at the bottom of the hill, following the wide, well-beaten track leading towards the fringes of the great forest that cloaked the southwestern body of Scotland north of Annandale. From that point on, as they passed through the hamlets and villages of their own lands, their numbers swelled constantly as other groups came from all directions to join them, and Rob came to think of their route through Annandale as a river with endless tributaries pouring new strength into its channel with every twist of the path.

Armies, in Rob's limited experience, were composed of disciplined military units. He thought of them in terms of blocks and phalanxes of armed men, usually dressed in uniform and marching in defined ranks—but he could see no semblance of organization in the swelling group around and behind him. This growing army moved freely, at its own pace and unconstrained by officers or sergeants of any kind. Each new party of newcomers tended to keep together, and the mounted men kept clear of the marchers for obvious reasons, and yet they made good time, moving quickly and efficiently as though by common consent, with only an occasional voice raised in command or reprimand.

His grandfather identified each group tersely for Rob's benefit as it arrived, a roll call of the vassal lairds of Annandale whom Rob had met the day before: Dinwiddies first, then Kirkpatricks, Johnstones, and Jardines, followed later by three separate groups of Herrieses and two of Armstrongs, late arrivals from the Jedburgh region, and finally a large contingent of Crosbies from the area surrounding Dumfries. Although his grandfather had estimated fifty men might come from each source, there were no fewer than seventy in the second group of Herrieses to arrive—and that was the smallest of all in number. The Crosbies of Dumfries alone had turned out a group of close to two and a half hundred.

They made camp that first night in a rocky meadow among the Lead Hills, on the bank of the wide, strong stream that would become the River Clyde within the next thirty miles, and Rob, duty free from the moment they dismounted, wandered through the encampment. He guessed that more than twelve and perhaps as many as fifteen hundred men had answered his grandfather's call to muster, and they seemed a mismatched crew at first glance. On closer inspection, though, he recognized how his grandfather's motley muster was comparable to the formal, English-defined norm of cavalry and infantry, rigidly segregated and organized in disciplined formations and cadres.

The Bruce force may have appeared to lack discipline. Yet both were readily discernible, evident in the extreme care the Annandale marchers all took to keep themselves spread far apart and cross through their own home lands without causing any depredations that could be avoided. They advanced on an extended front, close to a mile wide where the terrain would permit, because, as his grandfather explained to Rob, fifteen hundred men with horses and wagons moving in a compact body would destroy every field and every copse it crossed. These were the men of Annandale and this was their home, so they took great pains to leave few lasting signs of their passing.

By the time they were beyond Annandale and struck northwest towards Bothwell, their muster was complete, and any newcomers they saw kept well away from them, gathering on vantage points from which they could watch, and count, the passing Bruce forces.

From Bothwell, they left the widening valley of the Clyde and struck northeast again, towards Stirling and the River Forth that split the realm of Scotland into its two ancient divisions, northern Highlands and southern Lowlands. On that part of their journey they were contacted by couriers from the Earls of Lennox and Mar and Fife and from Sir James Stewart himself, the hereditary High Steward of the realm, all of whom promised Lord Robert armed support and offered encouragement and godspeed.

Rob's father caught up to them the day before they reached Stirling, adding a full seven score of newcomers from Carrick to their ranks. Rob was alone with Nicol when the earl arrived, and they were the first to welcome him back, and while his father made no reference to the changes in Rob's bearing and demeanour since their last parting, Rob felt sure that he was quietly pleased with his son's progress and he felt no need to prove anything further. His two immediate ancestors were serving their realm well, he believed, and he was determined to do no less when his turn arrived.

They arrived at Perth, less than ten miles from their final destination at Scone, and Lord Robert and some twenty of his most prominent followers rode into the town, leaving the main body of their following drawn up in the fields outside the town's walls, not wishing to alarm the inhabitants any more than they must. They were met in the marketplace by Robert Wishart, the Bishop of Glasgow, a dyed-in-the-wool Bruce supporter and a close friend and confidant of the Stewart, within whose holdings Glasgow lay. He was also a member of the council of Guardians, wherein his Bruce sympathies were well known. Even before Lord Robert and the Earl of Carrick had time to dismount, the bishop came striding to meet them, dressed in the full episcopal regalia of his guardianship. He nodded grimly to Lord Robert and the earl and curtly summoned them to confer with him. Without waiting for a reply, he stalked away towards the pavilion that had been erected for him in the middle of the marketplace.

Earl Robert swung a leg over the cantle of his saddle and slid to the ground, watching the bishop's retreating back. Beside him, his father dismounted with less agility, his face impassive as he handed his reins to one of his men. As Lord Robert stamped his feet, loosening his leg muscles, the earl turned to him, one eyebrow raised in a silent question. The patriarch shrugged slightly but said nothing as he turned to follow the bishop. The earl instructed Nicol to warn the others to stay in the square and form a cordon around the bishop's pavilion, far enough from the tent to keep prying ears at bay. As he turned back to make his own way towards the tent, the earl saw that his father was walking with one hand on young Robert's shoulder.

The earl entered the pavilion just in time to hear the bishop question the boy's presence.

"He's a Bruce," Lord Robert said. "He has to learn and earn his place and I intend to see to that myself. Thus he is here and will remain."

The bishop nodded solemnly, then waved young Rob to a chair. Rob returned the nod with equal solemnity and went to stand by his assigned seat. He and Wishart had met mere months earlier, in London, but there had been no question of status for Rob then. He had been a mere high-born boy, interviewed by a bishop who might one day have to deal with him as a man and wondered, in consequence, how much precocity the lad possessed. Today, with Rob's grandfather's brusque words, all of that had changed.

Dust-covered and sweat-stained from their long ride that day, the three Bruces seated themselves at the table, and several of Wishart's acolytes brought them food and drink. Lord Robert waved them away, but the earl raised a hand.

"Water," he said.

Lord Robert looked at him in mild surprise, but then nodded. "Aye, bring water. Cold."

Wishart, sitting opposite the old man, raised an eyebrow. "What, not a drop of wine, my lord?"

"Not until I find out why you have marched us in here without a word of welcome," Lord Robert said. "I doubt I'll like what you have to say, and if that's the case I would not wish to be beholden to you in advance for hospitality. So spit it out, Rab Wishart. What's afoot?"

Bishop Wishart looked at the waiting priests and nodded to the senior of them. "You heard Lord Robert, Father James. Set what you have on the end of the table and bring some fresh water from the well. Then leave us alone. I will summon you if I have need of you."

The priest ushered his assistants outside, and as soon as they were gone Wishart looked the Bruce patriarch straight in the eye.

"I'll tell you what's afoot," he said wryly. "*You* are, Robert Bruce. You are afoot, for the time being. But you rode in here at the head of an army and that places you squarely in revolt against the Guardians."

"Be damned to you, Wishart. What kind of sanctimonious claptrap is that? Are you accusing me of treasonous revolt? Against what King? I *am* the King of Scots, man—or I will be, soon, now that the

Maid is dead and the throne vacant again. How then can I be treasonous to myself?"

"I said no word of treason, Robert. I said revolt." The bishop's determination to be unequivocal was evident from the hard edge in his voice and the familiar use of the Bruce's first name. "When you come marching half the length of Scotland at the head of an army you put yourself in open, public defiance of the council and its concern for the welfare of this realm."

"Damnation, man, I have no wish to defy the council and you know that as well as I do. I have come here to attend the gathering at Scone, with the others, magnates and mormaers. And Guardians."

"Aye." The bishop's voice was suddenly wry again. "And you have come alone, you and yours, to mingle with your peers. Only a fool would think to question the well-known fact that you travel always with two thousand swords, requiring them to fan the midges off your brow when the sun sets."

Lord Robert ignored the sarcasm. "You exaggerate," he said bluntly. "I brought my swords to guard my back and protect my presence here because I had no wish to be waylaid and then dispossessed *in absentia* by a clutch of clawing Comyns. And don't try to wave away that statement, Robert Wishart, for you know it's the likeliest thing to happen, were I foolish enough to take the risk. This northland is Comyn territory, hoaching with them like fleas on a hedgehog, and none here would heed my voice at all were I not to raise it loud and long in my own cause. So don't talk to me about my shortcomings and my lack of respect unless you are prepared to condemn the Comyns equally."

"I am, Robert. We are … We, the council of Guardians."

The old man blinked. "You are? Prepared to condemn them?"

"Equally, as you said."

"Then what? I don't understand. Why are you accosting me?"

"*Equally* was the word I used, Robert."

"Aye, I heard you, but what does that mean?"

"It means that both of you—both factions, Bruce and Comyn— are equally guilty in this sorry affair."

"If I hear you aright I disagree. What is sorry about my being here?"

"Oh, for the love of God, man, have you no sense at all? Between your two houses you have the whole country on the brink of civil war! And we'll no' stand for that."

"Civil *war*? I am here to protect my valid cause, my claim."

"Aye, and there's the shame of it, for the Comyns are equally turned out to protect theirs, which they see as the cause of Balliol."

"Balliol's an Englishman! He has barely set foot in Scotland since he was a brat."

"I'll not argue that, but his mother, Devorguilla, was not, and since her death he has been Lord of Galloway and is now therefore richer, perhaps, than even you. And his claim to the Crown is every bit as valid as your own, despite his English upbringing."

"Horseshit! Mine is the stronger claim and has ever been so."

Wishart shook his head. "Only by the ancient Gaelic law of tanistry, Robert, which permits inheritance through the female side. Both you and Balliol lay claim through that, but your claim is stronger than his by one degree of cousinship. On the other hand, though, according to strict law of primogeniture, the right of the firstborn, Balliol's claim as senior heir in direct descent from Earl David supersedes yours." He held up a hand to forestall Bruce's response. "I know that primogeniture has no *de facto* place in Scotland's law, but it is none the less considered valid the length and breadth of Christendom with the backing of Holy Mother Church. And by that argument John Balliol's claim is arguably stronger than yours is."

Only the youngest of the three Bruces betrayed any reaction to that, turning his head to look uncertainly from one to the other of his elder relatives.

The bishop continued, calmly. "That is why we are so concerned. We fear injustice, to either one of you. Both of you, you *and* Balliol, have valid claims to the Crown, with strengths and weaknesses to each claim, and the matter cries out for judicious arbitration, for the continuing welfare and good conduct of the realm." He paused.

"I should not need to point out to you, of all men, Robert, that the needs of the realm take primacy over the mere welfare of any individual house."

Rob knew that Wishart had spoken the plain, objective truth as he perceived it. Unsettled, and reassessing this situation for the first time, he turned again to look at his grandfather, anticipating the old man's outrage, only to find himself confounded yet again by his mistaken expectations, for Lord Robert showed no trace of anger. He sat straight-backed and straight-faced, his eyes focused upon the embroidered cross on the prelate's green mitre. Beside Wishart, stretched out straight-legged in his narrow chair, the Earl of Carrick sat frowning, his hands clasped over the waist of his metal cuirass and his lips pressed into a thin line between his teeth. Rob held his breath, waiting for his grandfather to speak.

"Had any man but you said that to me, Rob Wishart, I would have taken it ill," the old man said eventually, his voice quiet and even gentle. "But since it was you and I know your loyalty, I'll take it as offered. You're right, and I admit it. But I doubt the Comyns might be so willing, and there's the meat of it." He sighed, loudly and deeply. "There are no Comyns here, though, so let me speak solely as Bruce.

"Arbitration, you said—this thing needs arbitration. But even though that be God's own truth, where, in the name of that same God, are we to find an arbitrator for this case?"

Wishart started to speak, but Lord Robert silenced him with an upraised palm. "Let me finish. Think about it, man. Who in all this land could arbitrate this dispute? It canna be the Guardians, for they are even-split, half for Bruce and half for Balliol, which in Scotland means Comyn. The council was set up that way, to keep a balance between our two houses, and in keeping with that, there is no presiding vote therein to break an even match. And even were the councillors themselves to elect another to their number, who would that other be? Any man you name would have a bias one way or the other, and you'd never get agreement from both sides. Surely you see the truth of that?"

Wishart pursed his lips, then bent his head slightly in acknowl-edgment. "It's true there may be no such man in Scotland," he said. "But that does not mean there is no such man at all. There is one man qualified to judge such a weighty matter."

Names tumbled through Rob's mind, but they were names of which he had only heard and he had little knowledge of the men themselves, and he admitted to himself that he had no idea who Wishart could be thinking of. And so, gritting his jaw, he waited for his grandfather's response, aware from the patriarch's frown that he was reviewing his own list of candidates. Eventually, though, Lord Robert sat straighter and eyed the bishop.

"One man, you say. And not in Scotland. Where, then? In England?"

"Aye."

"And fit to judge. Are you thinking of Edward?"

"The King himself, aye."

Lord Robert stood up abruptly and stalked away from the table to stand with his back to all of them. His right hand was clasped loosely in his left, at the small of his back, but his entire bearing radiated hostility, and the others knew better than to interrupt his thoughts. As they waited, the tent flaps opened and the acolytes came in with cups and a wooden pail of fresh water. No one spoke as the drinks were poured and distributed, and the silence lasted until they were alone again.

Earl Robert was the only one who was really thirsty, and as he drained his cup and set it down a heavy gust of wind buffeted the walls of the pavilion and rattled the venting flaps in the peaked roof. All of them glanced up in surprise, for the day had been calm to that point.

"Weather's changing," the old man said absently and then turned back to them. "It's true," he said to the bishop. "Edward could do this, render an even judgment where none else could." He returned to his seat at the table, still deep in thought, and sipped at the water that had been poured for him.

"He's done it before," he continued. "In Portugal, and then in brokering the peace between France and Aragon that ended the war in Sicily a few years ago—a brilliant feat of diplomacy, from what I've heard. But would he agree to do it again in this case? He has problems enough of his own to see to—in England with his barons and across the sea with his affairs in Gascony and his dealings with Philip of France. I doubt I would take the time, were I him … " He set down his cup. "How would we approach him, if the need arose?"

"The need is here already," Wishart growled. "My question is, would you trust him to adjudicate the matter, were he to profess himself willing?"

Lord Robert sniffed loudly, then pulled out a kerchief and wiped his nose. "For the good of the realm and to avoid a war? For those reasons I would set aside my reluctance, and aye, I would trust him. Providing, mind you, that the rules to guarantee fair-mindedness and a willingness to accept the settlement were clearly outlined and agreed upon in Scots law, and on all sides, beforehand. And that would lie within the jurisdiction of the Guardians' council. So aye, I would trust Edward of England's judgment. I have fought beside him when we were both younger and I respect him as a man. Besides, he is my liege lord under the ancient feudal laws of Christendom, since I owe him fealty for my lands and estates in England." He sat musing for a few moments. "But think you the Balliol people will agree? And if they do, how will your council proceed?"

"It is already done."

Rob watched as his grandfather stiffened and drew himself upright.

"*What* did you say?"

Wishart shrugged and spread his hands. "A letter has been sent to England, asking Edward to intercede."

The old man's eyes were wide with disbelief. "You sought the agreement of the Comyns ahead of mine?"

"We did not consult the Comyns. We but wrote to Edward, voicing our fears of civil war and asking him for assistance in maintaining the peace of the realm."

"Did you, by God? And who is this 'we'?"

The bishop's green chasuble shifted as Wishart shrugged his shoulders again. "The letter was drafted by Fraser of St. Andrews."

"Damnation, man, he is a Comyn. What kind of villainy is he plotting?"

"Shame on you, Robert Bruce." Wishart's tone was withering. "Above and beyond all else William Fraser is a bishop of Holy Church. He is also a former chancellor of Scotland. The man is a lifelong patriot, dedicated to the welfare and prosperity of this land and its folk—*all* of its folk. His reputation and his probity are beyond question, attested to by a lifetime of service and devotion to duty. That his name is Comyn has no relevance in this matter. He saw his duty to be as clear as it has always been: to protect the peace and stability of the realm. He drafted his letter to that end, with the ungrudging assistance of another Comyn, Lord John of Badenoch, a man whose rectitude matches Fraser's own. And neither of them thought to set the welfare of their house ahead of that of the realm. They drafted the letter as soon as word reached them of your preparations to march, for they perceived the predictable response of Balliol's supporters, most of them their own kin. They sent it first to me, for my input. I saw no need to improve upon what they had written and I endorsed the letter myself, for the good and the need of Scotland, Lord Bruce. That same need that led you to concede just now that you will abide by Edward Plantagenet's judgment in order to avoid civil war. The fact that most of those Balliol supporters are Comyns mattered nothing to either of the writers, for they believe that nothing—not family name or pride or reputation—supersedes the importance of their first priority, the realm and its folk."

The fire of Wishart's delivery left no one in any doubt of his belief in every word he spoke, and Rob could see that it had mollified the fierce old warrior to whom it had been addressed. Lord

Robert sat glowering, his jaw jutting pugnaciously, but he said nothing for a while, shifting his eyes from one spot to another without looking directly at anyone. Finally, though, he grunted and turned to his son.

"Robert, what think you of this?"

Earl Robert spread his hands. "I am here as a mere witness, Father. Your decision, whatever it may be, will affect my life henceforth, as it will Rob's, but yours is the claim and therefore this is your decision to make. I'll be content to stand at your shoulder and support you, whatever you conclude."

"Hmm ... " The fierce old eyes switched to Rob, who thought his grandfather was going to speak to him, but Lord Robert turned back to face Wishart.

"Fine," he growled. "I will retract that last remark about Fraser. It was unworthy. So the letter is sent. So be it. Where does that leave us now, the four of us here?"

The bishop cleared his throat. "Well, for one thing, it leaves me hoping that now you'll have a cup of wine with no ill will between us, for water does little to cut the fog in my gullet. For another, it leaves us to decide what's to be done to clear the air."

"Hmm ... Rob, pour us all some wine before the bishop dies of thirst."

Rob hurried to obey, serving each of the men and listening closely so as not to miss a word.

"Of what do we need to clear the air?" his grandfather asked.

Wishart blinked at him. "Why, this threat of civil war, of course ... the talk of it."

"Ah. And how will we do that?"

"By demonstration. Your departure with your men in train and no blood spilt will kill the talk."

There was a long pause, and then Bruce said, "Is that all you want? For me to turn tail and go home meekly, without a word to anyone, and leave the Comyns here to laugh at me and mine? Tell me, if you will, that that is not what you meant."

"It is precisely what I meant, though no one will laugh at you behind your back."

Bruce's deep-lined face was expressionless. "No, they might not. They'll be more like to wait until I emerge again from Lochmaben and then laugh in my face."

Wishart hissed, swiping the flat of one hand across the table, narrowly missing his cup. "In God's name, man, can you not see?"

"I can see them all laughing, aye. I swear, Rab Wishart, you men of God are never loath to make impossible demands on ordinary folk."

The bishop shook his head in frustration. "By doing this, as Bruce of Annandale, you will send a signal to the entire community of Scotland—the Guardians, clergy, earls, barons, and commons north and south of the Forth—to be mistaken by none. A clear signal that you are prepared to set aside your own legitimate rights in the interests of the realm until such time as that community itself can come to a just decision, in full parliamentary assembly and assisted by whatever powers of law, custom, and usage God will provide, upon the matter of whose claim is strongest. Surely you see the truth of that?"

"Aye, I can see it. But what if some folk disregard the signal? We need name no names, but what then, Master Bishop?"

Wishart slammed his hand against the tabletop. "Then they will be in rebellion no matter who they are and they'll face the wrath of the council and the assembled host of the realm of Scotland!"

"Aye, and so they should, of course," the patriarch said mildly. "But tell me, does that no' sound like civil war to you, Lord Wishart?"

The bishop glared at him, then nodded. "Aye, it does, Lord Bruce. But if that should come to pass—the which may God forbid—it will be for the good of the realm and at the behest of the council and community, not at the whim of some ambitious malcontent."

Lord Robert sucked at his teeth. "So be it, then. I'll do it. But I'll need to talk to my folk and tell them why we're turning back with nothing done after so long a march."

"No!" Rob flinched at the angry snap of Wishart's voice. "That's not true at all and you must not even think it. Much has been done, Robert, and that is how you should present it to your folk, for without a drop of blood being spilt or a blow struck, you have gained what you sought to achieve in coming here. Your cause is guaranteed an open judicial hearing by the community of the realm, arbitrated by a fair-minded judge of your own choosing, and you have set yourself above the ruck of your adversaries by keeping the peace and leaving them to do likewise. No failure there of any kind, old friend."

Lord Robert sighed. "Aye, well, mayhap. We'll see. I envy you your optimism, Robert. But it's done. We'll head back to Annandale come morning."

Wishart inclined his head soberly. "Thank you, my lord," he said. "Scotland is in your debt." His eyes moved to the two younger Bruces. "And you two should be proud of the restraint and good judgment your elder has shown."

The words, simple as they were, filled Rob's chest with a riot of unfamiliar sensations. He held his breath and looked across the table at his father, and watched as a small, rare smile transformed the earl's features. He was almost afraid to look at his grandfather, sitting beside him. He sat frozen, willing himself to master his pounding heart and his suddenly uneven breathing, but then he turned his head slowly, and found Bishop Wishart's eyes watching him closely.

He met the old bishop's look squarely, then turned to his grand-sire, whose fierce old eyes were filled with a look that Rob could not define. A great aching lump was in Rob's throat, and as tears spilled down his cheeks—tears he had not even known were there—he stood and pushed back his chair with his legs, then dropped to one knee and bent his head. How long he knelt there he could not have said, but he felt the outstretched hand settle upon his head as he tried to blink away his tears. Soon after, he stood up and stepped back, resisting the urge to wipe at his cheeks like a child, and found all three men gazing at him solemnly. No one spoke, but the old patriarch nodded to him kindly and with a wave of the fingers of his still-outstretched hand gave him permission to leave.

It was only as he walked away, straight-backed and with his head held high, that he understood why he had been weeping: he had been giving thanks for the miracle within himself that had transformed his grandfather, within the space of a single week, from the grim, threatening old troll Rob had always feared into the Noble Robert he knew he would always revere from that day forth. As he stretched out his hand to open the tent flap, he wondered if, should he ever become Robert Bruce the Elder, he would embody even a fraction of the nobility he had just witnessed.

"You didna like that, did you?"

His grandfather's voice came from close behind him, making him jump. He had not heard the old man approaching, for he had been lost in thought and watching the scene ahead of him, where the Annandale men yet sat their horses in a loose ring around the bishop's pavilion, facing outward towards the uneasy group of townsfolk watching from the edges of the market square.

"There was a lesson for you there, Robert. A lesson most men go to their grave wi'out ever having seen, let alone learnt. But I want you to learn it, here and now, for it could make a wise leader out o' ye, so heed me here. You don't aey need to spill blood to win a victory, nor swing a blade to win a dispute. There will be times ahead of you when all you'll need to do is make an appearance—a *strong* appearance, mind—prepared to fight gin the need arise. Just *bein'* there, ready to act, can sometimes win the day for you when the ruck o' folk would rather hang back and do nothin' than set their lives at risk. Some folk might call it recklessness, but it's far from being anything o' the kind, for it's never the choice that any wise man makes wi'out long, hard thought and consideration o' the consequences. That kind of effrontery—resolve, we'll call it—will aey set the strong leader apart frae the switherers, for it's the very soul o' leadership, and other men will follow you gin you show it. They'll take heart from your example and they'll rise to it."

Rob frowned. "That's all? The lesson? The mere need to *be* there?"

Lord Robert reached out and grasped his grandson's shoulder. "Aye, lad, that's all. The simple need to *be* there, from time to time. But it's never easy. And believe me, I've had plenty o' years to come to know the truth o' that. It goes against the grain o' human nature for a man to put himself deliberately in danger's way. The greater the harm he faces, the bigger the risk he takes and the more he stands to gain by it. But most would call him a mad fool. Others—a very *few* others—would see him as a God-inspired leader."

He loosened his grip and formed his hand into a fist, then punched the younger man's breast gently. "I think you might make such a leader, one o' these days. Wi' the help o' God, of course." He smiled. "It'll no' be soon, mind, for I've no plans to die afore my time, but I'm encouraged to think the day will come when you'll remember *this* day and make your own choice to *be* somewhere, to make a stand, for Bruce and for Scotland … Now, come back to the tent wi' me, for I have things I'll need you to do for me."

# CHAPTER NINE

# FAMILY TIES

"Master Bruce. Your turn, if it please you."

The words were expected, but Rob felt his chest tighten none the less. His friend John Bigod had just picked up his fallen sword and walked out of the whitewashed circle in the centre of the training ground, holding the weapon awkwardly in his left hand while he clamped his sore right hand, still in its mailed gauntlet, beneath his armpit and fought to keep his face free of any sign of the pain he was feeling. Sir Marmaduke Tweng, now alone at the centre of the circle, was waiting for Rob, waving his long sword gently, point down, from side to side in front of him.

Rob stepped into the circle, hoisting his blade as he went, and for a moment stood in a slight crouch, acutely aware of the weight and heat of the plate armour he was wearing over his mailed hauberk and of the padded stiffness of his heavily armoured gloves as he flexed his fingers on the sword's hilt. It was approaching noon on a hot day in late September, and he could feel sweat running down the channel between his shoulder blades to pool in the hollow at the small of his back before trickling itchily to the crack of his buttocks. His hair was soaked under the mailed cowl of his coif, and he knew that if a single bead of sweat ran down his temple to penetrate the corner of an eye it would sting unbearably and he would not be able to wipe it away … Not with a steel-backed gauntlet.

Sir Marmaduke, on the other hand, looked cool and fresh, notwithstanding that he had dispatched seven consecutive opponents within the past half-hour, all of them less than half his age. The only sign of his efforts was the slightest sheen of perspiration on his forehead, and even that seemed to dry up as Rob approached. The knight brought his weapon up to touch his chin with the cross-guard in a salute, then swept it down and out before bringing it back into the guard position.

Rob sucked in a deep breath and repeated the gesture, then fell into his fighting stance. Tweng had had them drilling in the blazing sun since daybreak, mercilessly running them through their paces with quarterstaff and heavy weights until their muscles were numb and their reflexes hammered into nothingness. This final test, blade to blade and without shields, had become a ritual, the last ordeal of each day, a ceremony religiously pursued at the close of every training session in order to remind the trainees that, though they were within days of achieving knighthood, none of them had yet managed to best their mentor and taskmaster.

There were eight trainees, all senior squires, and the swords they used were blunted, their edges filed flat and their central spines augmented with narrow strips of lead solder to increase their weight, making each one half again as heavy as a normal sword blade. But the solid weight of them on impact was barely less lethal than a keen-edged blow would have been, and John Bigod, nursing his bruised hand, was the last of seven who had been newly reminded of that. This was the final half day of formal training for the youths, and the knight seemed determined to sweat the last ounce of fight out of them before he released them for the last time at noon. By tradition, the night ahead would be theirs as soon as they were dismissed, an entire night in which to celebrate together in the knowledge that their training was complete and there would be no pre-dawn run and no soul-numbing drill the next day. Instead, the following afternoon, they would be ceremonially bathed and shriven in preparation for the solemn rites of the eve of their knighting. At sunset they would be escorted into the castle chapel to stand vigil, spending the entire night in prayer, in full armour, under the watchful eyes of priests. The next morning, ritually purified, they would be knighted by the King himself, their manhood and nobility formally acknowledged in the eyes of all the world.

Sir Marmaduke tilted his head slightly to one side, questioningly, and Rob gripped his sword more firmly and moved to the attack. He saw his opponent back away respectfully, his eyes watchful and his movements slightly tentative, but he knew from experience that the move was designed to tempt him to strike out. It had been successful in the past, but this time he ignored the invitation and concentrated on how he could change his established pattern of engagement. Tweng had taught them well, and Rob, at least, had finally learned that fighting patterns were predictable to a self-possessed antagonist, especially after months and years of familiarity with the fighters. And predictability, when the matter at hand was combat with swords, was invariably lethal.

Today, this last bout, Rob was determined not to be beaten as easily as he usually was—as all of them always were—and a thought flicked into his mind. He sprang forward, eyes and point centred upon his opponent's breast in a full frontal lunge, but before he committed himself fully he went down on one knee, almost as though his foot had slipped, opening himself up to a punitive rap from Tweng's ever-ready blade. As his knee touched ground, however, and the knight's sword came slicing towards him exactly as predicted, Rob thrust his blade upward, straight-armed, to catch the descending edge on the braced bar of his own. In the brief moment of Sir Marmaduke's surprise, Rob twisted with his entire upper body to sweep the knight's sword to the side with all his strength, then, with a two-fisted grip, whipped the blade down to land solidly on the outside of Tweng's knee. The knight stumbled sideways and back, off balance but already swinging his blade back awkwardly to defend his centre. He was too late, though, for Rob had immediately launched himself into a lunging, two-handed thrust, driving himself forward and up from his kneeling position with churning legs, his sword striking like a lance solidly against the very centre of the knight's armoured breast, with all of Rob's uncoiling strength and weight behind it. He heard the roar of approval from his fellows as Sir Marmaduke Tweng crashed full-length on the flat of his back. He was suddenly appalled at what he had done and stricken with fear by the stunned silence that followed.

In the distance, a bullock bellowed in outrage, but no one moved. Rob swallowed hard, feeling himself begin to shake, then bit down on his own teeth and thrust the blunted point of his sword into the ground, leaning on it to force it home. He stepped forward and stood looking down at Sir Marmaduke, one nerveless hand extended in a timid offer of assistance. The knight lay still, looking up at him with wide-open eyes. Then he blinked and moved his head to one side, to where the others of Rob's group stood staring in awe.

"I have never seen any of you from this viewpoint before," he said evenly, "but I must admit it is no more flattering than my normal view of you." Still no one moved and no one dared to smile. Tweng did, however, his strong white teeth showing suddenly in a bright grin. "That, gentlemen," he said, looking up at the seven gaping observers and then back at Rob, "is what these past months have been all about. That was the triumph of a fighting man. A stratagem that came from inside, unsought—and unplanned, I believe—and perfectly executed. Help me up." He gripped Rob's proffered hand and heaved himself to his feet. "Well done, Robert Bruce," he said, his smile still in place. "We'll make a fighting knight of you after this." He hesitated. "It *was* unplanned, was it not?"

"Aye, sir, it was. It came into my mind as we saluted."

"And what prompted it, do you know?"

"Aye, sir, I do … I was thinking about how to be unpredictable for once, and then it came to me that even you can be predictable. I didn't stop to think about it but I knew at once what you would do if I left myself open, even slightly."

Tweng was nodding judiciously. "Excellent. Truly excellent. Of course, the boy I first crossed swords with a few years ago could not have done it, nor even thought of it. But that boy has changed greatly in those years—as have all of you. Bigger by far, stronger by far, and sometimes, unfortunately, denser by far. Well done, Bruce. By knocking me down you have brought your training to a fitting end.

I wish you all well in future, gentlemen, and I know you will be worthy knights in the King's service. Go, then, and enjoy yourselves with my full blessing. Oh, wait." He reached into the pouch at his waist and pulled out a small leather purse, which he tossed to Rob. "In case you should have need of coin tonight, this should purchase a decent meal for all of you. Now be off."

He turned to walk away but stopped, his eyes on a figure running towards them. "Hold again," he added. "It looks as though someone here might be in demand."

The runner reached them, breathing heavily, and made a sketchy bow. "Your pardon, Sir Marmaduke," he gasped. "Is Master Robert Bruce among your number?"

"I'm Robert Bruce," Rob said.

The fellow was still labouring for breath. "You are summoned, Master Bruce. You must come with me at once. To meet the King. As you are."

Rob glanced at Tweng, wide-eyed with surprise, and the knight bowed his head.

"At once is the word. But I would counsel you to walk, not run. A knight must show dignity at all times, and it will not aid your case—whatever that might be—to walk into the royal presence panting like a dog and pouring with sweat. Go, then, and fare ye well, Robert Bruce."

Rob bent his head in acknowledgment and spoke to the messenger. "Lead on, then, but bear in mind what Sir Marmaduke has said. We will walk befittingly." He tossed the leather purse to John Bigod. "I've no idea what's afoot, so don't wait for me. But if you find any wenches worth spending time with, save one of them for me. I'll join you as soon as I may." He flipped a hand in farewell and turned away to follow the messenger.

He thought of the last time King Edward had sent for him unexpectedly, more than two years before, and he recalled quite clearly how apprehensive he had been about entering the royal presence then, not knowing what to expect and then finding the King surrounded by dukes, bishops, and barons, all of them looking at

Rob as if he were a beggar who had intruded upon them. Today he was even more ill at ease, because the Edward Plantagenet who summoned him now was a very different man. The King had lost his Queen to a sudden illness in November that same year of 1290 and had vanished from public view for months, shutting himself up with his grief for an entire winter, during which the governance of the realm of England was effectively suspended. When he re-emerged to take up his reign again, people immediately began to note the changes in him.

Eleanor of Castile had been Edward's wife for thirty-six years, and not only had they loved each other deeply and faithfully throughout that time but the Queen's advice and tolerant guidance had become indispensable to Edward, who trusted her above all others in matters relating to his own weaknesses. It had been she who advised him best in matters of policy wherein his own impetuosity and impatience might often have led him astray, and it was well known within his small circle of intimates that Queen Eleanor had, in many instances, been the actual source of Edward's more important regal decisions. The tragic loss of her had radically changed the man she had loved. Gone forever, it seemed, was the whimsical, frequently irrational, and self-deprecating sense of humour that had set Edward apart from other powerful men. Nowadays he was all careworn monarch, beset by swarming, never-ending duties, and it was said that he had not laughed aloud since.

Rob had greatly liked Queen Eleanor, and she had returned his fondness, often going out of her way to make him feel welcome at her court, for despite his family's great English landholdings, others still perceived him as something of an alien, a Scot among Englishmen. She it was who had encouraged him to take advantage of his differentness rather than try to conceal it; she had encouraged him to be more flamboyant in dress and manners than his peers, accentuating his status as a visiting guest from beyond the borders of the realm. Rob missed her greatly.

They were all far from Westminster on this occasion, in the formidable stone castle of Norham that belonged to the King's friend and sometime deputy for Scotland Antony Bek, Prince-Bishop of Durham. The castle, two hundred years old but recently rebuilt, lay at the northernmost reach of England, directly facing the Scots border, and for the past two years it had been the setting for King Edward's court of inquiry to decide which one among an entire cadre of claimants—fourteen of them in all and including Rob's own grandfather—held the strongest claim to the vacant Scots throne. That number of competitors had long since failed to impress Rob, for he knew, as did everyone, that there were only two serious contenders, his own grandfather and Lord John Balliol of Galloway, both of whom were southern Scots. Edward of England, though, as arbitrator in the affair, had been, as always, at great pains to be perceived as even-handed and judicious, and a gathering of 105 auditors, including the King himself as moderator and presiding judge, had been assembled at Norham. The court was modelled on the *centumviri* of the ancient Roman republic, the court of 105 formed to settle property disputes.

The entire affair had become known throughout Scotland as the Great Cause, though none could say who had coined the name. In the early days there had been much argument in Scotland about the wisdom of agreeing to convene what was in essence a meeting of the Scots parliament on English ground. In consequence, great care had been taken to assure the four estates of the Scots community—the earls, clergy, barons, and commons—that neither the Scots participants nor the realm of Scotland itself would be placed in any kind of legal jeopardy. It appeared deliberate, though, that the court of auditors should consist of eighty Scots lords and bishops—forty supporters from the ranks of each of the two principal claimants, Bruce and Balliol—with the remaining twenty-four being English, and thereby presumed neutral. Over the preceding year, amid exhaustive and exhausting legal wrangling, the lesser claims had been adjudicated and set aside, leaving only the matter of the Bruce/Balliol contention to be settled.

As he crossed the main courtyard of the castle towards the massive square central tower, Rob wondered whether that final decision might have to do with his being brought before the King. He dismissed the thought immediately. Whatever Edward required of him, it would have nothing to do with the case before the court of auditors, which was still in session, he judged, given the deserted courtyard. And that thought prompted another: the King himself should have been in the auditors' chamber. That he was not, that he had apparently left the court and sent for Rob, was ominous.

Rob slowed his pace in the last few steps towards the main doors of the tower, but the messenger ahead of him looked back and waved to him to hurry. Rob caught up to him by the time they reached the doors, which a pair of guards held open for them. The messenger led Rob quickly across the empty entrance hall and ushered him into a tiny cubicle, where an elderly man in long, dark robes had clearly been waiting for him.

The man stood up immediately, dismissing the messenger with a wave of his hand. "His Majesty awaits you," he said. "Come with me."

The man led him up a long, sweeping flight of stairs and along a short passageway lined with several identical doors. These were not, Rob knew, the official audience rooms. The man knocked on one of the doors and waited until a voice from inside bade him enter. He opened the door and leaned inside, announcing Rob's name before he stepped aside and allowed Rob to enter. The man pulled the door closed behind him.

The room was small and dimly lit by two windows that flanked a large stone fireplace directly across from him, but Rob saw that it was walled on three sides with oiled and polished oak that had been cunningly carved to resemble draped linen panels, and it contained few furnishings. The fireplace, empty and cold, was fronted by a wide, heavy table at which the King of England sat alone, staring at a parchment laid out in front of him and anchored at the corners by small stones. He looked up as Rob entered, then eyed him grimly as the young man bowed formally.

"Training," he said tonelessly. "It's a hot day to be wearing armour."

"Yes, my lord."

"Aye. For all that, I'd rather be out there myself, working up a sweat, than be stuck in the smelly courtrooms I live in nowadays." There was still no inflection to his voice, and Rob was shocked by the tired, deep-graven lines that now etched the face he knew so well. "You look well, young Bruce. Sir Marmaduke has not been neglecting you, has he?" The question was rhetorical, for Edward continued without waiting for an answer. "This was your last day of training, no?"

Rob nodded. "Yes, my lord. Your messenger arrived just as we were finishing."

"I gauged as much, though the timing was accidental. I sent for you as soon as I received word." The monarch waved towards one of the two chairs that faced him across the table. "Sit down. Pull that chair closer."

Rob's confusion grew stronger. With the sole exception of his very first encounter with the English King, eight years earlier in his father's earldom of Carrick, he had never seen Edward Plantagenet unaccompanied. There was always someone with him, even if it was only a cleric or two, no matter how informal the occasion. Alarmed, he lowered himself into the chair and waited.

Edward was nibbling at his upper lip, glowering, but then he placed both hands palm down on the parchment in front of him. "I will not be knighting you with the others."

It flashed into Rob's mind that the monarch had been called away, perhaps back to London. But then the full meaning of what he had said crushed Rob like a falling tree. He sat gaping, searching frantically within himself for anything, any fault or sin of dereliction or omission that could have brought about such a disastrous condemnation.

Edward, seeing the alarm in the young man's face, realized belatedly what he must be thinking and snapped up an open hand. "No! I did not mean I have decided *not* to knight you. Do not think such a thing. You have done nothing wrong and you are not being punished." He leaned back into his chair. "It is simply that it cannot be. You will not be here for the ceremony. That is all I meant to say and I could have said it better. Forgive me for alarming you thoughtlessly."

"But … But I *am* here, my lord King."

"Aye, but you will not be tomorrow. You must leave today." He braced his straight arms on the edge of the table, then laid his hands again upon the parchment there. "I received this today, Robert, and would give much not to have done so. It is from your father." He looked Rob square in the eye. "He informs me that your lady mother is gravely ill, her very life in peril. Some sudden affliction like the one that took my Queen. And of course he sought your release from duties immediately, so that you may go to be with her."

A hollowness grew inside Rob's head—*gravely ill, her very life in peril*—and the King's voice seemed to echo strangely within it, the words he now spoke empty of meaning. He saw his mother's face clear in his mind and heard her throaty, swelling laughter as she played exuberantly with his youngest sisters, radiating health and vitality to all the world. Marjorie of Carrick could not be *sick*! The very thought of it was ludicrous. She was his mother, her entire life dedicated to and thriving upon the welfare of her turbulent brood. He began to hear a roaring in his head and realized that he had stopped breathing, and as he released his pent-up breath he heard the King still speaking to him.

" … arranged. You'll find them waiting for you at the stables when you are ready to leave. I sent people to your quarters to pack up your belongings, so all you need do is take care of any last-moment matters that occur to you. A dozen men are set aside to ride with you, with food and spare horses for all. If you leave immediately, riding hard and bypassing Berwick, you should reach Dumfries by nightfall or soon after. From there, depending on how hard you drive your men and horses, you should be home sometime tomorrow night. Now go with God, Robert, and deliver my condolences to your father. I will pray you arrive in time to take your leave of your mother."

Barely aware of what he was doing, Rob stood up and went through the motions of thanking the King for his concern and kindness, then bowed, turned, and walked away, vaguely aware that he was walking stiff-legged and jarringly and that his most immediate concern was to remain upright and keep moving without falling down. The noises in his head were strange and alien, metallic reverberations and echoing fragments of words, and his senses threatened to desert him, but he closed the door behind him and leaned against it for a few moments, fighting to control his breathing.

In the times that lay ahead Rob would find it alarming, when he thought of it, that he had no recollection of the journey from Norham to Turnberry. He knew it had been a hard, unrelenting ride with little pause for sleep or even rest. He had no detailed memory of any part of the passage across the rugged, trackless Lowland hills and no remembrance at all of passing the border town of Berwick, where they had crossed the Tweed River that first day, before swinging west.

He remembered nothing, in fact, of what had passed between the moment when he heard the terrifying tidings from King Edward and the other, agonizing moment in the middle of the next night when the door of his parents' darkened bedchamber swung open to reveal his mother lying pale in her massive bed, the startling planes and hollows of her ravaged face and sunken cheeks rendering her unrecognizable at first look. The bed was flanked by racks of flickering candles that revealed the presence of his father and his grandfather, both of whom stood gazing down in silence at the woman who lay between them.

It was Lord Robert who turned towards the sound of the opening door and saw his grandson standing there, his eyes wide with terror. He swung away from the sickbed and strode to meet his grandson, reaching out to turn Rob around. He ushered him back out into the dimly lit hallway and pulled the door shut behind them.

"We didn't know when to expect you."

Rob turned to face the closed door at his back. "Is she—?"

"Aye, she is alive, praise God. And sleeping soundly. When did you leave Norham?"

Rob shook his head impatiently. "Yesterday, around noon. What's wrong with her?"

The old man harrumphed. "You made good time, then. Have you slept at all?"

Another headshake. "A little. There was no time. What happened to my mother?"

"Childbed sickness," he growled. "Nothing anyone could do. The child was born dead, six days ago, and the midwives could not stop the bleeding. And then your mother caught a fever. She is gravely weakened. Close to death, I fear, though none will come right out and say so. But the cleric physician, Ethelric, believes she may survive. It is in God's hands, but she has received the best of care and she appears to be regaining a little of her strength. She supped a bowl of broth this evening, for the first time since she fell sick, and now she is sleeping more easily than she has in days. And sleep, Ethelric says, is God's own balm and cure."

Rob tried to remember a time when his mother had not been with child. She had been surrounded constantly by a sprawling, growing, clamorous brood, her belly distended constantly either with the aftermath of one pregnancy or the burgeoning of her next, and none of that had hampered her for a single moment in her running of the massive household that was her ancestral home. He remembered the last time he had seen her, eight months earlier, before he had left to join King Edward at Norham. Then her face had been lovely still, full-cheeked and glowing with health, with no trace of the wrinkles any of the other women showed. He had smiled back into her loving eyes, enjoying her wide, generous smile as she kissed him by the gates and tied a leather purse of sweetmeats of honeyed almond paste—his favourite delight—to the belt at his waist. Her hair, too, had been lustrous and rich then, deep auburn and burnished with streaks of reddish gold, a far cry from the dank and colourless tangle of ropes that now lay twisted on her pillow.

"What was the child?" hc asked, plainly not caring.

"It was a boy. They would have called it Angus."

"It killed my mother."

"Now, now, boy. That's not so. Your mother is not dead, and besides, the childbed sickness has nothing to do with the child being birthed. The sickness comes on afterwards, the result of evil humours."

"I want to speak with her, Grandfather."

"Aye, I know you do, but now is not the time, hard as that may seem for you. This is the first restful sleep she's had these past seven days. It would be shameful to wake her from it merely because you lack the patience to wait until tomorrow, and you'll see that if you but think on it. She knows you're coming and has been waiting for you, as eager to set eyes on you as you are to see her, but if she sleeps though the night she'll waken tomorrow refreshed and stronger … I can tell from just looking at you that you're almost as tired as she is, so go you now and sleep and you'll scc her when you awaken."

"What's wrong with my father? He did not even look at me when I came in."

The old man sighed, his face creased with concern. "Your father is mourning for his love. Not for the loss of her life, mind you … rather for the loss of her youth and his own. He feels that he has betrayed her somehow and he is impotent to change anything. He would gladly leap to bear her sickness and her woes if he could. But he did not ignore you wilfully. Not in the way you thought. You have your life ahead of you and he knows that. All his attention, all his care tonight, is for his wife and for her life, which he is in terror of seeing disappear …

"Go now, and get some sleep. That is a command, Robert. I promise you, if anything goes amiss in the night—the which may God forbid—I'll send for you immediately. Go now, and pray to God for the strength to face your mother cheerfully come morning, for she'll need to see you smiling for her."

"Robbie, you're here."

Her whisper was barely audible, and he felt his throat constrict at the dry weakness of it as he stooped to take her hand and kiss her forehead, struggling to hold a smile that felt more like a rictus. His grandfather had told him, just before they entered the sickroom, that she had slept well and was stronger than she had been for days, and Allie had washed her face and combed out her hair before binding it with a silken ribbon that brought out the blue highlights of her startling blue-green eyes. But the brightness of the ribbon also emphasized the pallor of her skin and the high, hectic flush on her cheekbones above the hollows of her face.

Her grip on his fingers was strong, though, and there was no mistaking the joy the sight of him gave her. He blinked rapidly, willing himself to show no sign of grief or anguish, and knelt as close to her as he could come, bending forward to inhale the remembered scent of her and feeling it soothe him as it always had.

"I'm sorry I took so long, Mam. I came as soon as I heard."

"I know you did … All the way from England, at the gallop. You've grown up, Robbie … When you went away you were a boy, a fine lad and my pride and joy, but just a boy, and here you've come back in just months, a man grown. Stand up and let me look at you."

He rose and stepped back, watching her closely as her eyes swept over him. He had changed greatly in the previous eight months, he knew, but his gains in weight and bulk during that time were merely the end result of the process that had started two years earlier, when first he started living in England at the King's court, committed to the unrelenting discipline of training daily, brutally and diligently, for his eventual knighthood. Since then he had come home to Turnberry only three times, seeing the changes in his growing brothers each time but unaware of the changes in himself. And at that thought, he realized for the first time since leaving Norham that his friends in England had become men in fact since he left, formally dubbed and raised by King Edward to the exalted state of manhood as warriors within the order of knighthood.

"You're so *big*," she whispered. "Look at you, the size of you! You're bigger than your da."

He found it easy to smile at her now. "But not as big as my gransser," he said quietly, using the name he had given the old man before he learned to pronounce *grandsire* properly. Her eyes flicked immediately to where Lord Robert stood listening, his craggy old face for once lit by a smile of pure fondness for his good-daughter.

The countess smiled again. "No," she whispered. "Not yet, that's true. But you will be, someday soon. You've the same shoulders and you're still growing. You'll be a Robert Bruce to make him proud. You wait and see."

"He makes me proud already, my dear," the old man said. "But I believe you're right."

The countess nodded. "I'm glad you two are close now" was all she said, and then looked back at her son. "Have you seen your brothers? Allie told me you came home late last night. Were they here?"

Rob's smile widened into a grin. "Aye, Mam, but they were all abed by then."

"And you woke them up when you went upstairs, I expect."

He ducked his head to one side. "I did, but they werena sleeping very soundly. We talked for a while and then I ordered them back to bed."

"And what did you talk about?" She wiggled her fingers. "Come back to me."

He moved quickly to kneel beside her again and reached for her outstretched hand, feeling her grasp his fingers again far more strongly than he would have expected earlier. "About living in England and training for knighthood," he answered. "Are you surprised?" She had no need to know that he had talked with his brothers for hours about her condition and their fears for her—and for themselves, should she not recover.

His mother was watching him closely and he made himself smile again. "Edward can't wait for his turn to be a squire to someone, and he prays every night that he will find a master who loves horses as he does. And Thomas and Alec are in despair because they still have to wait years before they can even start."

His mother's chin dipped as she nodded gently, squeezing his fingers more tightly. "Aye," she said in that voice that sounded like a zephyr stirring dried leaves. "But the years fly by faster and faster as we grow older … And what seemed like a lifetime ago is no more than a flitting moment, seen from afar. Their time will come soon enough. Sooner than they would wish were they older and wiser. But for now they are just wee boys, aching to be men. So leave them to fret, Robbie. Remember yourself, how young you were when you were their age, and let them be. Let them learn at God's own pace. Now, when will you be knighted?"

His face must have fallen, for he saw the alarm in her eyes, and he quickly shrugged, discovering, to his own great surprise, that he really did not care about the temporary loss of his knighthood compared to the gift of being able to see her again.

"I missed it, Mam," he said. "This time at least. I was on my way here when the ceremony happened. It was today, this morning." He hurried on as he saw her eyes widen in horror. "Mam, don't fret. It doesna worry me, and that's God's truth. The King himself told me I have earned my knighthood and that he will gladly confer it upon me at the first opportunity that comes. For now I am a knight in all but name."

"I know you are, my son … You always have been, in my eyes, but it's a shame you had to miss the ceremony with all your friends."

He stooped and kissed her again on the forehead. "No, it's not, Mam. I'll see them all again soon enough and I'd rather be here with you right now."

She smiled. "I don't think you even expect me to believe that, Rob Bruce, but I thank you for that lovely thought. I'll—" She jerked violently, and suddenly her fingers were digging sharply into his hand and her eyes were wide with fright.

"Mam?" He could hear the panic in the single word. "Mam, what's wrong?" The pressure of her grasp increased and her mouth twisted into a rictus. Already his grandfather was at the door, calling loudly for Brother Ethelric, and he bent forward, scooting as close to her as he could on his knees, wrapped his arm around her shoulders and pulled her into his embrace. She was feather-light, it seemed to him, and he could feel the fierce heat of her skin through the thin stuff of her nightgown. He clutched her close, willing her to be free of this sudden agony, as the door swung open hard and the monk Ethelric swept into the room.

"Out!" the monk said to him, and there was no mistaking the urgency of his voice. "Up and out! In God's name, make way."

Rob remembered the rain that blew into his face that second morning of October in the year 1292. It chilled him to the bone befittingly as he stood among his family while they buried the Countess of Carrick. He remembered, too, that his father's eyes were swollen from weeping, and that the rain streaming down Earl Robert's face seemed like an extension of the man's grief. He also remembered the ghostly wailing of the bagpipes before and after the service, the music offered as tribute to the Countess Marjorie of Carrick by a tall, cadaverous Gael whose long plaid fluttered from his shoulders like a flag in the wind. He was from Arran, Rob was told long afterwards, related to the countess on her father's side. He had been in Maybole town when he heard of her sudden death and had come to pay his respects. He remembered, too, being surprised at the number of people, many of them strangers to him, who assembled at the graveside, more than a hundred of them, old and young, gathered from farmsteads and villages both local and distant, though no formal word had gone out and his mother had been dead for less than three days.

But he remembered little else—nothing of the service itself, not the words that were spoken or the priest who spoke them—and in truth only the storm that morning stayed firm in his mind, a feral thing slashing in from the icy western sea to howl around the forlorn, open grave on the shelf above the tiny beach in front of the castle. His mother had loved that spot all her life, for the view it offered in all weathers and most particularly when the great winter storms sent mighty waves hurtling on the rocks along the shore, often crashing up towards her in their final throes as though attempting to reach her. Knowing of her love for the place—for they had all shared it with her on countless occasions—it seemed fitting to everyone that it should be her resting place forever.

He stood alone, after the others had returned to the castle, watching Murdo's men filling in the grave, their hair and clothing buffeted by the blustering, icy wind as they bent and straightened relentlessly, replacing the dirt they had shovelled out the day before. He remembered the wind, buffeting him and snatching at his breath, but he had no recollection of feeling cold, for nothing could penetrate the vast emptiness that filled him. He remembered thinking that he was barely eighteen and was motherless, and that nothing the future held could possibly outdo the awful, crippling bereavement of that day. He remembered watching the men pile the cairn of stones over his mother's grave and waiting to place the last of them himself.

He remembered arriving back at the castle hours after that and finding Lord Robert in the entrance hall, muffled in his great black hooded cloak of thickly waxed wool.

"Robert! There you are. I wondered where you'd got to."

"I've been at the graveside. But where are you going?"

"Home, lad, to Lochmaben, as quick as may be. I mislike being away from Annandale and I've been gone too long. I was hoping I'd see you before I left."

"But surely you'll eat first? It's bitter cold out there and no time to be on the road with an empty stomach."

Lord Robert shook his head. "I've food enough. Allie knew I'd be away right after the funeral and she had food and drink ready packed for me and all my folk. We'll eat on the road. Alan should be here directly wi' my horse. But I need to speak wi' you." He glanced over his shoulder as a pair of men came into the hallway through a far door, and then he took Rob by the arm. "Come outside. Too many ears in here."

They went out, closing the main doors behind them, and Lord Robert looked to where his travelling companions were assembling, safely beyond hearing, before he turned back to his grandson, eyeing him keenly. "How are you feeling?" he asked.

Rob shrugged. How *should* he be feeling? was the question in his mind. He had just buried his mother and her absence would be a blight on his life forever.

"Well enough, considering the day," he answered quietly. "Don't worry about me, Gransser. I'll be fine." The childhood name fell easily from his lips, and he realized again what that showed of his comfort around the patriarch now.

"I know you will, lad, and I'm not worrying about you. It's your father I'm concerned about. You'll need to keep an eye on him this next while."

"On my *father*?" The disbelief in his voice was obvious even to him and so he hurried on. "Why so?"

"Because he's lost, that's why. And because he's your father, which means there's much of him—the real man, Robert Bruce, the Earl of Carrick—about which you know nothing, simply because you are his son. Sons seldom see their fathers as real people, and that's the tragic truth. You and I have spoken of this before, when we discussed my regrets about him. D'you remember that?" Rob nodded. "Aye. And when I was young I had my own difficulties with my father in his time. Sons only see in their fathers what they have learnt and been taught to see. They see no more than the stern pater-familias who rules and regulates their life, and they seldom have cause to consider the living, human man who lived and dreamed and hoped as a young man himself before he married and cares forced him to become that unforgiving figure."

He cleared his throat, and his eyes narrowed. "You feel betrayed and bereft because you've lost the mother that you loved, and that is right and proper, Grandson. The countess was your mother and a wondrously gifted woman in that respect, and now she's gone and you will mourn her with all the rest of us. But I want you to try to imagine how my son must be feeling now. Your mother was all the world to your father—his lifelong love, the woman he worshipped, his closest companion and most trusted friend. She was his inspiration and his salvation in this world. Her love formed the very core of his life as a proud and noble man. And now she's gone. He will never see her again or hear her voice or be able to seek her advice. His household now has no binding force to guide it other than himself, and he feels helpless. He is faced now with the sole responsibility for tending and guiding the family she reared so effortlessly, and he will see no way of living up to that trust, now that he is bereft of her counsel and wisdom, her guidance and her strength. In his own eyes at this moment, your father's life is over, his future, if he can see one, filled with emptiness and lacking a focus. He will get over it in time, as all men do, but the grief of it will be overwhelming to him for the next while. And that is why you need to keep an eye on him. I canna do it, nor would I even seek to try. There is too big a gulf between him and me still."

He fell silent again, and into that silence came a whistle and a loud voice calling his name. He snapped his head up and waved away the summons in annoyance.

"I have to go," he growled, "but I am not yet done, so listen. Take care of your father in the weeks ahead. He'll be like a rudderless boat in a heavy sea. And that means you'll have to look to your brothers, too, forbye your sisters. You'll have help with the lasses—Allie and the other women will see to that—but you will need to play the father with the boys. You need to be the man of the house these next few months." He cocked his head, raising an eyebrow. "Can you do that?"

Rob shook his head, his eyes wide. "I don't know, Grandfather." His voice was almost a whisper. "I don't know, but I'll try."

"That's all I need to hear, that you're willing to try. But you'll have help. Your mother's uncle Nicol will be there to guide you, and you can feel free to talk to him. He is a wise and canny man, Nicol MacDuncan. And forbye, your mother's people here are all solid folk. I'll be at Lochmaben should you have need of me. But I doubt you will. Everyone in your charge now has been raised by your mother, God rest her soul, and her teachings will bear fruit, you mark my words. I have no doubt that you can do this, Robert. You're a Bruce, and a fine one. And when this time has passed, I will knight you with my own hand, as is within my right as Lord of Annandale and a magnate of this realm. That is a promise. Come now and embrace me, for I have to be away."

Rob stood alone outside the castle gates in the pouring rain and watched his grandfather ride off with his escort into the lowering gloom of the bleakest afternoon of his young life.

Turnberry seemed an alien place without its castellan. Even Allie and Murdo, the two family retainers, were mute and listless in the weeks that followed the funeral, when the visiting mourners had all departed and left the big house strangely echoing and lifeless. They still carried out their routine tasks from day to day, supervising the workers who kept the house and the estate functioning, but as the days progressed and Rob began to notice things again, he became aware that the faithful couple had lost something of their own in the death of their beloved mistress.

The Bruce household had changed in many ways. For one, gone was the long-established ritual of the evening meal, presided over by the countess and governed by laws that had seemed immutable to Rob and his siblings. When there were guests in the castle, the children—those of them deemed old enough to behave themselves in front of company—dined in the great hall with everyone else, where they were seated apart from the adults and closely chaperoned by one of the countess's women. At all other times, though, the daily family supper was served in a lesser dining room, known for some long-forgotten reason as the Lodge, and no one was permitted to be absent unless they were too ill to leave their sickbed. Countess Marjorie was adamant about the need for everyone to be there, for it was the sole and jealously guarded time of day when the family would meet and share food and conversation together. Other meals in the day could be eaten wherever and whenever food and time might be available, but the family supper was sacrosanct, and lateness, or far worse the occasional failure to attend, was punishable by a wide range of penances, from drudge duties in the scullery to dire loss of privileges.

Within a week of Countess Marjorie's death that family ritual had begun to unravel, for Earl Robert had chosen the same means of mourning the loss of his wife that Edward of England had espoused two years earlier: he avoided all human contact and remained shut up in the quarters he had shared with his wife for more than twenty years. Rob found himself reluctantly, and resentfully, supervising the evening meals served in the Lodge, and it became clear to him very quickly that he lacked any authority to sustain his new status. The first few days after the funeral were naturally doleful. The children gathered in the Lodge each night, but for three entire days no one spoke at the table, and more than once the silence was broken by the sounds of sobs.

They were ten siblings—five girls and five boys—an astounding number of healthy children for one family, and they ranged in age from four to twenty. Christina, the eldest, was already married to Gartnait, the future Earl of Mar in the far northeast, and she had remained in Turnberry after the funeral to see her siblings over the worst of their mourning period. Rob's sister Isabel was almost exactly a year younger than him, at seventeen. After Isabel came the four younger brothers, Nigel, almost sixteen, then Edward, Thomas, and Alec, newly turned eleven. Behind them came Mary, Margaret, and Matilda, aged nine, seven, and four. Watching the three little girls in those first few days, Rob wondered how much they understood what had happened. Mary certainly knew her mother was gone, but Rob doubted whether she understood the permanence of it. Little Matilda cried constantly, but probably only because she saw the grief among her siblings.

His brothers, though, were a different matter. They were old enough to understand that their mother was gone, but not yet mature enough to deal with the tragedy as adults, and their obscure, confused feelings, allied with the absence from the table of their father, quickly resulted in bickering.

It was little Matilda who started an uproar towards the end of the first week by throwing a tantrum, screaming for her mother and refusing to be pacified. Her outburst upset her young sisters, who burst into tears, infuriating Edward, always the least patient of the brothers. Nigel shouted at him to shut up, and one word led rapidly to the next, so that in moments everyone except Christina was adding to the tumult, each of them trying to shout above the others.

Rob rose in a rage, snatching up the clay water jug and hammering it hard on the table as he bellowed for quiet. The jug shattered, water splashing everyone around the table and one whirling shard catching Isabel on the cheek, instantly drawing blood. For a few moments everyone froze, the only sound the loud splashing of water pouring from the table to the floor. Then Isabel sprang to her feet, one hand pressed to her injured face, wet with splashed water mixed with blood, and ran sobbing from the room, closely followed by Christina, who glared at Rob as she followed her sister. The three youngest girls started screaming again, and the harried nursemaid, pale faced and wide-eyed, snatched up little Matilda and shepherded Mary and Margaret out of the room, leaving Rob alone with his four younger brothers, the handle of the shattered jug still clutched in his hand.

Edward was white faced with fury, glaring at Rob as he flexed his fists.

"Don't even think of it," Rob warned, and then looked at the others. "Sit down, all of you."

"Where?" Edward's voice was a hiss. "Everything's soaked. Even our food. And you could have put Bella's eye out." He walked away towards the door.

"Come back here," Rob told him, but he was gone in a few strides.

"We're going, too," Nigel said, his voice barely recognizable.

"No, you're not," Rob said. "I need you to stay here."

Nigel looked him straight in the eye. "Edward needs us not to even more," he said, then glanced at the others. "Come on."

They followed him, and Rob stood watching them, his face twitching with anger. He looked at the wreckage of the table, wondering how things had come to such a pass and thinking that his brothers had become strangers. He came closer to weeping in frustration at that moment than he had in years. But then the truth hit him, and he had to clutch at the table for support. It was he who was the stranger here, not them. This was their home, their world, and it had been pulled down on their heads in the space of mere days, all their familiar anchors severed, leaving them without leadership or support. He, on the other hand, had been gone for two full years while they'd remained at home and grown closer to one another than he could possibly be to them by now. Nigel was their leader now, in age and rank, and he had just demonstrated his leadership by defying his man-sized elder brother. It had been Edward, though, always the mercurial one, who had been the first to rebel against the stranger who had been attempting to bully all of them.

Rob stood in the quiet of the Lodge, mulling those thoughts and listening to the random drops of water still falling to the floor, and then he snatched in a deep sigh and went looking for his uncle Nicol.

He was cold in the October chill by the time he finally found Nicol in the stables, grooming his horse by the light of a single lantern.

His uncle took one look at him and grunted. "Sit," he said, nodding towards a stool by the gate to the stall. "I'll be done in a minute."

He finished his task with a few more strokes, then led his horse back into its stall and piled some fresh hay into its crib. He came back out to close the gate and leaned against it, eyeing his nephew.

"You look like a jilted lover," he said. "What happened?"

Rob told him all about the fracas in the Lodge, and Nicol stood and listened.

"Hmm," he said. "It occurs to me that yon might have been a good place not to be. Thank God I was safe here, talking to my horse. The boys defied you, you said? And how did you respond?"

Rob shook his head. "I didn't. I had already done and said too much."

"Hmm. And the girls, Christina and Isabel, where did they go?"

"I don't know. To see to Bella's face, I suppose … "

"You didn't check? How badly was she cut?"

"Bad enough. I saw blood."

"And you didn't think fit to go and see how she was?"

"No. I was shamed."

"Where are the others now?"

"The young ones went with their nurse. I don't know where the boys went."

"Right. Well, we need to go and see to Isabel. After that, it seems to me the next question should involve what you have to do next. Did you speak to your father?"

Rob's eyes went wide with surprise. "No. He made his wishes plain two days ago. He said he wanted to be alone without being bothered by any petty squabbles. I never even thought to go to him. I came to you instead."

"Aye, probably just as well … So, what d'you intend to do to make matters right?"

"About Isabel, you mean?"

"No, Isabel's cut and can't be uncut. We can only hope it's not too bad and she won't be disfigured. I meant what do you mean to do about the others, the whole thing?"

Rob straightened on his stool and shook his head. "I don't know, Uncle Nicol. I don't know what to do about anything anymore. That's why I'm here … I hoped you might be able to tell me. Besides, I did nothing to make it wrong in the first place."

"That is true," Nicol agreed, nodding his head slowly. "But wrong it is, nevertheless, would you not agree?" The soft sibilance of his Gaelic speech was comforting to Rob.

"Yes," he whispered. "It's very wrong. Our mother will be weeping in Heaven."

A kindly smile lit up Nicol's face, and he waggled a raised finger. "No, lad, I doubt that. Your mother was never a weeper. She will be watching, though. No doubt in my mind about that. She will be watching to see how you handle matters now, on your own." He saw his nephew's baffled look. "It's the truth. What you are facing here, Nephew, is your first real test of manhood, in the sense of being responsible—the matter of whether or not you are capable of acting as both father and mother to your brothers and sisters."

"I'm not, obviously."

"Yes, you are. You simply haven't come to grips with it yet."

Rob frowned at him. "Come to grips with it? How would I even begin to do that? I'm a knight, not a nursemaid, and I don't even know how to begin to be different. That's why they all hate me."

"Och, Robert, there speaks a man who is feeling sorry for himself." Nicol heaved himself away from the stall door and tightened the belt at his waist, then shrugged mightily and bloused the front of his tunic until it hung comfortably again. "You saw how glad they all were to see you last week. How then could they have come to hate you so quickly? They're angry at all the world right now, that's all that ails them. It's only natural that they'll strike out at anyone they can rage at. But that will pass quicker than they or you might believe, I swear to you, for they are all young and life goes on, no matter what is lost. What *you* have to decide, and quickly, is what you can do to help them find their way again. What do they need that you can give them most easily?"

Rob shook his head. "I don't know, Nicol."

"Well, I know. And I know, too, how easily you'll do it once you see what's needed. You'll give them love, and leadership, strength, and guidance. They all look up to you, as they should. You're the eldest man in the family now, apart from your father, and you're grown up, forbye, a knight, fully trained and lacking only the tap of a blade upon your shoulder to complete you. You share their pain and their grief, but you must bear both of those as a man, while they are only boys and little girls.

"And so tomorrow you will preside at supper in the Lodge and you will do it properly, with the full dignity of your rank and status. You'll do it naturally and with kindness and you'll make no mention of today's debacle. Forget that ever happened, and if any of them should bring it up, dismiss it as forgiven and forgotten, a thing of no

significance. I will talk to each of them during the day and make
sure that they attend. And I'll warrant you they will all be feeling as
miserable as you are about what happened tonight. I think, though,
that it might be wise to have the youngest children sup with their
nurse for a few days, until everything settles down again." He
paused, then asked, "Do you understand what I'm saying to you?"

"I do, I think." Rob drew in a great breath, and then he sat
thinking for a few moments. "You want me to encourage them to
talk … And to listen to them rather than to talk to them. Is that
right?"

"Good man. That's it, exactly. Listen, and encourage them to
speak up. Once they start talking about their mother, the relief will
act as a poultice. The poison that's affecting them will drain away
like pus from a festering cut."

"But how will I get them to start?"

"By asking questions, lad, and by remembering they all look up
to you. Ask them what's been happening while you were gone. Ask
them about your mother, about what she did for them as children,
about what they remember most about her. It won't be difficult,
you'll see. But most of all, don't be afraid to let them see how much
you care yourself—how much you miss her and how much you
loved her. Tell them a few of your own favourite memories of her."

The beginnings of a smile flickered at Rob's mouth. "Like the
time she raised the big tents to house the Kings and surprised my
father so much that he couldn't show it?"

"Aye, things like that. Once you make a start, the rest will come
naturally, you wait and see. All you have to do is be yourself. Don't
preach at them and don't talk down to them … So, you can do this,
you agree?"

"Yes. I can do that."

"Good, then, because soon Christina must go home to her
goodman in Mar, and she should do that without feeling guilty for
leaving grief and misery behind her. Once she sees that the others
are in good hands with you, she'll be much relieved." He rubbed his
hands together. "Now, I suggest we go and find Isabel and see to her

wants if need be. Then we might go and find something to eat by the kitchen fire. I have the feeling you did not sup much tonight."

That won him a reluctant grin as Rob rose to his feet. "I haven't had a bite since this morning and I'm starving."

Nicol wet his fingers with saliva and crossed to where the lamp burned smokily. "Wait for me outside while I make sure this thing is out. It would be too bad to burn down the stable while solving a minor problem."

The result of it all was that the dam of sorrow and resentment and self-pity that had sprung into being in the previous week was completely broken, and the family suppers from that day forth became almost as carefree and enjoyable as they had been while Countess Marjorie had been there to adjudicate. They spoke of her constantly with love and longing.

It was Nigel who brought up the absence of their father for the first time.

"What will we all do now?"

His question brought silence and curious looks, for no one knew what he was talking about.

"About the house, I mean. We won't be able to stay here now, for Da isn't really Earl of Carrick. Not now. He only held the name because he was married to Mam. She was the true countess, and Carrick belongs to her family. It's their holding, not Bruce's. Now the earldom will go to the next heir in line, and that'll be a Gael, one of Ma's cousins. That's the law. So where will we go when the new earl comes to live here?"

Even Rob was stunned by what Nigel had said. But he saw the truth of it and saw, too, the worry on the faces of the two youngest boys, whose eyes were darting everywhere as though they expected the walls to collapse or the door to crash open as strangers burst in to dispossess them.

"No, that's not true," Christina said, drawing every eye to her. She looked at each of them in turn, briefly but commandingly. "We will all stay here." Her voice was more authoritative than they had ever heard it, the words of a countess coming from their big sister's mouth. "This is our home and nothing will change in that." She looked at Rob. "Uncle Nicol—who is really Ma's uncle—is the heir Nigel's talking about. Nicol stands next in line for the earldom. But he wants no part of it. He is content to leave things as they are. I've heard him talk about this with Mam, several times in the past few years, and I know what they agreed upon. Mam wrote it in a letter more than a year ago, before my wedding. She sent it to the Bishop of Glasgow as the senior bishop of the southern realm, and Uncle Nicol added his own wishes, as did both my goodman, Gartnait, and his father, Domhnall, Mormaer of Mar, when we were wed. Uncle James the High Steward added his approval, too, in writing, since our mother was his sister. All of them are staunch supporters of Grandfather Robert, and all of them felt that since Uncle Nicol was in agreement with his niece's wishes, our mother's wishes should be observed should such a need ever arise."

She broke off, her eyes filling with tears, but she swallowed hard and kept going. "Well, now that need has arisen, God help us all. But Gartnait believes that Da will be made Earl of Carrick in his own right, for the good of the Scots realm." She raised a hand, a mere flick of the wrist, to her oldest brother. "And before you can ask me if I'm sure it'll happen, I'm not. I only know what Gartnait told me his father said. But they both believe it's possible."

"He might be named earl, but will he ever come out of his room again?" Edward's voice sounded much older than his fourteen years, and it flashed through Rob's mind that his brother was attempting to be wryly humourous. But none of the others at the table found it amusing.

"He'll come out, never you fear." Rob felt all their eyes turn to him at once. He looked at none of them but spoke towards the centre of the table. "Da's mourning. We are all suffering from the loss of her, but Mam was Da's whole life, and he's dealing with her loss more quietly and privately than any of us is. So we must give him time, as much time as he needs." He looked from one to the other of them, missing none. "The best thing we can do for him is leave him to conquer it in his own way. He will come back to us."

# CHAPTER TEN

# ALARUMS

Their father did come back to them, even sooner than Rob had anticipated, but he was a changed man from the Da they had known a mere month earlier, and even the youngest girls remarked upon it. He had lost weight in the weeks since his wife first fell sick, and was gaunt and haggard-looking. The lines in his face, which had been there before whenever he smiled or grimaced, were now deep-graven and had a look of permanence about them. He had never been a garrulous man, not merry or jocular—the Scots word *jocose*, meaning both of those things and more, was one that no one would ever have used to describe him—but he had always been gentle and considerate to his children. Now, though, once he had reappeared to his family, Earl Robert was deeply melancholy. He spoke quietly and listened courteously when anyone spoke to him, but there was an unmistakable air of distraction about him, as though there were some other place he would rather be at any time.

Reassured by ten days of harmony among her siblings and confident that they would now be able to support one another in whatever lay ahead, Christina had made arrangements to return to her home in Mar by the time the earl reappeared. It was her final night in Turnberry, and she had made her farewells to her father before presiding over supper in the Lodge for the last time. They had finished eating and the remnants of their meal had been cleared away and, as usual, they remained seated around the table for what had quickly reverted to being the favourite ritual of the family's day, just as it had been when their mother was alive. Christina knew, however, that this would be her last chance, perhaps for a long time, to deputize for their missing mother, and she was haranguing them gently, reminding them of the importance of sharing their love and kinship with one another after she was gone and of being the family their mother had loved so dearly, when the door opened at her back and Earl Robert stepped into the room. His arrival took everyone by surprise, so that no one even thought to stand up as they all turned to stare at him. Looking slightly bewildered, he scanned the gathering.

"Forgive me," he said, then blinked. "For what?" he added. "Why should you forgive me? I'm your father." The merest suggestion of a smile tugged briefly at the corners of his eyes. "But you all looked so serious that I felt for a moment as though I were intruding …"

Rob sprang to his feet, pushing his chair backward with his knees. "Forgive us, sir," he said, feeling a flush on his cheeks. "We had no thought of your joining—" He checked himself, aware of the implied insult in his words, and his confusion deepened. But his father was already nodding.

"Quite right, of course. I've been neglecting you all, and for that I must beg your pardon. But it pleases me to see you all gathered together here, just as—" He hesitated, very briefly. "As you did when your mother was alive." He glanced around the table. "Is there a chair for me?"

Rob moved briskly to bring forward a heavy chair from against the wall, and Christina dragged her own lighter one from the head of the table around to one side, making room for the earl, who then seated himself with a nod.

For the next half-hour, he spoke to each of his offspring in turn, beginning with Christina and working his way down the table by age, and by the end of that time the atmosphere was again relaxed and comfortable. It was only at the end of things that he told them their eldest sister, Christina, would return home to her goodman, Gartnait of Mar, the following day. Her place at supper would be taken over, at least for the next few weeks, by their next eldest sister, Isabel. It would be her task, their father said, to supervise these family gatherings while he and Rob were away, for they, too, must leave the following day.

That provoked a storm of questions that the earl quelled by simply raising his hands, palms outward, until they were all silent again. When they were, he held his pose for several moments longer, then asked if any of them could tell him how many messengers had visited the castle that day. None of them could.

"Well then, I'll tell you," Earl Robert said. "There were two of them. One of them arrived this morning and one came late this afternoon, but it's the one from this morning I want to tell you about. Can any of you tell me what is meant by '*de jure uxoris*'?"

Rob raised his hand, as did Nigel and Christina, but it was Nigel to whom their father pointed for a response.

"Aye, sir. It means 'by right of his wife,' does it not?"

"It does. By right of his wife, or more commonly, by right of marriage. Your mother was the born Countess of Carrick and it was she who ruled the earldom. I was but her husband and as such, by tradition, I was given the name Earl of Carrick as a courtesy—since a countess may not be married to a common man.

"Your mother, may God rest her soul, often fretted that I would lose the title in the event of her ... of her death. And so she set out to see that it would never happen. It was your mother's wish—shared with her successor, your great-uncle Nicol—that should she die before I did, I should be named Earl of Carrick in fact."

All eyes were on the earl.

"The messenger who came this morning brought word from Bishop Wishart in Glasgow that he and other nobles had agreed to grant your mother's wish in this matter, so that I am now recognized, with the blessing of the lords of this realm, both spiritual and temporal, as the legitimate Earl of Carrick from this day on." He paused. "That means that we—that *you*—will not have to leave this place you call your home. Turnberry will remain yours and ours, and your uncle Nicol will be welcome here for the remainder of his life should he wish to stay with us. I thought you would all be glad to hear that."

He allowed the buzz around the table to subside. "The messenger who arrived this afternoon came from your grandfather. *His* message was that I must make my way directly to Lochmaben and bring your brother Robert with me." He smiled fully, permitting them a glimpse of the man he had been before their mother's death. "I have to obey that summons," he said quietly. "For Lord Robert is far more than your grandfather. He is my father, and only an ingrate or a fool disobeys his father. Would you not agree?"

They set out early the next morning, accompanied by a small party of fifteen retainers, and they rode hard, wasting no time on the road throughout the day. Rob was glad to see his grandsire's fortress come into view in the distance just before nightfall. He had been wondering about their summons ever since his father had mentioned it, and he was impatient to discover the reason for it.

Lochmaben's taciturn steward, Alan Bellow, met them at the main gates and ushered them directly to Lord Robert's den, where the old man threw down his pen as soon as they arrived and abandoned the parchment on which he had been writing. He rose to his feet at once and waved them to the three plain, high-backed chairs grouped around the brazier in the corner. The steward poured each of them a mug of beer and collected a platter of food from an oaken sideboard, placing it on a small table beside the chairs. Earl Robert sat down in one of the heavy chairs, eyeing the savoury tidbits laid out on the broad wooden platter.

"Eat, Robert, eat," Lord Robert said, waving a hand over the food. "I remembered some of the bitties you favoured as a boy and had Alan order them for you from the kitchens. Ye'll have been on the road long enough and without sustenance, so I thought I might as well tickle your tastes while I picked your mind. You, too, Rob."

Earl Robert, though, made no move to touch the food. Instead he looked at his father, and then spoke without inflection. "You called us here without warning, Father, aware we are in mourning. That made me think your summons must be urgent, and so here we are, but I can live without food for a few more hours, so be it you will put my mind at rest over why you must have us here in Lochmaben so suddenly. What has happened?"

The old man looked at his son, and Rob thought he could detect the beginnings of a frown, quickly suppressed as his grandsire glanced away towards the fire and then sucked in a great, deep breath.

"Life has happened," growled the Lord of Annandale, removing his elbow from the back of the chair on which he had been leaning and moving to stand in front of the glowing brazier, presenting his backside to the warming glow of the coals. "Life. Confusion and frustration."

Neither of his listeners moved, and he looked from son to father before speaking again. "I regret having called you away so urgently, but I had no other choice. How are the children?"

Earl Robert pursed his mouth, but his voice, when he spoke, betrayed no resentment. "They are well. Well enough, that is, considering the newness of their loss. But they are yet … fragile. That is, I think, the word most fitting to describe them."

"And so it should be," his father replied. "It's apt enough. But you'll find my reason for calling you here equally apt. When things are fragile, it behooves the prudent man to pay attention to the possibility of losing them, through accident or carelessness." Now the patriarch looked at his grandson directly, though his words were still addressed to his own son. "Our world is changing rapidly, Robert, and the worst thing we could do would be to accept those changes without demur."

"What d'you mean?" Earl Robert was all attention now, leaning forward. "What changes?"

"Several. Edward, and England."

"Has there been a decision, then, from Norham?"

Lord Robert shook his head. "Not yet. But I have heard that one is coming soon."

"And that disturbs you, evidently. What have you heard, exactly?"

The old man's nose wrinkled in distaste. "That Edward is inclined to favour Balliol."

"But how can that be, Father? Yours is the stronger claim." The earl's voice was high pitched, almost querulous, and his father nodded, curtly, Rob thought.

"It is, if you cleave to the ancient law of Scots succession through the female side. But you were there in Perth and heard what Wishart said about the old Scots tanist law being out of favour. This new law, this primogeniture, passing the rights to the firstborn son, rules out the female claim, and it appears it has been widely adopted throughout Christendom, as Wishart said. And particularly so in England. Edward and his delegates now favour it, and that bodes ill for me and mine."

Neither of the two younger Bruces responded, each of them thinking deeply on what those words entailed.

Lord Robert breathed in deeply. "The damnable part of that is that Edward's no' alone in his thinking. Some of our own bishops within the court agree with him, and of course the Comyn crew is eager to back his judgment therein, as you might jalouse." He frowned. "There's more to it than that, though. At least so I hae come to believe after weeks of thought on the matter. And that's why you are here. I have made a decision—decisions, in fact—that will affect you and young Rob directly."

"Based upon *your* thoughts?" Earl Robert's emphasis was barely discernible.

His father nodded. "Aye. That's what I said."

"And are we to learn what those thoughts are?"

Again Rob thought he saw a flash of irritation in the old man's eyes, but the moment passed and Lord Robert stood silent. "Aye," he said eventually. "You are … My thoughts are these. I now believe Edward will give the nod to Balliol, for diverse reasons, not all of them without prejudice. By favouring the law of primogeniture, he undermines my entire claim and he can argue legally that he is right to do so. God knows his English clerics will support him there, and they, with the added weight of the Balliol and Comyn faction, will outnumber the pro-Bruce voices in the proceedings."

Earl Robert was frowning. "'Not without prejudice,' you said. What do you mean by that?"

The old man frowned. "I have suspicions, nothing more—nothing on which I could rely for proof. But I believe now that Edward believes he might make more use of Balliol than he could of me, were I the King of Scots." He glanced at Rob, then swung his eyes back to his son the earl. "You've met John Balliol, Robert. He is a good man, douce and pleasant, but he will never make a strong king. He needs too much to be liked … craves the good opinion of everyone. And that is fatal in a king, if not to the man himself, then surely to the realm he governs. John Balliol is too weak for kingship. And I suspect Edward knows that well, and plans to use it for his own designs."

"What designs, Father? If Balliol becomes the King of Scots, he will be sanctified as such, anointed and crowned and unbeholden to any man or any other King. How then could Edward use him?"

This time the irritation broke through. "In God's name, Robert, are you deaf or simply stupid? *Weak*, I said. The man is a weakling, and because of that his kingship will be feckless, too. Edward Plantagenet now seeks to place a puppet on our throne. *His* puppet, on *our* throne."

"Never! The Guardians—"

"The Guardians stand as *guardians* in the absence of a king!" Lord Robert roared, his forbearance exhausted. "The *absence* of a king! *Think* about that, for the love of God!" He stopped and drew a long, deep breath, held it before releasing it. He spoke again, this time in a calmer voice. "Their function as Guardians expires once a new king is crowned, and they return to being mere advisers to that king, as they have ever been. And advisers can be ignored by a king who has no wish to listen to them. Thus rejected, they have no recourse within the law. They may bite their gums in fury but they can *do* nothing against their rightful monarch. Can you not *see* that? All they can do is *advise*, and if their king chooses to listen instead to the advice of another, somebody more powerful, more pleasing, more manipulative—somebody like Edward Plantagenet—then the

Guardians may fume and fret but they will be impotent. That. Is. The truth. So let there be an end to this protesting. Given a choice between Balliol and me in furthering his own kingship, Edward Plantagenet will never choose me, because he knows he'll never dominate me."

The earl stared into the fire for a while, and then asked, "Have you suspected this outcome from the first, Father?"

"No, not a bit. It came to me but weeks ago as I was returning here from Marjorie's funeral. It began with something I remembered Robert Wishart saying, something about the way men are talking of the changes in Edward since Eleanor died. That led to other memories, of things I had heard tell of England's King but had ignored because I thought them demeaning to him, and to me for listening to them. But I am now convinced I have the right of it."

"I see … " Earl Robert scratched his chin for several moments. "You said you had come to some decisions that would affect all of us."

Lord Robert nodded. "I have." He moved away from the front of the fire and angled the vacant chair to where he could sit and look at both of his listeners, and when he spoke again, in formal English, his voice was low and solemn.

"I am convinced that, one way or another, John Balliol will fail as King. He might stand up to Edward of England for a while, and I suspect he will try at first, but he is no match for the man in any sense. Edward will bully him, browbeat him, harass him, and keep him under constant pressure until he eventually controls him. And when he does, then Balliol will fall and we will go to war with England. The Guardians might regain their powers then, but mark me and take note … It might also be too late by then. Their position—their very puissance in defence of this realm—could be set at naught by time and circumstance if Edward has his way. I now believe, deep within myself, that Edward of England, unchecked, will seek to garner Scotland to his Crown as he did Wales, by war and conquest if need be. And Edward, left unconstrained, will perceive such a need, you mark my words."

Mark them they did, for both sat staring at him wide-eyed as he continued speaking.

"Our sole protection against that will be constant vigilance from this time forth, for though I said he will *seek* that goal, he will not be able to achieve it unless this entire land and everyone within it simply bends the knee to him and permits it. And therefore this realm of ours must remain strong, and we must be diligent to keep it so. The Plantagenet has but one weakness that I can see, but it is a large and public one, and our task will be to exploit it and keep it in plain sight of everyone. This is a King who must ever be seen to abide by the law—his own and God's—for he has built his kingship upon that. But England's law is for England's realm, and it makes no allowance for Scotland, and Edward's barons will be slavering for our lands. Therefore we Scots must work to keep the outside world—the Pope, his cardinals, and all the crowned kings of Christendom—aware of what is happening in our land. If we do that, and take great pains to do it properly and constantly, we might, just might be able to retain our freedom.

"But even so, if Balliol is chosen and he fails, for whatever reason, this whole debate on succession will open up again, and that is where I must count myself beaten."

"How so, Grandfather?" Rob's voice was barely louder than a whisper, and Lord Robert tilted his chin and narrowed his eyes.

"Because I am too old, Grandson. Balliol will have years ahead of him before he falls, if indeed he does. By then I will probably be dead … I should have died long ere now. And so I have decided to resign my claim to the throne, now, while I yet live, in favour of my son."

"No!" Rob protested. "You can't do that. There has been no decision! What if the court rules in your favour?"

The old man flashed a grin that was full of wickedness. "Then everything will change and I will be the King of Scots, and God knows I have heirs aplenty. But I doubt that is likely to happen. Besides, there's an alternative consideration, should Balliol be selected over me. If I do not renounce my claim in favour of your father, I'll be left as Lord of Annandale, a vassal of the King. That means I'd have no other choice than to bend the knee—on pain of treason—in humble obedience and servitude to Balliol, and to his Comyn cousins, and that does not appeal to me. I might bend the knee anyway, but that will be my own choice as my own man, and it could not easily be forced upon me under threat of death. So I'll resign and go to live in England, on my lands in Essex, and there's the end of it. No Comyn can tell me what to do there." He glanced at his son. "Robert, what will you do, now that you are no longer Earl of Carrick?"

The earl blinked. "But I am, Father. I am earl in truth. It has been ratified by the council of Guardians."

For a long moment Lord Robert remained motionless, and then a smile slowly lit up his face. "Excellent," he said, elongating the vowels. "That is truly excellent, for it gives additional weight to what I propose to do. But mind you make no mistake on what your new title means, my son. Half of the council of Guardians, by design, are Comyn and Balliol men. They would never have approved a new Bruce earldom—particularly here in the southwest—were they not absolutely certain of a Balliol victory. For with their own man crowned King, no Bruce will be a threat to them, no matter what his rank.

"And so it is confirmed—the die is cast and, as I thought, the throne will go to Balliol. It will take but days more, mark my words. And so as soon as I hear formal word of the court's findings, I will renounce my claim and name you two my heirs, with full rights to the succession should the need ever again arise. And if anyone dares to ask me for my reason for so doing, I will tell them truly I am nigh on seventy-five years old and do not expect to live much longer. So you, Robert, will be Lord of Annandale from that day forth, and as soon as that is done, you, in turn, will do the same for young Robert here, renouncing your earldom and naming him Earl of Carrick. You'll both have to kneel to Balliol, of course, but neither of you is as personally close to this as I am, and a bent knee from you will ensure your holdings." He looked directly at his grandson then, still smiling. "You would hae no objection to that, lad, eh?"

Rob shook his head, his eyes wide with excitement. "No, sir," he said. "But I'm not even knighted yet. How can I be an earl?"

"Hah!" Lord Robert barked. "By kneeling on the floor in front of me and being tapped upon the shoulders by my sword in front of an assembled body of my own knights. And the next step, from knight to earl, will be announced by your father, so put your mind at rest. It's done, bar for the event itself."

"But what of King Edward, Gransser? Will he not be angry? He told me he would knight me himself next time we met. He might see your resigning of your claim for what it is, and he could take umbrage at what he might call your disrespect for his station. Is that wise, to provoke him like that?"

"Wise?" The Lord of Annandale grimaced. "It is neither wise nor unwise, Grandson, nor is it provocation. Edward is King in England. Not in Scotland. Here he is regarded, at his own insistence, as feudal overlord to such as I, the nobles of this land who own English hold-ings under his royal grant. But I'll give no offence to him in either case. I will but exercise my right as a magnate of this realm, and also as your grandsire, to raise you to the knighthood for which he himself has named you fit, and thereby to man's estate, in honour of the memory of your dear mother. Apart from that, as his true liege-man and vassal, I will renew my oaths of loyalty and fealty to him as my feudal overlord. I have no difficulty there, for the ancient laws of feudal custom hold me to that course. Besides, I wish otherwise to remain as close to King Edward's goodwill as may be, in keeping with the need for vigilance of which I spoke. D'ye follow me, boy?"

"Yes, sir. I do."

"And so do I, Father." Earl Robert's tone was subdued, but he sat silent for a spell thereafter, nodding to himself as he mulled the thoughts in his mind. "So," he resumed. "We do and say nothing until a verdict is pronounced by the Norham court, and if you are chosen, this entire matter will be forgotten and we will continue as before. But if the court elects John Balliol, then you will renounce your claim and name me your heir." A sudden scowl darkened his brows. "You would not think to— You—" He cleared his throat roughly. "What of your reaction? In public, I mean. How will you respond if Balliol is chosen?"

"As a loyal subject should. Can you doubt that? I may dislike the result and distrust the choice, but the process is valid and accepted by everyone concerned. When, not if, John Balliol is chosen, then I shall attend his coronation and bend my knee to him as my lawful King, for that is what he will be."

"And will you support him truly?"

"No other man would dare to ask me such a thing and hope to keep the flesh upon his back. Of course I will support him—reluctantly, let that be acknowledged, but I will support him." The old man grinned. "But now I think on it, I might take matters further— create some tension, perhaps stir up some panic, make them wonder what I'm about."

"How so?" the earl asked.

"Today is what, the third day of November?"

"No, it's the fourth."

The patriarch's brow furrowed as he thought. "I'll have to talk with my spies in Norham again, just to be sure that nothing new is in the wind, but if they are intent upon choosing Balliol then we might as well let them get on with it. It will depend on what I learn tomorrow from Wishart. He'll be here in the forenoon, for he's in Jedburgh tonight, I know, and he'll come here before he travels on to Norham. He's no more keen on what's happening there than I am and he will tell me the truth, as he perceives it, about what has been going on these past few months."

"And if he agrees with your conclusions?"

"Then I'll withdraw my claim in advance of the verdict and throw everyone into confusion. They'll all be waiting for my reaction to the verdict, hoping for an excuse to set a formal watch upon me as a malcontent, and such a watch would include the two of you as well. But by withdrawing ahead of the verdict, claiming age and infirmity, I'll draw their teeth before they can bare them at me, and at the same time I'll establish my acceptance of Balliol."

"But what if Bishop Wishart does not agree with you, Grandfather? What if he believes you might win?"

Lord Robert's smile was wintry. "Then I'll hide my astonishment and wait to see what happens."

# Book Three

# Siblings

# 1292

# CHAPTER ELEVEN

# A SURFEIT OF ROBERTS

Rob was spent, gasping for air and aching from head to foot, when the visitors arrived at mid-morning the next day, the fifth of November. He grounded his heavy quarterstaff and pointed towards the party of men wending their way down from the tree-crowned hill to the west.

Lord Robert looked, then nodded. "Wishart," he growled, and strode away towards the entry gates, shouting for his steward. Rob wiped the sweat from his brows and grinned at the man who had been belabouring him without mercy.

"I thank God he came when he did," he said, "for I thought you were going to hammer me to my knees in front of my grandfather."

The man he spoke to, Rab Elliot, was in his prime—Rob gauged him to be in his early thirties—and he was Lord Robert's senior sergeant, master-at-arms to Annandale. Rob knew him by repute as a dour, hard-muscled fighting man who had gained his rank through dedication to his fighting skills, his sworn duties, and his master's service. Lord Robert had called Rab in early that morning. He had heard good reports of his grandson's prowess, the old man told them both, but he had never seen him fight, and so he wanted to watch him pit himself against Lochmaben's best and to draw his own conclusions.

That had been an hour earlier, and since then Rob had been fighting the hardest mock battle of his life, for Rab Elliot took his master's wishes literally and neither gave nor sought quarter. For a full half-hour the two had fought without respite, beginning slowly as they felt each other out, and then standing toe to toe, their whirling quarterstaves spinning and striking so quickly that their blurred shapes were barely visible at times. Rob was bigger than his opponent, young, strong, agile, and well trained, and that had stood him in good stead for a long time, permitting him to set the pace at first and even to take the initiative from time to time. But the other man was a hardened warrior, oak-solid and indefatigable, and inevitably Rob found himself increasingly on the defensive and struggling to stave off his opponent's never-ending and constantly changing attacks. He had been close to the end of his endurance when he skipped away from an unexpected lunge and caught the flicker of distant movement that had granted him respite.

Now he stood panting, shivering with sudden cold and feeling the sweat on his brows cool rapidly.

Elliot didn't even appear to be breathing heavily, but he drew himself erect and flipped the heavy staff, catching it by the centre, then nodded at Rob. "No' bad," he said. "There arena' many about here wha can stand that long agin' me. I wadna like to fight you on a muddy field, and you wi' a sharp blade. Ye'll be fine, young Bruce. I jalouse that men willna be feared to follow, gin you lead. Lord Robert's no' unhappy wi' ye." He nodded towards where the old man was now walking out to meet the approaching group of newcomers. "Ye'd better go now an' join him."

The party had arrived barely ahead of an incoming storm that brought icy, blustering winds and a scattering of snow from a bleak, lowering sky, and as Rob watched Bishop Wishart arrive, swinging down from his fine gelding to embrace Lord Robert, he knew from the solemnity of the prelate's expression that he bore few welcome tidings for Annandale and Carrick.

Wishart removed the close-fitting woollen cap that framed his face and covered his head and neck, and threw the folds of his heavy cloak back over his shoulders to free his arms, exposing the plain brown cassock he wore belted beneath a long scapula of dark green cloth. Then he held Lord Robert close, and the two men greeted each other by name alone.

"Robert."

"Robert."

The bishop released him to clasp hands with Rob's father.

"Robert."

"Robert."

Finally the bishop's eyes found Rob.

"Master Robert." He smiled, a wintry little smile befitting the chilly day. "We have a surfeit of Roberts here, it seems."

Lord Robert grunted, then waved an arm, indicating that they should go inside.

The table in the den below the stairs held flasks and a tall ewer of chilled wine, but no one wanted anything to drink and they went straight to the cluster of chairs fronting the welcoming brazier in the chimneyed corner of the wall. The bishop shrugged off his cloak and threw it over a chair back, then folded the cap he had been holding and tucked it into the belt at his waist. He then washed his hands in the heat over the coals before turning to Lord Robert.

"I can tell the news is not good," the Bruce patriarch said in Latin.

Wishart's pursed lips were eloquent.

"How?" Lord Robert continued. "The primogeniture matter?"

The bishop nodded. "You have informants, I see."

"They have decided, then?"

"No, not yet." Wishart looked at all three Bruces in turn. "You understand that I've been away, these past weeks … pressing Church affairs in Glasgow, for which I had to obtain King Edward's permission to leave the council still in session. But my people have kept me informed. The last word I heard, delivered to me just before I left the cathedral to return to Norham, is that Edward has been persuaded since my departure that the law favouring the firstborn son is pleasing to God, in that it correctly asserts the right of descent through the prime, male heir. He was leaning towards that opinion before I left, but since then he has been convinced beyond a doubt that primogeniture embodies the will of God Himself."

Lord Robert and the earl exchanged looks. "Who convinced him?" the old man asked bluntly.

Wishart shrugged and moved to sit down beside the Annandale lord. "I don't know, Robert," he said quietly. "I wasn't there. But I believe it was my brethren in Christ. And I believe, deep in my heart, that they were motivated—and will always be motivated—by the fears of men. Mother Church, as you well know, is ruled by men, few of whom hold high opinions of women." He hesitated. "That sounds harsh, but it is no more than the plain truth, though it could be deemed blasphemous."

"God created woman," my grandfather growled. "Since when did men acquire the right to question His design?"

Wishart heaved a great sigh. "Since men were left to tend His Church. Are we to speak of theology, then, Robert? Of philosophy? Will you debate with me?" He held up both hands, palms towards his host. "You asked me a question, I offer you an answer, one I have no wish to defend beyond this point. Women represent—have always represented within the Church—temptation and the weaknesses of the flesh. You and I have spoken of that often in the past and you know it is become a truth by definition and long-held beliefs. And you've pointed out to me before that those beliefs entail a contradiction in terms: God's own Holy Mother is without blemish and comprising all the wondrousness of woman wrapped up in God's intent for man to marry and procreate. The contradiction lies within this ingrained viewpoint I acknowledge: that women are vessels of sin and temptation, unfit for the company of holy men. It is an inconsistency that will never be resolved, a debate that will never die out. But it has become a fact of religious life and it has given rise, at this particular moment, to a need among certain of my brethren—and not all of them English—to impress upon King Edward the importance of the law of primogeniture. Bluntly put— and it would earn me much grief and no approval were this statement to be heard outside this room—but bluntly put, the law of primogeniture is one more means of denying power to women. It affects men, of course, but it is rooted in my colleagues' fear of women."

"Aye. It affects me in particular, for it will cost me a crown. When will the court's findings be proclaimed?"

Wishart waved that aside with a flick of a finger. "I can't tell you that, but it won't be before I return to Norham. They won't be able to proceed to a proper verdict without my presence as the senior prelate south of the Forth. After that, though, if the report I heard is true and the King endorses primogeniture, it could come at any moment. Your auditors will vote against it, but all our Bruce votes combined cannot prevail against Edward's influence upon his English auditors, allied with the will of Holy Church and the whole-hearted support of the Comyn championship of Balliol."

"Aye, the Comyns will be eager to agree with that decision … So the Bruce claim is done, then?"

"Aye, Robert, I fear it is, unless I am gravely mistaken."

Lord Robert grunted, deep in his chest. "When will you leave for Norham?"

"Tomorrow morning. Why?"

"Because I will be coming with you."

Wishart's frown was immediate. "No, you will not. Why would you even think of such a thing? It would be most unfitting. At any time. You are a claimant, Robert, a suitor. You have no place among the auditors and your presence there would sow discord."

"I doubt that. My intent is to resolve matters, to the satisfaction of everyone concerned."

The bishop's frown darkened to a glower. "That is impossible. Your intrusion would insult Edward himself, challenging his authority. The French call that *lèse-majesté*."

"No insult would be intended and none taken by the King of England, nor anyone else," the old man said wryly. "Not when my sole purpose is to withdraw my claim to the Crown in favour of my son's future right to press it, should such unlikely need ever arise again."

Wishart subsided into his chair, his face going slack with shock. "You would renounce your claim?"

"Gladly, and without another thought, for I am now convinced I cannot win. I'll renounce my title to Annandale, too. Robert will become Annandale and young Rob, Earl of Carrick."

The bishop floundered for some moments, searching for words, then shook his head as though to clear it. "And you? What will become of you?"

"Become of me?" The old man laughed. "It has already happened, Master Wishart. It is an established fact and will soon become self-evident. I am become old. All the close friends I loved and trusted in my youth are long since dead, long, long years dead."

"Not all of them, my lord of Bruce. I count myself among them."

The old man smiled. "I know you do, Robert, and rightly. But I was speaking of my old, *old* friends, the friends of my youth. You're too young to claim that status, for all your balding pate ... barely older than my son here. I am too old to be the king that this realm needs today in her present case." He grunted. "But I will go on living until God summons me, and I'll still be Bruce of Annandale. I simply will be *Lord* of Annandale no more, and I may go and live in Essex, where I can render fealty to England's King for his largesse."

"You are conceding defeat?" Wishart looked unconvinced. "What devilry are you planning, my lord Bruce?"

The smile on the old man's face remained unaltered. "None at all, my lord bishop. I am but conceding my age and the times in which we live. The crown will go to Balliol no matter what I do. You yourself have said as much. And so I'll bend the knee to him ahead of time. I have no other option ... In truth, though, I but seek to make the best of what must now be."

"I ... " The prelate's voice grew quiet, his brow creasing with concern. "You have me at a loss, Robert. I never thought to hear such words from the Bruce, and your true intent escapes me. To make the best of it, you said. The best of what?"

Before he spoke again, Lord Robert leaned sideways and tugged at Wishart's side, pulling the woollen travelling cap from the bishop's belt and holding it up so that it dangled by its peak between his pinched thumb and forefinger. "Tell me first," he said mildly, "who is asking me that question? Is it my old friend Robert Wishart who needs a cap nowadays to shelter his pate from the chill winds, or is it the mitred bishop, for whom politicking has become a necessary art?"

Wishart blinked across at him. "It pains me that you would even think to ask me such a thing," he said in the same low voice, "but I can see the times demand it. Will you give me your word you intend no mischief to the realm in what you do?"

"Aye. My solemn oath."

"Then I am Robert Wishart, your old friend, sitting in your den and by your fire … What has brought you to this decision?"

"Life, old friend. And its realities. Listen to what I tell you now."

For the ensuing quarter-hour, Wishart sat listening while the old man led him through all that he had told his son and his grandson in the previous days, and when he finished a long silence ensued while Wishart wrestled with the complexities of what he had been told.

"Are you truly so distrustful of Edward now?" he finally asked.

"I am. And I believe I am right to be so. Distrust is what I have come to feel. I fear the King of England is a changed man from what he was a few years ago. And a different man altogether from the young prince with whom I went to war so long ago."

"How changed, and to what extent?"

"That I do *not* know, Robert. I can't put my hand on what it is that bothers me, and that is the truth. But the changes are there. Look at what happened in June last year."

Wishart frowned, impatient. "I don't need to look at it. I know what happened. I took part in it."

"I know you did, but do me the favour now, if you will, of looking at it from my point of view."

"I've listened to you now for the better part of half an hour and your point of view escapes me utterly." He sighed and flapped a hand. "And to tell you the truth, my friend, I fear that much of what I have heard might be described by others as the effects of age."

"You believe me doddering in my old age?"

"No, far from it, indeed!"

"Well, humour me, then!"

Wishart flushed, though whether from shame or discomfiture Rob could not have guessed. "Very well, last June." He closed his eyes, recollecting. "The events of June last year arose from the matters of the previous months. In May the court of auditors assembled at Norham and began deliberations to resolve the matter of the succession. Prior to that, though, King Edward had requested that, in return for his commitment to act as arbiter, he be formally recognized as—"

"Requested?" Lord Robert interrupted. "Yon's a lily-livered word, my lord bishop. He *demanded* it, the *sine qua non* of his arbitration. He made no request. The man issued an edict."

Wishart, now every inch the senior bishop of the realm, waved the protest away. "Requested, demanded. Words to the same end. He stood firm, and with ample reason, based upon his experience with similar courts in France and Sicily when he settled the same kind of contentious matters there. An arbitrator—any arbitrator—is powerless if he lacks the authority to back his findings. Hence his claim to be recognized as overlord of Scotland—lord paramount, as he himself named it. That provided him with legitimacy as an arbitrator, beyond dispute."

"Go on, then."

"Fine. On May the tenth, the day the court proceedings began, Edward formally declared his right to the title of lord paramount in a letter, and the community of the realm then took three weeks to consider its response, submitting it on the last day of the month."

"And that response was capitulation."

"It was nothing of the kind. You know that, Robert Bruce. The community was at great pains to ensure that such a rank—as feudal overlord—could in no way affect the independence or integrity of this realm, since none but a duly crowned King of Scots could agree in full to such a commitment. No man, or gathering of men of lesser rank, had the authority to make such a decision."

"Aye."

"Aye, indeed. And Edward accepted that."

"And was made lord paramount of Scotland in spite of it. What happened next?"

"An English army moved to Norham on the third of June, to ensure the King's peace."

"The *English* King's peace."

"Norham is *in* England. Will you interrupt me at every point?"

"No. Go on, then. What next?"

"The following day, June the fourth, the competitors, yourself included, surrendered the Scottish royal castles to Edward for the protection of the realm, upon his solemn declaration that they will be returned to the royal possession within two months of the new king being chosen."

Bruce opened his lips as if to speak, but contented himself with a mere nod, and Wishart continued. "A week later, on June the eleventh, the council of Guardians resigned their positions and were then reappointed by Edward."

Lord Robert grunted. "Hmm. And two days later?"

Wishart glared at him. "June the fifth. The Guardians and nobles of Scotland swore fealty to Edward as lord paramount of Scotland. You were there. You took the oath yourself. Why are you insisting on this catechism?"

"Because I have reconsidered everything, every item you have named, in the seventeen months that have passed since then. And now it is November and I cannot believe how stupid we have all been."

"Stupid? My God, man, are you going mad indeed? Where was the stupidity? We did all that we had to, to ensure the future safety of this realm. Every man involved in the affair knew the truth of that and each one, in good faith, swore to set aside his own concerns, and those of his house, for the overall good of the realm of Scotland. Where is the stupidity in that?" Wishart waited for a count of five heartbeats, then demanded, "Answer me!"

"I'll answer you. I believe every Scots lord acted in good faith. But I believe, too, that their good faith was based upon a false premise. They acted—and I with them—out of fear, the fear of civil war. And in the grip of that fear they—we—opened a door that we might never be able to close again." The old man's brows drew together and he inhaled sharply before continuing.

"A moment ago it crossed your mind, your polite denial notwithstanding, that old age was causing me to lose my wits. Now, my mind is as firm as it ever was. But who can swear, with certainty, that the same is true today of the Plantagenet? He is a vastly changed man since the death of his wife two years ago." He quirked an eyebrow at the bishop. "We should ask ourselves, is he going mad as he grows old? Could it be dangerous to us, to Scotland? And if it is—if there is even a possibility it might be—then think of this *catechism*, as you named it, from that point of view. Do that, though, and you will be forced to concede that in May and June of last year, driven by our own fears and desperate to find a king while avoiding the threat of civil strife, we might have made a fatal error. We might have misjudged our man, counting too much on his former reputation and failing to see what he might have become in recent times."

Again the bishop waved him away. "Too many mights and maybes, Robert. Too much speculation and too little certainty."

Lord Robert hawked and leaned forward to spit into the fire, then wiped his lips with the back of his wrist. "Aye. Well then," he growled, "let us speak of certainties. It is a certainty that Edward Plantagenet is a king above and beyond all else. He revels in statecraft and there is no other king like him in all of Christendom, save perhaps Philip of France, of whom I know little—and little of that is good. With the sole exception of his Queen, Eleanor, nothing in Edward Plantagenet's life has ever been more important than his kingdom—his realm of England. Nothing at all. And Eleanor's was the only warning voice that held him in check. She ruled him with love and kept his vices manageable. She curbed his lust for power, his princely choler, intemperance, and regal impatience. She guarded him against his own lack of restraint throughout his life, advised him on matters of state. And he took heed of her for thirty years and more. But now Eleanor is dead, and he is grown more choleric, more impatient and irascible with every day that has passed. Those are certainties, widely observed.

"It is a certainty, as well, that his realm is wealthy and yet he never has enough money to conduct his wars and keep his armies paid and equipped. His barons are fractious and tight fisted not only with their money but with their men and their feudal service to the Crown. Edward had no need to conquer Wales and add it to England. To subdue it and control its rebels, yes, and to impose his peace upon it. But to make it part of England's realm? The Welsh are Welsh. They have never been English and never will be. But Edward needed the gold, the rents and revenue his rule of Wales could command. He needed the men and the resources of the Welsh archers, to use as a threat against his own barons. And so he is now building massive new stone castles throughout Wales—at Caernarfon, Conwy, Harlech, and Beaumaris, more of them at one time than ever before in history—to cow the people there and keep them in subservience and fear. Those are *certainties*, my lord bishop."

He did not wait for Wishart to respond. "And to this man, this King, I fear we may have made a gift of Scotland, to add to Wales and swell the bulk of his Crown. We have acknowledged him as overlord of Scotland. Our highest nobles have resigned their positions as Guardians of the realm to him and then accepted those same positions back from his hand as that same overlord. *Paramount*, Robert—we named him lord *paramount* of this realm. Think of what that means, or could be held to mean. His English garrisons now control our royal Scottish castles—Edinburgh, Stirling, Roxburgh, and all the others. They *hold* them. For another certainty they say they hold them for our own protection—against ourselves— but they man our castles this day, and all we can do is pray they will return them to us as they promised. We have placed ourselves in Edward Plantagenet's hands and now we are forced to hope and pray that he will do his best for us with no consideration of his own desires and wishes. That, too, is a certainty, and it frightens me."

Wishart mulled that over for some time before raising his head again. "And you believe he has selected Balliol for hitherto unsuspected reasons of his own, reasons that bode ill for this realm?"

"He had two options open to him—to elect a man he could influence and control to his own ends, or to pick one whom he knew would never submit to being bullied."

Another long pause followed that before Wishart shook his head. "That is your own opinion, Robert, and not without bias."

Lord Robert shrugged. "Perhaps, but it's not without logic, either. Of the two options, he chose the former."

"And Balliol will be a feckless king, you fear. On what basis—?"

"No, my lord bishop, I do not fear that. I know it. All my fear now is for this realm of ours. I believe Edward covets this land, as another jewel for his crown, like Wales. He had his goal achieved, if you'll but think of it, when his son was to wed our new young Queen. But when the lass died, his plans died with her, and Edward Plantagenet does not tolerate denial of his wishes, even when God's own hand is evidenced. You watch—he will seek now to govern through John Balliol."

"To *govern*? This realm? Do you have any concept of how mad that sounds, my friend?"

"Aye, Robert, that I do. But the madness is not mine. The madness is that no one else in Scotland cares to—or dares to—see the truth of it." He glanced at his son and Rob. "Look at these two, listening without a word to say. They and I have argued loud and long on every aspect of this thing and I was hard put to win them to my view. Now, though, they believe me, at least sufficiently to trust that I will not lead them into danger henceforth."

"Hmm. So what *will* you do?"

Lord Robert thumped a fist into his open hand. "I will do my duty to the realm and I will recognize Balliol as the rightful, anointed King of Scots, once he is crowned. But Edward of England is my feudal overlord by right, and I will do anything on his behalf that he legally requires of me as his loyal vassal. You heard what I told you of the need I see to keep him honest by directing the eyes of the world upon his behaviour. To do that, and to maintain my feudal duty to him, I will remain close to him, as will my son and grandson. Young Robert's presence in England will provide us with a listening post. Edward thinks highly of him, and I believe that esteem might serve us well in the days ahead." He stopped and cleared his throat. "Your part, old friend, will be to ensure that the other powers in this realm—the community of which you are so proud—work together diligently to ensure we do not suffer at Edward's hands in the time ahead. Every man of them, magnates and mormaers and the earls and nobles of the land, must work with Church and commons to ensure the realm's welfare comes first, ahead of their own. Will you do that?"

The bishop pursed his lips and tilted his head to one side, gazing back at Lord Robert through narrowed eyes. "Aye," he murmured eventually. "I will. And I'll be watching closely from now on, for I confess you've given me much to think about. And so ... Supposing for the moment you alone, in all of Scotland, have the right of this, how much time is left to us, think you?"

Lord Robert shrugged. "Years, but not many. Five years, perhaps six. Edward himself will see to that. He's growing old like the rest of us."

"But no more than that? Six years?"

"No, no more. Balliol will have shown his weakness by then, or Edward will have shown his strength to the same effect. The magnates will not tolerate it, no matter which be true, and there will be trouble. But what about you and Mother Church? What will you do if you see things moving as I predict?"

Wishart sniffed, and then in a subdued voice he responded, "We will do what we have to do for the protection of the realm and its community."

Rob noted the words and the tone of them but had little time to think more of it at the time, for Lord Robert rose to his feet immediately.

"Grand," he said. "That's what I wanted to hear. And now we must—I must—make haste. There's much to do before tomorrow."

He called for Bellow, and from the moment the factor came in, all was urgent activity. The talking had all apparently been done, and the arrangements to flesh it out and make it real would be set in place thereafter.

# CHAPTER TWELVE

# SILVER SPURS

Rob Bruce would remember that month, November of 1292, because it was the second consecutive month in which his life changed entirely, transforming him, when he looked back on it, into another creature altogether, enabling him to see that his first eighteen years had been the caterpillar stage, the formative and vulnerable years that had moulded him towards manhood and had ended with the death of his mother in October. November, and the months that followed hard on its heels, on the other hand, encased him in the drab and protective shell of a chrysalis, enabling him to stay hidden in plain sight and to remain relatively insignificant during the following four years, while steadily increasing storms and political upheavals threatened to bring the free kingdom of Scotland to an ignominious end.

On the seventh day of the month, Robert Bruce, Lord of Annandale, one of Scotland's greatest and most active magnates for more than half a century, formally renounced his claim to the Crown of Scotland on the grounds of advanced age. At the same time he transferred to his son, Robert Bruce, the sixth of his name, Earl of Carrick, and to his heirs the right to pursue that claim in future. He presented himself in person to Edward of England in Norham Castle that day, renewing his feudal oath of loyalty and fealty to the monarch as a vassal of the English Crown, beholden to Edward for the vast territories he held there at the King's pleasure. Edward, despite his surprise at this unanticipated turn of events, was mollified by the dignity and propriety of the veteran lord's behaviour and deigned to accept the Bruce capitulation, assuring Lord Robert that his lands in England would continue to be at his disposal whenever he so wished.

Two days later, in an informal ceremony that was duly witnessed by a number of distinguished observers, the younger Robert Bruce, now the legitimate Lord of Annandale, resigned his own title to the earldom of Carrick in favour of his son Robert, the seventh consecutive Bruce of that name.

For Rob, that day brought some of his life's most enduring memories, uniquely his own, though they involved his grandfather Lord Robert.

The first of them began in the late afternoon of the previous day, when Rob presented himself, slightly out of breath, at the den in answer to a summons from Lord Robert. He stopped at the threshold, though, seeing that his grandfather had company and wondering if he should interrupt, but as he hovered there the patriarch looked up and beckoned him inside, and the three churchmen he had been speaking with all turned to look at Rob. He recognized one of them as the young priest he had last seen accompanying Bishop Wishart, less than a week earlier, but he had seen neither of the other men before. His grandfather quickly made all three known to him.

The young priest was Father William Lamberton, of Glasgow Cathedral. He was here representing Bishop Wishart, who was detained in Norham, Lord Robert explained. The delegation of authority to represent a senior bishop was not idly bestowed, and Rob knew the young priest must have earned Bishop Wishart's trust, but Lamberton looked barely older than Rob himself. The other two men were both mitred abbots, John de Morel of Jedburgh Abbey and Robert de Selkirk of Melrose Abbey, two of the most august religious houses in the realm.

When they had all exchanged solemn greetings, Lord Robert explained that their purpose here, at his personal invitation, was to escort Rob through the rituals of the knightly vigil, which he would undertake immediately. He would go with the visitors directly to a private chamber where they would lead him through the steps of ritual bathing and purification before dressing him in the full suit of heraldic armour that had been made for him three months before, in preparation for his knighthood ceremony in England that was then postponed. Rob was justifiably proud of that armour, for it was a masterpiece tailored in steel and mail to fit him perfectly, but he had never worn it since the day he had taken delivery of it from the English master armourer who had made it for him. Tradition, and superstition, demanded that it must not be worn until his knightly initiation. Now he would dress in it and be conducted by the three churchmen to Lochmaben's private chapel at nightfall, and there he would spend the night as a supplicant, standing before the altar in ritual prayer and supervised at all times by one of the invigilating clerics, beseeching God to grant him the strength of character he would require to be a worthy, devout, and dedicated knight.

The next morning, moving as though in a dream from lack of sleep, Rob followed the robed trio of clerics in a haze of incense as they led him to Lochmaben's main hall, into the presence of the two Lords of Annandale, past and present, and the close-packed assembly of the Annandale knights with whom he had marched to Perth in his grandfather's train and who called themselves the lairds of Lochmaben. It was an all-male gathering, but as he looked about him, slightly bewildered, Rob saw his mother's face in his mind's eye, wearing a tremulous but proud smile and hovering between him and the armoured ranks facing him. He was aware of kneeling between the two abbots, with the bishop's young representative standing attentively at his back, and hearing the words his grand-father pronounced over him, but they barely penetrated his mind until a sharp double blow, once on each shoulder, snapped him back to reality and Lord Robert's voice, commanding now, barked out, "Rise up, Sir Robert Bruce, knight of Turnberry."

Rob rose, assisted by the abbots on either side of him, and was immediately surrounded by the assembled knights, all pummelling his back and shoulders and shouting in congratulation, welcoming him for the first time as an equal. When he could win free of them, he moved to embrace his father, whose eyes, he saw with astonishment, were brimming with tears, and then he turned to his grandfather, who awaited him with open arms. The fierce old warrior hugged him close for long moments, cuirass to cuirass, then held him at arm's length.

"Your father has a gift for you," he said, then beckoned Alan Bellow, who had been awaiting the signal and now stepped forward smartly, holding out a crimson cushion on which rested a beautifully crafted pair of ornate silver spurs. Earl Robert picked them up, one in each hand, and held them out to Rob. "You'll wear these from now on," he said, smiling through eyes that were still moist. "But you'll have to learn how to put them on yourself, later … For the rest, well, now that you're to be an earl, you'll need a sword befitting your rank."

He gestured with an open hand towards his own father, and Lord Robert slipped his thumb under the heavy leather sword belt that hung across his chest and shrugged it over his head, his left hand grasping the thick scabbard of the enormous sword it held. He had sheathed the weapon after knighting Rob, but now he seized the hilt and bared the blade again, holding the sword up for all to see. It was a massive thing, its hilt made from solid steel and bound with wire-wrapped rawhide, and its great, broad blade reflected the lights that filled the hall, silencing every man there. Lord Robert hefted it, then stabbed it upward, thrusting it high above his head and gazing up at its gleaming point.

"It's no' a delicate thing," he said to Rob in Scots, speaking loudly enough for everyone to hear. "Nor is it fancy. But men heed it and it has served me well for nigh fifty year and more." He brought his arm down and held the blade horizontally across his body, bracing it with his left forearm and gazing down at it as he continued speaking. "Afore that, though, it belonged to your great-great-grandsire on your grandmother's side, William the Marshal of England himself, master-at-arms and teacher to King Richard o' the Lion Heart." He slid the long blade back into its sheath and held it out hilt-first to Rob. "I'm near too old to lift it now, never mind swing it, but if I'm any judge o' what I saw the other day between you and Rab Elliot, it should serve you well, too. Wear it wi' pride,

Sir Robert Bruce. An' should you e'er hae cause to swing it in earnest, swing it hard and clean."

Speechless, and uncaring that his eyes were blurred with sudden tears, Rob tucked his new silver spurs awkwardly beneath his left arm and reached out to take the massive weapon in his right hand, feeling the solid weight of it threaten to drag his arm down as his grandfather released it. He tensed in time and shifted his grip, raising the sword to eye level with both hands on the scabbard, clamping his left arm hard against the suddenly superfluous spurs and holding the huge sword hilt uppermost like a cross between himself and the old man. He swallowed hard, forcing his tongue to form the words, and whispered, "I will, my lord. So help me God."

The deep hush in the chamber lasted five heartbeats before the hall erupted again with shouts of approval.

The day proceeded from that point as planned, but much of what was said and done went over Rob's head, for it was all policy and ritual and it held no further surprises for him. He heard his father's announcement of his resignation of the earldom and the succession of Rob himself as Earl of Carrick, and he smiled in acceptance of the applause of the gathering, but for some time he had accepted that as being important but already in hand. Far more important to him was the solid weight of metal hanging from the wide, supple, hundred-year-old belt slung across his chest. He could hardly wait to take it out to the training yard, but hours were to elapse before he could find an opportunity to leave.

When the ceremonies and speeches were at last all over and the assembled throng had settled in to eat and drink, Rob whispered an excuse to his grandfather, telling him what he wished to do, and the old man gave him leave, pointing out that the November afternoon was fading quickly and he had best make haste. Impatiently aware of the truth of that, Rob made his way unobtrusively to the back of the hall, still clutching his new spurs, and slipped quietly out, making his way directly to the training yard just inside the main gates of the fortress.

The area was usually one of the busiest places in Lochmaben, but now it was deserted, for this was a day of celebration and Lord Robert had proclaimed a general holiday. But then he noticed the single fellow loitering alone in the distance, close by the open gates. The man was unknown to Rob, though, and too far away for him to take more than a passing interest.

He went directly to one of the solid oaken posts the garrison used for sword practice, chipped and slashed now by a hundred thousand hard-swung blows, and drew his new sword. But the act of unsheathing the weapon brought the new spurs back to his attention, for he still held them clamped beneath his left arm. He straightened his arm and released them to drop into his left hand, then gazed at them for a moment, knowing that he should put them on, for if he laid them on the ground by his feet he might step on them. He sheathed his sword and examined the spurs more closely, this time taking note of how beautifully made they were. He had worn spurs before, of course, but those had been simple jags—mere spikes of hammered steel. These ones were vastly different, made in the French fashion and finely worked and chased, the ends of their longish shanks split like the nocked end of an arrow and then riveted to hold ornate rowels that spun freely when he flicked them with a finger. He looked around him for a footrest, and crossed to a low log where he spent some time—too much time, a part of him insisted— fastening the things securely over his heavy boots until they were properly in place and tightly strapped, and then he straightened up to return to the training post. As soon as he began to walk, though, he found the spurs forcing him to change his gait. Their long shanks and jingling rowels altered the natural rhythm of his walk so that he had to pick each foot up and place it carefully at every step. His booted feet now felt clumsy, and although he knew he would grow used to the sensation quickly, he was aware of a need to be careful at first.

Back at the practice post, he drew his blade again and began the preliminary exercises designed to loosen his arms, shoulders, and back muscles, moving slowly and concentrating on the range of motion involved before even considering swinging the blade in earnest at the post. He settled into the rhythm quickly, enjoying the feel of his new weapon and the way it changed at once from a heavy, inert weight of metal to a living, balanced force as he swung it, and soon he was belabouring the oak post, thrilling to the solid delivery of the keen blade and the way chips flew from the dense oak at every stroke.

Seeing how quickly he was shaping twin grooves into the sides of the target, he stepped to his right and began to circle it, varying the height and angle of his blows, and as he did so he found his new spurs hampering him. His right heel lodged solidly as its spur caught on a projection and threw him off balance; he lurched, and then fell sideways, landing with a crash that knocked the wind out of him. He lay on his back for long moments, mouthing curses until he regained his breath, and then he rolled over clumsily and pushed himself back to his feet, fighting for every inch against the unaccustomed weight and unyielding constriction of his armoured legs. He retrieved his sword with difficulty, bending awkwardly from the waist and managing to grasp it with scrabbling fingers, and then straightened up, breathing heavily and wiping the dust from the blade with his hand.

The stranger he had noticed earlier was now less than ten paces away, leaning on a heavy staff and watching him with a smile on his face.

"What in Hades are you grinning at?" The words, snapped out in Latin, were out before Rob knew they were in him, but the big stranger merely straightened and held up a hand, his expression stating clearly that he had had no wish to offend. Rob continued in Scots, "Your pardon. That was … uncalled for—and ill mannered. But I felt foolish."

"No need. They're awkward things, I can see. I watched you strap them on and I could tell you werena used to them. They're very fine, forbye new … They'll be silver, then?"

"Aye," Rob said, eyeing the man.

"New silver spurs. You'll be Lord Bruce's grandson, then, I jalouse. The new knight."

Rob nodded slowly and sheathed his blade. "I am," he said, managing to summon up a one-sided, self-deprecating smile. "Robert Bruce of Carrick, newly knighted this day. Who are you? I've never seen you around here before."

"No, I've only ever been here once. I'm from Jedburgh."

"Oh! Did you come with Abbot de Morel?"

"From the abbey, you mean?" The stranger shook his head. "No. I didn't even know he was here. I'm no' really from Jedburgh. I bide close by there, though, on Bishop Wishart's estate. I arrived but an hour ago, to pay my respects to Lord Bruce, but they told me he was busy with his grandson's knighting." He shrugged enormous shoulders. "I left word that I'd wait, so here I am, and since you're here, too, and no' cloistered with your grandsire, it appears I might no' have to wait much longer."

Rob cocked his head curiously at the fellow, caught by his way of speaking. "Cloistered? Are you a knight, then? You don't look like one … " He hesitated, eyeing the stranger's clothing, which was predominantly green, then smiled. "I mean … Well, you know what I mean. And I meant no offence. But you speak like a knight."

The big fellow matched his smile. "No, I'm just a verderer—woodsman and gamekeeper for Bishop Wishart. But I've a brother who's a knight with Sir James Stewart the Guardian and I'm nephew to Sir Malcolm Wallace of Elderslie, one of Lord Bruce's tenants." He switched effortlessly to Latin. "As for my speech, I blame the monks. I went to school in Paisley for a while, at the abbey there."

Rob found himself attracted by the man's openness and his air of easy confidence, and now his eye settled on the long cylinder of heavy polished leather that hung from the other's right shoulder. "Is that a bow case?" he asked, nodding towards it. He knew it was, even without the matching bag of arrows hanging from the other shoulder, for the man's enormous chest, arms, and shoulders proclaimed him an archer.

"Aye, it is." The big fellow reached back to touch the lower part of the case with his fingertips.

"It must be English," Rob said. "Too big to be a Scots one."

"Aye, it's a longbow—yew, from the mountains of Aragon. Better than any grown in England today. But it was made here in Scotland."

"Made here?" Rob looked at the case in surprise. "By whom?"

The smile flashed again. "I made it myself, but with much help from a friend who is half Welsh and all bowyer."

"Hmm. And what about that?" Rob nodded, indicating the heavy staff that now rested comfortably beneath the big man's left arm, the thicker end lodged beneath his armpit. "It has the look of long, hard use. Did you make it, too?"

"I did, a long time ago."

"As a walking staff or a quarterstaff?"

"A quarterstaff." A quick smile flickered, showing white, even teeth. "But you look as though you'd like to try me wi' it and I fear I canna oblige you, no' when Lord Robert might send for me at any minute." Even as the big man said the words, they heard a shout, and one of the household staff came running towards them. The big man held up a hand to the messenger and looked back at Rob. "Mayhap later, though, if you are still here. I shouldna keep Lord Bruce waiting."

Rob nodded. "No, that's never a good idea. Your name is Wallace, you say?"

"It is. William Wallace of Elderslie, though most folk call me plain Will."

"Well met, then, plain Will Wallace. I hope your meeting with my grandsire goes well."

The friendly smile flickered again, accompanied by another effortless switch to Latin. "It will, Sir Robert. I came but to express my thanks to his lordship and pay my respects as I said, nothing more." He pointed down at Rob's feet. "In the meantime, should we not meet again, I wish you well with mastering those spurs." He dipped his head slightly in farewell and turned away to follow the summoner. Then, alone again, Rob drew his sword and again faced the drilling post, highly aware of his spurred boots and the need to mind his footing.

He was still hammering away at the post, though moving his feet with far more confidence, when he heard his name being called and looked up to see his grandfather approaching him through the rapidly gathering November dusk. He sheathed his sword, marvelling at how fast the light had gone.

"Should I be back in the hall, sir?" he asked.

"What? Oh, no, no. It's gey smoky in there and I needed some fresh air, so I thought I'd come and see how you're getting along." He glanced down at Rob's feet.

Rob looked down himself and grinned. "Ah, those … I'm growing used to them, my lord, though they were … awkward, at first. Did your guest tell you about me falling on my arse?"

Lord Robert blinked at him. "Guest? What guest are you talking about?"

"The forester. Wallace, I think his name was."

"Oh, him. You met him, then. No, he never said a word. You fell down?"

"Tripped over my spurs and he was watching. Is he gone already?"

"No, he's getting something to eat. He'll probably stay in the stables tonight and head home tomorrow. What did you think of him?" He tilted his head sideways.

Rob shrugged. "I liked him, what I saw of him. We spoke for a little while until your man came to fetch him. Who is he?"

"A fine young man who almost came to grief over a woman. Was falsely accused o' a crime by a rival. Fortunately Wishart, who thinks highly of him, caught wind of it. He asked some questions and discovered a plot to have young Wallace arrested and hanged for slaughtering a herd of my deer. At the time the deed was done, though, I was in Glasgow myself and met Wallace there having dealings with the bishop, so it wasna possible for him to have done what he was accused o'. Turned out to be plain jealousy over some young woman in Ayr, and the man who accused him—one of my own woodsmen—had suborned another forester to lie under oath that he had seen Wallace do the killing. Parcel of lies from start to finish, but it would have served his ends had I not met young Wallace in Glasgow when he was supposedly down here slaughtering my beasts."

"So what did you do, Grandfather?"

"What would you expect me to do? The miscreant committed crimes while in my employ, black crimes that could have besmirched my name for hanging an innocent man had things turned out otherwise, and then he lied to me, bare-faced. I hanged him on two counts—for the attempted murder o' young Wallace and the probable murder o' his perjured witness, who vanished wi'out trace the day young Wallace was accused."

"He said he'd come to thank you and to pay his respects, but he mentioned nothing of what had happened."

"Aye, well … That's done with now. How are you finding the sword?"

Rob grinned and raised his arm stiffly and theatrically before dropping his hand to the hilt at his waist. "Heavy," he said.

"Aye, you'll grow used to it. Years of practice, lad, that's all it will take, and you have years ahead of you—fifty o' them at least, if you take after me." He looked back towards the lowering bulk of the dusk-dark buildings behind them. "I should be getting back," he said. "Come with me. It will do you no harm to mix wi' my folk, let them gauge your mettle. They've all had a dram or two by now, so they'll be eager to take your measure now that ye outrank them all. But tonight, when all is quiet again, we should talk more, you and I. I have things to tell you."

Rob hesitated, but then he nodded. "Of course, Grandfather. I'll come and find you after everything is quiet. You'll be in the den?"

"Where else would I be at that time of night? Now come away inside and let folk meet the new Earl of Carrick. But don't be gulled into staying too long. Ye've had no sleep since the night before last and I need ye to be sharp-eyed when we talk later. If ye're in bed

within the hour ye'll have had a good five or six hours of rest by
midnight."

He began to walk back towards the main hall, and as Rob fell
into step beside him he glanced sideways at his grandson, one
eyebrow twitching. "D'ye feel like an earl yet?"

"I've no idea, sir," the younger Bruce said quietly. "How is an
earl supposed to feel?"

That earned him a smile. "Humble at first," the old lord said.
"The arrogance comes later."

# CHAPTER THIRTEEN

# THE DANGERS OF IDEAS

It was after midnight by the time Lord Robert brought a horn cup of steaming toddy to where Rob sat in front of the glowing brazier, gazing into the coals. Rob straightened up and took the proffered cup with a word of thanks, reflecting briefly that since they'd last sat together like this, he had come to relish the fiery drink.

His grandfather angled the chair beside Rob slightly, so that he could look at him as they spoke, then settled into it. He raised his cup in a silent toast before sipping from it appreciatively and resting it on his knee. "Well," he said. "It's been a while since we two sat and talked like this."

A while indeed, Rob thought. Two years, in fact. He hitched around and glanced at the closed door. "Is my father not coming to join us?"

"No, he's been abed these two hours. How is he doing these days?"

Rob sipped his toddy slowly, rolling the tangy heat around his tongue and enjoying the sensation of warmth and comfort offered by his padded chair and the lively fire. He had slept well for several hours and now felt strong and refreshed.

"Better," he said finally. "He's better. He was always quiet, but now he's even more so. Still mourning Mam, I suppose, even now that a month and more has passed. He scarce speaks now unless he has to, but when he *needs* to speak or act, he does so as he did today, confidently, with strength and conviction. I believe he's improving with every day that passes, and so do the others—Isabel, Nigel, all the rest."

The old man nodded. "That's good to hear. I think the same. He's mending rapidly. Would to God that everything else besetting our house were doing as well."

"What do you mean, sir? Is there word from Norham?"

"No, not yet, but it will come soon, now that I've removed myself from the debate."

"And what will we do then?"

Lord Robert sipped from his cup again before responding. "What do *you* think we should do, my lord earl?"

Rob blinked, hearing his title used casually for the first time. "I … I don't know, Grandfather. Will we attend the coronation?" He stopped, frowning. "I suppose we'll have to, will we not?"

"No, we will not." Lord Robert smiled crookedly, seeing the surprise in his grandson's eyes. "They'll place the crown on Balliol's head whether we are there or not, lad, and I see no benefit in travelling all the way to Scone merely to watch the smiles of victory on every Comyn face in Scotland. By the time they do crown him, though—and they'll waste no time—I'll be in England and so will you. Your father might remain here for a time, but he'll have much to do in Turnberry, tending to the family and making arrangements for their future."

"What kind of arrangements?"

"The kind that must always be foremost in a father's mind, and especially so after the loss of his wife. But we'll come back to that, for we hae more important things to speak of right now. Remind me of it later, though, if I forget. Now, let's deal wi' Scone first, and the coronation. It will be a great celebration, and rightly so, for it will give this land a visible head again. We've needed a king in Scotland these six years now and not everyone believed that king should be a Bruce. The court at Norham has been thorough and its judgment long awaited by everyone. When Balliol's succession is announced none will question it, especially in the light of my withdrawal of my own claim."

"But won't our absence there be noted?"

"Aye, and remarked upon, ye may be sure o' that. But we will have legitimate reasons for being absent, no matter what the old wives make of it. I'll be withdrawing to my new life as plain Sir Robert Bruce of Writtle in Essex and you'll be accompanying me as my deputy, to learn at first-hand how I will live there and make do." He raised a hand. "Mind you, I'm no' saying we'll no' swear allegiance to the new king. We will eventually—we'll hae no choice. But better to do it later, when the crowds are all dispersed. Plenty o' time then. And it will be safer."

There was the merest suggestion of a hesitation before that last word, and Rob seized on it. "Safer, sir? How so? I can hardly think there might be physical danger in attending the coronation. More risk in not being there, I think, and having our absence noticed."

The patriarch's lips twitched wryly. "That's no' the kind o' safety I was talking about. For the moment, think of this: gin you were to attend the Scone affair, you would be forced to swear allegiance then and there, in front o' all the eyes of Scotland. You'd be seen to bend the knee to Balliol at the outset, and that might no' be to your advantage further down the road."

Rob's eyes again betrayed his puzzlement.

"Edward will be there in Scone, lad, taking note of how things unfold, and if my suspicions are anywhere near correct, he'll be marking how many men kneel to Balliol and how keen they are to do it. He'll be watching with great care to see whom he can mark among his friends and enemies there. Who will be apt to accept whatever he might do and who is likely to prove troublesome in future. For that alone I'd have you far from there and safely neutral in England. I have no wish to see you placed on either of those lists."

"But … But surely Edward wouldn't—"

"No, surely Edward *would*. And he *will*. Mark me, boy, and pay heed. You'll serve all o' us Bruces well by being absent from that place. D'you hear what I am saying?"

"Aye, Gransser, I do. But I'm still not sure I understand all of it."

"No, and how could you?" The patriarch's voice was a low growl. "I havena told you all of it yet. But I will now. At least, I'll try to … " He sat straighter, his voice becoming stronger. "Pour us some more toddy. The water's still hot and there's enough for two more. Then let me think about this, for in truth I'm no' quite sure what I want to say to you."

His grandfather sat squinting into the fire as Rob spooned the remaining honeyed spirits into the two cups and fetched the heavy iron kettle from where it simmered over the brazier's coals.

"I'm an old man," Lord Robert said quietly, "but I fear you might think me a daft old man when I try to say what's in my mind, for I'm going to talk of things I never even considered until recently and I'm no' sure I can even find the words to explain what I'm thinking … I would like to think, having lived as long as I have, that I have learnt to look at life and draw some truths from what I've seen."

"It's called wisdom, my lord," Rob said quietly, smiling.

The patriarch shook his head vehemently. "No, it's no' wisdom. It's experience," he said, his Scots pronunciation growing more assertive. "Or mair like, it's the insight that comes wi' experience. Wisdom's no' necessarily the result o' old age. Last night, while you were standing your vigil in the chapel, I spent a long time talking to yon young priest, Lamberton. Now there's a clever man, Robert, and I'd wager he's less than half a decade older than you. That yin is wise beyond his years and has a canny head on his shoulders. He'd have to have, to impress Robert Wishart the way he has at sich a young age." He half smiled. "Rab Wishart might no' be easy to talk wi', now that he's Bishop o' Glasgow, but he wasna always so straight-faced. Truth to tell, though, he never could stomach fools, and he's always had a keen eye for seein' talent in others. Young Lamberton will go far, I jalouse, wi' auld Rab as his mentor."

"What did he and you talk about?"

"Oh, this and that. I'll tell you about it later, but right now I want to speak my thoughts and have you sit there and listen carefully. Will ye do that?"

"Of course I will, sir."

"There's no 'of course' about it. Young men seldom pay attention to the haverings of old ones. They might *seem* to be listening, sitting there and bobbin' their heads frae time to time, but most o' the time their thoughts are miles away, thinkin' o' the kind o' things that young men think important. And I know how true that is, for I can remember being young mysel' and doin' exactly that … "

"I will listen, Gransser, I promise."

"Fine, then. It's important that you hear these … these things, even should you never have to act on them. They shook me when I first heard them. They were … worrisome, and persistent, wouldna go away and leave me to myself … Tell me," he asked, "are you familiar wi' the ancients, folk like Aristotle and Plato?"

"A little, sir. I've heard of them. Father Ninian used to talk about them. Thinkers, he called them, and another word, Greek, I think. Philosophers."

"Aye, that's it, 'philosophers.' It means lovers o' wisdom in Greek, but it's just another word for men who love *ideas*, talking about them and debating them. Dangerous men, philosophers, for the thoughts they think are never gi'en to ordinary men—ideas can be calamitous, and too often they contain the seeds of destruction."

"But what on earth can they destroy? They're but ideas, no more than notions. They're not *real*."

"Not so. They're real, Grandson. Make no mistake on that." Lord Robert frowned slightly. "And if they're profound ideas, new ideas, and if the men who dream them make them work, they spread to others and grow in the spreading. And once that happens, they bring changes, as sure as the sun brings daylight. Changes in the way folk think and behave. The old ideas and ways of doing things die, making way for the new. Believe me, Grandson, that is the way the world works. And I've been struggling with some new ideas these past few months, as I said." He stopped abruptly, looking vaguely alarmed as a new thought occurred to him. "None of them are *mine*, mind you. Don't go thinking that. I'm no great dreamer of new ideas. But they're there, for all that, all around us, waiting to be seen and believed by ordinary folk."

"Forgive me, sir, but I don't know what you're talking about."

"I'm talking about this world we live in now, about duties and responsibilities and loyalties, all the touchstone things that keep us anchored in our daily lives."

"And you think they're changing, all those things?"

"I don't *think* it. I *know* it. I believe it—canna deny the truth o' it. I've been thinking about it for months now, since a talk I had with Rob Wishart when I was last in Glasgow. It was he who first brought up the notion of a changing world, of our whole *system* changing, throughout Christendom—and him a bishop! I thought at first that he was havering. But young Lamberton had just come back from France after living there for near two years, and Wishart brought him in that night to talk to me about the things he had seen and heard over there, the things he'd learned.

"We talked long into that night, about a wheen o' things. By the time I left to come home a few days later, my head was spinning, and I've scarce had a minute's peace since. Ideas, Grandson. They can drive you mad, defying your belief and everything you had held to be common sense." He nodded, sombrely, letting the pause stretch. "And so tonight I thought to pass them on to you. You've your whole life in front of you, whereas I'm old and nearly done. You should be aware of what's happening in the world out there beyond our doors, and able to think about it all in times ahead. What's out there willna *stay* out there. These new ideas will come here, whether we will it or no'. And no' just here to Scotland. They'll spread everywhere."

"That sounds … terrifying, Gransser."

The old man barked a laugh. "Aye, I know. And daft as well, eh? I can see it in your face. You're frettin' for my wits." The laughter vanished as quickly as it had erupted. "I swear to you, Robert, I'm no' mad, nor am I lying. I told you before, the Bruce doesna deal in lies. Yet I can see you're having difficulty grasping what I'm talking about. Let me help. Young Lamberton gave me an example o' the way these ideas have the power to change things."

Lord Robert nibbled his upper lip between his teeth for a few moments, then emptied his cup in one great swallow. "Our Lord and Saviour, Jesus the Christ. An ordinary man—forbye bein' the Son of God, of course. But an ordinary man none the less, the scriptures tell us. A carpenter, from a wee village in Galilee. But he had an idea the like o' which no one had ever heard. He believed in mercy, in compassion and forgiveness, talked o' loving his enemies and turning the other cheek to them that struck him, talked about the all-forgiving mercy o' a single God to *all* men, no' just his own kind, the Jews, who looked down on everybody else and called themselves God's chosen. And, mark you, this was a time when there was no such thing as mercy or compassion in the world. Rome ruled the world then. Rome *was* the world and showed no mercy to anyone, anywhere. Roman law was brutal—oppressive and all-powerful, and anybody who dared to defy it was quickly dealt wi', usually by killing but sometimes wi' a floggin' that would leave a man unfit to work and live, or wi' a lifetime of hard labour in the mines or as a galley slave.

"And then along comes this one man, this carpenter, who talks about forgiving our persecutors and befriendin' foreigners, about a better life in a perfect world after death in this one. Mad ideas, every one o' them. Laughable. But he set the example and others began to follow him and to believe in what he was telling them. The Romans killed him eventually—they had to—but his ideas spread and grew sacred to ordinary folk everywhere who found a message o' hope in what he had preached. And his idea, o' simple love and *hope*, changed the whole world. Even the Emperor Constantine became a Christian. And Rome collapsed, rotten from the inside out. But long before it did, Roman soldiers everywhere was swearin' their oath o' loyalty to the Empire on the Christian cross, and the Christian Church had brought the eternal light that is hope to common folk everywhere. An idea, Robert, one man's idea, more powerful than kings or emperors. For once an idea has taken root, nothing, no power on earth, can destroy it or erase it from men's minds."

Rob sat quiet for a long time, absorbing what his grandfather had said, and then he stooped and set down his empty cup, having no memory of drinking the contents.

"I think I'm beginning to see why you're concerned, sir. What was this new idea the bishop and Lamberton revealed to you?"

The patriarch sat up straighter. "It wasna just the one, lad. They had several. A wheen o' them, but taken thegither they were … 'frightening' is the word that's in my mind, and that's no' a common word for me but it's the right one, for they fit frighteningly thegither and they suggest a future that none o' us could imagine."

"Like what, Gransser?"

Lord Robert looked at him, smiling faintly. "Oh, am I bein' too slow for you? Ah well, I suppose I can't expect a young man to sit there bobbin' his head much longer." He sniffed. "Let's start, then, with a few ideas about kings—an old idea about divine right and a new idea about nation-states. You've been in England, at Edward's court, so you know there is no love between him and young Philip of France. The two of them will go to war wi' each other o'er this Gascony dispute, sooner or later."

"Probably." The younger Bruce nodded judiciously. He was well aware, through the teachings of his erudite religious tutors, of King Edward's troubles with his English barons over the ruinous costs of maintaining and policing his rebellious Duchy of Gascony. Political discord was brewing as the contentious Gascon nobles made repeated appeals to the French King to come to their aid against the intolerable neglect of their absentee English duke.

Lord Robert was watching him with one eyebrow cocked. "Aye, but have you any knowledge of what Philip is attempting to do wi' France itself?"

"No, sir." Rob shook his head slowly, knitting his brows slightly. "I know little of him other than that he is the King of France, and that he might be tempted to risk Edward's wrath and intervene in Gascony for his own ends. I know, too, that he was very young when he was crowned five years ago and is comely enough to be called Le Bel—the Fair."

"Aye, and he's a clever young man, for a king. He's versed in law, I'm told, and surrounds himself with lawyers—has done so ever since before he took the crown. And he's determined to finish the job his father left undone—the task of making France what he wills it to be. Philip has proven to be a hungry king and he grows ever greedier. Young as he is, he has a dream, you see. An idea. And that idea underlies his quarrels with Edward." He saw his grandson's frown. "He's a Capet, lad, and that means that, like his forebears, he believes he rules France by divine right, wi' the direct will and blessings of God Himself. That's a frightening thing, to have such certitude." He cleared his throat with a deep, harrumphing cough. "Father Lamberton told me all about it in Glasgow, and what he had to say made me sit up and listen. France was aey a tiny kingdom in truth, a wee stretch of land along the river Seine from the coast to Paris, held these two hundred years and more by the family Capet, who trace their ancestry to Charlemagne and have aey believed, as I said, that God Himself has given them the right to rule in His name, and no mere man, be he king or even pope, can dictate to them. That makes them hard to deal wi', of course.

"Philip is the fourth of his name, and he is using lawyers and the law, manipulating men and words and history, to extend his kingdom. His father started it, but Philip works far harder at it, to bring the great duchies into his domain in much the same way that Edward took Wales and Man to add to England's realm. Now Anjou, Burgundy and Poitou, Navarre and Champagne and the Languedoc, along wi' others, are all set to become parts of *France*, and young Philip has his eye on Edward's own duchies—no' just Gascony but Aquitaine too. This man dreams of a single, united French kingdom, all the great duchies under one Crown—his own. He calls his dream a nation-state, a single country ruled by a central government wi' him as the sole head, ordained by God Himsel'. He covets all the riches of what was once Roman Gaul—all the taxes, all the revenues, and all the wealth his, by divine right. And Lamberton says he is likely to achieve it."

Rob raised his eyebrows. "Then we should wish him well of it. As you say, Gransser, he's a far-off king, no threat to us."

"You think so? Then did ye no' hear what I said about a central government wi' him the sole head? What about his barons and earls, and the dukes of the great provinces? Gin he has his way, they'll be reduced to impotence. And rebel though they probably will, there'll be little they can do about it, because Philip has very cleverly sold his idea to the common folk—the same folk who have been abused by the great ducal families for hundreds of years. The common people's loyalties are now sworn to the young King himself, Lamberton says. The French folk love him, all o' them, for what they think he offers them, and they canna see that there's little about the man himself to love … And you are frowning again because you canna see what I mean." He stared hard at his grandson, his eyes narrowing with the intensity of his need to convince the younger man.

"Think about it, Robert, and think like a priest, if you can, seeing the *whole* and no' just the glitter o' it. This King in France is in the act of destroying the very system that has supported Christendom since soon after the Romans left. *Our* system! Clerics and scholars call it the *feudal* system because it is based entirely on lands distrib-uted and held *en feu*—in fee, on trust, wi' every man dependent for his livelihood upon the man closest in rank above him, frae common peasants all the way up to the King himself, and wi' feudal obliga-tions—rents and taxation—working down through the same chain of duty and responsibilities.

"Now, with his lawyers fashioning his new nation-state, Philip is tellin' the folk that every man need be loyal only to himself and to the King, providing he pays his taxes directly to the royal coffers when they come due. He wants to weaken his nobles, by dispos-sessing them and taking away the livelihood that's sustained them for hundreds o' years—the feudal loyalty of their vassals. He wants to make them dependent on the Crown alone for their freedoms and liberties. That means the days o' the great feudal nobles over there are coming to an end, as sure as there's down on a goose."

Rob dipped his head. "And the same thing could happen here, is what you're saying ..." He paused. "Forgive me if I disagree, Grandfather, but I don't think it could. It might work in France, for Philip, but it won't work here, if only because we have none of their great, independent duchies."

"Oh, is that what you think?" Lord Robert's jaw tightened pugnaciously. "Well, *you'll* forgive *me* for saying so, but you think *that* because you're fifty years younger than I am, a bairn wi' eyes that are no' yet fully open. No great feudal duchies here, you say? And you the heir to one o' the greatest? What about Wales, then? Or the Isle of Man? For that matter, what of our Scotland? What about the great English dukedoms and baronies, Kent and Hereford, Essex and Cumberland, Norfolk and Northumberland, whose barons are so rich and puissant that they are a constant goad in Edward's side?"

"What about them? Edward is no Philip, Grandfather. He is King of England, yes, but not by divine right."

"Rubbish!" It was the first time the old man had raised his voice that night, and Rob stared at him, as the patriarch fought to restrain his temper. "Look, lad, I asked you to think, but you're no' *seeing* what I'm telling you. I'm no' talking about the Second Coming o' Christ. I'm talking about reality—today and in your lifetime. Philip's task will soon be done. He's scarce five years older than you but he's been King for that long and his dream is taking shape, and as long as he can see that, he'll never let go of it. He'll hae it done before he dies, you wait and see. A single, united French kingdom, massive and controlled by him alone, his every wish and whim carried out by willing lackeys backed by modern armies. His word will be law everywhere, in every duchy, every province, every town and city of a kingdom ten, twenty, fifty times larger than his ancestors controlled. It is beggaring him right now, from what I have heard—he owes more to the Temple bankers than his entire lands are worth—but once he succeeds, once it's all his beyond dispute, he'll be the wealthiest king in all Christendom and no one— *nobody*—will be able to gainsay him. His new nation-state, wi' its centralized control an' unimaginable wealth, will be invincible."

He fell quiet for a moment, breathing heavily, and then continued. "Now let me ask you this. Do you believe the other kings o' Christendom are ignorant o' what he is tryin' to do? Do you believe they're no' watching him like hawks? And do you believe they're no' envious o' what he hopes to achieve? There's no' a single one of them, includin' Edward Plantagenet, who isn't chafin' under the reins his barons place on him. No' one of them who isna close to beggary. So ask yourself, boy. Gin he succeeds and takes control o' everything, how long will it be, think ye, before other kings try to copy him wi' their own nation-states? And when they do, where will that lead?"

A long pause, and then Rob whispered, "War. Wars everywhere."

"Aye, war, and confusion and destruction throughout the length and breadth o' Christendom. War until Hell willna hold all the dead men. What is it? Ye're chewin' at something."

"*Ideas* … You said there were a number of ideas that were frightening *together*, but you've only spoken of the one, Philip's idea for his new France. What are the others?" Rob was talking to the old man as an equal now, speaking as a man with problems on his mind, and if his grandfather noticed it at all he paid it no attention, choosing to respond in kind.

"Aye, there are others. There's a Scots priest in England, a Franciscan in a place called Oxford, who is highly thought of for his scholarship, even though he, too, is no' much older than you are. He'd be the same age as Lamberton, I jalouse. His name is John Duns, and he's a theologian and a philosopher, and a teacher of both. They call him Duns the Scot—Duns Scotus. He went to France, to Paris, last year, to debate wi' the scholars there, and Lamberton was there at the time and spoke with him often. Often enough, in fact, to have come to think o' him as havin' the finest mind he's ever encountered. And comin' frae Lamberton, that's no small praise.

"Anyway, this Duns was raised hereabouts, on the Borders, and he's fierce proud o' bein' what he is, a Scot. But he's a deep thinker, too, and some o' the things he's thinkin' nowadays would earn him no gratitude from Edward o' England—or from me, were I king, come to think of it. John Duns has some strong views on freedoms, Lamberton tells me—freedom o' will and freedom o' conscience and the freedom o' a people to choose their own rulers—the freedom and responsibility, in fact, of the community of Scotland to appoint their own kings and to get rid o' them and replace them afterwards if they winna do what the community requires o' them. Lamberton heard the man say so last year in Paris, before the court at Norham even started its deliberations. Well, it wouldna please England's King to hear that voiced, even though to this point he's done nothin' but what we asked o' him, we bein' Rab Wishart's community o' Scotland.

"That doesna sound like much, I ken, but it's the kind o' thought that could stir folk up if it got about, an' it surely will. Men o' free will, in a free society, bein' free to choose their own leaders? Rubbish, you'll say, and so you should, considering who you are. But it's another o' these new ideas."

Rob shook his head. "Aye, mayhap it is, but where would these supposedly free men come from? No man today—here in Scotland at least, or even in England—is free of duty or obligation to someone, be it knight, lord, or baron. That's the way of the world."

Lord Robert smiled. "Is that a fact? Tell me, when were you last in a big town or city?"

"Any one?"

"Aye, any one. When was it?"

Rob shrugged. "London, I suppose," he said as he rose to add fuel to the dying brazier. "If you don't count our last journey to Perth. We werena there long enough to see anything—in and out the same day. I was in London with Da two years ago, though. We passed by Berwick on the way home that time, but we didn't stop there and I haven't been anywhere else since then, except for Norham, and that's no' much of a place, beyond the castle." He thrust a third log onto the two he had already placed and straightened up, dusting his hands against each other. "Why do you ask?"

"Because they're all filled wi' free men, Robert, every town and city in the land. And in France and England and everywhere else in

Christendom. We call them burgesses, the citizens o' the burghs. In England they're called burghers and the French ca' them bourgeois, but they're a' the same. They're merchants, living in towns and working for themselves, and the richest o' them, here in Scotland, anyway, are making themselves heard as part of the realm's community."

"I know that." Rob was frowning as he prepared to lower himself into his chair. "But I don't see—" He stopped and grasped the arms of the chair, his eyes suddenly gone wide, and then he subsided gently into his seat.

The old man smiled again, more widely this time, and dipped his chin. "You see it now, though, eh? They've slipped the leash. Vassals to no man, they're free to do whatever they want. I've seen it happening in my own lifetime, getting more and more noticeable frae year to year. We havena had a war here for nigh on eighty year—the tulzie at Largs wi' the Norwegians wasna a real battle, and there wasna really a war. Since then we've been at peace, throughout King Alec's reign, and when peace lasts for years like that, commerce grows strong.

"So now the burgesses are startin' to speak up as a group, and powerfu' folk are listenin'. They're forming merchants' guilds and trade associations everywhere—in the Low Countries, in Norway, Sweden, Germany—everywhere. The Dutchmen have formed a league, they call it the Hansa League because that's the name for a guild there, an' they've seen to it that they can trade freely wi' one another throughout their entire region at favourable rates. Our own wool merchants do the same here. Merchants are everywhere today, Robert, and they're growing stronger every year, growin' rich an' paying tribute or fealty to very few. They all owe fealty to the Crown, right enough, but that's as far as it goes. They live in the burghs, mainly for their own safety and the safety o' their warehouses, and they support themselves by what they do. They even lend money to noblemen like us, and that's how they steer clear o' trouble. They pay taxes, right enough, but to whom? I'll tell you: to the burghs themselves, for their upkeep and governance. And until now no one has challenged them, because they canna *be* challenged under the system we have. None o' the magnates can lay claim to the burghs. And every nobleman in the land relies on the burgesses to keep him supplied wi' goods. Do you see what I'm telling you? Another idea—free burgesses—and one that's already too well settled to be stopped."

He scratched his chin, and then went on as though speaking to himself alone. "It's a different world from when I was a boy. And it's changin' more and more wi' every month an' year that goes by. Had anyone tried to set himself up like that when my great-grandsire was alive—a self-supportin' merchant payin' no tithes or taxes—he would hae been arrested and flogged. But now it's commonplace. They're everywhere, and they hae power." He waved a hand. "I'm no' sayin' it's a bad thing, mind you. From what I've seen o' it, it could be good for everybody someday. I canna imagine it, but who's to say wi' certainty, one way or the other? But it's another *different* thing, another new idea that's already replacing the old way o' life."

"Where did the burghs come from, Grandfather? In the first place, I mean. All of them sit within someone's domain, so you'd think those lords would claim them as their own, would you not?"

"Aye, you might think so, but ye'd be wrong. The burghs were here afore the barons. Hundreds o' years afore, when the Norse Viking raids were at their worst an' men lived their whole lives in terror o' the dragon boats. Folk built the burghs for protection—fortified towns, gatherin' places wi' stout, stone walls where folk could shelter and defend themselves. That's why they're all by the sea, because that's where the threat came from. And they've always been free ports, since they were built, because they canna be taken. They're strongholds, no' just against invasion frae the sea but against attack frae the land, too. And no man, be he baron or magnate or king, can change that now.

"It's *all* about new ideas, Rob, and about where they come from," Lord Robert said. "New ideas and how a wise man might make use o' them someday. You'll need to stop being *Rob* now, for one thing, and that's going to be a new idea for you, too—mayhap even a hard one for you to grasp at first. Plain Rob Bruce was a laddie, a growing boy, and he belongs in your past now that you're a knight. Few men will think to call you Rob to your face from this day on, and if any does you'll have to put him in his place. Insist on your title and your full name always, from the moment you leave here this night. Men must call you 'my lord' if they're speaking to the earl, or 'Sir Robert' if they're speaking to the knight. And your friends, your real friends—for you'll have many now who'll seek that rank but never gain it—will call you Robert man to man. None but your closest kin can call you Rob now, and then only in private. Take it from me, Sir Robert—a man is as he is perceived to be, and too much familiarity from lesser men can mar that perception.

"So, new ideas and lessons. That's the first of them, but all the rest are related, and the gist of what I tried to tell you earlier is this: Your whole life as a man, as a knight and as an earl, will be defined by your own ideas, by your beliefs and the way you express them. You'll be judged by others, all the time and for the rest of your life, by the way those ideas reveal your true beliefs in what is fit and just and proper." He flipped a hand. "Of course it's true, too, that if you've no interest in any o' those things, fitness and justice and the like—if ye're a liar and a fool—folk will accept that, too, and you'll never amount to anything worthwhile. But I hae no worries over that. I've been watching you closely these two years and I believe you have the stuff o' a truly noble earl."

He sat up suddenly, looking at the brazier. "I'm thirsty. Is there enough water in that kettle to make us two more toddies?"

There was, and as Rob added fuel to the brazier and thrust the kettle directly on top of the coals, his grandfather busied himself with mixing the other ingredients from a stoppered clay flask and a covered pot of honey, so that only a short time later they sat back by the fire again, nursing freshly steaming cups.

"But it's no' just your own ideas you need to be concerned wi'," Lord Robert continued, unaware that he had slipped back into the Scots dialect. "You hae to be aware of other people's thinkin', o' the new ideas that folk are talking about, or believin' in, or even laughin' at. You hae to be open to such things, expectin' them, watchin', ready for them an' lookin' for the ways that they might change your life. You hae to keep your heid high an' your eyes wide, because there's nothin' more dangerous than change, Robert.

"Mind you, for some folk things like that dinna matter. Gin you're a farmer or a charcoal burner or a forester like young Wallace, changes can come and go and they'll no' bother you much, for you'll likely be none the wiser for their passin'. But gin you're a king or a magnate, a baron or a bishop or an earl—somebody whose very life depends on stability an' order among those wha follow him—those same changes that left others unaffected can sweep ye into ruin."

He sipped, inhaling the scented fumes, and his grandson sat gazing into his own cup, waiting for him to continue.

"So," the elder said eventually, setting his cup down carefully on the floor by his side and using his fingers to enumerate what he said next. "You have your name—the form o' it and how men use it. You have your beliefs, governing your thinking and behaviour. And you have your vigilance to what's goin' on about you, your openness to new ideas and the risks they present for you. What else, then, does an earl need? There is somethin', the most important thing of all, and I've left it to the end because it overarches everything else. Can you tell me what it is?"

His grandson twisted slightly in his seat to face him, holding the steaming cup beneath his nose as he looked at the patriarch, narrow-eyed and deep in thought. Then he shook his head almost imperceptibly and whispered, "No, sir, I can't. Tell me."

"Yourself, my lord earl, wi' all the burdens o' an earldom. Your family. Your ancestry, name, and heritage. Your loyalties and your understandin' o' your duties and responsibilities. The lands and properties you hold and the hundreds o' folk who live on them and who rely on you for their livelihood and safety. And every bit o' it affectin' your honour and integrity. All o' those things are easy to name, but there's no' a single one of them that's easy for a man to thole for a whole lifetime o' righteousness. And yet that's what lies ahead o' you, Sir Robert. And all o' it connected in a hundred ways to every other bit o' it.

"So let us start wi' loyalty, the two o' us. To whom should you be loyal, Bruce of Carrick? Name the folk."

His grandson blinked. "The King's grace. The King of England, too, as a dutiful vassal. You yourself, sir, as my grandsire … The Bishop of Glasgow?"

His grandfather grunted and nodded. "Aye. Questions like that to a boy who hasna considered them before are like questions frae the same boy about what goes on between men and women. Everybody expects somebody else to explain it but nobody ever does. Listen to me closely, then, for I might never hae the chance to tell you this again. Forget about the Church when you speak o' loyalty. You owe no loyalty to any churchman, includin' the Pope himsel'. Obedience, aye and certainly, but loyalty? A bishop's just a man in fancy robes whose concern should all be for your immortal soul. Your *loyalty's* required elsewhere.

"First an' foremost and heid and shoulders above all else, your surest loyalty must aey be to the Bruce—me, your father, yourself, and your house and heirs." His speech was faster and more guttural now, and he pronounced "house" as "hoose" and "shoulders" as "shoothers." "Never lose sight o' that, Sir Robert, for if you fail your house, you fail yourself, and then you can never serve anyone honestly. Your house comes first. Blood, family, and kinship—your honour and their welfare. Those are your prime loyalties. And along with that comes responsibility to, and for, all the folk who depend on Bruce. They, too, demand your loyalty, and on their loyalty in return will rest your success or failure in this life. Make no mistake on that, Sir Robert. Your folk depend on you for everything they have. But you depend equally upon them, and far more so, in fact, for without their loyalty to you, as man and leader, you'll achieve nothing that's worthwhile.

"After those, a distant second, comes your loyalty to the rightful King o' Scots, your liege lord. I said you willna be goin' to Scone and that might sound like disloyalty but it's no'. Once Balliol is crowned King, he'll *be* the King. But until then, he's just another man like you an' me and neither one o' us owes him a thing. After Scone it'll be different, but before that we can bid him kiss our arses, gin we wish. Ye ken my fears for his kingship. He'll go down before Edward o' England sooner or later, I'm sure o' that, and my biggest fear for you is that you'll get caught up in it and suffer for it."

"You think it will come to war, then, Grandfather?"

"It might, but God forbid. If it does it will be short and bloody, for we canna win."

Rob reacted as though he had been slapped. "What d'you mean? How can you say that?"

"How can I say it? You mean how can I even *think* such a thing? I've thought it now for months and I can say it loudly and honestly. I could shout it frae the walls and roofs, forbye, but nobody in Scotland would believe it." He stopped, frowning. "Think about it, Robert. And think wi' your heid, no' wi' your heart. I said a while ago we havena fought a war in eighty year. But Edward has been at war since afore he took up the crown these twenty year ago. He still has men among his barons and knights who fought wi' him on crusade. And he has fought in France and Gascony, forbye two wars in Wales in recent years. His armies are toughened, Robert. Battle hardened. They're tight and disciplined, and after years o' victory, they're confident.

"We're confident, too, in this realm, but ours is the confidence o' blowhards. We're deluding ourselves. We're just no' fit, the way things are, to take the field against an English host. We've no heavy cavalry an' we've no bowmen—none that could stand up against Edward's Welshmen, anyway. We wouldna hae a chance."

If the younger man was dismayed by what he had heard, he gave no sign of it. "And that's why you want me to withhold my allegiance to Balliol?"

Lord Robert looked surprised. "Is that what you think? No, I don't want that at all. What I *want*—what I need you to see—is that we owe more real allegiance to Edward Plantagenet than we do to John Balliol, and for the exact same reason that John Balliol himself

owes loyalty to Edward. We owe him homage for our estates in
England, which are worth more than all we have in Scotland—it's
our English lands that pay for our Scots ones. And mark me, that
same concern is what's going to bring Balliol down, for his English
lands are three times as big as ours and he'll no' want to lose them.
Our new King is about to find out that you canna be master in one
realm when you're duty bound to the master o' another."

"But—" Rob's brow creased. "But would you not have been in
the same situation, had you won?"

"No, I would not. I made up my mind long ago that, gin I won
the Crown and became King o' Scots, I'd surrender my lands in
England—gie them back to the Crown. It would hae been a painful
thing to do, but I'd have had no choice. It would hae been the only
way to keep Edward at arm's length—otherwise he'd hae been interferin' wi' everythin' I tried to do here. Only by forfeiting our lands
in England would I hae been free to be king in Scotland, and the
sacrifice would hae made it plain to Edward that he could never be
king here."

"Balliol might do the same."

"I doubt he will. As I said, he has far more to forfeit, and he spent
his whole life in England till his mother died. He's more English
than he is Scots and he willna want to give that up. He'll try to
handle both. That's the kind o' man he is, and that spells grief for
this realm. But it's no' just Balliol, Grandson. There's scarce a
nobleman in Scotland who's no' beholden to the English Crown for
lands an' privilege. That's why Edward can lay claim to being lord
paramount o' Scotland. Through grants o' lands and titles in
England, he commands the loyalty o' every baron in this land and
most o' the Highland mormaers, forbye."

"So he owns Scotland. Is that what you're saying?"

Lord Robert sat quiet for a moment, then shook his head. "No,"
he growled. "He doesna. What he owns, what he *possesses*, is a club,
a weapon both legal and lethal, and strong enough to cow the Scots
nobility, John Balliol among them, into lettin' him do what he wants.
And that bodes ill for this realm in years ahead. Ye'll hear folk talk

o' patriotism when it suits them, Grandson, when they feel the need to sound grand an' independent. But wealth has a bigger, louder voice. Wealth and the fear o' losin' it."

Rob shifted in his seat. "So what must we do?"

"We? You mean Bruce?" The old man grimaced. "We'll do what's right, for that's a' we can do, in honour. We'll keep to ourselves for the welfare o' our house, and we'll mind our own affairs and let the rest get on wi' what they must. I hae no need now to abandon what I hold in England, and I bent my head in renewed fealty to Edward, on behalf o' all o' us Bruces. And so I'll go to England, as will you and yours, to watch and wait and see what happens."

"And if it comes to war?" The question was hushed.

"Then so be it. It will be a disaster. I hope it willna come to that, but if it does, it will no' be o' my makin', nor yours, nor your father's."

"And if Scotland has need o' us?"

The old man smiled, his expression almost pitying, and responded quietly in words Rob Bruce would remember for the rest of his life.

"*What* Scotland, Grandson? Have you no' heard a word I've said? There's no Scotland today, other than the land itself. No' since Alexander died. There's an *England*, a puissant kingdom united under a hard and able leader, but there's no *Scotland* in the sense you mean. What we hae here now is a collection o' mixed bloods and peoples, an' most o' them at one another's throats—Gaels in the north and west and Isles, Norwegians in the far north and east, and others scattered everywhere north o' the Forth—and our so-called leaders, the barons o' the realm, are the descendants o' Norman Frenchmen who canna make up their minds where they belong. They're the ones who'll be the ruin o' this realm if things go as I fear they must—the ones who'll let Edward ride roughshod over them because they canna bear to think o' losin' their estates in England. They might ca' themselves Scots and strut about like Scots nobles, but their affairs in England are their main concern, and until they see things differently, Scotland will just be a place, an idea … just an old, done notion."

A pocket of resin exploded in one of the logs, making them both jump, and Lord Robert yawned and stretched his arms above his head, blinking owlishly. "It must be late," he said. "What hour o' night is it, I wonder?"

"Very late," Rob responded, eyeing him solicitously. "Do you want me to leave?"

"No, no' unless you want to."

His grandson grinned. "You sent me to bed at suppertime and I slept for hours, so I'm wide awake now. And you asked me to remind you about what my father needs to do for the family."

"Aye, I did … I was talking about marriages. Your sister Isabel is to marry Eric, the King o' Norway. The talk has been goin' back an' forth for years between your father and the Norwegians. But it's a fine match and a good thing."

It was the first Rob had heard of such a thing, but he found himself surprisingly unsurprised. King Eric of Norway had been married before, to another Scotswoman, Margaret Canmore, the sister of King Alexander, and their daughter had been the ill-fated Maid of Norway. And for the past few years, on his visits from England, Rob had heard mention from others about visiting Norwegians in his parents' household. He had been curious at times, but never greatly enough to ask questions. Isabel would make a fine queen, he thought, and smiled at the thought of having a queen for a sister.

"But what about the boys and the youngest girls, Mary and Margaret and wee Mattie?" he asked then. "Who'll be left to see to them, once Isabel's gone?"

The old lord smiled. "The same folk that would be left to see to them anyway. They'll move to England wi' your father. Better, though, that you should ask about yoursel'."

Rob tensed. "What is there to ask?"

"About your future wife."

His frown grew deeper. "Is there one? I knew nothing of it."

"Oh, aye, and you'll like her. I've met the lass and I havena a doubt in my mind. She's bright an' smart an' she's no' ugly—a quick wit, a sunny nature, an' a laugh that could set the world laughin'. Forbye, she's o' a good family, well connected."

Rob was having difficulty breathing. "Connected to whom?"

"To us. She's sister to your good-brother Gartnait of Mar. Her name's Isabella."

"I scc. How old is she? And when was this decided?"

"Oh, no' that long ago. Her father, old Domhnall, has been one o' my staunchest supporters for year, an' like me, he canna see much good comin' out o' our new King. He believes our house has a destiny and wants to align himsel' wi' us more strongly than before. So this marriage was his idea." He glanced shrewdly at his grandson then and held up a hand. "Before you say another word, lad, think o' this. You're eighteen now, wi' an earldom to run, and so you need a wife. This lass will be a good one for you." His face broke into a wide grin that lit his eyes from inside. "D'you think I'd saddle you wi' a hirplin' auld crow or an eyesore wi' hairy warts? You're my grandson, and the bairns you breed wi' her will be my great-grandsons, so I want them to be comely, just like me."

"But—" The Earl of Carrick sucked in a deep breath, looked about the room almost wildly, then sighed. "When will I meet this wonder?" he asked.

"No' for a while yet," Lord Robert said. "She's but fourteen, so she'll no' be ready for another wheen o' years. By the time you turn one and twenty, you'll thank me."

Rob's mind flashed back to London and the unknown young women who had ambushed him and held him down so delightfully, and he felt a swelling ache in his chest at the thought of never again experiencing such a thrill. He had had other sexual adventures since that day, but they had all been fumbling, hasty, and largely guilt-filled episodes of opportunities seized on the spur of the moment. None of them had been truly memorable or fulfilling or even really pleasant, and none of them had ever come close to matching the visceral excitement and pleasurable wickedness of that first, unexpected escapade. And now, faced with the prospect of an unknown wife, even three years in the future, it seemed to him that the chance of repeating that encounter was lost forever. Marriage would put an end to such things, he feared, feeling sorry for himself, but then he became aware of his grandfather again, sitting across from him and gazing at him in curiosity.

"Three years, then," he said. "And what will I do in the meantime?"

"Probably more than I'll want to hear about. But you'll be at Edward's court in London until then. Does that trouble you, three years in England?"

"No, sir, it does not. Not if you're there, and the rest of my family." Rob smiled. "My friends will be there too, much of the time—Norfolk and Surrey, Hereford and the others. I'll be well content there, I believe."

"Aye, I hope so. But mainly you'll be out o' Scotland and away from all the nonsense that's to come. Mind you keep on the right side o' Edward, though. He's an ill man to cross. As long as you're in favour, he'll keep you entertained and well provided for, but get you on his bad side and you'll rue it. An' now get you to bed, though I jalouse you'll hae enough in your head now to keep you awake for the rest o' the night."

His grandson nodded, and stood up to take his leave.

The old man stood, too, and pulled him close into his embrace. He held him tightly for a moment, and then released him and stepped back, watching in silence as the new Earl of Carrick, his noble house's future, walked out into the stillness of the sleeping household.

Ten days later, on November nineteenth, the court of auditors at Norham found in favour of John Balliol, Lord of Galloway, and declared him Scotland's rightful King.

Less than two weeks after that, on the thirtieth day of November in the year of our Lord 1292, Scotland's new King was crowned upon the ancient Stone of Destiny at the royal palace of Scone, near Perth, proclaiming himself John, King of Scotland.

# Book Four

# The English Lordling

# 1295-1297

# CHAPTER FOURTEEN

# THE POLITICS OF LOVE

Jennets, they were called, and for no reason he could discern, Robert Bruce found himself smiling as he looked at the four twinned beasts he was approaching, each pair supporting a litter delicately slung between them, front to rear. Designed expressly for the transportation of women, the litters were barely wider than the sturdy animals that bore them, and both were draped in shrouding curtains of the light and delicate Arabian fabric known as muslin. The term *jennet* came from a gentle, placid breed of horse native to northern Spain and widely famed for their gentle, rolling gait. But northern Spain was half a world away and these jennets were Scots, female donkeys bred and trained to be tranquil, dependable beasts of burden like their Spanish namesakes, and brought to England from Scotland several years earlier by his grandfather Lord Robert, for the convenience of his lady wife.

The ostler in charge of the closer of the two litters had paused with raised eyebrows as the brightly clothed young knight approached, and now Bruce swung his leg over the cantle of his saddle and slid effortlessly to the ground. Dropping his reins as he landed and leaving his horse ground-tethered, he strode forward, sending the ostler away with a wave before he raised the flap of the curtains between him and the litter's occupants.

As he did so, a heady waft of exotic perfume swept over him and he heard one of the two young women inside the narrow litter giggle. He ignored her, his eyes going automatically to the other occupant, a beautiful, imperious, and self-sufficient young woman who gazed coolly at him with lambent, green-flecked eyes.

"Sir Robert," she said, in a quiet, husky voice. "Is something amiss? Why have we stopped?"

Bruce stuck his head in through the hanging curtains and sniffed the perfumed air pleasurably and obviously. "No, my lady," he said easily. "Nothing is wrong. I but found myself desirous of the scent of you. And so I stopped our progress to refresh myself. I hope I have not inconvenienced you."

The young woman raised a languid eyebrow and shrugged delicately. "How could you?" she drawled, then glanced at her companion. "Estelle, your ears."

The other woman covered her ears with both hands and closed her eyes, twisting her head ostentatiously towards the far corner of the tiny space they occupied. Her mistress looked back at their visitor and, without raising her voice beyond a murmur, continued, "And have you scent enough to satisfy you now, sir?"

"No, my lady." His response was barely more than an expressed breath, even quieter than hers as he bent to speak directly into her ear. "Not all the Muses and their gifts combined could sate the need I have for the scent of you … that subtle, exquisite scent so long remembered."

Gwendolyn de Ferrers merely smiled and dipped her head very slightly, even as she felt her cheeks flush and her heartbeat increase. It was only recently that she had again encountered the young squire with whom she had once so shamelessly toyed. Since that far-off encounter, though, she had been joined in wedlock to Sir James de Ferrers, a wealthy knight more than twice her age, and the nameless but comely young squire had become a knight and a belted earl. Now a close and highly privileged favourite of King Edward, the dashing twenty-one-year-old dandy had a well-deserved reputation for gambling profligately, winning and losing with equal unconcern in the knowledge, according to the whisperers who disparaged him, that his losses would be covered by the King's privy purse and his winnings would be used for his own pleasure. And the pleasures he pursued fed the rumour makers constantly, ranging as they did from his love of outlandish and outrageously expensive clothing in all the newest fashions, colours, and fabrics that the royal tailors could provide, to his propensity for seducing every woman with whom he came into contact. No woman, it was said, was safe from his blandishments, and very few of those he chose resisted him for long.

Meeting him again unexpectedly after so long, she had been excited to realize that he remembered her. Of this he had left her in no doubt, having looked her directly in the eye and told her that he would know her anywhere, even were he blindfolded and pinioned on his back. She had felt the blood rush to her face, and yet the feeling that had swept over her had nothing to do with shame or confusion. It was far more like triumphant exultation, and she felt her heart take a great leap of pleasure.

Now, gazing at his face so close to hers, aware of the breadth of his shoulders and the richness of the long, open-fronted wine-red tunic that he wore over a rose-coloured shirt of fine cambric and matching hose, she became aware of the smell of him, a clean odour of light perspiration mixed with a mild scent that she could not identify. She forced herself to remain outwardly impassive and kept her voice as low as his. "Are you then incapable of being sated, sir?"

"With you, milady? Aye, I fear I could be." His head tilted towards her in the close confines of the litter and his lips brushed against her cheek. She hesitated only half a heartbeat and then moved towards him, returning his kiss, oblivious to her servant Estelle as she felt his hand settle firmly on her upper thigh and knead the soft flesh gently.

Bruce's eyes were closed and he could hear his own heartbeat drumming in his ears as he explored the soft wonders of her mouth and the soft flesh beneath his fingers, but she stiffened suddenly and pushed him away with an urgency that snapped his eyes open and brought him back to where he was. The seductive veil of lust fell away quickly as he realized that the pounding heartbeats in his head had been replaced by the thudding of approaching hoofbeats, and he muttered a quiet curse as he straightened quickly and took a half step back from the litter, turning to see who was coming so fast. For a guilty moment he half expected to see the lady's outraged husband galloping towards him, though he knew even as it came to him that the thought was ludicrous. It was his own man, Thomas Beg—Wee Thomas—from Turnberry, and Bruce saw at a glance that he was bringing ill tidings.

"Forgive me, my lady," he said, turning quickly back and speaking through the closed curtains. "I must speak with this man."

He stepped out to where Thomas Beg could see him in the bright, mid-morning light and raised an arm, and the big man swung his mount towards him and brought it to a sliding halt within arm's reach of where Bruce stood. He dropped his reins on his horse's neck and swung quickly down.

"Lord Robert," he growled, his face dark. "I need to talk wi' ye." He glanced at the litter and the watching ostler. "For your ears alone."

"Aye. Come."

Bruce headed for a dense tangle of head-high bramble bushes nearby, and Thomas Beg followed him closely. When they reached the clump of brush Bruce stood with his back to it. He swept his eyes over the two litters and their few attendants, just to be sure no one was paying too much attention.

"What is it?"

"Sodgers," the giant answered, his frown still in place. "And they're no' yours, though they're on Bruce land. They're gettin' ready to hang some folk. Our folk, I think. I heard the noises they were makin' an' went to see what wis happenin', but when I saw they wis strangers I came back here."

"Where are they? How far away?"

"Doon that way." Thomas Beg pointed southwestward. "About a mile frae here, just on the ither side o' the burn."

Bruce's chin came up. "On the other side o' the river?"

"Aye. I had to cross it to reach them."

"Then that's not Bruce land. That's Sir John Mowbray's territory, part of the Earl of Surrey's estates, so they must be his men. But you said they were getting ready to hang some people?"

"Aye. They had about ten folk there, under guard, and mair bein' brought in as I watched."

Bruce's mind was racing. "How many soldiers, Tom?"

The big man spread his hands. "I'm no' sure, but I had seen mair than a score o' them afore I lost count. They wis movin' about too much to count, but there must be half a hunnert there by now."

"Fifty men-at-arms? Who's in charge of them, did you see?"

"Three knights at least. Big horses, fancy armour."

"Damnation! How far are we from our campsite?"

"Less than a mile, but the other way, atop the ridge there. So there's likely a mile 'tween it an' the sodgers."

"And all is ready there for our arrival?"

"Aye, Sir Robert. Everything's ready."

"Good. Mount you up then and wait for me. I'll send the ladies on ahead to the campsite with the others and you and I will ride down there and find out what's going on."

Thomas Beg looked at his master askance, taking in the velvet doublet and hose and the sheathed ornamental dagger at Bruce's waist. He nodded towards it. "Is that the only blade ye've got?"

"It's all I'll need. I am on my own land. Why should I need any blade? Mount up and wait for me."

Less than twenty minutes later the two men were at the top of a small knoll on the far side of the river that bounded the southeastern edge of the Bruce lands of Writtle, looking down at the scene in the wooded dell a hundred yards below where a large number of well-equipped men-at-arms were assembling in order, their task evidently completed. Bruce counted forty-four of them, including three mounted knights.

"By God, they didna waste ony time. Look ower yonder." Thomas Beg pointed to where a staggered row of four mature oaks stood out against the lighter growth behind them, and Bruce felt himself stiffening as he saw the corpses dangling from their lower limbs. Fourteen of them, he counted, all of them dressed in rags and revolving slowly despite the lack of any breeze. They had been dead for only minutes, he realized, the slow spin of their bodies caused by the residual force of their struggles as they choked to death. He turned back, open-mouthed, towards the executioners, who had now formed themselves into two disciplined blocks, four ranks wide by five deep, then felt his throat constrict as a fourth knight, accompanied by a quartet of mounted sergeants, rode in to join the others, bearing a blazoned shield that Bruce recognized instantly.

He stood erect in his stirrups and cupped his hands around his mouth. "Below there!" he bellowed. "Bigod!"

The majority of the men swung around in concert to gaze up towards the knoll, but though they were plainly visible to him from above, the bushes surrounding him made him invisible to them. Moments later, the two outer ranks of each block of infantry peeled away to the left and right, trotting towards the flanks of the hill on which Bruce stood, while the four remaining files of men, all of whom carried crossbows, combined into a solid unit, arming their weapons and facing squarely up the hill.

"They're coming up," he said to Thomas Beg. "Squads of ten on either side, each led by a knight. Come with me."

He nudged his horse with his spurs and advanced until he could be seen clearly from below, then sat patiently, arms folded across his chest, as they came into view and surrounded him and Thomas Beg. Then he turned to the knight on his right, who had arrived slightly ahead of his counterpart on Bruce's left. The fellow was frowning fiercely, his flushed face visible beneath his raised visor, but he hesitated as he took in Bruce's appearance.

Bruce spoke first. "Robert Bruce of Turnberry, Earl of Carrick. My lands of Writtle lie the other side of the river. I saw my friend Sir John Bigod with you and sought to make myself known. Will you take me to him?"

The knight glowered and raised his hand to his men, tacitly warning them to wait but remain vigilant. He answered civilly enough, though, nodding as he named himself. "William de Hazelrig of Louth. You should have come down to us, my lord. It ill behooves an earl to shout like a huckster."

Bruce bit back the urge to put the newcomer firmly in his place. He merely shrugged, forcing himself to smile in spite of an instinctive dislike of the man. "Sometimes a shout is safer than an unannounced approach. You have crossbowmen down there." He turned to the second knight and found another stranger gazing at him, though this one with a smile. "And you, sir, are … ?"

"Gilbert de Coulle, Sir Robert. I've heard Sir John speak of you often. He will be most pleased to see you thus unexpectedly."

"That is my hope," Bruce answered, thinking about the hanged men and the legality or otherwise of their deaths. Of the small coterie of friends he had made in London as a squire, Bigod had been the closest, and he had never impressed Bruce as being bloodthirsty or brutal. But Bruce had counted fourteen dangling corpses with his own eyes. "Shall we go down, then?"

As they rode clear of the obscuring brush on the hillside, Bruce could see John de Bigod, backed by four mounted sergeants-at-arms, sitting his horse at the side of the twenty crossbowmen looking up at them, and he saw the sidewise, straight-armed gesture that ordered the men to lower their weapons and stand easy as soon as it became obvious that the returning parties showed no sign of conflict. Look as he would, though, he could see no sign now of the fourth knight he had seen earlier. The two groups were too far apart for either side to distinguish individual faces, but Bruce knew that Bigod would already have seen that neither he nor Thomas Beg wore armour and that their horses—and his own wine-coloured doublet—marked them as people of some consequence.

No voices were raised as the descending group approached, and Bruce saw the sudden quickening of interest as John de Bigod sat straighter in his saddle, tightening his reins and flipping up his visor as something in Bruce's appearance struck him as being familiar. The knight lifted one arm and called out an order, and the mounted sergeants at his back began moving, shouting to the men in their charge, who immediately broke ranks, disarmed their weapons, and formed up again in a twenty-man block, largely ignoring the newcomers now that their commander had accepted them as being harmless. Bigod spurred his horse to a trot until he was close enough to recognize Bruce, and then he hauled back on the reins and stood upright in the stirrups.

"Bruce! Damn me, where did *you* spring from?" There was no doubting the welcome in the knight's wide smile, and Bruce kicked his mount forward to meet him, arms spread wide, as Bigod bellowed, "Harry! Here! Look at this."

A thick bank of bushes on Bruce's right, less than forty paces distant and masking the row of oaks with their dangling corpses, stirred and split as the missing knight rode slowly into view, followed by a score of Welsh archers whose presence Bruce had neither seen nor suspected. The man's shield and surcoat bore an escutcheon that Bruce did not recognize, although elements of it were disconcertingly familiar to him—the blue lion rampant on a field of gold was almost identical to the ancient arms of the House of Bruce. Otherwise the knight was armoured in plain steel, from helmed head to booted feet. But the shouted name had prompted Bruce already to guess at his identity, and as the obscuring visor rose up from a swipe of a gauntleted hand, he saw the familiar face of Henry de Percy, another of his companions from his days of squiredom. Percy was frowning, plainly wondering what was going on, but then he recognized Bruce and his face, too, broke into a grin.

As the three came together, exchanging greetings, Bigod swung around in his saddle to address the knight called Hazelrig. "Get the men ready to leave. We're finished here. Send us word when you're ready, but in the meantime leave us alone. We are old friends here."

It had been three years since the three had last seen each other, the morning of the day before their knighting, when Bruce had ridden home to his mother's sickbed, and they behaved as old friends long parted always do, exchanging jibes and reminiscences while appraising the changes that had marked them all since last meeting.

Henry Percy, Baron of Alnwick, pulled off his heavy helmet and slung it from his saddle horn before pushing back his mailed cowl, baring his head and scrubbing at his matted scalp as he eyed Bruce's doublet and the lace trimming at the neck of his white shirt. His gaze slid down his friend's velvet-clad legs to the soft, brushed leather but thickly soled riding boots he wore.

"I'd heard rumours that you are become a ladies' man, Bruce," he said, "but I hadn't believed them until now. Do you always ride out dressed like milady's favourite minstrel?"

Bruce smiled. "On my own lands, and in the company of ladies, aye, I do. Much of the time, anyway. And my lands lie across the river there." He gestured over his shoulder.

"Of course," Percy said. "Writtle is Bruce land. It's been so long since I was here that I'd forgotten. Our grandsires' estates touch here."

"Aye. It *was* my grandfather's. But he died these three months since, may God rest his soul, and left it to me."

"The Competitor is dead? That grieves me to hear—though now that I think of it, I had believed him dead long since. He was a legend when we were boys, though he was not the Competitor then, not until after the death of King Alexander. I've always thought the new name suited him. How old was he?"

Bruce shrugged. "Older than anyone I've ever known. Eighty, or thereabouts. He was ready to go, he told me last time I saw him. But I missed his death by days. They had sent to summon me from the north but I was already on my way here and must have passed the messenger along the way. The old man was laid out for burial by the time I arrived and I didn't even know he had been sick. His second wife, the Lady Christina of Ireby, still lives here, under my protection." He waved a hand towards the finery of Percy's surcoat. "And what about you? I know the blue and gold are the colours of Warrenne, but a rampant lion azure? Where did that come from?"

Percy smiled smugly. "My wife. I was wed last year. Name's Eleanor, daughter to the Earl of Arundel. Their crest is a rampant lion, in gold. I adopted it in honour of my lady wife and changed it to the blue of Earl Warrenne. With the approval of both earls, of course."

Bruce nodded. "Of course, not to mention the King. And it is … striking. Makes a statement of authority."

"I believe it does … Why do you smile?"

"Because it's like my own." Bruce kept his voice low. "Or rather my grandfather's, which I have adopted. The ancient Bruce arms—a red saltire on a field of gold, surmounted by a red chief, with a blue rampant lion in the left corner."

Percy sat still, the colour draining from his face, and then he barked, "Damnation, Bruce. You jest with me."

Bruce shrugged and held up his hands, palms outward. "Harry, I would not do such a thing. I speak the truth. Those are the Bruce arms, though they're seldom seen today. My grandsire preferred the plain blue lion rampant. That was his personal standard. But those are Scots arms, Harry, not English, so few Englishmen will ever see my version. No need, then, to make a fuss about it."

"I am not *fussing*."

Bigod glanced at Percy, attracted by the sudden tension in his voice. Bruce and Percy both schooled their faces, betraying nothing, and after a moment Bigod grinned, and his eyelid flickered in the merest wink to Percy. "Ladies, you said, Bruce, did you not?" he drawled. "I see no ladies."

Bruce grinned again. "I sent them on ahead when I got word that there were strange doings afoot on the far side of the stream … What happened here today?"

Percy made a grimace of distaste. "What *happened* here was retribution, in the King's name and at his command. You know about the Welsh rebellion, this past year?"

"Aye, who doesn't?"

"But you were not involved?"

"No, I was in Ireland, acting as a liaison between Edward and de Burgh, the Earl of Ulster."

Percy nodded thoughtfully. "I heard something of that posting. It made quite a stir, I recall. The King forgave all your debts, did he not?"

Feeling his face flush slightly, Bruce shrugged his silk-clad shoulders. "Aye, that's true," he said. "But they were debts incurred in his service. And in taxes that fell due when we moved to England. When we failed to attend his coronation and swear our fealty as quickly as he and his Comyn friends wished, King John of Scotland sequestered—" He thought about that for a moment, his brows furrowed. "Aye, that's the word Edward's lawyer used—he sequestered our holdings. Didn't snatch thcm away from us completely, but withheld their revenues and rents, declared us forsworn to justify his doing so, naming us … not treasonous, exactly, but something of that ilk, designed to make our name stink in the nostrils of our countrymen. *Defectors*, that was it. He named us defectors when we came to England as Edward's vassals. That moved Edward to publicly forgive my debts to him, in recompense, since I was new-arrived and had never lived in England prior to that time, other than as a visiting knight in training."

"Hold you!" Percy stared at Bruce, his brows drawn into a deep furrow. "Your own King named you *forsworn* for coming to England? How can that be? You own lands here, as does he himself."

"Aye, but there was more involved than meets the eye. There are two great houses in Scotland, dominating all others between them, and one of those is Bruce, so for Bruce to be absent from his crowning displeased the King greatly. And when we moved south to England, still without declaring fealty to him, he—or more likely his Comyn kinsmen—decreed that we had defected to England and forfeited our rights within his realm."

"Why didn't you take the oath and stay in Scotland?" Bigod sounded mildly perplexed.

"What, and forswear ourselves and our patrimony, John? Mouth allegiance to a man I know to be less able than my own grandsire, whose rightful crown he wears? The oath would have been insincere, and Bruce does not deal in lies. That was my grandsire's watchword throughout his life, and no man doubted him. I intend to follow his example."

"But Balliol *is* King there, declared so legally, at Norham. Do you dispute Edward's judgment and the verdict of the auditors?"

Bruce grinned at him, shaking his head. "No, not the verdict—merely the tenor and good sense of it. But then I am a Bruce, and I believe my grandsire had the better claim, besides being the better man. That's why we are here in England, John. We consider our fealty to Edward to be of greater import than our loyalty to Balliol and the Comyns. For make no mistake, the Comyns rule in all but name in Scotland nowadays, and John Balliol is closely bound to them by ties of blood and marriage."

"But what of the realm, your loyalty to Scotland?" Bigod asked.

There was no trace of humour in Bruce's reply. "What realm? England is a realm, John, in the true sense of the word. A realm needs a strong king—a powerful leader whom all men will gladly follow to the death in that realm's cause if need arises. There is none such in Scotland today. The land is ruled by one dominant house nowadays and that house dictates to all the others. Some are content with that. Others not so. But as things stand there is no place in Scotland today for Bruce to live and prosper without bending the knee to Comyns everywhere. The sole alternative would be rebellion and civil war."

Percy grunted, bored with the topic. "So what did Balliol do then, when you came south?"

"Exactly what I would have expected him to do. He gave the oversight and governance of my grandsire's holdings in Annandale—though they were in truth my father's by then—and of my own earldom of Carrick to a royal kinsman, the Comyn Earl of Buchan. He did not grant them outright ownership, but they hold them none the less, albeit in the King's name." He gave a half-smothered, ironic chuckle. "Comyns running Bruce estates … We Bruces have never loved the Comyn breed, nor they us." He raised an eyebrow at Percy, then added, "You met one of them when he came to Westminster with Bek, you might recall, when we were there the last time. Came down with him from Scotland, that day he rode in with Robert Clifford in tow, what was it, six years ago? The heir to the Red

Comyn lordship of Badenoch. There are two branches of the Comyn family, the senior being the Red Comyns of Badenoch and the lesser the Black Comyns of Buchan."

"I remember him," John Bigod interjected. "Didn't like him, either. An arrogant whoreson."

"Aye, that's a family trait, I'm told. Anyway, his people now hold our lands in Annandale and Ayr, and so we—my father and my family—lived in England, at my grandsire's estate of Ireby in Cumberland, until the King dispatched me to Ireland and the court of Richard de Burgh. And there I spent the entire year, in the wilds of Ulster, while Comyns ruled my earldom and collected my rents. It is … isolated over there. The Welsh rebellion was stamped out before I ever heard about it, let alone was able to take part in it."

"Don't fret over that," Percy said. "You were fortunate. Bigod and I were there, and it was no fit place for any man of honour. No glory to be had in Wales—nothing but filth and treachery, bloodshed and bitter hatred and the constant threat of pestilence. But while that sorry tale was being spun, the south here was almost wholly stripped of fighting men. And knowing that, malcontents everywhere believed themselves at liberty to live like their betters. There have always been outlaws in the forests—hard, broken men—but while we were away in Wales they grew bolder everywhere, even here, this close to London. Some of them became a public menace here in Essex, making free with the local people, looting, raping, and murdering.

"When we came home from Wales at the end of April, the entire countryside around London was in chaos. Townspeople hid behind their walls, not daring to go out for fear of being robbed and killed. Edward was furious—never seen him so angry—and sent out groups in all directions—us under de Valence of Pembroke here in Essex— to scour the land free of the vermin. We've been harrying their nests now for more than a month." He waved a pointing thumb towards the distant oaks. "These were the last of them left organized. We caught up with them yesterday. Of course they knew we were coming by then and most of them scattered into the deep woods. These few here were the diehards. And die hard they did."

Bruce blinked, rattled by the mention of the Earl of Pembroke's presence nearby. It was de Valence's own granddaughter, the beautiful and willing Gwendolyn de Ferrers, who was lustfully awaiting Bruce's return to camp that night, and he felt a chill run over him as he imagined the old earl's vengeful fury should he ever suspect such a thing. He could not conceal his reaction or the involuntary frown of concern it brought, but he managed to disguise its origins by glowering at Percy and asking, skeptically, "And you did all this with forty men-at-arms and four knights?"

"And a score of archers. But no, we were more than that. Our group here is but the smallest of three. There's a larger group under Pembroke himself—de Bohun's among them, which might surprise you—conducting a sweep north of here, and a third force, larger again, commanded by Antoine La Pierre, one of Pembroke's Frenchmen, is scouring our perimeters, mopping up the escapees ..." He paused, almost squinting at Bruce. "Were you jesting? Do you really have women with you?" He laughed. "Of course you do. Why would I even bother to wonder?"

Bruce nodded absently, ignoring the jibe as he considered what he had been told. "Where are you going now?"

"To our rallying point, to meet up with Pembroke's force. They should be coming in later today. Might even be there now, depending on what they encountered to the north. De Valence chose the spot himself, a hamlet on the main London road, with open land, fresh water, and good grazing nearby. It's not far from here, about two miles north, along the riverbank. Why d'you ask?"

"Because I *do* have ladies here, and I should rejoin them—and no, Harry, I cannot take you with me. That would be ... indelicate, shall we say. I have a camp set up for them on my lands and have promised them a day of hunting tomorrow. It came to me, though, that I should see my guests fed and comfortable—they are well chaperoned and guarded, for despite my own unarmoured state I'm not completely irresponsible. Then later, when I am satisfied that all is well with them, I would like to join you by your campfire. Would that be acceptable?"

Bigod smiled wolfishly. "Aye, but far more so were you to bring the women with you."

Percy smiled, too, but waved Bigod's comment aside. "Into an armed camp, he means, to be frightened out of their wits by the sights and smells of half-wild men who have been campaigning for more than a month. But come yourself, by all means. We've an unweaned pig roasting on a spit—the unintentional gift of some farmer who failed to keep it carefully penned—so don't eat before you come, and don't waste any time. Your ladies will still be there when you get back, no?"

Bruce nodded, amused. "Yes, they will. They will await my coming. And so I'll leave you to your departures. Two miles from here, you say? And I'll find you if I stay close to the river?"

"Humphrey will be there by then," Percy said, his teeth flashing in a savage grin. "So even if you can't see our fires, you'll hear de Bohun." He stretched out his hand in farewell. "Until tonight, then."

"Is that right? Ye're goin' back there this nicht, to their camp?"

Thomas Beg's question brought Bruce out of the reverie in which he had been riding, and he looked around him, surprised to see that they were approaching the base of the low hill on which his people had set up their camp and would be there in a matter of minutes.

He nodded. "I am, for a while."

"An' whit aboot the lady?"

Bruce fought the urge to grin at the brusque impertinence of the question, which implicitly dismissed three of the four women they were riding to rejoin.

"What about her?" No point, he knew, in trying to dissemble.

The big man scowled. "She'll no' be happy gin ye up an' awa, an' her lookin' tae spend the nicht wi' ye."

"She'll wait," he answered, still resisting the smile that pulled at the corners of his mouth. "She has no choice. Besides, I'll be gone but a few hours and the matter's important. My need here is greater than her ladyship's, I fear."

"Aye. Tell *her* that. Better you nor me."

Now Bruce did grin. "I will, Thomas, never fear. I wouldna ask you to do that."

"No, an' a good thing, too, for I'd hae nothin' to do wi' it."

Bruce barked a laugh, marvelling again at the difference between Scots and Englishmen. None other among his people in Essex would ever dare to use such a tone to any of their so-called betters, let alone voice such questions and demand answers to them. The Scots, though, were vastly different in that respect—sternly intolerant of human foibles, without regard for rank or person. They might accord a nobleman the respect of a title, but only if they thought the man had earned it. They had no tolerance for bending the knee unwillingly or for paying lip service to a fool even if he was a titled fool. And they had no reluctance at all about cutting a fool's pretensions down to size.

Wee Thomas had earned every scrap of the authoritative familiarity that permitted him to take issue on occasion with his employer's behaviour. The giant man had been the younger Bruce's shadow—bodyguard, trainer, escort, and confidant—since the day the earl had committed the twelve-year-old boy to his care. Thomas Beg had been eighteen then, young for such a responsibility, but he had accepted it wholeheartedly, and since then the two had been apart only during Bruce's two-year sojourn in Westminster, training for knighthood in the royal household.

He spoke again. "So yon was Percy."

It was not a question, but Bruce treated it as though it had been. "It was. Sir Henry Percy, Baron of Alnwick and grandson of John de Warrenne, the Earl of Surrey. And with him another of the boyhood friends you've heard me talk about—Sir John de Bigod, no title, but firstborn nephew to the Earl of Norfolk. A third one, Humphrey de Bohun, heir to the earldom of Hereford, will join them tonight. He's riding with de Valence of Pembroke, whom Edward charged with stamping out the bandits they hanged today. Those fourteen were the last of them, Percy said."

"Ye dinna like *him*, do ye?"

"Who? De Bohun or de Valence?"

"De Valence. I've heard ye say as much."

"Hmm. I don't know the man at all, other than by name and repute. He's French and unfriendly and he's never given me a single nod of recognition, but he's well respected, if not well liked. He's one of Edward's oldest allies, too. Fought with him at Acre. It's his son, Aymer, I don't like, but he's not here, or Percy would have said so."

Thomas Beg harrumphed and pulled his horse to a halt, facing Bruce directly. "Right then," he said, his jaw set pugnaciously. "Three good friends, no' seen in a long time. But ye've a woman waitin' for ye. What makes *them* mair important than her, this minute? I've never seen ye choose the company o' a man ahead o' a willin' woman."

"It's about information, Tam," Bruce said, nudging his horse into movement again, and the big man swung his mount again to ride by his side. "I need the latest word on what's happening, here and in Scotland, and I'll get more truth out of de Bohun and Percy and Bigod in an hour than I'd get from anyone else in England in a month. They won't even know I'm pumping them. But I need to know what Edward has in mind these days regarding Balliol and his supporters. I haven't been invited to Westminster since I came down from the north, and Edward barely spoke ten words to me at my grandfather's funeral. I don't know what I've done to displease him this time, apart from having been born in Scotland—and now that I think on it, that's probably reason enough. He has troubles uncounted up there, I'm told. But then it never was hard to make Edward Plantagenet glower, so who can tell what's displeasing him from day to day?"

He shrugged. "For all that, though, these men are the best friends I have. They've been fighting in Wales for the past year and more and they're as much in favour with the King as I am out of it, it seems. So that leaves me with two options that I can see: to dally for pleasure with a woman tonight, or to spend that same time on an opportunity to find out what's really happening in the world. Sad that I can't have both, but there it is. My friends will be gone come daybreak."

"Fine. But now I think it wad be better for me just to ride in by mysel' an' tell the lassie ye've been detained by the Earl o' Pembroke, on the King's business. She'll no' be able to get vexed ower that. An' forbye, if you turn back now ye'll reach their camp damn near as soon as they do. Then later on I can go up there and tell ye ye're needed here." He saw the indecision in Bruce's eyes and cocked his head. "It's aey easy to come back and say ye're sorry ye was detained, but ye might look like a fool was ye to ride a' the way in there just to say ye had to go back again, when ye could hae stayed where ye wis i' the first place and done what ye had to do."

Bruce grimaced, unable to refute the simple, terse logic in that, but then he looked down at himself and shook his head. "I'm unarmed, Tam—dressed for womanizing."

"And why no'? Ye'll no' need to be armed anyway, ridin' in plain daylight wi' sodgers everywhere. But here, gie me that fancy dagger and tak my dirk an' awa ye go. I'll no' need a blade this close to camp, and I'll bring your sword and shield when I come to get ye, for the night ride back."

The earl nodded. "Go, then, and present the lady my good wishes and my regrets. And blame it on Pembroke, as you said. It's a small enough lie and worthwhile, to soothe her pride. But mind you tell her I'll be back soon after nightfall, and that you're coming to make sure I do. Go, then." He half smiled. "And don't be afraid to flee if the lady rounds on you. I'll be waiting for you later."

Bruce swung his mount around and kicked it to a canter.

# CHAPTER FIFTEEN

# THE POLITICS OF FRIENDSHIP

Bruce did not catch up to his English friends before they won back to camp, for they had clearly wasted no time moving out from the site of the mass hanging. The place was deserted by the time he reached it again, and he carefully avoided approaching the line of dangling bodies, all too aware of the sights and smells of violent death that would pollute this spot until the scavengers and the weather had cleansed it again and the dead men's fallen, insect-scoured bones had been covered by grass. Only in passing did he recognize that these were Englishmen hanged by other Englishmen, for they had been felons and had earned the justice meted out to them. Had he himself been sent to deal with them they would have fared no differently, for all his personal dislike of summary hangings.

He left them behind without another thought, following the broad, unmistakable path left by Percy's force, and within a few miles he found the English encampment spread out along the open lea flanking the river below the tiny settlement Percy had mentioned. A hamlet too small to have a name of its own, the tiny cluster of buildings had sprung up haphazardly on the crested flanks of a low knoll overlooking the crossing where the main London road forded the shallow, equally nameless river.

He drew rein before approaching the camp, far enough away to see it as a whole, and was surprised to find it larger and more

carefully organized than he had expected. It was square, in the fashion
of the old Roman marching camps, between three and four hundred
paces long on each side and cut into quarters by two broad, intersecting avenues, with the horse lines laid out in the two rear sections.

*Someone has strong notions of how to do things right*, he thought,
wryly acknowledging that the unapproachable Earl of Pembroke
must be responsible. More than three hundred men and their horses,
baggage, and attendants all in one spot created quite a scene.
Orderly lines of tents were already laid out in disciplined blocks
here and there in the two closest sections of the camp, while others
were being busily erected in the intervening spaces. He saw one
great pavilion in the centre, towering over all the others, that had the
colours of de Valence fluttering at its peak, and he determined to
avoid it, having no wish to meet the French-born Earl of Pembroke.
He turned his horse towards the line of guardsmen on his left and
rode forward to present himself.

The sergeant in charge of the detachment looked at the newcomer's rich appearance and waved him through, not bothering to ask
his business but raising an eyebrow at his lack of armour and the
single, belted dirk. Bruce halted anyway and asked him if he knew
where Sir Henry Percy might be found. The sergeant waved, indicating one of the new blocks of tents being built and saying he
thought he had seen Percy arrive earlier with Sir John Bigod's party.

Bruce made his way slowly in that direction until he spotted a
chevroned sergeant supervising a group who were labouring to put
up a knight's tent. The fellow wore Percy's new insignia on his left
shoulder, a gold patch bearing the blue lion rampant that so resem-
bled Bruce's own, and the look on his face as the earl approached
made it plain that he recognized him from earlier in the day.

Bruce drew rein again, nodding down at the man. "Bruce, Earl of
Carrick," he said. "Where will I find Sir Henry?"

"He's here somewhere, my lord, but I couldn't say where. You
*might* find him at one of the fires, in there somewhere." He lifted his
chin, and Bruce turned in his saddle, scanning the mass of bodies
moving aimlessly among the scattered campfires and the teams of

men raising tents all around. He could hear the staccato rattle of quarterstaves close by, but the press of bodies was so thick that he could see no sign of the fighters.

He swung down from his saddle and held out the reins. "Have someone look to my horse, will you? But keep him nearby, if you will, not in the horse lines. I'll be riding out again in an hour or two and I don't want to have to go looking for him."

The sergeant took the reins. "I'll keep him here, Lord Bruce, since you won't be staying."

Bruce nodded in thanks and turned away to walk into the crowded encampment where the noise quickly engulfed him, a riot of sounds and voices that hammered at his ears and made it impossible to really hear anything.

Within moments the press of bodies around him was dense enough to hamper his progress so that he had to shoulder his way forward carefully. And then, through a momentary eddy in the crowd, he saw Bigod's blazoned shield in front of a knight's tent not far ahead of him and veered towards it, realizing as he did so that Bigod had seen him at precisely the same moment and was waving to him. He started to wave back, but before he could even raise his arm the space ahead closed again and an abrupt change in the tenor and volume in the voices to his right warned him that something was going on there, just beyond his view. The crowd parted again, this time surging around him as men shuffled backward, shouting to each other, all eyes on whatever was happening ahead of them. He was aware again of the urgent clatter of quarterstaves nearby, but even more conscious of a new and ugly sound among the crowd, and though a voice in his head was telling him to be cautious, he reached out and grasped the two men directly ahead of him by their upper arms, prising them apart gently but firmly and stepping between them to find himself on the outer edge of a wide circle of cleared space.

Three men were fighting there, two against one, all of them armed with the thick, heavy poles of ash or oak that the English called the quarterstaff. He had a flickering impression of sullen hostility on the faces of the spectators ringing the space, and then his eyes were drawn to the activity in the ring itself as a vicious crack rang out, followed immediately by a woofing, explosive grunt and the dull, meaty sound of a heavy club smashing into a body. One of the three combatants went staggering, the quarterstaff spinning from his hands and into the packed throng as he reeled and stumbled, then fell heavily, face down, and lay motionless in a sprawl of mail-clad limbs.

The two other fighters ignored him, feet shifting warily as they crouched facing each other, but then one of them shook his head angrily and straightened up, throwing his quarterstaff to the ground and raising his hands high in surrender. His opponent, whose back was to Bruce, was a big man, almost as big as Bruce himself, dressed in a heavy gambeson that covered his arms down to the elbows and his legs to mid thigh. A chain-mail coif lined with padded leather covered his head, its flared tail protecting his broad shoulders. He, too, straightened up, but Bruce, who had expected the fellow to stand back and accept the surrender, was astonished when he spun the quarterstaff and lunged forward, slamming its thick end like a spear into the midriff of his defenceless opponent. The hapless victim whooped in shock, his eyes flying wide, and dropped to his knees like a stone before toppling sideways, too stunned even to clutch at himself. His attacker launched himself forward and kicked him viciously in the side of the head as he lay on the ground, then skipped back and raised his quarterstaff over his head in both hands.

Bruce was barely aware of moving but his fingers closed over the man's wrist and locked before he could begin his downward chop. "Enough," he said. "He's done." He felt the iron pressure of the wrist pulling against him, trying to break his grip, and he squeezed harder, tensing his arm to hold it motionless. Suddenly the fellow twisted, pivoting around the grip on his right wrist, his left hand scrabbling claw-fingered to grip Bruce's shoulder as he whipped his mailed head forward to butt his tormentor in the face. Bruce recognized the face immediately, even twisted with fury as it was, and almost hesitated in surprise to find himself confronting the knight Hazelrig from the hanging glade. His lifetime of rough-and-tumble training saved him, though, and he swayed backward, easily avoiding the clumsy attack, though he felt the fabric of his fine shirt give way at the collar to Hazelrig's wrenching. But he had to release the other's wrist to complete his move, and as soon as he was free Hazelrig grasped his quarterstaff in a fresh, two-handed grip and lunged, driving its end in a lethal thrust towards Bruce's throat.

This time, though, Bruce was ready, icy, familiar rage filling his breast. His right hand shot up and grasped the shaft, deflecting it almost scornfully as his other hand closed on it lower down. He stepped back with one foot and swung his powerful weight around to onc side, arching his body and pulling hard, using the other man's momentum to jerk him off balance so that he almost fell as Bruce completed the heaving pivot, releasing the thick shaft and leaping forward to kick the man hard behind the knee with the heavy sole of his iron-studded boot. The impact drove Hazelrig forward, and he lurched into the arms of the watchers at the front of the circle. There was no doubt now of their hostility. Rough hands seized the sprawling knight and spun him around before one burly soldier planted a boot at the base of his spine and propelled him back into the circle.

Bruce stood waiting, cradling one quarterstaff while standing over another. A silence fell as the two knights faced each other and the watching crowd held its breath in anticipation. Bruce stood easily, his face showing no sign of the tightly controlled anger that seethed in him. Hazelrig, on the other hand, was red-faced and glaring wildly, breathing loudly through his mouth. His shoulders were hunched forward and his arms outstretched, the large hands clenching and unclenching as he glowered at the unarmoured man in the open-necked tunic.

"You had no right to lay hands on me," he snarled. "I'll kill you for that."

Bruce flexed his knees and squatted to pick up the second quarterstaff, the down-and-up movement fluid and graceful. "With one of these?" He shook his head, a tiny, deadly smile playing across his lips. "I doubt it," he replied, deliberately emphasizing his Scots pronunciation. "You havena been fed well enough for that. But if you want to try it, go ahead."

He tossed the second quarterstaff across the circle, lightly enough for Hazelrig to catch it easily, and then fell into fighting stance, one foot ahead of the other and his staff in a two-handed grip, extended like a sword. Hazelrig stood unmoving, holding his own staff as he had caught it, his eyes narrowing and his wild anger fading visibly now as he took the measure of the elegant dandy across from him. He himself was a big, imposing man, a shade over six feet in height, broad in the shoulder and heavily muscled, his compact midriff hidden by the padded coat he wore.

The man he faced, though, was even bigger, taller than he by two or perhaps even three inches, and his shoulders were enormous even without padding or armour. The chest beneath the velvet tunic and soft shirt was broad and deep, the waist trim, the belly apparently hard and flat. The long legs, covered in brightly coloured hose, were like young trees, and the hands that held the extended quarterstaff were large and broad. The man reeked of confidence and competence, and now he was smiling more widely.

"Whenever you feel like it," he said quietly, and the watching crowd caught its breath again as Hazelrig grunted and slid into motion, extending his weapon and sidling to his right in the opening steps of the dance. Bruce watched him narrow-eyed as he, too, began to move, concentrating intently now and shutting the crowd out of his awareness, refusing to be distracted by the sudden surge of movement he caught from the left side of the circle. And Hazelrig sprang forward, his quarterstaff sweeping up in an axelike swing.

"Now, by the bowels of Christ! Enough!"

The shout was accompanied by a whistling arc of light as Sir Henry Percy leapt between the two men, landing nimbly and swinging a broadsword in a two-handed grip that drove the weapon's edge cleanly into Hazelrig's upraised staff. The blade cut deep into the thick pole and shattered it, driving the English knight back on his heels, where he dropped the severed stub and clamped both hands beneath his armpits, grimacing as he vainly tried to relieve the sting of the unexpected impact. He glared at the interloper and the other two knights who stood vigilantly behind him, John Bigod and a heavily bearded Humphrey de Bohun.

Percy hung there tensely for a moment, sword still upraised, watching Hazelrig through slitted eyes and poised for a reaction, then quickly took a half step back. He dropped one hand from the hilt of his sword and swung the long blade out and sideways, holding it horizontally between the two men.

Bruce had not moved since grounding his quarterstaff when Hazelrig lost his, and now he remained motionless as Percy turned his head to look at him, his eyes flickering down, then up, looking for damage. When he saw none, the knight looked away again, this time downward to where Hazelrig's two erstwhile opponents yet lay on the ground, the first of them unmoving, the other writhing feebly and groaning. Bruce saw him draw in a deep breath, then hold it, but Percy's face betrayed little of his thoughts before he stepped towards the huddled form of the first man. He knelt smoothly and felt beneath the chin, looking for a pulse, then stood up and scanned the surrounding crowd. He pointed with the tip of his sword.

"You four. Take up these two—carefully—to the Hospitallers' area. Carry them on poles and shields and be cautious. They may be gravely injured." His voice was flat and hard, and he raised it higher as he looked around at the watching throng. "As for the rest of you, we have a camp to set up here and no time for idleness. I will find ample work for any man still here by the time I count to ten. One. Two … " Before he reached four the crowd was scattering, men hurrying to appear busy and industrious. Percy kept counting none the less, and by the time the tenth syllable rang out the five knights were alone amid the bustle of normal camp activities.

Hazelrig had lowered his hands from beneath his arms and now stood staring blank-faced at Percy, whom Bruce supposed to be his nominal commander. Percy, however, ignored him for the moment, turning to look directly at Bruce and waving in the direction of the departing porters.

"Did you have anything to do with that?"

Bruce merely shook his head, and the knight looked from him to Hazelrig.

"Then why were you two fighting? Hazelrig?"

The Englishman drew himself up to attention, glowering towards Bruce. "Because that Scotch whoreson laid hands on me."

Percy did not react to the insult other than to purse his lips. Then he said, "That Scotch whoreson is a direct descendant of William the Marshall. Think you the Marshall, too, was a Scot?"

Bruce kept his face impassive, but he was surprised that Percy would know such a thing, let alone remember it. He kept his eyes on Hazelrig, though, and saw the fellow's brows twitch in surprise before settling into a sullen scowl. "You know what I mean, Baron Percy. He insulted me … Assaulted me in front of my men."

Percy's narrowed eyes flicked back to Bruce, whose slight shrug was barely perceptible.

"I stopped him," Bruce said. "From hitting a downed man. It seemed the right thing to do at the time. Unless he has some right I don't have to injure the King's men rather than his enemies."

"Two men were down," Percy said in the same, clipped voice. "One unconscious, one disabled." His eyes switched back to Hazelrig. "That was your work? You beat them both insensible?"

"We were training."

Percy's whole face tightened, and Bruce could almost feel him fighting not to give Hazelrig the lie, thereby precipitating a direct challenge. Instead the baron sheathed his sword deliberately and turned to where de Bohun and Bigod stood watching, beckoning them closer. "I need you to bear witness, my friends," he said, "lest mention of this incident arise again later." He turned back to Hazelrig, whose brows had come together again—less in anger this time than in perplexity.

"Sir William Hazelrig," he began, in the same flat tone he had used earlier. "I, Henry Percy, Baron of Alnwick and knight of this realm, should have no need to remind you that he who strikes down any loyal soldier of King Edward is guilty of offence against the

King himself, an act of treason against the King's majesty. Here, though, the need is clear, and this reminder therefore takes the form of an official warning. You are a knight in my command and this is not the first time I have been made aware of the tendency you have to be ... over*zealous*, let us say, in your treatment of the men with whose welfare you have been entrusted. I remind you now that they are my men and, by extension of the rules of command, the men of Lord Guillaume de Valence and of the King himself. None of them, I would suggest, would dare to treat you as you so evidently feel free to treat them, and you have set yourself perilously close to the point beyond which *training*, as you term it, becomes abuse and unlawful assault. Be warned accordingly. And be warned further, in this. Sir Robert Bruce is here in this camp as my guest, by my goodwill and at my invitation. He is also an earl, the Earl of Carrick, a rank that carries far more privilege than yours, as a mere knight bachelor. He has also come among us unarmoured and weaponless, save for a dirk, so I can scarce believe that the scene I found here when I arrived was really as violent as it appeared to be. That is correct, is it not? The appearance was misleading?"

Hazelrig looked as though he were fighting to swallow powdered glass, and the glare he directed at Bruce was one of smouldering fury, but he had the good sense to nod in agreement, one brief jerk of his head, and mumble, "It was," through wooden lips.

"So be it, then. You may return to your quarters, Sir William. Directly, I would suggest."

Hazelrig jerked his head again, his face flaming with rage, and turned stiffly and stalked away without a backward glance. The other four knights watched him go until the crowd had swallowed him up, and then Percy looked around the surrounding throng to see if anyone was watching them. None appeared to be, and he finally exhaled and relaxed visibly, the tension flowing out of his shoulders.

"Bruce," he said quietly, speaking half over his shoulder, "you might think yourself fortunate we came along when we did. That one is an ill man to cross."

Bruce grunted. "I had no thought of crossing him, Harry. But he would have maimed the man."

Percy sucked in air with a tutting, sibilant sound. "Aye, he's done the like before, although he's never yet been challenged for it. Nor has he ever been so open about it." He glanced at Bigod and de Bohun, who were listening and watching, and grimaced as though at a bad taste. "Ah well," he said. "Enough of this. Roast piglet. Evermore delightful than mere piggery. Dinner should be awaiting us by now, so let us see if we can find it."

"Tell me about Wales, Percy."

A good two hours had passed in banter and raillery, and the roast pig was now only a memory, save in the eyes of the servants who had cooked it and were now feasting on the remnants. The others who had shared the feast had all drifted away, leaving Bruce, Percy, and de Bohun alone by the fire. De Bohun was still gnawing at some bones, and Bigod had gone off somewhere, saying he would be back.

"Wales?" Percy asked, looking at Bruce with a frown. "What about it?"

"You said earlier that you hated being there. What made it so bad?"

The frown turned to a scowl as the faint breeze wafted a cloud of smoke from the campfire into Percy's face. "Bad?" He fanned the smoke away with one hand. "It wasn't merely *bad*, Bruce. It was hellish. I was there for almost five months, and they were … " He shook his head, still scowling as he searched for words. "They were the most futile, dangerous, and bowel-loosening months of my life. Never a moment to enjoy anything. Unrelenting tension all the time, waiting to be attacked or shot down from any direction, and no time, ever, to be truly at ease. It was impossible to tell friends from enemies among the locals. At least it was at first, until we learned that there *were* no friends among them. All of them, we learned to our cost, were enemies. You could trust no one but your own comrades. Everyone else, down to the women and children who waited on you and served you, was as likely as not to stab you in the vitals as soon as you turned your back. The only time I felt confident there was when we finally brought them to battle in Powys, in March, because then it was straightforward—them and us, kill or be killed. We smashed them, but their leader, Madog, escaped and no one has laid eyes on him since. Believe me, Bruce, it was a foul experience, and it will take a miracle or a direct royal command to send Harry Percy back to Wales again. You were fortunate to be busy in Ulster."

He twisted to look around him, and Bruce said nothing, content to wait for more. The encampment was finally beginning to grow quieter as close to three hundred men and their mounts, now fed and watered, settled in for the night. Bigod had told him that the veteran Earl of Pembroke, Guillaume de Valence—Gwillie, as he was irreverently known—had barely taken the time to acknowledge his subordinate commanders on his arrival. He had gone straight to his own pavilion, where he had dined alone as he usually did, catered to by his personal retainers. He was known to be disdainful and high-handed at the best of times, though, and his knights and officers accepted his truculence gladly, grateful to be spared the dubious privilege of his recognition or company.

"I never thought to encounter such hatred in my own country," Percy went on, still addressing Bruce but sounding now as though he were musing aloud. "I mean, I'm not describing mere dislike, Bruce. Who cares if they like us or not? But this was palpable *loathing*. Those people detest us with a passion that goes beyond anything I've ever encountered. Being among them, being in Wales at all, is … unnerving after a while."

Bruce straightened slightly, leaning towards the fire but looking at Percy as he did so, aware of de Bohun listening on his other side. "In sweet Jesu's name, Harry," he said quietly, "are you surprised? *Truly* surprised? Of course they detest you, and with good reason, at least in their own eyes. Think about what you just said—you never thought to encounter such hatred in your own country. Well, you didn't. You weren't in your own country—you were in *their* country.

Wales is theirs and always has been. To them, you were an invader.
They have been free since before the Romans came to Britain, until
Edward decided to add their red dragon to his English Crown.
Edward has no care for what the Welsh folk think of him. He wanted
Wales and he took it, by provoking the Welsh into rebellion, but the
Welsh *folk* were a mere nuisance, a distraction, between his decision
and its achievement. And now that he has the place, he'll hold it fast.
The castles he is building over there will see to that."

"By the *Christ*!" de Bohun had risen to his feet and now he
uttered an inchoate sound of pure disgust and hurled the bones
angrily into the fire, which collapsed upon itself, throwing an
inferno of sparks high into the evening sky. "That's treasonous talk,
Bruce, and I won't listen to it. *Provoking* the Welsh into rebellion,
in Christ's name! Since when have the Welsh needed to be provoked?
What kind of arrant shit is that? They rose up against the King of
their own free will, led by Llewelyn and his troublemaking brood,
and since they did, twelve years and more ago, they've run amok
and sent many a good Englishman to meet his God unready. They're
rebellious whoresons, one and all, and as a King's man I'd gladly
send them all to roast in Hell."

He was almost spluttering in his rage, his bearded chin slick with
grease from the pig he had been eating and his left hand brandishing
the wooden platter that had held his meal. "And what of you? You're
said to be a King's man, but from your words here I might doubt
that. Have you listened to yourself, spewing shit like that? You
would be well advised to keep such mouthings muted, Bruce, lest
you find yourself and your loyalties taken to task. By the Christ, I've
never heard such shit from the mouth of any King's knight. I'll bid
you a good night, sir, for I have no wish to listen further."

Bruce had leaned backward, looking up mildly at de Bohun from
beneath raised brows, his weight braced on straight arms against a
second log at his back, and now he smiled and shook his head from
side to side. "Humphrey, Humphrey," he said. "Hotheaded as ever
and wrong again to boot. I had no thought of being disloyal to our
King, my friend. Nor was I." He held up a hand quickly before

de Bohun could speak again, and as the burly English knight stopped, open-mouthed, he continued. "I merely stated the truth, as I perceive it, about the way the Welsh see things."

De Bohun blinked in perplexity. Bruce waved a hand towards the log from which the other had sprung up. "Sit down, man," he said gently. "Truly, you misread my meaning. I am Edward's man as surely as you are and as Percy is. I left my homeland to serve him as my liege lord and I owe him more than I can ever repay. How, then, could I be disloyal to him? My duty is to him and my life is his to command. He may not be my King by birth, since I was born in Scotland, but I have chosen to serve him willingly, ahead of Scotland's King, and you have known me long enough to know I do not deal in lies." He turned to Percy. "Harry, what say you? Will you not tell the man to sit back down? Or do you, too, think me treasonous?"

Percy, who had been gazing narrow-eyed at Bruce as he listened, grunted and waved a languid hand at the big, glowering knight standing over them. "Sit down, Humphrey, in God's name. And remember to whom you're listening. Bruce is Bruce and ever was. He says ungodly things from time to time, but he's a heathen Scot when all's said and done, and none of us has ever had cause to doubt him. Besides, he has the right of it in this. Now be a good fellow and sit down before I strain my neck from looking up at you."

De Bohun hesitated, his face a picture of scowling indecision, then slowly lowered himself back to sit on his log. "No matter," the big man muttered darkly. "Still don't like hearing things like that. Makes us sound like thieves and brigands and makes the King sound like some foreign tyrant. He's the King of England, Bruce. That means in England he can do what he likes, and it's our duty to make sure o' that."

Bruce merely raised his eyebrows, and it was Percy, again, who answered de Bohun's grumbling. "No one's contesting that, Humphrey. Bruce was but talking among friends, expressing an opinion with no thought of sedition in his head. Isn't that so, Bruce?"

Bruce nodded slowly. "Aye, it's so."

"There, you see?" Percy said, as though explaining something to a backward child. "So now let's talk of other matters." He paused then, eyeing Bruce. "Mind you, Humphrey does have a point. I can think of others who might be equally offended at hearing what you said, others less inclined to listen in friendship. We are all King's men here, but some beyond this fire would take those comments of yours ill, my lord earl. It's not the kind of thing that should be shouted out aloud. It could be bad for discipline."

"By causing other men to think in ways they're not supposed to see? Aye, you're right. It could. *Mea culpa*. I retract my words." Bruce rose to his feet and went to a nearby pile of fuel where he spent some time selecting a quartet of thick, well-dried logs that he carried to the fire, one by one, and threw onto the embers.

"That's a fine way to ruin an expensive doublet," John Bigod said, approaching the fire just as Bruce was brushing the dust and debris from his clothing. He peered at Bruce's garment again, then reached out and fingered one of its sleeves, dipping his head and pursing his lips appreciatively before subsiding, with a wry glance at Percy, to sit on one of the logs scattered around the rim of the fire pit. "Gwillie's in a fine old snit," he said. "Stopped me as I was passing by his tent and chewed on me for not keeping one or two of our bandits alive. As if they might have had aught to say that was worth hearing." He looked down at Percy. "Says he wants to talk to you."

"Shit. When, now?"

"No, no. When he sees you. So were I you, I'd keep away from him. There's nothing he can do now. They're all dead and there's an end of it, so all he can do is carp. Seems to think it would have been good for him had he taken back some guilty felons to show to the crowd in Westminster. It never hurts to keep the King happy, he thinks, though he didn't say it aloud. He's right, too, though Christ knows it's growing more difficult from day to day."

Bruce's ears pricked at that. "How so?" he asked. "Is the King distempered?"

"Don't even ask," Bigod answered him, his voice heavy with disgust. "Believe me, you've done well to be so far removed from things this past year, beyond the sea, in the Ulster wilderness." He waved a hand to indicate his two companions. "We, on the other hand, have had to suffer through all of it."

Bruce was frowning. "All of what, John?"

"He means all of the things that have happened to displease the King this past year," Percy explained. "Rattling like hailstones on a helmet. France set it off, back in May or June of last year—" He hesitated, then asked de Bohun, "When was it, Humphrey? When did Philip of France cut off our good King's beard?"

"May nineteenth. I remember it because it was the same day my grandmother died, God rest her soul. But that was ten years ago ... when she died, I mean."

Percy rolled his eyes and kept on talking to Bruce. "That's it. May nineteenth last year, it was. Of course, we heard nothing of it until weeks later, but on that day Philip of France had his lawyers declare Edward's stewardship of Aquitaine invalid because Edward refused to do him homage, or some such nonsense. Anyway, Philip marched his armies into Aquitaine and seized it, and Edward declared war as soon as he heard of it. That put us at war with France *and* the rebels in Gascony, both at the same time, and that set some of our own barons howling about the costs of it all. Then in July, your Scots parliament stepped on Edward's toes in earnest when he required a supporting levy of Scots knights and liegemen to accompany us to France. They told him to his face that your King John had no power, even had he willed it, to commit Scots knights to support an English war in France without their authority as parliament."

Bruce blinked in astonishment. "They told him that *in person*? Who dared do that?"

Percy waved the question away brusquely. "Well, they didn't tell him, exactly. They sent a letter, much beribboned and festooned with seals. It was sheer defiance, but cloaked with churchly decorum. Edward was livid, believe me. No one dared mention Scotland or Scots within his hearing for months."

"Balliol is not *my* King John, since you mention it," Bruce murmured. "Never was and never will be, which is the point of my family's presence here in England. But I did know something of that debate and its upshot. My grandfather said that parliament had behaved correctly. No Scots King has ever had the power to send an army beyond the seas without first consulting with all the magnates of the realm, and none of those would ever go, lacking some massive urgency. The costs are ruinous and the land is far less populous than yours. Scotland simply cannot spare the men. Not surprising, then, that they spoke as they did, but I can see why Edward would be displeased."

"Displeased!" Percy made a sound between a snort and a scornful guffaw. "Aye, 'displeased' might be a good word for it. About as apt as *dismayed* would be in describing a well-born maiden who finds herself confronted by a blood-mad pirate bent on tupping her. There was nothing he could do about it, though, short of going to war with Scotland atop all else. And then, as we finally made ready to embark for Gascony with an army in September, the mad Welsh dog Madog made a costly error. Costly for everyone. Someone had told him that the main part of our armies had long since shipped safely away to France and there was nothing but a holding force left behind to raise more Welsh bowmen. So up he jumped in rebellion, mouthing the same tripe: that Welshmen could not be conscripted by an English King—" He broke off, staring at Bruce with a strange expression. "But you must have heard all this, surely, here, if not in Ulster."

Bruce nodded. "A bit here, a bit there, and little of it about Wales. De Burgh had his own priorities to deal with in Ulster, though, and little time to sit around and talk about what might be happening elsewhere. And we heard nothing from the King himself. There were rumours, of course, particularly about the French treachery last year, but I've never heard the full litany listed quite like this."

"That's not the full litany. Merely the start of it," Bigod added. "And none of it grows better in the telling." He wrinkled his nose. "The Scots in general are a contentious issue. Never at rest, those people, and always arguing. They're like ants—there's order there, of a kind, but no mere man can say how it works or what controls it. Now they have a King who shifts about like a flag in an errant wind and whose temper can never be depended on for any length of time, and all of us wonder how he can ever hope to keep control of the savages he is supposed to govern. Which reminds me, d'you know a knight called Douglas? Sir William Douglas?"

Bruce dipped his head. "Of Douglasdale, aye, I've heard tell of him. Never met the man, but from what I hear he's a wild one, ungovernable, foul-tempered and … What was that word you used? 'Contentious'? Aye, that would fit what I've heard. How do *you* know him, John?"

"I don't." Bigod's denial was curt. "But I've met him, once, on May Day past. Now *there* is an arrogant whoreson. I detested him on sight. The King is well aware of the fellow, though. Calls himself William le Hardi, Lord of Douglas, and behaves as though he were King of all Scotland—and England, too, for that matter. Considers himself answerable to no one. He abducted an English woman some years ago—back in eighty-eight it was—a widowed woman of noble birth whom the King himself had dowered. She was living in the north at the time, under the protection of Lord Alan la Zouche, Baron of Ashby, and this lout Douglas laid siege to the baron's castle for some imagined grievance and captured the woman. Eleanor Something-or-other. Same first name as my wife and the late Queen. Carried her off to his castle, and before a ransom could be arranged, the silly woman married him and refused to be ransomed."

Bruce grinned. "Aye, I heard about that. It would seem the man's not as savage and uncivilized as repute would have him."

Bigod made a face. "Some females prefer beasts to men, I've been told—drawn towards the violent and savage. He was taken soon after that. Edward imprisoned him in Winchester for a spell, then let him go, upon his promise of good behaviour, which the fellow broke quickly enough. Since then he's been in and out of grace and favour constantly. But he's here now, close by, I'm told."

"You mean in England?"

"No, I mean here in Essex. You and he are neighbours."

"Are we, by God? I knew nothing of that. How might I find him?"

"If you've an ounce of sense in you, you won't. The man's name reeks of ill intent and sedition."

"He's imprisoned here, you mean?"

"No, not exactly. He is under parole of good behaviour."

"I see. And you expect him to break that."

"I think it's inevitable. It was the business with Hazelrig that made me think of him. Now there's a creature to beware of. He can be pleasant enough when he wants to be, and he's good at what he does, but what he does best is the kind of thing most men like us would choose to do only with great reluctance—and he does everything for Hazelrig before all else. He'll make a bad enemy. And he has the King's ear."

It flashed through Bruce's mind that Percy himself would make a far more dangerous enemy than Hazelrig ever could. He had watched Harry during the brief confrontation with Hazelrig and had no doubt that matter might have ended fatally had not Hazelrig backed down. Bruce himself had never killed a man. He had come close, particularly so in Ulster, where he had ridden out several times on sorties against bands of rebels and insurgents. None of those had ever come to action, though, and so the entirety of his experience in arms had been in mock battle and in the lists at tourneys, always using blunted weapons. Percy's experiences had been more practical, in Wales and elsewhere, and Bruce knew that when duty demanded it the Baron of Alnwick would be implacable, killing without a second thought. A man of impeccable honour, combined with probity, integrity, and finely honed military skills. A very dangerous enemy, indeed.

Percy did not notice the barely perceptible hesitation his comment had occasioned. Bruce cocked an eyebrow. "The King's ear, you say? You mean Edward can't see his faults?"

"No, I mean the King can *use* his faults. Hazelrig is an Englishman with certain peculiar talents, let us say—talents that not all Englishmen possess or favour—and the King has need, from time to time, of creatures of his stamp. This Douglas, on the other hand, is a Scot, and an uncouth, ungentle one. But an adder is an adder—venomous whether English or Scots." He stopped suddenly, then asked, "When did you last speak with the King?"

Bruce shrugged. "In April. He attended my grandfather's funeral. But we did not speak privately, merely exchanged civilities. He was under duress and had no time for anything more."

"That was months ago. You have not seen him since?"

"No, nor heard from him."

"How so? Did you offend him?"

Bruce almost smiled. "I have no memory of doing so. And you know Edward. Had I done so, he would have left me in no doubt of it. But no, I have given him no cause to be displeased with me." He shrugged. "Nor to summon me, either, for that matter … "

"Then you must go to Westminster and pay your respects," Percy said, his voice filled with conviction. "The King has much on his mind these days, and he may have lost sight of the fact that four months have elapsed and your mourning is over. Go and show your face, my friend. I'll warrant you'll be glad you did." The other two nodded, even the surly de Bohun scowling in what might have been encouragement.

"I will, then," Bruce said. "The worst he can do, if he is displeased with me, is have me hanged."

"No," de Bohun growled, "he could have your entrails drawn, too, and burn them there in front of you while you watched."

The big knight was jesting, Bruce knew, but he twisted his mouth wryly. "I doubt that, Humphrey. His name's Plantagenet. Only a de Bohun would come up with a punishment as refined as the one you describe."

As the others laughed, Bruce caught sight of Thomas Beg coming towards them, searching among the campsite fires and leading a horse loaded with Bruce's half armour, shield, and sword belt. "Here's my man," he said, rising to his feet and waving to attract his attention. "Come to lead me back home in safety, God bless him. Though why he should feel I have need of armour is beyond me. Thomas Beg, over here!"

He saw Tam veer towards their fire, then swung back to his three friends and thanked them for their hospitality and the pleasure of their company, promising to see them all again soon, most probably in Westminster. By the time his farewells were over, Thomas Beg had reached their campfire and stood waiting.

"Thomas," Bruce said, eyeing the armour piled on the horse Tam led. "Have I need of all that for the short ride to camp?"

"We're no' goin' to camp, my lord. We're goin' back to Writtle. Your father sent word while ye were here that he'll be there afore noon and expects you there to greet him … Him and the lady Isabella, your wife-to-be."

Bruce sucked in sharply and choked, then doubled over in a fit of coughing that delighted his English companions, and their guffaws rang in his ears throughout the time it took him to regain his composure. Bruce wiped his eyes with the sleeve of his tunic and blinked owlishly at his retainer, ignoring the splutters and snorts of his suddenly raucous friends. He forced himself to remain motionless until their chortling died away completely and then he cleared his throat gently and spoke in a calm voice. "Forgive me, Thomas. My reaction may have been stronger than you expected, but you took me by surprise. My … my lady *wife*, did you say?"

Wee Thomas nodded, his face inscrutable. "Aye, that's what I said. The Lady Isabella o' Mar, come in train wi' your father an' her ain, auld Earl Domhnall himsel'. They'll be stopping to collect you, on their way to Westminster to obtain the King's blessing on the match."

"By the holy rood, Bruce, that's a bit sudden, is it not? A quick end to your whoring days, no? You had no inkling?"

Bruce shook his head in mute response to Bigod's question, his eyes still on Thomas Beg, but then Percy slapped him on the upper arm.

"My felicitations, Bruce. Surprise or not, expected or otherwise, you are about to enter Paradise, if my own experience is anything by which to judge. But you must have known something of this, surely? It cannot be a complete surprise."

In spite of feeling as though someone had kicked him in the belly, he calmly answered Percy's question. "No," he said, sounding uncertain even to himself, "I had some inkling, a long time ago, but ... " He scrubbed his hand across his eyes again, then moved to resume his seat on the log by the fire, waving to the other three to join him. When they were settled, he sighed and shook his head ruefully. "My grandfather told me about this, years ago, when the lass was no more than twelve. Her brother Gartnait of Mar is already my good-brother, wed to my sister Christina, and her father, the Gaelic mormaer—that's their word for high chief—Domhnall of Mar, has been a lifelong supporter of the House of Bruce. Domhnall had no more liking for John Balliol and the Comyns than we Bruces did, and it was he who suggested this match soon after the child Isabella was born. I think he thought even then that my grandsire would be King one day. But when I first heard of it from my grandsire the possibility was long years away in the future. And then Balliol became King and we lost our status and our holdings in Scotland, and I thought no more about it. We could not return to Scotland, so how then could I be wed according to my grandsire's plan?"

Percy sat staring across the fire at Bruce, nodding slowly. "So you have never met the girl?"

"Never met her, never seen her. She exists, that's all I know. Clearly, though, my father seeks to make the old man's dream a reality, if he has gone to the trouble to bring her to England."

"Aye, and to involve the goodwill of the King in the matter. That bespeaks long consideration."

Bruce sighed, thinking wistfully about the other long-considered matter of the woman who would not, after all, be sharing his bed that night. "Aye, it does ... " He glanced to where Thomas Beg stood waiting. "I should be away, then, for I can see by my man's stance that he is impatient to be on the road."

"How long will it take you to get home?"

"Not long. We have about eight miles to ride … Two hours in the dark? But I had better change into my armour. May I use your tent?"

"Of course," Percy said with easy grace. "It should be ready by now."

"Mine certainly is," Bigod intervened. "And it's closer. I'll have your horse brought up from where you left it."

"My thanks. I will." He beckoned to Thomas Beg to join him, and they made their way to Bigod's tent, leading Tam's mount and the armour-laden packhorse.

"What did you do with the women?" Bruce asked as soon as they were inside the tent.

"Sent them on to Writtle. They'll hae been there afore it got dark. They werena happy, but they could see for theirsels what had happened. Lord Bruce's courier arrived no' long after me. It's Sir James Jardine, an' ye ken what he's like."

Bruce nodded, his mouth twisting wryly. He recalled the grim, unsmiling Annandale laird clearly. Jardine had been one of the Noble Robert's most loyal vassals, and he had evidently transferred his loyalty to the old man's son when the younger Bruce assumed the lordship, but his personality was less than sparkling. Bruce could not recall ever having seen the man smile and could not imagine him finding humour in anything.

"He wasna pleased to find you no' there when he reached Writtle," Tam continued. "And that didna improve when ye werena in camp, either, by the time he got there. He'd had a hard time findin' the place, an' he made no secret o' what he was aboot, either, so the whole camp heard him and kenned what was afoot, and it wis plain there wis naethin' else for us to do but pack everything up and leave. The ladies wis disappointed, but they went wi'out a fuss. Jardine went back to Writtle wi' them and I told him I'd hae you there, too, as soon as I could collect ye. Oh, an' the lady sent ye this." He reached into his scrip and pulled out a folded sheet of fine vellum, shaved to the point of semi-transparency and sealed with a blob of plain wax. Bruce took it and carried it to the nearest light, where he flicked the seal open and scanned the short note.

*It seems we are not meant to enjoy each other. A courier brings word that your wife-to-be will arrive tomorrow. I wish you both well. Someday, perhaps, we may meet again and begin again.*

No names, no signature. He sniffed, aware of a small feeling of regret, and that it was overshadowed by a small, growing excitement over what the morrow might bring. Tam was watching him, and he held the letter up to the flame of the lamp, holding it there until it caught, then watching it burn, twisting the parchment until the written portion had been completely consumed. He held it until he was in danger of burning himself, then dropped the last, still-burning fragment and ground it under his foot.

"Right," he said. "Help me get dressed."

# CHAPTER SIXTEEN

# NATURAL WRATH

Bruce and Wee Thomas arrived home in the darkness before midnight, when the moon was still high in the sky among a sparse scattering of clouds. They had expected to find the lights all out and the household fast asleep, but instead they saw the place lit up from a mile away, its square tower still visible against the green-tinged lightness of the western sky, and the sight of the unusual brightness glowing through the night from such a distance reminded Bruce that the place was astir with guests and visitors who would have set the place in turmoil, since no one had expected anyone to return from the festive hunting trip for at least another two days. He turned in his saddle to look at Thomas Beg and found the big man watching him, clearly waiting for him to say something. And so, being Bruce, he said nothing. But Tam was not to be put off.

"They're up late," he said, his voice hovering somewhere between disapproval and pleasure.

Bruce shrugged. "Not really surprising, if you think on it. You said the women would arrive back here before nightfall, and the sun set less than three hours ago. And they would have been tied to the pace of the lame jennet. We've made more than twice the speed they would, but even so, they'll barely have had time to eat, for Allie would be scandalized to send them to bed with naught but a cold, scant supper. So they might still be at table."

"A bit late for that," Tam said, and then his voice brightened. "But that means hot food for us, too."

Bruce grinned. "Aye, it might, provided someone said we'd be coming after them. Somebody as kind and considerate of others as Sir James Jardine … "

Even in the moonlight he could see Thomas Beg frown as he thought of that, and then the big man kicked his horse into a canter, the words "Better get there while it's still hot, then" drifting back over his shoulder.

The household was not quite at table when they arrived; the female guests were being shown to their accommodations by Bruce's harried staff, and the outer yard was bustling with activity as servants loaded the bulk of the ladies' baggage onto carts and wagons in preparation for an early departure in the morning. Bruce had seen the Lady Gwendolyn de Ferrers as soon as he stepped into the house. She had been going upstairs and turned to him, and he was glad to see that the swift smile she sent him was open and free of resentment. He would have been unsurprised had she withered him with a scathing sneer, and he was grateful for her forbearance.

"My lady," he called as she began to turn away, surprising himself since he had had no thought until that moment of approaching her. She stopped, as did her companions, and then she moved slightly closer, to the low wall edging the stairs, looking down at him with one hand laid on the decorative stone hand rail that topped the coping stones. Only then, as she looked down at him with that same gentle smile, did he realize how ill prepared he was for this encounter. He had removed his helmet on dismounting and now carried it upside down in the crook of his arm, its bowl stuffed with his riding gauntlets; he had also pulled off the mailed coif, flinging it carelessly across one cloaked shoulder as he scrubbed at his matted scalp with his free hand. Now, looking up at the lushly beautiful young woman above him, he imagined he could see himself through her eyes, awkward and clumsy, unwashed and unkempt and reeking pungently of sweat—his own and his horse's— and the ingrained stink of oily, leather-lined chain mail and rancid gambeson. The thought made him flush with embarrassment.

"Madame, I must ask you and your companions to forgive me for my neglect of you and for the disappointment I have caused you all—"

He stopped as she raised a hand to silence him.

"My lord Bruce," she said, her voice low pitched yet carrying clearly to all who listened, "you have no reason to apologize to anyone. Our lives are all dictated by conditions and circumstances that we can seldom control. Yours is clearly no exception. The Earl of Pembroke summoned you, and you had no choice but to obey. Tonight Sir James has told us of your betrothal years since, and of how tomorrow you will set eyes for the first time upon the lady who is to be your wife. We all are glad for you, Earl Robert, and wish you well. And—" She grinned a sudden, wicked grin and turned to eye her companions, inviting them to join in her banter, "we will all be gone again from here long before she comes, lest she should think she has competitors to fear. And now, sir, may God be with you this night and we will leave you to your duties, in the hope of meeting you again someday, with your lady wife." She smiled again and raised a hand in farewell, then glided up the stairs, already deep in conversation with one of the other women.

Bruce stood blinking at their backs, nonplussed by the thought of the scowling Annandale knight speaking to them at all, but then he shook his head as though to clear it and made his way into the main hall. He was confident that his path would cross hers again someday and next time, he was determined, they would enjoy settling the business that lay unfinished between them.

His musings were cut off by the sight of Sir James Jardine, still seated at one of the large tables in the hall and gazing at Bruce as he entered. There was no one else of consequence around—several men and women from the household staff were clearing away the debris of the meal, now that the other guests had departed, but none of them was anywhere close to where Sir James sat alone holding a drinking mug, his wooden platter pushed out into the centre of the table for collection. Bruce caught the eye of one of the servants as he crossed the room and pointed to the knight's abandoned platter, indicating with a flick of his hand that it should be cleared away. He reached the table and waited silently while the servant removed the platter, then nodded courteously to his guest.

"Sir James. You'll forgive me, I trust, for not being here to greet you when you arrived. Had I known you were coming … "

The Lochmaben knight nodded in acknowledgment, his face expressionless. But then he surprised Bruce by standing up and extending his hand.

"It's of no import now, Earl Robert," he said. "Though I'll admit I was vexed at first when you werena here. But ye're here now, so there's nae harm done. It's just that my bones are getting old and I'd been in the saddle ower long. My hip's causing me grief these days." He waved a hand at the tabletop. "Will ye sit wi' me? The ale here's better than the usual."

Bruce was hard put to disguise his astonishment at the man's affability, but he merely called to one of the servants to bring him a jug of ale and a tankard, and sat down. The Annandale knight had been one of Lord Robert's oldest, most experienced, and closest retainers. Jardine, Bruce knew, had been prepared to give up all he owned and accompany his master when Lord Robert retired to England, and he had had to be ordered to remain behind in Annandale to look after Lord Robert's interests. Middle-aged by the time Bruce first saw him, Jardine had impressed him as a sullen, glowering gargoyle; a sturdy, stocky, grim-faced, grizzle-haired veteran who had earned his place, the boy learned later, by dedication, example, and hard work. From their first meeting, young Bruce had considered him to be utterly without humour, truculent and surly, but even then, disliking the man intensely, he had never entertained the slightest doubt about the fellow's loyalty and dedication to Lord Robert. Jardine extended his intolerance to everyone else equally, and Bruce knew that the man's peers suffered his behaviour without rancour and accepted him, even amiably, in spite of it.

"What happened to your hip, that it pains you?" he asked.

The other man grimaced. "A horse. Kicked me three an' twenty year ago. Laid me up for a month, and there were times I thought it had crippled me for good. But it's near as bad now, frae time to time, as it was then. Six hours in the saddle these days and it starts to gowp, and once it starts it winna go away until I get back on two legs." He cleared his throat as the servant returned with Bruce's flagon and a fresh jug of beer, and when they were alone again he refilled his own mug.

"So ye ken your father will be here i' the mornin'."

"Aye. Tam told me. And he brings my betrothed."

Something, perhaps the hint of the beginning of a smile, improbable as that seemed, flickered in the other man's face before being eclipsed by his normal scowl. "Aye," Jardine said quietly. "The lassie frae Mar. D'ye recall her?"

"How could I? I've never seen her. Frankly, I never thought to hear of her again—had forgotten all about her, in fact."

One grizzled eyebrow twitched upward. "Why would you think never to hear o' her again? The two o' ye were betrothed soon after she was born. Lord Robert, may God rest his soul, would never stand forsworn on a thing like that, even in death."

Bruce noticed that Jardine still spoke of the old man as Lord Robert and that when he spoke of the son, Bruce's own father, he referred to him as "Annandale," his current title. To Bruce himself, of course, he spoke of "your father," and the earl found himself smiling inwardly at the difficulties in nomenclature caused by having an unbroken succession of seven Robert Bruces in the same family.

"I had no thought of forswearing anything, Sir James. I was speaking purely of the political reality in Scotland nowadays when Bruce is not a name regarded with fondness. I have no intention of returning there while Balliol rules, now that he has dispossessed us of our lands, and it had never crossed my mind that I might return there to be wed. The risk of being imprisoned made it inconceivable."

The other man squinted at him slightly, then nodded tightly. "Aye, to be sure. That's why her father brought her here to England. It's the match that is important, Earl Robert, no' the placement o' it.

Ye'll be as tightly wed here in England as ye'd be in Scotland, and your bairns will still be Bruce, wi' claims to Mar, Annandale, and Carrick, forbye Scotland itsel'."

"My bairns … Jesu!" Bruce could not imagine having children, and he turned his head aside, his eyes darting nervously around the darkened hall. The servants had all gone now, and most of the candles were out, the air heavy with the distinctive smell of smouldering wicks. On his side, set into the west wall, the great fireplace still pulsed with light from the last oaken logs, and flames cast leaping shadows on the ceiling high above his head. He imagined the shadows capered like faceless infants, reaching out to him and demanding his attention. He looked back at Jardine.

"My bairns," he said again, grimacing wryly to the other man. "Sir James, I will confess to you that yon notion brings frightening thoughts. I mean, who *is* this woman? What is she like? What does she *look* like?" He raised a hand to forestall any answer. "I know that's not supposed to be important, but she is to be my *wife* and I know *nothing* about her! She might be a hunchback, or cross-eyed, or hairy-chinned and plagued with warts and wens! Most of the married men I know had the opportunity at least to set eyes in advance upon the woman to whom they were to be attached for life. This … this *advent* tomorrow might undo my entire life—" He stopped suddenly, aware that he was raving. "Forgive me," he said. "I've been thinking such thoughts since first I heard of this today and I fear my terrors ran away with me there."

Sir James nodded, his expression unreadable. "I canna blame you," he murmured. "From where you sit, I might hae thought the same things mysel'." He sniffed. "But then, I've seen the lass, and I can tell ye there's nothin' o' the like for ye to fret about. Warts and wens and humphy backs, I mean. There's none o' that."

"You've *seen* her? When?"

"Yestreen, afore I rode out to come here. And twice ere that. Once when she was but a bairn, when I went north wi' Lord Robert for him to arrange the match. And then again when she came down to Annandale wi' her father, about five years ago."

"And is she—" Bruce hesitated, then plunged ahead. "Is she wholesome?"

"Wholesome? What does that mean? She's bonnie enough. A wee on the thin side for my taste, but bonnie ne'er the less. Ye'll see for yoursel', come midday." He lifted his flagon and drank deeply, emptying the pot before setting it down and then leaning back to belch comfortably. "Good ale," he said. "And gin the cot ye offer me is half as good, I'll sleep sound. God knows I'm ready for it."

"Of course, you must be. You've had a long day. Did Murdo show you your quarters?"

"Aye, he did. I've a room to mysel', in the back o' the house."

"Good. The Wee Room, we call it. I sometimes repair to it when I have guests whose need of the main bedchambers I deem greater than my own. Where will my father spend this night, do you know?"

"He's wi' an old friend o' his, Sir Roger Fitz Allen.

"They knew each other in Edinburgh when they were about your age. Sir Roger has a place on the main road north, about thirty mile frae here. They'll be up an' on the road afore dawn, if this weather holds, so that should bring them here about midday."

"Aye, it should. Let's hope this weather lasts, then, at least until tomorrow. Though it's June, which means you'd be a fool to bet on it. Before you go, though, tell me this, if you would. How do you find life in Annandale nowadays, with a Comyn overlord?"

Jardine sniffed, half grimacing. "We thole it. I canna say I enjoy payin' your father's rightfu' rents to Buchan, but that aside, it could be worse. He's seldom there, and when he is he keeps clear o' us most o' the time. He put in his ain factor when he took hold o' the place, as ye'd expect, a man called Hector Comyn—as ye'd expect again. And I have to say he's a good man at what he does. He's no Alan Bellow, but he minds his business and mainly leaves the rest o' us to our lives. And those are much the same as ever. The kine need keepin' and the lands need tendin' and the folk hae the same problems they've aey had. Where is Alan Bellow, by the way? I hinna seen him since I got here. Is he still wi' you?"

Bruce smiled. "He is, but he's in London at the moment. Something to do with a wine merchant there. It's one part of his duties that I never even ask about. He keeps us well supplied with good wine, which is really all I require of him these days, and I leave him to it, since he knows far more than I do about what's involved."

"He's a good man. Dour, but solid."

Bruce had to school his face to hide his amusement at the thought of Jardine calling anyone else dour. "What's happening in Scotland these days?" He saw the quirk of Jardine's eyebrow and added, "We don't hear much down here in the south, unless it be in Westminster, and I haven't been there in more than a year. The folk here are more interested in what's happening in France than anything that happens in the north."

"It's much the same in Annandale," Jardine growled. "Folk have enough to fret ower wi'out fashin' about what's happenin' in foreign parts … like Glasgow an' Linlithgow. But from what we hear it's like a wasp's byke anywhere close to where Balliol might be— angry at the best o' times, wi' wise men takin' pains to walk well clear o' it. The King's no' helpin', either. Winna make up his mind an' keep it set frae one day to the next. He blaws hot and cold, like a wind out o' a snowstorm gustin' o'er a fire. The magnates—some o' them, anyway, the ones who arena' Comyns—are champin' at the bit. They feel they canna rely on him for anythin'. He's too … " He paused, frowning.

"Inconsistent?" Bruce suggested.

The other jerked his head in agreement. "Aye, that's a good word … gin it means what I think it means."

"It means unreliable. Changing all the time, from one moment to the next."

"Aye, then. That's him. As I said, hot one minute, cold the next. Anyway, some o' them think he's too *inconsistent* in his dealings wi' England—though no' so much wi' England as wi' its King. Yon's a hard man and he has men around him who are just as hard as him. Folk like that Bek fellow—the Prince-Bishop he calls himsel'. Christ, he's mair like a king himsel' than any bishop I've ever seen."

He paused, then added, "Mind you, now that I've said that, I have to say the magnates themsel's are divided. Most o' them are Comyns—that goes without sayin', but even so they're split up amang themsel's. The main men, Buchan an' Badenoch, are fine wi' things the way they are. They like Balliol just the way he is, because it suits their purposes—Bek an' Buchan are close friends and Buchan doesna' want to upset England. But there's others, Comyns o' the lesser houses, who hae doubts, and some o' them hae thrown in wi' the non-Comyn magnates and want the King to show some backbone. An' the upshot is that the whole country is seethin' and bubblin' like a cauldron o' boilin' oats."

"Hmm. What about the bishops, Wishart and the others?"

"They're wi' the magnates like the Stewart, tryin' to make the King take a stand and stick by it. Ye ken Wishart an' what he's like. His concern is Scotland, the realm, ahead o' all else. He sees his sole duty bein' his flock—the folk first, and the nobles, the King among them, comin' after that. Him and Fraser is the two ringleaders."

"Fraser? St. Andrews' Fraser? He's a Comyn."

Jardine shrugged. "He's one o' them, but he's a churchman first, a bishop afore all else, and he doesna believe that Prince-Bishop Antony Bek, or England's King himsel' for that matter, has the right to appoint English clergy to Scots livings. He's been jumpin' up an' down in holy outrage ever since the Pope in Rome tried to foist *that* on Scotland.

"Ach, but I steer clear of it a'. I'm just a knight an' no' a magnate, thank God. Forbye, it's like any other game—dice or any o' them." He raised one eyebrow as he saw Bruce's incomprehension. "Ye canna lose if ye dinna play, lad. Ye canna win, either, mind you, but by no' playin', ye juke the chance o' bein' accused o' cheatin'. I play no games. I keep my head down, mind my ain affairs, and look after my folk."

Bruce could only purse his lips and nod, unable to dispute the man's logic.

The Annandale knight was looking at him speculatively, scratching one finger idly at his cheek, his fingertip lost in the thick, greying hair that covered it. "Lord Robert was right, though," Jardine added quietly. "As right as ever he was, and I never knew him to be wrong. Years ago, afore the English got brung in wi' their courts an' auditors, when there was need to take strong steps to secure the realm after King Alexander was killed an' afore the Maid was named to the throne, he said to me many a time that John Balliol would be a feckless king. 'The worst thing that could happen to this land o' ours,' was how he put it.

"Mind you, nobody imagined then that England would come into it at all. Lord Robert simply didna trust the man Balliol to do what needed to be done, gin he ever became King o' Scots. He swore even then, nigh on ten year ago, that Scotland needed a strong, guidin' hand, a Scots hand wi' a tight Scots fist. Balliol, he said, was an Englishman by choice who'd scarce set foot here afore his mother died an' left him the lordship o' Gallowa'. Lord Robert didna trust him to be man enough to wear the crown."

The craggy face broke into a grudging smile. "And he was right. By the crucified lord Jesus, he was right." He sat silent awhile, then heaved a heavy sigh and stood up, brushing crumbs from his shirt beneath the open sides of his leather jerkin. "I'm in need o' sleep now," he said, nodding to his host. "Stay you where you are, though. I'll find my own way back." He hesitated, glancing around the empty hall. "They never brought ye aught to eat."

"They were told not to. There's food set aside for me in the kitchens. I told Tam that I'd join him there later."

"Aye, well, then I'll bid ye a good night and a sound sleep, and I'll see you in the mornin'. Tell me, though, d'ye ever think about the things Lord Robert used to tell ye?"

Bruce almost smiled. "All the time, Sir James," he answered quietly. "And I remember all of it."

"Good ... aye, that's good. He was a wise man, God rest him. I never heard him talkin' nonsense in a' the years I spent wi' him. And that was nigh fifty." He nodded again. "Keep mindin' them then, and pay close heed to what they tell ye. God alone knows what's to come to pass in Scotland, but I dinna think John Balliol will hae a long reign. Keep yoursel' ready to come back. Ye're a Bruce, and Scotland will need a Bruce again someday."

Again a flickering smile tweaked at Bruce's cheek. "Then Scotland will have my father."

"No, I think not." There was a flat finality in the utterance. "Your father lacks his father's … What's the word? His strength? His foresight? Neither one of those is right. He lacks Lord Robert's sense o' *purpose*. Scotland will need a sure hand to guide it, stronger than his. Keep that in mind in time to come, and a good night to ye."

He stepped back on one heel, bowed, though not deeply, then turned and marched stiffly away, leaving Robert Bruce blinking after him and wondering if he had just been accepted by an unlikely ally or patronized in some obscure fashion.

Having discovered that he had no appetite for the food that had been set aside for him, Bruce told Thomas Beg about his unexpected conversation with Sir James and apologized for having kept him waiting pointlessly. He then sent him off to bed and sought his own, feeling ready to fall asleep quickly and soundly. But he found it impossible to relax and find oblivion.

It began innocuously enough with the realization, soon after he had climbed into his bed, that Gwendolyn de Ferrers was within a few paces of him, two doors away along the narrow corridor that connected the sleeping chambers on this second level of his house, and with that he found himself imagining her sleeping face and unbound hair and wondering if she truly would be asleep. It was easy, from that point, to imagine her awake as he was, thinking about him and how close he was, and his pulse quickened as he saw himself rising and going to her, warning her to be quiet with a finger on his lips, then leading her back here. He remembered the soft yield of her thigh beneath his fingers as he kissed her, leaning into the litter that morning. But he quickly smothered the sensations that aroused. The lady was not alone in that nearby room, he told himself, and even could he enter it stealthily—for at least one of the serving women would be sleeping on the floor inside the door—he would have little chance of picking Gwendolyn out among the other sleeping forms, let alone spiriting her out of the chamber in secrecy.

Annoyed with himself for indulging in such futile fantasy, he grunted and turned on his side, pulling the bedclothes up around his chin only to realize that a new phantasm had entered his thoughts: a faceless woman, wimpled and gowned in shapeless garments that cloaked her utterly, masking any hint of shape or colour and transforming her into a grey wraith, a spirit-being that stood beyond his bed, watching him with unseen eyes that made him want to squirm and hide himself. A part of him knew that what he was feeling was fear—not of the dream wraith but of the unknown threat that it had brought to hover over him. He felt no guilt, though, despite the whispers of the Church-shaped soul within him that muttered inchoately of sinful intent and covetousness. Would he have pursued Gwendolyn de Ferrers so avidly had he known his intended bride was coming to England? He knew he would have, and blithely—he would merely have taken pains to arrange the timing of things more fortuitously. He was an earl of Scotland and a favourite of the King, Edward Plantagenet, and he was young and healthy and tall and strong. He was also well educated and superbly dressed, with a deep and melodious voice and an easy air of confidence and good humour that made him generally pleasing and attractive in the eyes of women. He knew all of that to be true because he had been told it often enough by a very large number of women, young and otherwise, none of whom he had ever doubted was available for the asking. And ask he had, many times, cheerfully ignoring his confessor's exhortations on the pitfalls of concupiscence and lechery, the moral quagmires of adultery and the perils of promiscuity. He was one and twenty years of age and his life was one of privilege, wealth, and boundless freedom with no responsibility.

That, he realized with a flickering of dread, was what was frightening him.

The imminent arrival of the unknown young woman who was to be his wife—this unseen chit of a Scots girl, *a wee on the thin side*, as Jardine had described her, was a threat to his entire way of life—a life he had no slightest desire to change. He heard his heart thundering in his ears and he came close to choking in surprise as he found he had been holding his breath. He exhaled with an explosive whoosh and gulped again as he felt nausea surging upward from his belly. His head reeled and cold beads of sweat broke out on his forehead as he hurriedly forced himself up and out of bed to kneel on the floor, flailing one arm beneath the bed to find the chamber pot and barely managing to bring it into place before he vomited.

He huddled miserably over the clay pot and retched dryly long after there was nothing left in him to expel. Eventually the spasms passed and some degree of calm returned to him, though his whole body quaked still like a man with the ague. Raising himself cautiously on extended arms, he spat a few more times to clear his mouth of sourness, then pushed the chamber pot cautiously back beneath the bed and allowed himself to topple sideways to the floor, where he lay curled like an infant, uncoiling only slowly as his body gradually accepted that the agony had ended.

He slept then, or dozed for a time, until the chill of the stone floor woke him in pitch-blackness. The single candle that had lit the room was burned out, and his entire body ached from lying on the stones, though the muscles of his belly still felt strained from the effort of retching. Grunting, he forced himself to kneel and then to stand, and then he lowered himself slowly and gratefully to the softness of the straw-filled mattress and pulled the bedclothes over him.

Yet still he could not sleep. The faceless woman remained there at the edge of his awareness, and he found himself reviewing his recent life and wondering, belatedly, what might have happened if the Earl of Pembroke had discovered that his precious granddaughter, whose marriage he had personally arranged, had been within miles of him that day and bent upon an adulterous night in the arms of the Scottish Earl of Carrick, whose position as a spoilt favourite of the King was an offence to the old Frenchman's sensibilities. And then, from the unfocused contemplation of one old aristocrat, his chaotic thoughts swung without logic towards another, even older one, his own grandsire Lord Robert, patriarch of the

House of Bruce. He saw and heard Sir James Jardine speaking of the old man and then he saw and heard the old man speaking for himself, and all of it was infuriatingly dreamlike, a flowing stream of disconnected thoughts without cohesion that left him more and more frustrated because he could make no sense of it.

He fell asleep eventually, for when he opened his eyes light was streaming past the edges of the shutters and he could hear people outside his room, but he felt as though he had not slept in days, and where he would normally have leapt from his bed to meet the new day he chose instead to shun this one, flinging himself away from the insistent light and holding his eyes tight-shut as he drew the covers over his head. The movement outside persisted, and once a raised female voice penetrated the darkness of the covers, causing him to sit upright, listening intently. The sound was not repeated, though, and soon the passageway outside his room was silent. His guests, he knew, were preparing to leave, and he threw back the covers and swung himself out of bed, crossing to the room's single small window and cracking one of the shutters open far enough to enable him to look down into the outer yard, filled with horses and wagons and a bustling throng of people.

There were servants everywhere he looked, busily piling crates and chests of clothing and provisions into baggage carts and helping heavily muffled, well-dressed ladies into two large wagons with strong sides that supported thickly padded benches. Each wagon was harnessed to a team of four horses, and both vehicles were covered with a high canopy of tightly stretched leather panels mounted on a box-shaped frame, with tightly rolled side flaps that could be lowered against inclement weather. He watched as one of the ladies, a black-haired woman whose name he did not know, was helped up and into her seat. Just before she bent her head and disappeared beneath the canopy, she looked up at the sky then said something to one of the attendants. Bruce heard him shouting to some of his fellows, and in the yard beneath him, men began swarming over the women's wagons, pulling down the weather flaps and securing them tightly.

The knights and other mounted men of the party were moving into formation, preparing to ride out towards the road, and Bruce remained there watching as the cavalcade slowly creaked into motion, with much shouting and cracking of whips until the entire train began to wend uniformly through the outer gates like a giant caterpillar. He saw no trace of Gwendolyn de Ferrers before he lost sight of the cavalcade as it passed through the gates, but he remembered the feeling that had swept over him the previous evening when he stood looking up at her above him on the stairs. He had felt oafish, he recalled; smelly and sweaty and dishevelled.

He pushed the shutter closed and stepped back towards his bed, still thinking about that feeling, then crossed to the door and threw it open, leaning out to see if anyone was nearby. One man was, cleaning something at the end of the passageway, and Bruce sent him to fetch Thomas Beg immediately.

He was standing at the foot of his bed, lost in thought, when Thomas Beg's voice sounded from the doorway.

"I'm here. What d'ye need?"

"A bath." He waited for a response and then turned to find the other man watching him, his left eyebrow riding high on his forehead. A raised eyebrow from Tam was the equivalent of a roar of surprise from another.

Tam nodded. "A bath. Aye ... That'll be a *hot* bath, I jalouse?"

"Aye, it will. It came to me last night that I need one ... Something in the way the lady looked at me."

"Was she close enough to smell ye?"

"No, I don't think so. A good ten paces distant. But she was above me, looking down."

"Ye had a bath at Eastertide. So did I."

"That was in April, before Gransser died. This is June. There's a tub in the kitchens. I saw it a while ago at the back of the pantry. Have it brought up here and then send some people to heat water and fill it for me. And I'll need soap and towels."

"Towels … Up here … A bath. Aye. I'll do that. But what for? Ye'll pardon me for wonderin', I hope."

"Don't wonder. I'll tell you why, since you've obviously forgotten. I have a bride arriving here today. She may be as ugly as a mountain hag or as smelly as a farrowing sow—and it's possible she might be both—but I am determined that one of us, at least, will have no trace of stink about us when we meet. Will you fetch my bath now?"

Thomas Beg shrugged his enormous shoulders and nodded. "I'll see to it," he said, and left.

The bath made him feel whole again, though he could not have said how or why, and when Thomas Beg approached him after-wards, brandishing a pair of hand shears as Bruce was pulling on a clean shirt, he looked askance at the big man.

"You think that necessary?"

"If ye want the lass to see your face, aye."

"I'm not sure I do … Not until I've seen hers, at least." But he sat down obediently, none the less, and sat patiently as Tam trimmed his hair and beard. For all his great size, Thomas Beg could be surprisingly deft and gentle.

Eventually Tam took a step back, cleaning the gleaming edges of the sharpened shears abstractedly with an extended finger as he squinted at the results of his ministrations. He nodded once. "That'll do," he growled. "Now ye'll no' frighten her. An' don't you be expectin' sympathy frae me about how sad it is that ye've been saddled wi' a sow. Sir James Jardine telt me she's a fine-looking lass. Too skinny for his taste, he says, but he's a man wha thinks every woman should hae an arse like a horse."

He delivered one final flick of his towel end and stepped back again, dropping his arm to his side. "There! Is there anythin' else ye'd need? I've ither things to see to. Ye ken where I'll be gin ye hae need o' me again."

"I do. What hour is it? I've no idea."

That earned him yet another raised eyebrow, but the answer was mild enough. "It lacks about an hour to mid-mornin' an' it's been pishin' rain since daybreak … Ye havena eaten yet?" At Bruce's headshake he quirked his mouth. "Well, ye'd better see if Allie has anythin' left on the fire. It's no' like you to go hungry an' it winna do ye any good to meet your new countess on an empty stomach. I'll see ye later."

A half-hour later, having eaten a bowl of thick, honey-sweetened porridge with cream by the kitchen fireplace, Bruce trudged back to the house through smashing rain that had turned from a mere down-pour into a deluge. He made his way directly to the tower roof, to stare at the bleak prospect of the waterlogged countryside without a single thought for the train of departed guests from the night before, who had long since disappeared into the sullen mists.

The Essex house was no castle, but it was fortified none the less, sufficiently so to withstand any casual raiding party that might come its way, and from the top of the tower, thirty feet above the ground, he could hear the noise of the torrents of water from the roof drains crashing into the puddles below the walls. From up there, on any other day, he could have seen for more than a mile in the direction from which his father would approach. Thanks to the downpour, though, and the lowering clouds that shed it, the road to the north-east was invisible, and he was cursing himself for a fool for being out there in the storm at all, knowing that there was no possibility of the Annandale party arriving for hours, if they came at all.

The road they followed was an ancient one, strongly made and almost arrow-straight, built by the Romans a thousand years earlier and running all the way southwest from Colchester to London. Even so, had they left Sir Roger Fitz Allen's place at dawn and made good speed on the road, Bruce knew it would take them six hours to cover the thirty-mile distance. He knew, too, that the ferocity of the storm around him was too great for this to be any more than a local phenomenon. He told himself that it was far more likely that his father, with women in his train, would have enjoyed a leisurely breakfast with their host and then set out once the morning sun had dried the chill dew from the grass. By now, with less than two hours remaining before their projected arrival, they would most certainly have ridden into the fringes of the storm and perhaps might even have taken shelter in a roadside tavern, waiting for it to pass. Wherever they were, sheltered or not, he doubted that they would reach their destination much before mid-afternoon, and when they did they would be battered and travel worn.

The storm had passed when, an hour and more after noon, Bruce looked out again from the top of the tower, but it had lasted for more than six hours, a drenching downpour the like of which not even the eldest in the Bruce household could remember, and the entire countryside was flooded. He could see the north road this time, stretching arrow-straight to where the forest swallowed it a mile away, but it showed no sign of life, coming or going.

He walked around the perimeter of the square roof, staring out. As far as he could see in every direction, the new spring crops were drowning in vast, lake-like pools of water, and on the northeastern side, wide channels of brown, glistening mud reflected from the deeply rutted roads that met beyond the gates. Within the outer walls, the yard was a quagmire, churned into a glutinous morass that had sucked the boots off more than a few feet once people started to move around again. It was still raining heavily, but no more than was normal for a June day, and the clouds had retreated into the sky where they belonged, allowing the cheerless daylight to expose the devastation.

He had returned to his starting point, looking out to the northeast again, when he heard nailed boots scraping the steps in the tower behind him, and he turned to see who was coming just as a low, distant thunderclap rolled and rumbled somewhere to the eastward. Stooped in the narrow doorway of the entrance to the stairs, Sir James Jardine had heard it, too, and he paused with one hand on the door frame, looking up in wide-eyed surprise.

"What in God's name was that?"

"Thunder," Bruce answered, wondering what Sir James could want up here. "I'm surprised we haven't had more of it." He waved a hand to indicate the distant fields as Jardine straightened and stepped outside. "Look at this. Have you ever seen the like?"

The two men stood side by side for a while, gazing out at the scene and directing each other's attention to various sights that caught their eye. Neither man doubted that the damage they were looking at was catastrophic and neither wanted to be the first to acknowledge the probable cost of it. The crops, mainly oats and barley, were resilient, but even so their survival was in question. It was Jardine, a landowner all his life, who put the thoughts into words.

"You have good drainage here?"

"As far as I'm aware. We've never had a problem in the past. But I doubt we've ever been hit by anything like this, either."

"What's underneath? Sand or clay?"

Bruce shook his head. "I don't know. I've never needed to know."

"Well, ye'll find out now. If it's sand, this will sink an' settle quick enough. If it's clay, ye'll hae to ditch it to drain it, an' ye'll lose the crops." He straightened suddenly, lifting a hand to point. "What's yon?"

Beside him, Bruce drew himself up and looked to the northeast, along the line of Jardine's pointing finger. "Light on metal. My father's here, I think."

A few minutes later the approaching movement had resolved itself into a party of travellers accompanying several wheeled conveyances.

"Aye, it's Annandale right enough," Jardine murmured, hitching his cloak about him. "I should ride out to meet them."

Bruce turned to him in genuine surprise. "Why would you do that? Why would you want to plouter through all that, up to your arse in mud, when there's no need? They'll arrive when they arrive, whether you ride out to them or not. Better you stay here to welcome them with me and greet them civilly in clean, dry clothes, don't you agree?"

Jardine was about to speak when they heard a commotion swelling up behind and below them, on the eastern side of the tower.

Voices were shouting in a chorus that grew rapidly louder, and then the metallic sound of an alarm as someone pounded frantically on the steel triangle that hung from a cross-post in the yard below. Bruce strode quickly to the side of the tower and leaned over. Below, men and women ran from everywhere, converging on the alarm post with its clanging summons.

"Tam!" he roared, seeing the man's giant form immediately. "Tam! Up here!"

The big man heard him and looked up, craning his neck to see Bruce high on the battlements and then cupping his hands around his mouth. "The stables, sir!" he bellowed. "They're collapsed wi' the rain, and they're on fire!"

*That thunder*. The thought was instantaneous. *It was the building coming down*. He cupped his hands around his own mouth. "Is anybody hurt?"

"Aye, it looks like it. Horses and folk. Ye'd better come."

Bruce swung back to where Sir James stood watching him. "You heard that? A building came down. The thunder we heard. It was the stables. There's a fire and folk are hurt."

Jardine was already heading towards the stairs. "A fire, in this? I'll come wi' ye."

"No! I'll see to it." Bruce gestured sharply towards the approaching cavalcade. "My father's nearly here. Meet them at the gates for me, if you will, and welcome them. Tell them what's happened and take them inside, then see to their comfort for me. I'll be indebted to you. Tell my father I'll return as soon as I am able. Will you do that?"

Jardine merely nodded, his usual scowl firmly in place, and Bruce ran for the stairs.

The building that housed the stables was ancient, older than the house itself and built of heavy river stones, some of them man-sized, that had been mortared together in a time long past. It was two storeys high and windowless above the ground floor, its second level a hayloft and the roof space above that, accessed by a sturdy wooden ladder, used for various other kinds of storage, including extra harness and surplus or seldom-used farm implements. Men seethed around it, scrambling over piles of debris and coughing in dense, yellow-roiling smoke, but Bruce saw at first glance what had happened. A torrent of filthy water had come spewing down from what had been the little stream on the gentle hillside beyond, destroying the small pond by the stable wall and surging over its banks to batter at the stonework of the old building's corner where the mortaring between the stones had rotted. The pressure of the pounding water must have quickly found the weaknesses in the ancient walls, and over the course of hours it had destroyed the entire corner. The walls above had given way, too, pulling the entire structure down into crashing ruin. The floors of the upper levels, and all their stores, had crashed down upon the horses inside, and the screams of the trapped and injured animals—and perhaps of the people caught inside with them—were hellish. A lantern had smashed in the collapse, and smoke was already pouring from the piles of hay among the debris.

The farm manager had a bucket chain established within minutes, a string of sweating, cursing men battling to keep a supply of water flowing up from the still-raging stream. Bruce nodded to him grimly. He knew, though, that despite the tremendous rainfall that day, the tons of hay now feeding the fire had been warm and bone dry when they tumbled from the floor above, and that it was only a matter of time, perhaps mere moments, before the fire would erupt into an inferno.

He shrugged out of his heavy cloak and pulled off his shirt, crumpling it into a ball and then soaking it in the rushing water at his feet before wrapping it around his lower face against the thickening smoke. Scrambling to keep his balance on the treacherous stones that threatened to roll under his feet, he fought his way up to the top of the pile and stood looking down into the chaos of the interior. The fire was on his far right, a dense pall of yellow and black smoke that showed no hint of flame, though the fuel beneath the surface must have been burning like a charcoal burner's kiln. Directly below where he stood, the well of the floor was a mass of bales, hay and straw, most of them intact. In one spot, though, loose hay heaved alarmingly, and he realized that there must be a horse beneath it, struggling to free itself. Beyond that a section of the collapsed floor of the hayloft hung loosely, sagging from one corner and forming a sloping wooden wall that concealed the rear of the stables on that side. He could hear the panicked screams of horses coming from behind the rough partition, and he swung around, looking for someone he could trust.

"Patrick!" Bruce shouted, and a young man looked up. "Up here, quick!" Patrick Dinwiddie was one of the Annandale men who had come south to England with Lord Robert years before. Behind him, Bruce saw Thomas Beg bent over with his hands on his knees, head hanging as he coughed and spluttered, trying to clear the foulness of smoke from his lungs. Dinwiddie scampered up the collapsed stones on all fours, and Bruce took him by the shoulder and pointed. "See those bales? Get a team of men and haul them out of there, quick as you can." The young man turned away with a nod, but Bruce restrained him. "There's a horse there, too, under the straw. Try and save it." The young man dashed away, and Bruce looked back down the sloping scree of stones. "Tam! Come up here!"

Moments later Tam was there, still wheezing but no longer spluttering. Bruce pointed to the sagging upper floor. "There are horses back there. They're still alive and they may even be uninjured, so we need to get them out. Are you fit enough?"

Tam drew a shuddering breath and nodded. "Aye," he croaked. "I'll manage. What d'ye want to do?"

"I can't remember—is there a window back there?"

Tam squinted, then nodded. "Aye. Two o' them, but they're wee. Ye winna get a horse through."

"No, but we could knock out the wall beneath them. We'll need pickaxes or hammers big enough."

Again the squint of concentration. "The smithy. I'll get some. But we're like to bring the whole place down about our ears. These walls are done."

Bruce looked up at the remaining walls of the upper floors. The one to his right was almost completely gone, its fragile remnants tapering up to a point against the rear wall. The one opposite, on his left, was hanging drunkenly, wrenched out of true by the weight of the falling floors, and might come down at any moment. The rear wall looked stronger, but he knew that was only because he was looking at it full on and could see no evidence of it sagging in or out. He grimaced.

"It they fall, they fall. The horses are more important right now. We can't afford to lose any more of them. Go and get something to breach the walls with and meet me at the back." Tam grunted and turned away, passing Patrick Dinwiddie as he went at the head of a file of men armed with pitchforks and baling hooks.

"Good man, Patrick," Bruce said as the Annandale man reached him. "See to the horse first. Then get as many of those bales out as you can. But be careful, and set someone to keep an eye on that wall up there. Any hint of it moving, anything at all, get your people out of there. Understand?"

"Aye, my lord." They turned away together, Bruce down to the outside again while Dinwiddie led his men cautiously down to the mass of hay fronting the hanging floor.

Bruce ran round to the back of the stables, where he stood staring at the wall, trying to gauge its strength and its vulnerability. Four small windows were evenly spaced along its length, well above head height here at the back. He had already pulled himself up to peer in through the lowest one, but he had seen nothing but drifting smoke and a sullen glow of fire before he had to lower himself again. Now he was frustrated, for the sill of the rightmost window was a good foot beyond his reach, and there was nothing nearby he could use to stand on.

Thomas Beg came into view around the edge of the wall, closely followed by another man with an armful of tools.

"I need to get up there," Bruce said over his shoulder to Tam. "Need to see what's inside before we try to break in."

"Stand on my shoulders, then." Tam braced his back against the wall and cupped his huge hands to hold Bruce's foot.

"Be careful," the other man said in Gaelic, and Bruce whipped his head around in shock.

"Nicol!"

"Robert, you're looking fine, lad. But get up there quick—the fire's spreading and they won't be able to hold it much longer. Go!"

Bruce launched himself upward until he was standing on Tam's shoulders, then pulled the shutters open and leaned forward to peer through the open window. He could see nothing inside apart from the slowly pulsing yellow light of the fire on the far side of the fallen floor, but he clearly heard the sounds of the panicking animals in the darkness directly beneath him. He checked the thickness of the windowsill under his hands and then lowered himself to the ground.

"Three horses, perhaps four—none of them injured. The wall's thick, but not too thick—probably about four feet at the base here but tapering to two as it rises. Mortared stones front and back, with rubble in the space between. I'll start with a pickaxe."

He stepped back to check the alignment of the window above him. "The mortar's old and the stones are round. It shouldn't be too difficult to break the seal and chop out the first stone. After that the rest will be easier. Stand back."

He took aim at the plaster topping one stone at about the level of his eyes and swung the heavy pick in a short, sharp blow, shattering the ancient mortar easily and sending it flying in splinters. He hit again, below the stone this time and with the same result, and mere moments later he had pried the first stone free, leaving a gaping hole.

"Right," he said. "There's our start. We only need to bring it down to the floor, which should be about there." He pointed straight forward at about the level of his waist. "We just have to keep the opening narrow—wide enough for a horse, but narrow enough to keep the wall from coming down on top of us. Once we've punched a hole through, I can crawl in and work from the other side."

Nicol's hand grasped him by the shoulder. "How big is yon window? Could you get through it?"

"Aye, easily."

"Then do that. You can dig from inside while Thomas and I work out here. It'll cut the time in half."

It took only a short time to break the first hole open, and from that time on the work went more quickly, with Tam and Bruce pounding the stones free and Nicol MacDuncan shovelling the debris out and away as quickly as he could. Bruce found himself panting heavily, his mouth and nostrils stinging with the dust and smoke, and from time to time he could hear urgent voices behind him, on the far side of the hanging floor. He stopped and looked up at the wall ahead of him, then began to swing his pickaxe upward, smashing at the stones there and squinting narrowly against the flying chips until one mighty full-arm swing met no resistance and he overbalanced, falling to his knees. He regained his feet, checked the width of the opening they had made, then reached outside and pulled Tam and Nicol up until they stood beside him.

"Careful," he told them. "These beasts are terrified. They'd kick you to death without knowing it. Blindfold them if you can, and we'll lead them out one at a time."

There were five uninjured horses in the smoke-filled space beneath the sheltering floor, heaving in a frightened mass and pressed as close as they could come to the wall in their need to be as far away as possible from the noises and smells that threatened them. Bruce grappled with them one by one, covering their heads with clothes torn off and thrust at him by his companions, and calming them as best he could before passing each one along to one of the other two to lead outside. As he passed the fourth beast's rope halter to Tam, the dull glare of yellow light beyond the hanging wall exploded in a rising ball of brilliant flames that sucked all the air and smoke out of the space in a whoosh.

# CHAPTER SEVENTEEN

# THE FRENCH PHYSICIAN

Bruce drew in his breath with a sharp hiss when his eyes would not open properly. His body stiffened instantly in protest, and the reaction made him aware of multiple centres of pain throughout his upper body: on the left side of his chest; in his hip, also on the left; and in his right shoulder. His entire head felt as though it were on fire, and he had a flashing memory of exploding flames and a horse leaping past him, screaming, its tail a blazing torch.

He sensed rather than saw a blurred, dark shape leaning over him, and then a heavy hand pressed down on the centre of his chest, pinning him.

"Lie still, Robert. Don't try to move."

He recognized his father's voice and the day came whirling back at him: the storm, the stables, the fire. And the roar of the conflagration that he had barely noticed at the time. He fought down an urge to resist and forced himself to remain still. His nostrils twitched, inhaling a sour odour of charred wood and bitter smoke.

"I can't see," he said.

"Your head's bandaged. Covering your eyes. There's nothing wrong with them. You fell and hit your head—landed on stones."

... *Bandaged. There's nothing wrong with them* ... He felt a great relief welling up in him, and then his mind filled again with the image of the immense ball of fire that had filled the air around him. He had thought himself dead.

"Am I burnt?"

"No, just singed a bit ... your hair. It will grow back."

"Tam cut my hair," he said softly, remembering being sheared that very morning.

"I know." His father's voice was gentle, filled with concern. "And a good thing, too. There was less to burn."

"I can still smell the stink of it—the fire."

"We all can, but it's getting better. The smoke was everywhere. The whole house was full of it. How do you *feel*, though?"

A blink, feeling the roughness of cloth against his eyelids. "Sore," he whispered. "Chest and side and shoulder. I can see, though? Are you sure, Father?"

In answer, a finger probed somewhere above his right eye, prying at the bindings there.

"There … Try again."

He did, and his vision blurred as a great surge of gratitude swept up from deep inside him. He could *see*. He blinked rapidly, feeling again the lid of his left eyelid move against the roughness of its covering cloth, and what he was seeing came into focus. The room was night-dark, leaping with flickering light from fire and candles that brightened one half of his father's face and left the rest in shadow. Beyond his father's looming shape, closer to the fire's brightness, he saw two other men looking down at him, their faces grave. One was his great-uncle Nicol; the other, much older and white-haired, with a deeply lined face, was a stranger. Bruce felt a cough well up in him and released it. A flare of pain exploded through his chest and cut off his breath. His father winced in sympathy.

"Aye, that'll hurt, right enough. It's your ribs. We thought at first you might have stove your rib cage, but Father Baldwin tested them and thinks there's nothing broken. They're badly bruised, he says, and you'll be laid up for a week or so, but you're as healthy as a horse in prime and you'll recover quickly. That being," he added, "by the grace of God and the power of prayer. The same goes for the rest o' you. You're hairless on one side and skinned raw on the other, but nothing's broken." A tiny smile tugged at his mouth. "Mind you, we'll have to keep you out of Lady Isabella's sight until your brows and your eyelashes start to grow again—and the hair on your head and face, of course."

Bruce ignored the reference to his betrothed, his mind already busy with other things. "Who did we lose?"

His father looked up, his eyes on someone beyond Bruce's sight. "Thomas," he said. "You're better informed than I am. Tell the earl what you know."

Thomas Beg came into view, moving around from one side of the bed to the other. Bruce tried to twist his head to see him as he came, but the pain of his singed scalp flared again and he lay still, waiting until the huge man stood towering over him.

"There's six folk missin' frae the head count," Tam began without preamble, "three o' them stablemen. Five men was in the stables when it happened, we jalouse, and a woman."

Bruce lay stony-faced as Thomas Beg continued. "Forbye, we think at least six horses, though there might hae been more. We just canna tell. Auld Sammy the stablemaster's one o' the missin' folk and he's the only one who would hae kent how many beasts was in there at the start."

"Is the fire out now?"

Tam shook his head. "No, no' yet, but close enough now. It's rainin' again—heavy—and that should soak what's left."

Bruce sighed. "God rest their souls," he said. "The folk, I mean, though God knows the beasts are worthy of pity, too … I fear you'll have to send men in there tomorrow, Tam, or as soon as the ashes cool … to find the bodies."

Tam's left eyebrow flared high. "What bodies, my lord? D'ye mind tellin' me yon story about the Viking chiefs, when they died an' wis burnt wi' their boats?"

Bruce stared up at him, wondering what he was talking about, though he did have vague recollections of telling him one time about a Viking funeral.

"Well," Tam said, "this was a worse fire than any Viking ever saw. We'll no' find any bodies in there, Earl Robert. I doubt we'll even find the odd bone. And gin we do, the only thing that'll mark them as horse or human will be the size o' them. When that place finally went up it burnt like the fires o' Hell—a furnace stoked wi' straw an' hay an' wooden beams an' joists an' posts an' floors an' stalls, every bit o' it dry, well-seasoned fuel—wi' the walls actin' like a chimney."

The silence that followed was deep, every man there imagining what it must have been like.

Bruce drew a shallow, careful breath before asking his next question. "Is Dinwiddie safe?"

"Aye. He got out wi' a' his people just afore the fire exploded. He saved that horse you telt him to. There was three more under the straw, trapped there when the roof fell in on them. Two o' them was dead an' he had to kill the third. But him an' his men got a' thae bales safe out o' there, and there was more o' them than ye'd think. Mainly good hay feed, wi' a scatterin' o' straw."

"And no one else was killed, apart from the missing six you mentioned?"

"No' a soul. There was a few bangs an' bruises, that's a'. It could hae been a lot worse."

Bruce barely nodded, and Thomas Beg hovered for a moment, then turned to leave.

"Wait, Tam. Help me to sit up."

"No!" The senior Bruce stepped forward quickly, waving Thomas Beg away. "No sitting for you, Robert. Not until we know there's nothing broken inside you. Father Baldwin *thinks* you're merely bruised, but he's not certain of his own judgment and he's sent for help—another physician, from Sir John Mowbray's place a few miles from here. Until he comes, you are to stay flat on your back—tied down, if need be. We have no wish to see you die of a punctured lung from one of your own broken bones." He glanced at Tam. "Thank you, Thomas. Away you go now."

The big man nodded after a moment, cast a swift glance down at Bruce, and then left obediently, moving in silence for all his enormous size.

The silence lasted after his departure and grew long, broken only by the crackling of the fire in the grate. Bruce forced himself to breathe slowly and gently. The pain caused even by a too-deep breath was close to being unbearable. A snippet of memory flashed through his mind, a vague remembrance of a campfire comment made some long-past night, something about the degree of a wound's agony being in relationship to its severity. He had no idea who had said it or where.

He became aware then of the silence and turned his head slightly to look up at his father, who was staring emptily back at him from a face that lacked any expression.

"What happens now, sir?"

His lordship blinked, his eyes visibly coming back to focus. "What? Oh … We have to get you up on your feet again, and hale, before we press on to Westminster and the King." He almost smiled. "From the sounds of it, that ought not to take too long … " His father's face sobered again, and his eyes narrowed to slits. "You did well today, Robert. Your folk are speaking highly of you and they are more concerned for you than I ever remember mine being for me." His voice sank lower. "And that's as it should be. I'm proud of what you have achieved here in Writtle, my son."

"Managing to let half the place burn down about our ears, you mean?" He grimaced, embarrassed by his father's praise. "I knew that corner of the barn building was weak, Father. I saw it a year ago—the condition of the mortaring and the looseness of some of the bottom stones. I talked about it with Old Sammy and with Alan Bellow, but I did nothing about it, thinking it less urgent than other things. Old Sammy himself said that it had stood more than a hundred years and would keep until we had the time to mend it … He was wrong, and I was, too. But Sammy died because of it, and I'm still here."

Now his father was frowning. "You can't blame yourself for the fury of God's weather, Robert. That storm we had today was unlike anything in living memory. Not once in a hundred years does such a thing come along."

"That may be true, sir. But not once in a hundred years did anyone mend the corner of that wall. And now it has cost lives."

Light and darkness stirred as Nicol MacDuncan stepped forward, followed by the third man, who had not yet uttered a sound.

"It's as your father says, Rob," Nicol began in his flowing, liquid Gaelic. "And you are as right as he is. But what's done is done—the will of God. There is nothing to be gained by blaming yourself for something no one could have foreseen. Did you ever imagine a torrent strong enough to rip that wall apart and tear down the whole building? A day ago you would have said that was impossible. Well, today it's no longer unimaginable, and never will be again. But you will rebuild your stables and they'll last another hundred years, perhaps twice that long, because you'll know the strength they must have to withstand such things. Life goes on, Rob. And so must yours. We all have our appointed time, and who can flout God's right to dictate that?"

Bruce nodded, and his eyes moved to the stranger standing behind Nicol. "Your pardon, sir," he said, addressing the man in Gaelic. "I have not yet even greeted you or made you welcome in my house. I presume you must be the Earl of Mar, good-father to my sister Christina and soon, it would appear, to me myself."

Lord Annandale straightened up abruptly, plainly appalled that he had neglected to introduce the old man, but Domhnall of Mar was already standing above the bed, smiling down at Bruce, and when he spoke his voice was musical, reflecting the ancient Western Isles tradition in which he had been raised.

"You have no need of my pardon, Robert Bruce, or that of any other. Your father here has praised you, justly, for today's perfor-mance of your duties, and now I would add my own voice to his. You *might* have come to greet and welcome us, bowing to our supposed importance while your stables collapsed and buried your people. But what would that have told me about the man to whom I have agreed to give my last remaining daughter's hand?" His smile grew warmer. "No, Sir Robert, I would not change your welcome if I could. Any man who places his folk and their welfare first and above all else in his concern, ignoring mighty men and rank and station to do what he must do, might, I believe, be relied upon to see to the welfare and protection of an old man's favourite daughter, even were she not his wife."

He stood gazing down pensively at Bruce, but when he grinned, the lines bracketing his mouth stood out sharply through the whiteness of his beard. "You remind me of your grandfather at your age— bandages and all. The first time I set eyes on him I was ten years old and he was twenty, and he had taken a tumble from a horse, landing in thick brambles while chasing a boar. His face and hands were cut to ribbons and he was bandaged about the head just as you are now. When I saw how he laughed at himself and his own folly, I decided, even at the age of ten, that this was a man I wanted to know. I became his squire soon after that, and then his loyal friend and follower forever after … And I had hopes of serving him as my king one day, though that was not to be."

He began to nod his head rhythmically, his smile spreading as he switched from Gaelic to English. "I think your noble father has the right of things, though. We'll keep my daughter away from you until you've lost that wild, raw look and grown some hair. Before then, you and I have much to talk about."

Had Bruce been capable of moving at that moment he might have squirmed while he recalled the demeaning things he had said and thought about this gentle man's daughter—a woman whom he had believed had leapt out at him, as if by magic, at the whim of others. Now, witnessing the evident fondness of the father for his daughter, he recalled the disparaging things he had said about her to Sir James Jardine and Thomas Beg, suggesting, without the slightest reason other than his own inchoate fears, that she might be hump-backed or warty or facially disfigured.

Now, faced with the kindly, unassuming humanity of his dead grandfather's "disciple," he found himself unable to hold the old earl's gaze.

Earl Domhnall did not appear to notice anything and turned away to say something to Nicol MacDuncan, and while the two conferred

Sir Robert Bruce withered with shame. Self-loathing was a new experience for him, but he took to it with the zeal of a convert and shuddered at the prospect he now faced: the daunting task of facing the blameless young woman he had demeaned and reviled, with all the hypocrisy of keeping his simmering resentment and ill will hidden from her.

He was rescued from pondering his dilemma further by the arrival in his chambers of Father Baldwin and his invited colleague, Maître Reynald de Frontignac, who walked with a heavy limp. Father Baldwin, plainly in awe of his new companion, launched at once into a recitation of the man's qualifications and experience, but the Frenchman quieted him with an upraised hand and a self-deprecating smile.

"Please," he said, waving a hand in the direction of the bed. "I am here solely to examine the wounded man, and obviously this is he. Will you permit?"

He clearly took their agreement for granted, for he ushered Lord Annandale and the others towards the door and out, sweeping his arms upward as though herding geese.

The Frenchman was an eldritch-looking figure, emaciated, with unruly grey hair that had seldom known the touch of comb or shears save on the crown, where his tonsured pate marked him as a monk or a priest. The shoulders beneath his plain black cassock must have been broad once, Bruce thought, but now they were bowed in a pronounced stoop that emphasized the man's advanced age, though he still towered head and shoulders over his thickset companion Father Baldwin, the local village priest. He wore a thick belt, tightly cinched about his waist, from which hung a bulky and anciently supple leather bag that covered him like an apron from waist to knees, but it was his face and hands that held Bruce's attention. The face was arresting, dominated by large, wide eyes of the palest silver grey that gleamed out from beneath bushy brows on either side of a nose like a hatchet blade. The lower half was concealed beneath a riot of grey-white beard to match the profusion of hair on his head, yet Bruce could clearly imagine a determined jut of jaw and chiselled chin. The man's hands were huge, the knuckles pronounced and the fingers long and spatulate with wide, carefully tended nails. He stood wringing his hands absently, as though washing them, while his narrowed eyes roamed over Bruce from head to toe, and finally he grunted and looked the earl straight in the eye for the first time.

"You have pain, *oui*?" Bruce nodded, gently. "Of course you have. How far did you fall?" Bruce did not know, though he might have guessed around ten feet, but the Frenchman did not wait for an answer. "Onto stones," he continued. "Sharp stones? With sharp edges?"

"No. Rounded … River stones, smooth."

"But solid, *non*?" The beard twitched in what might have been a tiny smile. "But not sharp is good. And now we have to look." His bushy eyebrows twitched. "My friend thinks the ribs are merely bruised but not broken. I think he might be right, but first I have to … to probe. You will not enjoy. You understand?"

Bruce gritted his teeth. "I understand."

He felt his coverings being removed and then a long surge of fluctuating agony as the two men moved him around, working together to remove the bandages that swathed him. But that pain faded to insignificance beside the torment that followed as the Frenchman poked and prodded at Bruce's injured ribs, at his shoulder and his hip, while his patient fought, with clenched teeth, against the ever-growing need to cry out. Eventually, the old Frenchman inhaled deeply and straightened up, his grave grey eyes returning to meet Bruce's.

"It is as my friend thought. Nothing is broken. Cracked, perhaps, but no fractures, no splinters inside you waiting to bite. Your head is injured, too, from the fall, but also not broken. Thus, you will live and you will heal, quickly, one hopes … "

"*But?*" Bruce looked the old man in the eye. "You did not say it, but I heard it in your voice. But what?"

This time the quirk of the mouth was undeniably a smile, and the Frenchman nodded in acknowledgment. "But, with such injuries to the ribs, broken or bruised, the sole cure is the same. It requires time … Time and a lack of movement. A *complete* lack of movement. That is difficult for everyone, but for a young man like you, it might be close to impossible. To lie as still as is required for as long as is required would try the patience of a saint. We can … how does one say it? We can immobilize you, strap you down so that you *cannot* move—that is what we do with people who have badly broken ribs—but I doubt you would tolerate that for long. Would you?"

Bruce grimaced. "No, probably not. Is there anything else you can do?"

The grey eyes narrowed yet again, this time to slits as the maître's bushy eyebrows drew together. "Yes. We can make you sleep." He turned to his companion. "I will need a small bowl, Father, clean and dry. Can you find one for me?"

As the other priest hurried off, Bruce touched one hand gently to his aching side, feeling the skin hot over the throbbing pain. "You think to make me sleep for days on end? With this? That would not be possible, Father."

"That is *Brother*, Master Bruce. I am a monk, not a priest. And all things are possible. As a Christian and a knight you should know that."

Bruce said nothing, suddenly aware of a black patch of cloth on the old man's left shoulder that was less worn than the cloth surrounding it. It showed where another layer of cloth had once been removed, a layer in the familiar shape of the cross of St. John that marked its wearer as a Knight of the Hospital. He frowned, now curious about the tall old man. A monk's vocation, like a priest's, was a lifetime calling, not to be revoked, and he could not remember ever having heard about a Knight Hospitaller renouncing his membership in the order.

The old monk was holding his hanging waist bag open with one hand while he rummaged inside it with the other. The door at his back swung open, and Father Baldwin came back in with a number of small bowls of various sizes.

"Ah, excellent, Father," said the Frenchman. "You provide more than was asked." He picked one, weighing it in his hand. "This will be perfect. Now … " He turned to Bruce again. "You have good milk here, Master Bruce?"

Bruce began to shrug, but was instantly reminded of the unwisdom of that. "Good and ample, Brother. Cow's and goat's."

"Which would you prefer?"

"Goat's."

"So be it. Father Baldwin, would you assist me once again and bring me, please, a jug of goat's milk? Enough to fill this bowl will suffice."

The priest nodded and left again, and Maître de Frontignac returned to his capacious bag, drawing out a small, beautifully carved wooden box inlaid with what looked like nacre. He placed the box on the bed, glanced about him, and lurched quickly to a small table that sat by one wall. He carried it back to the bedside and set it down carefully before placing his box on the tabletop. Bruce watched him curiously as he prised it open with extreme care, then reached inside the box with a gently probing finger. He withdrew it slowly and held it up, its tip coated with a fine, whitish powder. He returned the fingertip to the box and held it there while he wiped fastidiously with his thumb at the stuff coating it, returning every grain to the box.

"What is it?" Bruce asked. "That powder."

The old monk was examining his fingertip to be certain that none of the contents of the box yet adhered beneath the nail, and when he was satisfied, he looked down at Bruce, his eyes twinkling.

"A treasure from the Holy Land," he said. "More precious than the Magi's gifts. I had a good friend there who was something of a Mage himself—of great wisdom but not holy. His name was Sayeef ad-Din and he was a muslim unbeliever, but a good man none the less, and a far better physician than I could ever be. I was wounded in battle and taken prisoner and he took care of me. He saved my life, beyond a doubt, for I was close to death." He held one hand in front of him, making the sign of the cross in the air.

"People here at home prefer not to think, or even hear, that the followers of Allah might be able to outdo the Christian world in anything, but truth, even when unacceptable, must be acknowledged. When it came to healing battle-broken bodies, we Franks, even among the ranks of the Hospital, had no physicians with skills that even approached those of our enemies. Thus it is true that had I not been taken prisoner, I would have surely died among my own kind. The Sultan's people held me captive for two years until I was ransomed, and Sayeef ad-Din and I became friends because my injuries had ensured that I would never be able to fight again. That, allied with the fact that I was a healer, albeit of limited skill, led to my being well treated while I was among the warriors of Allah.

"When I regained my freedom, Sayeef gave me this box, along with his blessings. I knew what it contained, for I had been studying its use under his guidance, and I was deeply conscious of the honour he paid me by parting with such a gift. In consequence, I have used it very sparingly and only in time of great need because it is genuinely irreplaceable." He smiled. "But I have been back now from the Holy Land for many years and I have used it but twice, so that even having it and guarding it with great care, I have been wasting it by failing to use it. That has concerned me recently, for I have been wondering if perhaps it might be losing its potency, as powdered herbs frequently do. Has it maintained its freshness, despite its age, or has it faded with the passage of years? Now, with you, I intend to find out."

Bruce had been staring at the wooden box as the old man spoke and now he looked up.

"What does it do?"

"It *does* nothing, but taken in a draught it causes sleep and relieves even the worst pain. I will show you."

"Is it … dangerous?"

The old man's hawkish smile gleamed again. "Not in the fashion that you mean," he said, shaking his head. "But it has a danger of its own. Men grow too fond of it, Sayeef told me, and overuse brings its own perils."

Father Baldwin returned with a jug of goat's milk, and those were the last words Maître de Frontignac spoke to Bruce for some time, for he turned away at once and with his back squarely towards the bed began issuing low-voiced instructions to the village priest. When he did return to the bedside, Father Baldwin moved around to assist him on the other side, and between them, ignoring his groans, they encircled Bruce within their arms and eased him up into a position in which he could swallow the concoction fed to him. His gorge revolted against the acrid taste, but the old man merely removed the bowl and waited for the shuddering revulsion to pass before bringing the bowl back to Bruce's lips. The injured man gagged the mixture down, his body quaking as the last bitter grains lodged at the back of his throat. He swallowed once more, clearing his mouth, and then relaxed limply as they lowered him flat again.

"Now what?" he asked.

"Now we find out whether the powder has retained its powers," the French monk responded.

"And if it has?"

"Then you will sleep without pain. When you awaken you will find yourself restrained. We will do that once you are asleep and you will feel nothing. That mattress is too soft for our purposes. We will replace it with a padded board and bind you to the board with wrappings of cloth lest you move and injure yourself further."

"And how long will I have to stay here?" The mattress on which he lay, a straw-filled palliasse, was already hard and thin.

"For as long as necessary. Father Baldwin and I will watch you closely, and when we think it safe for you to move we will permit you to. In the meantime, you will sleep."

"Now?" Bruce snorted gently at the mere thought of sleeping. "I'll ask you to forgive me, Brother, but I am nowhere close to … " As he spoke the words, though, he felt a strange sensation stir somewhere inside his head, and it seemed to him the room receded. He blinked and turned to look again at the physician standing over him, only to see that the man was wavering visibly, like a reflection in water. He opened his mouth to speak and found he had no words, and he was not even aware of his eyes closing.

He had little awareness of anything at all, including the passage of time itself, and the few scattered memories that would return to him later would all share a dreamlike quality. He vaguely remembered being manhandled and being unable to react as he was moved around like some inanimate object, and he remembered the bitter taste that seemed permanently lodged beneath his tongue; he remembered faces peering down at him, some of them, his father's and Thomas Beg's, distorted and fluid-looking, others no more than moving, featureless shapes; and he remembered, equally indistinctly, seeing and hearing young women; several of them, he thought, their differences coalescing into a single presence. He had memories, too, of being fed—warm milk-soaked, honey-sweetened bread being spooned into his mouth and the acrid taste of the white powder that had been mixed with it.

He opened his eyes and saw the old French monk standing by the foot of the bed, watching him. He lay still for a long moment, returning the silent scrutiny, questioning himself and examining his body with his mind. He felt no pain anywhere, and when he tried to move his arms they moved freely, unencumbered.

"How do you feel?"

"Awake," Bruce said. "And alive and well, I think." He moved a hand tentatively towards the injury he remembered, the spot over his ribs, and discovered that he was wearing a shirt of some kind. "There is no pain."

That brought a quick smile to the monk's fierce old face. "Oh no, do not deceive yourself on that, Master Bruce. There is pain there aplenty, should you provoke it. Sleep is a wondrous curer of ills, but miracles are the work of God Himself, and nothing miraculous has happened here. We have but given your body time to heal itself a little, and the worst of the pain has passed."

"How long have I been asleep?"

"Four days."

"Four *days*? How is that possible?"

"I told you before, everything is possible if one has faith."

"Your ... Your powder is still potent, then."

"It is, thanks be to God. And you are awake now because you appear to have no more need of it. Yesterday, beginning in the morning, I began reducing the amount you received. You will require no more. Do you feel hungry?"

Bruce thought about that and nodded.

"Excellent, then we shall feed you. Hot broth alone today, though. Perhaps something more solid tonight, but by tomorrow you should be eating normally."

"Is my father still here?"

The bushy eyebrows rose. "Of course! Where else would he be? I will send someone to tell him you are awake, as soon as you have eaten. And I will send you some broth from the kitchens now." He turned on his heel and went directly to the door, moving quickly for a man of his age with a bad limp, but he stopped on the threshold and turned back. "One thing. Do not try to rise from the bed alone. You are not strong enough, and should you try, you will most certainly fall and might injure yourself again. Lie where you are and be patient a while longer. I will come back later."

As soon as the door swung shut Bruce raised himself cautiously on an elbow. He counted to five, then he swung his legs over the side of the bed, noticing that the shirt he wore was a nightshirt of fine wool, plain white and ankle-length. The old man's warning served its purpose, though, for instead of launching himself up to his feet as he would have done mere days earlier, he sat on the edge of the bed for a time, the whole room reeling and swaying as he moved his eyes. He felt a warning stir of nausea and quickly swung his legs back up to the bed, then lowered himself to lie flat again, grasping the edges of his palliasse and closing his eyes tightly against the sickening sense of motion that came close to overwhelming him. He lay still, holding his breath, and waited for it to pass. The heaving rotation died away gradually and left him clammy with sweat and clutching at the mattress. Finally, when his heartbeat had died down and his head no longer felt as though it were spinning, he lay quiet, breathing deeply and regularly.

His father was still in Writtle. That surprised him, although he knew the purpose of this visit was to take him along to Westminster with the rest of the Bruce and Mar party. But in days not long past, before the death of his grandfather, he would never have believed his father would remain quietly in one place for days on end when he had plans of his own to prosecute, particularly once he was assured that his son was in no danger and would recover. The Earl of Carrick Rob had known as a boy would have ridden on ahead to do what he must do, leaving instructions for his son to catch up as soon as he was able.

But if the Lord of Annandale was yet in Writtle, so, too, must be Domhnall, the Earl of Mar, and his daughter Isabella. He felt his spirits plummet at that thought, then remembered the strange sensations he had had of young women here in this room. There were no young women in Writtle … Certainly none that would dare raise their voices in the earl's sickroom. And yet he was almost sure that he had heard them, perhaps even seen them. He had hazy recollections of differing colours, different shapes. And Nicol MacDuncan! If his father was yet here, then his great-uncle would be, too. He felt a surge of pleasure at that thought, and at that very moment the door to his chamber opened and Nicol himself stepped in, followed by Thomas Beg carrying a covered serving tray.

"We have brought you food, Nephew! Can you sit up? You can't sup lying on your back."

"You'll have to help me. I feel light-headed."

"From starvation, I don't doubt. Here, hold on to my arm. Now pull up … That's it. Slowly now, slowly."

Thomas Beg was holding the tray as though it were a diplomatic offering.

"What's under the cloth, Tam?"

"Soup," the big man said. "Clear soup. Ye're to drink it slow, for fear your stomach winna thole it. Gin ye get sick an' puke, ye'll hurt your ribs again. Here, I'll hold it for ye." He lowered himself to one knee with great care and held the tray steady while Nicol removed the covering, then watched as Bruce picked up the horn spoon with an unsteady hand.

The hot broth was delicious, rich and tangy with the flavour of venison and better than anything Bruce could ever remember tasting. He moved tentatively at first, spilling some because of the pronounced tremor in his hand, but after the first startling mouthful he lost all awareness of anything except the need to taste more of it.

Nicol had perched himself on the edge of the bed to watch his nephew as he ate, and when the spoon scraped against the empty wooden bowl he looked up at Thomas Beg with a raised eyebrow. "I think he could have eaten more," he said.

Thomas took the bowl away from Bruce, then placed the tray on the table nearby. "Aye," he agreed. "We should hae brought the whole cauldron. But if yon was slow, I wouldna want to be here when he eats fast."

Bruce ignored him. His body felt alive again, his head full of questions. "So," he said to Nicol, "tell me what's been happening while I slept."

The two men made him comfortable, propping him up against his pillow, and then they talked for a long time.

No human remains had been recovered from the ashes of the stables, they told him; Father Baldwin had set up a makeshift altar in front of the ruined building and on the second day after the fire had offered a Mass for the souls of the missing six. The next day, the remaining walls of the stable had been pulled down and a team of men set to cleaning the old mortar from the fallen stones and storing them in piles by size and weight, for use in rebuilding on the same site, which was already being made ready.

The flooded fields were drying well, Tam told him.

"So we have sand beneath us," Bruce murmured. "Now we know we have good drainage."

"Ye dinna think we'll lose them then, the crops?"

"I hope we won't. The decision is God's, though. All we can do is wait and see what happens. Speaking of which," he continued, turning to Nicol, "tell me about my father. Why is he still here?"

Nicol MacDuncan spread his hands. "He has his reasons, clearly, but he has not shared them with me. We had an ill time on the road, though, in that storm. None of us has ever seen anything like it. Twenty miles we travelled through it, and it was hellish every step of the way. Everyone needed a few days of rest and warmth by the time we finally arrived here."

"Twenty miles of it? I didn't think it could be that widespread. Still, a few days of rest I can understand, but four? That smacks of idleness."

Nicol gazed back at him with a quizzical arch to one eyebrow. "You had best ask him yourself for his reasons. I suspect they have much to do with the need he feels to have you with him when he reaches Westminster. But that's my own opinion and I might be wrong."

"Hmm. All right, then, I'll ask him that when I see him. Brother Reynald said he would send him to me as soon as I had eaten … Were there women here? I thought— It seemed to me I heard women's voices from time to time. Young women. Did I dream that?"

"No, that would hae been the lassies that ye heard." Thomas Beg answered him. "Lady Isabella's young women. Three o' them's even younger than she is. There's no' much here to keep young folk busy, and so the auld monk had them fetchin' and carryin' for him, runnin' to the kitchens and wherever else he needed, and sometimes keepin' an eye on you when he had to go out."

Nicol cleared his throat and stood up. "We'd best leave you alone again. Your father will be waiting for word to come and see you, and we've said all we have to say for now. Is there anything I can bring for you?"

There was nothing, so they went about their business, each of them nodding farewell as he left.

As soon as they were gone, Bruce pushed himself away from the wall, with more difficulty than he had expected, and stretched out full length upon his cot. The sitting posture that had seemed so comfortable at first had taxed him quickly after a short time, for the curvature of his body had placed increasing pressure on his injured ribs. Now, flat on his back again, he could feel the pain recede slowly from a throbbing fullness to a dull, steady ache and eventually, as he continued to lie still and draw slow, shallow breaths, it faded completely.

He must have dozed because he started awake at a sudden noise and found Brother Reynald standing over him, holding a steaming cup in his hand. Feeling absurdly guilty at having been caught sleeping in the light of day, he muttered something unintelligible, hearing the thickness in his own voice. Brother Reynald paid no attention.

"Drink this," he said, holding out the cup.

"What is it? More of that white stuff?"

"No, it is mulled wine, with something in it to make you sleep."

"I've been sleeping for days, Brother, as you know very well. I have no need of more."

"That is your opinion. Mine is different. Sleep is still necessary if you are to heal quickly. Drink." The old monk helped him again to a position in which he could drink without spilling, and when he was satisfied that his patient had taken as much as would be helpful, he stood to leave.

"Your father is here," he said. "Waiting outside. Are you strong enough to receive him?"

"I believe so. I feel much better than I did earlier. But will your wine permit me to?"

"It will. It is nowhere near as strong as the white powder and will take longer to affect you. I'll send him in." He went to the door and opened it, beckoned to Lord Annandale to come in and then left, drawing the door shut at his back and leaving father and son to face each other.

Bruce nodded, feeling awkward to be on his back looking up at his father. "My lord father," he said with a nod, "be welcome." He waved towards one of the room's two high-backed chairs. "Sit, if you would."

Lord Annandale's mouth parted in a smile. "I would not, as your lord, but I will, gratefully, as your father. I have been on my feet since dawn, without respite. You look better today, Robert. Not so pale." He stepped forward and bent to peer at the bandages that still covered his son's left eye. "And the burn looks fine … No scorching at all that I can see, though I can't see much beneath the wrappings."

He moved away and picked up one of the heavy chairs easily with one hand, returning to the side of the bed and angling it so that he could sit and look down directly into his son's eyes. "How do you *feel*, though?" he asked, then looked at the pillow that his son was reaching for with clawed fingers, though it was inches beyond his reach. "Here, let me do that." He pummelled the pillow and smoothed it before placing it behind Bruce's raised neck. "So you are well? No weakness from the potions?"

"No, Father, none at all." The pillow felt wonderful behind his head and he sighed and stretched his neck appreciatively.

He looked at his father carefully now, noting his high colour and the weight he had gained since last they had seen each other. The older Bruce looked tired and careworn. His cheeks and eyes, seen from beneath, were baggy and pouched, and the younger man wondered why that should be, since his father's duties and concerns were now far less onerous than they had been in Annandale.

"Uncle Nicol was here earlier, soon after I awoke, and when he told me you were still here I was surprised."

Lord Robert raised his eyebrows. "And why should that surprise you? Would you expect me to leave you sick and strapped to a board?"

Bruce did not know what to say, since that had been precisely what he'd expected.

"I came here to collect you in passing, thinking to let you meet your future wife and then ride with us to Westminster. God annulled my plans. But Brother Reynald tells me you should be fit to travel in a few more days, if all continues to go well."

"I know, Father … He said the same to me." He coughed nervously. "And how is the Lady Isabella?"

His father smiled. "Better than I had expected, after the misadventures she has had. That journey through the storm—the *cataclysm* as one of our priests called it—was the stuff of nightmares. But she's a sturdy lass, strong as an ox, for all her female charms. She came through it all well and is now eager to meet you, once you are well enough."

*God help me*, Bruce thought, glumly aware that his father's words echoed those of Sir James Jardine: *a wee on the thin side, but a sturdy lass and strong as an ox. With praises like those, I can but imagine her female charms.* He forced himself to nod in response and tried to keep his voice pleasant as he said, "I, too, look … forward to that meeting." Then, to conceal his growing discomfort, he changed direction. "When does the King expect us to arrive, Father?"

Lord Annandale gave a mildly scornful snort. "Expect us? The King does not *expect* us, Robert. Were that so, we would face the risk of keeping him waiting, and that would be sheer folly. He knows we will be visiting Westminster when we do arrive, because I sent him word that we would pass this way about this time and that I hoped to meet him again and renew my allegiance while we were here. But he has no *expectations* of us, and any expectation on our part would be presumptuous."

"Then there is no urgency to reach Westminster … "

"Of course not. Why should there be? But there is ample reason for our going there. Good policy and sound common sense both dictate that it will do no harm to show the King our faces again and remind him of our fealty and our family's obligation to his royal goodwill. He thinks highly of you, too, and has favoured you greatly since we lost our lands in Scotland, so it is fitting that you should extend him the courtesy of presenting your intended wife for his approval. Besides, I want Edward to meet Domhnall of Mar and be assured that not all the magnates in Scotland are anti-English."

"What does that mean, Father? Are you implying that most of the magnates *are* anti-English now?"

His father's right cheek twisted in a familiar grimace that had become a habitual tic. "Aye, so it would seem, from what I hear from north of the border. There's great unrest in Scotland these days and we Bruces are well out of it. The place is become a stewpot of politics wherein good men who seek but to mind their own affairs must scurry about like mice, lest they give offence to someone—anyone— who could have their life for it."

"Are things that bad?"

The elder Bruce scowled. "They're worse, from what I'm told. The realm is falling into anarchy and I wish I could lay the blame squarely at the feet of the Comyns, but I cannot. It's the King himself who is at the root of all of it, and he is Comyn only through marriage." His voice died away and when he resumed again it was low and bitter and hard-edged with resentment. "John Balliol of Galloway, may God preserve us all! The only King in Scotland's history to be called the King of *Scotland* and not the King of Scots. *Damn* the man! That distinction marks him clearly—he thinks more highly of the land itself, a place for him to possess, than of the folk who live there.

"My father called it rightly, years ago, when he named him a weakling unfit to rule. Not a coward, mind you, but his lack of *passion*—call it strength of will or assertiveness—will be the undoing of us all someday. The man is not capable of making a solid decision and then standing by it. He is forever changing his mind— swearing defiance against Edward at one moment, then grovelling for his forgiveness the next—and that, as you might imagine, is driving the magnates to distraction, since they themselves know not which way the royal cat is going to leap tomorrow."

That was almost exactly what Jardine had said earlier, and Bruce wondered if the knight had discussed the matter with his father. "What about the Stewart?"

"What about him? He is my main source of information, and he despairs of the situation." Annandale surged to his feet and began to pace the length of the room, his right hand clutching the hilt of the dagger at his waist as the words poured out of him.

"There is a move afoot, the Stewart says, to form a council of Guardians, officially, to *assist* the King in his administration of the realm. That assistance will entail guidance in forming policy, in establishing resolve, and in enforcing that resolve thereafter. Twelve Guardian councillors—four bishops, four earls, and four barons, equally drawn from north and south of the Forth. The Stewart will be one of them, of course, as will Bishop Wishart of Glasgow. Fraser of St. Andrews and Comyn of Badenoch will make two more. The others I know not at this stage."

Bruce was frowning. "And what if the King decides he has no need of such assistance?"

"He will be … persuaded to change his mind. The magnates stand convinced of his incapacity to rule. He has shown no slightest capacity to withstand the will of England's King and that has led to grave concern among the magnates that the future of the realm itself may be under threat of English domination." Lord Bruce had stopped pacing and now he stood behind his chair, grasping its high back, glowering.

"My God, Father. That is scarce believable. A council of Guardians usurping the King's authority."

"There is no usurpation involved, and the King is *demonstrating* no authority." Bruce had seldom heard his father sound so acerbic. "And that, God help us all, is the distilled truth at the heart of this entire matter. The King of Scotland for the time being is a feckless nonentity. He is incompetent! But there are those among his following who *see* that and stand prepared to set the cause of the realm above the weakness of the monarch. Any action taken by the council will be aimed solely at strengthening Balliol's royal presence and bolstering his status for the good of the realm."

"Aye. But whether he likes it or not is what you are saying. They have placed his kingly power under interdict. It sounds treasonous to me."

For a moment he thought his father would explode in anger, but with a visible effort of will the lord of Annandale moved around his chair and sat down again. The florid face lost its tension and his shoulders slumped against the chair's high back. "'Treason' is not a word to be lightly used by folk like us, Robert, dispossessed and exiled as we are. Besides, ask yourself what the land would have *without* such a council. It's easily named—anarchy. And I have already said we're close to that as things stand. Scotland is in turmoil, and unless there are changes in the near future—great changes—the country faces civil war. The men of goodwill, the leaders within the realm—people like James Stewart and Domhnall of Mar and Andrew Moray of Petty, along with others of their ilk from north and south of Forth—are seeking ways to make things better. And this council is the sole, honourable course open to them. The Church stands with them, as do most of the Comyns. They see no other way to guard themselves than by uniting behind the King *despite* the King, and forcing him, in time of need, to play his part convincingly and be monarch in fact as well as name."

"That will not please Edward Plantagenet."

"No, it will not. But Scotland is not yet an English fiefdom. Your grandfather was right about that, too."

"He was. And Bruce stands clear of all of this." It was not a question, but his father responded as though it had been.

"Of course. We have no choice the way things stand. You know that."

"Aye, I do ... I dislike it, but I understand. And we have made our choice long since, to stay in England."

"For the duration, aye."

"For the duration ... " Bruce's eyes narrowed. "The duration of Balliol, you mean? Would you change your mind were that to change, Father?"

The Lord of Annandale shook his head, the gesture studiously noncommittal, his eyes betraying nothing. "So," he said, "I believe King Edward will be glad to see us."

Bruce dipped his head, blinking rapidly against a surge of lethargy that told him Brother Reynald's new concoction was taking effect. "Let us pray it be so, Father." He could hear himself slurring the words though he forced himself to speak clearly.

"You're tired," Annandale said, leaning forward. "Brother Reynald told me not to stay too long. Try to sleep now. I have other things to do ... Domhnall, for one. I need to speak with him. Rest now, boy."

# CHAPTER EIGHTEEN

# ENCHANTMENTS
# AND INTRIGUES

When he opened his eyes again it was night, and the darkness of the room was relieved only dimly by a dying fire flickering weakly in the grate. He lay still for a while, allowing his eyes to adjust to the darkness as he listened to the silence, searching for the sound that had awakened him, but as he lay quietly waiting for it to be repeated, he began to believe that it might have been born of a dream.

Then it came again, a whisper, unmistakably feminine, followed by a stifled giggle from the darkest corner of the room, near the door.

"Who is there?"

Another muffled, furtive sound was followed immediately by the darkness in the corner growing blacker, and even as his eyes widened in surprise he knew what had happened. Someone had moved the wooden screen from the wall beside his cot and set it up in that far corner to conceal them from where he lay, and at the sound of his voice they had blown out the candle there. Now he heard the voices again, whispering urgently, and saw hurried movement; the door to his room swung open and a tall, slim shape, undoubtedly a woman, swung into momentary view in the dim firelight before vanishing into the passageway and pulling the door shut behind her.

Silence fell again, deep and unbroken, and Bruce lay still, his mind working quickly and clearly. Lady Isabella's young women,

Thomas Beg had called them, all of them younger than their seven-teen- or eighteen-year-old mistress, and all set to watch him at various times while his physician and Father Baldwin were other-wise occupied. Clearly they had been told to watch over him while he slept, and they had moved the screen or had it moved for them—it was a heavy, cumbersome thing made of carved wooden panels—to where they could do both with the least risk of disturbing him. If that were the case, though, they should have had no need to startle at his awakening and no reason at all to run away. But only one had fled and there had been two of them at least, whisperer and giggler, which meant that one was still there, hiding in the darkness.

He called again, expecting a response this time, but when nothing happened he felt the first stirrings of annoyance. On the point of raising his voice, though, he remembered what he was dealing with here. The young woman hiding from him was from the earldom of Mar, north of the river Forth, and thus it was more than possible that she might speak no language other than her own, the Erse tongue of the northern folk. Keeping his voice calm and level he tried again, this time in Gaelic.

"I know you are there, so come out now and bring your candle with you. Light it at the fire again and then light another one for me, over here."

Nothing happened for a few moments, and he was on the verge of speaking again when he heard the tiniest of rustling sounds and a child emerged into the dim glow of the firelight and moved slowly towards him. She stopped about five paces from the bed and stood there timorously, staring at him as he looked back at her. He could not see her clearly, but even so her waif-like form reminded him of his younger sister Mary and he reacted as would have done with her.

"You should be abed, child, at this time of night. What are you doing here? And what hour is it, anyway?" He flattened his hands on the mattress and tried to push himself up to sit, but he was rewarded with a blinding pain that made him gasp. He fell back and the pain passed quickly, but by the time he opened his eyes again the child was standing close, one arm stretched out as though to help him. He grimaced and waved her away.

"Leave me be," he said, hearing the shakiness in his own voice. "I have no need of help." He drew a deep, steadying breath, and when he spoke again his voice sounded normal. "It's too dark in here. I can't see your face. Light your candle at the fire, as I said. There's a taper there. Then light mine."

She moved to obey him, but his mind was already ranging elsewhere, wondering why the other, taller woman had raced away so guiltily. He thought he knew the answer.

The child came back, frowning in concentration as she held one hand protectively over the flame of the thin wax taper she was holding. She went to the table the physician had moved to the foot of the bed and stooped over the thick candle stub in the holder there, her frown holding steady until the wick caught. Then, with less of a frown and still without looking at him, she held up her taper and looked around until she saw the other candle in its tall, floor-standing holder on the far side of his bed. She went to it quickly, lit it, then blew out her taper and took it back to its place at the fireside. Then she set about replenishing the dying fire from the pile of logs in the fuel bunker beside the hearth before lodging the heavy iron poker securely among the logs in the fire basket.

Bruce watched her idly throughout, half amused that she avoided his eyes in everything she did, but he knew exactly why she was doing so; she believed her secret to be safe as long as she did not look at or speak to him.

When she had remade the fire, she picked up her candle holder but remained kneeling in front of the hearth with her back to him, leaning back on her haunches and staring into the flames.

"Come here, child. Place your candle on the table there and pull that chair across to where I can look at you." She obeyed willingly enough, dragging the heavy chair noisily over the stone flags. "No, come closer. I won't bite you and I want to speak to you without having to shout. Closer. There, that will do."

She sat down facing him, a tiny, frowning tic between her brows as she finally looked him in the eye, but then she squinted sideways and blew an errant lock of black hair away from her cheek before tucking it back demurely into the wimple from which it had escaped. When it was safely out of sight, she looked back at him and nodded. "My lord," she said, in a small, subdued voice.

"What is your name?"

She blinked at him and tilted her head slightly to one side. "Mary, my lord."

"Fancy that," he said, and smiled. Even without the Gaelic, her voice would have been unmistakably Scots from north of the Forth, but it had a pleasant, vaguely husky timbre, and he had a sudden certainty that her wit, when she chose to show it, would be quick and wickedly barbed. "The first thing that came into my mind when you stepped into the light was that you reminded me of my sister Mary. Mary what? I can see now, in the light, you're clearly not my sister Mary Bruce."

In fact he could see now, in the light, that she was not the child for which he had first taken her. She was small enough in stature, but now he could see she must be four or five years older than he had first thought her. And she was devastatingly pretty. *A heart-breaker, someday.* The tightness of the plain white wimple emphasized the heart shape of her face, and she had high, prominent cheekbones and a wide, generous mouth that looked as though it would laugh easily. But it was her eyes that drew his attention; they were large and brilliantly green in the light of the candle's flame.

Now she nodded her head slightly, as though reassuring herself that his question had been reasonable. "Mary Henderson, my lord. My father is Sir Gavin Henderson of Thorndell, knight in service to Earl Domhnall."

"I see. And how old are you, Mary Henderson?"

She hesitated, then quirked her lips ruefully. "I'm seventeen."

"Seventeen?" He managed to stop himself from smiling but let his voice express his gentle disbelief. "*Seventeen?*"

Now she flushed and tossed her head. "Well, then sixteen … But I'll be seventeen come July."

"Good for you. And how long have you been a companion to Lady Isabella?"

"Two years, come Martinmas."

"And how many of you are here?"

The black eyebrows drew together. "What d'you mean, my lord?"

"How many ladies did the countess bring with her?"

"Oh, five of us. But she's no' a countess, my lord. She's just Lady Isabella … Your own sister, Christina, is to be Countess of Mar."

"True, but your mistress is to be Countess of Carrick when she becomes my wife."

The green eyes blinked. "So she is … I never thought of that. Countess Christina is the only countess I've ever met."

"And do you like her?"

"Who, your sister?"

"No, your mistress."

"Why would I *not* like her?"

Bruce hitched one shoulder in a semi-shrug. "I don't know, Mary Henderson. You know the answer to that better than I do. The lady is to be my wife but I have never met her. I merely wondered whether you enjoy your life as her companion."

"I do, as a matter of fact." The girl's voice radiated a distinct coolness.

Bruce raised his hands in surrender. "Forgive me, Mary. I did not mean to pry, or to ask you to say anything improper." He gave her what he hoped was an engaging smile. "I have been stuck in this bed, in this room, since soon after she arrived here and I have yet to set eyes upon her. And so I am curious about her. But I'll ask no more questions of you … None, at least, that might take advantage of your position."

Mary nodded slowly, and Bruce returned the gesture equally slowly.

"Who was behind the screen with you when I woke up and spoke to you?" He saw her eyes widen and she looked away quickly. "Was it one of the others, your companions?"

She nodded her head, biting her lower lip.

"Or was it Lady Isabella herself, come here to snatch a stolen glimpse of the ogre she is to wed?"

The great green eyes widened instantly. "That's not true," the girl snapped. "Why would you say such a thing?"

"Because she ran away when there was no need."

"There was a need! But that wasn't Lady Isabella. The very saying that it was is an insult."

Bruce raised an eyebrow, surprised by the ferocity of the girl's defence of her mistress. "How so? I meant no insult—"

"Yes you did! You accused her ladyship of spying on you like … like some kind of thief, and then running away when she thought she might get caught."

There was no doubting the young handmaid's outrage, for her cheeks flushed and her eyes sparkled, and Bruce threw up both hands for the second time in as many minutes. This time, though, he made no attempt to plead innocence or justify himself; he merely waited for the young woman to calm down. When she did, eventually, he said mildly, "This is my house, you know, Mary Henderson."

A blink of incomprehension, then, "What does that mean?"

"What does that mean, *my lord*?"

A pause, more of a hesitation, followed that before she repeated, "What does that mean, my lord?"

He blinked slowly back at her, knowing the effect was largely lost with one eye covered by bandages. "It means, Mary Henderson, that I can say whatever I please, most of the time, beneath my own roof." He gave that time to reverberate before he added, "Of course, most of the time I don't have to worry about quick-tongued young women jumping down my throat. We have no such young women here in Writtle. Or we did not until you and your mistress came to stay."

"I don't— I didn't—"

"Jump down my throat? Did you not? Pardon me, then, I must have been mistaken, but I was sure … " He stopped, then snapped back with another question. "You said there was a need for your companion who was not the Lady Isabella to run away. What was it?" He saw the sudden, stubborn set of her chin and waited, counting silently to five, then resumed. "Look, you, I believe you when you say that it was not your mistress who fled, but who was it, and why was there a need? I hope you can see that there is a mystery here and that we need to resolve it between us. Because I am a Scots earl in England and this is my sickroom and I could scarce defend myself were someone to attack me." He saw her eyes grow large with consternation and added, "I am not saying I expect to be attacked and murdered in my bed, or that I fear you or your friends might be plotting against me, but I do suspect that you have fears of causing trouble for someone else by telling me, and that concerns me. If I am right and that is true, then put your mind at rest. Whatever you say to me here will go no further. You have my word on that. Now, who was she?"

She spoke a name. It was indistinct, almost inaudible, but then she cleared her throat and spoke it clearly. "It was Marian."

"And who is Marian?"

"A friend … My friend … One of us."

"One of the five, you mean? And why did she need to flee?"

Again the reluctant, almost stubborn pause and then the dam burst and the words came pouring out of her. "Because she was forbidden to be here—not her, exactly, or not really her, but any one of us at all who was not supposed to be here. The old man made it clear—he was very angry with us—but he told us all that whenever any of us was here we were to be alone. You were an earl, he said, and betrothed to our mistress, and you were sick, and if we could not be trusted to watch over you without the need of being watched ourselves, then all our being here was a waste of time and he would make other arrangements and we would not be needed … "

She was almost breathless by the time she finished, and Bruce stared at her, trying to make sense of what she had said. At length he raised a calming hand, palm out towards her. "Very well," he said, keeping his voice low and unhurried. "First, which old man are you speaking of? Brother Reynald?"

"Yes, the old French monk … The physician."

"And why was he angry at you?"

"Because—" She stopped, and her shoulders slumped. "Because we were being silly—*flighty* was what he said. Elaine was here with Marian and me and we were chattering while he was doing something. I think he was mixing your physick."

"And your chattering annoyed him?"

"Yes … " She stopped again, then shook her head. "No. It was more than that. Elaine pushed Marian against the table and it fell over."

Bruce's eyes widened. "She knocked the table over? With the box on it, the wooden box that held the medicinal powder? She spilt it?"

"Yes … and no. She knocked the table over and the box was on it, but it was closed and Marian almost caught it as it fell. She missed, but nothing spilt. But he was very angry. I picked the box up off the floor myself and it was tight-shut, but the old man snatched it away from me and railed at me as though I had been the one to knock it over." She pouted. "He does not like young women, that old man."

"He is a monk and a physician, Mary—a Knight of the Hospital, and he is *very* old. He has little patience with young people at the best of times, even with me, and I'm older than you are. Besides, his monkish training as a knight would have taught him long ago, before ever you were born and perhaps even before your parents were born, to avoid all women under pain of mortal sin. He would have sworn a sacred oath to shun *all* women—not merely young ones. Besides, that box of powder has more value than you could ever begin to calculate. It would be irreplaceable, were it lost, for it came from the Holy Land long years ago and its like does not exist in all of Christendom. Small wonder he was angry. So he banned you from the sickroom?"

She shook her head tightly. "No, my lord. He forbade us to be *together* in the sickroom. We could be here, he said, but no more than one at a time, alone. Otherwise we would be banished."

"So why did you not just leave? What made it so important for you to keep watch?"

The young, earnest face cleared suddenly as though it had been wiped clean, and Mary Henderson smiled at him, emitting a radiant burst of pure and innocent beauty. "And leave you to lie here alone?" She shook her head, dismissing any such possibility. "You are Sir Robert Bruce, the Earl of Carrick and our mistress's betrothed. Our welfare lies with you in the years ahead, so how could we neglect a chance to care for you?" She hesitated, briefly, and then shrugged. "Besides, there is nothing else to do here in England. Not in this place, at least. We would all die of boredom otherwise, waiting for you to heal, and that would do no one much good."

Bruce nodded, as gravely as he could, flat on his back. "I see … "

A sniff, small and dainty, followed by a fumbling and the appearance of a small kerchief to wipe a dainty nose. "Marian came with a message from Lady Isabella. She was to deliver it and leave, but we started talking and woke you up. You frightened us and Marian ran away."

"Hmm. And how long will you stay here, Mary Henderson?"

"Until midnight. Then the old man will come back. He sleeps over there." She pointed towards the corner to the left of the fireplace, and Bruce turned his head to see a plain cot that had escaped his notice.

"It must be nigh on midnight now, I reckon."

She bowed her head. "Aye, sir, it must."

"What next, then?"

"Oh! Your physick. I near forgot." She sprang up and crossed quickly to the table, where she picked up a large clay mug and took it to the fireplace. After wrapping her hand in a heavy cloth, she pulled the iron poker from the roaring fire and plunged its red-hot end into the mug, releasing a dense cloud of hissing steam. She waited until the hissing died away and then rose again and carried the mug carefully to where Bruce lay watching her. She hesitated at the bedside, eyeing him uncertainly.

"Can you sit up to drink this?" Somehow the "my lord" formality had been lost again, and Bruce felt no need to remind her of it.

"I think I can, if you'll help me." He raised an arm towards her. "Set the cup down and hook your arm under this one, then pull me up and let me lean on you until I'm stable." She did as he had said, and up close she was even smaller than he had anticipated. He felt her forearm hook into his armpit and sensed her bracing it with her other hand, and then she leaned back, throwing her weight against his.

"Gently," he said, grunting. "Don't try to lift me. All you need to do is take my weight and brace me a little to stop me from falling back. Now, on three. One, two, and—there! That should do it. Now let's have that devil's brew."

She sniffed at the mug before holding it out for him. "It does not smell like a devil's brew," she said.

He grinned at her as she brought the mug closer to his mouth. "You're an expert on the Devil, are you, Mary Henderson?"

She frowned slightly but said nothing until he had emptied the mug, and then she stepped back, holding the vessel in both hands and frowning at him in what was almost a squint.

"Will that make you sleep? It's different from the other stuff. That made you sleep like a dead man."

"And so will this. At least, it did this afternoon ... So what now? Brother Reynald will be here soon. Will I see you tomorrow, Mary Henderson?"

"No, sir. Tomorrow you will have Elaine in the forenoon and Margaret in the evening."

"Who are they, this Margaret and Elaine?"

"Elaine MacGregor of Tarbolton and Margaret MacWilliam of Mar, Lady Isabella's niece."

"Ah! Yet another of the House of Mar. They are a prolific family." He saw her frown at the unfamiliar word and added, "They breed a lot."

"And why not?" She sounded disapproving again. "That's what families are for."

He grinned at her, enjoying her pertness, but at that moment the door swung open behind her and Brother Reynald stepped inside, carrying a shielded candle. He stopped short when he saw the young woman standing over the bed.

"Brother Reynald," Bruce said in French. "We have been expecting you. The young lady has just fed me your latest brew and is about to seek her bed." He looked back at the young woman and switched back to Gaelic. "Away with you now, Mary Henderson, and sleep well. I will look forward to seeing you again one of these days."

The girl flushed red and bobbed a hasty curtsy before scuttling out.

Brother Reynald was watching him as a boy might watch a frog, waiting for it to leap. "You slept most of the day today," the old man said.

Bruce nodded. "I know. And having drunk another draught but moments since, I suppose I'll sleep throughout the night as well."

"That is the intent. Are you feeling well? No aches or pains?"

"No, Brother, but as you yourself reminded me, they are there, waiting to be provoked."

"Then do not provoke them. We are making progress. Can you see clearly?"

"Not with this blindfold wrapped round my head."

"We will take it off tomorrow. But you are not seeing double? Nothing appears blurred?"

"No, sir. My sight is well enough—what there is of it. Tomorrow when you remove the bandages it should be perfect."

"So we can but hope." He crossed behind the bed and blew out the candle there, then stooped to do the same with the smaller one on Bruce's table. "Sleep well." He moved away, blowing out his own candle as he went towards the cot in the corner, and left Bruce in darkness illuminated only by the flickering of the fire. Plainly it was time for rest, needed or not.

True to his word, Brother Reynald removed his bandages the next morning and pronounced his healing to be more than satisfactory, with no scarring and scarcely a scab. Bruce's eyesight was clear, and, after some careful experimentation, he found that he was able to sit up in a chair and take more solid food.

For the next half-hour the Earl of Carrick sat and watched as fragments of the life of the household beyond his chamber door spilled inside to where he sat alone. A group of servants arrived first, none of them quite daring to meet his eye, and he admired the speed and efficiency with which they cleaned the entire room, straightening his bedding and sweeping out the ashes from the fireplace before building and kindling a new fire. They worked in a kind of breathless hush, communicating with one another only in grunts, and they were finished and away again in a miraculously short time, it seemed to him. One of them, though, in backing away from the hearth as he examined it for flaws, caught his shoulder on Bruce's great sword, where it hung in its belted sheath from a peg on one of the room's supporting pillars.

"Wait," Bruce said as the man steadied the swaying weapon. "Bring me that, if you will."

When Thomas Beg and Nicol arrived a short time later, bringing more servants with an array of food set out on trays, they found their quarry seated by his bed, holding the big sword that had been William the Marshal's and was now his. He had unsheathed it, and the discarded scabbard and belt lay on the floor at his feet while the long, gleaming blade tilted upward, pointing at the mantel.

While the servants began to lay out the food they had brought, Thomas Beg stood in front of the fireplace with his back to the flames and his hands crossed behind him. "Are ye thinkin' o' using that?" he asked Bruce.

Bruce smiled faintly, lowering the point to rest on the floor between them. "No, not at all," he said. "In fact I was thinking of how *little* use I've made of it since I've owned it. I've never swung this thing in anger."

"And pray God you never have to, lad." Nicol MacDuncan had seated himself on the edge of the freshly made bed. "It's a vastly unrewarding pursuit, and killing men, no matter how deserving they might seem of being killed, is no way to find lasting satisfaction. What brought you to thinking about that?"

"Oh, I was thinking about my friends, the ones I chanced across just before you came—Harry and John and Humphrey de Bohun. They are all hardened warriors now—veterans, they call themselves—and you can see it in their faces and the very way they walk. They've all been in battle, in Wales, putting down Madog's rebellion."

"Words, Robert, *words.*"

Bruce looked up in surprise, unaccustomed to hearing Nicol MacDuncan sound so emphatic. "What d'you mean, *words*, Nicol? Did I say something that offended you?"

"Aye, you did, but the words were not yours. You were spouting words your English friends had used, without thinking about what they meant. *Their* words, and meanings that mask meanings."

Bruce was gaping now, and making no attempt to disguise it. "Nicol," he said, "I have no idea what you are saying."

"But I know full well what *you* said. You were talking about Madog Llewelyn's rebellion, and that makes me angry. Madog led no rebellion. He led an *uprising.*"

He stopped, glaring into Bruce's astonished eyes, and then he shook his head. "You don't understand a word I'm saying, do you, Nephew? Then listen and learn. The Welsh are not English. They never were. They were here before the English came to Britain and they were here before the Romans came. Wales is their ancient homeland. That's why the English call them Welshmen." His eyes narrowed. "Do you understand that, Robert?"

Bruce nodded. "Of course I do. I tried to explain it to Percy and the others, when they were bleating about the Welsh not liking them. What I am failing to understand is why you're saying it."

"Well then, maybe you will be able to answer a question for me." He glanced over at the servants preparing their meal, but he had been speaking in Gaelic, and unable to understand a word, none of them was paying any attention to him. The head man straightened up, scanned the tabletop one last time to ensure that everything was in place, then ushered out his crew with a wave, leaving the three Scots to themselves.

"Tell me, if you can," Nicol continued, "how Welshmen, defending their own land against aggression and outright invasion by foreign armies, can be said to be *rebelling* against the invader? To make that sound reasonable you'd have to be English, with an Englishman's particular view of things. Me, I'm a Scot, so I have no time for such blatant haverings. No more should you, for all that you live here in England. If a thing has an honest name, then use that name in truth and don't try to twist it into something else. An uprising is one thing and may sometimes be justifiable. Rebellion is another thing altogether—the treasonous disputation of legally established order and the rules by which it governs. Your friends may have won their spurs in Wales, just as you say, but I would argue against the validity of the cause in which they earned them. What say you, Thomas Beg?"

Thomas Beg had crossed to the table and was raising the cloth covers from the steaming bowls and platters to inspect their contents, narrow-eyed. "Hot porridge wi' fresh cream," he mused. "New-baked, crusty bread frae the oven, butter, salt, some kind o' eggs, mixed up, an' juicy fried slices o' thick pork. Ye'll be better served eatin' this than e'er ye will talkin' about shite like that." He glanced at the other two, wry-faced. "The English hae their own way o' seein' things, and what they want, they take. Wales is the proof o' that, an' nothin' the likes o' us can say or do is apt to change a bit o' it. So let's eat." He stepped back and stood beside Bruce's chair while Nicol returned Bruce's sword to its sheath and hung it back on its peg. "A hand here, if ye will, Master Nicol. This poor soul isna fit to walk yet, so we'll lift him, chair and a'. I'll get the arse o' it and you hold the back. Are ye ready? Right."

They stooped and took hold, then straightened, grunting in unison, and swung Bruce, chair and all, to a place at the table, where they set about demolishing the meal spread out there. Bruce ate heartily, enjoying real food for the first time since the fire, and he was grateful for the similar single-mindedness with which his two companions addressed themselves to their food, for he had much to think about.

Eventually his uncle pushed his empty platter away and poured himself a fresh glass of milk, while Thomas Beg was folding a slice of buttered bread in half over the last piece of fried pork.

"Well, I'm glad I didn't spoil your appetites," Bruce said. "Nicol, if I didn't know you better, I'd have thought you'd grown political since last I saw you."

Nicol dipped his head to one side. "Aye, and you'd be right," he said mildly. "I've never bothered with politics in the past, but the thoughts I've been having recently are troublesome."

Bruce frowned. "What thoughts?"

His uncle sucked at something lodged in his teeth. "This whole affair in Wales … The *rebellion* you mentioned. It's done now, and Edward's got what he wanted, for the time being."

"For the time being? You think he wants more from Wales?"

"I *know* he wants more from Wales. He wants Welsh gold and Welsh taxes for his treasury and Welsh bowmen for his wars in France. That's why he's building so many castles there, fortifying his position. But that's not what concerns me."

"You amaze me, Uncle," Bruce said slowly. "Since when have you paid heed of what goes on in Wales? Or of where Edward builds castles?"

"Since that same Edward garrisoned the royal castles in Scotland! Can you not see it, boy?"

"See what?" It had been years since Nicol MacDuncan had called him boy, and again Bruce was surprised at his vehemence.

Nicol slouched back in his chair, and Bruce raised an eyebrow towards Tam, who merely made a face, then stood up.

"You two hae things to talk about that I don't want to hear, so I'll leave you to it."

Bruce had not expected that. "No, stay and talk with us."

"Nah," Tam said, shaking his big head. "Ye'll be talking politics and I hae no need to hear it. In fact, I hae no *desire* to hear it. I'll no' be far away, gin ye hae need o' me for anythin'. But I'll take my leave now, gin ye'll permit me."

Bruce sat staring at the door after Thomas Beg had left. "Well," he muttered. "That was plain enough. Thomas Beg likes politics no more than you do. But why would he not stay and listen? He might have learnt something."

"I think he might have learned long since when to mind his own affairs and leave others to theirs," his uncle said.

Nicol sat for several moments longer, nibbling at the inside of his cheek, then drew a deep breath and began to speak. "There are men in Scotland, powerful men with much to lose, who fear that Edward's rebellion in Wales was merely an earnest of what he plans for us."

"For us? For us Bruces, you mean? No, you're not a Bruce. For Scotland, then? That is ridiculous. Edward would—"

"Be quiet, Robert, and listen to me. And recall what your own grandsire said four years ago, at the start of the Norham proceedings."

Bruce opened his mouth to reply just as strongly, but something in his uncle's eyes stopped him before he could summon enough outrage. He sat back, gripping the arms of his chair. "Remind me," he said, keeping his tone neutral.

"Edward made himself lord paramount of Scotland. You recall that?" Nicol's voice was now calm and controlled. "He *made* himself lord paramount, uncaring of the will of the Scots people, and no man dared deny him. And all the Guardians resigned on the day that took effect, and were reappointed immediately by Edward, acting *as* lord paramount. Your grandfather thought the whole thing was iniquitous, that Edward was doing things for hidden reasons of his own and that it was sheer folly to present him with the royal castles as bases for English garrisons within our country. But it was all passed off and smoothed over as being for the good and welfare of the Scots realm, since the castles would be returned as soon as a new king was chosen. You'll remember that, too, no doubt."

"Aye, I do. But they were not returned, were they?"

"Not yet, and that's a sore point with King John, though there appears to be nothing he can do about it short of declaring outright war on England, which is unthinkable. But Lord Robert, God rest his soul, also said with absolute belief on one occasion that Edward of England was a different man altogether from the young prince with whom he had gone to war so long ago."

Bruce sat up straight. "Have you been talking to Wishart? I was there when Gransser said that once, as was my father, and the only other person there at the time was the Bishop of Glasgow."

"That's not important. What is—"

"I disagree. It *is* important, Nicol. It's very important. Because it tells me Wishart of Glasgow is one of those powerful men you spoke of earlier—'powerful men with much to lose.' And if you are communing with the likes of Wishart then you must also be speaking with the High Steward and his friends among the magnates, all of whom are Bruce adherents." He stopped, his brow furrowing, and then said, almost to himself, "Unless it was my father himself who told you. Is my father involved in this?"

"No." Nicol's denial was emphatic.

"Why not? He should be. It concerns him."

"It does not concern him. The Lord of Annandale renounced his Scots concerns twice: when he elected to come here to England and when he swore fealty to Edward, offending and abjuring King John."

"I did the same thing, Nicol, at the same time and for the same reasons. So why are you telling me about this and not my father?"

Nicol looked uncomfortable for a moment, then flexed his entire upper body with a great sigh. "Because it has been ... decided that your father holds no answers for Scotland in this case."

"Decided." Bruce's voice was now ominously quiet. "By whom? These same powerful men with so much to lose? Scotland is a quagmire, from what I hear, and King John does naught but pour water into the mud, confounding everyone and adding to the mess. You'll recall, I have no doubt, that my grandfather Lord Robert prophesied that such would be the case. He knew Balliol was not the man Scotland needed as its king. And now the magnates see the truth of that for themselves. But he also prophesied that Balliol would not endure, and that is why he passed his rights and claims to Scotland's Crown on to his son, properly and legally. Who dares dispute that?"

Nicol answered, equally quietly, "No one disputes it, Robert. The question being raised is one of temperament … of suitability. Some people feel—believe—that Lord Annandale would fare little better than our present King were he, too, forced to deal with Edward of England's demands and arrogance. He is too close to Edward, they believe, too beholden to him."

"Some people! Who are these nameless, faceless someones? Those who think they might do better than a Bruce, given a chance to make their own ambitions a reality? That is outrageous perfidy. My father is a fine, upstanding man, trained to his duty, and he has never been found wanting in the execution of it."

"True, and I can attest to that myself. Your father and I have always liked each other. He did well by my niece and he mourned her deeply, and for that I will always admire him. He is a fine man, Robert, as you say, and a decent one. But *his* father, your grandsire the Competitor, was a *great* man, and that's a very different thing." He sighed again. "And it is greatness, men are saying, that our realm has need of at this time."

"And so these people—you among them, Nicol—have decided that my father is unfit to rule? Tell me," he said, making no attempt to hide his hurt, "how did you come to be in Durham with my father at this time, as he was preparing to leave?"

"I was not. I came south with the Earl of Mar. When he heard that Domhnall was coming south to England, Wishart sent me to join him, bearing a message."

"A message to my father, bidding him stand down?" The grin that accompanied the words was bitter, more rictus than smile. "I find it difficult to imagine what words would be required to couch such an order and make it appear like a request. What did it say, and how did my father react?"

"The message was not for your father. It was for Domhnall of Mar, to be relayed to you at the proper time."

"To me … " He remembered the old earl saying that they had much to talk about, and his own dismissal of the comment as mere sickbed pleasantry. He frowned again. "And my father knows nothing of this?"

Nicol MacDuncan shook his head.

"God's holy teeth, Nicol, how could you do this to me, giving me information that my father does not have, and on something that concerns him directly? D'you expect me to put up with that? You expect me not to tell him what you've said?"

The older man raised his hands, palms outward. "I expect nothing, Nephew, one way or the other. I am merely the bearer of tidings. Whether those be ill or not depends upon the viewpoint of their interpreter."

"No! That's a false argument and you know it, Nicol MacDuncan. What you have said puts an end to my father's expectation of ever becoming King of Scots."

"He has no such expectation and has made that plain, Robert. And you give credence to that, merely by remaining here in England. Scotland *has* a king. The question of whether he be a good king or no is immaterial. He is the King's grace and we are all his subjects, sworn to stand behind him until death. There can be no other king while King John lives."

"What about this council of Guardians? My father knows about that. From Wishart himself."

"Aye, I know he does. That was a necessary step. The forming of the council, I mean. Twelve good men and true, dedicated to assisting King John in the administration of the realm."

"By holding his hand and pointing him wherever they want him to face." He tossed his head impatiently. "Four earls, four barons, and four bishops, two of each from north of Forth and two from south. All very equitable and politic, and all designed for the protection of the King. Tell me, is my father in danger?"

"Danger? Good heavens, what kind of danger?"

"Danger of death. Is he perceived as a threat? Are there people up there who fear that he might plot to seize the throne?"

Nicol sat open-mouthed, and then brought his hands together as though in prayer. "I'll answer that by telling you exactly how your father is perceived 'up there,' as you call it. Robert Bruce the Sixth, Lord of Annandale, is judged to be like many another great man's son—a weak reflection of his father's puissance. Your father is regarded by most as what he is, a Scots magnate who has chosen to absent himself. He is seen as being too close to England's King in sentiment, and England's King is proving himself to be no friend to Scotland. On the other hand, though, in answer to your question, his life is in no danger. He lacks the following now to make himself a threat to Scotland and its King. At most, were he to make any attempt, he might raise the remnants of his folk in Annandale, although their loyalty at this stage still clings to the memory of his father. Beyond that, he'd find no sympathy for the cause he would be proclaiming. It would cause civil war, and Scotland has enough grief to face without the threat of that. Your father is seen, at best, as a toothless lion, posing no danger to King John or the realm … and thus his life is safe."

Bruce sat silent, keenly conscious that he could not refute a word of what his uncle had said. He became aware of his uncle's steady gaze and raised his eyes to meet it. "A toothless lion … That's a harsh judgment, Uncle, whether it be true or not. And it sets me clearly in my place, too, does it not?" He smiled again, though only one side of his face twisted to show it.

"No, Nephew, it does not. *You* could be a threat."

The younger man's mouth fell open. He shook his head, then looked about him helplessly. His hands fastened on the arms of his chair and he began to push himself to his feet, but his weakened legs would not support him and he subsided, scowling in angry frustration. "Help me up, if you will. I need to stand."

Moments later he was clinging stubbornly to the high back of his chair and forcing his quivering legs to bear his weight against the stabbing pain in his bruised hip. He ground his teeth as he waited for Nicol to sit down again and then he counted slowly to ten, inhaling deeply with each count and giving himself time to exhale fully before beginning again. On the tenth count he leaned his weight into the chair back and moved his feet farther apart, feeling them respond more naturally than they had moments before.

"So be it, then," he said. "I could become a threat." He paused. "Do you truly believe that? And if you do, would you object to telling me *how* I might do so?"

His uncle shrugged. "Why would you need to ask me that? You have already given me the answer."

Bruce inclined his head, slowly. "But I have no slightest idea of what it was … Can you explain it to me?"

"I can, but you should know the opinion was not mine. It came from Bishop Wishart. All I did was hear your confirmation of what he said."

"And what did I confirm?"

"That you are mentally prepared—and even anxious—to take up your sword in support of Edward Plantagenet." He nodded towards the great sword hanging from its peg. "You were fretting over how your friends had drawn ahead of you, fighting in Wales and winning glory while you have yet to swing your blade in earnest."

"That's true, I was. But how does that construe to make me a threat to Scotland?"

"Oh, Robert! In God's name, listen to yourself! *Edward Plantagenet* is the threat to Scotland. And those young friends you think so highly of are the weapons he will bring against us—the younger sons of England's great families, all of them hungry to win lands and glory for themselves in Edward's wars. When he calls you to serve him, you will be one with them, part of them, and part of the threat he brings against us. Can you doubt he will make prominent use of you, if only as a figurehead? A Scots earl, a *senior* Scots earl with an ancient title—a Bruce, no less—fighting in England's vanguard. That holds the seeds of dissension and defeat for everyone to see."

"Everyone except me, it seems. It would never happen. The King would never set me against my own like that."

"Sweet Jesus! Are you addled, boy? This is Edward Plantagenet. His sole concern is kingship. He cares for nothing more than his own realm—its welfare and condition—and nothing, *nothing*, be it man or ideal or fear of God Himself, will come between him and what he has determined will be that realm's destiny."

A timid knock sounded at the door and one of the household servants pushed it open and leaned in, opening his mouth to speak, but Nicol rounded on him. "Out!" he roared in English. "Leave us."

The hapless servant withdrew quickly, closing the door securely, and Nicol turned back to his nephew, speaking again in Gaelic. "This is the man your grandsire warned us of when Queen Eleanor sickened and died, years ago—the man who had been held in check for decades only by her good counsel and his love for her. With her gone, he lost all restraint, and no one dared gainsay him. And now it is plain he wants Scotland and seeks to rule it by browbeating and abusing Scotland's King, driving the poor, weak man mad and riding roughshod over everything with no regard at all for the demands of decency or courtesy. Do you truly think he will be swayed by your tender feelings if he thinks he has a need of your support, or that you'll be the only man alive whom he will not manipulate and put to use? Spare me!"

Bruce turned away and began to walk, very slowly and deliberately, towards his bed. It took three steps, and by the third one he was swaying dangerously, reaching out with both hands. He made it, though, and half turned, allowing himself to drop onto the bed's edge. He sat there, blinking his eyes against the dizziness he felt.

"I do believe that," he told Nicol then. "I believe it deeply. Edward Plantagenet is the very soul of honour. He would never make such a demand of me."

His uncle expelled breath loudly. "Well, then, if that's what you believe, I'll pray you're right, but I'll not be surprised if you're proved wrong. D'you want to hear Wishart's message?"

"Aye, I do." Both of their voices were subdued now.

"He is aware, he said, of your duties to your family and loved ones, and he knows you will fulfill them ably. He is appreciative, too, of how your family's fortunes have been undermined by the politics of our land, the enmity of the Comyns and the ill will—or ill judgment—of our King, John Balliol. But he fears the pressures that your chosen King will bring to bear upon you to assist him in his handling, his *mis*handling, of the affairs of Scotland's realm. Should you be persuaded to set foot in Scotland, bearing arms for England, the bishop says, it would be taken ill, not merely by himself but by all loyal Scotsmen everywhere. Knowing, then, that a time will come when Edward seeks to use you, he bids you bear in mind two things: that Edward of England is growing old and will not live forever, and that there might—and he says only might— come a day when Scotland itself has need of the House of Bruce. He bids you hold yourself in readiness for such a time and be prepared to return into your own."

"Is that all?" The scorn in Bruce's voice was palpable. "No more than that? That I should hold myself in readiness to play the poltroon and betray my sworn liege despite all his kindness and consider- ation, returning to a land that has belittled and dispossessed me and mine, casting us into exile for the sin of being who we are? You must be sure to inform the bishop, when you next meet with him, how honoured and pleased I was to receive his message, with its sugges- tion that my honour and my loyalty can be traduced and bought and sold with empty promises of someday and perhaps."

"I can't do that," Nicol said firmly. "The message is not mine to deliver. It's Mar's. I told you of it solely to save time, never thinking you might disagree."

"Damnation, then I'll tell Mar the same as I tell you. I won't be bought. My name is Bruce, and Bruce does not bite the hand that feeds him."

"Ach, sweet Christ! God weeps at the pride of rash young men. No one is asking you to betray Edward, Robert."

"No? Are they not?"

"No, damn it. You're but being asked to hold yourself in readiness."

"Aye, in readiness to betray Edward and perhaps, someday, to sneak back home to Scotland with my tail between my legs. Tell my lord bishop to find someone else to suborn. I will not betray Edward's trust and turn renegade simply because someone in Scotland expects it of me. Not for any man, and not for any scheming bishop."

"Renegade? You? In Christ's name, Nephew, think about what you are saying! It is not … *You* are not the one at fault in any of this, and no one is suggesting you should renege on anything. Edward of England is the renegade, if anyone is. He has reneged on every promise and commitment he has made to Scotland since this sorry mess began. He is the one who is blameworthy here, not you."

The younger man shook his head, his expression flinty. "I cannot see that, Nicol. I can see where it might seem so, to certain men whose ambition might prefer things otherwise, but I myself have seen no signs of any perfidy on Edward's part."

"Of course you haven't! That goes without saying, Rob. You've never looked for any, never thought of it. You refuse even to conceive of it. And yet the evidence is there, plain to be seen by any eyes but yours."

"Any eyes that choose to see it or want to see it or need to see it, you mean. Aye, that part of it I can understand, and I'm not fool enough to think there's any lack of such eyes in Scotland. But I'm not going to be swayed by such one-sided thinking—no matter how *obvious* it might appear to be to the thinker, be he bishop or magnate—and I'm damned if I'll bow my head meekly and submit to anyone's will who hasn't spared a thought for me or mine in the past eight years."

Bruce's voice had risen steadily as he spoke, the anger in it squeezing caution and discretion aside until he was almost shouting, and now Nicol, to whom Rob Bruce had never raised his voice before, waved him down, frowning. "Hush now," he said, his voice low and intense. "There could be ears pricked up, even here. And even speaking in the Gaelic, what you're saying might be overheard and used against you."

The younger man glowered fiercely, though he still breathed hard.

"Fine," Nicol said quietly. "In great part I agree with you. I can't argue against your logic, save on one front." He paused, frowning again, then rose and pressed a finger to his lips. He crossed quickly and silently to the door, where he grasped the handle and pulled it open, stepping outside to peer up and down the passageway to make sure no one was hovering out there. Reassured, he came back inside and pulled the door shut at his back before returning to his seat.

"But what you've been saying is one thing, Nephew, and what I'm trying to say is another altogether, so listen to me now." His voice was heavy with urgency. "I'm not talking about what some faceless bishop or magnate thinks. I can't govern what they think or how they behave any more than you can, and I can see how they might seek to use you for their own reasons, but that is neither here nor there. My thinking on this matter is far more concerned with our own welfare—yours and mine and our families', Bruce and MacDuncan—and there's more to it than your simple code of loyalty to Edward Plantagenet. The voice I'm hearing in my head, speaking of this very thing, is your grandfather's, and I've been hearing it for weeks. He has been dead for years, God rest his soul, but his opinions on Edward were clear and well expressed, and free of any of the bias that is rife in Scotland today—that selfsame bias that led you to say what you have just said."

Bruce's glower had faded to a mere frown now. "So what are you saying? I'm not following you."

"Think about what Lord Robert thought of Edward of England. Can you recall that?"

"Aye, but—"

"No buts, Rob. He warned us, did he not, to have a care to keeping Edward honest by making sure the world beyond our shores knew what he did, as opposed to what he *said* he would do. D'you remember that?"

"Aye, I do. But you were not there when he said that."

"I know. He told me of it himself, later. He and I grew close before he left for England. I think he came to trust me because of your trust in me. He told me of how he warned you and your father to beware of Edward's ambition. He said, and he believed, that Edward's *kingcraft* overwhelmed all else. And that his obsession with that same kingcraft, allied with his growing sense of destiny, his own and that of his realm, would make nonsense of friendships and personal loyalties wherever and whenever Edward the King perceived them to be in the way of his grand designs."

Bruce was nodding. "That's true and I remember it."

"Aye. And then he said we would have but one weapon left to us with which to control the man … the man Lord Robert recognized very clearly as not being the man with whom he had ridden out to war long years before. A changed man, dark and bitter since the death of his Queen, and oppressed by what he sees increasingly as the disobedience and obstruction of his wishes by his unbiddable barons. Here, he said, was a man who set great store on his need to be seen as a just and temperate monarch, acting in enlightenment in the eyes of God and man and inscribing his every law, command-ment, and decree for scrutiny by anyone who cared to examine them. You recall that, too? Lord Robert bade us keep a wary eye on what Edward said he would do, and upon *what he did in fact*, and he warned us to be prepared to seek assistance from the other kings of Christendom and from the very Pope himself should the need arise."

Bruce nodded again. "I remember. And so?"

"And so that need is here. We find ourselves where we are today, where Edward's promises to Scotland are but empty noises. He has deposed our King."

"No, the magnates forced his hand."

"Horseshit. He deposed the King of Scotland where he had no earthly right to do so, God-given or otherwise. And he has invaded Scotland to such ill effect that our abused and harried people cry out to Heaven itself for succour against the depredations of England's armies. Damnation, Rob, it's hardly an exaggeration that there are more Englishmen than Scotsmen in Scotland today."

"All of them are there legally."

"Legally? By whose law?"

"By Edward's and by Scotland's both. He is lord paramount of Scotland, by legal statute and the agreement of the Scots magnates, speaking for the people. And as lord paramount he has the right to make demands of those who owe him allegiance. There is no denying that—it is the law. And I can see no evidence of any legal wrongdoing on King Edward's part, much as I may mislike what is going on."

"In Christ's name, Nephew! He has betrayed every promise ever made to us! He has reneged on every pledge, every assurance, every commitment into which he ever entered. That's why I named him renegade!"

"God damn your arguments, Nicol! They are false." Bruce was on his feet, a hand on the bed. "You are ignoring the obvious. He is the *legal overlord* of Scotland. Argument over that is futile."

"I'm not arguing the legality of the thing, Rob! I am decrying its *morality*. Here is a man gone far beyond restraint, turning his people loose in another realm without regard—" He stopped himself, reining in his anger with visible difficulty and raising his hands, his fingers spread. "You'll pardon me, I hope," he said. "I have no right to rail at you and I have no wish to fight with you. Clearly you have your mind made up. And yet I have to ask this one thing of you. This alone. Look at the man more closely from now on, Rob. Mark what he says and does in the matter of Scotland and then take note of what he really does, or causes to be done. I'm not asking you to condemn him out of hand or to challenge him openly on my word alone. I am only asking you to make a more determined effort from now on to see both sides of what is there to be seen. Open your eyes wider and take note of what is going on here in England, and how it affects what goes on in Scotland. Who wields the power in Scotland, for a fact, and does it suit Edward's designs to have those people there, out from beneath his feet in Westminster? I do not ask this of you lightly. You have not been in Scotland recently, but I have, and I swear to you it is beyond belief. Believe as you wish to believe, from the evidence of your own eyes and senses, but in Christ's name do not delude yourself by being blind to the other side of what is happening. Will you do that for me, in recognition of what we have always been to each other?"

Bruce nodded gravely. "I will, Nicol, I promise you. And yet I have seen nothing, heard nothing, that would indicate to me that Edward is guilty of the things that you ascribe to him. And until I do, until Edward demonstrates such behaviour personally in ways I cannot misconstrue, he will have my loyalty and my trust. Tell Bishop Wishart that."

Nicol MacDuncan stood, his face an expressionless mask. "I will, if you truly wish me to. But keep your head up as you proceed from here, Nephew. You will be pursuing a new course by even looking for the kind of things you will seek now. And only a fool heads into the unknown burning all the bridges at his back."

"Then you may have a fool for a nephew, Uncle." He paused, frowning. "Nicol, I have known you all my life, and of all my family, you have been closest to me. You have said what you came to say today and I have listened to you, and I respect your viewpoint. I have raised my voice against you, too, as I never did before, but that sprang from my anger that Robert Wishart would propose such a course of action to me and use you to present it to me where he knew no other could or would. But that said, I see no need for you and me to quarrel between ourselves ... I would hate that."

"So would I, Rob, so would I." The older man stepped forward and extended his hand, and as they shook, he grinned ruefully. "No quarrel, then, between us two and I thank God for it. The world will make its own demands and we will all respond to them in our own ways, and only God can tell who will do what when any given day arrives. Be at peace, Nephew."

"And you, Uncle. May God watch over you. Will you ride with us to Westminster?"

"No, by Jesus! All those Englishmen and Frenchmen, and ne'er a Gaelic speaker among them? The heavens spare me that! No, I will head homeward tomorrow, if the weather holds. And when I see the bishop, which should be within the week, I will be frank with him. I might not bid him go to Hell, but neither will I underplay your response to what he had to say." He pointed at Bruce's ribs. "Your ribs seem sounder. I have not heard you gasp in pain today." He grinned. "In outrage, aye, but not in pain. And you walked."

Bruce harrumphed, but he was smiling, too. "Four steps," he demurred.

"Four more than you've walked in the week past. By this time tomorrow you'll be moving normally. It doesn't take long, once you're firm on your feet again. But I should go. I'll send that servant back to tend your fire."

"Give him a penny, too, in recompense for frightening him."

Nicol's grin grew wider. "I'll do that. And I'll come back and say farewell before I leave for home."

Brother Reynald returned in the middle of the afternoon, and when Bruce stood up to greet him he blinked in surprise. When the monk asked him if he could walk, he nodded and set off across the room, moving hesitantly at first but gaining confidence with every step from the moment his dizziness vanished.

"So," the old man said. "Speedy and laudable improvements since this morning, no? I am well pleased. God has been good to you, and I think I may return now whence I came. You will progress quickly from now on, without any more need of me." His old eyes flickered in what might have been a smile. "Go with God, Master Bruce, but take care not to throw yourself upon any more piles of stones in the next few days. Wait for a few months at least." He bowed and was turning away when Bruce stopped him with an upraised hand.

"Brother, may I ask you a question?"

"You may, and I may even answer it if I am able. Is it about your injuries?"

"No, Brother, it is about you."

The fiercely grizzled eyebrows rose, but the old man's response was mild. "Then ask it, Master Bruce."

"I know you were a brother of the Hospital and I know you were gravely injured, in Outremer."

"I was. Near Acre, four years before the city fell to Baibars and his Mamelukes. Did we not talk of this before?"

"No, Brother, not directly. You spoke of your physician friend Sayeef ad-Din and how he befriended you in your captivity, no more than that."

"Yes, I recall now. What more can I tell you of those days?"

"Nothing. My question is more concerned with your life now. As a monk and a Hospitaller, how can you now be inactive? Both, I thought, were lifelong commitments, but you no longer wear the insignia of the order, though I see the outline of its patch upon your cloak, and clearly you do not live in cloisters." Bruce shrugged. "I know it is none of my affair. I am merely curious and I will not be offended if you choose not to tell me."

Now the old monk smiled easily and tilted his head to one side. "Dispensations, Master Bruce, on both commitments. You are correct, of course. The vows we take are permanent. In my case, though, my superiors were … lenient and merciful. I served the order faithfully for more than forty years and was already far past youth when I was captured by the enemy. My wounds were severe and I have never fully recovered from them. I returned to France eventually, and to my monastic, though not my knightly, duties, but there remained one thing to be discovered about the nature of my injuries."

He smiled again. "Weak and debilitated as I had been in Outremer, I had thrived there beneath the desert sun. Only after my return to Christendom did I discover how badly the cold and dampness of my native France would aggravate my condition. My health declined steadily with every passing year, and in the seventh winter I came close to dying, in the monastery—they are not built as palaces, as I am sure you know.

"Hospitallers take great pride, perhaps even sinful pride at times, in their ability to heal ailments of all kinds, but mine defeated the entire fraternity. Only one of my brethren was able to define anything about my sickness with certainty. I was chronically sick, he said. You know this word, 'chronically'?" Bruce nodded. "Ah, good. I was chronically sick of unknown causes, or of causes we did not yet understand, and I would most certainly die, unnecessarily, were I to remain where I was. It was the climate and environment of our monastery, he said, that was keeping me sicker than I should have been—the coldness and the constant dampness of the stones that housed our cells. Monks choose to live a life of hardship and austerity, he said, but mine, my chosen life, was leading me unwittingly to suicide. And so I was relieved of my responsibilities and my membership in the order, in order to prolong my life.

"I have one blood relative in all the world, a younger sister who is wife to an English lord, Sir John Mowbray, a tenant of the Earl of Surrey. Sir John required someone to tend the hospice he set up on his lands when he returned from Outremer, long years ago, and he was happy to offer me a place. The friend who foresaw my impending death in the monastery arranged for everything, for he was, and he remains, active in our order and travels widely here and in France in the performance of his duties on its behalf." He spread his hands in a purely Gallic gesture, smiling gently. "And here I am, in England, for the sake of my health, though few in France might find that credible."

"And you enjoy it here."

"I do. I love the daily work with which I am blessed, and the life I live. I have a small cottage of my own, and it is warm and snug and dry, allowing me to pray according to the dictates of my former order."

"But it is not home, as you think of home."

The physician—for there was no trace now of the monk as he gazed at Bruce with narrowing eyes—pursed his lips, then pressed the tip of his index finger into the ledge of his nose before drawing it all the way down the beak's sharp edge. "No, Master Bruce," he said quietly, "I think I must disagree with you there. It *is* my home. This is my home now. England ... " His eyes drifted out of focus for a moment. "But it will never be, it *can* never be France." He drew a deep breath and laid an open hand on his chest. "The homeland can never be dislodged, Master Bruce. It resides here, always."

And then he bowed and turned away, limping towards the door, and as Bruce watched him go, he was highly conscious of the honour the old man had so casually bestowed upon him. Brother Reynald de Frontignac, Knight of the Order of the Hospital and aged in the service of that august order, was a man who would voluntarily bow to very few.

# CHAPTER NINETEEN

# CONFESSIONS

"D'ye feel strong enough to go out for a walk?" Thomas Beg asked. "It's a rare day."

At the mere thought of it, of stepping outside into fresh air and sunshine, Bruce felt a surge of energy. "Aye," he said, "I do … Providing it's not too far or too fast."

"We'll tak it slow. Here, let me get your cloak an' I'll help ye on wi' your boots."

As they stepped out through the main door of the house and stopped at the top of the steps leading down to the courtyard, Bruce threw back his head and spread his arms wide, inhaling the scents of the June day and feeling his troubles of the past week fall away from him. The sky was a bright, brilliant blue with only a few scattered, woolly clouds, and the air was warm and balmy, rich with the scents of summer. There were people everywhere he looked, going about their usual business, and though most of them failed to notice him, several acknowledged him with passing nods or smiles, and he saw none of the tense and careworn frowns he had seen everywhere the day of the fire. He inhaled again, deeply, sniffing the air for the telltale stink of charred wood and smoke, but there was nothing to mar the calm beauty of the day.

"Where d'ye want to go first?"

Bruce tilted his head and met Tam's eye. "The stables. Let's see what's happening there."

What was happening there, he soon discovered, was an astonishing rebirth. No slightest sign remained of the building that had burned, save for the cleared and levelled space it had occupied. Even the newly riven channel scoured by the floodwaters had been filled in, and the pond that had been washed out had been re-banked and deepened, its earthen sides now lined with heavy stones that would channel any future spate downhill and away from the stables themselves. There were huge piles of round stones everywhere, graded by size, and mountainous piles of sawn lumber.

Thomas Beg pointed with his thumb towards a deep, broad trench on the far side from where they stood.

"There's masons down in there, layin' foundations. That trench is three steps wide there at the back, an' it's even deeper than the old one was. They're linin' it wi' boulders set in cement, the kind the Romans used to use—harder than mortar an' made to last forever. Nae fear o' that washing away."

"Cement? What's that?"

The big man shrugged. "God knows, but it's hard, as hard as granite once it's set. I'd never heard o' it afore, either. The mason in charge there knows where to get the stuff that's in it, but he wouldna tell me where or say what it is. He mixes whatever it is wi' lime an' sand, like ordinary mortar, but it's far frae ordinary, accordin' to what his folk say."

"And he keeps the source secret? Wise man."

"Aye. A secret passed frae father to son. Like one o' they ... " He frowned, unable to find the word he was looking for.

"An inheritance, you mean?"

"Aye, that's it, the very thing."

Bruce looked out at the miles of fields beyond the stables, marvelling at all he could now see from this vantage point, for the old stable building had hidden this view and the new one would soon do so again. "Hard to believe that was all under water a week ago."

"It still was six days ago, but aye, it is. But that's what comes o' haein sand underneath instead o' clay."

Bruce smiled to himself, enjoying the big man's unconscious assumption of knowledge and authority. "That reminds me," he said.

"Is Sir James Jardine still here? I haven't seen him since the day of the fire."

"Aye. He spends most o' his time wi' your father and the Earl o' Mar. They're out huntin' … unless I didna see them comin' back. But they wis up an' away this mornin' early, the three o' them wi' some local folk as guides." He glanced sideways. "How are ye doin'? Are ye ready to go back?"

"Not yet. We can go a little farther."

"As ye wish, but it's your first time out. You shouldna overdo it."

"I won't, Tam. Just a little longer."

They walked for another quarter of an hour and were nearing the house when a young woman emerged, wearing a full, long-waisted kirtle of pale grey cloth and clutching a basket piled high with linen. She was a lively-looking lass, tall and straight-backed, with curling hair and bright, flashing eyes that widened suddenly as she saw the two men approaching. Thomas Beg surprised his earl greatly then by stepping in front of him, bowing low and doffing his cap with a muttered "Mistress Mary, good day to you. Let me take that for you." The big man moved quickly and, more gracefully than Bruce would ever have believed, relieved the young woman of her burden before she could protest. He watched in amazement as they left him there without another glance, walking in the direction of the outbuildings, with the young woman hurrying to keep up with Tam's long stride.

"Another Mary … Two out of five," he mused, smiling at a pleasant recollection of little Mary Henderson with her great green eyes. The departing pair vanished around a corner, and Bruce turned to enter the house. In the space of a single step, though, with his hand outstretched to push open the door, the smile withered on his lips and he froze.

He was no longer sick but up and moving about again, growing stronger with every passing minute. And that meant, inevitably, that sometime very soon, possibly within the next few hours, he was going to come face to face with Lady Isabella of Mar, his betrothed bride. The woman had been here in his own house for a full week already, unmet and unseen thanks only to the grace of God and a fortuitous injury. But now he would have to face her, accompanied by her father and his own, and acknowledge his commitment to a lifetime of having her by his side, bearing his children and judging his every move and motive …

Bruce had never thought of himself as being a coward, but at that moment he wanted to run to the stables, mount a horse, and flee into the forests. Dizziness swept over him again, a swooping vertigo, and then he stiffened himself defiantly, clamping his jaw as he pushed open the door. *Duty*, he told himself. *Face up to it!* He drew a deep breath and held it, then walked stiffly into the house.

It was dark inside after the brightness of the late-afternoon sun, and it seemed to his dazzled eyes that the stone-flagged hallway was full of people and busier than usual. As his sight adjusted, however, he saw he had been mistaken; there might have been a few more people there than usual, but they were all household staff and they were congregated in the long room to the right of the main entrance. He could not begin to guess what they were doing, but it was evident they were organized and working hard. Then he caught a flash of bright-coloured movement above him and glanced up to see two more of the Lady Isabella's young women climbing the staircase to the upper floors. He recognized one of them immediately, little Mary Henderson herself, his sole contact with the imponderable quandary that lay ahead of him.

He was unaware of calling her name aloud, but he knew he must have, for she turned to look down in surprise, hesitating before saying something to the other girl with her. She stepped closer to the edge of the staircase as her companion continued up the stairs. And with an eerie sense of foreknowledge Bruce found himself where he had stood a week earlier, gazing up at a young woman who looked back at him from above, one hand resting on the polished stone rail of the staircase. Where Gwendolyn de Ferrers had smiled warmly at him, however, Mary Henderson was eyeing him with concern, the line between her brows visible even from where he stood.

"My lord?" she said, turning the salutation into a question. "Is aught amiss?"

Reality returned and he looked around quickly to see who might be listening, but no one seemed to be paying him any attention, and he looked back to where the girl stood staring down at him, her wide green eyes appearing disproportionately large in her pale face. He raised a hand as though to say something, then found he had no words, either in mind or mouth, and so he stood there, his lips moving silently while a voice in his mind berated him, *What are you doing, you fool? What can you say to the girl? Where will you go with this?*

But then she was coming down the stairs towards him, hesitantly at first and then more quickly, still with that vertical line of concern etched between her brows, and he went to meet her. She stopped before she reached him, hovering on the third step above the floor, and he drew a gulping breath, incapable of speaking or of looking away from those fascinating eyes. He had been close to panic moments earlier but he was unprepared for the soaring wave of mingled pleasure and guilt that now engulfed him to see her looking back at him with such transparent concern. She was the most beautiful creature he had ever seen and he wanted, more than he had ever wanted anything, to reach out, pick her up by the waist, and lift her to where he could smell the scent of her.

"My lord," she said in her native Gaelic, "what is the matter? Are you unwell?"

Again he opened his mouth and again he was unable to speak. He stood stock-still, hearing a distant thundering in his ears and comprehending, finally, the enormity of what he had come close to doing. And then his shoulders slumped and he dropped his hands to his sides.

"No, Mary Henderson," he heard himself say as if from a great distance. "I am not unwell at all … But I am utterly undone."

She blinked at him, and as her frown grew deeper, his crushing misery deepened with it. He raised his hands again, palms forward in supplication, then, horrified to feel his eyes starting with tears, he stepped back quickly and whispered, "Forgive me, lass. I am a fool and I am damned. Forgive me."

He spun on his heel and marched away, stiff-legged and straight-backed, holding his head high and sighting on the high point of the archway ahead of him that led to the main hall. He could see it only vaguely through the tears that now flooded his eyes and ran unchecked down his face, but he was in his own house and knew where he was going, and as he went, he could hear his own voice asking, *Why am I weeping? In Christ's sweet name, what have I done?*

He sensed rather than saw the arch pass above his head and he swung sharply to his right, where he could brace his back against the wall out of sight, and there he stood with his hands cupping his forehead, pressing the heels of his palms painfully against his eyes to stop his tears. He raged at himself for his unthinking stupidity and foolishness, but then a tiny, other voice welled up, pointing out that he had had no notion of what was happening. That was followed by a vision of Mary Henderson's face, the sweet innocence of her expression causing an explosion of aching grief in his breast, and that gave way to a wave of shame that made him writhe with self-revulsion at the thought of how the blameless Lady Isabella of Mar would react when she discovered the truth: that her betrothed husband had betrayed her with, or abandoned her in favour of, one of her own serving women.

A hand grasped his left wrist and tried to pull his hand down and he tensed against it, but then his other wrist was encircled and his hands pried apart and down. He could not resist. He opened his eyes and looked down at the small, fiercely beautiful woman glaring up at him. She said nothing, but the look in her eyes required no words and he had none of his own. He blinked rapidly until his own eyes were clear again, and gazed back at her, immobilized by his own shame. She glared at him for a few more moments and then, when she was sure he was not going to move, she released his wrists slowly and took a half step back.

"So, my lord," she said in a calm, flat voice. "The French monk was right. That knock on the back of your head was clearly more dangerous than it appeared. He warned us that it might affect you strangely, even after many days. He had a name for it, but I cannot remember what it was … a long, priestly name. You should return to your bed, for another day, at least."

There was no censure in her voice, no discernible judgment, and Bruce felt an instant conviction, against all logic, that were he to nod his head and simply return to his sickroom, no more would be said on the matter and it would be forgotten. He blinked again, rapidly, and as he did so Mary Henderson drew a kerchief from her bodice and held it out to him. He took it with a nod of thanks and dried his eyes, then leaned his head back against the wall and snorted—half sob, half disbelieving laugh.

"No, and I thank you, Mary Henderson, but I cannot return to my sickbed." He brought both hands up to his face again and dragged his fingertips down from his forehead to his chin before he added, "My behaviour here has nothing to do with a mere bang on the head, but—" he pointed over her shoulder to the nearest hall table, "if I could sit over there for a while, and if you would sit with me, I would like to talk to you. Tell you something."

She looked around the empty hall. "How long a while would you need, my lord? It's quiet now, but that won't last long. It's getting close to dinnertime and they'll be wanting to set up soon. Better we walk outside, if you agree. It's a fine evening and we can find a place to sit in public view, yet far enough removed to speak without being overheard."

He walked beside her as if in a dream while they returned to the entrance hall and crossed to the high doors. He pulled one side open and held it while she passed through, then closed the door behind them, grateful that no one had as much as glanced their way as they passed. They walked together down the short flight of steps to the courtyard, and she moved slightly ahead of him as she went to the crude seat of squared logs beside the mounting block that faced the open gates.

"Will this serve, my lord?"

He nodded, then waited until she seated herself on the lower end of the uneven bench. Somewhere above his head a skylark was singing joyously, and off in the distance beyond the gates a black-bird added its own music to the air. He hung there, motionless again, his stomach churning, his head awhirl with meaningless words and phrases and his heart pounding with an awful fear.

"Will you not sit, my lord?"

He moved awkwardly to sit on the other end of the seat, aware of how its sloping surface highlighted the difference in their heights so that he loomed above her, close enough to reach out and touch her had he so wished. And the silence between them grew and stretched to the point where he started to despair of ever finding his voice again.

"You said you had something you wanted to say to me, my lord."

He straightened with a jerk. "Aye … Aye, I did … And I do. It's just that I … I don't know how to start."

She smiled up into his eyes. "Then start by telling me how much you like the colour of my kirtle. It's new and I've never worn it before today."

Without another thought he blurted, "I can't do that, Mary. It would be wrong and I have wronged you enough already." He cursed himself instantly.

Her eyes went wide, the entire lovely circle of her irises visible in her astonishment. "You have wronged me? How, sir?"

He steeled himself and charged ahead. "In several ways, I fear. Ways you could not imagine."

She nodded, as though to herself. "I see. But I have been told I have a rare imagination, Lord Bruce. What have you done?"

He stared straight ahead. "I have cost you your position, ahead of all else."

"My position?" He heard the uncertainty in her voice. "You mean as Lady Isabella's companion?"

"Aye, lass," he said abjectly. "That is what I mean."

Another long silence ensued and he did not dare even glance in her direction, but eventually she spoke again. "How could you do *that*?" The question was one of genuine perplexity, with no hint of protest or outrage, and he shuddered with a fresh wave of self-loathing.

"I've grown too fond of you," he growled. "And I can't live with the shame of it."

"You are ashamed of feeling fond of me? Of *liking* me? How can that be bad, my lord? It surprises me, surely, for you know me not at all. We have met but the once ere now, and for how long was that? An hour? The half of one?" He imagined he could feel the coldness dripping from her words. "What you say makes no sense, sir."

"Ah, but it does to me, and there's the hell of it!" He swung to look down at her directly and was momentarily unsettled to find the wide eyes gazing at him steadily with self-composure and no sign of contempt. "I have wronged you grievously and I have wronged your mistress Lady Isabella even more, offering hurt where no hurt was deserved."

"But you have never met my mistress."

"I know that, child!" He stopped himself instantly, knowing his anger was directed at his own shortcomings and she had done nothing to deserve the slightest disrespect. She was no child; he knew that well enough now and he had no desire to scold her as though she were. When he continued it was in a far more gentle tone. "But your mistress is my betrothed, has been for years, and I have betrayed her like a brute, destroying her good name without ever setting eyes on her. I cannot see God Himself forgiving me for that, so how could she?"

The girl was frowning. "My lord, you make no sense. How have you betrayed her? What have you done?"

Bruce was on the point of barking at her again like an angry dog, and then he slumped, feeling the strength run out of him, and simply said, "I have met you, Mary Henderson."

Colour now surged into the heart-shaped face beneath the snowy wimple, two bright patches of crimson that flushed the high cheekbones beneath suddenly sparkling eyes as she turned her face away from him, raising the hand that yet held the kerchief she had lent him earlier. He sat quaking with shame as she dabbed at her eyes, and when she spoke again, her voice barely above a whisper, he had to bend forward to hear her.

"You have done nothing wrong, my lord, neither to me nor to Lady Isabella. You have not said an improper word or behaved in any way that could be called less than honourable. All you have done is to be human, and therein lies the whole of your fault. You think yourself wrong in liking me, a simple servant."

"Not simple, Mary. Far, far from simple." The words, spoken in a hushed tone, were out before he was aware of them, but Mary Henderson might not have heard them. She drew a long, deep breath and turned to face him, squaring her shoulders and thrusting her breasts into prominence, so that his mouth fell open.

"That is the first time that you've noticed those, is it not?"

He was incapable of speech and equally incapable of looking away.

Her breasts sank back to their former position, and she draped an edge of her white shawl over her bosom. "You are a young man, Lord Bruce, and you were sick. And you were ill at ease with the thought of being saddled with an unknown bride for life. Mine was the first strange face that came to you from my lady's party and you found it … pleasing. There is no sin in that. Nor was there lust in you—not for me or for anyone else. Believe me, had there been, I would have known. You call me child, but I am far from childhood … " She added, irrelevantly, "You will like Lady Isabella, I can promise you. And she already knows she will like you."

"How—?"

"Because I told her so." Again he could only blink at her. "You have been afraid of meeting her, have you not? That seems strange to me, after all the other things we have heard of you. According to the repute in which men hold you, you are afraid of nothing, and yet you are unnerved by the thought of meeting an unknown woman because you see her as a threat to all you are and to everything you hope to do." She tilted her head to one side. "Did you ever stop to think that she might feel the same, might have the same fears, the same dread of being tied to someone she could never love?"

She leaned towards him suddenly, and her hand shot up to grasp him by the chin, her fingers tightening and holding him firmly against his shocked reaction.

"Look in my eyes and tell me. Did you? Did you think of that? Did you think for one minute of *her* fears, a woman's fears, against your own?" She released him as quickly as she had reached out for him. "No, it did not occur to you. Because you are a man. Pfft!" She flicked her fingers, dismissing all men as fools. And then she sat straight up, looked at him levelly, and her voice softened as she smiled, tremulously. "But you may thank God that *she* did, Robert Bruce, because she came to see you for herself."

"What … What d'you mean? What are you saying, Mary?"

"I'm telling you that Mary Henderson is not my name, you blind, silly man. I am Isabella of Mar."

Slowly, slowly, as he gazed stupefied at Isabella of Mar and mouthed unintelligible words, he saw that her smile remained in place below the compassion that filled her eyes, and he felt the first, faint stirrings of recognition that she had delivered him from his anguish and rescued him from himself.

"*You* are Isabella of Mar?"

Even to his own ears it sounded inane, but she laughed, though the laugh hitched into a half sob. "Of course I am, and you are the only person here in this entire house—in this entire *village*—who has not known that for days."

"But … Why didn't you—?" He caught himself and closed his eyes, vainly trying to order his thoughts. "Forgive me," he said after a moment. "A moment, I beg you."

She dipped her head in compliance but continued to gaze at him with those compelling eyes while he fought for a semblance of composure. He shut his eyes tight again and breathed deeply and regularly, calling upon all the self-discipline he possessed. The pounding in his ears died down gradually and he found his breath returning to normal; the world around him steadied and stopped swaying. When he opened his eyes again, she was still watching him, her face stoic and unreadable.

"Who was that other person, then," he asked her. "The one who ran away?"

Her eyes widened slightly. "*That* was Mary Henderson. The real one."

"No. Forgive me if I seem to doubt you, but she could not have been. I saw Mary Henderson myself, not long since. She was carrying a basket of linen and went off with my man. I heard him call her Mistress Mary. A dark-haired girl. The woman I saw running away that night had yellow hair."

The heart-shaped face across from him broke into a wicked grin. "No, my lord, that was Mary Beaton, and she and Thomas Beg have been making cow eyes at each other since we came here. Mary Henderson has yellow hair."

"So two of your five women are called Mary?"

"They are. It is a common name."

"I know. I have a sister Mary, Mary Bruce … But you know that."

"I do. A younger sister, of whom I reminded you when you first saw me."

"Aye … But why did you not simply tell me who you were when first we met?"

"I don't know," she said simply. "I've been asking myself that same question ever since, and all I can think to say is that I was afraid."

"Afraid? What on earth were you afraid of? You had every right to be there."

The big green eyes flashed, warningly, he knew, though he could not have said how he knew. "I was afraid of you," she said tartly. "You called out in the dark, and I sent Mary running off. Then I sat there, hoping you might fall back to sleep, but you did not. And then you called again in Gaelic, calling me to come out, and you sounded angry."

"I wasn't angry."

"You called me child! Made me feel like a silly, wilful little girl again. That was what really frightened me and spurred me to the lie."

"That frightened you? How, in God's name?"

"Because I am *not* a child!" The great green eyes crackled with indignation. "I was—I am—betrothed to you, your wife to be. And I did not want your first impression of me to be one of childishness, of a little girl." She caught herself and glanced away. One corner of her mouth curled in a wry half smile, and she shrugged her dainty shoulders. "I chose the lie and it was done and over. Or so I thought at the time. It was only afterwards that I began to see the problems that arose from the deception. I had no thought of lying—not wilfully, at the time."

"I understand," he said, realizing with mild surprise that he did. "Sometimes we find ourselves in situations that spring into being without our being aware that anything's going on. So … you're not angry with me?"

"For what?" She was smiling again. "For liking me even though you thought me someone else? *Should* I be angry?"

He thought about that, feeling better by the moment as his mind adjusted to the fact that all his fretting of the previous week had been for naught. But then he recalled what she had said about her own fears of being wed to someone whom she could not love, and he recalled, too, her high-handed dismissal of his claim of having liked her too much in too short a time.

"You are frowning again, my lord."

"Don't call me my lord. I'm your betrothed husband. My name is Robert. You can call me Rob, if it pleases you."

"Rob, then. Tell me, Rob, if you will, what would you have done had I indeed been plain Mary Henderson?"

He looked back at her quickly, sensing the trap in the question, but having skirted the abyss thus far he was determined to avoid the edge and be completely honest. "In all conscience I don't know, my lady. I was greatly taken with Mary Henderson despite having spent but a short hour with her as company. The time I spent seeing her face and hearing her in my mind thereafter was vastly longer than the brief moments I spent looking at her and listening to her. But in the end, faced with the choice I had set myself, my duty was to Lady Isabella of Mar, and I would have been loath to wrong her. In fact, I doubt I could have, even had she been a warty crone with wens." He could smile now, saying that, since he knew it would be taken for what it was, an exaggeration made in jest. "Yet the temptation was there, right enough—to run away with Mary Henderson and live with my guilt forever afterwards."

"And might you truly have done that? Run away with a chit of a girl who knows nothing of the world you've been living in for years? A servant girl who had none of the"—she searched for the right word—"the *worldliness* of all the other women you've known?"

"No, I would not. You know that already."

Her right eyebrow rose slightly and he looked away, towards the open gates, unwilling or unable to meet her look with equanimity. Somewhere beyond the gates, out of his sight, the downward-spiralling skylark returned to earth and its song was cut off. The blackbird sang yet, but it had moved, too, its liquid voice more distant than when he had first heard it. A bullock bellowed far off, and the sound made him aware of how he felt, awkward and stubborn and vaguely foolish, a gelded simulacrum of his former vital self.

"What now, then, Rob Bruce?"

The question, softly spoken, brought him back, and he turned quickly to look at her, feeling the sudden stab at his heart as her beautiful face filled his awareness again. And then, before he could lose heart, he spoke the words in his mind.

"Will you have me, lass?"

Her brows came very slightly together, and then she shook her head in a tiny gesture that, while not refusal, was not yet acceptance. "I am sworn to you, sir. I have no choice."

"No, by God's holy dominance, you do! That choice is yours and freely given. I might be as selfishly unthinking as you said a moment since, but I heeded what you had to say about being married to a man you could not love. If that's the way you feel I'll let you go, for I doubt I could face a future with you, knowing you had no wish to be wed to me."

"Oh … " She watched him closely. "And you would do that willingly, for my sake?"

He felt as though his tongue were coated with coarse sand and the words emerged as a guttural, growling croak. "Aye, lady, I would. And will, if you but say the word. But not willingly … I have no wish to let you go, now that I've found you. None at all."

"And what of your fears of being chained and tamed?"

He dipped his head to one side, smiling for the first time since he had stepped outside with her. "They vanished, my lady, dried up and disappeared as soon as I saw them for the boyish things they were. Now the fears that plague me are all fluttering around my dread of hearing you ask me to release you."

"Then let them go, Sir Robert, and be rid of them. But ask yourself, before you say another word, if you are sure of what you want. You asked if I will have you, and I will, gladly. But now *I* ask, will you have *me*?"

He had once heard one of his grandfather's men explain relief by saying that he felt as though the cares of all the world had been lifted from his shoulders, but he had been very young at the time and had puzzled over the meaning of those words. Now, in a flash, he understood them perfectly and felt the radiance in his own face as he smiled.

"Isabella MacWilliam of Mar, I will have you above and beyond all others if I can, and for all time."

His reward came in the way she rose up from the seat and looked at him, her eyes glowing and then sparkling as they filled with tears. She reached out a hand to him and he took it and rose to stand beside her, drawing her close to his side and marvelling at the way the top of her head came barely to the centre of his chest. He stooped to kiss her, but she shrank back quickly and pressed her hand against his breastbone.

"Have a care, my lord," she said, but through a smile. "There are folk around and we are betrothed, not *wed*."

He laughed, throwing back his head and feeling the joy surge through him as he spun to see who had been watching them, but they were alone there in the open yard, and the lark had begun its upward spiral again, refreshed and strengthened by its rest, singing its heart out anew as it climbed towards the heavens. He spun back, pulled her forward before she could resist, and kissed her full on the wide, red lips that parted slightly in surprise as his hands closed upon her waist. It was a brief embrace and a briefer kiss, but the wonder of it lingered once they were apart again. He looked down at her, smiling, started to speak, then stopped.

"What?" she asked. "What is it?"

"Nothing, a mere memory … When we are wed, or even sooner if I behave well, will you show me again that vision I had never seen before?"

Colour surged into her cheeks and she gaped at him half-scandalized. But then she slapped him lightly on the arm and laid her other hand on his forearm, and together they walked slowly back into the house.

They met again at dinner that same night, and though Bruce marvelled that no one even thought to ask them how they had come to meet each other, he was far too busy staring at the wonder of her to pay attention to anything else that was going on in the great hall. He had taken care to look his best, in a dark blue quilted doublet of the rich French fabric known as damask, worn over hose of lighter blue and boots of fine doeskin. Isabella had changed into a gown of pale green, edged in gold, and her ebony hair, free of restraint save for a net of golden filigree studded with tiny green gems that matched her eyes, enhanced her beauty in a manner that took his breath away each time he looked at her.

He paid no attention at all to the food laid out for him and he heard little of the conversation around him, although at one point he had to rally himself to agree without demur when his father suggested that, since his condition had improved so remarkably within a single day, they might be able to leave for Westminster in two days' time. He was entranced by the vision Isabella presented for his admiration; enchanted by the smiles she sent his way; bewitched by the play of light upon her face and skin and hair. He was in fact, though he did not know it, the very picture of a man hopelessly in love.

Only at the end of dinner, when Isabella's father led him aside to talk with him in private, did reality descend to bother him again. He expected Earl Domhnall to talk about his daughter at first, but the old man had apparently accepted the pair's evident satisfaction with their situation as a matter requiring no further comment. His purpose in sequestering his future good-son was to bring up the matter of Bishop Wishart's message, and even in his euphoria Bruce retained sufficient presence of mind to conceal the fact that he had already heard the gist of it.

He listened gravely, nodding from time to time, and when the old earl had finished, he told him what he had already told Nicol MacDuncan earlier, though this time he felt less of the resentment that had angered him then.

"Forgive me for being blunt, sir, but this *communication*, the message it contains, has nothing in it that I find attractive. Frankly, I'm greatly vexed. But I must ask you, is this an invitation, or is it an instruction?"

Domhnall blinked, taken aback. "It is not my place to judge that, Earl Robert. I am but the messenger, acting in good faith."

"I don't doubt that, my lord, nor would I dream of holding you accountable. But I fear Bishop Wishart may have miscalculated my priorities in the face of his own. He would have me hold myself in readiness, he says. In readiness for what? A return to Scotland at some undetermined time? In the event that the currently anointed King might fail in his duty? And to the insulting and disloyal exclusion of my own father, to whom this message should have been rightfully directed? Is my father even aware of this communication?" The other man did not respond. "As I suspected. No, my lord, I can agree to none of that."

"But— In God's name, there's nothing wrong in what the bishop asks. No insult intended. He's merely thinking of the realm's welfare—and your own, as Bruce."

"Aye, I can see that. But Bruce stands banished from that realm today. Banished, my lord—our holdings forfeit to the ill will of our enemies, our very name tainted by lies and slurs. We chose to leave Scotland at my grandfather's urging, and his reasons—our family's reasons—were, as you well know, based soundly on the undying enmity of the Comyns, who are now all-powerful under King John. Since then we have renewed our oaths of fealty to England and its Crown—an oath that must equally apply to every man and woman in Scotland who holds lands in England. And yet, for taking it, we have been dispossessed of all our Scots holdings."

Bruce eyed his future good-father, trying to gauge how deeply he might have offended him, and then continued, keeping his voice pleasant and level. "Those are my concerns in this. And the disloyalty to my father, whether intentional or no, is the greatest among them. I wonder how deeply Bishop Wishart considered them before asking you to come to me like this. And I wonder, too, if he thinks me ambitious enough to betray my own father. But here is my answer, for you to take to him. My loyalty—the Bruce loyalty—lies with Edward Plantagenet and is bound by oath. And neither my father nor I has seen any reason to doubt the goodwill or motive of England or its King—a thing we cannot say of Scotland."

Domhnall had listened with pursed lips. "Aye, well. That's not what I'd expected you to say, and I'd like to talk about it further, just between ourselves as family. But here's neither the time nor the place."

"That's fine with me," Bruce said quietly. "But my father must be included in the discussion—as family, as you say." The Earl of Mar nodded, and Bruce felt relieved, for he had been dreading the inevitable airing of this subject with his father; he could easily imagine the anger and wounded dismay his report would provoke.

And yet he could think of no way to lessen the blow he must deliver to his father's pride.

He laid a hand on Domhnall's shoulder. "But before we join the company, my lord of Mar," he went on, "I want to tell you something privily, as your good-son. No man can know with any certainty what lies ahead for him or his, but I will swear this to you in person. No matter what the future holds for all of us, I will cherish and revere your daughter for as long as we both shall live. She will be my wife and my countess, honoured and loved above all else in my life, and wherever I may go, so, too, will she, at my right hand."

Domhnall of Mar inclined his head graciously. "I would expect no less," he said. "But I am glad to hear you say it. So be it."

# CHAPTER TWENTY

# THE EARL OF CARRICK'S IDYLL

arry Percy had been right, as it transpired. Bruce was welcomed back into the royal favour without question, other than a momentary flicker of surprise on the part of King Edward when he first saw the young earl enter his royal presence. That brief hesitation, unnoticed by everyone but Bruce himself, who had been watching for it, confirmed what Percy had surmised: that the King had had too much on his mind in the past year to be aware that the young earl's period of mourning for his grandsire's death had passed and that it was time he returned to the world again.

Edward, being the man and monarch that he was, behaved as though he had been patiently awaiting the Bruce party for some time. Noticing them the moment they were ushered into the audience chamber, he stood up from his throne and welcomed them loudly and with apparent pleasure, dismissing with a wave the group surrounding his seat, the foremost of whom was a resplendently dressed, dark-faced man with whom Edward had been speaking when they entered. The man, whom Bruce had noted immediately as a foreigner by his dress, backed away with a deep bow, accompanied by the others of his group, but he did not quite succeed in concealing a scowl at being interrupted in his dealings with the King. Edward did not so much as glance in his direction after waving him away. Instead he watched the Scots visitors bow deeply, and as they straightened up again he called to the younger Bruce in

423

a loud voice, stilling the crowd as he proclaimed his delight at seeing the young man there and demanding that he come directly to the throne and kiss his royal hand.

Bruce did so obediently, bowing low over the royal fingers and reflecting that Edward, with his gold, bejewelled crown resting naturally on his regal head, knew better than anyone how to put a faithful servant at his ease and bathe him in the welcoming warmth of the King's favour.

"You're well, boy?" the King growled. "I must say you *look* well, though your hair is … different."

"I am well, my liege. Better than I have ever been, in fact."

"Is that so?" One royal eyebrow rose in a query. "It pleases me to hear that. And to what is that due?"

"To my lady, my liege. I am to be wed."

"Are you, by God?" The question emerged as an incredulous roar, filled with gladness and disbelief in equal measure. "You'll take a wife who makes you smile like that?" All the crowd now watched. "By St. Alban's martyrdom that's something few men are fortunate enough to find, though Christ Himself knows you've done enough winnowing among the female wheat and chaff around here to have learnt to recognize value when you encounter it, eh? Where is this paragon? Is she here? She *is*? Then bring her to me."

Bruce stepped back, bowing and turning to obey, but Edward stopped him with a quick hand on his sleeve, his voice now quiet. "No, wait. She comes." He raised a hand towards Isabella, who had started forward uncertainly, and crooked his finger. "Come forward, my dear," he called. "I would look upon the face that has transformed my long-faced young earl here."

The lord of Annandale and his party were still at the rear of the audience chamber, a good twenty paces and more from the dais where the King sat, and as Isabella moved forward alone the people between her and the throne drew aside to clear her way, bowing deferentially. She walked regally, her small head held high, and once again Bruce felt his throat swell with love of her.

"By God, she looks like my Eleanor when first I met her," the King said quietly, for Bruce's ears alone. "You have a treasure here, young Carrick." He rose to his feet and draped the sides of his light cloak of blue-lined, pale gold silk back over the shoulders of the blue robe that covered him from neck to ankles and then he stepped quickly down from his elevated throne and went to meet her, arms stretched towards her to take both her hands in his own before she could dip into a curtsy. "Now, now, enough of that, young woman. It is I should be kneeling to you, for I have just finished telling the Earl of Carrick that you remind me forcibly of my dear wife Eleanor, God rest her soul. In her youth, she had that same flashing-eyed beauty and that regal bearing that you now own. Tell me your name, then, milady, and place me in your debt."

Bruce could see the truth in what the King was saying; there was a discernible resemblance between Isabella and the Queen he had known, though he could not have described what it was had his life depended on it. Something about the eyes and the cheekbones and the wide and generous mouth, he thought. The Queen had not been young when Bruce first met her, but she had retained sufficient of her youthful beauty to remain striking. As he listened to Edward's honey-tongued flattery, he felt nothing but pleasure at the effect his beloved was having on the King. It would do Isabella no harm at court for people to know the monarch had been taken with her.

Lost in thought for a moment, he had missed something of what the King was saying, but now Edward turned back to him and beckoned. "Come, Robert, we will welcome both of your fathers together." Bruce obediently fell into step at King Edward's right as the monarch, still holding Isabella's hand in his left, walked between the pair to where the Lords of Annandale and Mar stood waiting with their small entourage. The audience chamber was silent, Bruce noted, though no fewer than threescore people crowded it, and the assembled courtiers parted and stepped aside for them, bowing and curtsying, the only sounds the rustling of clothing and the occasional clack of a heel on the hard, wooden floor.

Despite the formality of the audience chamber, Edward welcomed his visitors warmly, congratulating Domhnall of Mar on his daughter's beauty and on the fitness and excellence of the proposed match between his own house and the House of Bruce.

He turned his head to Bruce. "And where and when will this event take place?"

"We have arranged no date, my liege. Lord Domhnall and my lady are but newly arrived from Scotland, and we came directly here from Writtle in the hope that you would welcome us as you have and deign to look kindly upon our match."

Edward almost smiled as he glanced again at Isabella. "And how could I do otherwise? You have my heartfelt blessings and it will be our royal pleasure to attend the nuptials, here in the Abbey of Westminster if that should please you."

Bruce's mouth fell open.

"FitzHugh, our faithful seneschal, will see to the arrangements and it will be done within the month—unless there be some pressing need to wait beyond that time?" The King turned to Lord Domhnall. "Would that be suitable, my lord? You have no pressing urgency that must take you back to Scotland 'twixt now and then?"

It was the King of England who had spoken there, though with Edward Plantagenet's most cordial voice, and no one listening had any doubt of it. Lord Domhnall inclined his head gravely. "None at all, my lord King," he said. "My place is here until I see this matter done and I am greatly sensible of the honour you do my house."

"So be it, then." Edward looked about him now, gauging the distance between himself and listening ears, and then waved the nearest courtiers away. He waited as people withdrew to a discreet distance, then beckoned Sir Robert FitzHugh to come closer. Dropping his voice to a gentle murmur, he spoke directly to Lord Bruce.

"I am engaged at this present time with Frenchmen, from France itself and from my Duchy of Gascony. Always a nuisance but never to be neglected. Matters with which I have to deal privily and quickly, concluding them this night if that is possible, so I have no time to talk with you at length. I do, however, wish to talk with you and soon as may be done. FitzHugh will inform you of the appointed time when he has made arrangements. He will also attend to your lodgings while you are with us." The seneschal bowed, giving no indication that those matters had already been dealt with, and Edward nodded, indicating that he knew they had.

"Again, then, I bid you welcome here, and you, young lady, most particularly so." He bowed and kissed the fingers he still held in his own, then nodded sideways, indicating Bruce. "Keep Carrick smiling, if you will. He seldom does so and never sufficiently, so I must lay this upon you as a solemn charge."

Isabella curtsied prettily, her head high as she looked into the fierce old eyes of the greatest King in Christendom. "And solemnly will I accept it, my lord King." She paused, and then added mischievously, "Although solemnity sits ill with smiling, I find."

Edward laughed, a double bark of pleasure, and drew her across in front of him, handing her off to her betrothed. "May God bless your coming union, my lady of Mar and Carrick. I have no doubt He will." His eyes scanned the small group again and he nodded. "Until tomorrow, then, for I must return to my Frenchmen. FitzHugh will look after you. Sleep well beneath our roof this night."

He moved away, back to his throne on its high dais, and as he went the focus of the entire room shifted to follow him, leaving the Scots party to make a discreet departure, shepherded by the old seneschal.

The gathering assembled promptly the next morning in the room assigned to them, a smaller group on this occasion, with none of the attendants who had accompanied them the day before. Bruce found his father and Earl Domhnall already present when he arrived, and within moments they were joined by Nicol MacDuncan and Sir James Jardine who, as senior member of the Gaelic lords of Carrick, continued to serve as Bruce's unofficial watchdog within his confiscated earldom.

Lord Bruce brought them tersely to attention by voicing the thoughts uppermost in his mind. "Right, we have a quarter-hour, no more, so let's address ourselves to what might be required of us. I expect Edward will be in need of information about what's going on in Scotland, probably to confirm or enhance what he currently knows or suspects. That means he'll have little to ask of me or Robert, since we are as far removed from Scotland as he is himself. Which means he'll be questioning the rest of you—most probably you, my lord of Mar, since by your rank you're the one most likely to be privy to the information he will want. Does that disturb you, that you'll be asked to discuss Scotland's politics and express your own opinions to England's King?"

Earl Domhnall shrugged. "No. Should it? It's because of Scotland's politics that I am here, as far removed from the stink of it as I can be and looking to the welfare of my own house."

Annandale looked at the others. "What about you, Nicol? And you, Sir James?"

Sir James, as usual, was frowning as he growled, "Gin he doesna ask me to forswear mysel' or betray my own folk, I care no' what else he asks me. He'll get the truth as far as I ken it."

"Nicol?"

The Gaelic shrug was close to being French in its expressiveness. "I say the same. This King has treated you and yours with more respect and honour than our own King has, to his black shame. I'll take no ill of anything he asks me, given the same provisos that Sir James has named."

"Good. He will know, from his eyes and ears in Scotland, of everything we know about, but what he will seek from you is confirmation, from the Scots' point of view, of what he has heard. Most, if not all, of his reports will have come from English sources in Scotland, and the likelihood of their being deliberately misinformed cannot be ignored. He was greatly vexed, this past year, by Pope Celestine's decree absolving the Scots lords from any requirement to conform to oaths undertaken under duress. Edward sees that as utmost perfidy, on the part of the Pope no less than on the part of the

Scots. He'll want to know about that—about how the community of the realm perceives it. About what difference, if any, it has made to the lives of the folk there. About how the lords themselves have received it. And most important of all, I jalouse, has it resulted in any real strengthening of Scotland's will to defy him?" He looked at the three visitors from Scotland. "Can any of you speak to that?"

Before anyone could respond, however, someone knocked at the heavy door, and FitzHugh stepped in and smiled at them, then drew aside without a word as Edward Plantagenet himself strode into the room, followed by two of his ubiquitous recording secretaries, both wearing the plain white robe and black scapula of their Cistercian Order.

"Ah," he said. "At it already, eh? Good, then let's sit down and be about it. I have an hour before those damned Frenchmen come pounding at my door again." He went directly to a high-backed seat at the head of the long table and waved to the others to take their seats beside him while the two secretaries busied themselves at the far end setting up inkhorns and jars of pens.

"Pay no attention to the scribes," Edward began. "They are here for my own requirements. I like to keep a record of everything being said, by me and to me, lest I forget important details afterwards. But if you are concerned, you have my royal oath that nothing you may say within this room today will ever be used to your disadvantage. I am here alone, save for these two, to speak with you as friends and guests without formality, in the hope of gaining insight—uncluttered and unfettered by the presence of courtiers and functionaries— to what you and your fellow countrymen of similar rank are thinking nowadays. I hope you will honour me by speaking as freely here as you would among yourselves. So, may we proceed?"

He began, almost exactly as Lord Annandale had guessed he would, by expressing his outrage at the arrogance of Pope Celestine in daring to meddle in England's external affairs by declaring the oaths sworn to him by Scotland's leaders to be invalid. When he had spat out his disgust he sat glowering from one to the other of them.

"That said, my friends, I hope I will have no need to say more other than this. I am lord paramount of Scotland, duly acknowledged by these same magnates who now have papal authority to flout me. That recognition of my rights, embodied in the title itself—lord paramount—was part and parcel of their acceptance of my fitness to judge in the matter of the King's succession. They swore a sacred oath to that effect, as magnates of Scotland, in full recognition of my feudal rights in granting the possession of their lands within my own realm of England. Those oaths were freely given by free men, in recognition of my feudal status as their overlord in England. They sought a bargain—my arbitration in return for their acknowledgment of my neutrality in the matter being judged. My terms were straightforward and they were met—acceptance of my judgment and the temporary secondment of the Scots castles to my control to combat the possibility of future rebellion should my judgment be disputed. There was no enforcement involved, no underhand designs, and no threat or duress of any kind."

*And that is true*, thought Bruce. *Unless you happen to perceive the threat of complete withdrawal of support thereafter, and the subsequent reality of civil war and anarchy beneath the guns of foreign-held fortresses, to be a threat or to deserve the name of duress of the most urgent kind.*

His point made, and plainly uncaring of what his audience thought of its validity, Edward moved on to question the three new arrivals, quizzing them minutely on their observations of the life around them in the aftermath of the Pope's decree and ending with the very question Annandale had anticipated, the matter of the stiffening of resolve among the Scottish people to withstand what they perceived to be English interference in the realm's affairs. He did not phrase his question quite that baldly, but it was not an easy one to disguise. His guests expressed the common view with which each was familiar in his own region, the northeast, the southwest, and the border lands respectively, that the populace would gladly stand united behind their King were that King seen to be willing and able to assert himself sufficiently to justify their faith. Bruce observed that none of the three committed himself to any local judgment that might conceivably affect his own people or their lands, and he was convinced that Edward, too, had been aware of it.

From there, Edward switched to an unexpected topic.

"I'm told on good authority that there's a move afoot to constitute some kind of council of Guardians to keep a close eye on King John's behaviour—those same Guardians, incidentally, who now find themselves papally relieved of the responsibility to adhere to the oaths they formerly swore to me. Can any of you enlighten me on that?"

He eyed each man in turn, observing their discomfiture. Bruce's own surprise was short lived, for his grandfather had always been fond of quoting the old adage that a secret shared is a secret no longer. Two, at least, of the three visiting Scots had spoken about the proposed council. Besides, the arrangements would all have been handled by clerics, and Edward's priests and bishops were forever moving in and out of Scotland, servicing the spiritual needs of the English soldiers garrisoning the Scottish royal castles, making it inconceivable that news of such potential magnitude should have failed to reach the King's ears.

Edward's eyes had finally settled on Earl Domhnall, and the old man shifted in his chair. "I've heard some talk of it," he admitted. "But nothing I could swear to with authority … Though I can say that nothing has come of it, as far as I'm aware."

"Nothing yet. But there has been talk of it," Edward prompted. "Among your peers, at least?"

"Aye, sir, there has. But there are peers and peers. I am known as being a follower of Bruce's interests, and this matter of the council, should it ever come to pass, has been a Comyn notion. That fact alone would keep me uninformed, officially, if only to be sure I could make no report of it to my lord of Annandale. The little I know has come from others like myself, outsiders known to be Bruce adherents."

"A Comyn matter, you say … What about the Church? The information brought to me described the idea as a Church-inspired notion."

Domhnall shrugged. "The two are not exclusive, my lord King. Bishop Fraser of St. Andrews is a Comyn, as are several other Scots bishops."

"Hmm. Where is Bishop Fraser, by the way? No one has seen or heard of him in many months."

The question seemed to vibrate in the air as Domhnall of Mar blinked. "Where *is* he? Sir, I have no idea. I pay but scant attention to the affairs of bishops at the best of times, and St. Andrews seat is far removed from my lands."

Bruce was aware that Sir James Jardine was studying his fingernails as though they held some great significance to him, but his preoccupation appeared to go unnoticed by the King as Edward looked at the elder Bruce. "And you, my lord of Annandale, were you aware of this matter of a new council?"

Lord Bruce shook his head gently, lying effortlessly. "No, my liege, I was not." His voice tailed upward on the last word.

"You have a reservation in your voice. What else are you thinking?"

Lord Bruce inhaled deeply. "It came to me, my liege, that even were such a council being formed, it could only be for the good of the Scots realm—as the magnates perceive that good, of course."

Edward's eyes narrowed and he plucked at the hairs on his upper lip. "I think you should enlarge upon that thought, Lord Bruce," he growled. "Are you bidding me look to my own affairs?"

"God forbid, my liege. I would not presume that far. I was but thinking of the skeins of conflicting loyalties that can torment the Scots folk."

"Go on." Edward hitched himself sideways in his chair to rest an elbow on the arm and cover the lower part of his face with an open hand. Bruce sat holding his breath, acutely aware that his father was treading dangerous ground.

Lord Annandale tilted his head slightly to one side. "I believe, my liege, that the issue of the two realms is obscured by the ordinary man's misunderstanding of your status as lord paramount."

"What is there to misunderstand? The name explains itself."

Bruce could not tell whether Edward had been angered by his father's observation, but Lord Bruce merely shrugged. "It does to men like us, my liege, but the common man has no regard for subtleties of the kind with which we must contend. If I may be so bold, sire, they see them but in terms of black and white."

Bruce did not fail to note the King's flicker of an eye at hearing his father's use of the word *sire*. The monarch then flicked his fingers impatiently.

"Go on, man, I'm listening. What are you saying? What of this black and whiteness to this common man? I'm supposing that you speak of the Scots?"

"Yes, my liege, of course, although the Scots are not alone in believing no man may serve two masters. Not that I am saying that need bother them," he added hastily, "since it is patently untrue in the present case. John Balliol is King of Scotland, duly demonstrated by your own court to be the true heir. His is the realm. But I am speaking of *appearances* and of confusion caused by lack of understanding that these *are* merely appearances. Your overlordship is well understood by every man in Scotland who holds lands in your own realm under your goodwill. They openly acknowledge that your rights therein, pertaining to those privileges, are sacrosanct. And upon those terms you have their loyalty as feudal overlord, from the King's grace himself down to the meanest landholder with small estates among your English possessions. All are beholden to you for the privilege entailed." He paused, collecting his thoughts.

"Not all men see it thus, though, and that is what I wished to bring to your attention. Few Scots below the rank of baron, earl, or bishop hold any English possessions, and while that might go without being said, I speak of it because it bears upon what I said about a man serving two masters. Those other, lesser men, lacking a place in England, also lack, perforce, any understanding of what such holdings entail. They cannot see why their leaders are beholden to you as overlord. Their own loyalty, if not their personal devotion, is committed to their King and his realm which is their home, and so they fail to see why their highest leaders should appear subservient to you and, in effect as they see it, to England. And human nature being what it is, the magnates have been … reluctant to explain the reasons to them, believing such things to be their personal affairs and no business of anyone else. And so their followers are confused and frightened, perceiving a threat to their own future where no such threat exists."

Edward still sat with his hand obscuring part of his face, but the scowl that Bruce had seen forming there had faded, replaced by a pensive frown.

"You know, my lord Bruce, no man has ever pointed that out to us before, and I confess that despite your damned impertinence in thinking to teach me my lessons, you make much sense." There was no venom in his words, and Edward was nodding his head, gazing towards the ceiling. "Fear and misunderstanding *do* breed resentment and unrest, as any man above a fool may know. But how would we redress this matter, to make it plain that we intend no threat to Scotland's realm?"

"I know not, my liege," Lord Bruce said. "But the mere recognition of it would seem to me to indicate that it can be solved, with thought and careful planning."

Edward looked down the table to where the two secretaries sat scribbling furiously. "You have all that, Brother Aylward?"

One of the two monks glanced at his companion for verification and then inclined his head towards the King. "We do, sire."

"Good, then go at once and make me a fair copy. The last part, containing my lord of Annandale's thoughts, will suffice. Bring it to me as soon as it is done." He waved them away, and the two Cistercians gathered up their implements and scrolls and left immediately. Edward watched them as far as the door, then swung back to his guests.

"How much time has elapsed?"

"I would say less than an hour, my liege," Bruce said. "And more than half."

"Hmm. Those damn Frenchmen will be howling for my ear any moment now, but they can wait until I've done here." He looked then at each man individually. "The Greens," he said. "What can you tell me about those people? Anyone."

"Who or what are they, my lord King?" asked Domhnall of Mar. "The name is unknown to me."

Edward squinted at him, then jerked his head in acceptance. "Aye," he growled, "it would be, you being from north of Forth. Sir Nicol?"

Nicol smiled and spread his hands. "I am no knight, lord King," he said. "I once owned a lordship, though, albeit one of the ancient Gaelic ones, but I gave up my succession to enable my good-nephew here to inherit the title. But the Greens?" He shrugged expressively. "I have heard of them, but only through rumour and exaggeration. They are outlaws, bandits and broken men, supposedly based in Selkirk Forest, though that's like saying north of Forth—a small name for a huge place. Yet the reports I have heard speak of discipline and much coordination. Strange words, applied to broken men."

"Selkirk Forest. That is by Annandale, is it not, Sir James?"

"Close enough, Your Grace." Jardine, conscientious in his use of the English language so foreign to his tongue, was unaware of having used the Scots form of royal address, and no one sought to correct him. "It's a full day's ride on a good horse frae Annandale to the Forest fringes. But aye, it's close enough for word of the Greens to hae reached us." He cleared his throat portentously. "There is great argument on who leads them, for Nicol is right, they appear to be disciplined, against all you might expect, and if rumour is to be believed, they are well led. Nobody can say for sure how strong they are, how many of them, and the same goes for their leader. He'd have to be a warlock to be in as many places as he's said to be all in one day, so folk are saying that it's no'—not—one single man. Two, mayhap three of them, all dressed alike, to make folk think they're all one and the same."

"And their name. They all dress in green?"

"A lot o' them do, aye, but no, they got their name for a different reason. We're told they keep a careful eye on the common folk o' the Forest, protecting them, and it seems that's true. They're quick to kill any man they think is guilty of abusing them. And on every corpse they leave behind a scrap of green cloth, pinned to the dead man's chest wi' a knife blade. It doesna happen much these days, but that's how they began and that's what gave them their name." He cleared his throat again. "But that's all I know, Your Grace."

Edward thanked him brusquely, then turned to stare through slitted eyes at Lord Bruce. Then he straightened suddenly and rose to his feet, speaking more loudly than he had to that point.

"In this instance, Sir James, we know more than you do. These Greens kill more than so-called miscreants. They have been killing Englishmen for months, attacking our loyal troops about the execution of their duties. They have even laid rough hands upon our bishops, despoiling them when they were passing through the Forest in pursuit of God's holy work. We have had enough of it, and the days of the Greens are numbered. Within the past three days I have dispatched a strong force northward in the command of our new Sheriff of Lanark, Sir William de Hazelrig, who is charged with rooting out and destroying the outlaw vermin of Selkirk Forest precisely as our forces commanded by the Earl of Pembroke did with their nameless counterparts last month in Essex. They, too, were outlaws, broken men who by their own misconduct had forfeited all claims to being English. These Greens, too, will be taught the folly of defying England's strength." He stopped abruptly, remembering perhaps that these were Scots to whom he was speaking so vengefully about deploying English soldiers in their lands.

"You have my thanks and gratitude, my friends, and I will detain you no longer. And now farewell." He nodded with finality and deliberately turned his back on them, relieving them of the need to walk backward from the royal presence. As they clustered at the door in leaving, however, the King's voice halted them.

"My Lord of Annandale! One more thing, if you will. And you, my lord of Carrick."

The two Bruces turned back, leaving the others to depart, and as they neared him Edward sat down again.

"Tell me, my lord Bruce, have I your loyalty?"

Bruce, from the corner of his eye, saw his father draw himself erect, and Edward raised a hand. "Be at peace, Lord Bruce. I had no wish to insult you, but the question was necessary."

Bruce saw the tightening of his father's lips as the older man nodded. "Yes, my liege," he said stiffly, "you have my total loyalty, given freely and under oath."

"Good. I have a task in mind for you, and Robert here will witness my request, for I will not order you to do it. Will you renew that oath, publicly?"

"Of course I will, my liege."

"It will do you little good among the Scots, I warn you."

"I can do little good among the Scots as things stand now, sire."

"Excellent. Then here is what I have in mind." He surged up out of his chair and turned to stand behind it, leaning against it and looking keenly from one to the other of his two listeners. "I need a man whom I can trust absolutely in a certain place in time to come. Not today and not for several months, in fact. But the need is there and urgent." He paused, eyeing the elder Bruce. "I would like you to accept an appointment as my royal Governor of Carlisle Castle. It is the only gateway to this realm's northwest, and as it sits today it is vulnerable." He raised a hand, holding up two fingers to forestall anything Lord Bruce might think to say. "I mislike this notion of a new council in Scotland, and Christ Himself knows the magnates have caused me grief enough up there already. And therefore there are things—the safety of the realm in that whole region—that I dare not trust to mere blind chance.

"I have to leave for France as soon as I may, with an army large enough to win a war there. That need is far beyond debate. But some of my own barons are set to cause me trouble, the last thing I need. They *disagree* with my assessment of the need to bring the war in France to a quick, decisive end." The contempt with which he emphasized the word was withering. "They can see no farther, in truth, than the insides of their sweaty purses, but they have somehow convinced themselves that *my* French concerns will look after themselves, without *their* stirring from their fat arses and wasting money in what they think to be a needless cause. They seem content with the debacle going on over there. Our armies barely hold their own and the barons acknowledge that, but their argument, God save the mark, is that at least our leaders in France are persistent in striving for success—even if they achieve nothing—and as things stand their current needs are not likely to bankrupt the treasury. And so my nearest and supposedly most trusted are disputing the need for me to go, and though I will stamp out their opposition, one way or another, I am left unable to trust many of them in the moment. If trouble should then break out—serious trouble—with this new council in Scotland, Carlisle Castle will hold the fate of England in its hands, and the man who governs it will wield the kind of strength I dare not allow into the grip of any man who might defy me. You see my point, I trust?"

Both Bruces nodded, and Edward eyed them as he weighed his next words.

"The closest lands to Carlisle are Bruce holdings, as you are well aware—Annandale and Carrick, *your* lands, but no longer home to Bruce. My trust in you was strong enough without that, but with it, with the knowledge that you face your own usurpers, I know beyond a doubt that you will fight to keep them outside my gates while I am occupied elsewhere. You will stand firm there while another, less contented man might seek to make alliance for his own purposes. You hear what I am saying, my lord of Annandale?"

"I do, my liege."

"And will you take the post? I said before I will not force it upon you."

"I will take it gladly, my liege."

"Good man. Earl Robert, have you anything you wish to say?"

Bruce shook his head slowly and emphatically. "No, my liege. It is my father's decision. I will support him, come what may."

"So be it. Here, then, is what we'll do. Your wedding will take place within the month, Robert, and that will keep you here as Earl of Carrick, preparing for your nuptials. Lord Bruce, you, on the other hand, may fill that time most usefully with a visit to Carlisle. No one will question your interest in seeing from close by the depredations being carried out in your home lands. In reality, though, you will be there to decide what you will need in the way of provisioning, strengthened defences, and garrison improvements. You will then return here for the wedding celebrations at month's end, and in the course of those, in company with your son and his young wife, you will renew, publicly, your oath of fealty to me as your liege lord. That might provoke reaction from the Scots—indeed I hope it will, for we will be watching closely and may read much from it. You will be recompensed for any losses you incur from that, of course, and I will increase your holdings here in my domain in recognition of your dedication to our cause. All being well, towards the end of August you will assume your place as governor in Carlisle and I will be able to make my arrangements for France with an untroubled mind—about the northwest, at least. Are we agreed?"

"Yes, my liege."

"So be it, then. And now I really must go. Farewell, my friends."

Father and son bowed together as Edward, every inch the careworn king weighed down by affairs of state, nodded sombrely to each of them and walked to the door, leaving them alone together in silence. The door had barely closed when the two turned to look at each other speculatively, each waiting for the other to speak.

"Now that was the Edward I remember best," Bruce said quietly. "The man I first met and admired that time he came to Turnberry. I confess I like him better than the distant and forbidding king he has become since Queen Eleanor died, may God rest her soul."

His father nodded. "God bless her soul, indeed." He spoke on without a pause, but the tone of his voice cooled noticeably with his next words. "But are you saying you mislike him? I hope not, for we have much to thank him for."

"No, sir, I meant no such thing."

"And what think you of this new appointment? You may speak plainly."

"Governor of Carlisle Castle. A great honour, Father, on the face of it."

"On the face of it?" Lord Bruce's frown was instantaneous. "What is that supposed to mean?"

"It means I believe the King is exercising kingcraft, Father. That was what Grandfather Robert called it. He said there was none in Christendom better at that craft than Edward Plantagenet. He is forever involved in it, to the exclusion of all else. He never stops, never neglects it, and never relents. Everything he does, every decision he makes, every step he takes is done in that cause and with great deliberation."

"Have you gone mad, boy?" The elder Bruce glanced over his shoulder, as though expecting to find someone listening. "Those words are impious! They impugn the King's majesty. You could be thrown in prison for mouthing them."

"Forgive me then, sir, but you did invite me to speak plainly, and the plain truth is that ever since Grandfather Robert brought that observation to my attention, I have been paying more heed than ever before to what King Edward does. And I have come to believe Grandfather was right. Edward Plantagenet does nothing without forethought, and most particularly so when he is manipulating those about him, those in power, with an eye to the welfare of his realm. Your appointment is a great honour, Father, beyond a doubt, and it will bring even greater honours with it. I merely wondered what, in fact, it portends. Will it prove to be a blessing or a curse? There's nothing you can do about that, either way, for you accepted it and now we must all live with it."

"We must all live with it … " The repetition of his son's words was cold and flat. "You sound as though you resent that. As though you think it an imposition of some kind. As though, in fact, you believe I should have refused the appointment."

"No, Father, with respect I believe no such thing. I wondered only about its ultimate intent. You could not have refused the appointment, sir—not after the way in which it was put to you. Had you done so, in the face of such apparent personal trust, you would have appeared selfish, ungrateful, and undependable. But that is precisely my point. You could *not* refuse, Father. You were used— manipulated and perhaps even abused into having no other choice. It was magnificently done, masterfully presented, and, I would take my oath on it, most carefully engineered long in advance." He shrugged, without even a glance at his father. "I was reminded, too, of something else Gransscr said about Edward, as both man and king. He liked and admired him in some ways, but he warned me once never to let down my guard in my dealings with him, least of all when I was unsure of what he wanted. And he drove home that lesson the next day, by taking me to watch the Lochmaben potter at his wheel. Edward, he said, could mould and shape men as easily as that potter shaped wet clay, making of them what he would and sometimes spinning them too far until they collapsed upon them- selves in ruin. It was a powerful lesson." He shrugged again, very gently this time. "That is Edward, master of his kingly craft, bending all men to his royal will and to his own ever-mysterious ends. Nothing wrong with that—it's what kings must do, I suppose. But it leaves simple men like us shaking our heads, perplexed at the layers between layers in the plainest, seemingly least important things."

He had been lost in his own thoughts as he spoke and now he became aware of his father's silence. He glanced over almost appre- hensively and found Lord Bruce looking at him with an expression Bruce had never seen before.

"Forgive me, Father," he said quickly. "I was havering—"

Lord Bruce waved him to silence. "How long have you thought that way?"

"What way, sir? I don't understand."

"Of course you do." There was asperity now in Lord Bruce's tone. "You understand far more than I ever suspected you could. You speak like a philosopher, a theorist, not like the son I thought I knew. You have insights I never saw or heard until now. You make me feel a fool, though I believe you had no thought of doing so. Where did you learn to think this way?"

"I have no idea, Father … unless it was in listening to and being around my grandfather. He had no tolerance for fools or dimwits, and he hated to waste time. And he was never silent when he was with me." He stopped, smiling suddenly. "He was teaching me constantly, about a thousand things at once, yet all of them were built around my own need to learn to read men, discerning their characters and motives, their weaknesses and strengths, their foibles and their follies. How to read men and how to trust in my own mind, its perceptions, its observations, and its conclusions. He taught me, I suppose, that a man with a supple mind—" Again he broke off, smiling again. "That a man with a supple mind can find perfect clay for the potter's wheel. Gransser taught me to trust in my own judgment."

A long silence followed that before his father said, "Remind me, should I ever appear to be tempted, never to ask what you think of me." He disregarded his son's astonished look as he continued. "So, then, we must take stock of our position. We are committed, as you say, for better or for worse. All that remains for us to do is make the best of what we have. I will ride north to Carlisle at once and take Jardine and Nicol with me. They can cross the border easily from there without being noticed and both of them will be better off at home. Domhnall is too old to be galloping about the country at the kind of speed I hope to maintain, and even in Carlisle he would still be hundreds of miles from Mar, with no retainers to escort him safely home. So he will stay here with Isabella until after you two are wed, after which he may do as he chooses. He holds no lands in England so I doubt he will wish to remain here, though that will be determined by Balliol's reaction to the news of your marriage. Your own part is preordained—you must remain here and take care of

Isabella and her father. Were you to come north with me it might cause questions that I see no need to excite. Good, then. That's it."

"What about the boys, Father?"

"What boys?"

"My brothers. And the girls, too. If you're to be in Carlisle, they'd best be here with me."

"Damnation, that would have come to me, but to this point I haven't given it a thought. I'll have them sent down."

"No, leave that to me. I'll send up a suitable escort for them as soon as I return to Writtle."

"That should suffice. Can you think of anything else?"

Bruce shook his head. "No, nothing. But I do have a question that has nothing do with any of this. The Earl of Mar looked perplexed when Edward asked about Bishop Fraser of St. Andrews, and it seemed to me Sir James took pains at the same time to look at no one. Do *you* know where Fraser is, Father? It does seem strange that no one should know the whereabouts of the senior bishop in Scotland."

Lord Bruce shrugged. "I have no idea. Bishops are bishops, as secret in their dealings and movements at times as any other magnate. Why should we care where he is?" He looked around again, gazing for a moment at the lower end of the table where the two scribes had sat. "Some good might come of this morning, if Edward truly means to make known what we talked about—the misunderstanding in Scotland of his role as lord paramount." He sighed, sharply, and moved towards the door with Bruce in tow.

"I've much to do, if I'm to take the north road tomorrow, and I think I should. The more time I can spend in Carlisle, the better the picture I can form of what's there and what's lacking. I'll be obliged if you would find Domhnall and Jardine and ask them to meet me at the stables within the hour."

Bruce said he would, and closed the high doors carefully at their back as they left the room.

# CHAPTER TWENTY-ONE

# KINGS' PLEASURES

Sir Henry Percy had said something, during that brief encounter as they dined around the fire, about the astonishing difference in the way time passed depending on what one was doing and the amount of enjoyment involved. He had been talking about his recent marriage, and how the months following his wedding had gone by in a complete whirlwind of activity and pleasure. He had been a married man for nigh on six months already, he said, but it seemed to him as though only a week had passed, because his military commitments—the campaign against the Forest outlaws being just one of several—had combined with the domestic upheaval of plunging into married life to leave him with no more than a blurred series of vague impressions of unaccustomed domesticity to recall, instead of the store of pleasant, cumulative memories he had expected.

Bruce had smiled at the time, he remembered, mildly surprised at the wistfulness that had underlain those words, for Percy, with his humourless dedication to duty at all times, was the last person he would ever have expected to hear complaining, however gently, about the personal sacrifices involved.

Now, at the end of July, with all the pomp and ceremony and the blinding, confusing brilliance of the wedding ceremony in Westminster Abbey behind him, he knew exactly what Percy had meant that evening. The month between Edward's decision to host the wedding at Westminster and the event itself had simply vanished, engulfed by the headlong urgency of preparation. He had laughed, at first, at the mere idea of an entire month being insufficient time to prepare for a ceremony that would last less than an hour, but that laughter had been short lived as other people's urgencies quickly began to press in on him. Within two days he had lost count of the multitude of people who converged on him from every direction, clamouring for his attention to an incomprehensible plethora of niceties and trivia to do with the ceremony itself. There were preparation and content to consider; protocol and seating arrangements and form and substance, each petty but pressing detail the be-all and end-all of existence for the swarm of functionaries charged with their responsibility, and every last one of them required his personal attention. On top of that, there had been the ridiculous amount of time he was forced to spend with the royal tailors, since it had been tacitly agreed by everyone save him that the sacrament of marriage demanded the provision of an entirely new wardrobe for the bridegroom—Isabella's involvement in her own wardrobe arrangements had been far more intense and time consuming than his, but from what he had gathered in passing, she had enjoyed the experience far more than he had.

Less than two weeks into those hectic days, the train of escorted wagons carrying the entire Bruce brood arrived at Writtle and settled in, and as soon as word came to him of their arrival, Bruce mutinied against the tyrants surrounding him. He had made swift arrangements, brooking no argument, for things to continue without him for a week, and had then abducted Isabella, along with her father and her ladies, and taken them directly to Writtle to meet his siblings.

There, for two full days, he had enjoyed himself thoroughly among his own kin, wearing Isabella on his arm like a trophy the entire time. It was the first time in weeks that the two of them had been able to spend more than a jealously snatched hour or two a day in each other's company, and they were determined to make the most of every moment they could spend together.

This gathering marked the first time in years that all the siblings had been together in one place, and the changes in all of them delighted Bruce. The girls were too young to hold much interest for him for any length of time, but his four close-grouped brothers,

Nigel, Edward, Thomas, and Alexander, more than made up for that. The only two missing were the eldest, Christina, who Bruce hoped would soon be joining them from her home in Mar, and Isabel, who was in Bergen on the far side of the North Sea where, at the age of twenty, she had been Queen Consort to King Eric II of Norway for two years.

Those two days in the company of his family had flown by, too, but the experience had rejuvenated Bruce and brought him and Isabella closer together than anything before, and it was there in Writtle, on the first evening of their stay, that the simple, chaste kisses they had grown accustomed to changed suddenly to a raging fire of need.

It had begun simply enough. The youngest children were long abed, the household servants had been dismissed for the night, and the remaining group, including Isabella and two of her five young women, had sat up, talking and laughing, enjoying some mulled wine, until Bruce realized how late it had grown. He jumped up and stopped Nigel before he could throw any more fuel on the fire, then announced that the following day would be a long one and it was time to make an end of this one. He then hovered over everyone until, with much good-natured grumbling, they got up and made their way to their various beds, still talking loudly enough among themselves to wake the household.

Isabella waited with him while Bruce doused the candles and lamps and looked to the safety of the dying fire in the big hearth, raking it and banking what was left of it so there would be no danger of stray embers falling loose. He then took the last remaining candle and set out to conduct Isabella to the large room she shared with her ladies.

He kissed her halfway up the stairs, turning her easily to face him from the step above him and holding the candle safely at arm's length, and she had come to him willingly, making a little sound of happiness as she raised her lips to his. But then, in an instant, the lighthearted, loving kiss changed and she was locked in the crook of his arm, her arms tight around his neck and her small, pliant body pressing against him fiercely enough to send him reeling down to the step below as her mouth blossomed into a moist and hotly demanding thing that covered his own and threatened to bruise his lips. He protested with an agonized moan and then, one-handed and with surprising difficulty, he pulled her arms from around his neck and stooped quickly to place the candle holder on the stair, safe against the wall. He wanted to extinguish it completely, but it was the only light left burning in the house, and he felt a ludicrous burst of fear as he imagined them stumbling and fumbling afterwards, trying to find their way along the passageways to their rooms in the pitch-darkness. So he left it burning and returned to her, and her hands locked behind his head and pulled him down to her mouth again.

What followed was a conflagration of sudden passion that took no heed of anything other than its own urgencies; a fiery blaze of lust and longing; ravening mouths and groping hands that dug in frenzied efforts to thrust cloth aside and find the living heat of naked, straining flesh and welcoming warmth, until a blinding flash of self-awareness caught him in the glare of his own folly and he froze and thrust himself back and away.

"Christ Jesus, lass! This is madness." He could hear the over-wrought tension in his own voice as she, too, froze into immobility, her breath caught in her throat. He forced himself to turn away from her, reaching for the candle, and as he picked it up he noted how the flame, the very candle itself, shook in his grasp. Isabella exhaled explosively, and he sensed rather than heard her sit up straight on the stairs at his back. Then came a rustle of clothing followed by the pressure of her hand on his shoulder as she pushed herself to her feet and stood above him, breathing raggedly. As soon as he was sure she was standing firmly he flexed his legs and straightened up beside her, aware of his thighs quivering strangely as he hooked his free arm around her waist and drew her against him, her head on his shoulder. He held her close for long moments, feeling her shaking die away slowly, and then he kissed the top of her bowed head.

"Oh, my dear," he whispered, speaking into her hair and only realizing then that her head covering was no longer in place. "That was wonderful, but folly … Aye, and dangerous." He chuckled. "Suppose someone had come while we were at that? From above or below, there we would have been, rutting like a country lover and his lass caught in the byre." He laughed again. "Now there would have been a story to tell the cooks in the morning … The earl and his countess on the stairs, doing what should be done between the blankets."

Then Isabella whispered, "But we are a country lover and his lass, my lord. Or we were then … So close. And it was so beautiful—" She held her breath for an instant, and then she, too, giggled. "It might have been worth being caught, just to see the reaction."

Suddenly they were both laughing madly, fighting to keep quiet and hugging each other for support. Eventually, when he felt fit enough to speak again without laughing, Bruce disengaged himself and leaned back, holding up the candle as he looked about him at the articles of clothing scattered on the stairs.

"Amazing how quickly those come off," he mused, "considering how long they take to put on. Here, let me help you." He stooped and gathered up her discarded head covering, its formal wimple now no more than a loose square of cloth, and by the time he straightened she had the remaining bits and pieces folded over one arm. He looked at her then, still holding the candle high, and smiled. "Well," he said easily, "at least we know now that we like and want each other. That's going to make our wedding night less frightening."

Isabella of Mar looked back at him wide-eyed. "Had it been frightening to you, my lord of Bruce?" She shivered. "Lah! It came on so *quickly*! I had no intent—"

"No more had I, my love. But right you are, it came on quickly."

"And it was wonderful—frightening, almost, but *wonderful*."

His smile had widened. "Aye, but the best part, the even more wonderful part, is that it will do the same again, time after time, now that it knows us vulnerable to it. But within the month we'll be wed and nothing—no one—can stop us from enjoying it whenever we please ... And now let's get you to bed, lass."

He turned her easily back towards the ascent before dropping his hands to her buttocks and urging her forward and up.

Three days later the young pair were back in Westminster and swept up again in the myriad preparations for the wedding, this time involving rehearsals for the ceremony and the rituals surrounding it as a royally attended event. Informal at first as they were carried out under the eyes of various dignitaries, the rehearsals grew progressively more complex and ritualized, until Bruce began to think his entire life revolved around the mere repetition of meaningless patterns of movement accompanied by music. He had always enjoyed music, but overfamiliarity with the music involved here quickly dulled his appreciation of it and he grew bored, and finally annoyed, with the mind-numbing sameness of the incessant practicing. Equally predictable—as he reflected ruefully far more than once—was the virtual impossibility of finding time alone with Isabella, for she was even busier than he, with a multitude of bridal things to do when she was not caught up in practice and rehearsals.

He was distracted from the now chronic annoyance at the interference in his daily life by the unexpected reappearance of his father, back from his scouting expedition to Carlisle, and he found it hard to believe at first that Lord Bruce had been gone for almost four whole weeks. A fortnight in surveying the town and its requirements, with a week of travelling on either side, had sped by.

They shared one meal alone together, two nights after his lordship's return, and in the course of it his father outlined all that he had discovered—and all that he achieved and hoped to achieve—about conditions in and around the fortress town he was to govern. He was to meet with Edward the following day, he said, to make a full report on his tour of inspection, and he was quietly confident that it would be well received by the King. It was his royal belief, the King had told Lord Robert prior to his departure for the north, that Carlisle was in sore need of refurbishment should there be any possibility of hostile actions from the Scots army under Balliol. Lord Robert could now confirm Edward's suspicions to be accurate, and he felt sure his recommendations would be put into practice.

The cloudless dawn sky was pink through the open shutters of his bedroom window as Robert Bruce, propped up on his elbow, gazed down at his sleeping wife. Exhausted from a night of making love, she was exquisite, her hair tousled and tangled, her cheeks flushed with health, and one perfect, surprisingly large breast exposed by the way she had thrown off the coverings at some point. She was his at last, he thought, smiling. At last, indeed … Two short months before, he had been panting like a hound in pursuit of Lady Gwendolyn de Ferrers, and when he had found out about Isabella's arrival, he had done everything in his power to avoid her.

He should be up and abroad by now, with the sky brightening rapidly and promising another brilliant summer day, and on any other day of his life he would have been; how many times in the past had he cursed himself as a slug-abed at the mere thought of wasting a moment of such a magnificent morning? But this morning was different from any other. This morning was his and Isabella's, to be shared with no one else, for this morning was the very first of their married life; they could spend the entire day in bed, naked and entwined, if they so wished. Indeed, it was expected of them. Nigel had promised him the previous night, before the wine and festivities took hold completely, that he would personally ensure that food and drink would be discreetly left for them on the other side of their locked doors.

God, she was beautiful!

On the point of yielding to a compulsion to bend forward and kiss that innocently bared, berry-tipped breast, he paused instead and then leaned backward gently, lowering himself until he lay beside her again and linking his fingers behind his head. She slept on, oblivious to his presence, and the swell of tenderness in his chest precluded any possibility of disturbing her rest. He himself had barely slept that night; he had dozed from time to time, but sprung awake each time Isabella moved, so unaccustomed was he to sharing a bed with anyone. Not that he had never shared a woman's bed, he thought then, for he had, perhaps too many, but he had seldom slept in them. He had enjoyed them, used their occupants and been used by them, but always he had risen afterwards and crept away under the concealing cloak of darkness.

Those days, and nights, were past now, and Robert Bruce, Earl of Carrick, long celebrated as a night-prowling tomcat, would stray no more. He knew that now beyond a doubt. Thinking back to the ceremonies of the previous day, he examined again the two clear memories he had retained; two sharply focused memories among a sea of formless impressions. He could recall being awed by the daunting magnificence of the abbey church, its slender, soaring columns sweeping up to the arched and vaulted roof so far above the heads of the worshippers, and by the mitred splendour of the robed bishops and abbots as they moved pontifically among the clouds of precious, sweet-smelling incense that filled the sanctuary; could recall, too, the haunting beauty of the choirs, the solemn, majestic chant of the abbey monks and the lighter, younger singing of the choristers. And, as clear in his mind now as it had been at the time, his bride had emerged from a light-filled haze, gowned and veiled in mists of green and golden fabrics as she came forward to meet him with one hand on her father's arm. There had been music, he knew, loud music that had been sustained throughout the nuptial Mass, but his awareness had been focused tightly on her approach and on the veil that concealed her face, hiding the smile that was the sole thing in the world that he wanted to see at that moment.

When at last she raised the veil as he bent to kiss her as his wife, the sight of her pure and stainless beauty struck at his heart and robbed him of all breath, and he had thought he might die happy at that moment. That was all the memory he needed of his wedding day, he knew.

Edward had come forward to greet them as they left the high altar, and behind him came a host of well-wishers, eager to meet the King's new favourite liegewoman, and as expected, a long and tedious course of introductions followed as Isabella and Bruce accepted the congratulations of all there. At one point, as he straightened up from kissing some unknown woman's hand, he saw the King beckoning to him.

"You have a treasure there, young Robert," Edward had growled. "A perfect pearl beyond price. Nurture her and she will nurture you. You have my word on that as one who spent four decades in the company of such another. May God bless your marriage and make it fruitful. But you'll need money more than ever now, if you're to treat your new countess the way she should be treated. Talk to Walter Langton. Tell him I said to fund you from my privy purse. A hundred pounds should see you on your way." He raised a hand abruptly, cutting off Bruce's startled thanks before they could be uttered, for a hundred pounds was a staggering sum, the equivalent of a full year of Bruce's lost rents in Scotland. "My wedding gift to you, intended for your wife. Now go and save her from those slavering hounds surrounding her."

In the week before the wedding the young pair had met twice with Edward, both times privately, and Bruce knew beyond a doubt that those privileges stemmed directly from the King's touchingly spontaneous and surprising paternal affection for Isabella. On the first occasion, purely on impulse, he had invited them to share the meal that was being served for him, for he had been working alone and planning to eat while he continued working. The unplanned sharing of an intimate meal with the monarch was an unheard-of honour that had gone unnoticed by no one at the court of Westminster.

The second meeting, the very next afternoon, had been private in name only, for the King had been accompanied by several dignitaries, few, to be true, but among the most powerful in the realm. As Bruce discovered afterwards, the business with which they were dealing had concluded and Edward had begun telling them about the enjoyment he had gained "from young Bruce's amazing wife," as he himself put it. And then, presumably still filled with goodwill from the previous evening, he had promptly summoned the young couple to come at once, as they were, and meet his ministers.

Foremost among them all, Bruce knew, was Master Walter Langton, Master of the Wardrobe until a few days previously and now newly appointed Lord High Treasurer of England. Bruce had met Langton several times over a period of years and liked the man, finding him refreshingly open and amiable despite the grave responsibilities he bore. As Master of the Wardrobe, Langton had controlled the privy accounts of the royal household for five years, including the so-called wardrobe treasure of gold and jewels that was funded by the treasury—but crucially free of the control of parliament—and used to fund the private and often urgent personal needs of the monarch, from secret diplomatic endeavours to waging war.

Now, as Lord High Treasurer, Langton would play another role, akin to but vastly different from his former one. Both involved the stewardship of vast amounts of money, but as Lord Treasurer, Langton was now nominally answerable to parliament for all monies disbursed by the exchequer. One of his duties would be to dispute and confound the wiles and wishes of his own successor, the new Master of the Wardrobe.

Bruce knew, without being told, that Langton's advancement to the treasurer's post had been a master stroke of policy on Edward's part. Bruce had in fact met briefly with Langton, within days of their arrival in Westminster, merely to pay his respects to the friend of an old friend. Langton, now in his fifties, had been a protégé of Robert Burnell, the Bishop of Bath and Wells, and before Burnell died he had recommended Langton's services to the King. Now, four years later, Langton had replaced his former mentor as one of the King's few real friends and most trusted advisers. His advancement from Master of the Wardrobe to the post of Lord High Treasurer had been Edward's political equivalent of deliberately setting a fox to watch the henhouse. By placing a trusted friend to safeguard his privy funds against the jealous interference of parliament and its tight-fisted, fractious barons, Edward had ensured the safety of his own continued funding. Were Langton to carry out the task as skilfully as

Bruce was sure he would, he would be guaranteed a wealthy bishopric one day as his reward.

There were two other clerics with the King at that second meeting, one of them the newly appointed Archbishop of Canterbury, Robert Winchelsea. Bruce knew nothing about this man, and he suspected that Edward Plantagenet might know little more than he, for the King was uncommonly reticent when speaking to the archbishop, and Bruce sensed that might be born of not yet having gauged the fellow's mettle. The mutual dislike between Winchelsea and Langton, however, was painfully obvious, communicated openly in the way they tended to sneer at each other, as though each was trying to outdo his rival—and rival for what? Bruce wondered— in superciliousness. Edward ignored their barely cloaked hostility, and Bruce knew the King had reasons for pretending blindness to it.

The third churchman there that evening was Walter de Wenlock, the Abbot of Westminster, a man incapable of posturing or pretense. This was the man who later officiated at the wedding, a plain, good-natured, and genuinely pious man, tall and stooped and elderly, without a trace of malice in his soul. Isabella delighted him by approaching him immediately and enthusing over his magnificent church, and he was her willing slave within moments, enchanted by her innocence and her complete lack of guile. Nor was he alone in being entranced by her; without exception, every man in the room fell quickly under Isabella's spell, and she manipulated them all artlessly and with equal ease, even drawing laughter from the Archbishop of Canterbury with one of her quips. Edward, of course, had been completely under her control from their first meeting; now it looked as though the three most influential men at court would share his fascination.

The Earl of Carrick and his new countess returned to Writtle two weeks after they were married, glad to leave the glittering but exhausting world of Edward's Westminster safely behind them at a distance of some twenty miles, and to have an opportunity now to set about establishing their own home in Essex during the long, mild autumn that must surely follow such a glorious summer. In the serenity of the countryside surrounding their home, they wrought miracles in the four months that followed, transforming the old Writtle House that had seen little change in the previous hundred years.

Thanks to the munificence of the royal wedding gift, they could afford to hire stonemasons and fine carpenters, and so with the help of the King's seneschal, Sir Robert FitzHugh, and the agreement of the King himself, they had temporarily hired the young Jeffrey of Canterbury from the currently suspended work of reconstructing St. Stephen's Chapel at Westminster. It had been an inspired choice on Isabella's part, because under the enthusiastic young mason's guiding hand, the ancient house was quickly rebuilt into a thing of beauty, with wide, soaring windows of leaded glass through which the light poured in to illuminate rooms, staircases, and even nooks and corners that had known nothing but darkness before then. The outer buildings were rebuilt as well, in keeping with the functional strength and rugged solidity of the newly resurrected stables, and as the new outbuildings rose, so did the crops that had survived the flooding, maturing into a finer, healthier crop than anyone could remember ever having seen.

In the neighbouring village and the surrounding lands, peace and prosperity were all-pervading, the people showing their contentment and ease on market days, when visiting merchants made sure to include the village on their rounds and the stalls were laden with a bewildering array of goods and produce that sold quickly and profitably.

In all that time, only two matters arose to ruffle the placid surface of life in Writtle. Bruce of Annandale had renewed his oath of fealty to King Edward at the time of his son's wedding in Westminster, as indeed had the Earl of Carrick himself, and the official proclamation of the elder Bruce's appointment to the governorship of Carlisle had come soon after that, at the beginning of August. Lord Bruce was gone within days of the announcement, riding at the head of a specially raised contingent of reinforcements for the Carlisle garrison and accompanied by Isabella's father, with his own escorting bodyguard, who rode with him as far as his new posting before continuing across the border and returning to his home in Mar.

Then, towards the end of that same month, Sir John de Bigod stopped briefly at Writtle on his way north to Suffolk and Norfolk, carrying messages from the King to the barons there. His visit lasted no more than an hour, sufficient time for him to feed his men and rest their horses, but his tidings caused Bruce some concern, because the royal summons he was carrying was a call to arms, the signal to begin assembling a fresh army to reinforce the faltering, poorly led one already in France. Edward would lead this expedition in person, to settle the question of the mutinous Gascon Duchy once and for all. The message being what it was, Bigod had no compunction in discussing it with Bruce, since it would soon be common knowledge, but it was a sharp reminder to the Scots earl of his recently renewed oath of fealty to Edward and the obligations it entailed. He might be called upon to join the armies, and the thought of leaving Isabella so soon after their wedding distressed him. He did not really believe Edward would call upon him for military service—the following he might levy from his few English holdings would be tiny—but the possibility was there and it nagged at him, though the threat of it grew dimmer as the time passed by without a personal summons.

The latter part of September and the first two weeks of October brought a flurry of communications, the most important of which was delivered in person by a special courier come all the way from Scotland. John Comyn, the young Lord of Badenoch, son of the Earl of Buchan, the senior Guardian of the new Scots council, arrived unannounced at Bruce's gates in late September. He came dressed as a royal herald, in a thickly padded, extravagantly decorated tabard bearing the royal arms of Scotland stiffly embroidered in silver and gold wire. He had been charged with conveying a formal summons from Scotland's King to Robert Bruce VII, living in England. The heavy parchment scroll was encased in a polished cylinder of thick bull hide stamped with the royal crest, and the missive itself was encrusted and festooned with seals and ribbons. Cumbersome to open, it was none the less quickly read, once stripped of its fulsomely convoluted flourishes: Robert Bruce, Earl of Carrick, was commanded forthwith, upon pain of forfeiture of all he held in Scotland, to conscript all the fighting men at his disposal as afore-said earl and present them, with himself, for duty in the assembled host of his royal grace, John I, God's anointed King of Scotland.

Bruce stood silent after he had read the thing, bowed head-down over the table on which he had spread it with its corners heavily weighted. Across from him, tapping his foot, Comyn waited for a reaction, but Bruce allowed no trace of emotion to show on his face; nor did he raise his eyes to meet the condescending sneer that had not left the Comyn's face since the moment he arrived. There were others present, member's of Comyn's escort and a few of Bruce's own retainers, but both principals were aware only of each other.

Beyond the gates, Bruce knew, the men of Comyn's escort yet sat their horses, eyeing the heavily armed and armoured household guard that Thomas Beg had turned out as soon as the newcomers were seen in the distance. They were less than thirty strong and tired after a long ride, and the Bruce guards outnumbered them even without the vigilant cadre of longbow archers who watched them suspiciously from the tower roof, arrows already nocked.

Bruce understood all too well the motive underlying this delivery—what had prompted it and what it was meant to achieve. His father would already have received a similar dispatch, in Carlisle, and would respond appropriately, Bruce knew. His own sole cause of hesitation was the contempt he felt towards the messenger, and even that, he knew, had been predesigned, the Comyn selected purely on the grounds of that dislike. His mind made up, he stepped back from the table and looked Comyn straight in the eye.

"This is ... unexpected," he drawled, careful to keep his voice flat. "It is also impossible. There can be no sane response to such an insult, and well you know it. Now you have done your duty as charged. Return to your King with this answer. I am Earl of Carrick in name only since he himself confiscated my lands and holdings. As such, I hold no sway among my former people and I command no men eligible to fight in Scotland's armies. The men I command here are all English, duty bound to England's King as am I myself, by oath, by free will, and by natural loyalty. I swore no such oath to Balliol or Scotland and for that I stand dispossessed." He flicked a hand dismissively towards the ornate scroll. "This is a nonsense, buffoonery trumped up for the sake of appearance and the needs of the moment. I reject it as invalid and unjust. And that is all my answer. Tell it to your King."

"You will write in response, as befitting to the dignity of the King's grace. Write it. I will await your answer."

Bruce had to turn away to conceal the fury that swept over him at the loutish arrogance of the words, more intolerable even than the disdainful look on the speaker's face, but with his back squarely presented to his would-be tormentor he controlled his anger quickly, gazing at his sheathed sword leaning in a corner formed by the wall and a finely carved, head-high armoire of burnished oak that held his papers and writing materials. He unclenched his fists and turned back.

"My lord of Comyn," he said quietly, half turning again to point at the armoire at his back. "Look you at this cupboard. I find it soothing to look at it. It is made of English oak. So, too, is the floor upon which you stand, and every wooden item within sight here."

"I care nothing for your furnishings, Bruce."

"I know that. I was but pointing out that they are all of English construction. So is everything about you. This house itself is English and the laws that prevail within it and outside it are all English, too. You are in *England*, man. And you are in *my house*. What kind of fool would think to command Bruce in his own house, even in Scotland? Do I make myself clear? You have no status here. I need do nothing at your self-presumed command. Nor will I suffer your ill manners or your ill temper herein. You are here on sufferance— *my* sufferance—and on my goodwill, and both have expired. Your duty here is done and you have my answer to you and to your King. Go you now and deliver it like a faithful messenger."

"Christ God! I'll have—" Comyn's eyes glared in fury and his hand swept into the gap of the heavy tabard, exposing the briefest glimpse of a dagger hilt there.

Bruce sprang away, but even as he moved the blade was drawn, though its withdrawal was hampered by the stiff bulk of the tabard itself. He continued his spin, snatched the sword from the corner at his back and pivoted again, whipping the sheathed weapon around towards Comyn. Such was the controlled fury of his two-handed swing that the scabbard dislodged itself and flew across the room with a metallic hiss before the point of Bruce's long blade came to a sudden halt, then pushed forward to press against the base of Comyn's throat, the Scots lord still tugging to free his weapon beneath his tabard.

"On your life. Drop it. Take it out slowly and drop it where you stand."

Comyn took a step backward, his face deathly pale, and Bruce pursued him, holding the polished steel sword tip against his neck as he spoke through stiff lips.

"Step back again, Comyn. You're close to the wall. After that, you're like to have a throat full of my blade. *Drop* it!"

The concealed hand came free of the tabard and the weapon it had held clanged solidly on the oaken floor. It was a Highland dirk, a heavy, ornate, single-edged weapon with a blade too long to clear its sheath in the confined space beneath the tabard. Bruce did not even glance down at it.

"An assassin's blade. A fitting weapon for a Comyn fool. Was that part of your orders from your father? To kill me if I would not come with you?"

So fast had been the sequence of events that no other person in the room had moved, but now they began to shift, their eyes taking in the fallen weapon even as their minds caught up with what had taken place. There was no doubting the crime that had occurred, even among the Scots of Comyn's escort. The breach of protocol was flagrant, the violation of the simple but immutable laws of hospitality self-evident.

Comyn's face was a study in rage and humiliation, but he could do nothing with the sword tip pressing against his throat, and none of his companions showed the slightest sign of moving to support him. Bruce removed his left hand from the hilt and lowered his sword slowly, keeping his arm extended, the weapon's point now resting on the floor. His eyes remained fixed on Comyn, narrowed to slits, and not a man there doubted that he would spill blood without a thought if he were provoked further.

"Now," he said softly, "curb your ill tongue and get your Highland arse out of my sight and out of my house. Take your servants with you and go with as much dignity as you can muster. But open your mouth again within my hearing and I swear by the living Christ I'll cleave you where you stand. Go. *No!* Leave that where it is."

Comyn had made a halfhearted move to collect his dirk, but the sudden shout and the sweeping slither of Bruce's blade across the floor stopped him at once.

"I'll go. But this is far from done. One day I will have my due of you, I swear."

"So be it, Comyn. But on that day you'll die. Now, out!"

Rigidly, John Comyn swung away and stalked to the door, his minions following like sheep. Bruce followed him out through the main hallway and into the courtyard, where Comyn's horse had already been brought forward.

"Thomas Beg," he called. "Our guests are leaving now. Forthwith. See that they do not tarry."

He cast a quick glance up to the tower roof, where he found the captain of his archers looking down at him. Bruce nodded at him, managing, in that one swift exchange, to convey the urgency of the need for continued vigilance. The veteran bowman nodded back, then hefted his own bow and looked towards the Scots escort beyond the gates.

Bruce had no doubt of the reception his rejection of Balliol's summons would receive in Scotland. There had never been any question of that. The simple confiscation of his lands and title, in effect a minatory rap on the knuckles rather than a punitive condemnation, would now become solid forfeiture. He would be legally stripped of rank and holdings and placed among the ranks of outlaws, alienated from royal favour and from any hope of restitution until such time as he prostrated himself before the Scots King and swore abject allegiance, denying the allegiance he had already sworn to Edward Plantagenet. His earldom and his people would be given to someone else, one of the current royal favourites or perhaps even to Comyn of Badenoch, though it would doubtless go to the elderly father rather than to the hotheaded son whom everyone was calling Red John nowadays.

Bruce knew he would be resentful of such injustice, but another part of him recognized a certain relief that this crisis had been resolved. He had already lost his rents and revenues from Scotland; this latest fiasco merely made the loss final, and he found he could accept that philosophically. His father, he presumed, would have received the same peremptory summons and would have reacted similarly; perhaps more temperately, he suspected, since Lord Bruce lacked the fiery temperament that appeared to have passed directly over him from his father to his son. Notwithstanding that, though, Bruce had no doubt that Balliol's other messenger would have journeyed home from Carlisle with a similar response to the one carried from Writtle. Lord Bruce was even more closely bound to Edward by ties of duty and responsibility than was his son, and thinking of that, his son resolved to ride northward soon with his wife to visit his father's new domain in Carlisle. And thus he resolved to waste no more time thinking about the anti-Bruce faction in Scotland.

Within the week, he received word from his father, warning him to be on guard for the arrival of a Scottish envoy bearing unacceptable demands. The letter, written some two weeks earlier, summarized Lord Bruce's refusal and rejection—precisely what the younger Bruce had expected it to be. His closing sentence, though, marked what was new between them: *I trust you are well, my son, and that my delightful good-daughter Isabella is by now soundly pregnant.*

She was not, but Bruce smiled at the thought that it was not from the lack of trying, and when he told her of his father's enquiry he laughed aloud at her reaction and permitted her to drag him early to their bed.

Soon after came a letter from Domhnall of Mar, a single piece of heavy parchment folded and sealed with wax bearing his personal stamp of a Scots thistle and covered in a tiny, meticulous script that Bruce knew was written by a priestly hand, for Domhnall was quite incapable of writing anything that small. The old man was there in the letter, though, his voice unmistakable.

*Robert:*

*Ill doings here these past few weeks. That council of which we spoke is now in place. Twelve magnates, Church and nobility from north and south of Forth, to assist the King's grace in the governing of the realm. The King himself, they say, is in a rage and bent on satisfaction. They say, too, though, that you—and not the council— are the cause of his vexation. You know, I jalouse, that they are those who will not speak to me directly, so I am left to hear their words through the ears and mouths of others. I heard that Comyn went to you straight from the King and that you spurned him; refused the King's command and abused Comyn forbye, turning him out of your house. I felt no great surprise to hear it. But the upshot of it all is you have been legally proscribed, your lands and goods seized in forfeit. That is not new, I know; has not been so for years. But the Comyn brood have been given full possession of your rights, as a reward for faithful service to the Crown. It makes me sick to have to send the word to you, but there it is. You are landless in Scotland now. But far from friendless.*

*Take care of my child, and should you ever need me, I will be here, at your service.*

*Mar*

Autumn had come later than usual, but its fruitful bounty stretched so far and so slowly towards winter that it sometimes seemed as though no winter would appear at all that year, and Robert Bruce was more content than he had ever been before, utterly besotted with his young and beautiful wife and blissfully grateful for the frequent and always happily willing urgency with which she responded to his satyr-like demands upon her body and her love, throwing off her clothes with an eagerness to match his own once they had reached the safety of their bedchamber. And sometimes, quite frequently, their pleasure was enhanced when they failed to reach the bedchamber or even to disrobe at all, overtaken by their all-consuming need to enjoy each other. He was twenty-one years old, blissfully wed and without a care in the world, and he assumed, with the natural arrogance of youth, that that condition would last forever.

And like every man before him, he was wrong.

# CHAPTER TWENTY-TWO

# A BRIEF AND DISTANT WAR

On a late-November day like no other he could remember, Robert Bruce sat lounging between the embrasures at one corner of the low wall that topped the tower of his house in Writtle. He was facing the sun, which was climbing towards its zenith in the southeast, and one long leg dangled over the rooftops of the outbuildings below him as he basked in the unseasonable warmth and fretted over his own inadequacy. Isabella had awakened that morning with her monthly courses flowing and had plunged headlong into grief that would brook no comforting from her husband. Four months they had been wed, she had cried; four months of faithful perseverance and wholehearted striving and fervent prayer—and nothing! No quickening; no pregnancy; no sign of ever being blessed with a child to bear her husband's name. She was a failure as a wife and would never be a mother.

Bruce had tried to soothe her, but every attempt he made succeeded only in increasing her despair. No matter what he said, the words had barely left his mouth before he knew they were precisely the wrong ones, and eventually, like all men, he came to accept that there were times when the best refuge for a simple man lay in plain flight. And so he had found himself on the tower roof, the only place in the house where he might find solitude.

He had no idea how long he had been sitting there mulling, but the day was gentle, the sunlight warm and pleasant, and the air about him was silent, not even a skylark's song breaking the stillness. He pushed himself up from his seat and turned to look behind him, seeing how the low-hanging sun set the late-autumn colours of the woods there in a blaze, and as he stared in admiration a distant flash of light in the open country beyond the trees caught his attention. He straightened, attentive now, and waited for the gleam to be repeated, knowing it had been reflected from metal—from a weapon or a piece of armour or harness. He folded his arms on the top of the parapet in front of him, eyes narrowed as he scanned the distant fields.

A quarter of an hour passed before he saw a far-off dot that soon resolved itself into three tiny specks. Three mounted men, coming from the southwest, along the road from London and Westminster. He checked an impulse to alert his people below, since there was nothing they could do but hurry to make ready and then wait thereafter; besides, there was nothing to fear from three men, armed though they were. The single flash that had alerted him was now repeated constantly from all three sources, undoubted evidence that the approaching men were not merely armed but armoured, which indicated in turn that their business must be official. Whoever they were, they were wasting no time, approaching now at a gallop.

He lost sight of them as the woods between them blocked his vision, but he knew now how far away they were. He crossed the flat roof to the other side of the building, overlooking the gates, where he leaned over the battlements and shouted to the guard below, warning him that people were approaching, then strode towards the stairs and went down quickly to his chambers.

Isabella was there alone, white faced and subdued but no longer weeping, and she rushed towards him as he entered, starting to tell him she was sorry, but he laid a finger on her mouth to silence her, kissed her fleetingly on the brow, and told her what was happening, bidding her make ready. He changed his simple tunic for a more elaborate one and shrugged into a supple leather jerkin, belting it about his waist. He ran his hands flat over his crown to straighten his hair, then made his way downstairs to meet the newcomers.

They had arrived and dismounted by the time he reached the inner yard and went out to meet them. All three were armoured officers-at-arms. Two wore the bronze emblems of corporals on their cuirasses and helmets, and their leader, a rock-faced veteran with the unmistakable bearing of a man who had commanded other men for many years, wore the insignia of a senior sergeant of King Edward's personal guard.

The leader snapped to attention and brought his clenched fist to his left breast in salute. "Lord Bruce," he said in a voice as hard as his expression. "The King requires your presence in Westminster without delay."

Bruce nodded. "Then he shall have it, Sergeant. A moment to alert my wife and we will join you." He turned to Thomas Beg, who had materialized by his side. "Thomas, Lady Isabella's carriage, quick as you like. You heard the sergeant."

Thomas nodded, but before he could turn away the sergeant stopped him with an upraised hand, though he spoke directly to Bruce. "Your pardon, milord. Your lady wife was not included. Without delay means what it says. We will be riding hard and we don't have sufficient men to guard your lady. His Majesty made himself clear. Not milady Bruce. Just you, with no delay."

Bruce frowned, but nodded again, tersely. "Very well. But I must still explain, and change my clothes."

"No, my lord, begging your pardon. You may explain your summons, certainly, but you are to come just as you are. At once, sir. There is much urgency."

The frown deepened. "That's plain enough," Bruce growled. "I will be quick, but even so you will have time to snatch a bite of food while I am gone. Thomas will take you to the kitchens before he brings my horse. I will be ready to leave within the quarter-hour."

The sergeant saluted again, then, leading his horse, he went with Thomas Beg, the two corporals behind him.

Isabella's dismay at the tidings was distressing for Bruce to see, for this was the first time the call of duty had intruded upon their peace, but she recovered quickly and helped him stoically as he threw some additional small clothes into a saddlebag. He pulled on a pair of thick-soled, well-worn riding boots, exchanged his light jerkin for a more substantial, fleece-lined one, then slung his sword over his shoulder to hang at his back. No shield, no armour, nothing much of anything, but at least he would have his sword and dagger. He kissed Isabella one more time, fiercely, and then snatched a heavy riding cloak from its peg on the wall as he swept out, calling farewell to her over his shoulder.

He had a few minutes alone in the yard, for his horse was not yet there and the sergeant and his men had not emerged from the kitchens, and he used the time to think about this summons. Its urgency was self-evident, but he was unlikely to know anything of the reasons for it until he reached Westminster. Normally, his summoner to an audience—if any such summons could be considered normal—would be a knight, and there would be nowhere near this urgency. And a knight, in common courtesy, would have been able to give him some inkling about what might be involved. The sergeant and his two corporals were royal guards with seniority, which meant they were both competent and trusted by the King; Bruce could trust them to escort him safely and quickly to Westminster, but he had little hope of conversation along the way.

A clatter of hooves on cobblestones brought awareness of everyone arriving at the same time, but rather than merely leading Bruce's saddled courser, Thomas Beg was mounted, too, on his great bay gelding, and neither the sergeant nor his companions appeared to have any objections to his riding with them.

They were on the road within minutes, watched by a forlorn Isabella from the tower roof, and by the time Bruce turned back in his saddle to wave at her for a second time, she and the house had vanished behind the screen of trees.

They travelled fifteen miles before the short November day ended, and spent the night in a roadside inn, the same one the soldiers had used the night before on their way down. It had been mid-afternoon when they were dispatched the previous day, the sergeant told

Bruce, and the setting sun had overtaken them ten miles out from Westminster, close by the inn called the Spotted Cow. The place was clean, though primitive, and the food was edible. The five men went to bed early, for lack of anything better to do, and were up and on the road by dawn, with ten miles left between themselves and Westminster and no real traffic to impede their progress, so that by mid-morning they arrived at the palace.

Bruce was surprised to see Sir Robert FitzHugh pacing anxiously on the flagged area fronting the main entrance when they clattered through the gates, and from the way the seneschal grew still at their approach it was plain he had been waiting for them. No sooner had Bruce dismounted and thrown his reins to Thomas Beg, leaving him to stable the horses at the guards' barracks and await him there, than FitzHugh signalled for him to follow. Bruce had to move quickly in order to keep up with the old man, and that did little to dispel his misgivings over this summons. They had swept through the ante-room of the Great Hall and into the warren of passageways that surrounded it before either spoke a word.

"This way," said FitzHugh, heading diagonally across a wide junction.

"What's amiss, Sir Robert?"

The seneschal did not even glance at him. "The King is vexed" was all he said.

"With me?"

That earned him a sideways glance and the hint of a wintry smile. "No, my lord," FitzHugh said. "With your countrymen."

"With my countrymen! I don't follow you."

"You will, in moments. The King is with the barons—as many of them as were here to find. Others are coming."

"The barons. I see." But in truth he saw nothing. "Why send for me, then?"

Another sardonic, sideways glance. "I am the seneschal, Lord Carrick, not the King. Here we are." He led the way up a wide flight of shallow steps that Bruce had climbed before.

"The Painted Chamber?"

"The King awaits you."

The entrance to the Painted Chamber was an enormous set of double doors guarded by six pikemen under the command of a sergeant, and before they had reached the top step the guardsmen's pikes were already in motion. The two men on the ends maintained their weapons upright; the pair inside those brought theirs forward at an angle as the bearers straightened their arms, pointing their weapons towards the newcomers; the pair in the middle changed their grips and drew their weapons inward across their bodies, forming a cross and barring entry. FitzHugh nodded to the sergeant in charge without slacking his pace and a quiet word of command brought the guards to attention again as they stepped aside, two of them opening the doors. Directly beyond those, in a narrow foyer lit by a brace of torches mounted on the walls, lay another set of identical doors, these unguarded. FitzHugh paused, his gaze sweeping Bruce from head to foot before he nodded and knocked with the side of a clenched fist, then pushed the doors wide and stepped inside.

The sound of raised voices, which had become audible only after passing the outer doors, died away quickly as men turned to look at the newcomers. Bruce had a quick impression of great tension as he saw the crowd inside, some sitting, others standing, all of them glaring at him as though resenting the interruption. But then he realized how the soaring, brightly painted walls of the great chamber dwarfed its occupants, reducing them to less than human size. Now he took in the large, open-ended square of tables that had been drawn up at the midpoint of the vast room. The barons, a brightly coloured throng of them dressed in clothing that ranged from courtly dress to full heraldic armorial trappings, were arranged along the outside of the tables on two sides; the far side was occupied by clerics, all of them scribbling busily; and in the middle of them stood Edward of England, in flowing robes of saffron and pale purple and wearing his light workaday crown of solid gold with a solitary square-cut ruby at its centre. He had been speaking, evidently, haranguing his listeners if the storm of voices Bruce had heard was any indication, but now his gaze was directly set on Bruce.

"My lord of Carrick," he barked. "We have been awaiting you. Come forward."

Bruce wondered briefly at the use of that "we." Was Edward referring to himself and the assembled barons, or was he being regally formal? Holding himself stiffly erect, he marched forward to the edge of the rectangular space where the King stood, then stopped and dropped to one knee, bowing his head.

"My liege, I came as quickly as I could."

"We do not doubt it. Rise, man. How many men can you supply from Writtle?"

Bruce almost blurted, "From *Writtle*?" but caught himself just in time and frowned instead, calculating quickly. "Fifty at once, my liege. Perhaps a hundred, given time."

Edward nodded. "Fifty will suffice for now. What calibre of men are they?"

"Fit enough to march and fight, my liege, when called upon. I have a force of thirty men-at-arms, armoured and equipped. The others would be tenants, variously equipped." He carefully said no more.

"We have a task for you, my lord earl, one we can think of none more suited to perform. You will return to your home and raise those men. At the same time, you will send word to your closest neighbours—eleven knights whose holdings lie within a day's ride of you. FitzHugh will give you a list of who they are. You will bid each of them, in my name and with my full authority—a writ to be supplied to that end by FitzHugh, too—to raise a similar force to your own and bring it to Writtle to join yours. Eleven knights with fifty men apiece. Then, in command of a force six hundred strong, you will execute my royal decree."

He looked around slowly at the listening barons lining the tables, and it seemed to Bruce that there had been something approaching scorn in the King's eyes as he turned to scan them.

"As you may see, we are in conference here, upon matters of state. And you must be confused about what we seek of you. Had word yet come to you of what has been happening elsewhere recently?"

"No, my liege. No word has come to us of anything new or unusual. Writtle is a quiet place where little happens and few men visit."

"Hmm. Would I could take your place for a month or two … Scotland is in turmoil," he continued, his tone suddenly harsh and hostile. "A group of troublemakers has emerged up there, though God Himself knows that is far from new. These call themselves the council of Guardians, or the council of Twelve, depending upon whom one listens to … What is it? If you have anything to say on that then spit it out. We need to hear it."

"Forgive me, my liege, it but crossed my mind that there is nothing new about a council of Guardians in Scots law. Such a council has existed since the death of King Alexander, during the interreg—" He cut himself off, seeing Edward's displeasure.

"The interregnum. Aye, we know that well," Edward made no attempt to hide his impatience. "But at its strongest such a council comprised six of their so-called magnates. This newest body is made up of twelve, and all of them are traitors. They have usurped their King's authority and now contrive to run the country. And Balliol, King though he calls himself, has ceded his power to them, submitting cravenly to their demands and dancing now to the tune they set for him. Faugh!" He stopped short, then resumed in a slightly moderated voice. "They came to prominence in October, though we know they had been plotting secretly for months. And when they did unmask themselves this so-called King stepped meekly to one side and let them do as they wished. To our great harm, be it said.

"He had agreed, long months before, to lend assistance to us for our war in France. Now he has reneged, refuses to fulfill his promise, for all he knows it to be his feudal duty. And the magnates are at fault, but not for that alone. Ever since they came to power last month, they have been *cleansing* their accursed land of Englishmen.

Their bishops, working in collusion with this upstart council, have dispossessed no fewer than four and twenty English clerics—abbots, priests, and bishops—from their duly appointed livings. Those unfortunates have been forced to return here to England, heaped in ignominy, to seek new appointments. We have reports, too, of diverse men of station being removed—expelled—from their own lands, to be replaced by Scots. And now we have reports of English merchants being killed in the town of Berwick—murdered and robbed by Scots while in the prosecution of their own legal affairs."

Edward turned away to address his next words to the listening barons.

"It is insufferable and it *will* be remedied. These damned Scots are now to find that two may play this new game of theirs."

This was all news to Bruce. He had had no inkling of the speed with which affairs had developed. No word of any of this—clerics dislodged from their benefices; landowners dispossessed; merchants assaulted, robbed, and killed—had reached him.

The King was pacing now, his eyes moving from one to another among his barons. "The granting of lands within a realm lies in the purview of its king and no one else, and those lands, once granted, may not be rescinded without just cause. Scotland is a small realm compared with ours, and nowhere near as rich, with fewer worthwhile lands to grant. And that is a lesson we must hammer home to these ingrates. Our realm is *full* of Scots. We have whole *towns* of Scotsmen living in our northern domains. But as of this day, that changes!"

He swung back to Bruce, extending a pointing finger. "You, my lord Bruce, will, with your six hundred men, embark upon a circuit of this region, the very heartland of our realm. You will ride north through Essex and thence into the shires of Suffolk, Cambridge, and Northampton, whence you will return by way of Warwick, Oxford, Berkshire, and Middlesex—the richest lands in all our realm, mark you. FitzHugh will arm you with the documents and authorization you need, as well as clerics to record your passage. In every county that you pass through you will find fine estates—magnificent estates—held in the name of Balliol, the puling King of Scotland. But now as he treats me and mine, so shall I treat him. You will haul down the standard of Balliol above each and every one of those houses and castles, replacing them with our own royal standard. I, Richard Plantagenet, now dispossess John Balliol and declare all his possessions in this realm forfeit to the Crown of England. His days of English wealth are at an end, and you, whom he himself betrayed and dispossessed, will be my instrument in demonstrating that."

His brows twitched in a frown. "Mind you, I want no blood spilt, Bruce. The lands and houses therein may be nominally his but all their folk, from soldiery to servants and tenantry, are English. Once they see the way of things, they will cause you no trouble. But to be sure, you will leave a score or two of men—more, if you see fit—at each place you seize, replenishing your force from the people in place there, so that your strength will remain constant at six hundred. Is that clear?"

"It is, my liege." Fighting to keep his face expressionless, Bruce dared say no more. His mind was reeling at the scope of the task he had been set, scrabbling to form some notion of the time it would take to complete the circuit Edward had described. And it had barely penetrated his awareness that the execution of his charge would incorporate his own profound revenge for the ill done to him and his kin by the very man he would now impoverish.

"And you accept the charge?"

"Of course, my liege."

"Well then, go off and do it. A day of preparation here with FitzHugh, ten days to raise your own cadre and warn your fellow knights, ten more to assemble their five hundred. Within four weeks, by Yuletide, you will be on the road. Are we agreed?"

"Yes, my liege."

"Excellent, then. We will be keen to hear of your success, and in the meantime we have much else to achieve. Go now with FitzHugh. He has everything in hand, and fare ye well, young Bruce."

"Thank you, my lord King."

The seneschal already had everything in hand. Within the hour, Bruce had met the quartet of recording scribes who would accompany him on his travels, four Cistercian monks from the same monastery that appeared to supply all the King's requirements in the matter of keeping records. They had a spacious wagon at their disposal, covered by a leather canopy and drawn by two of a complement of eight mules. The rear section of the vehicle was packed with chests containing everything the clerics might need to perform their tasks, in addition to three smaller chests containing the officially signed and sealed writs that Bruce would need in the course of his travels. Each property he was to repossess in the King's name as he progressed was named in sequence and described, along with directions for where to find it. A second, smaller wagon contained ceremonials: royal standards and the ropes with which to raise them, and a plethora of additional materials that Bruce was content to leave to the attention of others. There was also a wagon containing a fully stocked field kitchen and another heavy dray loaded with bags of feed grain for the draft animals.

Best of all, though, in Bruce's opinion, was the discovery that this headquarters unit, as he thought of it, was under the command of the same royal guard sergeant and corporals who had brought him here, and that they had two score of their own men with them, in full royal livery, to bolster Bruce's credibility—should ever that be needed—as a personal representative of King Edward.

Immediately upon his return to Writtle, he split his royal guard detachment into three ten-man squads, each with an officer and an attendant cleric, and dispatched them to deliver the orders for his knightly neighbours to assemble, each with his fifty men, and place themselves under his command within a week of receiving their instructions.

He knew only five of the eleven knights, and those five but slightly, having met them briefly in company with his grandfather during his intermittent filial visits from the north in the previous two years. He anticipated no trouble from any of them, though, for his mandate from the King was absolute. They might dislike him individually, might even resent him for his youth or see him as an interloper, but Bruce was genuinely surprised to recognize his own indifference to that. It was their obedience and cooperation he required, not their approval, and he was content to know they would obey him without question as the King's agent. Of far more concern to him was the force he would command.

He needed this to be a single force, united and dependable, looking to him for leadership rather than to their individual liege knights, and that, he knew, would be the greatest difficulty facing him from the moment they started to assemble at Writtle. The little military training most of these men might have would have been dunned into them by the knights to whom they were bound in service. Some would be well trained, but others would be less so, and some, inevitably, would be pathetic and inept. But the fact was that he would have no time to train them to work together. His orders were precise: to begin his sweep of the heartlands before Yuletide.

Not unusually, Bruce realized afterwards, it was Thomas Beg who proposed the only workable solution, offering it offhandedly when nothing was expected of him. They had been idly watching the remaining ten men of the King's Guard as they sat around their two tents, keeping themselves busy by cleaning their armour and weapons and mending whatever needed mending.

"Which o' them d'ye think will get here first?" Thomas Beg asked. The summons had gone out three days before.

Bruce shrugged. "Montmorency, I would guess. He's closest, less than six miles from here."

"An' what think ye o' him?"

"Barely know the man. But he's young enough to look respectable. Well put together and with an appearance of competence, I thought."

"Ye liked him, then?"

"I didn't *dis*like him. Why do you ask?"

"Because he's one o' eleven, and among them they could cause you grief."

"How so?"

"Their men and how they treat them. Together wi' ours, they'll be an army o' six hundred, but in truth they'll be a wheen o' different gangs—fifty in each. It'll take a fell, dour hand to keep them a' in order."

Bruce had been thinking the same thing for days. "Aye, and it won't be mine, for I can't take the time to do it. I'll confess, though, I don't know who it might be, and I do know it needs to be someone capable. The damnable part is that I don't even know most of these knights by sight. One of them might be capable of doing what we need, but until I've met them all I won't know, yea or nay."

"Beltane."

"Beltane? The old pagan festival—the one that's Easter now? What about it?"

"It's a man's name. The King's sergeant. He's your man."

"He's a sergeant, Tam."

"Aye, he is. And one o' the best in this land. I spoke wi' him the other day, when we were in Westminster. He's a good man. He's been guardin' Edward's back for years, since he was a boy. Saved his life twice in Wales and then refused a knighthood. Content to stay as he is, he said. A dour man, but ye winna find better anywhere."

Bruce eyed him curiously. "I don't doubt it, but I need somebody for this task that the other knights will heed. And they won't heed a common sergeant, no matter how good he is at what needs to be done."

"They will, gin you tell them to frae the outset. An' make him a captain. They might no' like it, but they'll hae no choice." He paused, reading the doubt in Bruce's face. "Think about what ye said, man. They're knights, wi' grand ideas o' themsel's, no doubt. But you're an earl an' you're Edward's own choice to lead this thing, and any fool knows this King winna thole anything that thwarts his will. If you say Beltane is to be your choice to train this rabble that they've brought to be your troops—to drill some sense into them— then hell mend the lot o' them if they dinna like it. What can they do, complain to Edward that they'll no' go because ye've insulted them?"

"By the sweet Christ, Thomas, you might be right." Bruce held up a hand to silence whatever might come next from the big Scot. "That's how the Romans did it, when they ruled the world. One man, the senior centurion, commanded an entire legion in matters of discipline, training, and procedures. Six to ten thousand men he commanded. They called him the *primus pilus*, the First Spear, and he answered only to the commander of his legion. By Christ, that might work! Why not?" He stopped short, his face falling. "But would Beltane accept such a position? You said yourself, he refused advancement from the King, so what's the likelihood of his accepting this? No point in us even thinking of it if he won't stand for it."

Thomas Beg grinned. "Have you ever *looked* at the man? Then do it next time ye see him. I don't know what your fancy Romans looked like, but scarce a single one o' them could outface Beltane in matters o' pride and appearance. I think he'd jump at this, were you to offer it—the chance to make an army out o' a rabble. It's his life, as well as his callin'. And wi' you to back him up an' keep the other knights frae interferin', I think he might work magic for ye. The other two, the corporals, I think he might like to promote them, make them sergeants, too, gin ye agree, and then they could make up some new corporals to replace them. It's a wee enough army, but it could be a fine one by the time we're finished."

"Tam, you're an inspiration. Send him to me as soon as he gets back and we'll get started on it. He's been gone what, three days? He should be back directly. By the time the first contingents get here, we can have the plan in place." He grinned wryly. "Thomas Beg, if this works out I will be greatly in your debt."

"Aye. Again," said Tam, turning away.

The matter of Sergeant Beltane's duties was quickly settled. It transpired that the stone-faced veteran was a great admirer of the Roman legions and their discipline and tactics. Beltane took to Bruce's notion instantly, and by the time they both stood up, more than three hours had fled and the newly promoted captain was counting off reminders on his fingers. Indeed, he appeared to relish the challenge of welding the incoming levies, within a few short weeks, into a functioning military unit. It would be a thankless task at first, they both knew, but not impossible.

Their little army never did become a proficient fighting force, but it quickly learned a basic discipline and became at least outwardly cohesive, able to march in good order and to present the crisp appearance Bruce demanded. The knights were sceptical at the outset, some of them openly resentful at having to defer to an unfamiliar subordinate in the handling of their own men, but within days they saw the advantage to themselves in having someone else perform the daily tasks of drill, training, and discipline, and they had sufficient brains among them to recognize the simple truth that no harm would come to them from having the behaviour and performance of their people thus enhanced. The royal guards were the only group who looked uniform, thanks to the King's livery they wore, but the other groups, motley as they were, formed natural divisions, each fifty strong and marching under a knight's banner. They marched in double groupings, a hundred men to each unit, the paired elements marching abreast where space permitted and alternating front and rear where it did not. Bruce was not unhappy with the result.

He was less than happy with the expedition itself, though, for its day-to-day sameness in the first two months of the new year of 1296 was debilitating to everyone, and by the end of January they had not yet reached the northernmost point of their route. They made fair progress, for the roads in that region were uniformly good; long, straight, and well drained, they had far outlived the Roman engineers who had built them a millennium earlier. But the men constantly had to strike away from those roads and into the countryside, in search of the places they had come to find, and winter had settled about their ears since they'd left home. The trees were bare, the incessant wind had that sullen chill that penetrated even the warmest of garments, and the grass underfoot was long and rank and wet from the constant rain and foggy drizzle. A sudden cold snap in Northampton had brought snow to add to their discomfort, and the rank and file of their soldiery grew bored and fractious as their armour chilled and chafed at them.

Most of the Balliol houses they visited were simply what the name implied, wealthy, strongly built places surrounded by several acres of land, but some were castles, and three of those were surrounded by vast estates. They had encountered no difficulty anywhere, the King's writ and Bruce's authority accepted without demur, but those larger estates had required detailed surveys and reports to be compiled by the recording clerics, and so three times Bruce had been forced to spend a week or more in one place while the infuriating records were drawn up. And throughout everything it seemed as though they rode and marched in utter isolation.

He found the dearth of news from beyond their route to be the most frustrating element of their sortie, the truth of it soon borne home to him by the very dullness of their progress. He had expected at first that, sooner or later, the news of his little army's advent would precede them as word sped from one to another of the Balliol holdings along their route, but it never happened, and he was forced to conclude that the urgency of his mission existed in his mind alone. The houses and estates he repossessed in the name of King Edward were simply that—individual and self-centred. None of their occupants had any thoughts of other, similar holdings beyond their own; each small group lived in its own little world, self-contained and self-sufficient. Each household showed initial surprise at being summarily repossessed, but they all adjusted quickly. Most of the occupants had never even seen, let alone met, their titular owner, the foreign King of Scotland, and since the repossession seldom entailed anything other than the changing of the royal standards above the roofs and parapets and the removal of anything that visually asserted Balliol's presence, the household staff invariably shrugged philosophically and carried on with their routines, so that Bruce had not even needed to leave any of his own men in place.

These houses were all English, after all; their people were English for the most part and they had no slightest difficulty in transferring their allegiance back to the English Crown.

More than any other thing that tugged at him, though, he missed Isabella savagely, often tossing and turning late into the night as he pined for her and wondered how she was faring without him. He had no real misgivings over her safety, though he often thanked God that he had decided to leave Thomas Beg behind to care for her, but he fretted constantly about their enforced separation and he was haunted by his memories of her despair over her failure to become pregnant. He began to fear that at his present rate of progress he might never win back to her.

It was not until they reached Oxford, homeward bound on the last day of February, that Bruce heard anything of what had been going on in other parts during his wanderings. They found an elderly Scots knight in residence at the last great house they stopped at. His name was Crawford, Sir Hector Crawford of Bootle, and Bruce guessed his age at seventy and perhaps even older. He was delighted to welcome Bruce, apparently attaching no significance to the purpose of his visit, and made a point of telling him that he had once served with old Lord Robert for ten years, when they were both young and hale.

Speaking alone with Sir Hector mere hours after his arrival, Bruce was perplexed at first by the old knight's enthusiasm and garrulity, for living in a Balliol house as he was, the old fellow must have known that this visit from a Bruce, representing England's King and claiming possession of the estate, could bode nothing but ill for his master. The old man's pleasure was unfeigned, however, and listening to his prattling and the way it went without logic from one topic to another, it gradually became clear to Bruce that the old man's mind had been somehow impaired, perhaps by his age. Whatever the reason, Sir Hector spoke out freely on whatever came to mind and showed no reticence about discussing things that would have been held close by a younger, fitter man. At one point, he confided that his eldest son had come to visit him from Scotland, privily, mere days before and had brought news of great, exciting portent. Scotland and France had made a treaty of alliance against England, he said, negotiated in France by several earls and bishops.

Bruce sat up straight as his mind snapped back to Edward's question months earlier on the whereabouts of Bishop Fraser of St. Andrews. He recalled how Sir James Jardine had very carefully not looked at anyone. The old man was still babbling away, and Bruce leaned closer, afraid now to miss a word. The two realms had aided each other in such matters before, the old knight was saying; for more than a hundred years now they had been close, but this new alliance would see England's power set at naught. A wapinschaw— a council of war—had been held earlier, and the summons had been sent out to the entire Scottish host, from north and south of Forth, to assemble at Caddonlee, near Selkirk, by the eleventh day of March.

*War!* Caddonlee was the traditional rallying ground for armies preparing to invade England. Bruce could barely contain himself, for this was information of incalculable worth, and he had to sit still, forcing himself to smile and nod in pretended innocence as he thought frantically of how quickly he could pass this news on to Edward in Westminster. He reviewed the mental list of the knights under his command and chose two of them to send directly. Ralph de Montmorency would be one, he decided, and Sir Ranulf Mortimer, whom he had come to know and like, would be the other. Two men, each making his own way alone and accompanied by a ten-man escort. That should be sufficient.

It was another hour before he could find two of the Cistercian clerics and dictate his tidings to King Edward. He signed both copies, noting that neither monk had betrayed the slightest interest in what was being written, then sent for Mortimer and Montmorency. He gave them their orders and told them to be on the road by dawn, knowing that each of them would do his utmost to reach Westminster ahead of the other and deliver the letter personally to the King.

He would not discover, until he reached Westminster again in mid-March to find the King long since departed, that word of what Edward called the foul Scotch perfidy had already reached the monarch ahead of Bruce's letters and had incensed him to a towering fury the likes of which no one could recall. He had immediately cancelled his plans to leave for France and reassigned his armies, the strongest in Christendom after years of war in France and victory in Wales. He would lead them to Scotland himself and, faced with the threat of this new alliance, his barons would support him to a man. The Scottish host would have gathered at Caddonlee by the eleventh of March, but Edward's armies had been at Newcastle, poised to attack, on March the first.

When they left Westminster, Bruce led his little army to Montmorency's castle, which lay between London and Writtle, and disbanded it there on a sunny, blustery day in the last week of March. Before he dismissed the men he thanked them for their support and commiserated with them that they had missed seeing the King at Westminster, for he had led them there to do precisely that, hoping that Edward would deign to recognize their service over the past three months. Captain Beltane and his guardsmen had remained behind at the palace, already preparing to march north to join the King, whose armies must have marched past them unseen on their way to Scotland, and it was left to Bruce to thank the eleven knights in whose company he had spent so much time. They were all as eager to return to their homes as he was, so the farewells were brief. Then, left alone with his own men, he gave the signal and spurred his horse towards Writtle and Isabella.

He spent the final two miles in a fever of expectation and fighting against the urge to whip his horse into a gallop and simply leave his men to follow at their own pace. But that, he decided, would be both disloyal and demeaning; he was not the only one impatient for the sight of a loving face after so long a journey, and he owed it to them, at the very least, to share their last hour of anticipation and anxiety.

He sensed the moment when they were first seen from the house, and soon he heard the warning horn blaring from the walls, announcing their arrival. And then at last they were approaching the gates and he was looking for Isabella among the bustling throng ahead of him. It was only when he saw she was not there and the pain began to well up in him that he thought to look up at the roof of the tower, and there she was, waving to him.

Thomas Beg stepped forward, smiling up at him. "Welcome home, my lord. Her ladyship's waitin' for ye. I'll see the men dismissed. Away ye go."

Bruce swung his leg over the front of his saddle and dropped easily to the ground. He handed Tam the reins and punched him on the shoulder. "Good to see you, Thomas," he growled, then made his way directly to the house, noticing that Isabella had already left the roof.

The words were churning around in his head as he ran up the stairs, but he forgot them all as soon as he saw her smiling at him from the landing by their rooms. She was even more beautiful than he had remembered, and she was laughing and reaching for him and ... By God, she was pregnant! He stopped dead, gaping at her, at the difference three months had wrought in her, her belly rounded and prominent and her face radiantly happy.

"Robert," she said, shy now as he stepped wide-eyed towards her. "I ... I had a surprise for you."

"By God you did, lass." His voice was thick and guttural, his windpipe choked by a swelling lump. "The best surprise a man could have. Come here."

She sprang forward into his arms, and as he swept her up, his senses spinning with the well-remembered, long-desired smell of her, he thought his legs might betray him and send them both crashing to the stone flags of the floor. But they held, and they bore him and his cherished burden effortlessly in long strides towards the open bedchamber door. He carried her inside, kicking the door shut behind them, and kissed her as he had dreamed of kissing her for months, aware of the yielding, pliant weight of her filling his arms and the feel of her fingers hooking into his hair as though she would never let him go. His heart hammering, he bore her straight to the bed and lowered her there, following her downward into a wonderland of groping, clutching hands and insensate hunger as they sought all they could find of each other.

Suddenly he thrust himself away and froze.

His wife pushed herself up from the bed on one elbow, a strange look on her face. "Robert? What ails you? What is it, my love?"

"I don't want to hurt you," he said quietly, his voice filled with bewilderment.

"Hurt me? How could you possibly hurt me?" Her voice faltered. "Unless by rejecting me? Is that what's wrong? Do you not want me? Do I disgust you?"

"Disgust me? Christ Jesus, Izzy, I've dreamed of nothing but this for months, of holding you and feeling you around me. But ... I don't want to hurt the baby."

"The baby?" Her face cleared suddenly and she laughed, the sound a mixture of relief and joy. But then she raised herself up strongly, hooking an arm around his neck and making hushing, crooning sounds as she pulled him gently down to where she could cover his face with fluttering, down-light kisses. "We cannot hurt the baby, my love," she whispered into his ear as her kisses became nibbles and moist licks. "Not by loving each other. Not now, nor in the months to come. There's ample room for both of you together inside me, and I can think of nothing I want more than that. So come now, take off all those smelly clothes and fill me up and show me how you love me."

He rose hesitantly to his knees, looking at her askance. "Are you sure? How can you know that?"

She laughed again, gazing up at him with adoration in her eyes. "Because it's true, my love. Every woman knows it. Quick now!" She reached for his belt but he evaded her hand.

"That sounds like old wives' nonsense. How can we be sure? There's ... " He waved a hand at her belly. "There can be little room in there."

Her smile was surer now. "There's more room than we need, Robert Bruce, believe me. And besides, it's true! No old wives' nonsense about it, though old wives are better placed to know such things than any man. Think you every man goes without love throughout the time it takes his wife to bear a child? That's silly, my love. Besides, I talked of it with Allie, and she knows everything about such things. Come here." She reached for him again and again he deflected her grasp.

"But what if I hit it with … What if I injure it, or you?"

"It's not an *it*, my love. It's a *him*, perhaps a *her*, and you can't injure either one, I swear." Her eyes were alight with mischief now. "And you know in your heart and head that nothing you can do to me like that will injure me … Though you can hurt me by denying me what I need and want. I want to feel you moving in me, loving me. I want to feel your need and draw it out of you."

"But—"

"No." She pushed herself upright and placed her fingers on his lips. "No buts."

Afterwards, between the soaring need of their first coupling and the subsequent stirrings of slowly renewed desire, as she lay cradling his shrunken maleness in her hand, he thought he heard her giggle— a gentle, muffled snort that she could not quite conceal—and he peered at her sleepily.

"What?" he murmured. "You find your goodman laughable?"

"No, my love, I find you adorable … It but struck me as strange that a knight champion, an earl of the realm and a leader of men who carries the sword of a famed ancestor—such a heavy, massy thing with a long blade of shiny, lethal steel—" She snorted again.

"Damn it, woman, you are laughing at me."

She snuggled closer, kissing his shoulder, her fingers squeezing gently. "No, truly, my lord of Carrick, I am not … " Her fingers moved again, knowingly but almost absently. "I would never laugh at you, my love. But it amuses me that such a puissant knight, with such a great, long, steely sword, should be afraid to stab with such a gentle dagger as this in my hand, for fear of doing damage."

He lay still, enjoying for a while the play of her fingers.

"It was … inexperience and ignorance caused my fear," he said finally. "Bear in mind, woman, that this knight champion, as you alone deem him, has never killed a man. Nor has that weighty blade he bears spilt blood since the death of its former owner, William the Marshal. In all such things I am a neophyte, as virgin as were you on our wedding night."

She rose up over him, leaning again on one elbow as she looked down into his face and stooped to kiss his eyes. "I know, my lord," she whispered, "and I revere you for that. Killing is not in you." He grunted, enjoying her lips on his closed lids, and she drew back to look at him again. "What are you sounding so gruff about? Would you have it otherwise? Do you regret that innocence?"

He opened his eyes and looked at her gravely. "No, Izzy, I don't, but it's not like to last. We are at war with Scotland. Did you know?"

She stiffened, but then he felt the reaction pass and she lowered her head to his chest again. "Aye," she said, almost inaudibly. "Thomas Beg told me weeks ago, when first the word arrived from Westminster. The armies had already left to march north by then." She lay silent, but by glancing down with lowered eye Bruce could see her gnawing at her knuckle.

"Your father will be safe," he said softly. "Edward knows who he is and is obliged to him, not least for having sent you here."

"It's not my father … It's the whole thing. War … I fear for Scotland."

He rolled away from her and swung his legs to sit on the edge of the bed. "Scotland can look to itself," he growled. "The magnates prepared for war and called out the army. They brought this folly on themselves. By making treaty with the French behind his back they thought to disarm Edward, render him impotent. Fools that they are, they'll rue it. Edward Plantagenet is no man's dupe, and their madness, underestimating him, has given him the one thing he had needed most to strengthen his position. In defying him like this they have united the barons of England in his cause. Few of them would support a war in France, but a war in Scotland, with land and titles to be won and no great way to travel? They'll fall on the magnates like swarms of angry wasps. It won't last long, you'll see."

Isabella was staring at him now, her face as troubled as his own. "Are you saying Scotland cannot win?"

"Against Edward's might and righteousness? They have no chance."

He was thinking of his grandfather again, remembering the old man's scornful dismissal of the true strength of Scotland's armies, and he repeated Lord Robert's words without thinking of the effect they might have on his wife. "Scotland has not fought a war in more than thirty years, not since the fight at Largs, against the Norwegian King Haakon. And that was more a skirmish than a battle. The Norwegians were ready to leave by then and put up little fight. Since then the Scots have fought no one, not even themselves. They haven't fought a *real* war since the days of King David, more than sixty years ago, and since then they've forgotten anything they ever knew of warfare. Except in their own minds. They remember glories past fondly enough, but they've done nothing to prepare for fights to come."

"But they will fight," Isabella said. "My father sent me word. The host was to meet at Caddonlee, this month."

He sprang to his feet and began to pace, unaware of his nakedness. "Aye, and so it would. And they will fight, but with what, and for what? They have no cavalry to match the English heavy horse, no fighting leadership, no battle commanders with experience. England has ten times the men Scotland can raise, and fighting men to lead them. Its armies are fat and strong with victories in France and Wales and think themselves unbeatable. And they are, as far as Scotland is concerned. This war is madness."

"There will be slaughter done, then." He heard the tone of her voice and turned quickly to look at her, only then seeing her tears, and he moved quickly back to the bed to comfort her, holding her close and kissing her eyes.

"Sweet Christ, lass, there, there … " He rocked her in his arms, speaking to her gently, as if she were a child. "Edward is no monster.

There might be one big battle—almost surely must be—but it will be swiftly won, and after that the magnates will lose heart and beg for peace. You'll see. Edward is feudal overlord. Most of the magnates are his legal vassals, in feudal and in canon law. They are in rebellion, surely, but for what they mistakenly believe to be just cause. Their loyalties have faltered because of Balliol's damnable lack of backbone. But misled though they are, they can't have lost all their sanity, and it would be to Edward's great disadvantage to be too harsh on them. You wait and see. They'll sue for terms as soon as they realize they cannot win, and Edward will take them back into his peace. He'll punish them, for they deserve punishment, but he'll forgive them once they swear their fealty to him again.

"Aye." Her voice was a whisper. "The magnates will survive. But what about the folk?"

He hugged her even tighter. "Aye, some of them will die in battle, certainly, for that's the way of war. But the real folk of Scotland— ordinary people like Thomas Beg and Allie and their ilk every- where—will overcome their troubles and continue as before, Izzy. They care little for the caperings of the magnates, just so be it they are left alone to live their lives as they always have in the past. They'll disperse when the truce is called and return to their homes. You'll see."

"I pray you are right, Robert … " She still sounded distant and unsure. "So you believe Edward will be merciful? Truly?"

"Why should he not, my love? He has nothing to gain, else. He doesn't seek Scotland's Crown for his own realm. He but seeks to bring the magnates to heel and settle matters for the good of his own peace. Once that's achieved to his satisfaction, he'll relent. He has too many other matters on his mind, in France, to waste his time in Scotland." He kissed her again, this time on the forehead. "Trust me," he whispered. "I know my King."

Spring warmed the air and melted into summer before any word reached Writtle of the war in the north, and when it did start to trickle in, the details were more rumour than fact, patchy, piecemeal, and incomplete. There had been a battle and a great victory, it seemed, at some place called Dummar, where hundreds of Scots knights and nobles had been captured and were being held for ransom. Bruce doubted the little he heard about it, mistrusting popular enthusiasm, though the place might have been Dunbar, he thought. There was a Scottish stronghold there, one of the strongest in the country, it was said, but even then, such an explanation made no sense to him, for no pitched battle could involve a fortress. A siege, yes, that was a different thing. But sieges were slow and complex affairs—campaigns rather than battles—and insufficient time had passed for the mounting of a successful siege.

Within the following week, though, tidings arrived of yet another confrontation, this one far more likely, involving an assault on Berwick, on the border. Berwick was the gateway to southern Scotland, a coastal town with a mercantile trade, extensive docks, and impregnable defences centred upon a strongly built castle. It was arguably Scotland's strongest and most thriving burgh, the maritime centre where cargoes of wool were assembled from all of southern Scotland before being shipped off to the manufactories of the countries across the North Sea. The source of this report was the eyewitness testimony of a crew of seamen from the English ship *The Fair Lass*, who had been lying off Berwick on the thirtieth of March and had witnessed the English capture of the town. Later they had been caught in a storm in the North Sea and blown far off course. Their stricken vessel had struggled into the port of Maldon, less than ten miles from Writtle, for repairs.

Bruce heard the story from Thomas Beg, who had ridden into Maldon to trade a wagonload of grain for ropes and cordage and overheard the story being told in a tavern there. The next day Bruce himself rode to Maldon to discover what he could for himself.

He found *The Fair Lass* easily, high and dry and under repair by an army of shipwrights and carpenters, but her captain was not there and Bruce had to seek him in a nearby tavern, where the seaman was meeting with the man in charge of the repairs to his ship. Both men looked up impatiently when Bruce appeared beside their table, but a single glance at his clothing served to stifle any protest they might have made, and when Bruce asked which of them was captain of *The Fair Lass* they exchanged glances and one stood up to leave, saying he would return later. The other, a thickset fellow in his thirties with a deeply weathered face, made no move to stand but nodded pleasantly enough to Bruce and indicated the chair the first man had vacated. Bruce nodded back, equally pleasantly, and sat down across from him as the tavern keeper came bustling over to look after the well-dressed newcomer. Bruce ordered ale for both of them, but the seaman waved a hand over his tankard to indicate that he needed no more. As the tavern keeper hurried away he cocked a bushy eyebrow at Bruce.

"How can I help you, sir? Or should I say my lord?"

Bruce's mouth quirked. "Sir will do well enough for now. I'm here for information and prepared to pay for it."

The cocked eyebrow levelled out. "Then you have questions. Ask away, but I can't promise to be able to answer them, not having any notion of what you're looking for ... "

Bruce waited until a foaming tankard was set in front of him by the officious tavern keeper. He flipped the man a silver coin he had been holding since he entered and then watched the fellow scuttle away before he lifted his flagon. "Is this worth drinking?"

The seaman shrugged. "It's said to be the best in Maldon. But that's not saying much."

Bruce sipped, then drank, enjoying the cool bite of the ale. "Good enough," he said, setting the mug down. "A man of mine was in town yesterday, in one of the taverns. He told me he had heard some member of your crew talking about King Edward's attack on the Scots town of Berwick at the end of March. That's all he heard, or all that he could trust, so I decided to come and find you for myself in the hope that you might tell me more."

"Hmm. Why? Who are you?" He watched Bruce's eyes and his eyebrow rose again. "You'll pardon me, I hope, but there's a war going on and I have no need, and no wish, to go spouting off opinions that could be taken amiss. I'm a loyal English seafarer, not a soldier or a plotter."

Bruce shrugged. "I am Robert Bruce, Earl of Carrick. And you?"

"Samuel Cromwell, mariner, as you know … Carrick? That's in Scotland, is it not? And I know the name of Bruce. Are you not a Scot yourself?"

"I am by birth, though outlawed by the King of Scots for holding loyal to King Edward. In all else I am English."

The brown face remained impassive save for a tiny wrinkling of the skin about the eyes, and Bruce found himself warming to this cautious but forthright man.

"Then why are you not in Scotland with the King? He'd want his earls about him, I should think."

"I would be, but he himself set me a task before he left for Scotland and I've been working on it ever since. I've been repossessing the Scots King's English holdings in King Edward's name."

The inquisitive eyebrow flickered again. "Then what can I tell you, Lord Bruce?"

"Was the report my man heard true? Were you in Berwick when the attack occurred?"

"Not in it, but I was close offshore. Our army had been sighted to the south the day before and the entire town reacted. We were barely half-laden, with a cargo of wool for Norway. Everything went mad from the moment the first alarm went up and I lost more than half my loaders. They all ran to the walls to see the English army for themselves. If you know Berwick, you'll know the quays are on the northeastern shore, inside the arc of the walls and supposedly out of sight—and reach of attack—from the south."

"Supposedly, you say. Were the Scots afraid? Did you sense that?"

"No, they were … jubilant was the word that occurred to me at the time. They thought they were safe behind their walls. Me, I was angry. I'd been hoping to be laden early and to make the tide. Took me three hours longer than it ought to have to finish taking on cargo and I had to use some of my own crew to get it done. All to no end.

We missed the tide and I was stuck out in the shallows, a quarter of a mile offshore with the supply fleet that came up in support of our army.

"And what happened? What did you see?"

Cromwell inhaled deeply. "More than I wanted to. Our forces took the town before the day was out."

"They stormed the walls in a single day?"

"They didn't need to. They went around the side, to where the endmost walls along the shore were wooden palisades that hadn't been maintained. The townspeople were up on the stone walls facing the main army, but the flanking forces went around unobserved to the weak point. They pulled a section down within an hour and that was that—it was all over. Our people fought their way inside from there and it was as though they had an open gate. Hell, it *was* an open gate. And once they were inside, the inhabitants gave up without a fight. Someone opened the main gates and let the army in." His mouth twisted in a humourless grin. "For a place that was supposed to be untakeable, it didn't last long."

"Did you go back into the town?"

"Go back? Do I look mad? My ship is called *The Fair Lass*, not *The Fearless*. No, I stayed right where I was. The army went in under the red flag. I caught the morning tide and cleared the place as quickly as I could." He shuddered and waved a hand as though to thrust the memory away.

"But your ship is English, and I presume your crew is, too, so what would you have to fear by going back?"

Cromwell looked around the room, but there was no one watching them or sitting close enough to hear. Nevertheless he hunched forward over the table and lowered his voice when he spoke again. "Understand this, my lord. My ship was laden, ready to go, and my crew was safe aboard. All I lacked was water under my keel, to carry me over the sandbars of the estuary. I wasn't even tempted to return, and especially not after the screaming started."

"What screaming?" Even as he asked the question Bruce knew he did not want to hear the answer. He knew full well what the dreaded red flag meant—it was the signal to annihilate the enemy. "Tell me."

"We were close inshore, remember, and the sound carried over the water. There was great slaughter done that night, throughout the night and into the dawn. They burned the town, all of it, even the Dutchmen's Hall where the traders gathered. I saw that with my own eyes and it was no accidental fire. There was fighting there. Some people, perhaps the merchants themselves, had locked themselves inside before the sun set and were fighting back. We watched a large body of men attack the place and be turned back, and then the fire was set to burn out whoever was in there ... "

"And did they come out?"

"You tell me, for you know as much as I do now. None of us saw what happened at the end, once the sun went down. We heard the roar of the fires, and the screams, but we could see nothing from where we were."

Bruce was unable to believe what he was hearing.

"How many—?" He stopped and cleared his throat. "Were you to guess ... How many deaths think you there might have been?"

The seaman sighed. "Did you have people there?"

"No, thank God. But I know the town."

"No, my lord, you knew it once. It was still burning when we sailed away. As to your question, with the red flag flying ... " His shake of the head was slow, ponderous. "Thousands, I would say, from what we heard that night. Perhaps the entire town. I simply don't know, Lord Bruce. But I know I have nothing more to tell you. We left on the tide and we were glad to be gone."

There was nothing more to say. Bruce thanked the man for his time and offered him a gold piece, but Cromwell shrugged it away. "I haven't earned that," he said flatly. "All I have done is speak of things that shouldn't be mentioned. I've been to Berwick many times and knew the people there. They were as much like us as any other Englishman could be. It sickens me enough to think that English soldiery could act that way anywhere, but to do what they did, where they did? That makes me ashamed of my own folk."

The eleventh of July marked Bruce's twenty-second birthday, though the event went unacknowledged by everyone except Isabella, who presented him with a magnificent pair of riding boots, ordered months earlier from London to mark the occasion of his first birthday as her husband. He wore them daily thereafter because they were not only beautiful but practical, soft and supple despite their weight and substance, and perfectly suited to the way he walked, which could not always be said of riding boots.

Several more weeks elapsed with no word from Carlisle, though, and by that time Bruce had grown seriously worried about his father. The Lord of Annandale had never been a letter writer, but even so Bruce felt that Carlisle's situation on the very border of the south-western invasion route from Scotland should have merited a communication of some kind, if only a word to let his family in the south know that he was alive. He himself had intended to write to his father, but in the aftermath of returning to Writtle and finding Izzy pregnant he had let the matter slide, telling himself that Carlisle would have been relatively unaffected by the hostilities thanks to Edward's pre-emptive strike into Scotland. Now, though, with so much time having elapsed in silence, he acknowledged guiltily to himself that he might have been less than perfectly filial in not contacting his father.

The end of July was approaching by the time he finally gave in to his uncertainties and decided to ride to Westminster in search of substantial news and information. Isabella was seven months into her carrying term by then, her tiny body made to look even smaller by the grotesque hugeness of the burden she was carrying inside her, and even though the road between Writtle and London was an excellent one and the weather appeared to hold no threats, Bruce and Allie both agreed, over Izzy's outraged protests, that the potential hazards of a fifty-mile return journey in a poorly sprung coach were far too high to justify the risks. She finally relented and agreed to remain in Writtle when Bruce pointed out that the journey would be pointless for her even in the best of circumstances, since Edward himself was still in Scotland. Without his royal presence and with all his glittering entourage accompanying the monarch on campaign, Westminster would be an empty shell, inhabited only by those senior ministers of the Crown whose duties kept them in place, running the kingdom in the King's absence.

Two days later, Bruce and Thomas Beg arrived in Westminster to find the place surprisingly busy, though in a way that Bruce had never seen before. The precincts surrounding the main buildings were crowded with soldiers and their officers, and scores of saddled horses were drawn up in ordered ranks in the great courtyard within the main gates. Bruce had never seen horses in the inner yard before, but judging by the dried manure scattered all over the cobblestones, this had evidently become a commonplace with the King not in residence and the constant comings and goings of mounted personnel. The guards were still in place where they always were, though, and Bruce presented himself to the guard sergeant on duty, asking to be announced to Sir Robert FitzHugh. The sergeant nodded, apparently recognizing Bruce, and sent a guardsman to accompany him to where he could wait for FitzHugh to receive him. A short time later he was shown into an anteroom where a good half score of other people were already waiting.

Waiting turned out to be the operative word, because Bruce sat there in silence for two hours while others came and went, though none of them was sent for by the seneschal. He was thoroughly bored and out of sorts by the time the door opened and FitzHugh crossed directly to him with an outstretched, welcoming hand, apologizing for having kept him waiting for so long. He had been in conference, he said, but was now free, at least for the moment, to spend some time with Bruce. He waved in invitation, and Bruce followed him from the room, all impatience banished by the warmth of the old man's welcome.

Sir Robert's private quarters were located close to the centre of palace activity, as was fitting for the seneschal, and he led Bruce into his small, private room at the rear where, in spite of its being high summer outside, a cheerful fire blazed in the grate. He went directly to a small table in one corner and uncovered a tray that held a jug of cold ale and two mugs, with new-baked, crusty bread, fresh butter, cold sliced meats, and two dishes of pickled onions and raw chopped carrots.

"Join me, my lord, if you will. I'm famished. Talking for hours on end breeds thirst and hunger both and I have been talking since dawn about one thing after another. Come, help yourself. I told them I would have a guest with me, so there is ample for both of us, and as you can see, there are two cushioned seats there by the fire ... Unless you are too warm?"

Bruce grinned and moved to the table. "Never too warm in this place, my lord FitzHugh. No matter how hot the day, the warmth never seems to penetrate the stone of castle walls ... And there were no cushions on that seat in your anteroom."

The old man smiled back at him. "Nor will that ever change. The last thing one needs in such a place is comfort for one's supplicants. Hard seats keep them suitably anxious. Sit down, sit down. I trust your countess is well?"

They talked while they ate of Isabella and her pregnancy and of how a mere man feels useless and foolish in the face of such female mysteries, and eventually they came to the purpose of Bruce's unheralded visit.

"So, I confess I was surprised to hear of your arrival this morning, my lord. It has been months since last we spoke on your return from your circuit of the Balliol estates, on which, in retrospect, I should offer my deepest congratulations. Everything is precisely as it should be there and your attention to even minor details in what you achieved—details that many another might have deemed unimportant—has not passed unnoticed. But I am sure you did not come all the way from Writtle simply to hear that. How, then, may I help you? Is there something you require?"

Bruce wiped his mouth and set his empty platter carefully on the small table by his side. "Yes, my lord, there is. I need information."

The old seneschal smiled. "Information is the most precious commodity in the world, my young friend, sought after equally by kings and paupers. May I presume you are asking about the war in Scotland?"

"Aye, sir, you may. And in Carlisle. I have heard nothing from my father since hostilities began. I know not whether he is alive or dead, and that does not sit well with me."

"Nor should it. Your father is alive and well. I had a lengthy report from him the day before yesterday, although he had written a preliminary report which I received last month. Carlisle was attacked at the outset of the war, while our main army was in the east, but thanks to Lord Robert's preparations the assault was beaten off. Since the Scots had no siege weapons and the defenders were ready for them, they turned back and went to raid elsewhere in the region—to little effect, I am glad to say. They set fire to some of the buildings in Carlisle, but the fire was quickly contained and the damage has been repaired." He took another swig of his ale.

"In his first report your father mentioned that the Scots leadership had appeared to be disjointed, which had resulted in their lack of cohesion in pressing the attack on his position, but obviously, in a report written in haste in the aftermath of the action, he had had access to little concrete information about the situation. Since then, though, the details have become more clear. The force that attacked Carlisle contained no fewer than seven earls, apparently, each with his own retinue of followers and each thinking himself the paramount leader, though the Earl of Buchan would have been in nominal command. In consequence, their invasion, as they thought of it, foundered quickly and resulted in little more than isolated raids on several nearby communities, civil and religious. As for the Scots war in itself, it is over … Has been for months."

Bruce blinked. "For months? When did it end?"

FitzHugh shrugged his shoulders eloquently and rose to carry his own empty platter to the table. "On the twenty-seventh of April," he said. "Three months ago. There were some skirmishes beyond that date, but nothing in the way of threat to our campaign."

"Sweet Jesus, that was quick. In God's name, Sir Robert, what happened?"

"From what I have been able to gather from all the reports we have amassed—not merely I myself but the other ministers in residence here—what happened was a repetition of the folly that turned the assault on Carlisle into such a shambles—incompetence and inadequacy on a staggering scale. The Scots leadership was overconfident from the start, and they showed a dismal lack of leadership on every front. No Scots leader, in fact, led anything, anywhere, other than uncoordinated and overconfident advances. Once challenged, they fell to pieces everywhere."

"And what happened to end it all on the twenty-seventh of April?"

"A battle, of sorts, at a place called Dunbar. A cavalry engagement of some kind."

"Dunbar. I heard something about that, but discounted it as idle rumour. What happened there?"

"A fiasco. Dunbar Castle belongs to the Earl of March, who has been a steadfast supporter of King Edward, as I'm sure you know. But the earl's wife, Marjory, a sister to the Earl of Buchan, was chatelaine during March's absence and took her brother's side rather than her husband's. She turned over Dunbar Castle to the rebels.

"The King was marching north from Berwick at that time and he dispatched the Earl of Surrey, Lord John de Warrenne, with a strong force of cavalry to take the castle back. But the Scots garrison, knowing we would be about their ears very quickly, had sent an urgent appeal for help to the Scots King, who was, unknown to our forces, encamped nearby, at a place called Haddington. The Scots dispatched a cavalry force as powerful as Warrenne's, although their King himself remained safely behind in his camp. The two forces met each other with very little warning. The Scots had the advantage, for they were on high ground and well disposed to repel any attack." He stopped suddenly and cocked his head, looking at Bruce inquiringly. "May I speak freely? This will go no further than this room?"

"Of course not, Sir Robert."

"Good, because I am about to voice a personal opinion, something I normally do solely to King Edward. I am no soldier, as you know, but even I can recognize folly when I see it—or read of it. As I said, the Scots had the advantage of a vastly superior position, sufficiently so for there to have been no question of attacking them. But Earl Warrenne attacked them anyway. He dispatched a large part of his forces to take the hill, and he should have lost his army then and there. But here is the tragic folly of the Scots. In order to attack the Scotch position, Warrenne's men had to turn their backs to the enemy and retrace their steps for a quarter of a mile to a spot where they could most safely climb down into a semicircular defile that lay between them and the enemy, and watching them ride away and disappear, the Scots believed they had quit the field. So what did they do? They left the high ground and charged down as a rabble to pursue and plunder the supposedly fleeing enemy. By the time they reached the bottom of the hill, they found Warrenne's cavalry advancing towards them in perfect order." He shook his head. "I cannot believe any leader could be so stupid. They were an undisciplined rabble as they streamed down from their heights and they were even more so when they encountered Warrenne's squadrons on level ground. They scattered and collapsed at the first charge. We took more than a hundred Scottish lords, knights, squires, and men-at-arms as prisoners. The rest fled westward to the great forest there."

"Selkirk Forest."

"Aye, that's the name. In any event, those prisoners are all now safely contained in England, some of them, the most notable ones, in the Tower itself."

"Here in London! Is that why there are so many soldiers about?"

"Here and everywhere else, aye. The war may be over, but the army has not been disbanded. The King himself believes Scotland is safe now, but he has yet to deal with France, and so he keeps the army ready."

"So what is happening in Scotland now? What about Balliol?"

"Balliol is no more—"

"Dear Jesus! He's dead?"

FitzHugh shook his head quickly. "No, I started to say he is no more the King of Scotland. He has been deposed."

"By Edward?" Bruce sat blinking. "But how can that be? Cretin and fool and dastard Balliol may be, but he is Scotland's anointed King. Has Edward seized the Crown, then?"

"Certainly not, nor has His Majesty any intention of so doing. Having solved the problem in Scotland and established the peace again, he is even now on his way back here."

Bruce sat back, frowning. "Pardon me, Sir Robert, but I am confused. In fact I am completely at a loss. I know I am only a simple knight, with little of a head for such affairs of state, but how can this be?"

FitzHugh smiled tolerantly. "Frankly, I can understand your confusion, my lord earl, but it really is quite a simple matter, in terms of feudal constitution. As you know well, King Edward is feudal overlord of Scotland, ratified as such by the Scots nobility several years ago. The King of Scotland, who was party to that ratification, was, and remains above and beyond all else, a feudal vassal of House Plantagenet. You yourself repossessed those assets that he held in that stead here in the south. This brief, unfortunate war we have lived through was precipitated by the actions of John Balliol— with the aid of his council of advisers, certainly—but Balliol was King there at the time, and in seeking alliance with Philip of France, King Edward's mortal enemy, and thereafter declaring war against England, he rebelled flagrantly against his feudal overlord. It was on those grounds that His Majesty dispensed his justice, proceeding not as one king against another, but as lord paramount of Scotland against a rebellious vassal who happened to be a king and used that circumstance to foment both war and rebellion. In feudal law, King Edward's hands were tied by the legalities of the situation. He had no other option in law than to insist that the delinquent vassal resign his fief. And that resignation had perforce to entail the loss of his kingship and the breaking of the seal by which he had committed his subjects to join him in his rebellion. That forfeited fief will remain in the King's hands henceforth."

"But what about the realm? The kingdom?"

"The rule of that is held in abeyance until another monarch be chosen. In the meantime, King Edward will rule directly from England, through an apparatus established to make that possible."

Bruce slowly shook his head, his eyes still wide with incomprehension, and the old minister continued.

"I know what you are thinking. This has all happened very quickly. But that victory at Dunbar, despite the folly of the move that sent our cavalry where it should not have gone, was the decisive moment of the war. King Edward moved immediately and took Dunbar Castle, then struck north with the utmost speed, and as he went, the Scots castles all fell before him. Edinburgh held out for nigh on a month before surrendering, but in Stirling, the strongest fortress in all Scotland, our scouts found the castle being held by a single gatekeeper, who fled when they approached. Fiasco was the word I used, and it's an apt one.

"King John fled northward, to beyond the River Forth, demonstrating to the world that he was even less effective as warrior and leader than he had been as monarch. He sued for peace terms soon after the fall of Edinburgh and was finally brought to trial for his crimes, at a place called … Brechin? Does that sound correct to you? My memory is not what it used to be and these alien Scots names can be devilish."

"Brechin Castle. Aye, it's in the east, in Fife, close to Montrose on the coast there. What happened at Brechin?"

"King John was arraigned there, no more, by Bishop Bek. And your memory is correct. He was then moved to the nearby burgh of Montrose. On July the seventh, he annulled and abjured the French alliance publicly and formally—his last act as a King. He was then legally deposed and taken into custody the following day, stripped of his royal arms, his seal broken, his monarchy abolished and annulled."

"Good God! And the Scots stood by for this?"

The old man spread his hands, palms up. "What else could they do, with their army defeated and the front rank of their nobility in custody? But privily I have been told that they were massively relieved to see the end of him and his unfortunate reign."

"July the eighth, you say? That was mere weeks ago. The news reached you quickly."

"It had to, for the good of England's realm and government. But the news is not yet widely known. That was the content of the meetings I have been conducting these past two days. Strictly speaking, I should not have informed you of any of this, but it will be common knowledge within the week and there will be great celebrations when King Edward returns home."

Bruce began to thank Sir Robert for his time but then hesitated, struck by another thought. "Berwick," he said.

"What about it?"

"I heard a tragic tale from a seaman who was offshore there on the day of the King's attack. He spoke of great loss of life and the town being burned. I found that scarcely credible, but he was there, he said, and insisted he had seen what he had seen. Was slaughter done there? And if so, why?"

FitzHugh shook his head solemnly. "The King commanded there in person, my lord of Carrick. I can only report what I have learned from his dispatches. The townsfolk resisted, believing themselves secure behind their walls, but once again they were overconfident. The walls fell and the defenders were overcome. Merchants and burghers were killed and there were some fires, but the town is now being rebuilt and will be the headquarters of a new administration for Scotland. A team of able officers and administrators is being assembled even now. Berwick will flourish in the coming years." It was his turn to hesitate then, and he smiled as though at a passing thought. "As will you and yours."

Bruce frowned briefly. "What mean you by that, Sir Robert?"

FitzHugh's smile widened. "Why, you will regain your own, of course. The King who dispossessed you is no more, and the family to whom he gave your lands is here in London, in disgrace and safely penned up in the Tower."

"Buchan is here?"

"He is, and with many of his Comyn kin. The Badenochs, father and son, to be sure. Thus Annandale and Carrick are both redeemed and will be returned to you by a grateful King when he returns."

"My God, the Earl of Buchan in the Tower of London!"

"And not alone. We have four earls in residence: Buchan himself, and the earls of Athol, Ross, and Menteith. Indeed there are Scots magnates and … what is their other word? Mormaers, that's it— magnates and mormaers under lock and key throughout the length and breadth of England. Will you be returning to Writtle tonight, my lord?"

Bruce jerked upright. "I will, if there be time. I do not care to leave my wife alone at night nowadays if it can be avoided. But I had lost track of the time."

FitzHugh gestured with a finger for Bruce to remain where he was and then crossed to the door, where he leaned out into the neighbouring room to speak to someone there. He returned immediately. "Between the second and third hour of the afternoon, so you have plenty of time, with the sun setting so late. Is there anything more you might require of me?"

It was a dismissal, but of the kindliest kind from a man so obviously pressed for time. Moments later, Bruce was in the outer yard again, making his way towards the barracks where Thomas Beg would be awaiting him.

"They deposed Balliol."

The two men were more than halfway home to Writtle, having passed the sign of the Spotted Cow a good hour earlier, and were cantering easily, knee to knee along the soft verge of the road to save their horses' hooves. The sun had just passed the midpoint of its descent and would fall more quickly now, but they were making excellent time and were optimistic that they would be back in Writtle, if not in time for supper, at least in time enough to find the food still warm enough to be palatable. Bruce had been reviewing his talk with FitzHugh and wondering for some time whether he ought to tell Thomas Beg what he had learned, and now that he had delivered the news he began to think that the other man was not going to respond at all.

"Aye," the big man growled eventually. "A good word, that, *deposed* … Sounds genteel, does it no'? It's no' the word I would hae used."

"What d'you mean?"

"I mean that, frae what I heard, the man was gutted. They stripped him o' everythin', and I dinna mean just his dignity, his good name—however little he might hae had left o' that. They brought him up in front of Edward in his full regalia, the poor, benighted whoreson, an' then they stripped him o' everythin'. Ripped the royal coat o' arms off his tabard and threw it on the floor for folk to trample. Broke his royal seal. Took his crown and ither jewels as trophies, everythin' they could lay hands on. They even broke his sword so he could never wield it again. As if he ever had! The preenin' prince-bishop, Bek o' Durham, was in charge o' every bit o' that and he milked the whole thing like a swollen udder … And him supposed to be Balliol's friend and kinsman. Pious whoreson hypocrite!"

"Where did you hear all this?"

Thomas Beg eyed him scornfully. "Where d'ye think? It was the talk o' the sergeants' barracks. Half the men in there today are new back from Scotland, and believe me, they hae some tales to tell … Two o' the fellows there—King's Guard, like Beltane—had been on duty when Balliol was shamed and saw it wi' their own eyes. They just got back here yesterday and they're still talkin' about it as though it *was* yesterday. One o' them said it was the worst thing he'd ever had to stand and watch. Like watchin' a dog gettin' whipped, he said."

"Jesus! And Edward took the crown and jewels?"

"Aye. Shipped them back to London. But that's no' even part o' what he took."

Bruce looked sideways at him, frowning. "What's worth more than Scotland's crown and jewels?"

"The rest of the realm's regalia and the royal plate. They emptied the treasure house. And then there's St. Margaret's own Black Rood, Scotland's holiest relic, and the Stone o' Destiny itself. The rood lifted frae Edinburgh and the other frae Scone Abbey, both to be shipped to Westminster Abbey for veneration by the English."

Bruce had reined in his horse, his face blank with shock. "That is blasphemy, Thomas Beg."

"Aye, it is, but don't glower at *me*. I wasna there and I'm no' responsible. But blasphemy it is, right enough, to steal one country's holy relics for the adornment o' another."

Appalled was not a word that would have come to Bruce at any time, but that was how this news affected him. The Stone of Destiny was the literal seat of Scottish kings. Every Celtic king from time immemorial had been seated upon it when he was crowned. The thought of its being taken to England, and as a trophy, in that moment made nonsense of all Edward Plantagenet's claims of judicious tolerance and strictly legal and constitutional deliberation. Scotland was now without a king, and by removing the physical trappings of kingship—crown, sceptre, robes, and treasury—and seizing the Stone of Destiny, obliterating centuries of tradition and ritual, Edward of England was plainly determined to ensure that it would remain without one.

"I heard somethin' else in there, too, and ye're no' goin' to like it."

"Tell it to me quickly, then. What else did they take? What else *could* they take?"

"No." He sensed Tam shaking his head, and as he turned to look at him the words came at him. "It's nothin' like that. It's about your father."

That brought a sudden dull ache to Bruce's midriff, despite FitzHugh's recent assurances. "What about him?"

"He wis in Scotland, just after the fight at Dunbar. But Edward sent him back to Carlisle wi' a flea in his ear."

"In Scotland … ? No, you're wrong, Tam. You have to be. FitzHugh would surely have mentioned it."

Thomas Beg twisted his mouth and dipped his head to one side, managing to give the impression of an elaborate shrug of doubt. "Different frae what I heard, then. But what I heard was definite, and the man that spoke o' it didna know me and didna know I kent anythin' about what he was sayin'. He was a northerner an' he named your father by name—the Lord o' Annandale, son of that Auld Bruce whit was near made king instead o' Balliol."

A worm of dread was beginning to roil in Bruce's gut. It didn't seem unfeasible on the face of things. The distance between Carlisle and Dunbar was not too great to preclude a swift sortie for Bruce—fifty miles or so across his own former lands of Annandale by Hawick and Melrose to the Lammermuir Hills and the coast; three, perhaps four days of hard riding each way. But what could have possessed his father to go there, quitting his own strategic post on the border in time of war? Bruce had a growing conviction that he did not want to hear the answer, but he kicked his horse into motion again and asked for it, clenching his guts against whatever the response might be.

"Go on, then. What did he say?"

"That even the mighty, stupit at the best o' times, could sometimes be as prancin' daft as a droolin' halfwit. An' he was laughin' at the thought o' it. He said Annandale chose ill on every front—ill timing, ill judgment, and an ill-phrased answer to the question o' why he was there at a' when he should be in England tendin' to his duties wi' the Scots still up in arms."

"Jesus God! The very question I would have asked him, too. And how did my father respond?"

"Ill, as I said. As poorly as he could have, in fact. He telt Edward to his face that he had come, now that Balliol was done, to claim the kingdom that was now his by rights."

"Oh, Jesus!" Bruce kept his face rock still, though he wanted to grind his teeth at his father's rash foolishness, seeing now, as Lord Robert had evidently been incapable of seeing, the reality of Edward's hardening will to keep the throne of Scotland vacant. The Scots regalia had not yet been seized at that point, but his father's provocation might well have been a determining factor, if not in fact the *sole* determinant, in Edward's decision to proceed with it. "And what was Edward's response to that? Did your fellow know?"

"Well, aye, he was standin' right there, on duty, watchin' and listenin'. He said Edward laughed, as though he couldna believe what he had heard. And then he went from laugh to rage in half a heartbeat an' roared, 'God's hoary balls, man! Have I no more to do in the middle of a war than find kingdoms for every pulin' supplicant who comes to me on his knees in search of favours?' Somethin' like that, anyway, though I've nae doubt the God's hoary balls bit was word for word. That's the kind o' thing Edward would say an' it's the kind o' thing folk remember."

"Ah, Father, Father, Father … " Bruce closed his eyes in horror at the thought of his father's humiliation. It felt like an age before he could continue. "And did my father have a response?"

"Shamed silence, was what I heard. No' a word o' protest or self-defence. He just knelt there, wi' his head down. And Edward let him wait there on the floor while he attended to other things. Nobody spoke, save for the King himsel', issuin' orders here an' there. But everybody was watchin' your father like corbies starin' at a dyin' beast."

"Oh, God … And how did it end?"

"The King ordered Sir Robert Clifford to tak a hundred men and ride at once wi' the Lord o' Annandale as far as Melrose, there to see his lordship safely an' speedily on his way back to his neglected duties in Carlisle. An' that was it. Your father left, wi' his tail between his legs."

"Clifford must have loved that, the arrogant pup. He's even younger than I am—barely one and twenty. One more humiliation atop the rest … " A silence stretched between the two men, broken only by the sounds of their horses, until Bruce spoke again. "This is sad news, Thomas. And not merely sad but threatening, in its way. Edward is a great bearer of grudges, and I think my father might have placed us all in jeopardy with this folly. God! How can any son grow up to be so different from the man that fathered him?"

# CHAPTER TWENTY-THREE

# LOCHMABEN REVISITED

"**C**arrick! There you are! I thought we'd have to start our parliament without you. Come forward."

The shout soared above the other voices, and many of the heads in the grand chamber of Berwick Castle that late-August day turned in response to it. Berwick town was swamped with people summoned to the parliament convened there by Edward Plantagenet to formalize his absolute victory over the Scots and to determine the matter of how the delinquent realm would now be ruled, since most of its nobility was under guard in England. Bruce had received his summons ten days earlier and had been riding for a week. He had arrived that same afternoon.

As an earl, he had been assigned quarters in the castle, and had stopped there briefly, taking only sufficient time to wash off the worst of the road dirt that had coated him and to exchange his smelly riding gear for clothing more suitable for greeting a king. He had been ushered into the royal presence as an honoured guest and had stopped just inside the door to scan the crowded assembly, looking for anyone he might recognize, and he had been there mere moments before the King's voice came to him over the surrounding throng. He nodded as he caught the King's eye, then wove his way among the densely packed bodies towards the high dais that gave the King, tall though he was, the extra height he needed to survey the monstrous chamber from where he stood.

Edward was being fitted for a new garment of some kind, for he stood in the centre of the platform between two kneeling tailors, with his arms extended to both sides as they fussed and tugged,

inserting pins and adjusting drapes of cloth. As Bruce approached
the dais, keeping his face expressionless and avoiding all eyes but
the King's, he was wondering what the immediacy and the auto-
cratic sharpness of the summons portended. Edward had called him
Carrick, not Bruce or Robert, as he sometimes did, and not even the
more cordial my lord of Carrick. Did that mean Edward was angry
with him? It might; it could easily mean that, though for what cause
he had no idea other than the King's lingering displeasure with his
father's behaviour. On the other hand, though, the size of the crowd
and the din of conversation might simply have demanded a louder,
sharper tone. The sins of the fathers, he thought, his mind still on his
father's folly as he slipped adroitly between two older men, idly
noting that there were no women present at this assembly.

He was almost at the lowest step leading to the dais when the
King spun in a fury, his arms still high in the air like a village
dancer's. "God's holy arse, fool!" he roared. "Will you bleed me to
death with your accursed pins? You've drawn more blood from me
in half an hour than the entire Scotch army was able to in the course
of a war! Get this thing off me and get out of my sight!"

The tailor who had pierced the royal skin was ashen faced, his
mouth stuffed with pins and his eyes starting from his head as he
sought to obey the royal command without provoking further wrath.
Between him and his equally shaken companion, they managed to
divest the monarch of his unfinished outer robe and to scurry away
to safety as Edward eyed the Earl of Carrick cannily, probing with
one hand at the left side of the royal ribs where the pin had evidently
pricked him. Bruce, bowing his head in greeting and preparing to
either drop to one knee or mount the steps if bidden, tried to analyze
that look and failed. He still could not tell if Edward was angry with
him.

"Come up," Edward said, extending his hand. Bruce mounted the
three steps and dropped to one knee, kissing the large ruby of the
ring on the King's hand.

"My liege," he said. "I rejoice to see you again, after such a long
time."

"Aye, and a long time it has been. You look well, young Bruce. And how is your countess, the beautiful Isabella?"

"She was well when I left her a week ago, my liege. Growing lovelier every day."

The King's mouth twitched. "Lucky man. And *bigger*, too, I suppose. How much longer now?"

"Two months, my liege. Early November, I am told."

"Excellent. And she is well otherwise?"

"She is, sire. Wonderfully well, by the grace of God. But she looks as though she is carrying a foal, so big is the child and she so small."

Edward nodded, but his eyes were already scanning the room again.

"Forgive me, my liege, but what is it that you require of me, to bring me all the way from England?"

The King came back to attention. "Your signature on the Scottish instruments of fealty."

"On the *what*?" Bruce stood gaping at the monarch like a landed fish.

"The instruments of fealty—for Scotland! You have not heard of this in all the time you have been travelling? Then by God's ancient bones that place of yours in Writtle is *really* far removed from the centre of things. How could you not have heard? No matter. You're here now and I have no concerns about your willingness in this. You renewed your oath of fealty on your wedding day and since then you've demonstrated your commitment to our cause, so I'll be brief.

"These past two months I have been the length and breadth of Scotland, while my people laboured here in Berwick and elsewhere. We have established new sheriffdoms throughout the Scots realm and have been at pains to collect written and sealed instruments of homage and fealty from everyone in Scotland—and I do not mean from the Scots alone. There are landholders and churchmen aplenty here who are of English, Italian, German, French, and other blood, and they, too, have signed such instruments. The folk are calling the collection process the Ragman Roll, I am told. I care not what they term it, but I must have the thing complete within this month of August—a complete written record of the sworn acknowledgment of every man with holdings in the realm of Scotland. It will be the greatest single volume of its kind since the Domesday Book.

"I need your name on that list, signed and sealed. You may do it here, while you are with us, and it will be added to the others. Your father has already signed. The documents were sent to him in Carlisle and executed there. It is a formality, but a legal one, to gather the sworn attestations of loyalty to us in person from all men of note in Scotland. We have been clement in Scotland, where we could have exacted greater vengeance had we wished, but these new articles and instruments require a personal commitment to me, not as lord paramount but as Edward, King of England, Wales, and Ireland."

Bruce kept his face blank as he nodded. "Very well, my liege, I'll do that before I do anything else." He glanced around. "Should I speak to Sir Robert FitzHugh?"

"FitzHugh's not here. I thought the journey might be too harsh for him. See Cressingham instead. He'll take care of it. You know Cressingham?"

"No, my liege."

"Hmm. An able man. You'll find him—he's big and fat and hard to miss, but he knows how to organize things the way I like them. He'll be my new treasurer for Scotland." He paused then, and tilted his head to one side. "I'm glad you're here, and now that you are here, I'll need you to stay a while." He raised a hand. "Aye, I know. Your wife has need of you. But not for two months, eh? What did you do for her from day to day before you left?"

Bruce floundered. "I … I tried to see to her needs, as a dutiful spouse."

"And were you successful?" There was humour in Edward's tone now, and Bruce grinned shyly.

"Not always, my liege."

"That's because you are a man. Earl you may be, but a mere male in the scheme of things and therefore useless in every woman's eyes during a pregnancy. They have no need of us once the beginning is achieved. But *we* have need of you, my lord of Carrick, as your liege lord. You have responsibility here, too, as a dutiful vassal." He did not wait for Bruce to respond. "The lady Isabella will do well enough without you for a while. You can do my bidding and return in plenty of time to pace the floor and fret about the coming of your child.

"Now. I need men I can trust today in Scotland, and you are one I can trust further than most. Your earldom of Carrick is restored to you, as of this moment, and your father's lands of Annandale to him. But he cannot yet go home. He still has work to do in Carlisle. And so I require you to go at once into your home lands and repossess them formally as forfeited by the House of Comyn. You will assure the loyalty of your own people there—both to yourself and to us. And when you have done there in Carrick, you will do the same in Annandale, on your father's behalf. You can be back in Writtle within six weeks of leaving, so be you waste no time."

"Thank you, sire." He hesitated. "Am I permitted to ask what you intend to do with the Comyns, my liege?"

"You are, my lord of Carrick." Edward spoke quietly, scanning the crowd as he did so but acknowledging none of the looks directed back at him. "I intend to forgive them their transgressions, on condition that they supply their full support to my endeavours in France. We hold four earls in London and several more elsewhere, and their manpower and contributions will be most useful. Once they have all agreed to my terms, I will issue a general amnesty and release all prisoners. The King of Scotland himself will remain in custody for the time being, until I decide how best to deal with him for the good of all. I cannot simply turn him loose to be used as a rallying symbol, though I doubt that would be likely to occur. In the meantime, I have a campaign in France to prepare and I will need strong men to back my administrative officers here in Scotland. There are taxes to be levied and collected and such things are seldom popular, and the men who would normally see to such things are all in

England now." He stopped again, head tilted. "You brought men with you, did you not?"

"I did, my liege. The same fifty I took with me when you sent me to tour the heartland. They did well on that occasion and the experience was good for them, so I thought to repeat it."

"Good. You'll be able to strengthen them with men from your own lands in Carrick. Dine with us tonight, my lord. Tomorrow you can meet with Cressingham, sign those articles, and then spend the remainder of the day preparing what you'll need to take with you. No need for you to stay here for the duration of the parliament. It will be dull, hammering out the rules of government. You'll leave the following day … "

He turned casually, sweeping his eye over the crowded floor.

"You are aware, I suppose," he said from the corner of his mouth, "that every man in this chamber now hates you for keeping me occupied with you for so long and not with them. Were I you at this moment I would bow and take my leave and walk out of here in the glow of the King's evident affection. We will speak again at dinner tonight."

Bruce bowed and did as he had been bidden, but as he left, looking straight ahead and avoiding all eyes, he had difficulty swallowing his resentment at having been so abruptly deprived of weeks spent in the company of his wife as her time approached. But that, he thought, was manipulation, and Edward of England was the master of it.

The Earl of Carrick's return to his earldom was hardly triumphal, but it was satisfying none the less, and along the route, his first sight of the grim old fortress of Lochmaben brought a lump into his throat with a startlingly vivid recollection of his grandfather. Bruce and his party had seen very few local inhabitants along the road, but that was hardly surprising. Fifty armoured marching men in the aftermath of a lost war offered little hope of goodwill towards locals, and wise men took care to stay well out of sight.

There was an English garrison at Lochmaben, commanded by a
Yorkshire knight called Humphreys, and Bruce made himself known
to the man but made no effort to assert his own or his father's
restored ownership of the place. He was merely passing through on
his way to his own earldom of Carrick, he informed Humphreys, and
showed him the King's writ of repossession. He would return after
his visit to Carrick, once order was re-established there, at which
time he would wish to meet with his father's vassals here, the
knights of Annandale. Humphreys raised no objection. The lord of
Annandale's loyalty to King Edward was well known and respected,
and the Earl of Carrick's activities on his father's behalf were
accepted as normal filial duty.

Two days later, Bruce rode into Carrick by way of the small town
of Maybole, where he stopped to gather what news he could from
the townsfolk. His unexpected arrival caused quite a stir, and he was
soon surrounded by a growing crowd of well-wishers eager to know
what the future would hold in store for them. None of them knew
that he himself was as anxious for such information as they were.

The town's provost owned the only house in the entire town with
an enclosed yard big enough to hold the crowd that quickly gathered
and kept growing, and Bruce quickly commandeered it, then
arranged with the two innkeepers to have food brought in to feed the
townspeople and thronging visitors who were still arriving. He also
had some men set up a small dais against the wall of the provost's
house and place a large chair on it, so that he could sit and overlook
the entire yard.

The town meeting that followed was the liveliest that had been
held there in years, since before the time of Bruce's replacement by
the new Comyn landlord, and Bruce set the tone by calling everyone
to order and then showing them the King's writ.

"Here's a thing you've never seen before," he began, holding the
writ up so everyone could see it. "I know it doesn't look like much,
but none of us has ever seen its like. Look at the official seals and
ribbons." He held the scroll horizontally, allowing the brightly
coloured fabric strips to dangle. "They look important, do they not?

But they're nowhere near as important as the words on the scroll itself." He held the scroll higher and pulled it open it with his other hand, spreading it for them to witness. "This is a king's writ, signed by Edward of England himself, as overlord of Scotland, and it returns to the House of Bruce—to my father and myself and our Bruce heirs—all the rights and possessions that were taken from us by King John Balliol and his Comyn supporters. I am now, once more, the rightful Earl of Carrick."

When the storm of applause and conversation caused by that began to abate—and by then Bruce estimated that there must have been close to a hundred people in attendance—he moved on quickly, telling them about the parliament currently under way in Berwick and outlining the plans that were being put in place for the ongoing governance of the realm. The matter of the kingship was being held in abeyance, he explained, but Edward had no intention of taking the Crown for himself. There would be an interim period—an interregnum of sorts—until the lord paramount should decide how to proceed.

He was aware that everyone in the crowd was listening avidly. These were the ordinary folk of Scotland—farmers, fishermen, herders, and small merchants—and they were unaccustomed to hearing such matters being laid out for their understanding.

There were three options open to the English monarch, he told them, and all were governed by feudal law. The first was the possible restoration of John Balliol to his throne, after a suitable period of penance and expiation for his rebellion against his feudal overlord. That possibility did not come without difficulties, Bruce pointed out. He explained that King John, a prisoner and convicted rebel as he was, could not simply be forgiven and reinstated. His former supporters, the magnates and mormaers who had driven the revolt, were still in custody in England, too dangerous to be released until they had given public and irrevocable declarations of their own guilt and undertaken to honour the King's peace in future. Once that had been achieved, Edward could decide what he would do about his vassal Balliol and the Scots Crown.

The second option, he continued, involved the folk of Carrick directly, by mere association. If Balliol's loss of the Crown was confirmed, then another claimant might be put in place, and the only suitable claimant was Robert Bruce of Annandale. He waited out the lacklustre reaction to that. Robert Bruce of Annandale was Edward's man, every bit as Balliol had seemed to be, and it was clear in the faces around him that these people were seeing the exchange of one weak leader for another. Bruce was neither surprised nor upset. He had his own doubts about his father's fitness to be king when that position entailed, as it inevitably must, unending eye-to-eye confrontation with England's intractable and domineering monarch. His father had never been, and would never be, a match for Edward Plantagenet.

As the buzz of speculation began to fade, the town miller, Gibby Rankin, raised his hand. "That canna happen afore the Balliol question's settled, can it? So is there any more o' these options ye're talkin' about?"

"Aye, Gibby, there is another one." Bruce glanced around the assembly, aware of the silence. "A third option is for Edward to name himself the King of Scots." He held up a hand quickly, to dispel the growing storm before it could become overwhelming. "But he won't," he shouted, and rose to his feet. The increase in height he gained by standing up forced men to look up at him, and they quickly fell silent.

"He won't do that," he said into the stillness. "If that was what Edward wanted, it would be done already."

The silence stretched as they considered that, and he sat down again, deliberately, knowing he had regained their full attention. When he resumed, he pitched his voice to carry and spoke slowly. "The King of England has had the ability to seize our throne ever since the fight at Dunbar. But he is content to be feudal overlord, lord paramount of Scotland. For him that is enough, and I believed him when he told me so. Edward Plantagenet has no wish to be King here in Scotland.

"And so a compromise is in place and the rules are being worked out at the parliament in Berwick as we speak. Government of the realm must go on, and so it will, though with some changes. For the most part, little will change in your lives here. Your rents and taxes will still be collected as before, and by the same folk who have always seen to that. The folk who make Scotland run from day to day will keep on doing what they do. But above them, working on King Edward's behalf, will be a new layer of government—ministers and officers appointed by the Crown in England for the governance of Scotland.

"The Earl of Surrey, John of Warrenne, is named Lieutenant of Scotland and will act as Edward's military viceroy in charge of the royal castles. A man called Hugh Cressingham is named Treasurer of Scotland, charged with the fiscal welfare of the realm. Another, William Ormesby, has been made justiciar, the Chief Justice of Scotland. His main task for the next few months will be to track down and arrest those who are still in revolt against Edward. So that should keep the Comyns busy and out of our hair."

That earned a laugh, and he allowed it to die away naturally before concluding. "That is as much as I can tell you for now. There are changes ahead for all of us, but they should not be threatening. Life will go on as it always does, and though this is but a short visit to show my face here again, I will be returning soon for good, bringing my new wife and child to live in Turnberry thereafter.

"In the meantime, though, I have been too long away and now I need to hear what *you* have to tell *me*, about how life has been here in Carrick these past few years. So let everyone now take their ease and talk. I have ordered food and drink from the inns and those will be brought here as soon as they are ready. I will join you throughout, and you may tell me anything you think I ought to know … And here comes the food now."

He rose to his feet as the people closest to the gate began to move aside, making way for a group of newcomers who entered in pairs, carefully carrying vast amounts of food laid out on portable breadboards slung between each pair. Others stepped forward to help roll two barrels of ale to where they could be set up and broached, and for a time everything appeared festive as the assembly turned its collective attention to satisfying hunger and thirst.

As Bruce moved among them afterwards, his people spoke to him as he had asked them to, telling him the things they thought he ought to know, and though he was gratified by this sign of their trust in him, he nevertheless heard much that caused him more concern than he had anticipated. He heard stories of outright abuse by English soldiery that surpassed anything he had expected to hear; stories of ordinary folk being mistreated and humiliated for no reason other than the malicious and vindictive pleasure of Edward's men-at-arms. He heard reports of robbery and battery, assaults and thefts, evictions and lootings, and of the hanging of an entire family who had lived together on a smallholding less than two miles from Maybole itself. They had been an unlovable crew, he was told, fifteen in number including several half-grown children, and they were well known as thieves, subsisting on the very edges of the law, but they had done nothing that anyone in Maybole knew of to justify their being taken out and hanged.

At first he believed these reports to be exaggerated and told himself that they were born of simple discontent and self-interest, but as the afternoon wore on and these tales were repeated and multiplied, he was forced to acknowledge that what he was hearing must be true. Too many honest folk were involved in the telling to permit any kind of collusion or conspiracy. And besides, he had to ask himself, to what end would they lie to him? They spoke of deeds done, some of them long since, knowing he could do nothing to redress any of their wrongs.

Not everything he heard during that afternoon was unwelcome or depressing, but the overwhelming impression that he was left with by the end of the meeting was one of serious *wrongness* within his earldom.

Later that same day he discussed all of what he had heard with Nicol MacDuncan, whom he had been delighted to find in residence at

Turnberry, surrounded by a number of familiar, well-remembered retainers, many of whom had been in service here during the time of his mother. The two men dined together alone that night and they had much to talk about, reviewing the status of the Turnberry estate as well as the earldom in general.

Nicol reassured Bruce that the Comyn tenancy had been a relatively lenient one, under the supervision of a cousin of the Earl of Buchan, and the affairs of the earldom had suffered little, save that the rents and revenues for the upkeep of Carrick had gone north to Buchan. Some of the household staff had inevitably been displaced to make room for Comyn counterparts, but Nicol had restored those as soon as the Comyns moved out and he himself had moved back in. Faced with the need since then to replenish the workforce in the absence of the fighting men who had been marched away by the Comyns to the war, he said, he had brought in people from the Isles, men and women of his own and Bruce's mother's clan; hard-working, hard-dirt farmers and fisherfolk who cared little for the wars of distant kings and to whom the mainland's bounty seemed like Eden. These new men were all fighting men, of course, he pointed out, well able to protect and hold their own, and since their fathers had all stood behind their countess while she lived, so, too, would their sons be loyal to her son. Carrick was in good hands.

They talked late into that first night, and once they had dealt with everything pertaining to the earldom, they moved on to discuss the war itself and the effect it had had, and was still having, on Scots life in general, with particular regard to what Bruce had heard said earlier in Maybole.

"I didn't like what I was hearing, Nicol, and I could hardly believe my ears at times, but it was plain that no one was lying. How bad is it, in truth?"

"It's bad," his uncle replied, "but no worse here than elsewhere, from what I'm told. It's the same everywhere. The English victory stunned the whole of Scotland, and the destruction of the supposedly unbeatable feudal host left the folk everywhere doubting themselves and all they had been told since they were born. Those they

had looked to as leaders were all imprisoned and there was no one
to replace them, so the folk left here were easy prey for the English
soldiery."

"Prey?"

Nicol looked at him askance. "Is it difficult to understand? The
folk didn't have a chance against the English attitude. They had been
conquered, Rob, invaded and defeated by people who plainly think
they are superior to any Scot, and who behave accordingly."

"But Edward's word is clear on that. No mistreatment of the
Scots folk—no raping, no pillage, no abuse."

Nicol sniffed. "That may be so officially, but the English soldiery
take their standards of behaviour from their knights and officers, not
from the King in Westminster. And believe me when I say that these
same knights and officers are more than merely slightly contemp-
tuous of all things Scots."

Bruce instantly remembered what his grandfather had so often
said about the power of men's perceptions: men believed what they
thought they saw to be true. If the English leadership, the earls and
barons, cared nothing for the welfare of the Scots people, too intent
on their own selfish ambitions, then their folk would behave accordingly, and all the written orders of the English administrators were
no more than a waste of ink and parchment. The English soldiery
would behave as lawlessly and brutally as their leaders permitted
them to behave. That was the way of soldiers everywhere—to take
ruthless advantage of everything they could, for their own benefit
and without being caught doing it. And if their leaders didn't care
what they did, why should they?

He decided there and then that the King of England needed to be
told about this directly, although he was not at all sure how Edward
would react to hearing it. Perhaps he might do something about
it—take drastic steps to enforce his stated will—but he found
himself forced to admit that the odds were equally good that he
might not.

He spent the next eight days with Nicol, visiting every bit of the
earldom and taking careful note of changes and repairs to be made.

He spent much of that time speaking with his tenants, long-familiar cottagers and fisherfolk for the main part, who were genuinely pleased to welcome him back home even though the men were gone and many of the women did not know whether their sons and husbands were alive or dead.

He left the earldom in Nicol's care and returned to Lochmaben, where, as he had promised, he summoned his father's knights to meet with him. He spent an entire day with them, listening carefully to all they had to say and making sure the elderly cleric who had served his grandfather took careful notes on matters that Bruce judged his father would deem important. Other than that, there was not much to be done in Lochmaben, since the knights were masters of their own lands and required no outside help with their activities.

The following day, he sought an audience with Sir Miles Humphreys, the temporary custodian of the fortress, and relieved him of his responsibilities. The knight sat blinking in astonishment.

"I don't think I can do that, my lord of Carrick. My orders are to hold this place until further notice, and I doubt if my superiors would recognize your authority to relieve me of my duties here. We are still legally in a condition of war, you know."

Bruce smiled and shook his head. "No, Sir Miles, the war has been over for months. The royal Scottish castles are held by English garrisons, and that is according to the King's wishes at the close of the hostilities. But Lochmaben is not a royal castle. It is an ancient fortress owned by my father, whose loyalty to King Edward is beyond doubt. Look you here." He reached into his doublet and pulled out the letter he had dictated the previous night.

"This is a formal letter of instruction, signed by me as an earl of Scotland and my father's deputy, relieving you of any further responsibility as custodian and freeing you and your men for duty elsewhere, where you can be put to good use. I have given permission for Sir James Jardine to occupy the castle in my father's stead for the time being, and if you know Sir James at all, you know the place could not be in better custody. I will be leaving to return to Berwick the day after tomorrow, and I suggest you and your men ride with me. There I shall speak personally with King Edward and absolve you of all responsibility in this matter"—he smiled— "because I am an earl and I left you no choice but to obey. I am here, after all, because His Majesty sent me directly, to reclaim my father's property. Should the King disagree with what I have done in good faith, though, I'll bear the brunt of it and no discredit will reflect upon you. And if he *strongly* disagrees, why then you may return and resume your post with nothing lost except a few days of travelling time. Does that convince you?"

The Englishman eyed the letter in a way that suggested to Bruce he might be illiterate, but then he sucked in a great breath and nodded. "So be it, my lord of Carrick. I'll take you at your word. We will be ready to accompany you when you leave for Berwick."

Edward was still in Berwick when they arrived, and he professed himself well pleased with Bruce's report on the status of Carrick and Annandale, assigning Humphreys and his score of men to other duties in Berwick. On the matter of Bruce's concerns over the behaviour of his troops in Scotland, however, the monarch was disconcertingly noncommittal. He listened to what Bruce had to say, frowning with what Bruce assumed to be displeasure at what he was hearing, and then mumbled something about looking into it. But where Bruce had looked for outrage he saw nothing but annoyance, and he could not tell whether it was directed at him or at the miscreants he had denounced. Edward then gave him permission to return to his home and his wife.

Two days later, Bruce was back in England, pushing his little following hard in his eagerness to win home.

# CHAPTER TWENTY-FOUR

# DEATH AND RESURRECTION

The time went quickly after that, the weeks flitting by until the day when Izzy jerked upright at the dinner table and clutched at the great mound of her belly, her huge green eyes going wider than he had ever seen them.

"Robert—?" she said, the word wrenched out of her, and Bruce's world disintegrated into a blur of being ignored and waiting, waiting, waiting, pacing the floor and praying, muttering to himself. It was fifteen harrowing hours before Allie approached him, beaming with smiles.

"You hae a dochter, my lord," she said, "and her ladyship is fine. Exhausted, poor lamb, but that's to be expected. The bairn's a bonnie wee thing, an' gin ye'd like to see the two o' them I'll tak ye up. Come on wi' me now."

Even newborn, the child was beautiful, a tiny, lovely thing with long, dark hair that Allie said would soon fall out. Bruce hoped it would not, but said nothing, content, after having kissed and cosseted his wife until she fell asleep, to gaze in fascination at the tiny being in his arms, wrapped in her new swaddling clothes. Izzy had long since agreed that, should their firstborn be a girl, her name would be Marjorie, after Bruce's mother, and now, looking down at the perfect, pink-faced mite, he felt that the name suited her well. Marjorie Bruce, future Countess of Carrick, would have a life of ease and beauty combined with duty and would be a credit to the grandmother for whom she was named.

She was a fractious child, though, screaming all night long every night so that neither of her parents could sleep properly. Allie grew more and more concerned as each day passed and finally, at the end of the first week, she drew Bruce aside.

"I think the wee mite's hungry, sir."

"How can she be hungry? She's forever at the tit."

"Aye, I know, but I'm startin' to doubt she's drawin' any strength frae it. That happens sometimes. Gin you agree, sir, I'd like to bring in a local lass who's nursin' one o' her ain. She has plenty o' milk to spare, and if that's what's wrong we'll notice it gey quick."

"Do it," he said. "But say nothing to Izzy until we know if you're right."

The baby stopped crying within minutes of feeding from the wet nurse, and within a week of that Isabella's own milk dried up. There was no reason for it that anyone could see; she simply stopped producing suck. Allie brought in the wet nurse permanently. Izzy was inconsolable.

A week after that, Bruce sprang up from the table as his wife entered the room. It was mid-morning, and the light pouring in from the open window revealed the shocking chalk-white pastiness of her face. He cursed aloud and leapt to her side, putting one arm around her shoulders and cupping her chin in his other hand, tilting her face towards the window and peering anxiously into her eyes. "Izzy, what's wrong? You look sick … Pale as wax and big, dark rings under your eyes. Are you tired? Are you in pain?"

She shook her head wanly, leaning into him. "I don't know, my love," she said in a fragile, whispery voice. "I don't feel sick … just *odd*."

"Christ Jesus. *Allie!*"

They put her to bed and sent for the physician, but nine nights later, in the early-morning hours of the fourth of December, while her exhausted husband slept upright in a chair by her bedside with her hand in his, Isabella Bruce, Countess of Carrick, died in her sleep.

There was no pain, or none that he could recall later. When he awoke and found her small hand cold and stiff in his own, Robert Bruce simply receded, like his father before him, into a limbo where nothing could reach him or touch him. He knew, because he was told when he asked long afterwards, that he attended the burial and threw earth onto the oaken coffin they had made for her, but he had no memory of being there or of doing anything else thereafter. For a full six weeks, encompassing Christmas and the unobserved New Year festivities, it was as though he had simply ceased to exist. The Earl of Carrick was there in body, but his mind and all his consciousness were elsewhere. He ate and drank and functioned physically, he knew, because by the end of that six weeks, when he began to return to the world, he was still alive though he had lost a frightening amount of weight. But all else was blank. He had no recollection of anything other than that moment of awakening to find himself clutching that small, cold hand.

Then, one morning in mid-January, he awoke to find his brother Nigel shaking his arm and calling him by name. He was irritated at first, then mystified when Nigel leapt into the air, grinning and shouting, and ran from the room, leaving him to go back to sleep.

That was the beginning of what Alec, his youngest brother, called the Emergence. All four of his brothers were there in Writtle, and had been there throughout almost the entire course of his withdrawal, and he supposed that in a way he must have known that. From that day on, he began to mend, emerging more and more each day from the protective shell within which he had been hiding. It was not a speedy process, and some days were better than others, but by the middle of February he was well enough to converse normally on almost any topic, the sole exception being the matter of Isabella, and to question what had been going on in the world during his "absence." His father had been here, he learned, and had brought the four boys with him, having obtained a leave of absence for Nigel from his squiring duties. Lord Robert had stayed in Writtle for an entire week before his duties called him north again, and throughout that time he had tried unsuccessfully to engage Bruce's attention.

King Edward had issued a general amnesty late in the year, having obtained the pledges of the Scots earls to participate in his French campaign, and the remaining captives had been allowed to return to their homes without grave penalty, though there had been no question of the Comyns keeping their control of Bruce lands. Yet Edward had sent no word of sympathy over Bruce's loss. Nigel pointed out that in all likelihood the King had failed to hear of Bruce's bereavement; he was busy even for a monarch, travelling all over England, amassing the army for his French campaign and deeply involved in the logistical details of transporting, maintaining, and supplying an invading army over vast distances involving sea travel.

Bruce listened without interest. He knew beyond question now that he had put all his faith and hopes for the future in God's hands the previous year, and those hands had proved to be either powerless or uncaring. That trust had evidently been misplaced, and in consequence, his belief in God's very existence had died … And if a man were sufficient of a fool to believe in a just and merciful God, how much greater a fool must he be to put faith in the constancy of kings? And so he simply closed his mind to Edward Plantagenet's indifference, refusing even to think about the man's supposedly high regard and affection for the blameless young woman.

Those who dared mention her death at all around him spoke in hushed tones of "childbed fever" and its associated maladies, but Bruce knew that was nonsense. She had been weeks clear of the childbed when she began to fail, and for the first two of those weeks at least she had been as beautiful and delightful as ever, her burgeoning health a cause of rejoicing. He refused to think at all about her malnourished daughter and the failure of her milk, or to consider any possibility that those might have been connected to, or had influence upon, her eventual death, and he refused, resolutely, to consider the possibility that she might have died of the same causes that had taken his mother from him years before.

He did not often have time, however, to ruminate upon such things, for his brothers conspired to shake him out of his brooding.

He had just emerged from a steaming bath one day and was towelling himself when the door opened and Nigel and Edward stepped inside, stopping one on either side of the open door to lean back against the wall and look at him.

"Shut that damn door. It's cold enough in here without adding a February gale."

They glanced at each other instead. "What do you think?"

Edward cocked his head, squinting at Bruce. "Not good," he drawled. "Good morning, brother Rob. Did you hear what King Edward said to John Warrenne as they were leaving Scotland last year, with the war neatly finished and the Scottish question settled?"

Bruce merely stared back at him, straight-faced, and Edward continued undaunted. "This is true, I swear it. Warrenne himself repeated it to others. They had just crossed the border at Berwick when the King drew rein and looked back into Scotland. 'Well,' he said. 'That's done. A man does good business when he rids himself of a turd.'" He stepped a pace closer and grasped Bruce's upper arm, squeezing it between his fingers before raising the unresisting limb for Nigel's inspection. "This arm has the consistency of shit. Nigel, do you agree?"

"It seems to have that feel to it. I agree."

"And therefore?"

"A man would do good business to rid himself of it."

"Exactly what I think ... " He dropped his hand to Bruce's forearm and gripped it, turning it until he could look down at the open palm. "The muscle's almost gone," he said. "Your hands have lost their calluses. The whites of your eyes are yellow. You, my dear brother, are a mess." He nodded towards the still-steaming tub. "Not as great a mess as you were earlier, but you need toughening up. Nigel and I have decided to undertake your retraining and get you back into fighting condition, and you are going to be bruised with many colours until you start to hold your own with us again. So put on clothes and cladding and come outside to the yard. We'll be waiting for you. Am I right, Nigel?"

"You are right, Edward."

"Good. That pleases me. I enjoy being right." He winked at Bruce. "You have the quarter-hour. After that, we come and carry you out."

The Earl of Carrick was dancing despite being swathed in heavy practice armour, hopping lightly and lithely from foot to foot, his shield solidly firm beneath his chin and the long, lethal beauty of his blade moving constantly as he faced his two younger brothers, neither of whom looked as blithe or as comfortably confident as he. Nigel's padding was mud stained, from landing on his arse when he had failed to anticipate his elder's next move, and Edward, the slightest of the three young men, was breathing heavily through his open mouth, having barely survived taking a fatal stab in an extended exchange with the earl while Nigel was sprawled in the mud.

"Somebody's coming," Nigel said, lowering his sword, and Bruce turned to look. One of the gate guards was running towards them.

"Strangers, my lord, coming from London. They just emerged from the woods, a mile and a half away. A mounted troop and three knights' colours." Bruce nodded, and the guard turned and ran back to his post.

"Three knights? I wonder who they are, riding with a mounted troop … " He shrugged. "They probably will not be coming here. Headed for Colchester would be my guess. But we'll find out soon enough. In the meantime, brethren, thank you for the diversion. I am really glad you decided to retrain me, and I am more than pleased with your success. I have not had a bruise in weeks. Have you two?"

He turned away, smiling. Even his smile had changed since Izzy's death; it was quieter somehow, less brilliant and far less frequent. But his eyebrows rose in surprise as he saw the guard running back towards them, shouting, "My lord, there's more of them, bearing the King's standard!"

"Christ God! Get back and sound the alarm, man! Turn out the guard! And send someone to the kitchens to find Allie and have her light cooking fires. Damnation, man, away with you! Run!" He turned to his brothers, both of whom stood open-mouthed. "You two, away with you and change your clothes, quick as you can. And tell Tom and Alec to be ready." He glanced down at himself, then started stripping off his bulky coverings. "Ah well," he muttered, "even a King must expect surprises if he calls on people unannounced, but can we feed half a royal army?"

The next half-hour went by in a turmoil of last-moment preparations, and the royal escort, rank after rank after rank of them, rode up and deployed themselves in the field beyond the road, facing the gates of Writtle House. Bruce estimated their number at somewhere close to a hundred and fifty men, with more solid blocks, perhaps as many men again, still approaching in the distance. As he was watching, a group of riders in brightly coloured surcoats and carrying lances with bright pennants turned and surged towards the gates, and among them Bruce saw the golden glint of the coronet surmounting Edward's helmet. He strode forward quickly and waited as the royal party approached, and Edward's voice boomed out even before they came to a halt.

"My lord of Carrick, be at peace. We have not come to beggar you or ruin your fields or eat all your provisions."

Bruce dropped to one knee, his head lowered, so that he heard rather than saw the courser's hooves approach and stop and its rider swing himself down from the saddle like a man thirty years his junior.

"Up, man, and greet me as a friend! Since when has Bruce had to kneel in the dirt for me?"

He rose, reflecting cynically to himself that all men sooner or later knelt in the dirt before Edward Plantagenet, and found himself face to face with England's King, who stared at him with narrowed, appraising eyes, a frown bisecting his brows. Then Edward reached out and grasped him by the shoulders, pulling him into an embrace.

"I'm on my way to Colchester," he said quietly, hugging Bruce to his chest. "I've been in the north and in Wales and returned to Westminster four days ago. And only then did I hear the word of your loss, my friend. Three months and more too late. You must have thought me cruel indeed to send no word of comfort or condolence."

He pushed himself back, but kept his hands on Bruce's shoulders as he continued in the same, quiet voice. "We will not stay to tax your hospitality, but I could not pass by without stopping to spend an hour with you privily. Will you invite me into your house?"

"Most certainly, my liege."

"No, not your liege today, Robert. I am here as your friend, albeit belatedly."

He swung to face the tall, helmeted knight closest to him. The man was a stranger and Bruce had never seen his livery before.

"I shall remain here with my friend of Carrick for an hour or so, Despencer. We have much to talk about. Take you the others and wait for me by the crossroads." He raised a hand quickly to stop another knight before he could dismount. "No, Brough, I need no guarding here in the house of Robert Bruce of Carrick. Go with the others. I will join you when I am ready."

Bruce saw the armoured knights exchanging glances and almost smiled because he could sense their confusion, faced with an unprecedented situation. The King went nowhere unaccompanied, ever. None dared challenge Edward, though, which went without saying. There was but one man in all England who would defy the royal wishes at a time like this.

"My lord of Norfolk is not with you, sire?"

Edward raised one eyebrow and stared at him. "No, he is not. What made you ask?"

Now Bruce did smile slightly, for he knew Edward understood precisely what had made him ask. He shrugged one shoulder. "I was remembering the time you came to Carrick, to Turnberry. That was long ago, but my lord of Norfolk would not have left you alone then and I doubt he would now, were he here. I trust he is well?"

"Oh, he's well enough. Hale and hearty and as stubborn as ever. But now he threatens to leave me alone indeed. Let us go inside. Who are these young men?"

Bruce had forgotten that his four brothers stood behind him and now he turned to see them all gazing raptly at the King of whom they had heard so much throughout their lives. "My brothers, sire," he said. "May I present them to Your Majesty?"

Edward greeted them graciously, speaking to each of them in turn and putting them at ease before dismissing them easily. Then he took Bruce by the arm and steered him towards the house. "The eldest one," he said, when the boys were out of earshot. "He's almost as big as you. Is he still a squire?"

"Finished training, my liege, but not yet knighted. He dreams of riding with you."

"Does he, by God? Then let's encourage him. I can use all the loyalty I can find." He spun on his heel and shouted at the retreating brothers. "Nigel! Nigel Bruce, come here."

Nigel approached quickly, his face alight with eagerness.

"Your brother tells me you are awaiting knighthood and would ride with me. Is he correct?"

Poor Nigel was incapable of speech, but he nodded rapidly, his eyes like a puppy's.

"Well, then," the King said, pointing. "You see that fellow over there, in the black armour with the silver crest? That's Sir Lionel Despencer, the commander of my guard. Tell him I said he is to take you with us. You'll stand vigil in Colchester while we are there and I'll knight you myself the following day. After that, we'll find you a place where your abilities will serve you well. You're a Bruce, so you must have abilities. Run, now. There's not much time."

He turned back to Bruce, who was as open-mouthed as Nigel, and began to walk again. Neither of them spoke until they were inside the house and sitting by the fire in Bruce's private chambers. There the King sat mute while Bruce recounted the details of the previous months as he had learned to reconstruct them, and when the younger man finally fell silent, he grimaced and shook his head.

"There is nothing I can say to you that will ease your grief, Robert. I know that from personal experience. All any man can do in such a pass is offer his regrets and suffer feeling futile and helpless. I, too, did what you did when I lost my Eleanor, and all the realm of England went begging until I found myself again. But I still feel the pain from time to time. Memories take you unawares forever afterwards, and each time they do, the pain seems just as fresh and raw as when you first felt it. But it does grow better, I can promise you that. The gaps that separate the pangs of pain grow longer as months pass. How is the child?"

"She's well enough. Well tended, with no lack of love."

"You blame her for her mother's death?"

"What? No, no such thing. It was no fault of hers, poor thing. The fault was mine alone."

"Yours?" Edward's eyebrows peaked upward. "How were *you* at fault?"

"I killed her."

"You *killed* her? How so, man? You mean you murdered her? You loved her, did you not?"

"More than life itself, but I got her with child. That killed her. Which means I killed her."

"That is horseshit, my lord of Carrick. The getting of children is the reason for our being here. To compare it to doing murder is blasphemous."

Until that moment Bruce had forgotten to whom he was speaking, addressing Edward as an equal with no thought of titles or proprieties. Now, hearing the familiar truculence in the King's voice, he pulled himself together.

Edward was still talking, almost grumbling to himself. "Damned nonsense, boy. You spend too much time alone out here, miles from anywhere and brooding about things you can't change. You need something to occupy your mind, get you out of yourself." He stopped, as if struck by a sudden thought. "And I have just the very thing to do it. A task for you—the perfect task, in fact. Are you familiar with the name of William Douglas?"

"You mean *Sir* William Douglas, le Hardi, as he calls himself?"

"That's the man."

Bruce shrugged. "I know a little of him. He was governor of Berwick when you took the place, was he not?"

"Aye, he was. And he arranged advantageous terms for himself when he surrendered the castle town to us. He was released with all his ilk in the amnesty late last year."

"And?"

"And now he's rebelling again, safe back in Scotland, damn the man." He waved a hand dismissively. "Not that anything he could do will amount to much, but he's causing dissension everywhere he goes, and he's interfering with the work of my people in his district. Nothing too damaging, as I have said, but his nuisance value is beyond all proportion to what he does. I cannot have him running around free, defying me wherever and whenever he chooses so to do. So I have dispatched a force to arrest him."

Bruce cocked his head. "And you wish me to join that force?"

"What? Christ, no. I have other plans for you. His castle in the Dale of Douglas lies close to your earldom, does it not?"

"Near enough, sire, but it really lies in Galloway."

"Aye, and Galloway is Percy's territory now. He's the one I dispatched to take Douglas, but he won't look for the old fox at home. Douglas is up by Glasgow, conspiring with that other wily creature, Wishart … But his wife remains in Douglas Castle. You know about Douglas's wife?"

"The willing abductee. I do, sire. She's English."

"She's a witch. I want you to go home and bring her back here. That will get Douglas's attention. Go and collect your men from Carrick and from Annandale, and burn down Douglas Castle. But get the woman first. I want her here in London, in the Tower if need be, because if there is anything in this world of ours that might bring this Douglas wolf to heel, I believe it might be her, the she-wolf with whom he mates."

"Very well, my liege, I'll do that. But Douglas Castle is strongly fortified and I have no siege engines. My Carrick men will not be much use against high stone walls."

"No, they won't, but I have siege engines in Berwick. You rouse your men, I'll see you well equipped. The prime intent is to bring back the woman, and that's why I'm sending you. You're Scots, by birth and speech at least, and you're an earl, and you're young and believable. Offer her whatever you think necessary, but get her to abandon that castle and surrender for her goodman's sake, to save his life. And once she's out, burn down the rats' nest. Will you do that for me?"

"I will, my liege. I'll start preparing to leave immediately."

"Good, but don't take too many men from here. Travel light and quickly and raise your own men up there. I want Scots involved in this, not an army of Englishmen against a single rebellious Scot."

Half an hour later, watching the last of the royal cavalcade move off along the road to the northeast, Bruce was deep in thought and failed to hear Thomas Beg come up behind him until the big man's voice startled him.

"That wis … unusual. Ye'll have folk callin' you the King's cata-mite, gin this keeps up. What did he want?"

Bruce raised an eyebrow. "To offer his sympathy."

"Oh aye? Nice o' him to wait so long."

"He didn't know. He was up north."

"Fine, and what does he want you to do now? Where are we goin'?"

Bruce looked at him and grinned. "Why would you even ask me that, Thomas? It makes you sound cynical. Do you truly think the King came here apurpose, with something already set in his mind?"

The big man shrugged, his eyes on the columns of departing horsemen. "If he didna, it would be the first time ever. So where *are* we goin'?"

The Earl of Carrick filled his lungs with air, smelling the over-powering scent of the great body of horses that had just gone by, and punched his companion gently on the shoulder.

"Scotland, Tam," he said. "We're going back to Carrick, rebel hunting."

# CHAPTER TWENTY-FIVE

# LESSONS IN LOYALTY

Eight days after receiving his instructions from King Edward, Bruce was again in the familiar fortress of Lochmaben. He had ridden first into his own Carrick earldom to raise his men there and advise them on what was afoot, and only then had he travelled back to Annandale. Now he was a supplicant, seeking aid. The lairds of Lochmaben and Annandale were his father's liegemen, not his, and although he knew his father would abide by Edward's expressed wishes to raise the Annandale men against Douglas Castle, the fact remained that his father was still bound by duty in Carlisle, and Bruce had not had time to go there and request the earl's authorization to raise Annandale. Instead he had sent word to Sir James Jardine, asking him to summon the Annandale knights to confer with him, as his father's representative, when he arrived. That had been several days earlier, and now the lairds were assembled. They had listened respectfully enough to what he had to say, and had then turned in unison towards the knight of Heriot, the senior among them, inviting him to answer for them.

Now John Armstrong of Heriot sat frowning, seemingly unaware that the eyes of every man in the room were fixed upon him, awaiting his opinion. Bruce forced himself to sit motionless, keeping his face blank to betray no slightest sign that he had much to lose should the old man's stern ponderings result in what the Earl of Carrick feared they might. When he delivered his response, Bruce knew, the others, representing the Annandale tenantry of Dinwiddies, Johnstones, Jardines, Crosbies, and Elliotts, would accept his pronouncement as a verdict. Armstrong, he knew, was barely literate, but that would in no way affect the old man's judgment; a lifetime of probity and conscientious duty in the service of the Noble Robert had given the old man an undisputable gravitas that was backed by a faultless record of dedication to the welfare of his folk.

The room in which they had gathered was the hall everyone called the Assembly, the half entrance hall and half common room inside the main doors of the central tower of the Lochmaben keep. Furnished with an open-centred arrangement of half a score of heavy oak tables where the sixteen men were seated haphazardly, it lay just outside the old lord's former den. On Bruce's right, separated from him by two other occupied chairs and flanked on his right by his son Andrew, Sir James Jardine sat stone faced, his lips a thin line beneath his grizzled beard.

Armstrong sniffed sharply and straightened up, tilting his head slightly as his pale brown eyes swivelled to meet Bruce's. His lips pursed into a pout as though he were tasting something sour in his mouth.

"This doesna sit right," he growled, looking straight at Bruce. "On the face o' it, it's straightforward enough, an' at any ither time I'd say nothin' an' just accept what ye're askin' o' us … I'll no' dispute your right to be here as your father's spokesman. But there are things happenin' here, circumstances naebody could hae foreseen, that winna let me agree to what ye want—no' without direct instructions frae his lordship in person. Gin ye had that, a letter o' some kind, I wouldna hae a choice. But that's no' the case, and so—"

"I understand, Sir John," Bruce said, cutting in before the old knight could deny his request outright. "I was aware of that lack when I set out to come here, trusting your goodwill in recognizing my duty to my father. But I came straight from Writtle by way of Berwick at King Edward's direct request and had no time to meet in person with my father in Carlisle. In truth, though, I have no idea of what you mean by what you have just said. 'Circumstances nobody could have foreseen'? Explain that to me, if you will. What are these 'circumstances' and how do they affect my request on my father's behalf?"

The old knight nodded judiciously. "It's no' easy to explain, Earl Robert, but I can see I need to try, so I'll start by remindin' ye in the first place o' what you're askin' o' us. You're here in Scotland upo' King Edward's business and for King Edward's ends, and that's fine. You and your faither are both liegemen to Edward and your duty's clear—your faither is to bide at his task in Carlisle and you're to obey the King's edict to tak Douglas Castle and put it to the torch, then tak the Lady Douglas back wi' ye in custody to Edward's court. To that end you're to raise your men o' Carrick to your bidding an' use them to do what ye must. An' as Earl o' Carrick, that's your right an' they're your folk. Naebody can argue wi' that.

"On the ither hand, though, we here are a' Annandale folk and our earl, your faither, is the only man who can command the like obedience frae us. Maist o' the time, that's straightforward, but there are times, an' nae man can foretell them, when things winna line up the way they should, and that's what we have here … "

Bruce gritted his teeth, waiting for the old chief to come to the point.

"Ye'll hae heard about what happened in Lanark, I jalouse, wi' the sheriff. "

"In Lanark? No." Bruce sat up straighter, suddenly more alert. "That would be Hazelrig. The sheriff. What has he done?"

"We don't know … No' yet. But he's deid, murdert by a Scot, they say, and there's hell to pay up there."

"Sweet Jesus! Murdered, did you say?"

"No, I said he was deid. It's the English who say he was murdert."

"And was he? Is it true? Who did it?"

The old knight shook his head. "We canna say for sure, except for the fact that he's deid. But it's true, like enough. He was hell-bent on hangin' Will Wallace, a forester livin' as an outlaw in Selkirk Forest, and the word we heard is that he took Wallace's wife an' bairn and they wis killed while in his custody. Next thing onybody knew, Hazelrig was deid, too. Some say Wallace went right into

Lanark and killed him in his ain court while he was playin' the judge there, but I doubt that's the way o' it. There would hae been too many guards around for that to happen easily. Others say he went lookin' for Wallace in the Forest and was found shot fu' o' arrows wi' a' his men. An' Wallace is kent to be an archer, i' the English style, so that's mair likely true than the other tale, it seems to me."

"Good God … So where's this Wallace now?"

"Your guess would be as good as mine, Lord Carrick. He's disappeared. Some say he's out now wi' the Lord o' Douglas, but I canna swear to that. Wherever he is, though, he's set the whole o' southern Scotland heavin' like a pot o' boilin' porridge, and the English are runnin' mad everywhere, searchin' for him. It's an ill time for the folk around here."

"I see … That makes things … difficult for you. I can see that. And that's the source of these circumstances you spoke of?"

Sir John's shrug was restrained. "The source? Aye, I can see why you might say that. But ye'd be wrong. The *source* o' it's the English themsel's an' the way they treat the folk around here, tramplin' them like dirt and kickin' them aside wi' ne'er a blink o' concern or care. An' I'm no' talkin' about the odd insult. It's happenin' a' the time, frae day to day, an' gettin' worse. Folk canna even trust they'll hae' their ain roof ower their heads frae one day to the next. It's like we're a conquered folk, an' the Englishry despise us as though we wis cannibals."

"Cannibals my arse," one of the others interrupted. "Gin we wis cannibals they'd keep clear o' us, for fear o' bein' ate. But they treat us nae better than sheep—to be kicked and herded and shorn for what they can get frae us. Rab Dinwiddie's place was emptied the ither day. Some English fool's buildin' a watchtower at the crossroads and a squad o' men just marched into Rab's yaird and arrested his three sons an' anither fower men wha wis working there. Just lined them up, threatened them wi' a floggin' gin they objected, an' then marched them awa an' set them to work buildin' their whore o' a tower. Rab wis too auld, so they left him alane, but he fell doon in a fit a wee while after and now he's no' expected to live. What kind o' shite is that?"

A man at the far end of the room stirred, sat up straighter, and then leaned forward urgently. His face was flushed, his features twisting into a scowl. Bruce had never set eyes on him before this meeting, but the man, whoever he was, had been the last to arrive, interrupting the proceedings a good half-hour after they had begun. He had entered the hall silently, nodding in stern-faced apology to Sir John as senior there, but had offered no explanation of why he was late and no one had sought to question him. Since then he had sat fidgeting and listening, his frowning gaze switching from face to face as various people spoke.

"I'll tell ye what kind o' shite it is," he growled. His voice, though low pitched, was filled with sufficient anger to draw every eye in the room. "It's the kind o' shite that starts up wars, and I'm ready to do somethin' about it." He turned his eyes unexpectedly to Bruce. "Lord Carrick," he said, nodding curtly. "I kent ye wis comin' here to meet wi' us and I was set to be here early, but I had ill news reach me just afore I set out." He straightened in his chair and looked around at his fellows, then stood up. "I'm Alexander Armstrong o' Jedburgh. My father died last year—November—and I was raised to take his place. I've been listenin' here and I've never spoken out like this afore now, but I canna stay quiet on this."

He gestured with a thumb towards the previous speaker. "Ye've heard Alastair's story about Rab Dinwiddie an' how he's like to die o' a fit. But vexed though he was, auld Rab fell down on his own, wi' naebody near him. I hae a different tale to tell ye." He swept his eyes around the assembly, all of whom were watching him raptly.

"I had word this mornin' that a wheen o' our folk was found slaughtered yesterday. They was cut down like beasts. Men, women, and bairns—three families o' ordinary, law-abidin' folk who never harmed a soul ... and no' a sign, supposedly, o' who could hae done such a thing." He paused, waiting for the outburst of shock to die down, and Bruce, as the only magnate there, had to fight to keep his own face expressionless.

"They had set up a place, about seven years ago," Armstrong continued. "Three houses for the families and some pens for pigs an' the like, and for the first five years they worked to clear new fields. They planted their first crop last year and brought it in wi'out help frae us. Their wee place hasna got a name, it's just a bit o' hard-won land about two miles frae Jedburgh. The eldest—the headman, if ye like—was my cousin Broderick MacRae. Him and his wife had three grown sons who lived there wi' them. Two o' them was married and had houses o' their own, and between them seven bairns, the eldest o' them about eight ... They're a' deid ... Fourteen folk."

The silence stretched for a long time until one man said in a stunned voice, "Christ Jesus, Alec, that's awfu'. That doesna stand belief. Who would do such a thing?"

"Nae human worthy o' the name," someone else added.

"Aye," the first man said, his eyes agog, "but *somebody* must hae done it. Ye must hae *some* idea o' who it was, Sandy, surely?"

Armstrong swung towards the speaker, his face suffused with rage. "Some *idea*? I don't *need* ideas, Johnston, I know damn well who did it. The God-cursed Englishry did it. But I havena got a name to put to anybody, an' no' a shred o' evidence to show, and a' the folk who could point a finger o' accusation hae been murdered."

"But ... " It was the man Johnston. "But how d'ye *know* that if they're a' deid?"

"Because I was *telt*!" he howled. "They wis *seen*!" Armstrong reined himself in abruptly and drew in a deep, shuddering gulp of air. He turned to gaze wide-eyed at Bruce, and when he resumed his voice was calmer, almost matter-of-fact. "The lad that brought us the word saw them, less than twa miles from where it happened. He was on his way to see my cousin Broderick, wi' a load o' hay. He saw them comin' out o' the forest into a glade by the river there. Nine or ten o' them, he said. English sodgers, wearin' leather hauberks and steel hats. He was above them, lookin' down the hill, and he hid as soon as he saw them."

"Why?" Bruce asked, cursing himself for his stupidity even as the word left his mouth.

"*Why*? Because he kent better than to let them see him. He drove his cart into the bushes out o' sight and hid himsel' and watched them go by, waitin' till they was out o' sight."

"And he was sure they were English?"

Armstrong ignored the question, clearly deeming it unworthy of response, and Bruce added, "Ten of them, you said?"

Armstrong shrugged. "Nine, ten … He didna try to count them. It was enough to see them there, wi' naebody in charge o' them. The boy kept out o' sight and waited till they was past and then went on his way. And then he smelt the smoke as he got near Broderick's place. Every buildin' in the place was on fire and everybody was deid. The women were a' naked, their throats cut … And the men and bairns had a' been cut to bits … He couldna do a thing, he said, an' he doesna ken how long he stayed there, no' knowin' what to do or where to turn. And then he came lookin' for us."

"So what did you do?"

Armstrong looked at him with eyes that were utterly blank. "What *could* I do? Nothin' that would change a thing. I sent some men along with our priest to clean the place up and bury the bodies. And then I came here to bring the news."

"But ye have a witness," old Sir John Heriot said, speaking for the first time since Armstrong had begun. "The boy. Who is he?"

"Adam Westwood, they call him. He's sixteen. But he didna see anythin' to *witness*, ither than a rabble of Englishry comin' out o' the forest frae the direction o' Broderick's place. He wasna close enough to see their faces or even what crests they was wearin' and he wouldna ken a single one o' them gin he was standin' in among them. I can just imagine what the English would say about that, the bastards."

The Earl of Carrick nodded. "There's nothing I can say to ease your grief or your anger. They might be anywhere by now, safe among their own kind. They might even have been deserters, but we'll never know." He frowned. "You say the boy said they were a rabble. They were not in formation, marching?"

"No. A rabble was what the boy called them. No' marchin', just daunderin' along wi' naebody in charge, laughin' and shoutin' to one another like laddies wi' no' a care in the world."

"Hmm … So what will you do now?"

Armstrong simply stared at him. "Had ye asked me that afore I cam here this mornin' I wouldna hae been able to tell ye," he said in a low voice. "But I ken now." He turned away to address the gathering. "Justice for my folk," he said. "I'm goin' out to the Forest. To join the outlaws, join Wallace. If I canna depend on the law for help, then by Christ I'll make my ain law. I'll take my boys wi' me, the twa eldest and a handfu' o' my men. Twelve o' us a' thegither, single men wi' nae families to fret about. Them that stays behind will be enough to see that there's nae repeat o' what happened the day afore yesterday." He glanced from face to face as though expecting opposition, but no one spoke. "My mind's made up," he said. "I've had enough o' sittin' on my arse an' sayin' nothin', twiddlin' my thumbs like some eejit. I'm goin' lookin' for English sodgers. I'm no' askin' for help frae any o' ye, no' askin' ye to come wi' me. This is my business and I'll see to it. I'm just tellin' ye so ye'll ken when ye hear tell o' it frae other folk." He hitched his jerkin closer about him and looked at Sir John Heriot. "That's all I have to say, and now I'm goin' home. But I'll be awa in three days frae now, and after that, God knows. We'll see. Good day to ye all." He nodded one more time to Sir John and then to Bruce, and then walked out, pulling the main door shut behind him.

The sound of the door closing seemed to echo in the silence before a sullen murmur erupted among those left behind. Sir John Heriot quelled them with an upraised hand and a sharp call for quiet. When the room was still again, the elder turned to look at Bruce.

"There you have it, my lord earl," he said. "Better and more sudden than I could have told you. That's the kind o' thing that's goin' on in this sorry land these days." He paused. "I hope ye'll no' mind my sayin' so, but you and your faither hae no idea o' what it's like up here. Ye're both secure in England, magnates who hae sworn oaths o' fealty to Edward, livin' in England's peace an' doin' your duty by England's King. Ye see nothin' o' what's truly happenin' here. For us, though, it's a different story. We hae to live wi' that kind o' arrogance and anger—frae the English, I mean, no' frae the likes o' poor Sandy Armstrong. And that's no' easy to thole at the best o' times. Never was. For years we wis worried about civil war, Bruce against Comyn, but that never cam to pass, thank God. Now, though, it's far worse, and that's why I canna agree to what ye ask, no' wi'out a letter o' instruction frae Annandale himsel', and I doubt, gin he knew what was goin' on here, he'd write such a thing."

Bruce was sitting straight-backed now, frowning deeply, and he threw out his hands in exasperation. "Forgive me, Sir John, and all of you. I hear what you are telling me, and God knows this is not the first time I have heard such things. It is, though, the first time I have truly seen how bad things really are, all across this land—the first time I have really *believed* it. You must think me stupid indeed, but—"

"The fault's no' yours, Lord Carrick. It comes frae the life you've lived in the south. Down there, you're a Scots earl, loyal to the English King for good and ample reason. Naebody here questions your allegiance—the lack o' it, I mean—to Balliol. That was aey understood frae the outset, and ye behaved wi' honour throughout all o' that. But now Balliol is gone, and Scotland should be a better place … Except it's no'. But here's what ye need to think o' now.

"Up till now, we was a' Bruce men wi' a duty to do Bruce's biddin', and that's no' changed. But now it's no' about Bruce's will in Scotland—no' completely or as clearly as it was in the past. Now it's about England's *bein'* in Scotland, when they've nae right to be here. It's about the depredations o' the English sodgers an' the way they treat the folk—rapin' and murderin' wi' nae restraint and nae fear o' reprisal. An' it's about the way the folk here look at what's goin' on. To them—to men like Sandy Armstrong an' a host o' others—it's us and *them*, *them* bein' the English. This Lord o' Douglas whose castle ye're sent here to burn isna rebellin' against the English King. He's up in arms about the damage bein' done to his lands and his folk by people who shouldna be there in the first place. To them that lives hereabouts, he's mair hero than rebel and mair patriot than outlaw—is that the right word, patriot?" He saw Bruce's reluctant nod and grunted. "Aye. Anyway, ordinary folk hae nae interest in the high obligations o' the magnates. To them, it's a' about their wives and bairns, their goodmen and kinfolk, about house and hearth and livin' frae day to day wi'out fear o' being hung or trampled on. And to them, that's what Douglas is tryin' to protect. There was a word your grandsire used to use. It was 'perceptions,' gin I recall it right. D'ye ken what that means, Lord Carrick?"

"Aye, I do, Sir John. I understand it well."

"Aye, well the *perceptions* here in Scotland this day, among ordinary folk, is that there are Scots folk, livin' on their ain lands, and then there's Englishry, actin' as though thae lands are theirs. The folk winna thole it, my lord. And I winna order my men, be they Armstrongs or any other here in Annandale, to ride out barefaced and be *perceived* to be helpin' the English in puttin' down their ain folk. Ye may think what ye will o' me, but there it is."

Someone among the silent knights sighed, but Bruce did not look towards the sound. Instead he sat chewing on what he had heard and eventually, reluctantly, he nodded.

"Thank you, Sir John," he said, then lapsed back into silence. No one stirred, their stillness reflecting the gravity of what had transpired here, and Bruce wiped the corners of his mouth with a spread hand before continuing. "This—session—has given me much to think about, and none of it expected." He rose to his feet and began to pace, his gaze moving now among all the listeners. "*Much* to think about. And though I would never have believed yesterday that I would say what I am going to say, I say it now without reluctance and without hesitation." His formal tone announced that he spoke not as Robert Bruce the younger but as the Earl of Carrick. "My grandfather taught me well on the importance of perceptions, and having listened now to Alexander Armstrong and the rest of you, I can see not only what you mean but also that you are correct. In my own defence, I can only say that my blindness to the truth of what I've heard was—like my father's own—born of our isolation in England. My father and I have had no idea of the situation you have to live with. And so I withdraw my request in the belief that my father would, too. I will ask no man of Annandale to place himself against the judgment of the folk in Scotland for what could look like treasonous behaviour in their eyes.

"My own men of Carrick have told me the same kind of thing, but until I came here this day I had chosen to believe they were speaking only of local occurrences. Carrick is far removed from here, after all. But now it seems that no place in Scotland is too far removed to be unscathed. The task I have to do at Castle Douglas can be accomplished with the men I have at hand. It is mine alone to perform and I will do it, as I must, with my Carrick men, under the blue banner of Bruce and the gold of Carrick."

He looked around the room, meeting the gaze of each man. "I am grateful, then, for your patience in listening to what I have had to say and I thank you for allowing me the time in which to say it, foolish as it might have seemed to you even without the horror of the tale we have heard this day. And that said, I will detain you no longer. I will send a report to my father in Carlisle, and I give you my word it will contain my full agreement with your concerns and no hint of criticism of you or your beliefs in this matter. Once again, my thanks, and God be with you all."

When they had gone, Bruce sat musing for a while, then pushed himself away from the table and walked the few steps to his grandfather's den. There he paused in the doorway, leaning against the jamb and frowning at the chair where the old man had sat working for so many years by the fire. Things had changed greatly since the old man left. There was no fire burning in the grate now, and the place looked dusty and unused. He could never remember having seen that fire dead before, and that single detail struck home to him, making him realize that had Alan Bellow been in Lochmaben, that fire would still be burning, if for no other purpose than to keep the old man's memory alive. He made a mental note to reinstate Bellow as factor as soon as he returned to London and had an opportunity to send the word to Writtle. Alan was part of the fabric of Lochmaben and was practically useless in England, with nothing better to do than keep the little-used Writtle cellars stocked; besides, he was aging rapidly, and Bruce knew it would be good for the taciturn old servant to return to the place that had been his home for most of his life.

That thought conjured an immediate image of his grandfather sipping hot toddy by the fire. Bruce straightened up, seeing the old iron kettle still in place, its singed handling cloth suspended on a nearby nail, and he wondered suddenly if the battered wooden cupboard against the wall still held his grandfather's toddy ingredients. He crossed the room quickly and stooped to open the cupboard doors, knowing even as he went that the shelves would be bare, but as he turned away, disappointed, he decided to have the fire lit and fresh toddy ingredients brought in. He knew he still had much thinking to do, for he did not feel comfortable with some of the things he had learned in the previous two days and was aware of some new, niggling, formless doubt. A toddy by the fire would do him good, he thought, for until he could point his finger firmly at whatever it was, this canker that was gnawing at him, he would fret himself into inaction. And inaction, with the looming raid upon Douglas Castle, was something he could not afford.

After going to the kitchens and issuing orders to have the fire lit in Lord Robert's den and a fresh supply of spirits, honey, hot water, and fresh cups taken there, Bruce went for a walk in the late-afternoon air, wandering wherever his feet took him while he allowed his thoughts free rein.

Half an hour after that he re-entered the assembly hall from the courtyard and almost bumped into Sir James Jardine as they both stepped into the doorway from opposite directions. Bruce stopped, stock-still.

"Sir James! You startled me." He had completely lost sight of the fact that the veteran knight was now the castellan of Lochmaben and had thought him long departed with the other knights.

"Aye, I can see that. I didna mean to." Jardine stepped back, giving Bruce room to come in and close the door. "I've been thinkin' about what was said here earlier an' came to talk to ye, but ye werena here, and I was just about to go lookin' for ye. D'ye hae a minute or two to talk?"

"Of course." Bruce smiled. "Better yet, though, will you join me in the den for a toddy? The fire should be going by now, and if it is the kettle should be hot."

They sat by the fire for a while in companionable silence, sipping at their drinks and staring into the flames, before Jardine came out with what was on his mind.

"I can let ye hae fower hunnert men. Jardines and Dinwiddies. For your task."

"Four hundred? My God … But why? I've already said you don't need to."

"I ken. But it's the thing to do. The right thing, I think. No' because o' duty to the English, God knows, nor even yet to your faither—mair for your grandfaither, God rest his soul. He thought well o' you and he wouldna hae let ye leave Annandale wi'out support o' some kind. Ye'll ride wi' Jardines, just as he did himsel' … But I'm noticing the size o' these wee cups. Mine's empty already."

"I was thinking the same thing," Bruce murmured, smiling crookedly. "But they're as easily filled as emptied." He took both cups and went to the fire, where he measured and mixed the ingredients carefully while Jardine watched him.

"Something's troublin' ye," the older man said shrewdly. "Was I wrong to make that offer?"

"What? No, by God's holy teeth, that's not what I was thinking at all … " He folded the scorched old pad over the kettle's handle and lifted it off the coals, then carefully poured hot water into each cup. "You're right in thinking something's troubling me, but it has nothing to do with your offer. I appreciate that more than you could imagine, but as I said earlier, I think I have enough men of my own to do what has to be done at Douglas." He paused, frowning.

"But ye're still no' sure about somethin', am I right?"

Bruce pursed his mouth. "Aye, you are. But I don't know why and that makes it even worse. It's … It's in my mind that I'm being used here, for some reason, and it makes me … uneasy. And I'm not even sure why I should think so … "

"Hmm. Well, here's as good a place as any on earth to talk about it, right here in your grandsire's den, where you and me hae both heard him talk about such things for years." He paused, then went on. "Ye're here on Edward's business, are ye no'?" He watched Bruce nod and raised his cup. "Then ye're bein' used."

He inhaled the fragrant vapour, then held the bowl of the cup in both hands, gazing into it. "There's no' a doubt o' that in my mind." His eyes moved back to the young earl. "Nor should there be in yours. Edward o' England uses *everybody* to get what he wants. It seems to me, then, that what ye hae to decide is just *how* ye're bein' used … And to what ends. An' what the costs o' that might be to you in times to come. Have ye thought on that?"

"Aye. There's been little else in my mind for the past two days."

"Why? What happened twa days ago?"

Bruce sucked air between his teeth, a short, sibilant sound. "I met with the Englishmen sent from Berwick with the siege engines. I'd met their commander before, in Berwick, on my way up here, but there was nothing then that troubled me. Now there is. Something changed in the interim."

"And ye think it has somethin' to do wi' Edward?"

"I know it has. No question of that. What I don't know is the how or why of it. Do I suddenly find myself mistrusting Edward? No, not at all. Edward is Edward. I trust him well enough and I accept him for what he is. But he's set a guard on me for some reason. A cleric called Benstead, a younger brother, I am told, of a man called John Benstead whom Edward has appointed to some position of importance. This priest is a loathsome slug, and Edward has seen fit to appoint the man as watchdog of some kind to keep an eye on me."

He took a sip of his drink. "Edward has a passion for keeping clerics hard at work recording everything that happens around him, but now he has extended that need to cover me, it appears, and I have this creature hovering by me every time I turn around."

"He's the leader o' the Englishry that's here wi' you?"

"No, that's Sir Christopher Guiscard. He's well enough disposed towards me and he commands a hundred mounted men-at-arms whose task is to support the sappers he has with him. Guiscard's a siege engineer above all else, and his concern is all about his engines and their fields of fire, and so he's content to leave command of the men-at-arms to his subordinate, Sir Roger Turcott. And Turcott's what you might expect him to be—a stolid, unimaginative turnip head."

"Then what's your difficulty with this clerk Benstead?"

"I detest the man. He offends everything that's in me. I would love to send him packing back to Berwick, but I can't."

"Why no'? Ye're the Earl o' Carrick. Are ye no' in charge o' the whole thing?"

"Yes, according to Edward's instructions. I am."

"Then send the whoreson packin'."

"I can't. He's given me no real reason to dismiss him and he was appointed to his task, whatever it really is, by Edward himself. I cannot simply send him home because I mislike the man."

"Hmm. Then why d'ye dislike him so much, gin he's done nothin' wrang?"

Bruce took another sip from his cup, rolling the liquid around his mouth before answering. "Thomas Beg told me all about him in Berwick when first we heard he would attach himself to us. He's a crawling toady, bowing and fawning to everyone he deems his superior or whom he senses might be useful to him. That's bad enough, but on the other side he is a vicious, overbearing bully to anyone he feels is beneath him. God help the hapless servant who falls afoul of that humble priest. Even his looks offend me. He's big and burly and yet cowering. Broad shouldered and ugly, with a face like a hatchet, all bumps and lumps and eyebrows and nose—a great, long, lumpy nose that should have been flattened when he was a babe in arms, if ever he was."

"Aye … And how does he behave when he's around you?"

"Well, I'm an earl, you see, so he oozes and bobs up and down, rubbing his hands as though he were washing them and practically quivering with pleasure when I notice him."

"Aye, so the best thing ye could do is ignore him. There's nothin' ye have to trust him wi', is there?" Bruce shook his head. "Well then, he canna betray ye, can he? Stay aware o' where he is and what he does, then, and just ignore him ayont that. Ye'll be glad ye did."

"It's like feeling someone is standing at your back with a dagger in his hand."

Jardine grunted. "Well then, I dinna ken what mair to tell ye. Ye'll just hae to watch him like a hawk … " He put his mug down on the small table beside him. "So ye'll no' be needin' my men?"

"I don't know, my friend, and that's the truth of it … I might not, but then again I might, and if I do I'll need them badly—some of them, at least."

Jardine frowned. "I hope *you* ken what you're talkin' about, Lord Carrick, for I don't."

"How familiar are you with the countryside around Douglas Castle? Do you know if there's a place nearby where you could hold two hundred men unseen and get them to me quickly should the need arise?"

Jardine's eyes narrowed in thought. "I'm no' that familiar wi' it, but I ken o' one place that might suit. There's but one road leadin' there frae here, an' it crosses another road about a mile short o' the castle hill. The crossroads is in the middle o' the woods, so it's well out o' sight of the castle, even frae the top o' the hill. They're hawthorn woods for the maist part but there's a big auld ash tree there, blasted wi' lightnin' years ago, that ye canna miss. We could wait there, I jalouse, and gin ye need us we could be wi' ye in a half-hour o' gettin' word. What's in your mind?"

"My gransser. He used to say a good commander keeps his mind on what *might* be needed, forbye what's clearly needed. And that's what I'm trying to do." Bruce stooped and placed his long-empty cup on the floor by his feet. "I'm not convinced I'm right—not by a long stretch—but I've learnt to trust my instincts when they shout at me. If I'm wrong, there will be no harm done and your men will be in no danger. I still believe what I said earlier about placing no demands on the Annandale men. If I'm right, though, and there's treachery of any kind afoot, I'll send Thomas Beg to bring you back to join us. You can be sure from the moment you see him that there's something far wrong. Will you do that for me?"

"Aye."

"Good. The English force is of a size with my own, two hundred and fifty in all, but of those only a hundred are a fighting force, the mounted men-at-arms. The others are sappers, tasked with manning and handling the siege catapults. My Carrick force is infantry, a hundred and a half of those, backed up by a hundred bowmen. How many bowmen could you bring with you?"

"Another hunnert, I jalouse, mayhap half as many again gin I had time to raise them."

"How much time?"

"A day or so. They're a' close by. I just need to send for them."

"Good. Send for them at once, then. I'll be gone from here by dawn tomorrow, to meet with my Carrick folk and the English force half a mile from Douglas Castle. We'll meet in council tomorrow and make arrangements for the following day. Can you have your men in place by tomorrow night?"

"Aye, easy."

"Right, then so be it. If all goes well, you'll have a night in the open and no harm done, and then you can return to Annandale. But if I need you, I'll need you at the English rear. With my hundred bowmen in front and your hundred and fifty behind, we'll outnumber them by more than two to one and disarm them, then send them home. Guiscard won't fight once he sees the number of bowmen against his riders. He's a steady man and a good soldier, not at all hotheaded. He'll withdraw and report back to Berwick for further orders."

Jardine nodded. "Aye. An' what will you do then? It'll look like rebellion against Edward's wishes. Your favourite priest there will see you suffer for that."

"Let him. All I'm doing here is trying to foresee all possibilities and have reserves in place against the worst of them, and that sanctimonious whoreson is my sole reason for being suspicious. I'll put him in his place tomorrow and that should be an end of it. Thereafter I'll expect no trouble."

Jardine shrugged and rose to his feet. "Fine, then. I'll thank ye for the toddy and be on my way. And I'll send men out wi' the word for the bowmen right away. Five an' seventy bowmen each frae Jardine and Dinwiddie and as many others as might want to come wi' us. Three or four hours' travel should see us at the big ash tree by mid-afternoon tomorrow."

Bruce was up and away more than an hour before dawn the next day and made excellent time, despite his early fears for the weather. The sky remained overcast the entire time, but the clouds were high and the threatened rain never fell, so that he found his Carrick men, under Nicol MacDuncan and Thomas Beg, waiting for him when he arrived at the meeting spot, close by but out of sight of Douglas Castle. Everything was ready, and Nicol reported that they had met or seen no one on their way south from Carrick, and so they set out immediately to where the English force had gathered less than half a mile away.

The officer in charge of troop dispositions had already set out the lines of a camp for the Scots contingent some two hundred yards beyond the horse lines on the far side of the main English encampment, and as soon as he had dismissed his men to set up camp, Bruce made his way towards the large pavilion that was Sir Christopher Guiscard's command post. The first thing he noticed on his arrival, much to his surprise and delight, was that the English cleric Benstead was nowhere to be seen. All the English knights were already there, though, and so as soon as he had greeted

Guiscard and his officers he called them to order and launched directly into their reasons for being there.

There were sixteen knights in attendance, with a scattering of senior sergeants from the siege-engine division, and they listened attentively to Bruce's plan to surprise the Douglas household the next morning. As soon as it was light enough for movement, the Carrick contingent would surround the castle, throwing a ring of bowmen into place where they could scour the battlements with arrows should the need arise. The mounted English men-at-arms would be held in reserve but assembled in plain sight before the gates, their threatening siege engines in readiness, their implicit double menace a highly visible deterrent against resistance. Then, with the risks of resistance clearly demonstrated, Bruce himself would ride out to parley with the castle's castellan and make his best efforts to persuade her to surrender. If she refused, then they would attack the castle, which could not hold out for long against the English catapults, and the surrounding Carrick men, backed by the mounted English, were a guarantee that no one inside could escape.

There was no argument of any kind; everyone knew why they were there and understood the situation, and Bruce, watching closely, could see no sign of disgruntlement among the English knights. Only when everything had been agreed upon did he ask about Benstead's whereabouts, and Guiscard told him that the cleric and his assistant, Father Robert Burlington, had been unexpectedly summoned early that morning to attend upon the prior of the nearby Monastery of St. Gildas. No reason for the summons had been given, and Guiscard, apparently happy to be rid of the odious priest, had asked no questions.

When the two English priests arrived back shortly after noon, Bruce saw them passing in the distance, but made no attempt to acknowledge them. Benstead seemed to be glaring at him, but he paid the fellow no attention. He gave the man no further thought at all until later that afternoon, when he was talking with his uncle on the inner fringe of the Scots camp. The drizzling rain that had been threatening all day had begun to fall, and Bruce was about to return to his tent for his cloak when Nicol raised a hand and murmured, "I think someone's lookin' for you."

Bruce turned to see an English man-at-arms, wearing a corporal's insignia, coming towards him.

"Forgive me, Lord Carrick," said the man after he saluted, "but I couldn't find you. They told me you were somewhere else."

"Well, you've found me. To what end?"

"You are to attend a gathering in Sir Christopher's pavilion, my lord. A command meeting. I think it might have started already."

"A *command* meeting?" Bruce made no attempt to hide the disbelief in his voice, and he bit down hard upon his anger. "Very well," he said. "I'll come. Who sent you, by the way?"

"The priest, sir. Father Benstead."

"Thank you, Corporal. Go about your business." He turned to Nicol, one eyebrow raised high as the corporal stalked away. "You were right," he said softly. "It seems I am being summoned. Well, well." He raised a hand, seeing that Nicol was set to go with him. "No, Nicol, I'll collect my cloak and go alone."

When he entered the pavilion, still racking his brains for what could possibly have justified the extraordinary summons, he stopped no more than a few paces in, seeing Benstead there watching and obviously waiting for him.

"Ah, young Master Bruce, there you are, and late as usual. Come in, come in. You know everyone … "

Bruce gawked about him like an idiot, swaying from side to side and ducking and raising his head exaggeratedly as he swung this way and that to peer into the shadowed corners of the great tent. Apparently satisfied at last that the corners were all unoccupied, he then turned to gaze keenly, with eyes narrowed to slits, at the men assembled in the semicircle of folding chairs around the pavilion's open central space.

"Master Bruce?" Benstead said. "In God's name what ails you, sir? Are you unwell?"

The question, and the alarm in the voice that posed it, brought an end to Bruce's strange behaviour. He turned and looked frankly at his questioner.

"Unwell?" His voice was strong and calm and filled with assured self-confidence. "No, if it please you, I am very well. I simply thought to see this fellow you were talking to, somewhere behind me. But he's not there."

"*What* fellow?" There was no missing the querulous asperity in Benstead's voice now.

Bruce straightened his shoulders and drew himself up to his full height. "The young *Master Bruce* you were speaking to. Where did he go?"

Some of the seated knights traded uneasy glances. The cleric, seated at the table, continued to frown in annoyance.

"Where did *who* go?"

Bruce threw the edges of his rain-wet cloak back over his shoulders, peering down with lowered chin and draping the folds to his satisfaction before he reached to his waist and unbuckled and removed the belt that hung there, supporting a plain, sheathed dagger on one side and a well-worn leather purse on the other. He hefted the thing in both hands, for it was heavy, and walked forward to the desk, where the now disconcerted cleric sat watching him.

"Do you know what this is?" he asked.

Benstead flushed. "It's … ehh … it's a sword belt."

"No, not so." Bruce's voice was mild. "No sword belt, this. Notice the gold on it, if you will." He hefted the belt again. "The weight and worth of it, I mean. See the crest of Carrick on each of the fifteen lozenges. This is an earl's belt, and it is mine." His voice hardened, not by much but sufficiently to add an edge to his next words. "Bear that in mind from this moment on, Benstead. If you ever address me in future by any title less than my lord of Carrick or my lord earl, I will have you lashed to a wagon wheel and flogged until your bones are bare. The right and privilege of doing both lie well within my power and pleasure."

The stillness in the pavilion seemed unnatural, and no one, including Benstead, so much as stirred. This was a new Robert Bruce they were witnessing; a stone-faced Robert Bruce whose existence no one there had suspected until that moment. And no man there cared to be the first to try to test him. Benstead sat ashen, his bulbous eyes wide with dawning horror.

"Is that clear to you now, *Master* Benstead? You will address me as befits my station and with keen regard to your own. You are a clerk—an ignoble functionary raised above your proper station solely because you are a younger brother to a better man, who holds a post and title given him by King Edward." He gazed at the loathsome man with a stare that made his eyes glitter like ice. "Hear me clearly. *I* will decide if and when I wish you to speak to me in future, and I find no temptation to have you do so any time soon." He lowered his voice to an intimate, conversational level. "You have seen fit his day to usurp my authority as commander of this expedition by summoning this meeting. More than that, you had the gall to summon me like a lackey to attend it. I could have you hanged for that, you fool. Or do you doubt that?"

Benstead appeared to shudder and then raised his head in a gesture of defiance. "I am here on the order of my superiors, and what I have done I have done at their command."

"Your *superiors*? This is Carrick, you blockhead, and I command here in my own earldom!" He stopped, willing himself to say no more, and when he spoke again he sounded weary and disgusted. "You are not a pleasing man, Master Benstead, and I am not alone in finding you offensive. And *offensive* does not even *begin* to describe my feelings towards you. You are a toady and a lickspittle, grovelling to everyone you think superior to you, while to those unfortunate enough to have you think of them as inferiors, you are a ruthless, abusive, and unrelenting bully. Look about you as you move throughout this encampment today and from now on. You will see few friendly faces, and fewer yet with any sympathy for you in your new estate. And make you no mistake, Master Benstead, your estate *is* new now. Your days of lording it around here are over. You will perform your allotted task in recording the conduct of this excursion we are on, but you will take no further part in anything having to do with its conduct and you will *never* again think to cross me and expect to live afterwards. Do I make myself clear?"

"But ... but you can't do that! I am here at King Edward's direct command."

"And so am I, you stupid man. Which of us, think you, will have the louder voice in the King's ear?"

He allowed the silence to lengthen beyond comfort before he added, "I am waiting for your acknowledgment of what I have said, Benstead. Did you understand what I said to you?"

Benstead opened his mouth and made as if to speak, but nothing emerged.

"Well, did you? And have a care to that angry look in your eye before you answer."

Bruce's face remained cold and flinty as Benstead squirmed. Finally, though, the cleric nodded, his voice emerging as a strangled squeak.

"I ... I heard you, Lord Carrick—*hear* you."

"Excellent. Then let us be rid of you for a while." He looked to where Benstead's deputy, Burlington, sat head down, his eyes fixed on the table in front of him. "We have nothing to discuss here, since we settled everything this morning while you were absent. But Father Burlington will record what we do say and present you with his documents when we are done. From them you may compile your own report and then you will bring it to me to read before you send it off. Now get out of my sight."

When the man had gone and the flaps of the tent closed again, Bruce reattached his sword belt, meanwhile looking from face to face among the others, though taking care to keep his eyes away from the priest Burlington. They all stared back at him, two of them approvingly, four blankly, and the remaining half dozen with quiet hostility that might, Bruce mused, have stemmed from resentment of his youth, or from what they thought of as his high-handed arrogance, or merely from the fact that he was a Scots earl asserting seniority over a group of Englishmen. He was slightly surprised to discover that he did not care. They all loathed Benstead, he knew, but he wondered whether any of them might take the cleric's side against him later, for political reasons. And he discovered that he did not care about that, either.

"Does any of you wish to question what I did?"

The only answer came from Sir Roger Appleton, the man whom Bruce had come to like best of all the English knights attached to the expedition. Appleton spread his hands. "I thought it was excellently done," he said, then grinned. "The only thing I failed to see was why you didn't come out and simply tell the fellow what you really thought of him."

If he had expected the others to laugh at his sally he must have been disappointed, for there was no lessening in the general air of disapproval.

Bruce nodded, firmly. "Well then, shall we get on with this, even though it be a waste of time? We're all here now, so let me verify that we are still in agreement on what tomorrow holds." He looked at Sir Christopher Guiscard, who commanded the English forces sent to join Bruce from Berwick. "Sir Christopher. If you would be good enough to outline the plan we agreed upon earlier, we can make short work of this. I must presume that Master Benstead intended to alter what we had decided, but I cannot begin to guess at how he might have done so, though I doubt it could have been for the better. The man is a priest with not an ounce of military training or knowledge. I doubt he could erect a tent, let alone direct an action."

Guiscard was one of the few who had not shown hostility to Bruce since this began, and now he smiled lopsidedly, though Bruce could see no humour in his eyes. "His plan was to seize some children from one of the villages nearby and threaten to hang them in front of the castle, one at a time, until Lady Douglas surrendered."

"Christ Jesus! Is the fellow insane? He discussed this with you?"

Again the half smile flickered at the corner of Guiscard's mouth. "He ... mentioned it. No more. Master Benstead is not a man to discuss much with anyone. He thinks, he decides, and he acts, rightly or wrongly. As when he misjudged your … youth, my lord of Carrick."

The tiny hesitation had been barely noticeable, but Bruce grinned wryly. "I fear Master Benstead misjudged far more than that, Sir Christopher. He misjudged how far he could push his scant officialdom." He glanced around the gathering. "So, are we agreed there will be no butchering of children come tomorrow?"

"It might have worked," Sir Roger Turcott muttered. "Not that we'd really have hanged them, of course. But the threat of it might have been enough to move the woman."

"Hmm. Have you heard much of Sir William Douglas, Sir Roger?"

Turcott stirred, stretching his legs. "Aye. The man's a traitorous, untrustworthy lout from what I hear. A wild animal, ungovernable and uncontrollable by anyone."

"Aye, well, the woman we are threatening to frighten here is his wife, and she is English. He abducted her from the castle of Lord Alan de la Zouche and kept her forcibly confined. And then she married him willingly and refused to be ransomed. She has been with him ever since, equalling him in everything. Does that suggest she'll be paralyzed by compassion at the threat of seeing a peasant child hanged?"

Turcott shrugged sullenly. "I but said it might have worked. Might have … I knew nothing of the woman involved."

Bruce nodded. "No more do I, but I know enough to know she won't be easily cowed." He looked again at Guiscard. "Well, Sir Christopher, what think you?"

Guiscard sniffed and sat straight up in his chair. "I think we should proceed as planned. You, my lord earl, will handle the niceties of the negotiation, as one Scot to another." He stopped, smiling again. "Not quite, though. Apart from being born here, I believe you are no more Scots than I am. And her ladyship is English, you said. Still, she is married to a Scot, and a rebellious one at that, so she should be open to discussion, at least. Your Carrick bowmen will be in place and prepared to sweep the walls clean should her ladyship decide to fight. Our hundred mounted men-at-arms will back you up—an added show of strength. Should the lady prove stubborn, we will attack the place with our engines and bring it down about their ears. Should she decide to be wise, however, we will take her and her people into custody and march them back to Berwick, and burn the castle once they are all out."

"So be it. Let's hope to God the woman sees sense. I have no wish to spill Scottish blood. I'll have my folk ready at dawn."

# EPILOGUE

Thursday, May 16, 1297

T homas Beg was hauling at the last of the buckled straps at Bruce's waist when the roaring drum rattle of the heavy downpour abruptly died away, leaving only the sluicing sound of running water being shed from the sloping roof.

"Well," Thomas growled, "thank the Christ for that. We'll still be arse deep in mud out there but at least we winna get soaked on top. Unless it starts up again." He stepped away and opened the tent flaps, and stood peering out for a while and listening to the splashing sounds of unseen people moving around in the darkness. A loud clatter of falling pikes and a bark of profanity announced that someone had blundered into a pile of stacked weapons in the dark, and he turned back to Bruce. "Darker than it should be," he said, "but there's no use in carryin' a torch, even if we had one. The clouds must be awfu' thick. Are ye set?"

"As close as I'll ever be," Bruce answered, tugging at his sheathed sword until it hung comfortably. "Let's see if we can find that clerkly, whining bastard Benstead, then, and make a start to this *auspicious* day."

Thomas Beg looked askance at him, ignoring the heavy irony in Bruce's emphasis. "Benstead?" he asked instead. "I thought ye put him in his place yesterday, for good. Why would ye seek him now?"

Bruce grunted, the sound heavy with distaste. "Because of what his true place is. He's Edward's official representative. I can't change that, nor can I ignore it, much as I'd like to. So we'll go and find him before we set anything in motion, see if he has anything to say. I doubt I'm going to like whatever comes out of his mouth, for the man's a venomous reptile. But this is a matter of duty, and I owe it not to him but to his master. Come on, now, lead the way."

"Fine, but first I'll see to the candles." Thomas Beg stepped back, releasing the tent flaps, but before he could reach the nearest candle the flaps were raised again from the outside and Nicol MacDuncan stepped in, dripping wet and frowning.

"Wait, Tam," Bruce said, but Thomas Beg had already stopped. In the act of cupping a hand behind the closer wick he had half turned, eyeing the newcomer, and Bruce heard his muffled, "Uh-oh."

Bruce spoke to Nicol in Gaelic, his tone apprehensive. "Was that you who knocked over the pikes?"

"Aye. It's blacker than the pit of hell out there. I walked right into them."

"What's wrong?"

His uncle looked at him strangely. "I don't know, Rob, but the English camp's empty. I couldn't sleep with the noise of the rain, so I went for a walk to clear my head. There's not a soul in the camp, not even guards. Everything's in place, so they are still around somewhere. They must have left in the middle of the night and nobody heard a thing."

"Hell's fire," Tam swore, but Bruce stood stock-still.

"Benstead," he whispered eventually. "He must have spent the night threatening Guiscard. I should have flogged the whoreson yesterday while it was in my mind."

Nicol blinked at him. "What are you talking about?"

"Treachery is what I'm talking about, and hanging children. God damn the wretched man! Tam, quick as you can. Mount up—don't waste time with a saddle—take the road east for Annandale. You'll come to a crossroads, less than a mile from here, marked by a big, dead tree. Jardine says it's impossible to miss. He'll be camped there, waiting. Bring him here. Tell him there's no time to waste. He'll have two hundred men with him—more, if we're lucky. Tell him we've been betrayed by the English priest and I need his bowmen in an arc at the Englishry's backs, with the others he could muster as a solid block in the centre. He'll know what I mean. Go, now!"

Thomas Beg was through the flaps and away almost before Bruce had finished speaking.

"Nicol, get our people moving now. Armed and ready. We'll go straight to the castle. God knows there's no reason now to move quietly. Have your men form up on me. I'll be waiting by the English horse lines. Quick, man!"

The men of Carrick had no need to waste time forming into disciplined blocks and ranks like English soldiers. They found Bruce in the strengthening pre-dawn light and arranged themselves behind him, watching him for instructions, and when he estimated most of them were there he gave the signal and rode forward, leading them out, knowing the stragglers would catch up quickly.

Half an hour later, with the Carrick men all soaked to the waist from running through long grass after the overnight downpour, they came in sight of the ancient keep of Douglas Castle and found the English drawn up there, facing the main gates. The great siege engines, mainly catapults capable of throwing man-sized stones that would quickly breach any but the very strongest walls, were being manhandled into their final assault positions by the sappers who tended them, and each of them was already stocked with a large pile of missiles, with more being brought up by wagons. But it was the rhythmic sound of heavy hammering that attracted Bruce's attention, and as he turned to look for the source of it his eye was drawn to where twin teams of straining men were hauling on ropes, erecting the framework of a tall set of gallows. Even from a distance, he could see that the thing was prefabricated and knew that it had been there all along, brought north from England with the siege engines.

Nicol MacDuncan was close by his side, and behind Nicol, in the grey morning light, Bruce could sense the dozen Carrick lieutenants watching him. He gave his orders without taking his eyes from the men erecting the gibbet, watching as it reached the vertical and dropped into the slotted holes that had been dug to secure the uprights.

"Nicol, take the men forward as we arranged yesterday. Place them between the English and the castle, facing the walls. No man to look back, except you. You keep your eyes on me. I'm going to talk to Guiscard. I'll need a standard-bearer with my colours but no one else. I don't know if I can stop what's happening here but I'm going to try, until Jardine's men get here. When you see my standard wave from side to side, turn the men around and have them move towards me. At the walk, mind you. No attack, no charge. Keep your approach slow and steady and have your bowmen ready to shoot, but stop when you're a hundred paces distant, within easy killing range for your bowmen, yet far enough away to remain clear of a sudden sally by Guiscard's horsemen. It's a threat I want to present here, not a challenge or provocation. We'll spill no blood if it can be avoided. Is that clear?"

"Aye. But how will we know if we need to attack?"

Bruce grunted, then took his eyes from the gallows to look at him. "If you see me taken, or if I fall dead, attack. Otherwise wait. I am about to discover whether I'm as good a talker as I hope I am. The rest remains with Guiscard. If he's the man I think he is, he'll see the truth of his position when Jardine arrives and he'll hold his men in check. I'm going now. Wish me well."

He lowered the visor on his helmet, noted the immediate loss of vision beyond the narrow eye slit, and raised it again before he turned to face the English knights and men-at-arms. But he made no move to start towards them. Instead, he sat looking in their direction, highly aware that they were watching him, too.

The light was growing stronger with each moment, and he felt a growing tension in his chest as he stared into the distance, waiting. He was twenty-two years old, approaching twenty-three, and as he sat there he told himself he was not the callow twenty-one-year-old who had ridden to his marriage in Edward's abbey at Westminster a lifetime earlier. He had grown since then; learned much of life and loss; he had trusted in God and been deluded, and now, today, he knew he had been used by people he had trusted. Edward of England had used him as an unwitting dupe, without regard for his honour, his station, or his esteem. He had been sent here purely as a nominal Scot, his rank and name exploited for the most cynical of English purposes. His presence here was a sneering jest, and every vestige of authority he had believed he possessed had been scorned and belittled. He might refuse to hang Scots children here this day, but his attendance would be noted by all of Scotland, his integrity impugned beyond salvage. He thought again, fleetingly, of his grandfather and his warnings about perceptions and how powerful they were, and felt a wave of self-loathing at his own gullibility. God! Edward must have laughed inside the last time they had met, to hear the Earl of Carrick pleading for his Scots folk.

Something moved in the distance ahead of him, at the farthest limit of his sight, and he straightened slightly, peering intently until he could make out the low-lying line of heads approaching the English rear. He turned and nodded to his standard-bearer. The lad was a nephew of Nicol MacDuncan, which must have made him some kind of cousin to Bruce himself, and he found the young man looking back at him expectantly.

"Well, young Ewan MacDuncan," he said. "We'll take a walk over and meet Sir Christopher Guiscard. And we'll do it slowly, since I'm in no rush to die this day. Have you noticed yet that there are men approaching from the English rear?" The young man nodded. "Good. They're ours, so take one last good look at them and then ignore them. The English will be watching us approach them. Don't let them see you looking at anything beyond them. Right, let's go."

He kicked his horse into motion and then held it to a tight-reined walk as they crossed the two-hundred-yard distance to where the English knights and their men-at-arms sat waiting for them, and as they went Bruce kept talking to the younger man. "Mind you," he said, "I doubt they'd be concerned even if they saw our fellows coming up behind them. These are the victorious Englishry who mere months ago routed the entire Scots army and won a war within three weeks. They'll have little fear of another rabble of Scots peasantry. Now, before we reach them—I'll tell you when to do it—I want you to sway the standard you're carrying from side to side. Don't brandish it like a blazon. Let it sway, as I say, and gently, no more than that, as though you're having difficulty keeping it upright. Do it twice. Nicol will be watching you, so that will be enough. Do you have that? Good lad."

They reached the halfway point of their approach, no more than a hundred yards from the English, and Jardine's men were clearly visible now, moving towards them through the long grass at the rear of the English horsemen. Sir James Jardine rode in the centre of the advancing line, flanked by two other riders Bruce presumed to be his sons, and they drew rein less than two hundred yards behind the mounted force. The Annandale bowmen were already within killing range and now they began to spread outward in a wide arc to cover the English rear.

"The standard. Do it now," Bruce said, then kicked his mount to a canter over the few remaining yards to where Guiscard and his fellows waited. He pulled his horse to a halt in front of them and sat quietly, waiting for some kind of greeting. When none was forthcoming and he was quite sure that no one would speak to him, he turned his head to glance towards the gallows, where a man was throwing long ropes up to another who straddled the crossbar. Then he looked back at Sir Christopher Guiscard.

"You brought it with you, all the way from Berwick—or was it all the way from England? I thought at first this morning that the priest had threatened you, to bend you to his will, but I see now I was wrong. This plan was settled from the outset, and all your reluctance was sheer mummery. You gulled me, Guiscard. You used me, led me by the nose, and the more fool me for permitting it. And so here I am, outwitted and condemned by my own folly in trusting an Englishman's word on the matter of anything Scots."

He saw stirring among the ranks of the men-at-arms before him and saw from their frowns that they were watching Nicol's Carrick men forming up at his back, but he kept his eyes on Guiscard, smiling now and surprised that he could do so.

"I do not see his oiliness, your slimy priest, but I doubt he's far away. He would be loath, I'm sure, to miss the chance of seeing children swinging from a rope. Give him a message when next you see him, from me, Robert Bruce, Earl of Carrick. Bid him stay well away from Scotland, for when I see him again, he will hang that same day, on my oath as an earl of Scotland." He raised his voice slightly. "I see you counting the men at my back. They are but two and a half hundred, mostly bowmen. A small number for a mounted force as puissant as yours, but they will empty a lot of saddles before your men can close with them, I promise. You have a hundred men-at-arms and what, sixteen knights? But I believe you are a clever man, Guiscard. Too clever by far to commit your force without looking behind you. You'll see three hundred men back there, too, with arrows drawn, if you but look."

It was highly gratifying to see the reaction his words invoked, for Guiscard uttered a startled curse and swung his mount around, pulling it up onto its hind legs as he sought to look over the heads of the men at his back, but he saw enough to bring him wheeling back to face Bruce, his face reddening in outrage.

Bruce could not disguise his smile. In truth there were more than three hundred at their backs—far more, Bruce saw, now that he had time to look more carefully. Jardine had brought fully the four hundred he had promised in the first place, and they were now pouring forward, bows at the ready, to encircle the hapless English who were milling in confusion like a herd of sheep.

"Have you gone mad, Bruce?" Guiscard's voice was a disbelieving roar. "This is rebellion! This is perfidy!"

"Hah! Perfidy?" Bruce shouted back, curbing his mount. "*You* speak to *me* of perfidy? This is not rebellion, Guiscard, nor is it perfidy." His voice rose to a roar that matched Guiscard's. "This is *Scotland*, you dissembling whoreson, and your kind are not welcome here."

Guiscard kneed his horse forward so that he had no further need to shout. "Not welcome here?" he hissed. "And what of you? Think

you these Scots folk will flock to you? You who are Edward's favourite dancing boy?"

Bruce nodded. "I was Edward's favourite, once, I suppose. But
now I see I am a Scot before all else. You taught me that, Guiscard.
You should not have come to hang children. I would have taken
anything else but that. But to watch my own folk hanged because an
Englishman thinks he can control me thereby? That is the line I will
not cross." He raised his voice to a shout again, smothering any
response Guiscard might have made. "*Listen now!* Here is what you
will do, to appease me and protect my honour."

He waited, watching the other man's eyes for the blink he knew
would be forthcoming, and when he saw it he spoke again, more
quietly this time.

"You will take your men and ride away from here, back to
Berwick. There you can report me to whomever you please—say
what you must say. Call me rebel, traitor, what you will. But what I
am this day, you made me—you and your lying, treacherous, arrogant ilk. So take your men and your sappers and go and do not look
back. If you resist, I'll wipe you out, here in this place, and I swear
by the living, breathing Christ not one of you will survive. Make
your choice now. No more talk. Go, or die."

"I could have you killed now."

"I don't care, Englishman. My wife is dead and I have no great
wish to live. Your King—the King to whom I gave my fealty—has
used me shamefully, and I have betrayed my own people enough to
welcome death for that alone. So *have* me killed. Then die with your
men. Else be gone within the quarter-hour. And leave the engines
here. We'll burn them before we move on."

"And what about the woman?"

"She'll come with us, north, to join her rebel husband. You're
wasting time."

"Edward will have your head for this, you fool."

"Then let him come and get it. He has better and more needful
things to do, in France. And I meant what I said about Benstead.

When I set eyes on him again I will hang him, for he is an insult and a shame to Holy Church."

He swung his horse around and spurred away, expecting at any moment to be challenged and attacked, but nothing happened, and eventually he reined in and turned back to watch as Guiscard's little army reformed itself and marched away to the east.

Three days later, outside the town of Ayr, just north of his own earldom of Carrick, Robert Bruce sat on a low wall and watched as Sir William Douglas ran to greet his wife and his young son, James, newly and surprisingly delivered to him through the good graces of the pampered, foppish favourite of Edward Plantagenet. Being reputedly a churlish, fearsome creature at the best of times, Douglas paid no slightest attention to their rescuer, but Bruce was not offended and was more than glad to be quit of Lady Douglas, who had treated him with glowering suspicion and disdain since he presented himself at her gates and explained what he had done, then offered to transport her north in safety to her husband. She had acquiesced, for she had little choice, but she had made no effort to be pleasant to her saviour. The child, James Douglas, had not spoken a word to Bruce since the day of their rescue, but Bruce had been aware, much of the time, that the boy, whom he gauged to be eight or nine years old, stared at him constantly.

Douglas finally took his family off to wherever he was living, hugging each of them under one arm, and Bruce watched them go. His own men—the forty he had retained as an escort after his return to Carrick—had already scattered, released by Nicol, and only as he began to notice the growing stillness around him did Bruce realize that he had nowhere to stay that night, though he presumed there must be an inn or a hostelry somewhere close by. He rose to his feet and arched his back as well as he could beneath the armour plate he was wearing, pushing his thumbs into the soft spot under his rear ribs beneath his corselet.

"So you would be the great English traitor Robert Bruce, the best-dressed dandy in King Edward's court. Is that right?"

There was no trace of truculence in the voice, and he turned slowly and found himself facing a man who dwarfed him without being taller than he was; a bearded giant, massive with muscle, with enormous shoulders, solid thighs, and a great, deep chest.

"It might be," he said easily. "I would hope to seem better dressed than the others at Edward's court, for they're a dreary, uninspiring crew. But as for being a great traitor … Are you saying I am a traitor to England because I came to Scotland, or a traitor to Scotland because I went to England?"

The big man smiled back, a warm, humorous grin, and Bruce felt, oddly, that he had seen it before. "Either way, it's too deep for me. I'm but a simple verderer. But I'm glad to see you've learned to walk, at least, without tripping over your spurs." He ignored Bruce's shocked expression and held out a big hand. "I'm William Wallace. We met once before, at your grandsire's estate."

"I remember." Bruce's own smile was wide and sincere. "At Lochmaben, on the day I was knighted. That seems a lifetime ago."

"Aye, doesn't it." The great head cocked sideways. "So, Sir Robert, are ye a magnate in truth, or will ye deign to drink a cup o' ale wi' a mere woodsman?"

"Right now I'm thirsty and I'm an unwelcome stranger here, it seems. So I'll be glad to drink with you, William Wallace—plain Will, if I remember aright—and you can tell me about what life is like in Scotland nowadays. I'll be a magnate on another day."

On the point of moving, though, the man Wallace stopped at those words and looked curiously at his new acquaintance. "No," he said quietly in Latin. "It's not that simple. You cannot have the luxury of choice. Either you are a magnate or you are one of us, the plain folk. And your name alone precludes you from being that. You are a magnate, I fear."

"Why would you fear it?"

"I distrust magnates."

Bruce blinked at him. "Do you, now? Why then are you here with Douglas and the others, Stewart and Atholl and even Wishart? They're all magnates."

Wallace was unapologetic. "Aye, but they're among the few that have proved themselves worthy of trust."

"Ah … And you would deny me a chance to do the same, merely because I'm Bruce and I've been in England?"

The other shrugged. "Those seem like two good reasons to me," he said mildly.

Bruce nodded tersely. "Fine," he said. "So will we drink together or no? And will we talk reasonably together or no?" He eyed Wallace's massive shoulders and added, "I might argue with you, Will Wallace, but I'm not stupid enough to fight with you."

Wallace barked an unexpected laugh and turned away, extending his arm in an invitation for Bruce to walk with him. "So be it," the big archer said. "We'll talk of Scotland, for I fear you know little of it, and you and I will decide how to save it from the English. The howff is up the hill here."

The two men walked up the sloping roadway side by side, already feeling comfortable with each other, and not a living soul took notice of their going.

# GLOSSARY

aey: always; ever (pronounced "igh" as in night)

ayont: beyond

corbies: crows

douce: gentle, sweet-natured

fashing: worrying, fretting over; being concerned about

fell: dire; implacable; resolute

forbye: besides, in addition to; except

gey: quite

gin: if

gowp: throb

haverings: ravings; maunderings; nonsense outbursts

hirpling: limping; doddering; lurching

hoaching: swarming; infested

kine: cattle

mind: recall; remember

mormaer: magnate; Celtic landholder and clan chief

swither: dither; be inconclusive, indecisive

thae: those

thole: tolerate; bear; put up with

tulzie: fight; struggle

wheen: a number; several